AMERICAN SHORT STORIES

REVISED EDITION

American Short Stories

1820 TO THE PRESENT

EUGENE CURRENT-GARCÍA
Hargis Professor of English and American Literature
Auburn University

WALTON R. PATRICK
Head, Department of English
Auburn University

SCOTT, FORESMAN AND COMPANY
Chicago • Atlanta • Dallas • Palo Alto • Fair Lawn, N.J.

KEY EDITIONS • JOHN C. GERBER, GENERAL EDITOR

Our basic aim in preparing this revision of *American Short Stories*, as in the first edition, was to assemble a collection of representative American short stories which, while illustrating the development of the short story in America from Irving's day to the present, could also be studied and enjoyed individually as examples of a complex literary art. To carry out this purpose, our first consideration was to update the contents of the volume to include the works of prominent new writers who were either unknown or unsung a dozen years ago. The addition of five stories by Flannery O'Connor, John Updike, Bernard Malamud, Peter Taylor, and Truman Capote fulfills this purpose.

Our second consideration was to strengthen, so far as possible, the offerings of older writers represented in the original text. This has been done by adding five other stories by Mark Twain, Stephen Crane, Willa Cather, Kate Chopin, and William Faulkner. To provide space for these ten new stories, we have dropped seven stories which, on the basis of a decade's teaching experience, seemed most readily expendable. The net result, a volume containing three more stories than its predecessor and brought up to date through revision of the introduction and headnotes, preserves, we believe, the character and virtues of the original edition while at the same time eliminating its less useful features.

As before, our aim has been to exhibit the broadest possible range of significant story types and methods. Thus, the carefully plotted story may be studied successively in the work of such writers as Poe, Bierce, Chopin, and O. Henry; the local color story, in either its humorous or serious vein, in that of Irving, Harris, Twain, Jewett, Freeman, and Garland; the realistic character study in that of Howells, James, Dreiser, Lardner, and Updike; the symbolic story in that of Hawthorne, Melville, K. A. Porter, Welty, Malamud; and so on. But our aim has also been to draw attention particularly to those writers who have contributed something of permanent value to the growth of the short story as an art form in America. Not all of the forty-three stories included in this volume are intended to stand as the best or best-known stories written by their authors. Copyright restrictions in the case of certain contemporary authors, notably Faulkner, Hemingway, and Fitzgerald, make it impossible for the anthologist to reprint the particular stories he would like to: he must make the best of what is available. By the same token, certain authors—Salinger, for example—cannot be represented at all. So far as possible, however, we have carefully selected each story as being representative of the special techniques of its author.

These techniques are discussed briefly in the introduction and the biographical sketches, where in each instance an attempt is made to point out their most significant features and to relate them to the stories in the text. Believing that the interpretation and evaluation of these stories are properly the function of the individual teacher and his students, we have made no attempt, however, to thrust forth our own judgments on the structure and meaning of the stories in the form of elaborate critical analyses. To avoid also the inflexibility of categories, we have arranged the stories chronologically according to the birthdates of their authors. The stories may thus be taken up successively as examples of a sequentially developing form, or they may be rearranged under a variety of other classifications and studied in any order desired to suit the teacher's convenience.

In preparing this text we have again profited much from the suggestions of Professor John C. Gerber and from those of various members of the editorial staff of Scott, Foresman and Company. Revision of the introduction has been done mainly by Eugene Current-García; that of the author headnotes, by Walton R. Patrick. But the editorial material, as well as the selection and substitution of the stories, is the result of cooperative effort.

Auburn, Alabama
June 1964

Eugene Current-García

Walton R. Patrick

CONTENTS

Note: The author's signatures preceding the headnotes are authentic with the exception of G. W. Harris' and Kate Chopin's.

the short story in america

romanticism and the beginnings: 1800-1860

Although the short story as we know it today springs from a tradition
buried in the distant past, its history in the United States goes back
less than 150 years to a time when the young nation was becoming
culturally self-conscious. In 1815, as the second successful war against
England ended, Americans could boast of their military and political
achievements and look forward confidently to a great economic future
for their country, but their pride in these things was somewhat
dampened by the feeling that they had as yet no independent literary
tradition. Ever since the Revolution the patriotic desire to establish a
native literature had spurred many an American into energetic, though
largely amateurish, writing of poetry, drama, and fiction; yet, as late
as 1820, their failure to impress foreign travelers and critics, who jeered
at their lack of artistic and intellectual development, could be summed
up in Sidney Smith's contemptuous wisecrack: "In the four quarters
of the globe, who reads an American book?" Significantly, it was
the short story which gave the first effective answer to this famous
question, for Washington Irving's *The Sketch Book* (1820) proved
that American writers could produce a literature which would command respect abroad.

A single book, however, even though a classic, does not make
a literature. For many years after 1820 the United States, while
developing rapidly in other fields, continued to lag culturally behind
Europe, its literature overshadowed by England's. The cutting away
of literary dependence upon England was especially difficult, first
because Americans naturally kept on reading English books, and second
because they had little time or monetary incentive to write many of
their own, as both book and magazine publishers understandably filled
their pages with the more popular English literary works (which they
could pirate freely) and often ignored the prior claims of American

writers, whom they would have had to pay. Nevertheless, during the forty years between 1820 and 1860 the short story flourished in America, for although the country remained predominantly an agrarian republic with no large cities and a rural population thinly scattered over a million square miles, hundreds of literary periodicals were founded, many of them sincerely dedicated to bringing the work of American writers before the public. Among the most noteworthy of these were the *North American Review, Knickerbocker Magazine, Graham's,* and *Southern Literary Messenger.* Next to poetry, the short story was perhaps the type of literature most adaptable to magazine publication, and, as it quickly proved to be the most popular, developed as a distinctive art form with extraordinary rapidity. By 1860, thousands of short stories had been written and published in America, and the technique of the short story had been raised to the highest level of nineteenth-century literary art.

As with other types of literature, the writers of short stories followed European fashions, imitating the literary forms and conventions popular abroad. The prevailing movement in European literature at this time was the romantic revival, a movement in thought and expression embracing a sense of newness and wonder, which Americans found particularly appealing and quickly turned to their own uses. Though difficult to define precisely, romanticism was characterized by: (1) an ardent interest in the emotions and the imagination, an awareness of the mystery, ecstasy, and yearning locked up in the human heart; (2) a fondness for the picturesque, exotic, and sensational manifestations of these feelings; (3) a belief in the greater goodness of simple, unspoiled humanity, and a humanitarian sympathy for the joys and sorrows of the common man; (4) a marked enthusiasm for external nature, the wilder and more primitive the better, since many romanticists tended to assume that nature in its pristine state taught unmistakable lessons of wisdom, beauty, and truth; (5) a fascination for remote times and places, which possessed exotic charms in the form of picturesque legends, superstitions, and adventures; and (6) a tendency to manipulate all these materials so as to idealize both nature and human nature without too much regard for "truth to life." Romanticism, in short, implied a search for new realms of experience, a thirst for novelty, and a desire to live intensely.

American writers naturally turned to popular European romantic literary types for inspiration and strove to convert them to the uses of American materials. Their efforts were often too slavishly imitative to be wholly successful; but they quickly demonstrated considerable originality in the short story, possibly because European romanticists had only begun to work out the techniques of this type of fiction when the Americans themselves began to experiment with it. In form the short tale was partly an outgrowth of the eighteenth-century sketch and periodical essay, and the possibilities of its development into a type of fiction distinct from the novel, yet containing most of the elements which gave the novel its strong popular appeal, were just coming to be realized when Irving took it up and fashioned it into a species of narrative that brought him immediate fame.

Nearly all the short tales in Irving's three most important volumes—*The Sketch Book, Bracebridge Hall,* and *Tales of a Traveller* —are the result of his borrowings from older European literatures. Even his most famous stories, "Rip Van Winkle" and "The Legend of Sleepy Hollow," are directly traceable to German legends which he found ready made during his travels on the continent. In refashioning the source materials of European legends, Irving simply followed the standard practice of most of his contemporaries, but the difference between their transparent imitations and his successful adaptations lay in his artistry, which made these old materials uniquely his own rather than obviously derivative.

Irving had both a professional attitude toward the materials of fiction and a highly developed skill in shaping them within a preconceived framework in order to produce a finished and pleasing work of art. He had a keen eye and ear for the significant details of everyday life and human character, the look on a face, the tone of a voice, the meaning of a certain gesture; he understood his own limitations as a writer and knew how to work within them to the best advantage in short units; and he possessed a feeling for words, knowing how to choose and combine them to arouse in his readers the emotions he wished to produce. Irving's artistry may be summarized as the realization of a fundamental principle of art, later to be forcefully reaffirmed by Poe and James, that "manner" or execution rather than choice of subject matter is the criterion of a writer's worth. This principle is clearly set forth in the letter Irving wrote to his brother-in-law in 1824, explaining his refusal to attempt a novel:

. . . I fancy much of what I value myself upon in writing, escapes the observation of the great mass of my readers: who are intent more upon the story than the way in which it is told. For my part I consider a story merely as a frame on which to stretch my materials. It is the play of thought, and sentiments and language; the weaving in of characters, lightly yet expressively delineated; the familiar and faithful exhibition of scenes in common life; and the half-concealed vein of humour that is often playing through the whole—these are among what I aim at, and upon which I felicitate myself in proportion as I think I succeed. . . .

I have preferred adopting a mode of sketches and short tales rather than long works, because I chose to take a line of writing peculiar to myself; rather than fall into the manner or school of any other writer: and there is a constant activity of thought and nicety of execution required in writings of the kind, more than the world appears to imagine. . . .

However strongly later critics have objected to the looseness of structure implicit in Irving's idea that a story is merely a frame on which to stretch materials, none has ever questioned that an especial "nicety of execution" distinguishes the short story from longer forms of fiction. Irving's realization of this fact establishes him as our first conscious literary artist in the short story.

But by twentieth-century standards of short story technique even the best of Irving's stories betray faults which the critical reader may find disturbing. Action develops slowly, impeded by long passages of description and chatty editorial commentary, which the reader accustomed to the swifter pace of today's stories grudgingly tolerates or skips altogether. Besides lacking tension and that sense of "immediacy" which we have come to regard as almost necessary attributes of the short story, Irving's stories often betray an objectionable quality of languorous softness, most prominently displayed in such tearful tales as "The Broken Heart" and "The Pride of the Village." But the fact that Byron wept over "The Broken Heart" and pronounced it good is evidence that such softness was a characteristic of the romantic age in which Irving wrote.

No adverse criticism, however, can destroy the enduring values which Irving's contemporaries were quick to recognize in his work. The perfection of tone in his best stories, the pictorial quality of his prose, and the pervasive humor, subtly blended with a nostalgic, dreamlike atmosphere, coalesced in a style which a whole generation of younger writers sought to duplicate. Taking their cue from Irving's success with *The Sketch Book*, many of them tried to imitate both its style and methods, with the result that their stories often revealed even more obvious technical crudities and unevenness of form than were apparent in Irving's. But like him these writers were also striving to make vivid the characters, scenes, customs, and legends of American life. Among the most noteworthy of these minor contemporaries were William Austin, J. K. Paulding, R. H. Dana, James Hall, Catharine Sedgwick, Albert Pike, and A. B. Longstreet, men and women from widely scattered areas of the United States, yet all imbued with a common desire to capture in story form the charm and picturesqueness of their own communities. From the beginning, "local color," one of the chief virtues in such a tale as "Rip Van Winkle," has been a prominent motif in the development of the American short story.

The mounting popularity achieved by our earliest short story writers soon raised a problem—the commercialization and standardization of literary art—which has remained central in American literature down to the present, particularly in the short story. Professional authors in America have always had to meet the demands of a commercial market; at first they had to compete with pirated British authors for space in the magazines, and, if they hoped to succeed financially, they had to write the kind of stories which magazine editors would buy and publish. Commercialization of the short story came to the fore as early as the mid-1820's with the appearance of the annual or gift book, a new publishing phenomenon that created a wide vogue lasting more than a quarter century. An ornate volume containing a variety of literary fare, the gift book quickly proved both a popular and profitable medium for the distribution of short stories. The demand for stories kept pace with the burgeoning gift books, and as more and more publishers brought out many new editions of them between 1830 and 1850, the shrewd author who managed to place each year a number of his stories in several gift books could count on a moderate income from his efforts. While these annuals created a market for short stories and offered encouragement to even the most talented of our early writers (nearly thirty of Hawthorne's earliest stories first appeared in *The Token,* an annual published in Boston beginning in 1827), they also served to direct the course of the short story's development. The fact that gift book requirements were geared to a popular demand for frothy, romanticized treatment of such current interests and fads as pseudo-science, the Indians, hair-raising deaths and premature burials, unrequited love, and the great American rags-to-riches theme, necessarily brought about a certain degree of standardization in the product—or at least standardization skillfully blended with only enough novelty to meet and surpass competition.

Such literary conventions naturally resulted in a flood of ludicrously pretentious writing, which rapidly increased in volume as more and more writers strove to satisfy the almost insatiable demands of the American public for light literary entertainment. The success of the annuals prepared the way for the still greater success of the ladies' books, which offered a monthly instead of a yearly harvest. *Godey's Lady's Book*, founded in 1830, became the first of the great "slicks." This new magazine was so astutely tailored to fit the demands of its feminine audience that despite the swift growth of competition it boasted, by 1836, the largest circulation of any monthly in the United States and continued to dominate the field for half a century. Fiction in the *Lady's Book* during its early years consisted largely of sentimental tales culled from British magazines and annuals. But financial success soon led to the bolder and more constructive policy of soliciting "original" American stories and paying their contributors the highest rates in the country, so long as they could satisfy its editor's plea for

> . . . short, racy, spirited essays; stories and sketches that embody pages of narrative and sentiment in a single paragraph, and by a few bold touches paint rather than describe, the characters they exhibit for the instruction and entertainment of our readers.[1]

The most successful literary men were those like Nathaniel Parker Willis who could readily satisfy these demands. Willis' fabulous success (his yearly income during the early 1840's, when both Poe and Hawthorne were struggling desperately to earn a livelihood from writing, ranged between $8,000 and $10,000) was due largely to his mass production of sentimental tales, "crowded with duels, intrigues, disguises, escapades, masked balls, lost heirs, and all the stock properties of the romancers' art."[2] Obviously a degeneration of Irving's style of writing, this sort of thing predominated in the annuals and ladies' magazines, with the result that not even Poe or Hawthorne could escape its influence altogether. The demands of the age help to explain the lush, rococo quality in much of Poe's writing as well as the pale, feminine tint in .some of Hawthorne's. But at the same time the movement toward sprightlier dialogue, faster action, purposeful description, and other such techniques of the short story was given impetus by the *Lady's Book*, as its remarkable success bred a host of imitators, all eager to exploit its materials and methods. The influence of the annuals and ladies' books was both bad and good, but they

[1] Mrs. Sarah Josepha Hale, quoted in F. L. Pattee, *The Development of the American Short Story*, New York, 1923, p. 71.
[2] *Ibid.*, p. 80.

deserve acknowledgment for having occasionally published the work of the two greatest artists of the short story of their day, Hawthorne and Poe.

Long before Irving had ceased writing, these two emerged, almost simultaneously, to challenge and presently to surpass his pre-eminence. The publication of Hawthorne's *Twice Told Tales* in 1837 emphatically proved that the young nation need no longer apologize for its literature, but if further proof were needed, Poe's short stories, appearing regularly during the 1830's and 1840's, supplied it. Like Irving, both Hawthorne and Poe were literary craftsmen; but they differed markedly from each other—and from Irving—in that Hawthorne's stories, generally unfolding against a New England background, were often symbolical and almost always stressed a moral theme, while Poe's usually depended on no particular locality, generally avoided allegory, but revealed an extremely tight and unified construction, as well as an astonishing power to evoke atmosphere. In the work of these two men, the short story in America reached a high level of art, though the nation at large scarcely realized that fact.

Hawthorne's active career as a short story writer fell roughly into two periods of nearly equal length covering a span of about twenty-five years. The first period, sometimes called his "anonymous years," began with his graduation from Bowdoin College in 1825 and ended with the publication of his first noteworthy collection in 1837; the second ended shortly after the publication of *The Scarlet Letter* when, his fame now assured, Hawthorne issued in 1851 his last significant collection of tales, *The Snow Image and Other Twice Told Tales*. By this time he had published over one hundred tales and sketches, including two other important volumes, his second series of *Twice Told Tales* (1842) and *Mosses from an Old Manse* (1846).

To *The Snow Image* Hawthorne affixed a short preface which casts an oblique but penetrating light upon both the evolution of his own art and the status of the writing profession in New England during the formative years of his career. Looking back a quarter century from the vantage point of 1851, he could now survey his earliest efforts with cool detachment. The first twelve years of heartbreaking struggle and frustration, during which he had made at least three abortive attempts to publish a collection of tales, he quietly summarized with the simple statement that he had then been "the obscurest man of letters in America." He called attention to the slender success his first volume of stories achieved when it finally appeared in 1837 and modestly admitted that, although their reputation "was not such as

would have gratified a craving desire for notoriety," the stories themselves "made no enemies." But neither had they taken the country by
storm because, he now believed, they were too shadowy and insub-
stantial:

> They have the pale tint of flowers that blossomed in too retired a shade,—
> the coolness of a meditative habit, which diffuses itself through the feeling
> and observation of every sketch. Instead of passion there is sentiment;
> and, even in what purport to be pictures of actual life, we have allegory,
> not always so warmly dressed in its habiliments of flesh and blood as to
> be taken into the reader's mind without a shiver.

In this incisive self-criticism Hawthorne touched the core of
the objections raised against his short stories by both his contemporaries
and subsequent critics. As early as 1830, Samuel Goodrich, editor and
publisher of the annual in which some of Hawthorne's earliest stories
appeared anonymously, said that his tales were "too mystical to be
popular"; and Poe repeated much the same charge in his famous review
of *Twice Told Tales* in 1842, when he found in them "a somewhat
too general or prevalent *tone*—a tone of melancholy and mysticism."
Hawthorne himself acknowledged this deficiency in confessing to
Longfellow: "I have seen so little of the world that I have nothing
but thin air to concoct my stories of, and it is not easy to give a lifelike semblance to such shadowy stuff." It was a weakness which he
felt he never fully overcame.

What Hawthorne and his critics alike meant by the terms
"mystical" and "shadowy" was simply that his stories did not capture
the surface texture of life in the way that Irving's did; for instead of
working from human types or individuals whom he had observed, he
usually began with an imagined problem or situation involving human
destiny and then invented characters to fit it. Since he was more
interested in human motives than in human actions, he chose to delve,
like a modern psychologist, deep into the hidden springs of human
nature rather than dwell lightly, like Irving and his imitators, upon
the surface features of life. His stories, therefore, revealed a persistent
quest for the "inner" meanings of human nature which made its surface action understandable. In following this path, Hawthorne was
living up to his Puritan heritage; when he admitted that strong traits
of his ancestors' grim nature had intertwined themselves with his
own, he did not mean simply that he had inherited a "New England
conscience," but that he had been bequeathed their sense of a "calling"

—the need, in his case, to confront and express the life of the mind. As a true scion of the Puritans he could not have been satisfied merely to portray externals of scene or character. But by rendering anew in nineteenth-century symbolic terms the grim moral vision of his fore-bears he might re-enact in the forms of romance the old truths of seventeenth-century Puritan religious thought. Thus, the moral idea which forms the basis of virtually all his tales is often set forth in a manner analogous to that of the old seventeenth-century sermons, by means of signs and symbols, carefully selected and elaborated for the purpose of driving home a complex theme.

Only within recent years, as critics have begun to free themselves from the demand for purely realistic fiction and to appreciate the values of symbolic treatment, has it become apparent, first, that Hawthorne deliberately chose the symbolic in preference to the realistic because he wished to "manage his atmospherical medium [so] as to bring out or mellow the lights and deepen and enrich the shadows of the picture"; and second, that the recurrence of images signifying guilt, isolation, self-contemplation, and emotional frigidity, interwoven into the texture of his stories, was intended to dramatize the several basic themes which summarize his views and attitudes toward life. The most frequently noted of these themes are the inescapable presence in the world of evil as a positive force; the alienation or isolation of the individual from his fellowmen; the necessary dependence of the present upon the past; and the interdependence of the intellect and the emotions in the make-up of a normal human being. Most of Haw-thorne's significant stories offer variations upon one or another of these themes, although central to all of them is the conviction that life is essentially tragic, and that therefore "a loving heart is better than wisdom." The theme of isolation, for example, finds such frequent and varied embodiment in his stories that almost all his major char-acters are made to feel its influence. Similarly, the problem of sin and its manifold effects upon human life receives consistent emphasis in his fiction. For, in direct contrast to the prevailing optimism of his age, Hawthorne felt deeply the ubiquitous presence of evil in the world and strove not only to penetrate its mystery but also to portray its corrosive influence. To most of the comforting beliefs of men like his friend Ralph Waldo Emerson—beliefs in the innate goodness of man, in the assurance of moral lessons to be derived from nature, in the inevitable rightness of impulse and the virtue of self-reliant individ-ualism—Hawthorne countered by depicting repeatedly in his stories the disastrous effects of pride and hardheartedness.

The problem of evaluating these stories, therefore, is not simply a question of deciding whether they are too "mystical" or too allegorical, as Poe and other contemporaries regarded them. It is rather the more complex question of determining whether and to what extent Hawthorne succeeded in fusing in them the worlds of fact and idea. He probably failed oftener than he succeeded because he tended to neglect the visible, tangible surface of life which provides a necessary support for the inner spiritual realities informing it. He knew well enough that every story risks failure if it does not "possess enough physical substance to stand alone"; and although he reminded himself that "human nature craves a certain materialism," still he fixed his attention so unwaveringly upon those spiritual realities that he did not at times heed his own warning, with the result that many of his characters strike us as merely personified abstractions, neither their actions nor their speech possessing vitality enough to move us with the force of convincingly real persons. Moreover, many of his poorer tales betray weaknesses in structure and technique which indicate a lack of both power and effort. Some are mere fragmentary sketches, undeveloped outlines; others suffer from the conventions of the gift book trade for which they were written. A sprawling, imprecise, leisurely style, and an overuse of the hackneyed devices of sentimental fiction—Gothic terrors, fiendlike villains, supernatural portents—are sufficiently prominent in these poorer tales to remind us that Hawthorne, like Poe, frequently lowered his standards to thrill the crowds.

But Hawthorne's best stories succeeded in capturing with astonishing power both the inner and the outer reality of his subject. In "Young Goodman Brown" and "Rappaccini's Daughter," clearly among the finest examples of his work, allegory is abundantly present too, but the important difference is in the spontaneity and control of its employment. It does not give the impression of having been groped and fumbled for; so skillfully blended are image and idea, meaning and form, that it would take longer to explain either story's total effectiveness than it does to tell the story. These and fifteen or twenty other stories of nearly equal quality were so powerfully wrought that Hawthorne's own generation and later ones barely recognized their explosive potentialities; whereas a generation like ours, nurtured on Freudian psychology and inured to the presence of evil in the modern world, is perhaps better prepared to accept and evaluate them. For all of them show unmistakable evidence of finished craftsmanship: the rounded development of a central theme; the evocation of a single, poignant mood; the economy and density of revelatory detail; the meaningful integration of parts; the detached, unobtrusive style; and the richness of imagery. Up to 1850 Hawthorne was still unsure of his medium, his grip on reality less firm than it might have been or than he wanted it to be. Yet from the beginning of his career his stories demonstrated how the genius of Puritanism, when channeled into an unfamiliar realm of art, could develop into a rare growth altogether unlike that of the short story elsewhere in the United States.

No two contemporaries similarly dedicated to the creation of enduring literature could have been further apart than Hawthorne and Poe in background, training, and temperament: one, the typical offspring of a deep-rooted New England Puritan heritage; the other, rootless, erratic, brilliant, and psychologically insecure. Where the one was relatively democratic, the other was blatantly anti-democratic; where the one distrusted the claims of science, the other admired, perhaps above all else, the orderly processes of rational analysis. Interested almost exclusively in probing the nature and destiny of the human soul, Hawthorne had fashioned his art into a delicate instrument for that purpose. Determinedly anti-moralistic, Poe was interested primarily in achieving brilliant effects and therefore studiously devoted his talent in the short story to the creation of novelty, variety, and surprise. In view of these basic differences in their character, it is not surprising that the works of the two men present startling contrasts. Yet in several significant respects their careers as short story writers followed parallel lines of development. Both began to experiment with the form at approximately the same time; both underwent preparatory periods of solitary study; both knew the bitterness of popular neglect and the pinch of penury, despite repeated efforts to suit their product to popular demand; and both persevered, despite repeated discouragement, in their devotion to literature.

Poe's earliest stories consisted of a group of sixteen, probably written between 1830 and 1835, which he hoped to publish as a volume entitled *Tales from the Folio Club*. But like Hawthorne, he had to draw what satisfaction he could at first from having the stories published separately in annuals and magazines like the *Courier* and the *Southern Literary Messenger*. As he became better known he succeeded in publishing in 1840 a two-volume edition called *Tales of the Grotesque and Arabesque*, containing all but one of the twenty-six stories he had written up to that time; and again in 1845 there appeared another selected edition of twelve *Tales*. These were the only book-length collections of his stories issued during his lifetime, though he wrote in all nearly seventy prose tales and sketches.

From the beginning of his career Poe clearly had his eye on the market and attempted to meet its demands by exploiting the sensational devices then current in popular magazine fiction. Chided in 1835 by the publisher of the *Messenger* for his questionable taste in "Berenice," he admitted frankly that some details in the story were "far too horrible"; but to him the question of taste was irrelevant, since "to be appreciated you must be *read*." He knew, or thought he knew, precisely what sorts of material would appeal to the public; and the variety of subject matter and treatment in his earliest stories indicates that he was striving to make his own appeal as broad as possible. "The ludicrous heightened into the grotesque: the fearful coloured into the horrible: the witty exaggerated into the burlesque: the singular wrought out into the strange and mystical"—these, said Poe, were the types of stories the public would buy; hence these he would write. His early stories, accordingly, were done in the popular Gothic manner of the time: they were morbid horror tales, full of the supernatural, of madness, premature burial, mutilation, and weird, unearthly scenes. Throughout his career Poe worked in these and other startling modes, notably the analytic detective story; and his success in the editing of various leading magazines as well as his subsequent reputation in the field of the short story suggests that he had gauged his public pretty accurately.

Poe's reputation rests, however, not only on his virtuosity as an artist, but also on his brilliance as a critic and theorist of the short story, for he was the first American writer who attempted to define its technical requirements. In critical essays published from time to time, he gradually evolved his aesthetic theory of *effect* based upon the principles of brevity and unity, the best known statement of which (as regards the development of the short story) occurs in his review of Hawthorne's *Twice Told Tales*. The three central ideas of his theory may be summarized as follows: (1) that since "unity of effect or impression" is of primary importance in any form of imaginative expression, the most effective poem or story is one that can be read at a single sitting; (2) that the short prose narrative, as exemplified by Hawthorne's tales, offers the greatest opportunity next to the poem for the exercise of artistic genius, provided the writer deliberately subordinates everything in his story—characters, incidents, style, and tone—to the bringing out of a single, preconceived effect; (3) that the prose tale may be made the vehicle for a greater variety of these effects than even the short poem. This abridgment of his theory makes clear that Poe's main concern focused sharply upon matters of design, proportion, composition; for what he meant by *effect* was largely the impact which a work of art would make upon the reader. Speaking of the artist's obligation and reward, he added:

> If his very initial sentence tend not to the outbringing of this effect, then he has failed in his first step. In the whole composition there should be no word written, of which the tendency, direct or indirect, is not to the one pre-established design. And by such means, with such care and skill, a picture is at length painted which leaves in the mind of him who contemplates it with a kindred art, a sense of the fullest satisfaction.

Given this dominant preoccupation with effect, one is not surprised to find Poe paying unabashed tribute to Hawthorne's artistry, while at the same time misinterpreting almost entirely the latter's equally significant moral purpose. As both critic and artist, Poe's interest in the short story was that of the craftsman, not that of the moralist; but by insisting upon standards of literary excellence, calling attention repeatedly to the need for effective presentation, and demanding that the finished work of art be judged on its own merits rather than on its author's well-meant if unfulfilled intentions, he probably performed his greatest service to American literature.

Many argue that Poe's stories are little more than a tissue of cleverly wrought impressionistic effects—of horror, fear, melancholy, disgust, or analytical agility—and that his vaunted aesthetic theory is merely a means of rationalizing his own limitations as a literary artist. They admit his skill in the manipulation of incidents, his inventiveness in plot construction, and his vividness in the depiction of intense situations; but they find no evidence in his stories of an imaginative power to re-create life and human feeling through characters. His characters seem to them mere pawns in a game which Poe, the master mind, plays with his audience. Poe's apologists, on the other hand, are more inclined to take at face value his declaration that the terror in his tales was "not of Germany but of the soul." Ultimately, the issue can perhaps be settled only by the individual reader, who must decide for himself whether Poe's fantasies and abnormalities, along with his morbid, narcissistic heroes and decadent damsels, are simply sensational Gothic devices, or whether they reflect, however inadequately, genuine, deeply felt emotions. The problem is not easy, since even Poe's most unsympathetic critics grudgingly acknowledge the imaginative power in a few of his stories, such as "Ligeia," "William Wilson," "The Masque of the Red Death," and "The Fall of the House of Usher." Ruin and the disintegration of human life are the prevailing themes in these stories, and it is difficult to read any of them sympathetically and still affirm that Poe's own sense of suffering is not mirrored there, since much the same preoccupation with evil, the same "haunted mind" that troubled Hawthorne, hovers over them. Indeed, since recent studies have disclosed unsuspected levels of meaning artfully concealed beneath Poe's elaborate façades, perhaps all his stories—even his detective tales—should be read as allegories of dream experience and neurotic states of mind. But however they are interpreted, Poe's impact upon our literature was that of an original creative force; the kinds of fiction he wrote—detective, pseudo-scientific, lurid adventure—have become the staple of millions who have never heard of his theories.

During the 1840's and 1850's many other American writers entered the field of short fiction, but the fact that the short story still went unrecognized as a distinct literary form was evident in the almost total neglect of Poe after his death, as well as in the prevailing notion that short fiction belonged chiefly to the popular ladies' books and magazines. The 1850's, in fact, deservedly earned the title "feminine" as a result of the orgy of sentimental, didactic, sloppily written fiction produced during that decade by a group of popular writers whom Hawthorne despairingly characterized as "a damned mob of scribbling women." The short story, therefore, struggled along with little purposeful guidance in the absence of any other first-rate practitioners except Herman Melville, whose *Piazza Tales* (1856) was virtually the only collection of short pieces of the decade which was fit to put beside those of Hawthorne and Poe. Melville treated symbolically in these tales a number of the powerfully tragic themes, such as the endless struggle between innocence and evil, the paradox in the dualism of man's nature, and the pain of loss and despair suffered in the effort to reconcile ideals and worldly values, which he had developed more fully in novels like *Moby Dick* and *Pierre*. Unfortunately, however, Melville had not as yet mastered the technique of the short story, so that not more than two or three of the stories in this volume bear comparison with Hawthorne's best work. Yet it is perhaps fitting that one of the best of them, "Bartleby," may be interpreted as Melville's symbolic response to the commercialization of art in America at the fag end of its romantic period.

The impact of the Civil War upon the United States was so powerful that after 1865 virtually a new nation came into being, and so numerous were the changes wrought by the war's aftermath that the basic patterns of thought and expression in the generation between 1860 and 1890 necessarily contrasted sharply with those of the preceding one. The dislocations and disillusionments produced in the South, for example, kept that area depressed for over thirty years, creating almost insurmountable social and economic problems. Elsewhere in the country equally pressing problems arose, though from other causes, as three significant forces, operating concurrently, changed the face and the psychology of the nation more rapidly and more radically than ever before. As an outgrowth of the North's victory and the post-war expansion of its industrial system, great railroad lines spanned the continent, filling its vast empty spaces in the West with a polyglot multitude of European immigrants who had been lured there by the promise of land, wealth, and political freedom. The westward movement, reaching the climax of its surge in this period, thus became one of the dominant forces in reshaping national life. No less significant, a second force engendered by industrial growth was the rapid mass movement of population, both native and foreign, from farms to cities, creating a new American phenomenon— the metropolis—with its motley social fabric and its extremes of wealth and poverty symbolized by the skyscraper and the slum tenement. As a result of this increasing mechanization and urbanization, new tensions, reflected first in the nation's changing mores and ultimately in its cultural expression, produced a gradual but decisive shift in the basic assumptions of the age. In place of the older romantic optimism founded on the assumption of the individual's central significance and infinite progress in a world of moral values, there began to appear now a more critical realistic mood, as the pressures of modern society, economic warfare, and the power of the machine made the individual less certain of his destiny. This drift toward a pessimistic determinism was further accelerated by a third important force, the rapid advance of scientific knowledge, particularly in geology and biology, which profoundly modified man's understanding of life and undermined his former certainties. For out of the welter of this new knowledge emerged the concepts of evolution, natural selection, and scientific materialism, which effectively destroyed the foundations of an older belief in nature as the visible manifestation of an indwelling, benevolent spiritual reality. Thus, science and industrialism, by changing America's thinking and living habits, prepared the way for a gradual shift in the prevailing national outlook from romanticism to realism.

As reflected in the literature of the period, this shift of emphasis from a romantic to a realistic interpretation of life was achieved only after much wrangling over the ultimate purpose of literature; for the romantic impulse persisted far into the new era, and romantic themes and moods continued to influence, often to dominate, American writing. At bottom, the issue between romanticism and realism was a philosophic conflict over the basic purpose and function of literature. The romantic believed that literature should idealize life by emphasizing its more picturesque or desirable features, while the realist tried to give a faithful representation of all the prosaic facts of actuality exactly as they appear to the senses. Between these two extreme views lay many varying attitudes concerning the proper use of the materials of fiction and the most appropriate techniques for rendering them artistically; but since most authors kept on writing for cash, not for the ideals of art, the vast majority of short stories in the popular magazines remained as before on the "boy-meets-girl" level of mass entertainment. Rather than venture too far afield, the popular magazines then as now tended to perpetuate the standardized romantic devices because these had proved to be the most profitable literary commodity; while the controversy over realism raged mainly among the few artists and critics who took literature seriously. Nevertheless, a gradually developing tendency to present life with greater fidelity to the facts of actual experience could be discerned, even at the popular level, in several types of stories which gained currency during the period. Though the movement toward pure realism was exceedingly slow, it became evident first in the regional "local color" stories, acquired new technical precision in the "well-made" story, and reached its fullest development before 1890 in the type of psychological fiction based on ethical problems that was written by Howells and James.

Of these three types, the first furnished the greatest variety of stories and was decidedly the most popular, as well as the least realistic. Elements of local color writing, which may be defined loosely as the representation in fiction of the distinctive features, customs, and modes of life in a particular area or locality, were present even in Irving's stories; but as a type which dominated American fiction from 1870 to 1890 these local color stories grew out of two distinct streams of earlier romantic fiction—the comic tall tales of the Western frontier and the genteel, didactic stories of the ante-bellum East and South—which were fused by Bret Harte and others in the 1860's. Tracing its source to A. B. Longstreet's *Georgia Scenes* (1835), the first stream sprang naturally out of the free, unregulated life of the back country, and in most respects presented a striking contrast to the refined product of the Eastern seaboard. For the high-mindedness, correct behavior, and polite tone of the latter, it substituted a frankly unethical, amoral tone and glorified in vigorous, gusty language the rough features of frontier life. Its heroes were braggarts, bully boys, and rascals, whose exploits, modeled upon the fabulous deeds of Davy Crockett and Mike Fink, furnished the materials for the yarn-spinning talents of writers like Johnson J. Hooper, T. B. Thorpe, J. G. Baldwin, and George Washington Harris. In the main the stories written by these men discarded the rhetorical "literary" manner of conventional fiction and adopted in its place a method derived from the old folk tale, namely, the device of placing within the story a narrator who recounted in his own untutored but racy speech the principal events of the story. Called "mock oral tales" because they were written adaptations of yarns that were told or might have been told by fireside yarnspinners, these stories, though often crudely contrived, delighted a vast audience, chiefly masculine. But since they flouted the established conventions of polite literature, they usually drew censure rather than encouragement from the literary critics of their day and consequently flourished mainly on the sub-literary level of newspapers and sportsmen's magazines. Recent scholars, however, have found in their authentic American types and indigenous backwoods idiom some of the myth-making sources of a native literary tradition—the "Big Bear" or tall-tale tradition—from which Mark Twain, O. Henry, Faulkner, and others have drawn models and inspiration.

Less readily discernible in its early development, the second stream of local color writing came down through the work of writers like Catharine Sedgwick in New England and William Gilmore Simms in South Carolina, who had consciously employed the scenes and legends of their respective localities as background for the romantic action of their characters. These decorous, didactic tales gradually acquired further realistic touches from other writers in the 1840's and 1850's, notably Harriet Beecher Stowe, but remained relatively undistinguished until the merger between them and the uninhibited, amoral Western yarns produced a type of local color story which marked a decisive turning point in the history of the American short story. Credit for bringing about this union belongs largely to Bret Harte, who took hold of the more picturesque materials and methods of frontier humor and rendered them palatable for sedate Eastern appetites. The stories he wrote for California periodicals in the 1860's gained nationwide fame when they appeared later in his small volume *The Luck of Roaring Camp and Other Sketches* (1870) and thus bridged the gap between East and West, giving impetus to a trend which had already begun. Harte's achievement may be explained in part by his awareness of the importance of humor in the short story; in part by his skill in exploiting it, together with irony and sentiment, through his compression of incident and terseness of phrase. Having discovered in the humorous newspaper anecdotes such qualities as extravagance, freshness, conciseness, and originality, Harte went so far as to insist that native American humor was alone responsible for them. Exaggerating somewhat the importance of humor, he argued that the newspaper yarns had provided not merely the distinctive new elements, but also the only new techniques and disciplines which made the American short story of the 1880's a native product, free at last from the dominance of foreign influence. But despite this overemphasis, there is little doubt that the technique of the frontier humor yarn was largely responsible for Harte's own success in the short story, as his best stories were essentially frontier narratives which had been smoothed, polished, and sweetened with a coating of sentiment to make them attractive to the national audience of his day.

In the wake of Harte's success, but not necessarily in imitation of his methods, scores of writers, including G. W. Cable, Mary E. Wilkins Freeman, Sarah Orne Jewett, Mary Murfree, Kate Chopin, Joel Chandler Harris, and Thomas Nelson Page, fashioned the trend of the local color story. Quaintness of scene, character, dialect, and local customs, carefully purged of their grosser elements, thus became a staple in the short story from 1870 to 1890, as the nation was deluged with stories about life in the hinterland. Realistic only in externals, these stories were rather like folk idylls than truthful representations of events in the contemporary scene, for an air of nostalgia pervaded most of them, as if their writers were seeking to preserve a bygone era which the expanding industrialism of the post-war period was destroying. By the late 1880's the local color story had run its course. Having become fully as standardized as the sentimental romances that Hawthorne had condemned thirty years before, it elicited both the scorn of the "veritists" and the sarcasm of bored editors who had grown surfeited with the reign of dialect in "corrupt English." But before the vein played out, the many writers of local color stories had clearly demonstrated as never before how infinitely varied were the materials of fiction in America and how handily the short story form could make use of them. It is hardly coincidental, therefore, that at the peak of its local color vogue the short story was officially "discovered" by writers and critics who now resurrected Poe's theories and reapplied them.

The writers most prominently associated with this rediscovery of the short story were Thomas Bailey Aldrich, H. C. Bunner, and Brander Matthews, who formulated anew in 1885 the so-called laws governing the form and for the first time used the term "short story" to designate it. These laws, though apparently new at the time, were merely Poe's principles rephrased and extended; but more significant than the mere restating of the principles were the new technical effects which these writers produced. Their "well-made" story was interesting chiefly for its emphasis on technique, the consciousness of form implicit in it, rather than for its subject matter, which was realistic only to the extent that representative individuals from two or three social groups could be identified in it. Stories of this type ranged in content and tone all the way from the light foolery of Frank Stockton's "The Lady, or the Tiger?" to the tartly ironic cross purpose of Aldrich's "Two Bites at a Cherry"; yet all shared a quality which was new to the fiction of the time, a deliberate concern over the manner of presenting the story most effectively. To achieve their aims, leading writers applied to the rich body of American materials being exploited by the local colorists methods originally adapted from Poe by French artists like Daudet and De Maupassant. Ingenuity in contrived situations and dexterity in manipulated incidents, along with compression, vivacity, and wit in characterization, became the hallmarks of the "well-made" story—as opposed to the somewhat greater emphasis placed on setting and dialect in the local color story. The chief emphasis of the "well-made" story lay upon a carefully worked out pattern of events moving swiftly toward a sharp climax and sudden denouement, with suspense as the *sine qua non*. Aldrich's "Marjorie Daw," an ingenious tale dating from the 1870's, served as the model for similarly contrived stories by Matthews, Stockton, and Bunner; the "amusing twist of surprise at the end of it" was the supreme mark of dexterity which inspired them. Such stories were less numerous during this period than the local color variety, partly because they required greater skill to bring off successfully; partly, perhaps, because at first their relatively sophisticated make-up lacked the broad democratic appeal of local color stories. However, as more and more writers caught on to the trickery and artifice needed to produce sharp, dramatic effects, and paid less and less attention to characterization and theme, the type degenerated into the standardized "plot story," which dominated the popular magazines of succeeding generations.

Since the full flowering of realism depends on the truthful portrayal of individual human character, the foremost realists will be those who have imaginatively created the largest number of most fully realized individuals. By this criterion the short story form is almost ruled out of consideration in the ultimate reaches of realism because its limited scope prevents the writer from developing even in one character the multitudinous minutiae required to set that character apart from all other individuals, let alone enabling the writer to create a social pattern of such individuals. For this reason the three major writers of the period, Twain, Howells, and James, owe their reputation as realists to their novels rather than to their short stories. It would be hard to find within any five-year span three greater American masterpieces of realistic fiction than James' *The Portrait of a Lady* (1881), Twain's *The Adventures of Huckleberry Finn* (1884), and Howells' *The Rise of Silas Lapham* (1885); but while all three of their authors figure prominently in the rise of realism, neither Twain nor Howells devoted much attention to the short story. Twain was altogether too dynamic a figure to be roped and branded by a single tag. He was humorist, realist, local colorist, romanticist, and satirist all in one, and thus uniquely representative of the America of his time. And although Howells became the high priest of realism, setting forth its canons with utmost clarity in his *Criticism and Fiction* (1891) and vigorously championing its cause during his long editorial career, as a practicing realist he is remembered chiefly for his thirty-odd novels, which showed a deepening interest in human character—particularly in character confronted with ethical problems. The story "Editha," an excellent example of the analysis of conflicting ethical values, is one of the very few shorter pieces he attempted in the third type of realistic problem fiction. James, on the other hand, gave virtually as much study and care to the art of the short story as to that of the novel. Beginning in the 1860's and working steadily for forty years, he produced an imposing number of stories of such finished artistry that his reputation, especially among writers, stands higher today than ever before.

James, however, has never been a popular writer, even to the extent that Poe and Hawthorne were popular in their day; for the problem he set himself, to create flawless stories embodying and

dramatizing the subtlest of psychological conflicts, proved to be too fastidious an aim for the general public. James regarded fiction as a form of art and the writer of fiction as an artist, whose obligation was to create a nearly perfect illusion of life. To do this would be to produce stories whose form and substance were inseparably fused and indistinguishable from each other. Going beyond terms like realism and romanticism, he argued that the imaginative writer should strive to catch the color and texture of life and convert "the very pulses of the air into revelations"; for only by such means could he hope to achieve in story form a work of art which would be "a living thing, all one and continuous, like any other organism." In his own efforts to achieve such a harmonious union of meaning and form, James' short stories, though less rich in texture than his novels, often show him at his best, besides offering sharper insights into the underlying purpose of his art. This purpose, like Hawthorne's, is the revelation of some psychological truth hidden beneath the surface facts of life in the motives and actions of the human mind and heart. Having posited a world in which moral values are not merely of primary but almost of exclusive importance, James' major interest did not center upon the obvious clashes of temperament and passion which go on all about us in everyday experience; it centered rather upon the undisclosed reasons which cause highly civilized men and women to think and act in certain ways when confronted with inescapable moral problems. His heroes and heroines, accordingly, do not strive for the ordinary prizes of everyday life—money, glory, prestige—but instead for the much greater prizes of self-realization and the preservation of their individual integrity, which can only be won by submitting to the most rigorous of tests and making difficult decisions entirely on their own responsibility. This was the essential reality of life as James saw it. To create a faithful illusion of it in fiction which his readers would be compelled to accept as meaningful and interesting, he gradually worked out a method that managed to convey dramatically both the external action involved in a complex experience and the inner significance of that action.

In order that the reader might get the feeling of looking directly at a significant bit of life unfolding before his eyes, everything that happened in the story and the meaning of everything that happened was to be presented from a single point of view, or center of revelation. Ordinarily this center of revelation was fixed in the mind of one of the characters who, at the outset of the story, possessed no more knowledge of the situation which was about to develop than

did the reader himself. Thus the reader, as though standing directly behind this observing character, would discover for himself both the events occurring before his eyes and the complex implications of those events in the same way as the observer because there would be no gratuitous information about them supplied during the story's unfolding, no help from the author, explaining the meaning of this or that character's real intentions in saying or doing a certain thing. Every turn of events must fall logically within the range of this observing character's impressions; every meaning and every evaluation must grow organically out of his own process of discovery. By means of this method James could direct the course of the story entirely from behind the scenes and achieve simultaneously both an objective presentation of situation, characters, and events, and a subjective evaluation of their significance. It not only preserved the illusion of reality, but also communicated with the fullest immediacy every sensation evoked by the experience.

To achieve both the illusion and the fullness of lifelike situations James strove constantly to design plots packed with significant incidents, yet firmly contained within a shapely, uncluttered form, so that his short stories might become "like the hard shining sonnet, one of the most indestructible forms of composition in general use." For him, therefore, the writing of every story posed the problem of reconciling the opposing thrusts of matter and form, and in his efforts to deal with this problem he worked out another dramatic technique—the "scenic" method—which has since become a standard feature of serious contemporary fiction. Many of his stories are comparable to stage plays in that their most significant action occurs in a series of scenes which bring several characters face to face with the problem at hand, and it is thus conveyed to the reader through the dialogue. Essentially the same method is employed by Hemingway in "The Killers," in which nearly all the climactic tension is developed and communicated through several conversations, although the clipped, monosyllabic dialogue of Hemingway's lowbrow characters is quite different from the elaborate conversational fencing of James' refined sophisticates. More than any other single element, perhaps, this circumlocutory quality of James' style, which becomes so involved in his "later manner" that many readers find it disturbing, has severely restricted his audience to a small circle of enthusiasts. Once this difficulty of style is mastered, however, there is little tendency to question either the permanence of James' artistic achievement or the importance of his contribution to the development of fiction in the

short story. For his best stories are perennially absorbing, capable of being reread many times with profit and amusement; moreover, his technical innovations, such as the restricted point of view and the subjective inner drama, have remained standard in the serious fiction of today. Virtually every significant writer of the twentieth century owes something to his craftsmanship.

The fiction of Howells and James, with its emphasis on the highest ideals of both ethical motivation and artistic craftsmanship, brought more sharply into focus than ever before the cleavage in American fiction between serious art for the few and standardized entertainment for the many. While the popular magazine story remained essentially the same rehash of old formulas, the work of serious artists continued developing experimentally from the point to which James, Howells, and Twain had brought the realism of their day. This development proceeded in two parallel paths: first, the artists' increasing concern over socio-economic problems, which extended the concept of realism into the realm of social protest; and second, their reaction against the genteel formalism and exclusiveness in the art of the older realists.

from realism to naturalism: 1890-1920

In the period from 1890 to 1920, the machine age developed fully, intensifying along with its growth all the problems common to an urban industrial society. During these years the United States nearly doubled its population again, shifting meanwhile from a predominantly rural and agricultural nation to a great industrial power; during the same period the nation emerged through two more wars from relative isolation and self-centeredness to a position of involvement and eventual leadership in the affairs of the whole world. Inevitably, the vast expansion in all lines of activity which accounted for these fundamental changes made itself felt directly and indirectly in the work of American writers, augmenting on the one hand the volume of their product and requiring on the other a reassessment of their values. With the advent of the five- and ten-cent weekly magazines, supported by advertising and brightened by modern methods of printing and illustration, the reading public in America multiplied, and the demand for short fiction increased accordingly. A mass market was created for the short story, just as it was for the automobile, and both products became

increasingly standardized. The financial rewards to successful writers in this highly competitive field kept pace with its growth, so that in time the author whose stories appeared regularly in *Collier's* or the *Saturday Evening Post* could flaunt the income of a bank president. But more and more American writers were forced to choose whether they would serve art or mammon, for the price of success in the popular commercial field was an inflexible pattern of writing which led eventually to sterility. Thus, the struggle to reconcile these conflicting pressures, to maintain high standards of craftsmanship and artistic integrity despite the lure of profit in mass entertainment, has been one of the most characteristic phenomena in twentieth-century American literature.

Above the level of sheer entertainment, the serious fiction of this period reflected the stresses and strains of modern life in other ways, taking on deeper tones of pessimism and determinism as well as extending the implications of realism to include harsher and more unpleasant aspects of life than earlier realists had cared to investigate. Realism, in short, developed a tendency to pry beneath the smiling surface of the average which Howells had characterized as typical of America and to expose to view conditions which he and James in particular had preferred to leave unexplored. In its progress toward the ultimate extreme of unabashed frankness, realism thus passed through two further stages, one growing out of the other. The first stage, identifiable in the fiction of social and economic protest, may be seen at its best, perhaps, in the early stories of Hamlin Garland, with their emphasis upon the injustices suffered by Midwestern farmers in the 1880's under the tyranny of corporate ownership, or in Howells' later novels, which attempt to dramatize specific instances of industrial strife, such as railway strikes and lockouts. The second stage introduced into American fiction a new literary movement called *naturalism,* which has remained till now a disturbing yet highly provocative force in modern literature.

An offshoot of modern scientific inquiry, naturalism promulgated a concept of man and his relation to nature and society totally different from the older view of the nineteenth century and thus became responsible for changing both the content and the form of contemporary prose fiction. In place of the artistic and moral standards of the earlier period, which were grounded in a philosophy of optimistic idealism, naturalism substituted a set of standards based on a skeptical, deterministic view of the universe. Under the older system of belief, carefully plotted stories emphasizing moral and spiritual themes—beauty,

faith, ethical purpose—were the norm, since the universe itself had been conceived of as a divine and purposeful plan, in which man's actions were inspired by divine motives and judged on the basis of his "free will" choice between good and evil. Stressing the moral conduct of the individual, such stories could be made to dramatize conflicts which proceeded logically to a climax and resolution consistent with the accepted moral code for distinguishing between right and wrong: goodness, truth, and beauty might be made triumphant, evil and ugliness suppressed, because God's eternal verities were believed to work out that way. From the naturalistic point of view, however, any such attempt to re-create divinely inspired patterns of human behavior in literature became meaningless, as the naturalist saw the universe itself as a purposeless complex of blind forces, a vast mechanism of which man is a very insignificant part. Far from being accountable for his actions, the individual in a naturalistic world has no control whatever over his destiny but must follow the inexorable pattern designed for him by his heredity and environment. His actions might be interpreted in terms of these controlling factors, but since "free will" has nothing to do with his behavior, to propose moral judgments on it or to label some men good and some bad would be patently absurd. Strictly speaking, there can be neither heroes nor villains in naturalistic fiction, since there are no longer any spiritual values for differentiating between them.

Having thrown overboard the traditional ideals of human conduct, the naturalists therefore sought and found new modes of expression for the patterns of behavior which they regarded as significant. Pretending to take a detached, scientific view of life (like that of a chemist or biologist examining matter under a microscope), they analyzed men's actions on the basis of the inner, biological forces or the external social and economic forces controlling them. Like the scientist, too, they believed *all* life to be equally significant and therefore determined to examine all the facts, the unlovely and ignoble, the revolting and the coarse, as well as those which had heretofore been socially acceptable. Naturalism, in short, refused to recognize the sacredness of old taboos, literary or otherwise, with the result that the form as well as the content of modern prose fiction was torn apart and subjected to all manner of experimentation. Whereas formerly the characters in fiction could be defined as consistent human beings, acting in accordance with the normal human patterns of behavior common to their station in life, they were now presented as mere fragmentary bundles of impressions, delusions, or frustrations, victims of the outer forces of industrialism or the inner forces of biological necessity. And since the individual had ceased to be a whole person and was no longer regarded as a responsible agent of society, the methods of re-creating him in fiction became widely exploratory, varying in each case with the writer's own preconceptions as to which were the facets of his personality most deserving of portrayal. For some writers such portrayal meant a relatively objective presentation of men and women driven by their impulses into open violation of social conventions; for others, it implied a subjective study of the mazes of the human mind itself. But whether predominantly objective or subjective in method, the new fiction brushed aside all restraints as irrelevant, becoming by turns bold, reckless, brutal, cynical, bawdy, tender, and sympathetic. Accordingly, the most obvious effect of naturalism in American fiction was to make readers more intensely aware of the animalistic side of human nature than they had ever been before; and as a result the guardians of traditional morality, clamoring from pulpit and editorial page, denounced the more extreme naturalists as pornographers and sensation mongers. From the artistic point of view, however, a more important effect of naturalism, too often ignored by conventional moralists, is apparent in the increased vigor, honesty, and sensitivity which characterize the serious short story today as compared with that of 1900. Because of the influence of naturalism, few areas of American life have been left unexplored and no realms of being can any longer be regarded unworthy of creative representation, for the philosophy of naturalism has broadened the scope and deepened the perception of living American writers, regardless of whether they subscribe to its basic tenets or not.

In the short story the first steps toward the goal of a franker realism were taken in the 1890's by Hamlin Garland and Mary E. Wilkins Freeman, whose work represented a new, if not very daring, departure from the conventional local color fiction of that era. Garland consciously rebelled against the implications of this type of writing and the restrictions imposed by the genteel tradition upon its realism, a term he scorned and tried to replace by the word "veritism." Feeling that both the local colorists and the genteel realists had falsified or sentimentalized the American scene, especially that part of it which he knew best, the raw, unlovely Midwestern prairies of his youth, he was determined to tell the truth about it. He remembered that life, not as a picturesque round of pastoral episodes engaged in by happy farming folk, but as a heroically tragic, almost futile struggle against great odds. Endless, profitless drudgery, grinding poverty, loneliness, and the abuses of grasping landlords and monopolies—these were the characteristics of rural life on the plains which Garland felt impelled to exhibit, "not as the summer boarder or the young lady novelist sees it—but as the working farmer endures it." His burning resentment against such a life found expression in the two volumes, *Main-Travelled Roads* (1891) and *Prairie Folks* (1893), which contain almost the only enduring stories of his long, prolific career. The distinction of the thirty stories in these collections is due to both their passionate sincerity and their freshness of execution. Written without obvious concessions to sentimentality, each records honestly an episode in the drama of western settlement; each is an attempt on the writer's part to stand "alone before Nature and before Life" with no thought of embellishing either to suit the conventional tastes of his reading public. Yet, implicit in all of them is that strain of humanitarian zeal which has often moved the American creative writer to protest in periods of economic stress. Garland was one of the first to turn the short story into an instrument of social significance, but the measure of his success as an artist may be judged by the fact that while the propaganda of the 1880's is now dead, these few stories of his are still readable.

What his "veritism" did for the local color portrayal of the Middle West, Mrs. Freeman's art accomplished for New England, though with less emphasis upon social protest. Her forte was depicting the granitic characters of ordinary New England village folk in a style as flinty as their own lives. During a long career she wrote well over two hundred stories, most of them characterized by careful workmanship, sincerity, and sympathetic insight into human motives; but like Garland, her fame rests primarily upon the achievement of her first two collections, *A Humble Romance and Other Stories* (1887) and *A New England Nun and Other Stories* (1891). The distinctive qualities of the fifty-odd stories in these volumes are of two sorts: their accuracy of portraiture, aided by an abundant use of dialect, which is skillfully employed as a dramatic characterizing device; and their incisive presentation of those ineradicable vestiges among New Englanders of the Puritan inner life, its inhibitions and smouldering passions, as well as its rigidly Old Testament standards of loyalty, honor, and integrity. Thus, they record with quiet effectiveness the somber side of a declining civilization, which yet clung tenaciously to old values and mores.

During the same decade of the 1890's the work of two other writers, Ambrose Bierce and Stephen Crane, demonstrated even more clearly than that of Garland or Mrs. Freeman how the infusion of naturalistic attitudes and methods was deepening the tone of the short story and turning its course into newer paths. Bierce gathered much of his material from Civil War experiences, working it up somewhat in the manner of Poe with an eye toward achieving sensational, melo-dramatic effects. So mordant was the bitterness of these stories, how-ever, that magazines of that day refused to print them. Physical suffering and death, unrelieved by any saving grace of pathos but accentuated rather by a kind of sardonic diablerie, comprised their major substance; and Bierce's chief concern appeared to be a pitiless, almost sadistic revelation of human weaknesses. Many of the stories in his two collections, *In the Midst of Life* (1891) and *Can Such Things Be?* (1893), show the touch of a skilled craftsman. His ability to bring into focus many carefully chosen details which lead swiftly but inexorably toward a horrifying revelation, points unmistakably back to Poe; while the sudden, ironic surprise of his endings and the economy of his method point forward to O. Henry.

A similarly mordant attitude toward human nature and the forces controlling its destiny colored and conditioned the work of Crane, the more significant artist of the two. As seen in his two best collections of stories, *The Open Boat and Other Tales of Adventure* (1898) and *The Monster and Other Stories* (1899), life represented to him an endless series of ironic contradictions, which he strove to re-create objectively through the medium of symbol and paradox. There were seldom any plots of the conventional sort in his stories, just as there were no heroic figures, no leaders or ideal types. Often name-less, his characters, like Bierce's, are often defeated in an unequal struggle against the superior force of an indifferent universe; but the question of how they face up to this struggle at a moment of crisis is their story. Moreover, while Bierce's mannerisms and his unvariedly sardonic tone make his treatment of similar materials seem contrived, Crane's intensity of vision and his determination to keep aloof from his characters impart to his best stories that illusion of actuality which James described as "a direct impression of life." His achievement of this illusion is due to his style, a seemingly loose collection of brilliant fragments which, on closer inspection, turns out to be based on a carefully patterned arrangement of images and symbols disclosing interrelated meanings which add up to a convincing re-creation of experience. Crane did not attempt either to paint the whole scene with all its documentary minutiae or to tailor the situation and events into a "well-made" plot; instead, he presented the total experience in terms of those fragmentary portions of it which his characters were able to comprehend, often dimly or mistakenly, at any given moment. By minimizing the importance of plot construction and at the same time suggesting the inscrutable complexity of a universe in which human beings are helplessly involved, Crane became one of the first naturalists in American literature, blazing a trail for such later writers as Theodore Dreiser, John Dos Passos, and James T. Farrell. But in his use of precise, colorful imagery, as well as in his economy and respect for point of view, he also pointed the way toward the widely varied styles of writers like Willa Cather and Ernest Hemingway. By virtue of both temperament and technique, therefore, Crane revealed a closer affinity with diverse twentieth-century writers than any other artist of his time.

During Crane's brief career various other writers ventured into naturalistic fiction, notably Frank Norris and Jack London, but among those whose work has left the deepest impress upon contemporary fiction the names of Theodore Dreiser and, a little later, Sherwood Anderson stand pre-eminent, the one for his massive handling of objective detail, the other for his sensitive analysis of personality. Dreiser saw life as a gigantic but utterly purposeless struggle in which men and women are all "more or less pawns . . . moved about like chessmen by circumstances over which [they] have no control." Everyone, he felt, was driven by a love of power or a desire for self-realization through sexual or artistic achievement, but for most men, even the strongest, either defeat or frustration was to be the inevitable goal of all their striving. In Dreiser's world, a grim, humorless place, the race is always to the swift and the battle to the mighty; but while he depicts with scrupulous honesty and a mass of convincing detail the dominance of strong-willed characters over their weaker or less fortunate competitors, their triumph offers no grounds for exultation, since it is achieved at the expense of the many who fail. For these, Dreiser manifests a deep, abiding pity, buttressed by his dogged accumulation of objective facts which leave little to the reader's imagination to surmise or misinterpret. As a result, Dreiser's primary virtues, honesty, sincerity, and a massive power of expression, cannot be effaced by what is regarded by some critics as the clumsiest style in modern American prose. The sensitive reader is often annoyed by his tortured, ungrammatical sentences, his inelegant, cliché-ridden phrasing, his pointless repetitions and undiscriminating choice of detail. Yet despite these artistic flaws—serious enough to have sunk any lesser writer—the overall effect of Dreiser's stories is profoundly moving.

A more conscious artist than Dreiser, Anderson likewise accepted to a certain extent the naturalistic interpretation of modern industrial society as a huge swindle in which the sensitive individual is tricked and robbed, his normal instincts distorted by the artificial restraints and materialistic standards of his environment. But where Dreiser tended to dramatize the outer scene of conflict responsible for these frustrations, Anderson sought instead to objectify the inner warpings of personality produced within the individual by the clash between his urges and the mores of his society. To present this inner experience dramatically Anderson felt that he must find a new form which would avoid the artificiality of the obviously plotted story, for he was certain that "there were no plot short stories ever lived in any life I had known anything about." In his search for a form he was aided and encouraged by Gertrude Stein, who showed him how form, through the skillful selection and arrangement of words in common speech, might be made to grow "out of the materials of the tale and the teller's reaction to them." The first noteworthy result of this discovery was his *Winesburg, Ohio* (1919), a collection of interrelated stories hailed by many critics as a landmark in the development of the contemporary American short story, not so much because of the radical departure from traditional forms which Anderson thought he had achieved in it, but rather because it revitalized and combined older methods of storytelling which had fallen into disuse. In the *Winesburg* stories Anderson revived the methods employed by Hawthorne and Melville in their efforts to probe the recesses of the human mind, but he made those methods more flexible by combining with them a technique similar to that of the apparently artless narrator device in the frontier "mock oral" tale. In Anderson's best stories, therefore, the quality of the narrator's personality and the way he tells a remembered experience are as important to the total effect as are the events he has to tell. As the narrator begins to tell his story, he often confesses a mixed feeling of oppressiveness and bewilderment, and as he proceeds in the telling he may have to pause occasionally to reassure himself that his recollection of the events is correct, that his mind has control of their significance. But Anderson himself, the creative mind outside the story, does have this control; so that what results as the story unfolds is a complex structure developing along several different levels at the same time: the events themselves, the feelings and memory of the narrator who recalls his involvement in them, and the underlying related significance of all three which, though present for the reader, lies outside the narrator's awareness.

Unfortunately, Anderson could not keep such a firm grip as this on his medium; but in a few of his later stories, such as "The Egg" and "Death in the Woods," he did fulfill the promise of his early hopes.

Whatever their limitations, Dreiser and Anderson stand together with Crane as pioneer figures whose efforts to liberate American fiction from the shackles of conventional attitudes and methods encouraged the widespread experimentation in form and technique which has characterized the last forty years of the short story's development and kept it vigorously alive as an art form. Their efforts were all the more noteworthy in that they had to overcome persistent, often violent opposition, for up to 1920 and beyond, both the tenets and the exponents of naturalism were bitterly assailed in the United States. And yet, even though few of our present-day writers can be ticketed as naturalists pure and simple, the pervasive influence of this movement is plainly visible in the work of many. As new experiences arising from the widespread violence and suffering of contemporary life have brought a new awareness of impending chaos to larger numbers of the reading public, the extreme attitudes and the sensationalism for which our early naturalists were censured no longer seem quite so abnormal, while the methods they devised for expressing themselves have been quietly appropriated, even by our popular writers.

post-naturalism — tradition and experimentation: 1920 to the present

Living conditions in the United States since World War I have altered so radically and often that only a decade-by-decade summary of specific changes could hope to achieve a reasonably accurate generalization of the underlying patterns of social and literary development growing out of them. As the feverish "jazz age" of the 1920's gave way to the grim depression years of the 1930's, and those in turn to the anxious war years of the 1940's, the nation's ups and downs presented anything but a sense of orderly, progressive growth. All these rapid developments, however, were but a prelude to the feverish pace of economic expansion in the 1950's and to that decade's counterbalancing anxieties produced by the "cold war" between East and West. Recurring national hysteria over such things as the McCarthy spectacle and the civil rights "freedom rides," though offset by spectacular advances in nuclear physics, space exploration, and national defense, pointed unmistakably to the menacingly divisive forces at work in both the nation and the world at large—forces symbolized by the Berlin Wall, our commitments in Southeast Asia and Africa, the Castro problem in Latin America, and our agonizing problem of racial disharmony at home, and climaxed by the shocking assassination of President Kennedy. Only the perspective of time, therefore, can disclose whether there has been during this period any dominant literary movement to match those of earlier periods, or whether the period has been merely an uneasy transitional stage between one great age and another. But while it would be premature to attempt any precise generalizations about American life and literature in the past forty years, it is evident that certain new influences, both foreign and domestic, have been at work altering still further the living and thinking habits which were standard in 1920. One obvious result of America's participation in two world wars, for example, has been to make the nation bigger, richer, and more powerful than ever before. The psychological implications of this growth, however, are perhaps even more important than the sociological and economic ones, for besides forcing millions of its citizens to readjust their personal aims and hopes, the nation's rise to its present stage of perilous pre-eminence in the world has developed among many of its writers a mature sense of international ties such as only a few of their predecessors possessed. This broadening awareness of America's increasing involvement in world affairs has been accompanied by a correspondingly greater receptivity to European intellectual currents, which have had much to do with shaping the imaginative literature of our time. After World War I the impact of Sigmund Freud's ideas and methods in the field of psychoanalysis became noticeably prominent in American writing, and the Freudian interpretation of character and experience has continued as a dominant strain in our fiction down to the present. Out of this broad influence have come such others as the "stream of consciousness" technique inherited from Marcel Proust and James Joyce, and the freedom of form contributed by Chekhov. Still another powerful influence, its force greatly augmented by the severity of a world-wide economic depression in the 1930's, was the proletarian movement initiated by Karl Marx and fostered by the rapid growth of Soviet Russia. Scarcely a piece of serious American fiction written between 1920 and 1950 can be fully understood without some awareness of the import of these influences, as one or another of them (sometimes several at once) has had something to do with the nature and presentation of American materials in the short story.

As a result of these and other influences already noted, the short story now presents a bewildering array of attitudes, philosophies, forms, and styles. Out of this welter of conflicting modes and methods of expression several dominant patterns may yet be traced, but the underlying drift which gives meaning to most of them is apparently a search for positive values to take the place of those lost in the breakdown of nineteenth-century assumptions. Clearly one of the most prevalent attitudes in contemporary fiction is the growing concern, expressed or implied, over the shrinking of the individual's role in a modern, mechanistic world. This feeling that the individual, becoming more and more submerged in the mass, has lost or is losing his identity and importance as a person, doubtless accounts for much of the somberness, as well as the violence and starkness found in today's fiction. What ideals can a man safely live by and still survive in a push-button, atomic age? This is a major problem haunting not only the Faulkners, Hemingways, and Steinbecks, pioneers in extending the range of the modern short story, but also the younger craftsmen who have followed their lead. At bottom, therefore, the serious short story of today may be regarded as a search for truth in twentieth-century terms.

The truth often differs for different writers, however, and their methods of truth telling vary widely, depending upon their individual biases and backgrounds. Consequently, no simple classifications or distinguishing labels can be applied to any of our major contemporary short story writers, as the individuality of their styles makes each a special problem in analysis and appreciation. Yet, several broad categories may be discerned among them. In one group, for example, there are the conservatives or traditionalists, writers like Edith Wharton, Willa Cather, F. Scott Fitzgerald, and Wilbur D. Steele, who carried on the Poe-De Maupassant-James tradition, refining the techniques present in the older "well-made" plot story. In another group there are the experimentalists like Hemingway, Faulkner, William Carlos Williams, and Eudora Welty, who have been much the more influential in extending the range of the short story as a literary form. A still larger group, however, falls somewhere between these two extremes, writers like Lardner, Kay Boyle, Steinbeck, and Shaw inclining rather toward the conservative group, and others like Caldwell, Nelson Algren, Katherine Anne Porter, William Saroyan, and J. F. Powers, toward the experimental one. But even such a loose classification as this may be too inflexible to suggest the occasional deviations which most of these writers have made from their usual methods. The youngest writers especially, such as Truman Capote, Peter Taylor, Bernard Malamud, Flannery O'Connor, and John Updike, have shown remarkable versatility in presenting the human scene with sharpened insights and from fresh points of view. In their eagerness to avoid the trap of imitation and to develop individual styles of their own, they have published stories ranging in mode all the way from the literally representational to the allegorical and the grotesque.

Of the three groups, the aims and methods of the traditionalists are easiest to identify and describe because their basic intention has remained consistently understandable: namely, to write interesting, well-wrought stories without departing radically from the conventional plot framework and standard devices for evoking suspense through the interaction of character and incident. Their stories are thus more nearly like the standardized commercial stories, though elevated above the mediocrity of the popular magazine types by virtue of the more careful artistry and the greater degree of honesty informing them. Willa Cather's stories, for example, of which "The Sculptor's Funeral" is one of the most satisfying specimens, are marked by a deftness in the handling of expository material and a depth of feeling for character which tend to hide the conventionality of their structure. Moreover, her style, based upon a consciously developed theory of restraint and selectivity, transforms the most commonplace materials into enduring prose. At the hands of Fitzgerald and Boyle, likewise, the traditional type of short story gained distinction, freshness, and occasionally moral depth and power. And yet, for all the ingenuity displayed by these writers, their type of story, has lost its former sure-fire appeal as the more daring innovations of the experimentalists have gradually shouldered aside the constructed plot story.

Except insofar as these experimentalists share a common antipathy to the formally plotted story, their aims and methods are not so readily classifiable as those of the traditionalists, for their reaction against prescriptions and rules has taken many forms. Some of them incline toward naturalism, extending the themes expressed by Dreiser and Anderson and employing variations of their methods; others disavow all connection with that or any other movement and yet have devised daring new methods of their own to interpret the life they know as honestly and effectively as they can. Some are primarily objective in their approach to it, relying chiefly on realistic devices; others are primarily subjective, consciously employing such nonrealistic devices as fantasy, symbol, and dream sequence to enrich their interpretation; and still others combine the two methods, often in the same story.

Among the primarily objective writers the most familiar name, of course, is that of Ernest Hemingway, whose stories reveal a strong undercurrent of compassion and admiration for the people he created, together with an equally strong determination not to parade these feelings but to convey them cleanly and directly (without "cheating," as he liked to put it, meaning void of lofty preachments) in terms of sharp reactions to physical sensations. In Hemingway's stories one finds almost no concern for the ordinary practical situations of business and family life, possibly because he regards these as secondary activities, incidental to the more urgent need felt by the individual to wrest what satisfactions he can from a universe devoid of meaning. Determined throughout his career to put down on paper only what he really felt, not what he was supposed or expected to feel, Hemingway demonstrated his hatred of sham and hypocrisy by reducing life to its barest terms and judging it on the sole basis of primary emotions—love, hate, fear, hunger, thirst, pain, sex. With simplicity and truth as his double aim, he has created a world in which morality is measured, not by conventional standards, but in these same primary terms ("I know only that what is moral is what you feel good after"); and he has peopled this world with characters whose worth is apparent by what they leave unsaid in the presence of fundamental situations involving love, danger, and death. To maintain one's courage, dignity, and integrity; to keep a "stiff upper lip" against overwhelming pressures; to salvage something of basic human worth out of a messy world, if only one's self-respect—these are the distinguishing marks of Hemingway's heroes. In a style deliberately contrived to dramatize this attitude of tight-lipped suppression of feeling, ironic understatement and simple but subtle repetitions furnish the keynotes. Hemingway has reduced everything in his stories—description, narrative, exposition, characterization, dialogue—to the status of the simple predication. Subordinate clauses and modifications, the language of logic and intellectual sophistication, are seldom found; for Hemingway's aim is to record brusquely yet sensitively the behavior and speech of people who are either nonintellectual or anti-intellectual. Hence the tone and idiom of these characters, their vocabulary as well as their syntax, flavor the narrative portions no less than the dialogue of the story. Their speech is colloquial and low-brow, their dialogue, lean and bare; the things they talk about are few and commonplace and undeveloped. Yet these things are set forth in subtly varied rhythms, suggesting implications cunningly woven into the tone and texture of a casual remark, which heighten the mood or emotion and intensify the effect desired. As a result, in the best of Hemingway's stories powerful irony and deep sentiment are communicated forcefully and dramatically, with few overt hints from the author.

During the depression years of the 1930's many other writers used variations of Hemingway's objective method to dramatize the evils of poverty and unemployment in both urban and rural settings. Algren, Farrell, Dos Passos, Halper, and Weidman all helped develop the vein of proletarian fiction that characterized the violence and degradation of metropolitan life during that decade, while Erskine Caldwell, the most prolific of the lot, exploited all the shocking social conditions prevalent among the rural poor whites and Negroes of backwoods Georgia. As artist, Caldwell was more successful than most of his contemporaries because he adroitly dramatized the ignorance, filth, superstition, disease, cruelty, and perversion of these unfortunate folk in situations and incidents that make their outrageously unorthodox behavior seem both horrifying and ludicrous at the same time. But the difficulties of maintaining Hemingway's or Caldwell's detachment of tone and point of view in the treatment of such material evidently proved too great to master, since little of the relatively objective fiction of those years any longer carries the weight of conviction it was thought to have upon first appearance. Except in the hands of a first-rate artist, the technique does not appear to lend itself too readily to a convincing depiction of life; for as soon as it becomes too closely allied to social purpose it runs the risk of degenerating into sheer melodramatic propaganda, and even when used with a frankly satiric intent, as in the manner of Ring Lardner, it fails to satisfy a normal human craving for the heroic and the ideal. Accordingly, many of the writers employing this method have wisely modified it with an element of the subjective. Steinbeck, Kay Boyle, William Carlos Williams, and Irwin Shaw have all demonstrated this tendency.

On the whole, the inner world of the human mind has proved a more fruitful field for experimentation in recent fiction than the outer world of social action for the simple reason that the life of the mind presents infinitely more varied nuances of being than does the external scene. Consequently, as Freud's seminal ideas regarding the nature of human personality gradually gained wider circulation, more and more writers seized upon the myriad possibilities offered by those ideas for dramatizing the conflicts of the psyche, and the methods open to such exploitation have been as varied as the richness of the material itself. Among the devices employed by writers working in the subjective, for example, are fantasy, symbol, myth, allegory, reverie, dream processes, and the telescoping of past and present, all of which are adaptable to the technique of a free association of ideas and can be used in many different ways to achieve a richer illusion of life than is possible in objective fiction alone. Thus a writer like Faulkner, one of the most versatile of modern artists in prose fiction, developed through these means a great many stories in which the power, intensity, and richness of human experience are felt on every page.

Faulkner's pre-eminence in contemporary fiction, however, results not so much from his technical versatility as from the boldness of his creative imagination. Yoknapatawpha County, Mississippi—"Area, 2400 Square Miles: Population, Whites, 6298; Negroes, 9313: William Faulkner, Sole Owner & Proprietor"—is his own imagined world, a microcosm of individuals who live fully in their own right, their lives elaborately documented with genealogical evidence, but who also serve, like stones in a mosaic, the purposes of a grand design. There is thus a symbolic value in this "legend of the South," which some critics have interpreted as a commentary on the contrast between an older way of life based on a code of traditional values and disciplines and a modern one in which those values and disciplines have been lost sight of, a commentary that might well be extended beyond the borders of the South and applied to our modern world as a whole. And there is in it likewise a deeply felt tragic theme, intricately bound up with the lives and relationships of these men and women, Negroes and whites: it is a theme of virtually Biblical proportions and significance involving the timeless myths of race conflict and mankind's perennial struggle to fulfill its destiny on earth and to rid itself of ancestral guilt. To embody this theme in dramatic human action Faulkner created whole families of individual characters—Sartorises, Sutpens, Compsons, McCaslins, Edmondses, MacCallums, Bundrens, Snopeses, Beauchamps—who are so completely delineated and so exhaustively explored from one story to another that the casual reader may often despair of mastering their complexities. The fact that characters in one story will reappear at different stages of their lives and under different guises in other stories, and that cryptic references are made in one story to situations and events lying outside the context of that story but clarified in others, necessarily leads to the mystification of readers who are not acquainted with the whole panorama of Faulkner's unfolding legend. A major obstacle of this sort, for example, is presented in "A Rose for Emily," which might be misread as a mere horror tale of the sort Ambrose Bierce produced in "The Coup de Grâce"; for unless the reader carefully notes the narrator's subtle reference to the passing of time—and especially to the community's changing attitude toward Emily over a long period—he may have some difficulty orienting himself within the environment and period of the story. And he may very likely miss the depth and complexity of Faulkner's vision—the very meaning of the story—whereas one who is familiar with Faulkner's patterned world will recognize that Miss Emily's triumphant pride and independence are among the values that all his heroic figures share.

Many other obstacles besides these are strewn in the reader's path because Faulkner, an incorrigible experimenter, developed numerous methods for handling his narratives, as well as a style which is sometimes so heavily freighted with poetic imagery or psychological speculation that one cannot hack a way through the chaos of his syntax. And yet, for all the difficulties he raises, Faulkner is indeed a born storyteller, who knows how to fascinate his readers with the implied promise of some breathless disclosure to come and to keep them guessing what it will be. In some stories he accomplishes this purpose by the fairly conventional method of characters objectively presented within the framework of a tightly organized plot leading up to a shocking climax, as in "A Rose for Emily." In others he renders the narrative entirely in terms of the mental processes of the characters themselves, making such daring use of the stream-of-consciousness technique that even the disorganized impulses of idiots and imbeciles become organic parts of the story. And in still others, he employs an episodic method which is unified by means of what has been called the "sense of a voice," a narrator who remembers and tells the story as it was told to him but who is not present in the story as a narrator in the formal sense. Like Henry James, Faulkner often demands a great deal from his reader, expects him to become as fully absorbed in the reading as Faulkner himself was in the writing of the story; and more often than not the careful reader is amply rewarded for his pains.

Whatever the technique employed, the best of Faulkner's stories have the quality of being lived and remembered experiences which combine a feeling of mingled compassion, pride, love, and understanding of and for the people and the land he is a part of. For too long a time Faulkner was misunderstood and misrepresented as a kind of literary psychopath, diabolically serving forth a witches' brew compounded of nightmare horrors, sexual abnormalities, violence, bloodshed, and mental derangement. The horror in Faulkner—psychological horror—is certainly there, as it is in the work of Poe, Hawthorne, Melville, and Henry James; but it is balanced by a species of rich, earthy humor, which has become more and more mellow in Faulkner's later stories. No one can read attentively all the episodes in *The Hamlet* or *Go*

Down, Moses and fail to catch this strain in his writing. The humor of "Was" is of the essence of Mark Twain and the frontier tradition in American literature, just as the horror of violence and decadence in "A Rose for Emily" is of the essence of Poe. The one deserves as much emphasis as the other, for the right key to an understanding of Faulkner must be sought in two of his favorite words—"doom" and "endure." Echoing throughout his stories and re-emphasized in his Nobel Prize Award speech, as well as numerous utterances made during his tenure as artist in residence at the University of Virginia, they symbolize his deeply tragic, ambivalent view of humanity and help to explain why his works are so powerful.

The tragic view, however, is only one of many attitudes which may be forcefully conveyed by means of subjective materials and methods. As an instance of two contrasting extremes to which the subjective may be carried, the short stories of Truman Capote and James Thurber spring to mind: Capote's for their flavor of innocent, childlike delight in wish-fulfillment, Thurber's for their ironic exposure of humanity's zaniest moods and antics. Capote manifests something of the same richness of feeling for simple humanity that is to be found in Faulkner, together with a like sympathy for the lowly and deprived and a scorn for the inhuman, but these attitudes are overshadowed by a delicate haze or irony that masks the subtlety of his technique, making it appear as though the story he has to tell is a matter of no great import or literary skill. And yet, much of the beauty in a story like "Jug of Silver" is embedded in the seeming artlessness of its telling: that is, in the clever management of point of view, the choice of a small-town narrator who speaks in his natural, colloquial idiom, slightly stiff and stilted at times, slightly vulgar at others, as he recalls the foibles and peculiarities of a number of wonderfully individualized small-town acquaintances involved in a related series of small-town events remembered from the distant past. The story of Appleseed and his miraculous powers of concentration is thus doubly delightful precisely because it seems to flow effortlessly from the mind of one who makes no pretension to story-telling abilities whatever. In contrast to this studied carelessness, however, the discipline in Thurber's work is felt in the slightest details—the choice of a phrase, or even a single verb or noun, to strike off precisely the right shading of irony which he is trying to achieve. His style itself is thus a source of pleasure to the reader who appreciates the quiet mastery of recalcitrant language, but the quality which makes such control all the more appreciable is the wildly comic imagination to which it is applied. In Thurber's world there are no limits of riotous excess to which the minds of men may go in their efforts to adjust to a crazy-quilt pattern of existence; yet the underlying seriousness implied in their behavior gives a sharp edge to his humor.

Between the two extremes presented in the materials and methods of Faulkner and Thurber can be found numerous other examples of individual talent expressing attitudes of widely varying complexity and intensity in forms ranging from the boldly experimental to the nearly conventional. As is true of the established classics, however, what distinguishes the work of the best of these writers is not so much the novelty of their effects or the boldness of their technical ingenuity, but rather their honesty in confronting the world they know, their sensitivity and sharpness of perception, and their mastery of the materials perceived. Among the several who consistently aim at the highest of these standards are four women writers, Kay Boyle, Katherine Anne Porter, Eudora Welty, and Flannery O'Connor, each in her own way an artist of unmistakably superior rank. Of this group, Miss Boyle's work perhaps comes closest to the standards of the "quality" magazines; it is less daringly experimental in method, though it seldom falls below a high standard of artistic finish. A widely traveled writer, keenly perceptive, Miss Boyle has shown herself to be equally versatile in dealing with materials chosen from Continental or American backgrounds; but her preferences appear to be centered chiefly in metropolitan life, especially in the complex emotional problems of artists and other sophisticated types rather than in the more elemental concerns of simple or primitive life. In developing these materials, she employs both subjective and objective techniques, sometimes shifting from one to the other in the same story as a means of securing the sharpest possible effects with the least expenditure of creative energy.

By contrast with her work the short stories of Katherine Anne Porter are intensely subjective and often super-subtle in effect. An uncompromising perfectionist, Miss Porter is among that small group of serious writers who will release nothing for publication which they feel has not satisfied the highest standards of art. Her work accordingly gives the impression of having been shaped with extraordinary patience and attention to minute detail, scene by scene and incident by incident painstakingly enriched until all the parts have been cunningly and precisely fitted together and every phrase has been made to yield the utmost in poetic suggestiveness. Because such great devotion to the principles of craftsmanship necessarily exacts a high price in the limitation of one's output, Miss Porter has produced scarcely more than half a dozen volumes and a handful of occasional pieces in thirty years, and she has had to wait till the 1960's to achieve the widespread popular acclaim (ironically on the basis of an inferior work, *The Ship of Fools*) which her consummate artistry deserved many years ago. But, such artistry as hers likewise brings its reward in a sense of fullest satisfaction with the experience rendered, as in a story like "Flowering Judas," which sets forth a significant moral theme enriched through the characterizations of Laura and Braggioni by a wealth of subtly suggestive ironies and overtones clothed in symbolic terms.

Symbolic imagery, paradox, and fantasy—present to some extent in the work of many twentieth-century writers, including even primarily objective ones like Hemingway—are among the most distinctive elements employed by those writers who deal in the subjective. Since the subjective is often intangible and abstract, and thus cannot stir the emotions very effectively, symbols are of especial value in providing the necessary link between inner and outer reality. They are the means of reconciling the general and the concrete and, depending upon the skill and subtlety with which they are used, of giving both a broader meaning and a deeper emotional tone to human actions and events. The densely woven fabric of religious symbolism in "Flowering Judas" amply demonstrates why its author has long been reckoned among the foremost short story writers of our time.

Eudora Welty, though differing markedly in her approach to the problems of fiction, has shown equally varied power and skill in her craft. Her first collection, *A Curtain of Green*, received high praise, not only for the freshness and individuality of style which marked all the stories in it, but also for the surprising variety of both subject matter and method presented in them. Combining comedy, pathos, satire, horror, and fantasy, these stories revealed a singleness of purpose, however, in their varied emphasis upon the contrast between external reality and the world of dreams, between the individual's social relationships and the realm of his inner life. Miss Welty's later stories have indicated an increasing interest in this life of the subconscious, which she often renders with great delicacy and charm by means of symbolic representation. At times bordering on the allegorical, as in "Livvie," these later stories are often a tissue of symbols which, when successful, give one simultaneously a double view of life, the vivid pattern of the actual world of time and space, of field hands, cosmetic saleswomen, and aged, dying husbands, inextricably tied to that other world of timeless myths and meanings embodying ancient wisdom and desires.

Still another marked contrast may be seen in the work of Flannery O'Connor, a newcomer to the field during the past decade, whose powerful stories have deservedly brought her reputation to the front rank of contemporary American writers. Firmly based upon the theological doctrines of the Roman Catholic Church, these stories almost invariably concern themselves, as Hawthorne's do, with fundamental problems of the human soul in its quest for salvation. Unlike Hawthorne's, however, the souls of Miss O'Connor's characters are embodied in recognizably three-dimensional human folk, whose problems of adjusting to the violence and conflict within themselves and the world around them are problems inescapably shared by all of us. There is thus a touch of Dante's inferno in all their private hells and a rugged path to trod before attaining the peace of mind that passes understanding. And there is more than a touch of Dante's uncompromising austerity and firm control in this author's portrayal of the human predicament. The full force of "Good Country People" and the beauty of its construction may not at once strike the casual reader unless he discovers the close linkage between its explosive climax and the pattern of character relationships that make such a climax inevitable. For the pathetic Joy Hopewell, her fatuous mother, the diabolical Bible salesman, and the grubby Mrs. Freeman, though quite recognizable as ordinary individuals anywhere in America, also offer a profoundly moving symbolic commentary on a basic dilemma in our modern wasteland. Shared alike by the educated and the ignorant, it has to do with the lack of genuine spiritual conviction amid the artificiality of our functional trappings.

Artistry such as Eudora Welty's, Katherine Anne Porter's, and Flannery O'Conner's may be too fastidious to withstand the corrosion of time, but for the present it cannot be doubted that they have achieved in the short story many subtle effects which would have delighted their most fastidious predecessors before 1900. Together with other established writers like Hemingway, Faulkner, Irwin Shaw, Bernard Malamud, Peter Taylor, and John Updike, they have enriched the form and opened new avenues for its development. These, together with many other fine short story writers who can scarcely be acknowledged by name in this brief context (e.g., J. D. Salinger, John Cheever, Jessamyn West, Shirley Jackson, John O'Hara), find their materials today, as good writers have always done, among the most fundamental concerns of the human race. The individual's desperate need for love and understanding, the pathetic disparity between his ideals and his practices, the dilemmas he must face in adjusting to a world he never made—these are the basic problems. And out of the individual's courage and subterfuges, his versatility and pretentiousness, his follies and failures (as well as his triumphs) in meeting the challenges of daily life in an age of automation and Polaris missiles come the stories which, when they are well done, shock us into laughter and tears by making us see ourselves as others see us. When they are well done, the shock may be as brutal as a blow on the head, such as Malamud delivers in "Take Pity"; or it may come like an ominously reverberating toothache, as in Updike's "The Doctor's Wife"; or from a totally different direction it may bring thoughtful laughter through the medium of light irony such as that developed throughout Taylor's double exposure of "true romance" pretense and practical reality in "Reservations: A Love Story." But there are many more ways than these whereby the serious fiction writers of our time have extended the range and deepened the impact of the short story. Through their efforts the modern American short story has fulfilled the high hopes with which Irving ventured into the creation of this new art form nearly 150 years ago.

Washington Irving

RIP VAN WINKLE

THE STOUT GENTLEMAN

Washington Irving was born in New York City, in 1783, the eleventh child of a prosperous merchant. A frail boy, he traveled abroad (1804-1806) to improve his health and further his education. Although he read for the law, and was admitted to the bar in 1806, he soon abandoned any serious thought of making law his career, preferring instead to turn to writing. His first significant work, *Salmagundi* (1807-1808), written in collaboration with his brother William and James K. Paulding, drew some attention; but it was with his next work, *Diedrich Knickerbocker's History of New York* (1809), that he won literary recognition. He did not immediately follow up this success, however, being occupied during the next half-dozen years with such miscellaneous activities as lobbying in Washington for his brothers' hardware firm, editing the *Analectic Magazine,* and serving as an aide-de-camp to Governor Tompkins. In 1815, he went to England to work in the Liverpool branch of his brothers' firm, but its failure in 1818 caused him to resume writing, this time with the added incentive of earning a livelihood. The first result of his renewed effort, *The Sketch Book,* published serially in England and America in 1819-1820 and in book form in 1820, was an immediate success. Continuing his foreign residence, where he enjoyed the friendship of the leading European writers of the day, he exploited the popularity of *The Sketch Book* in later volumes of similar tales and sketches. When he finally returned to the United States in 1832, after seventeen years abroad, he was internationally famous. He continued an active literary career until his death in 1859, but devoted his energies principally to biographical and historical writing. Among other volumes of his tales and sketches are *Bracebridge Hall* (1822), *Tales of a Traveller* (1824), and *The Alham-*

bra (1832). None of these equals *The Sketch Book* in merit or originality, so that in importance as well as in point of time, *The Sketch Book* is the initial landmark in the history of the American short story.

The first American writer to produce stories of genuine merit, Irving was also among the first to recognize the short story as a distinct form of literature. By asserting that a nicety of execution is required in writings of this kind "in which every page must have its merit," and by embodying this quality in such stories as these two, he demonstrated that the manner of writing fiction is as important as its matter. Although his manner permits him to loiter over detail and to infuse his own genial personality into the story, it also demands that everything in the story fit a broad design and that he keep the reader interested. Most of all, possibly, "nicety of execution" suggests Irving's grace of manner that enables him to transform a German legend into an enduring American story in "Rip," and to fabricate a compelling narrative from trivial material in "The Stout Gentleman."

rip van winkle

a posthumous writing of Diedrich Knickerbocker

> *By Woden, God of Saxons,*
> *From whence comes Wensday, that is Wodensday,*
> *Truth is a thing that ever I will keep*
> *Unto thylke day in which I creep into*
> *My sepulchre*—Cartwright

[*The following Tale was found among the papers of the late Diedrich Knickerbocker, an old gentleman of New York, who was very curious in the Dutch history of the province, and the manners of the descendants from its primitive settlers. His historical researches, however, did not lie so much among books as among men; for the former are lamentably scanty on his favorite topics; whereas he found the old burghers, and still more their wives, rich in that legendary lore so invaluable to true history. Whenever, therefore, he happened upon a genuine Dutch family, snugly shut up in its low-roofed farmhouse under a spreading sycamore, he looked upon it as a little clasped volume of black-letter, and studied it with the zeal of a book-worm.*

The result of all these researches was a history of the province during the reign of the Dutch governors, which he published some years since. There have been various opinions as to the literary character of his work, and, to tell the truth, it is not a whit better than it should be. Its chief merit is its scrupulous accuracy, which indeed was a little questioned on its first appearance, but has since been completely established; and it is now admitted into all historical collections as a book of unquestionable authority.

The old gentleman died shortly after the publication of his work, and now that he is dead and gone, it cannot do much harm to his memory to say that his time might have been much better employed in weightier labors. He, however, was apt to ride his hobby his own way; and though it did now and then kick up the dust a little in the eyes of his neighbors, and grieve the spirit of some friends, for whom he felt the truest deference and affection; yet his errors and follies are remembered "more in sorrow than in anger," and it begins to be suspected that he never intended to injure or offend. But however his memory may be appreciated by critics, it is still held dear by many folks whose good opinion is well worth having; particularly by certain biscuit-bakers, who have gone so far as to imprint his likeness on their new-year cakes; and have thus given him a chance for immortality, almost equal to the being stamped on a Waterloo Medal or a Queen Anne's Farthing.]

Whoever has made a voyage up the Hudson must remember the Kaatskill Mountains. They are a dismembered branch of the great Appalachian family, and are seen away to the west of the river, swelling up to a noble height, and lording it over the surrounding country. Every change of season, every change of weather, indeed, every hour of the day, produces some change in the magical hues and shapes of these mountains, and they are regarded by all the good wives, far and near, as perfect barometers. When the weather is fair and settled, they are clothed in blue and purple and print their bold outlines on the clear evening sky; but sometimes when the rest of the landscape is cloudless, they will gather a hood of gray vapors about their summits, which, in the last rays of the setting sun, will glow and light up like a crown of glory.

At the foot of these fairy mountains, the voyager may have descried the light smoke curling up from a village whose shingle-roofs gleam among the trees just where the blue tints of the upland melt away into the fresh green of the nearer landscape. It is a little village of great antiquity, having been founded by some of the Dutch colonists in the early times of the province, just about the beginning of the government of the good Peter Stuyvesant (may he rest in peace!), and there were some of the houses of the original settlers standing within a few years, built of small yellow bricks brought from Holland, having latticed windows and gable fronts, surmounted with weather-cocks.

In that same village, and in one of these very houses (which, to tell the precise truth, was sadly time-worn and weather-beaten) there lived many years since, while the country was yet a province of Great Britain, a simple good-natured fellow, of the name of Rip Van Winkle. He was a descendant of the Van Winkles who figured so gallantly in the chivalrous days of Peter Stuyvesant, and accompanied him to the siege of Fort Christina. He inherited, however, but little of the martial character of his ancestors. I have observed that he was a simple good-natured man; he was, moreover, a kind neighbor, and an obedient, henpecked husband. Indeed, to the latter circumstance might be owing that meekness of spirit which gained him such universal popularity; for those men are most apt to be obsequious and conciliating abroad who are under the discipline of shrews at home. Their tempers, doubtless, are rendered pliant and malleable in the fiery furnace of domestic tribulation; and a curtain lecture is worth all the sermons in the world for teaching the virtues of patience and long-suffering. A termagant wife may, therefore, in some respects be considered a tolerable blessing; and if so, Rip Van Winkle was thrice blessed.

Certain it is, that he was a great favorite among all the good wives of the village, who, as usual with the amiable sex, took his part in all family squabbles; and never failed, whenever they talked those matters over in their evening gossipings, to lay all the blame on Dame Van Winkle. The children of the village, too, would shout with joy whenever he approached. He assisted at their sports, made their playthings, taught them to fly kites and shoot marbles, and told them long stories of ghosts, witches, and Indians. Whenever he went dodging about the village, he was surrounded by a troop of them, hanging on his skirts, clambering on his back, and playing a thousand tricks on him with impunity; and not a dog would bark at him throughout the neighborhood.

The great error in Rip's composition was an insuperable aversion to all kinds of profitable labor. It could not be from the want of assiduity or perseverance; for he would sit on a wet rock with a rod as long and heavy as a Tartar's lance and fish all day without a murmur even though he should not be encouraged by a single nibble. He would carry a fowling-piece on his shoulder for hours together, trudging through woods and swamps and up hill and down dale, to shoot a few squirrels or wild pigeons. He would never refuse to assist a neighbor, even in the roughest toil, and was a foremost man at all country frolics for husking Indian corn, or building stone-fences; the women of the village, too, used to employ him to run their errands and to do such little odd jobs as their less obliging husbands would not do for them. In a word, Rip was ready to attend to anybody's business but his own; but as to doing family duty, and keeping his farm in order, he found it impossible.

In fact, he declared it was of no use to work on his farm; it was the most pestilent little piece of ground in the whole country; every thing about it went wrong, and would go wrong, in spite of him. His fences were continually falling to pieces; his cow would either go astray or get among the cabbages; weeds were sure to grow quicker in his fields than anywhere else; the rain always made a point of setting in just as he had outdoor work to do; so that though his patrimonial estate had dwindled away under his management, acre by acre, until there was little more left than a mere patch of Indian corn and potatoes, yet it was the worst-conditioned farm in the neighborhood.

His children, too, were as ragged and wild as if they belonged to nobody. His son Rip, an urchin begotten in his own likeness, promised to inherit the habits, with the old clothes of his father. He was generally seen trooping like a colt at his mother's heels, equipped in a pair of his father's cast-off galligaskins, which he had much ado to hold up with one hand, as a fine lady does her train in bad weather.

Rip Van Winkle, however, was one of those happy mortals, of foolish, well-oiled dispositions, who take the world easy, eat white bread or brown, whichever can be got with least thought or trouble, and would rather starve on a penny than work for a pound. If left to himself, he would have whistled life away in perfect contentment; but his wife kept continually dinning in his ears about his idleness, his carelessness, and the ruin he was bringing on his family. Morning, noon, and night, her tongue was incessantly going, and everything he said or did was sure to produce a torrent of household eloquence. Rip had but one way of replying to all lectures of the kind, and that, by frequent use, had grown into a habit. He shrugged his shoulders, shook his head, cast up his eyes, but said nothing. This, however, always provoked a fresh volley from his wife; so that he was fain to draw off his forces, and take to the outside of the house—the only side which, in truth, belongs to a henpecked husband.

Rip's sole domestic adherent was his dog Wolf, who was as much henpecked as his master; for Dame Van Winkle regarded them as companions in idleness, and even looked upon Wolf with an evil eye, as the cause of his master's going so often astray. True it is, in all points of spirit befitting an honorable dog, he was as courageous an animal as ever scoured the woods—but what courage can withstand the ever-during and all-besetting terrors of a woman's tongue? The moment Wolf entered the house his crest fell, his tail drooped to the ground, or curled between his legs, he sneaked about with a gallows air, casting many a sidelong glance at Dame Van Winkle, and at the least flourish of a broomstick or ladle, he would fly to the door with yelping precipitation.

Times grew worse and worse with Rip Van Winkle as years of matrimony rolled on; a tart temper never mellows with age, and a sharp tongue is the only edged tool that grows keener with constant use. For a long while he used to console himself, when driven from home, by frequenting a kind of perpetual club of the sages, philosophers, and other idle personages of the village, which held its sessions on a bench before a small inn, designated by a rubicund portrait of His Majesty George the Third. Here they used to sit in the shade through a long lazy summer's day, talking listlessly over village gossip, or telling endless sleepy stories about nothing. But it would have been worth any statesman's money to have heard the profound discussions that sometimes took place when, by chance, an old newspaper fell into their hands from some passing traveller. How solemnly they would listen to the contents, as drawled out by Derrick Van Bummel, the schoolmaster, a dapper, learned little man, who was not to be daunted by the most gigantic word in the dictionary; and how sagely they would deliberate upon public events some months after they had taken place.

The opinions of this junto were completely controlled by Nicholas Vedder, a patriarch of the village, and landlord of the inn, at the door of which he took his seat from morning till night, just moving sufficiently to avoid the sun and keep in the shade of a large tree; so that the neighbors could tell the hour by his movements as accurately as by a sun-dial. It is true he was rarely heard to speak, but smoked his pipe incessantly. His adherents, however (for every great man has his adherents), perfectly understood him and knew how to gather his opinions. When anything that was read or related displeased him, he was observed to smoke his pipe vehemently, and to send forth short, frequent, and angry puffs; but when pleased, he would inhale the smoke slowly and tranquilly, and emit it in light and placid clouds; and sometimes, taking the pipe from his mouth, and letting the fragrant vapor curl about his nose, would gravely nod his head in token of perfect approbation.

From even this stronghold the unlucky Rip was at length routed by his termagant wife, who would suddenly break in upon the tranquillity of the assemblage and call the members all to naught; nor was that august personage, Nicholas Vedder himself, sacred from the daring tongue of this terrible virago, who charged him outright with encouraging her husband in habits of idleness.

Poor Rip was at last reduced almost to despair; and his only alternative, to escape from the labor of the farm and clamor of his wife, was to take gun in hand and stroll away into the woods. Here he would sometimes seat himself at the foot of a tree and share the contents of his wallet with Wolf, with whom he sympathized as a fellow-sufferer in persecution. "Poor Wolf," he would say, "thy mistress leads thee a dog's life of it; but never mind, my lad, whilst I live thou shalt never want a friend to stand by thee!" Wolf would wag his tail, look wistfully in his master's face, and if dogs can feel pity, I verily believe he reciprocated the sentiment with all his heart.

In a long ramble of the kind on a fine autumnal day, Rip had unconsciously scrambled to one of the highest parts of the Kaatskill Mountains. He was after his favorite sport of squirrel shooting, and the still solitudes had echoed and reëchoed with the reports of his gun. Panting and fatigued, he threw himself, late in the afternoon, on a green knoll, covered with mountain herbage, that crowned the brow of a precipice. From an opening between the trees he could overlook all the lower country for many a mile of rich woodland. He saw at a distance the lordly Hudson, far, far below him, moving on its silent but majestic course, with the reflection of a purple cloud, or the sail of a lagging bark, here and there sleeping on its glassy bosom, and at last losing itself in the blue highlands.

On the other side he looked down into a deep mountain glen,

wild, lonely, and shagged, the bottom filled with fragments from the impending cliffs and scarcely lighted by the reflected rays of the setting sun. For some time Rip lay musing on this scene; evening was gradually advancing; the mountains began to throw their long blue shadows over the valleys; he saw that it would be dark long before he could reach the village, and he heaved a heavy sigh when he thought of encountering the terrors of Dame Van Winkle.

As he was about to descend, he heard a voice from a distance, hallooing, "Rip Van Winkle! Rip Van Winkle!" He looked round, but could see nothing but a crow winging its solitary flight across the mountain. He thought his fancy must have deceived him, and turned again to descend, when he heard the same cry ring through the still evening air; "Rip Van Winkle! Rip Van Winkle!"—at the same time Wolf bristled up his back, and giving a low growl, skulked to his master's side, looking fearfully down into the glen. Rip now felt a vague apprehension stealing over him; he looked anxiously in the same direction, and perceived a strange figure slowly toiling up the rocks, and bending under the weight of something he carried on his back. He was surprised to see any human being in this lonely and unfrequented place; but supposing it to be someone of the neighborhood in need of his assistance, he hastened down to yield it.

On nearer approach he was still more surprised at the singularity of the stranger's appearance. He was a short, square-built old fellow, with thick bushy hair, and a grizzled beard. His dress was of the antique Dutch fashion: a cloth jerkin strapped round the waist, several pair of breeches, the outer one of ample volume, decorated with rows of buttons down the sides, and bunches at the knees. He bore on his shoulder a stout keg, that seemed full of liquor, and made signs for Rip to approach and assist him with the load. Though rather shy and distrustful of this new acquaintance, Rip complied with his usual alacrity; and mutually relieving one another, they clambered up a narrow gully, apparently the dry bed of a mountain torrent. As they ascended, Rip every now and then heard long rolling peals, like distant thunder, that seemed to issue out of a deep ravine, or rather cleft, between lofty rocks, toward which their rugged path conducted. He paused for an instant, but supposing it to be the muttering of one of those transient thunder-showers which often take place in mountain heights, he proceeded. Passing through the ravine, they came to a hollow like a small amphitheatre, surrounded by perpendicular precipices, over the brinks of which impending trees shot their branches, so that you only caught glimpses of the azure sky and the bright evening cloud. During the whole time Rip and his companion had labored on in silence; for though the former marvelled greatly what could be the object of carrying a keg of liquor up this wild mountain, yet there was something strange and incomprehensible about the unknown, that inspired awe and checked familiarity.

On entering the amphitheatre, new objects of wonder presented themselves. On a level spot in the centre was a company of odd-looking personages playing at ninepins. They were dressed in a quaint outlandish fashion; some wore short doublets, others jerkins, with long knives in their belts, and most of them had enormous breeches of similar style with that of the guide's. Their visages, too, were peculiar: one had a large beard, broad face, and small piggish eyes: the face of another seemed to consist entirely of nose, and was surmounted by a white sugar-loaf hat, set off with a little red cock's tail. They all had beards, of various shapes and colors. There was one who seemed to be the commander. He was a stout old gentleman, with a weather-beaten countenance; he wore a laced doublet, broad belt and hanger, high-crowned hat and feather, red stockings, and high-heeled shoes, with roses in them. The whole group reminded Rip of the figures in an old Flemish painting in the parlor of Dominie Van Shaick, the village parson, and which had been brought over from Holland at the time of the settlement.

What seemed particularly odd to Rip was, that though these folks were evidently amusing themselves, yet they maintained the gravest faces, the most mysterious silence, and were, withal, the most melancholy party of pleasure he had ever witnessed. Nothing interrupted the stillness of the scene but the noise of the balls, which, whenever they were rolled, echoed along the mountains like rumbling peals of thunder.

As Rip and his companion approached them, they suddenly desisted from their play, and stared at him with such fixed, statue-like gaze, and such strange, uncouth, lack-lustre countenances, that his heart turned within him, and his knees smote together. His companion now emptied the contents of the keg into large flagons, and made signs to him to wait upon the company. He obeyed with fear and trembling; they quaffed the liquor in profound silence, and then returned to their game.

By degrees Rip's awe and apprehension subsided. He even ventured, when no eye was fixed upon him, to taste the beverage, which he found had much of the flavor of excellent Hollands. He was naturally a thirsty soul and was soon tempted to repeat the draught.

One taste provoked another; and he reiterated his visits to the flagon so often that at length his senses were overpowered, his eyes swam in his head, his head gradually declined, and he fell into a deep sleep.

On waking, he found himself on the green knoll whence he had first seen the old man of the glen. He rubbed his eyes. It was a bright, sunny morning. The birds were hopping and twittering among the bushes, and the eagle was wheeling aloft, and breasting the pure mountain breeze. "Surely," thought Rip, "I have not slept here all night." He recalled the occurrences before he fell asleep—the strange man with a keg of liquor, the mountain ravine, the wild retreat among the rocks, the wobegone party at ninepins, the flagon. "Oh! that flagon! that wicked flagon!" thought Rip. "What excuse shall I make to Dame Van Winkle?"

He looked round for his gun, but in place of the clean, well-oiled fowling-piece, he found an old firelock lying by him, the barrel incrusted with rust, the lock falling off, and the stock worm-eaten. He now suspected that the grave roisterers of the mountain had put a trick upon him, and, having dosed him with liquor, had robbed him of his gun. Wolf, too, had disappeared, but he might have strayed away after a squirrel or partridge. He whistled after him, and shouted his name, but all in vain; the echoes repeated his whistle and shout, but no dog was to be seen.

He determined to revisit the scene of the last evening's gambol, and if he met with any of the party, to demand his dog and gun. As he rose to walk, he found himself stiff in the joints, and wanting in his usual activity. "These mountain beds do not agree with me," thought Rip, "and if this frolic should lay me up with a fit of the rheumatism, I shall have a blessed time with Dame Van Winkle." With some difficulty he got down into the glen: he found the gully up which he and his companion had ascended the preceding evening; but to his astonishment a mountain stream was now foaming down it, leaping from rock to rock, and filling the glen with babbling murmurs. He, however, made shift to scramble up its sides, working his toilsome way through thickets of birch, sassafras, and witch-hazel, and sometimes tripped up or entangled by the wild grapevines that twisted their coils or tendrils from tree to tree, and spread a kind of network in his path.

At length he reached to where the ravine had opened through the cliffs to the amphitheatre; but no traces of such opening remained. The rocks presented a high, impenetrable wall, over which the torrent came tumbling in a sheet of feathery foam, and fell into a broad, deep basin, black from the shadows of the surrounding forest. Here, then, poor Rip was brought to a stand. He again called and whistled after his dog; he was only answered by the cawing of a flock of idle crows, sporting high in air about a dry tree that overhung a sunny precipice; and who, secure in their elevation, seemed to look down and scoff at the poor man's perplexities. What was to be done? The morning was passing away, and Rip felt famished for want of his breakfast. He grieved to give up his dog and gun; he dreaded to meet his wife; but it would not do to starve among the mountains. He shook his head, shouldered the rusty firelock, and, with a heart full of trouble and anxiety, turned his steps homeward.

As he approached the village he met a number of people, but none whom he knew, which somewhat surprised him, for he had thought himself acquainted with everyone in the country round. Their dress, too, was of a different fashion from that to which he was accustomed. They all stared at him with equal marks of surprise, and whenever they cast their eyes upon him, invariably stroked their chins. The constant recurrence of this gesture induced Rip, involuntarily, to do the same, when, to his astonishment, he found his beard had grown a foot long!

He had now entered the skirts of the village. A troop of strange children ran at his heels, hooting after him, and pointing at his gray beard. The dogs, too, not one of which he recognized for an old acquaintance, barked at him as he passed. The very village was altered; it was larger and more populous. There were rows of houses which he had never seen before, and those which had been his familiar haunts had disappeared. Strange names were over the doors—strange faces at the windows—everything was strange. His mind now misgave him; he began to doubt whether both he and the world around him were not bewitched. Surely this was his native village, which he had left but the day before. There stood the Kaatskill Mountains. There ran the silver Hudson at a distance. There was every hill and dale precisely as it had always been. Rip was sorely perplexed. "That flagon last night," thought he, "has addled my poor head sadly!"

It was with some difficulty that he found the way to his own house, which he approached with silent awe, expecting every moment to hear the shrill voice of Dame Van Winkle. He found the house gone to decay—the roof fallen in, the windows shattered, and the doors off the hinges. A half-starved dog that looked like Wolf was skulking about it. Rip called him by name, but the cur snarled, showed his teeth, and passed on. This was an unkind cut indeed. "My very dog," sighed poor Rip, "has forgotten me!"

13

He entered the house, which, to tell the truth, Dame Van Winkle had always kept in neat order. It was empty, forlorn, and apparently abandoned. This desolateness overcame all his connubial fears. He called loudly for his wife and children. The lonely chambers rang for a moment with his voice, and then all again was silence.

He now hurried forth, and hastened to his old resort, the village inn. But it, too, was gone. A large, rickety wooden building stood in its place, with great gaping windows, some of them broken and mended with old hats and petticoats, and over the door was painted, "The Union Hotel, by Jonathan Doolittle." Instead of the great tree that used to shelter the quiet little Dutch inn of yore, there now was reared a tall naked pole, with something on the top that looked like a red night-cap, and from it was fluttering a flag on which was a singular assemblage of stars and stripes. All this was strange and incomprehensible. He recognized on the sign, however, the ruby face of King George, under which he had smoked so many a peaceful pipe; but even this was singularly metamorphosed. The red coat was changed for one of blue and buff, a sword was held in the hand instead of a sceptre, the head was decorated with a cocked hat, and underneath was painted in large characters, *General Washington*.

There was, as usual, a crowd of folk about the door, but none that Rip recollected. The very character of the people seemed changed. There was a busy, bustling, disputatious tone about it, instead of the accustomed phlegm and drowsy tranquillity. He looked in vain for the sage Nicholas Vedder, with his broad face, double chin, and fair long pipe, uttering clouds of tobacco smoke instead of idle speeches; or Van Bummel, the schoolmaster, doling forth the contents of an ancient newspaper. In place of these, a lean, bilious-looking fellow, with his pockets full of handbills, was haranguing vehemently about rights of citizens, elections, members of Congress, liberty, Bunker's Hill, heroes of seventy-six, and other words, which were a perfect Babylonish jargon to the bewildered Van Winkle.

The appearance of Rip, with his long grizzled beard, his rusty fowling-piece, his uncouth dress, and an army of women and children at his heels, soon attracted the attention of the tavern politicians. They crowded round him, eyeing him from head to foot with great curiosity. The orator bustled up to him, and, drawing him partly aside, inquired on which side he voted. Rip stared in vacant stupidity. Another short but busy little fellow pulled him by the arm, and, rising on tiptoe, inquired in his ear, whether he was Federal or Democrat. Rip was equally at a loss to comprehend the question; when a knowing, self-important old gentleman, in a sharp cocked hat, made his way through the crowd, putting them to the right and left with his elbows as he passed, and planting himself before Van Winkle, with one arm akimbo, the other resting on his cane, his keen eyes and sharp hat penetrating, as it were, into his very soul, demanded in an austere tone, what brought him to the election with a gun on his shoulder, and a mob at his heels, and whether he meant to breed a riot in the village.

"Alas! gentlemen," cried Rip, somewhat dismayed, "I am a poor quiet man, a native of the place, and a loyal subject of the King, God bless him!"

Here a general shout burst from the bystanders. "A tory! a tory! a spy! a refugee! hustle him! away with him!" It was with great difficulty that the self-important man in the cocked hat restored order; and, having assumed a tenfold austerity of brow, demanded again of the unknown culprit what he came there for, and whom he was seeking. The poor man humbly assured him that he meant no harm, but merely came there in search of some of his neighbors, who used to keep about the tavern.

"Well, who are they? Name them."

Rip bethought himself a moment, and inquired, "Where's Nicholas Vedder?"

There was a silence for a little while, when an old man replied, in a thin, piping voice, "Nicholas Vedder! why, he is dead and gone these eighteen years! There was a wooden tombstone in the church-yard that used to tell all about him, but that's rotten and gone too."

"Where's Brom Dutcher?"

"Oh, he went off to the army in the beginning of the war; some say he was killed at the storming of Stony Point. Others say he was drowned in a squall at the foot of Antony's Nose. I don't know. He never came back again."

"Where's Van Bummel, the schoolmaster?"

"He went off to the wars, too, was a great militia general, and is now in Congress."

Rip's heart died away at hearing of these sad changes in his home and friends, and finding himself thus alone in the world. Every answer puzzled him, too, by treating such enormous lapses of time, and of matters which he could not understand: war, Congress, Stony Point; he had no courage to ask after any more friends, but cried out in despair, "Does nobody here know Rip Van Winkle?"

"Oh, Rip Van Winkle!" exclaimed two or three, "Oh, to be sure! that's Rip Van Winkle yonder, leaning against the tree."

15

Rip looked and beheld a precise counterpart of himself as he went up the mountain, apparently as lazy and certainly as ragged. The poor fellow was now completely confounded. He doubted his own identity, and whether he was himself or another man. In the midst of his bewilderment, the man in the cocked hat demanded who he was, and what was his name.

"God knows," exclaimed he, at his wit's end; "I'm not myself. I'm somebody else. That's me yonder. No, that's somebody else got into my shoes. I was myself last night, but I fell asleep on the mountain, and they've changed my gun, and everything's changed, and I'm changed, and I can't tell what's my name, or who I am!"

The bystanders began now to look at each other, nod, wink significantly, and tap their fingers against their foreheads. There was a whisper, also, about securing the gun and keeping the old fellow from doing mischief, at the very suggestion of which the self-important man in the cocked hat retired with some precipitation. At this critical moment a fresh, comely woman pressed through the throng to get a peep at the gray-bearded man. She had a chubby child in her arms, which, frightened at his looks, began to cry. "Hush, Rip," cried she, "hush, you little fool; the old man won't hurt you."

The name of the child, the air of the mother, the tone of her voice, all awakened a train of recollections in his mind. "What is your name, my good woman?" asked he.

"Judith Gardenier."

"And your father's name?"

"Ah, poor man, Rip Van Winkle was his name, but it's twenty years since he went away from home with his gun, and never has been heard of since. His dog came home without him; but whether he shot himself, or was carried away by the Indians, nobody can tell. I was then but a little girl."

Rip had but one question more to ask; but he put it with a faltering voice, "Where's your mother?"

"Oh, she too died but a short time since; she broke a blood-vessel in a fit of passion at a New England peddler."

There was a drop of comfort, at least, in this intelligence. The honest man could contain himself no longer. He caught his daughter and her child in his arms. "I am your father!" cried he. "Young Rip Van Winkle once—old Rip Van Winkle now! Does nobody know poor Rip Van Winkle?"

All stood amazed until an old woman, tottering out from among the crowd, put her hand to her brow, and peering under it in his face for a moment, exclaimed, "Sure enough! it is Rip Van Winkle. It is himself! Welcome home again, old neighbor. Why, where have you been these twenty long years?"

Rip's story was soon told, for the whole twenty years had been to him but as one night. The neighbors stared when they heard it; some were seen to wink at each other and put their tongues in their cheeks; and the self-important man in the cocked hat, who, when the alarm was over, had returned to the field, screwed down the corners of his mouth and shook his head—upon which there was a general shaking of the head throughout the assemblage.

It was determined, however, to take the opinion of old Peter Vanderdonk, who was seen slowly advancing up the road. He was a descendant of the historian of that name, who wrote one of the earliest accounts of the province. Peter was the most ancient inhabitant of the village and well versed in all the wonderful events and traditions of the neighborhood. He recollected Rip at once and corroborated his story in the most satisfactory manner. He assured the company that it was a fact, handed down from his ancestor the historian, that the Kaatskill Mountains had always been haunted by strange beings. That it was affirmed that the great Hendrick Hudson, the first discoverer of the river and country, kept a kind of vigil there every twenty years with his crew of the *Half Moon;* being permitted in this way to revisit the scenes of his enterprise and keep a guardian eye upon the river and the great city called by his name. That his father had once seen them in their old Dutch dresses playing at ninepins in a hollow of the mountain; and that he himself had heard, one summer afternoon, the sound of their balls, like distant peals of thunder.

To make a long story short, the company broke up and returned to the more important concerns of the election. Rip's daughter took him home to live with her; she had a snug, well-furnished house, and a stout, cheery farmer for a husband, whom Rip recollected for one of the urchins that used to climb upon his back. As to Rip's son and heir, who was the ditto of himself, seen leaning against the tree, he was employed to work on the farm, but evinced an hereditary disposition to attend to anything else but his business.

Rip now resumed his old walks and habits; he soon found many of his former cronies, though all rather the worse for the wear and tear of time, and preferred making friends among the rising generation, with whom he soon grew into great favor.

Having nothing to do at home, and being arrived at that happy age when a man can be idle with impunity, he took his place once more on the bench at the inn door and was reverenced as one of the patriarchs of the village and a chronicler of the old times "before the war." It was some time before he could get into the regular track of gossip or could be made to comprehend the strange events that had taken place during his torpor. How that there had been a revolutionary war, that the country had thrown off the yoke of old England, and that, instead of being a subject of His Majesty George the Third, he was now a free citizen of the United States. Rip, in fact, was no politician; the changes of states and empires made but little impression on him, but there was one species of despotism under which he had long groaned, and that was petticoat government. Happily that was at an end; he had got his neck out of the yoke of matrimony, and could go in and out whenever he pleased without dreading the tyranny of Dame Van Winkle. Whenever her name was mentioned, however, he shook his head, shrugged his shoulders, and cast up his eyes; which might pass either for an expression of resignation to his fate, or joy at his deliverance.

He used to tell his story to every stranger that arrived at Mr. Doolittle's hotel. He was observed, at first, to vary on some points every time he told it, which was doubtless owing to his having so recently awaked. It at last settled down precisely to the tale I have related, and not a man, woman, or child in the neighborhood but knew it by heart. Some always pretended to doubt the reality of it, and insisted that Rip had been out of his head, and that this was one point on which he always remained flighty. The old Dutch inhabitants, however, almost universally gave it full credit. Even to this day they never hear a thunderstorm of a summer afternoon about the Kaatskill, but they say Hendrick Hudson and his crew are at their game of ninepins; and it is a common wish of all henpecked husbands in the neighborhood, when life hangs heavy on their hands, that they might have a quieting draught out of Rip Van Winkle's flagon.

Note

The foregoing Tale, one would suspect, had been suggested to Mr. Knickerbocker by a little German superstition about the Emperor Frederick der Rothbart, and the Kypphäuser mountain: the subjoined note, however, which he had appended to the tale, shows that it is an absolute fact, narrated with his usual fidelity.

"*The story of Rip Van Winkle may seem incredible to many, but nevertheless I give it my full belief, for I know the vicinity of our old Dutch settlements to have been very subject to marvellous events and appearances. Indeed, I have heard many stranger stories than this, in the villages along the Hudson; all of which were too well authenticated to admit of a doubt. I have even talked with Rip Van Winkle myself, who, when last I saw him, was a very venerable old man, and so perfectly rational and consistent on every other point, that I think no conscientious person could refuse to take this into the bargain; nay, I have seen a certificate on the subject taken before a country justice and signed with a cross, in the justice's own handwriting. The story, therefore, is beyond the possibility of doubt.*

"*D. K.*"

Postscript

The following are travelling notes from a memorandum-book of Mr. Knickerbocker.

The Kaatsberg, or Catskill Mountains, have always been a region full of fable. The Indians considered them the abode of spirits, who influenced the weather, spreading sunshine or clouds over the landscape, and sending good or bad hunting-seasons. They were ruled by an old squaw spirit, said to be their mother. She dwelt on the highest peak of the Catskills, and had charge of the doors of day and night to open and shut them at the proper hour. She hung up the new moons in the skies, and cut up the old ones into stars. In times of drought, if properly propitiated, she would spin light summer clouds out of cobwebs and morning dew, and send them off from the crest of the mountain, flake after flake, like flakes of carded cotton, to float in the air; until, dissolved by the heat of the sun, they would fall in gentle showers, causing the grass to spring, the fruits to ripen, and the corn to grow an inch an hour. If displeased, however, she would brew up clouds black as ink, sitting in the midst of them like a bottle-bellied spider in the midst of its web; and when these clouds broke, woe betide the valleys!

In old times, say the Indian traditions, there was a kind of Manitou or Spirit, who kept about the wildest recesses of the Catskill Mountains, and took a mischievous pleasure in wreaking all kinds of evils and vexations upon the red men. Sometimes he would assume the form of a bear, a panther, or a deer, lead the bewildered hunter a weary chase through tangled forests and among ragged rocks; and then spring off with a loud ho! ho! leaving him aghast on the brink of a beetling precipice or raging torrent.

The favorite abode of this Manitou is still shown. It is a great

19

*rock or cliff on the loneliest part of the mountains, and, from the
flowering vines which clamber about it, and the wild flowers which
abound in its neighborhood, is known by the name of the Garden Rock.
Near the foot of it is a small lake, the haunt of the solitary bittern,
with water-snakes basking in the sun on the leaves of the pond-lilies
which lie on the surface. This place was held in great awe by the Indians,
insomuch that the boldest hunter would not pursue his game within its
precincts. Once upon a time, however, a hunter who had lost his way,
penetrated to the Garden Rock, where he beheld a number of gourds
placed in the crotches of trees. One of these he seized and made off with
it, but in the hurry of his retreat he let it fall among the rocks, when a
great stream gushed forth, which washed him away and swept him
down precipices, where he was dashed to pieces, and the stream made
its way to the Hudson, and continues to flow to the present day; being
the identical stream known by the name of the Kaaters-kill.*

the stout gentleman

a stage-coach romance

I'll cross it though it blast me! — Hamlet

It was a rainy Sunday in the gloomy month of November. I had
been detained, in the course of a journey, by a slight indisposition, from
which I was recovering; but was still feverish, and obliged to keep
within doors all day, in an inn of the small town of Derby. A wet
Sunday in a country inn!—whoever has had the luck to experience
one can alone judge of my situation. The rain pattered against the
casements; the bells tolled for church with a melancholy sound. I went
to the windows in quest of something to amuse the eye; but it seemed
as if I had been placed completely out of the reach of all amusement.
The windows of my bedroom looked out among tiled roofs and stacks

of chimneys, while those of my sitting-room commanded a full view of the stable-yard. I know of nothing more calculated to make a man sick of this world than a stable-yard on a rainy day. The place was littered with wet straw that had been kicked about by travellers and stable-boys. In one corner was a stagnant pool of water, surrounding an island of muck; there were several half-drowned fowls crowded together under a cart, among which was a miserable, crest-fallen cock, drenched out of all life and spirit, his drooping tail matted, as it were, into a single feather, along which the water trickled from his back; near the cart was a half-dozing cow, chewing the cud, and standing patiently to be rained on, with wreaths of vapor rising from her reeking hide; a wall-eyed horse, tired of the loneliness of the stable, was poking his spectral head out of a window, with the rain dripping on it from the eaves; an unhappy cur, chained to a doghouse hard by, uttered something, every now and then, between a bark and a yelp; a drab of a kitchen-wench tramped backward and forward through the yard in pattens, looking as sulky as the weather itself; everything, in short, was comfortless and forlorn, excepting a crew of hardened ducks, assembled like boon companions round a puddle, and making a riotous noise over their liquor.

I was lonely and listless, and wanted amusement. My room soon become insupportable, I abandoned it, and sought what is technically called the travellers' room. This is a public room set apart at most inns for the accommodation of a class of wayfarers called travellers, or riders; a kind of commercial knights-errant, who are incessantly scouring the kingdom in gigs, on horseback, or by coach. They are the only successors that I know of at the present day to the knights-errant of yore. They lead the same kind of roving, adventurous life, only changing the lance for a driving-whip, the buckler for a pattern-card, and the coat of mail for an upper Benjamin. Instead of vindicating the charms of peerless beauty, they rove about, spreading the fame and standing of some substantial tradesman, or manufacturer, and are ready at any time to bargain in his name; it being the fashion now-adays to trade, instead of fight, with one another. As the room of the hostel, in the good old fighting-times, would be hung round at night with the armor of wayworn warriors, such as coats of mail, falchions, and yawning helmets, so the travellers' room is garnished with the harnessing of their successors, with box-coats, whips of all kinds, spurs, gaiters, and oilcloth covered hats.

I was in hopes of finding some of these worthies to talk with, but was disappointed. There were, indeed, two or three in the room; but I could make nothing of them. One was just finishing his breakfast, quarrelling with his bread and butter, and huffing the waiter; another buttoned on a pair of gaiters, with many execrations at Boots for not having cleaned his shoes well; a third sat drumming on the table with his fingers and looking at the rain as it streamed down the window-glass; they all appeared infected by the weather, and disappeared, one after the other, without exchanging a word.

I sauntered to the window, and stood gazing at the people, picking their way to church, with petticoats hoisted midleg high, and dripping umbrellas. The bell ceased to toll, and the streets became silent. I then amused myself with watching the daughters of a tradesman opposite; who, being confined to the house for fear of wetting their Sunday finery, played off their charms at the front windows, to fascinate the chance tenants of the inn. They at length were summoned away by a vigilant, vinegar-faced mother, and I had nothing further from without to amuse me.

What was I to do to pass away the long-lived day? I was sadly nervous and lonely; and everything about an inn seems calculated to make a dull day ten times duller. Old newspapers, smelling of beer and tobacco-smoke, and which I had already read half a dozen times. Good-for-nothing books, that were worse than rainy weather. I bored myself to death with an old volume of the *Lady's Magazine*. I read all the commonplace names of ambitious travellers scrawled on the panes of glass; the eternal families of the Smiths, and the Browns, and the Jacksons, and the Johnsons, and all the other sons; and I deciphered several scraps of fatiguing inn-window poetry which I have met with in all parts of the world.

The day continued lowering and gloomy; the slovenly, ragged, spongy clouds drifted heavily along; there was no variety even in the rain: it was one dull, continued, monotonous patter—patter—patter, excepting that now and then I was enlivened by the idea of a brisk shower, from the rattling of the drops upon a passing umbrella.

It was quite *refreshing* (if I may be allowed a hackneyed phrase of the day) when, in the course of the morning, a horn blew, and a stage-coach whirled through the street, with outside passengers stuck all over it, cowering under cotton umbrellas, and seethed together, and reeking with the steams of wet box-coats and upper Benjamins.

The sound brought out from their lurking-places a crew of vagabond boys, and vagabond dogs, and the carroty-headed hostler, and that nondescript animal ycleped Boots, and all the other vagabond race that infest the purlieus of an inn; but the bustle was transient; the coach again whirled on its way; and boy and dog, and hostler and Boots, all slunk back again to their holes; the street again became silent, and the rain continued to rain on. In fact, there was no hope of its clearing up; the barometer pointed to rainy weather; mine hostess's tortoise-shell cat sat by the fire washing her face, and rubbing her paws over her ears; and, on referring to the Almanac, I found a direful prediction stretching from the top of the page to the bottom through the whole month, "expect—much—rain—about—this—time!"

I was dreadfully hipped. The hours seemed as if they would never creep by. The very ticking of the clock became irksome. At length the stillness of the house was interrupted by the ringing of a bell. Shortly after I heard the voice of a waiter at the bar: "The stout gentleman in No. 13 wants his breakfast. Tea and bread and butter, with ham and eggs; the eggs not to be too much done."

In such a situation as mine, every incident is of importance. Here was a subject of speculation presented to my mind, and ample exercise for my imagination. I am prone to paint pictures to myself, and on this occasion I had some materials to work upon. Had the guest upstairs been mentioned as Mr. Smith, or Mr. Brown, or Mr. Jackson, or Mr. Johnson, or merely as "the gentleman in No. 13," it would have been a perfect blank to me. I should have thought nothing of it; but "The stout gentleman!"—the very name had something in it of the picturesque. It at once gave the size; it embodied the personage to my mind's eye, and my fancy did the rest.

He was stout, or, as some term it, lusty; in all probability, there-fore, he was advanced in life, some people expanding as they grow old. By his breakfasting rather late, and in his own room, he must be a man accustomed to live at his ease, and above the necessity of early rising; no doubt, a round, rosy, lusty old gentleman.

There was another violent ringing. The stout gentleman was impatient for his breakfast. He was evidently a man of importance; "well to do in the world"; accustomed to be promptly waited upon; of a keen appetite, and a little cross when hungry; "perhaps," thought I, "he may be some London Alderman; or who knows but he may be a Member of Parliament."

The breakfast was sent up, and there was a short interval of silence; he was, doubtless, making the tea. Presently there was a violent ringing; and before it could be answered, another ringing still more

23

violent. "Bless me! what a choleric old gentleman!" The waiter came down in a huff. The butter was rancid, the eggs were overdone, the ham was too salt; the stout gentleman was evidently nice in his eating; one of those who eat and growl, and keep the waiter on the trot, and live in a state militant with the household.

The hostess got into a fume. I should observe that she was a brisk, coquettish woman; a little of a shrew, and something of a slammerkin, but very pretty withal; with a nincompoop for a husband, as shrews are apt to have. She rated the servants roundly for their negligence in sending up so bad a breakfast, but said not a word against the stout gentleman; by which I clearly perceived that he must be a man of consequence, entitled to make a noise and to give trouble at a country inn. Other eggs, and ham, and bread and butter were sent up. They appeared to be more graciously received; at least there was no further complaint.

I had not made many turns about the travellers' room, when there was another ringing. Shortly afterward there was a stir and an inquest about the house. The stout gentleman wanted the *Times* or the *Chronicle* newspaper. I set him down, therefore, for a Whig; or, rather, from his being so absolute and lordly where he had a chance, I suspected him of being a Radical. Hunt, I had heard, was a large man; "who knows," thought I, "but it is Hunt himself!"

My curiosity began to be awakened. I inquired of the waiter who was this stout gentleman that was making all this stir; but I could get no information: nobody seemed to know his name. The landlords of bustling inns seldom trouble their heads about the names or occupations of their transient guests. The color of a coat, the shape or size of the person, is enough to suggest a travelling name. It is either the tall gentleman, or the short gentleman, or the gentleman in black, or the gentleman in snuff-color; or, as in the present instance, the stout gentleman. A designation of the kind once hit on, answers every purpose, and saves all further inquiry.

Rain—rain—rain! pitiless, ceaseless rain! No such thing as putting a foot out of doors, and no occupation nor amusement within. By and by I heard someone walking overhead. It was in the stout gentleman's room. He evidently was a large man by the heaviness of his tread; and an old man from his wearing such creaking soles. "He is doubtless," thought I, "some rich old square-toes of regular habits, and is now taking exercise after breakfast."

I now read all the advertisements of coaches and hotels that were stuck about the mantelpiece. The *Lady's Magazine* had become an abomination to me; it was as tedious as the day itself. I wandered out, not knowing what to do, and ascended again to my room. I had not been there long, when there was a squall from a neighboring bedroom. A door opened and slammed violently; a chambermaid, that I had remarked for having a ruddy, good-humored face, went downstairs in a violent flurry. The stout gentleman had been rude to her!

This sent a whole host of my deductions to the deuce in a moment. This unknown personage could not be an old gentleman; for old gentlemen are not apt to be so obstreperous to chambermaids. He could not be a young gentleman; for young gentlemen are not apt to inspire such indignation. He must be a middle-aged man, and confounded ugly into the bargain, or the girl would not have taken the matter in such terrible dudgeon. I confess I was sorely puzzled.

In a few minutes I heard the voice of my landlady. I caught a glance of her as she came tramping upstairs—her face glowing, her cap flaring, her tongue wagging the whole way. "She'd have no such doings in her house, she'd warrant. If gentlemen did spend money freely, it was no rule. She'd have no servant-maids of hers treated in that way, when they were about their work, that's what she wouldn't."

As I hate squabbles, particularly with women, and above all with pretty women, I slunk back into my room, and partly closed the door; but my curiosity was too much excited not to listen. The landlady marched intrepidly to the enemy's citadel, and entered it with a storm: the door closed after her. I heard her voice in high windy clamor for a moment or two. Then it gradually subsided, like a gust of wind in a garret; then there was a laugh; then I heard nothing more.

After a little while my landlady came out with an odd smile on her face, adjusting her cap, which was a little on one side. As she went downstairs, I heard the landlord ask her what was the matter; she said, "Nothing at all, only the girl's a fool." I was more than ever perplexed what to make of this unaccountable personage, who could put a good-natured chambermaid in a passion, and send away a termagant landlady in smiles. He could not be so old, nor cross, nor ugly either.

I had to go to work at his picture again, and to paint him entirely different. I now set him down for one of those stout gentlemen that are frequently met with swaggering about the doors of country inns. Moist, merry fellows, in Belcher handkerchiefs, whose bulk is a little assisted by malt-liquors. Men who have seen the world, and been sworn at Highgate; who are used to tavern-life; up to all the tricks of tapsters, and knowing in the ways of sinful publicans. Free-livers on a small scale; who are prodigal within the compass of a guinea; who call all the waiters by name, tousle the maids, gossip with the landlady at the bar, and prose over a pint of port, or a glass of negus, after dinner.

The morning wore away in forming these and similar surmises. As fast as I wove one system of belief, some movement of the unknown would completely overturn it, and throw all my thoughts again into confusion. Such are the solitary operations of a feverish mind. I was, as I have said, extremely nervous; and the continual meditation on the concerns of this invisible personage began to have its effect—I was getting a fit of the fidgets.

Dinner-time came. I hoped the stout gentleman might dine in the travellers' room, and that I might at length get a view of his person; but no—he had dinner served in his own room. What could be the meaning of this solitude and mystery? He could not be a radical; there was something too aristocratical in thus keeping himself apart from the rest of the world, and condemning himself to his own dull company throughout a rainy day. And then, too, he lived too well for a discontented politician. He seemed to expatiate on a variety of dishes, and to sit over his wine like a jolly friend of good living. Indeed, my doubts on this head were soon at an end; for he could not have finished his first bottle before I could faintly hear him humming a tune; and on listening, I found it to be "God Save the King." 'Twas plain, then, he was no radical, but a faithful subject; one who grew loyal over his bottle, and was ready to stand by king and constitution, when he could stand by nothing else. But who could he be? My conjectures began to run wild. Was he not some personage of distinction travelling incog.? "God knows!" said I, at my wit's end; "it may be one of the royal family for aught I know, for they are all stout gentlemen!"

The weather continued rainy. The mysterious unknown kept his room, and, as far as I could judge, his chair, for I did not hear him move. In the meantime, as the day advanced, the travellers' room began to be frequented. Some, who had just arrived, came in buttoned up in box-coats; others came home who had been dispersed about the town; some took their dinners, and some their tea. Had I been in a different mood, I should have found entertainment in studying this peculiar class of men. There were two especially who were regular wags of the road, and up to all the standing jokes of travellers. They had a thousand sly things to say to the waiting-maid, whom they called Louisa, and Ethelinda, and a dozen other fine names, changing the name every time, and chuckling amazingly at their own waggery. My mind, however, had been completely engrossed by the stout gentleman. He had kept my fancy in chase during a long day, and it was not now to be diverted from the scent.

The evening gradually wore away. The travellers read the papers two or three times over. Some drew round the fire and told long stories about their horses, about their adventures, their overturns, and breaking-down. They discussed the credit of different merchants and different inns; and the two wags told several choice anecdotes of pretty chambermaids and kind landladies. All this passed as they were quietly taking what they called their night-caps, that is to say, strong glasses of brandy and water and sugar, or some other mixture of the kind; after which they one after another rang for "Boots" and the chambermaid, and walked off to bed in old shoes cut down into marvellously uncomfortable slippers.

There was now only one man left: a short-legged, long-bodied, plethoric fellow, with a very large, sandy head. He sat by himself, with a glass of port-wine negus, and a spoon; sipping and stirring, and meditating and sipping, until nothing was left but the spoon. He gradually fell asleep bolt upright in his chair, with the empty glass standing before him; and the candle seemed to fall asleep, too, for the wick grew long, and black, and cabbaged at the end, and dimmed the little light that remained in the chamber. The gloom that now prevailed was contagious. Around hung the shapeless, and almost spectral, box-coats of departed travellers, long since buried in deep sleep. I only heard the ticking of the clock, with the deep-drawn breathings of the sleeping topers, and the drippings of the rain, drop—drop—drop, from the eaves of the house. The church-bells chimed midnight. All at once the stout gentleman began to walk overhead, pacing slowly backward and forward. There was something extremely awful in all this, especially to one in my state of nerves. These ghastly great-coats, these guttural breathings, and the creaking footsteps of this mysterious being. His steps grew fainter and fainter, and at length died away. I could bear it no longer. I was wound up to the desperation of a hero of romance. "Be he who or what he may," said I to myself, "I'll have a sight of him!" I seized a chamber-candle, and hurried up to No. 13. The door stood ajar. I hesitated—I entered: the room was deserted. There stood a large, broad-bottomed elbow-chair at a table, on which was an empty tumbler, and a *Times* newspaper, and the room smelt powerfully of Stilton cheese.

The mysterious stranger had evidently but just retired. I turned off, sorely disappointed, to my room, which had been changed to the front of the house. As I went along the corridor, I saw a large pair of boots, with dirty, waxed tops, standing at the door of a bedchamber. They doubtless belonged to the unknown: but it would not do to disturb so redoubtable a personage in his den; he might discharge a pistol, or something worse, at my head. I went to bed, therefore, and lay awake half the night in a terribly nervous state; and even when I fell asleep, I was still haunted in my dreams by the idea of the stout gentleman and his wax-topped boots.

I slept rather late the next morning, and was awakened by some stir and bustle in the house, which I could not at first comprehend; until getting more awake, I found there was a mail-coach starting from the door. Suddenly there was a cry from below, "The gentleman has forgotten his umbrella! Look for the gentleman's umbrella in No. 13!" I heard an immediate scampering of a chambermaid along the passage, and a shrill reply as she ran, "Here it is! here's the gentleman's umbrella!"

The mysterious stranger then was on the point of setting off. This was the only chance I should ever have of knowing him. I sprang out of bed, scrambled to the window, snatched aside the curtains, and just caught a glimpse of the rear of a person getting in at the coach-door. The skirts of a brown coat parted behind, and gave me a full view of the broad disk of a pair of drab breeches. The door closed—"all right!" was the word—the coach whirled off; and that was all I ever saw of the stout gentleman!

Nath. Hawthorne

YOUNG GOODMAN BROWN

RAPPACCINI'S DAUGHTER

Nathaniel Hawthorne was born in 1804, in Salem, Massachusetts, the son of a sea captain who died in Dutch Guiana when Nathaniel was four years old. Through the aid of an uncle, Hawthorne entered Bowdoin College, numbering among his friends there the poet Longfellow and Franklin Pierce, a future president of the United States. While still an undergraduate he decided to follow writing as a profession, and upon receiving his degree in 1825, he returned to Salem, where he spent the next twelve years in a virtually monastic study of literature and of the history and legends of his native region, chiefly those of the Puritan era. During this period of literary apprenticeship, Hawthorne grew to maturity as a writer, for his first volume of stories, *Twice-Told Tales,* published in 1837, is obviously the work of a finished writer. This volume caused so little stir, however, that he worked on in semiobscurity, engaging in hack work and serving in various posts, such as surveyor of customs for the port of Salem from 1846 to 1849. The publication in 1850 of the novel *The Scarlet Letter* brought him some fame, and a campaign biography he wrote of his friend Pierce secured for him the appointment as consul in Liverpool, England. He held this post from 1853 to 1857 and continued to reside abroad until 1860, when he returned to live in Concord, Massachusetts, until his death four years later in 1864. The best of some 120 short tales and sketches he wrote are contained in *Twice-Told Tales* (first published in 1837 and expanded into a second series in 1842), *Mosses from an Old Manse* (1846), and *The Snow Image* (1851).

Unlike Irving, who was content if his writing kept "mankind in good humor with one another," Hawthorne wrote with a high seriousness of purpose, concerning himself primarily with fundamental problems of character and conscience. "Young Goodman Brown," for example, centers on the destructive effect of man's loss of faith in his fellow man: after his grim discovery in the forest, Goodman Brown is unable to take comfort in the general predicament of human society and becomes the victim of a corrosive skepticism. "Rappaccini's Daughter" deals with the tragic consequences of putting intellectual, or scientific, interests over emotional, or human, values. In caring "infinitely more for science than for mankind," Rappaccini "would sacrifice human life, his own among the rest, or whatever else was dearest to him, for the sake of adding so much as a grain of mustard seed to . . . his accumulated knowledge." Hawthorne's finest stories, like these two, are developed, however, on more than one level of meaning. There is first the surface level of plotted narrative, and second the abstract level of moral consciousness, conveyed through a pattern of interconnected symbols. Ultimately the story's effectiveness depends on the successful fusion of both levels. One risk in attempting such a fusion is that even the characters may become merely lifeless symbols. Thus, it is worth considering whether "Rappaccini's Daughter," which carries symbolism further than "Young Goodman Brown," is the less effective of the two, even though a supernatural element is introduced into "Young Goodman Brown."

young goodman brown

Young Goodman Brown came forth at sunset into the street at Salem village; but put his head back, after crossing the threshold, to exchange a parting kiss with his young wife. And Faith, as the wife was aptly named, thrust her own pretty head into the street, letting the wind play with the pink ribbons of her cap while she called to Goodman Brown.

"Dearest heart," whispered she, softly and rather sadly, when her lips were close to his ear, "prithee put off your journey until sunrise and sleep in your own bed to-night. A lone woman is troubled with such dreams and such thoughts that she's afeard of herself sometimes. Pray tarry with me this night, dear husband, of all nights in the year."

"My love and my Faith," replied young Goodman Brown, "of all nights in the year, this one night must I tarry away from thee. My journey, as thou callest it, forth and back again, must needs be done 'twixt now and sunrise. What, my sweet, pretty wife, dost thou doubt me already, and we but three months married?"

"Then God bless you!" said Faith, with the pink ribbons; "and may you find all well when you come back."

"Amen!" cried Goodman Brown. "Say thy prayers, dear Faith, and go to bed at dusk, and no harm will come to thee."

So they parted; and the young man pursued his way until, being about to turn the corner by the meeting-house, he looked back and saw the head of Faith still peeping after him with a melancholy air, in spite of her pink ribbons.

"Poor little Faith!" thought he, for his heart smote him. "What a wretch am I to leave her on such an errand! She talks of dreams, too. Methought as she spoke there was trouble in her face, as if a dream had warned her what work is to be done to-night. But no, no; 'twould kill her to think it. Well, she's a blessed angel on earth; and after this one night I'll cling to her skirts and follow her to heaven."

With this excellent resolve for the future, Goodman Brown felt himself justified in making more haste on his present evil purpose. He had taken a dreary road, darkened by all the gloomiest trees of the forest, which barely stood aside to let the narrow path creep through, and closed immediately behind. It was all as lonely as could be; and there is this peculiarity in such a solitude, that the traveller knows not who may be concealed by the innumerable trunks and the thick boughs overhead; so that with lonely footsteps he may yet be passing through an unseen multitude.

"There may be a devilish Indian behind every tree," said Goodman Brown to himself; and he glanced fearfully behind him as he added, "What if the devil himself should be at my very elbow!"

His head being turned back, he passed a crook of the road, and, looking forward again, beheld the figure of a man, in grave and decent attire, seated at the foot of an old tree. He arose at Goodman Brown's approach and walked onward side by side with him.

"You are late, Goodman Brown," said he. "The clock of the Old

South was striking as I came through Boston, and that is full fifteen minutes agone."

"Faith kept me back a while," replied the young man, with a tremor in his voice, caused by the sudden appearance of his companion, though not wholly unexpected.

It was now deep dusk in the forest, and deepest in that part of it where these two were journeying. As nearly as could be discerned, the second traveller was about fifty years old, apparently in the same rank of life as Goodman Brown, and bearing a considerable resemblance to him, though perhaps more in expression than features. Still they might have been taken for father and son. And yet, though the elder person was as simply clad as the younger, and as simple in manner too, he had an indescribable air of one who knew the world, and who would not have felt abashed at the governor's dinner table or in King William's court, were it possible that his affairs should call him thither. But the only thing about him that could be fixed upon as remarkable was his staff, which bore the likeness of a great black snake, so curiously wrought that it might almost be seen to twist and wriggle itself like a living serpent. This, of course, must have been an ocular deception, assisted by the uncertain light.

"Come, Goodman Brown," cried his fellow-traveller, "this is a dull pace for the beginning of a journey. Take my staff, if you are so soon weary."

"Friend," said the other, exchanging his slow pace for a full stop, "having kept covenant by meeting thee here, it is my purpose now to return whence I came. I have scruples touching the matter thou wot'st of."

"Sayest thou so?" replied he of the serpent, smiling apart. "Let us walk on, nevertheless, reasoning as we go; and if I convince thee not thou shalt turn back. We are but a little way in the forest yet."

"Too far! too far!" exclaimed the good man, unconsciously resuming his walk. "My father never went into the woods on such an errand, nor his father before him. We have been a race of honest men and good Christians since the days of the martyrs; and shall I be the first of the name of Brown that ever took this path and kept—"

"Such company, thou wouldst say," observed the elder person, interpreting his pause. "Well said, Goodman Brown! I have been as well acquainted with your family as with ever a one among the Puritans; and that's no trifle to say. I helped your grandfather, the constable, when he lashed the Quaker woman so smartly through the streets of Salem; and it was I that brought your father a pitch-pine knot, kindled at my own hearth, to set fire to an Indian village, in King Philip's war. They were my good friends, both; and many a pleasant walk have we had along this path, and returned merrily after midnight. I would fain be friends with you for their sake."

"If it be as thou sayest," replied Goodman Brown, "I marvel they never spoke of these matters; or, verily, I marvel not, seeing that the least rumor of the sort would have driven them from New England. We are a people of prayer, and good works to boot, and abide no such wickedness."

"Wickedness or not," said the traveller with the twisted staff, "I have a very general acquaintance here in New England. The deacons of many a church have drunk the communion wine with me; the selectmen of divers towns make me their chairman; and a majority of the Great and General Court are firm supporters of my interest. The governor and I, too—But these are state secrets."

"Can this be so?" cried Goodman Brown, with a stare of amazement at his undisturbed companion. "Howbeit, I have nothing to do with the governor and council; they have their own ways, and are no rule for a simple husbandman like me. But, were I to go on with thee, how should I meet the eye of that good old man, our minister, at Salem village? Oh, his voice would make me tremble both Sabbath day and lecture day."

Thus far the elder traveller had listened with due gravity; but now burst into a fit of irrepressible mirth, shaking himself so violently that his snake-like staff actually seemed to wriggle in sympathy.

"Ha! ha! ha!" shouted he again and again; then composing himself, "Well, go on, Goodman Brown, go on; but, prithee, don't kill me with laughing."

"Well, then, to end the matter at once," said Goodman Brown, considerably nettled, "there is my wife, Faith. It would break her dear little heart; and I'd rather break my own."

"Nay, if that be the case," answered the other, "e'en go thy ways, Goodman Brown. I would not for twenty old women like the one hobbling before us that Faith should come to any harm."

As he spoke he pointed his staff at a female figure on the path, in whom Goodman Brown recognized a very pious and exemplary dame, who had taught him his catechism in youth, and was still his moral and spiritual adviser, jointly with the minister and Deacon Gookin.

"A marvel, truly, that Goody Cloyse should be so far in the wilderness at nightfall," said he. "But with your leave, friend, I shall take a cut through the woods until we have left this Christian woman behind. Being a stranger to you, she might ask whom I was consorting with and whither I was going."

"Be it so," said his fellow-traveller. "Betake you to the woods, and let me keep the path."

Accordingly the young man turned aside, but took care to watch his companion, who advanced softly along the road until he had come within a staff's length of the old dame. She, meanwhile, was making the best of her way, with singular speed for so aged a woman, and mumbling some indistinct words—a prayer, doubtless—as she went. The traveller put forth his staff and touched her withered neck with what seemed the serpent's tail.

"The devil!" screamed the pious old lady.

"Then Goody Cloyse knows her old friend?" observed the traveller, confronting her and leaning on his writhing stick.

"Ah, forsooth, and is it your worship indeed?" cried the good dame. "Yea, truly is it, and in the very image of my old gossip, Goodman Brown, the grandfather of the silly fellow that now is. But—would your worship believe it?—my broomstick hath strangely disappeared, stolen, as I suspect, by that unhanged witch, Goody Cory, and that, too, when I was all anointed with the juice of smallage, and cinquefoil, and wolf's bane—"

"Mingled with fine wheat and the fat of a new-born babe," said the shape of old Goodman Brown.

"Ah, your worship knows the recipe," cried the old lady, cackling aloud. "So, as I was saying, being all ready for the meeting, and no horse to ride on, I made up my mind to foot it; for they tell me there is a nice young man to be taken into communion to-night. But now your good worship will lend me your arm, and we shall be there in a twinkling."

"That can hardly be," answered her friend. "I may not spare you my arm, Goody Cloyse; but here is my staff, if you will."

So saying, he threw it down at her feet, where, perhaps, it assumed life, being one of the rods which its owner had formerly lent to the Egyptian magi. Of this fact, however, Goodman Brown could not take cognizance. He had cast up his eyes in astonishment, and, looking down again, beheld neither Goody Cloyse nor the serpentine staff, but his fellow-traveller alone, who waited for him as calmly as if nothing had happened.

"That old woman taught me my catechism," said the young man; and there was a world of meaning in this simple comment.

They continued to walk onward, while the elder traveller ex-horted his companion to make good speed and persevere in the path, discoursing so aptly that his arguments seemed rather to spring up in the bosom of his auditor than to be suggested by himself. As they went, he plucked a branch of maple to serve for a walking stick, and began to strip it of the twigs and little boughs, which were wet with evening dew. The moment his fingers touched them they became strangely withered and dried up as with a week's sunshine. Thus the pair proceeded, at a good free pace, until suddenly, in a gloomy hollow of the road, Goodman Brown sat himself down on the stump of a tree and refused to go any farther.

"Friend," said he, stubbornly, "my mind is made up. Not another step will I budge on this errand. What if a wretched old woman do choose to go to the devil when I thought she was going to heaven: is that any reason why I should quit my dear Faith and go after her?"

"You will think better of this by and by," said his acquaintance, composedly. "Sit here and rest yourself a while; and when you feel like moving again, there is my staff to help you along."

Without more words, he threw his companion the maple stick, and was as speedily out of sight as if he had vanished into the deepen-ing gloom. The young man sat a few moments by the roadside, ap-plauding himself greatly, and thinking with how clear a conscience he should meet the minister in his morning walk, nor shrink from the eye of good old Deacon Gookin. And what calm sleep would be his that very night, which was to have been spent so wickedly, but so purely and sweetly now, in the arms of Faith! Amidst these pleasant and praise-worthy meditations, Goodman Brown heard the tramp of horses along the road, and deemed it advisable to conceal himself within the verge of the forest, conscious of the guilty purpose that had brought him thither, though now so happily turned from it.

On came the hoof tramps and the voices of the riders, two grave old voices, conversing soberly as they drew near. These mingled sounds appeared to pass along the road, within a few yards of the young man's hiding-place; but, owing doubtless to the depth of the gloom at that particular spot, neither the travellers nor their steeds were visible. Though their figures brushed the small boughs by the wayside, it could not be seen that they intercepted, even for a moment, the faint gleam from the strip of bright sky athwart which they must have passed. Goodman Brown alternately crouched and stood on tiptoe, pulling aside the branches and thrusting forth his head as far as he durst without discerning so much as a shadow. It vexed him the more, because he could have sworn, were such a thing possible, that he recognized the voices of the minister and Deacon Gookin, jogging along quietly, as they were wont to do, when bound to some ordination or ecclesiastical council. While yet within hearing, one of the riders stopped to pluck a switch.

"Of the two, reverend sir," said the voice like the deacon's, "I had rather miss an ordination dinner than to-night's meeting. They tell me that some of our community are to be here from Falmouth and beyond, and others from Connecticut and Rhode Island, besides several of the Indian powwows, who, after their fashion, know almost as much deviltry as the best of us. Moreover, there is a goodly young woman to be taken into communion."

"Mighty well, Deacon Gookin!" replied the solemn old tones of the minister. "Spur up, or we shall be late. Nothing can be done, you know, until I get on the ground."

The hoofs clattered again; and the voices, talking so strangely in the empty air, passed on through the forest, where no church had ever been gathered or solitary Christian prayed. Whither, then, could these holy men be journeying so deep into the heathen wilderness? Young Goodman Brown caught hold of a tree for support, being ready to sink down on the ground, faint and overburdened with the heavy sickness of his heart. He looked up to the sky, doubting whether there really was a heaven above him. Yet there was the blue arch, and the stars brightening in it.

"With heaven above and Faith below, I will yet stand firm against the devil!" cried Goodman Brown.

While he still gazed upward into the deep arch of the firmament and had lifted his hands to pray, a cloud, though no wind was stirring, hurried across the zenith and hid the brightening stars. The blue sky was still visible, except directly overhead, where this black mass of cloud was sweeping swiftly northward. Aloft in the air, as if from the depths of the cloud, came a confused and doubtful sound of voices. Once the listener fancied that he could distinguish the accents of townspeople of his own, men and women, both pious and ungodly, many of whom he had met at the communion table, and had seen others rioting at the tavern. The next moment, so indistinct were the sounds, he doubted whether he had heard aught but the murmur of the old forest, whispering without a wind. Then came a stronger swell of those familiar tones, heard daily in the sunshine at Salem village, but never until now from a cloud of night. There was one voice, of a young woman, uttering lamentations, yet with an uncertain sorrow, and entreating for some favor, which, perhaps, it would grieve her to obtain; and all the unseen multitude, both saints and sinners, seemed to encourage her onward.

"Faith!" shouted Goodman Brown, in a voice of agony and desperation; and the echoes of the forest mocked him, crying, "Faith! Faith!" as if bewildered wretches were seeking her all through the wilderness.

The cry of grief, rage, and terror was yet piercing the night, when the unhappy husband held his breath for a response. There was a scream, drowned immediately in a louder murmur of voices, fading into far-off laughter, as the dark cloud swept away, leaving the clear and silent sky above Goodman Brown. But something fluttered lightly down through the air and caught on the branch of a tree. The young man seized it, and beheld a pink ribbon.

"My Faith is gone!" cried he, after one stupefied moment. "There is no good on earth; and sin is but a name. Come, devil; for to thee is this world given."

And, maddened with despair, so that he laughed loud and long, did Goodman Brown grasp his staff and set forth again, at such a rate that he seemed to fly along the forest path rather than to walk or run. The road grew wilder and drearier and more faintly traced, and vanished at length, leaving him in the heart of the dark wilderness, still rushing onward with the instinct that guides mortal man to evil. The whole forest was peopled with frightful sounds—the creaking of the trees, the howling of wild beasts, and the yell of Indians; while sometimes the wind tolled like a distant church bell, and sometimes gave a broad roar around the traveller, as if all Nature were laughing him to scorn. But he was himself the chief horror of the scene, and shrank not from its other horrors.

"Ha! ha! ha!" roared Goodman Brown when the wind laughed at him. "Let us hear which will laugh loudest. Think not to frighten me with your deviltry. Come witch, come wizard, come Indian pow-wow, come devil himself, and here comes Goodman Brown. You may as well fear him as he fear you."

In truth, all through the haunted forest there could be nothing more frightful than the figure of Goodman Brown. On he flew among the black pines, brandishing his staff with frenzied gestures, now giving vent to an inspiration of horrid blasphemy, and now shouting forth such laughter as set all the echoes of the forest laughing like demons around him. The fiend in his own shape is less hideous than when he rages in the breast of man. Thus sped the demoniac on his course, until, quivering among the trees, he saw a red light before him, as when the felled trunks and branches of a clearing have been set on fire, and throw up their lurid blaze against the sky, at the hour of midnight. He paused, in a lull of the tempest that had driven him onward, and heard the swell of what seemed a hymn, rolling solemnly from a distance with the weight of many voices. He knew the tune; it was a familiar one in the choir of the village meeting-house. The verse died heavily away, and was lengthened by a chorus, not of human voices, but of all the sounds of the benighted wilderness pealing in awful harmony together. Goodman Brown cried out, and his cry was lost to his own ear by its unison with the cry of the desert.

In the interval of silence he stole forward until the light glared full upon his eyes. At one extremity of an open space, hemmed in by the dark wall of the forest, arose a rock, bearing some rude, natural resemblance either to an altar or a pulpit, and surrounded by four blazing pines, their tops aflame, their stems untouched, like candles at an evening meeting. The mass of foliage that had overgrown the summit of the rock was all on fire, blazing high into the night and fitfully illuminating the whole field. Each pendent twig and leafy festoon was in a blaze. As the red light arose and fell, a numerous congregation alternately shone forth, then disappeared in shadow, and again grew, as it were, out of the darkness, peopling the heart of the solitary woods at once.

"A grave and dark-clad company," quoth Goodman Brown.

In truth they were such. Among them, quivering to and fro between gloom and splendor, appeared faces that would be seen next day at the council board of the province, and others which, Sabbath after Sabbath, looked devoutly heavenward, and benignantly over the crowded pews, from the holiest pulpits in the land. Some affirm that the lady of the governor was there. At least there were high dames well known to her, and wives of honored husbands, and widows, a great multitude, and ancient maidens, all of excellent repute, and fair young girls, who trembled lest their mothers should espy them. Either the sudden gleams of light flashing over the obscure field bedazzled Goodman Brown, or he recognized a score of the church members of Salem village famous for their especial sanctity. Good old Deacon Gookin had arrived, and waited at the skirts of that venerable saint, his revered pastor. But, irreverently consorting with these grave, reputable, and pious people, these elders of the church, these chaste dames and dewy virgins, there were men of dissolute lives and women of spotted fame, wretches given over to all mean and filthy vice, and suspected even of horrid crimes. It was strange to see that the good shrank not from the wicked, nor were the sinners abashed by the saints. Scattered also among their palefaced enemies were the Indian priests, or powwows, who had often scared their native forest with more hideous incantations than any known to English witchcraft.

"But where is Faith?" thought Goodman Brown; and, as hope came into his heart, he trembled.

Another verse of the hymn arose, a slow and mournful strain, such as the pious love, but joined to words which expressed all that our nature can conceive of sin, and darkly hinted at far more. Unfathomable to mere mortals is the lore of fiends. Verse after verse was sung; and still the chorus of the desert swelled between like the deepest tone of a mighty organ; and with the final peal of that dreadful anthem there came a sound, as if the roaring wind, the rushing streams, the howling beasts, and every other voice of the unconcerted wilderness were mingling and according with the voice of guilty man in homage to the prince of all. The four blazing pines threw up a loftier flame, and obscurely discovered shapes and visages of horror on the smoke wreaths above the impious assembly. At the same moment the fire on the rock shot redly forth and formed a glowing arch above its base, where now appeared a figure. With reverence be it spoken, the figure bore no slight similitude, both in garb and manner, to some grave divine of the New England churches.

"Bring forth the converts!" cried a voice that echoed through the field and rolled into the forest.

At the word, Goodman Brown stepped forth from the shadow of the trees and approached the congregation, with whom he felt a loathful brotherhood by the sympathy of all that was wicked in his heart. He could have well-nigh sworn that the shape of his own dead father beckoned him to advance, looking downward from a smoke wreath, while a woman, with dim features of despair, threw out her hand to warn him back. Was it his mother? But he had no power to retreat one step, nor to resist, even in thought, when the minister and good old Deacon Gookin seized his arms and led him to the blazing rock. Thither came also the slender form of a veiled female, led between Goody Cloyse, that pious teacher of the catechism, and Martha Carrier, who had received the devil's promise to be queen of hell. A rampant hag was she. And there stood the proselytes beneath the canopy of fire.

"Welcome, my children," said the dark figure, "to the communion of your race. Ye have found thus young your nature and your destiny. My children, look behind you!"

They turned; and flashing forth, as it were, in a sheet of flame, the fiend worshippers were seen; the smile of welcome gleamed darkly on every visage.

"There," resumed the sable form, "are all whom ye have reverenced from youth. Ye deemed them holier than yourselves, and shrank from your own sin, contrasting it with their lives of righteousness and prayerful aspirations heavenward. Yet here are they all in my worshipping assembly. This night it shall be granted you to know their secret deeds: how hoary-bearded elders of the church have whispered wanton words to the young maids of their households; how many a woman, eager for widows' weeds, has given her husband a drink at bedtime and let him sleep his last sleep in her bosom; how beardless youths have made haste to inherit their fathers' wealth; and how fair damsels—blush not, sweet ones—have dug little graves in the garden, and bidden me, the sole guest, to an infant's funeral. By the sympathy of your human hearts for sin ye shall scent out all the places—whether in church, bedchamber, street, field, or forest—where crime has been committed, and shall exult to behold the whole earth one stain of guilt, one mighty blood spot. Far more than this. It shall be yours to penetrate, in every bosom, the deep mystery of sin, the fountain of all wicked arts, and which inexhaustibly supplies more evil impulses than human power—than my power at its utmost—can make manifest in deeds. And now, my children, look upon each other."

They did so; and, by the blaze of the hell-kindled torches, the wretched man beheld his Faith, and the wife her husband, trembling before that unhallowed altar.

"Lo, there ye stand, my children," said the figure, in a deep and solemn tone, almost sad with its despairing awfulness, as if his once angelic nature could yet mourn for our miserable race. "Depending upon one another's hearts, ye had still hoped that virtue were not all a dream. Now are ye undeceived. Evil is the nature of mankind. Evil must be your only happiness. Welcome again, my children, to the communion of your race."

"Welcome," repeated the fiend worshippers, in one cry of despair and triumph.

And there they stood, the only pair, as it seemed, who were yet hesitating on the verge of wickedness in this dark world. A basin was hollowed, naturally, in the rock. Did it contain water, reddened by the lurid light? or was it blood? or, perchance, a liquid flame? Herein did the shape of evil dip his hand and prepare to lay the mark of baptism upon their foreheads, that they might be partakers of the mystery of sin, more conscious of the secret guilt of others, both in deed and thought, than they could now be of their own. The husband cast one look at his pale wife, and Faith at him. What polluted wretches would the next glance show them to each other, shuddering alike at what they disclosed and what they saw!

"Faith! Faith!" cried the husband, "look up to heaven, and resist the wicked one."

Whether Faith obeyed he knew not. Hardly had he spoken when he found himself amid calm night and solitude, listening to a roar of the wind which died heavily away through the forest. He staggered against the rock, and felt it chill and damp; while a hanging twig, that had been all on fire, besprinkled his cheek with the coldest dew.

The next morning young Goodman Brown came slowly into the street of Salem village, staring around him like a bewildered man. The good old minister was taking a walk along the graveyard to get an appetite for breakfast and meditate his sermon, and bestowed a blessing, as he passed, on Goodman Brown. He shrank from the venerable saint as if to avoid an anathema. Old Deacon Gookin was at domestic worship, and the holy words of his prayer were heard through the open window. "What God doth the wizard pray to?" quoth Goodman Brown. Goody Cloyse, that excellent old Christian, stood in the early sunshine at her own lattice, catechizing a little girl who had brought her a pint of morning's milk. Goodman Brown snatched away the child as from the grasp of the fiend himself. Turning the corner by the meeting-house, he spied the head of Faith, with the pink ribbons, gazing anxiously forth, and bursting into such joy at sight of him that she skipped along the street and almost kissed her husband before the whole village. But Goodman Brown looked sternly and sadly into her face, and passed on without a greeting.

Had Goodman Brown fallen asleep in the forest and only dreamed a wild dream of a witch-meeting?

Be it so if you will; but, alas! it was a dream of evil omen for young Goodman Brown. A stern, a sad, a darkly meditative, a distrustful, if not a desperate man did he become from the night of that fearful dream. On the Sabbath day, when the congregation were singing a holy psalm, he could not listen because an anthem of sin rushed loudly upon his ear and drowned all the blessed strain. When the minister spoke from the pulpit with power and fervid eloquence, and, with his hand on the open Bible, of the sacred truths of our religion, and of saint-like lives and triumphant deaths, and of future bliss or misery unutterable, then did Goodman Brown turn pale, dreading lest the roof should thunder down upon the gray blasphemer and his hearers. Often, awaking suddenly at midnight, he shrank from the bosom of Faith; and at morning or eventide, when the family knelt down at prayer, he scowled and muttered to himself, and gazed sternly at his wife, and turned away. And when he had lived long, and was borne to his grave a hoary corpse, followed by Faith, an aged woman, and children and grandchildren, a goodly procession, besides neighbors not a few, they carved no hopeful verse upon his tombstone, for his dying hour was gloom.

rappaccini's daughter

from the writings of Aubépine

We do not remember to have seen any translated specimens of the productions of M. de l'Aubépine,—a fact the less to be wondered at, as his very name is unknown to many of his own countrymen as well as to the student of foreign literature. As a writer, he seems to occupy an unfortunate position between the Transcendentalists (who, under one name or another, have their share in all the current literature of the world) and the great body of pen-and-ink men who address the intellect and sympathies of the multitude. If not too refined, at all events too remote, too shadowy and unsubstantial in his modes of development, to suit the taste of the latter class, and yet too popular to satisfy the spiritual or metaphysical requisitions of the former, he must necessarily find himself without an audience, except here and there an individual or possibly an isolated clique. His writings, to do them justice, are not altogether destitute of fancy and originality; they might have won him greater reputation but for an inveterate love of allegory, which is apt to invest his plots and characters with the aspect of scenery and people in the clouds, and to steal away the human warmth out of his conceptions. His fictions are sometimes historical, sometimes of the

*present day, and sometimes, so far as can be discovered, have little or
no reference either to time or space. In any case, he generally contents
himself with a very slight embroidery of outward manners,—the
faintest possible counterfeit of real life,—and endeavors to create an
interest by some less obvious peculiarity of the subject. Occasionally a
breath of Nature, a raindrop of pathos and tenderness, or a gleam of
humor, will find its way into the midst of his fantastic imagery, and
make us feel as if, after all, we were yet within the limits of our native
earth. We will only add to this very cursory notice that M. de
l'Aubépine's productions, if the reader chance to take them in precisely
the proper point of view, may amuse a leisure hour as well as those of
a brighter man; if otherwise, they can hardly fail to look excessively like
nonsense.*

*Our author is voluminous; he continues to write and publish
with as much praiseworthy and indefatigable prolixity as if his efforts
were crowned with the brilliant success that so justly attends those of
Eugene Sue. His first appearance was by a collection of stories in a
long series of volumes entitled "Contes deux fois racontées." The titles
of some of his more recent works (we quote from memory) are as
follows: "Le Voyage Céleste à Chemin de Fer," 3 tom., 1838; "Le
nouveau Père Adam et la nouvelle Mère Eve," 2 tom., 1839; "Roderic;
ou le Serpent à l'estomac," 2 tom., 1840; "Le Culte du Feu," a folio
volume of ponderous research into the religion and ritual of the old
Persian Ghebers, published in 1841; "La Soirée du Chateau en
Espagne," 1 tom., 8vo., 1842; and "L'Artiste du Beau; ou le Papillon
Mécanique," 5 tom., 4to., 1843. Our somewhat wearisome perusal of
this startling catalogue of volumes has left behind it a certain personal
affection and sympathy, though by no means admiration, for M. de
l'Aubépine; and we would fain do the little in our power towards
introducing him favorably to the American public. The ensuing tale is
a translation of his "Beatrice; ou la Belle Empoisonneuse," recently
published in* La Revue Anti-Aristocratique. *This journal, edited by the
Comte de Bearhaven, has for some years past led the defence of liberal
principles and popular rights with a faithfulness and ability worthy of
all praise.*

A young man, named Giovanni Guasconti, came, very long ago,
from the more southern region of Italy, to pursue his studies at the
University of Padua. Giovanni, who had but a scanty supply of gold
ducats in his pocket, took lodgings in a high and gloomy chamber of
an old edifice which looked not unworthy to have been the palace of a

Paduan noble, and which, in fact, exhibited over its entrance the armorial bearings of a family long since extinct. The young stranger, who was not unstudied in the great poem of his country, recollected that one of the ancestors of this family, and perhaps an occupant of this very mansion, had been pictured by Dante as a partaker of the immortal agonies of his Inferno. These reminiscences and associations, together with the tendency to heartbreak natural to a young man for the first time out of his native sphere, caused Giovanni to sigh heavily as he looked around the desolate and ill-furnished apartment.

"Holy Virgin, signor!" cried old Dame Lisabetta, who, won by the youth's remarkable beauty of person, was kindly endeavoring to give the chamber a habitable air, "what a sigh was that to come out of a young man's heart! Do you find this old mansion gloomy? For the love of Heaven, then, put your head out of the window, and you will see as bright sunshine as you have left in Naples."

Guasconti mechanically did as the old woman advised, but could not quite agree with her that the Paduan sunshine was as cheerful as that of southern Italy. Such as it was, however, it fell upon a garden beneath the window, and expended its fostering influences on a variety of plants, which seemed to have been cultivated with exceeding care.

"Does this garden belong to the house?" asked Giovanni.

"Heaven forbid, signor, unless it were fruitful of better pot herbs than any that grow there now," answered old Lisabetta. "No; that garden is cultivated by the own hands of Signor Giacomo Rappaccini, the famous doctor, who, I warrant him, has been heard of as far as Naples. It is said that he distills these plants into medicines that are as potent as a charm. Oftentimes you may see the signor doctor at work, and perchance the signora, his daughter, too, gathering the strange flowers that grow in the garden."

The old woman had now done what she could for the aspect of the chamber; and, commending the young man to the protection of the saints, took her departure.

Giovanni still found no better occupation than to look down into the garden beneath his window. From its appearance, he judged it to be one of those botanic gardens which were of earlier date in Padua than elsewhere in Italy, or in the world. Or, not improbably, it might once have been the pleasure-place of an opulent family; for there was the ruin of a marble fountain in the centre, sculptured with rare art, but so wofully shattered that it was impossible to trace the original design from the chaos of remaining fragments. The water, however, continued to gush and sparkle into the sunbeams as cheerfully as ever.

A little gurgling sound ascended to the young man's window, and made him feel as if the fountain were an immortal spirit that sung its song unceasingly and without heeding the vicissitudes around it, while one century embodied it in marble and another scattered the perishable garniture on the soil. All about the pool into which the water subsided grew various plants, that seemed to require a plentiful supply of moisture for the nourishment of gigantic leaves, and, in some instances, flowers gorgeously magnificent. There was one shrub in particular, set in a marble vase in the midst of the pool, that bore a profusion of purple blossoms, each of which had the lustre and richness of a gem; and the whole together made a show so resplendent that it seemed enough to illuminate the garden, even had there been no sunshine. Every portion of the soil was peopled with plants and herbs, which, if less beautiful, still bore tokens of assiduous care, as if all had their individual virtues, known to the scientific mind that fostered them. Some were placed in urns, rich with old carving, and others in common garden pots; some crept serpent-like along the ground or climbed on high, using whatever means of ascent was offered them. One plant had wreathed itself round a statue of Vertumnus, which was thus quite veiled and shrouded in a drapery of hanging foliage, so happily arranged that it might have served a sculptor for a study.

While Giovanni stood at the window he heard a rustling behind a screen of leaves, and became aware that a person was at work in the garden. His figure soon emerged into view, and showed itself to be that of no common laborer, but a tall, emaciated, sallow, and sickly-looking man, dressed in a scholar's garb of black. He was beyond the middle term of life, with gray hair, a thin, gray beard, and a face singularly marked with intellect and cultivation, but which could never, even in his more youthful days, have expressed much warmth of heart.

Nothing could exceed the intentness with which this scientific gardener examined every shrub which grew in his path: it seemed as if he was looking into their inmost nature, making observations in regard to their creative essence, and discovering why one leaf grew in this shape and another in that, and wherefore such and such flowers differed among themselves in hue and perfume. Nevertheless, in spite of this deep intelligence on his part, there was no approach to intimacy between himself and these vegetable existences. On the contrary, he avoided their actual touch or the direct inhaling of their odors with a caution that impressed Giovanni most disagreeably; for the man's demeanor was that of one walking among malignant influences, such as savage beasts, or deadly snakes, or evil spirits, which, should he

47

allow them one moment of license, would wreak upon him some terrible fatality. It was strangely frightful to the young man's imagination to see this air of insecurity in a person cultivating a garden, that most simple and innocent of human toils, and which had been alike the joy and labor of the unfallen parents of the race. Was this garden, then, the Eden of the present world? And this man, with such a perception of harm in what his own hands caused to grow,—was he the Adam?

The distrustful gardener, while plucking away the dead leaves or pruning the too luxuriant growth of the shrubs, defended his hands with a pair of thick gloves. Nor were these his only armor. When, in his walk through the garden, he came to the magnificent plant that hung its purple gems beside the marble fountain, he placed a kind of mask over his mouth and nostrils, as if all this beauty did but conceal a deadlier malice; but, finding his task still too dangerous, he drew back, removed the mask, and called loudly, but in the infirm voice of a person affected with inward disease.

"Beatrice! Beatrice!"

"Here am I, my father. What would you?" cried a rich and youthful voice from the window of the opposite house—a voice as rich as a tropical sunset, and which made Giovanni, though he knew not why, think of deep hues of purple or crimson and of perfumes heavily delectable. "Are you in the garden?"

"Yes, Beatrice," answered the gardener, "and I need your help."

Soon there emerged from under a sculptured portal the figure of a young girl, arrayed with as much richness of taste as the most splendid of the flowers, beautiful as the day, and with a bloom so deep and vivid that one shade more would have been too much. She looked redundant with life, health, and energy; all of which attributes were bound down and compressed, as it were, and girdled tensely, in their luxuriance, by her virgin zone. Yet Giovanni's fancy must have grown morbid while he looked down into the garden; for the impression which the fair stranger made upon him was as if here were another flower, the human sister of those vegetable ones, as beautiful as they, more beautiful than the richest of them, but still to be touched only with a glove, nor to be approached without a mask. As Beatrice came down the garden path, it was observable that she handled and inhaled the odor of several of the plants which her father had most sedulously avoided.

"Here, Beatrice," said the latter, "see how many needful offices require to be done to our chief treasure. Yet, shattered as I am, my life might pay the penalty of approaching it so closely as circumstances demand. Henceforth, I fear, this plant must be consigned to your sole charge."

"And gladly will I undertake it," cried again the rich tones of the young lady, as she bent towards the magnificent plant and opened her arms as if to embrace it. "Yes, my sister, my splendor, it shall be Beatrice's task to nurse and serve thee; and thou shalt reward her with thy kisses and perfumed breath, which to her is as the breath of life."

Then, with all the tenderness in her manner that was so strikingly expressed in her words, she busied herself with such attentions as the plant seemed to require; and Giovanni, at his lofty window, rubbed his eyes and almost doubted whether it were a girl tending her favorite flower, or one sister performing the duties of affection to another.

The scene soon terminated. Whether Dr. Rappaccini had finished his labors in the garden or that his watchful eye had caught the stranger's face, he now took his daughter's arm and retired. Night was already closing in; oppressive exhalations seemed to proceed from the plants and steal upward past the open window; and Giovanni, closing the lattice, went to his couch and dreamed of a rich flower and beautiful girl. Flower and maiden were different, and yet the same, and fraught with some strange peril in either shape.

But there is an influence in the light of morning that tends to rectify whatever errors of fancy, or even of judgment, we may have incurred during the sun's decline, or among the shadows of the night, or in the less wholesome glow of moonshine. Giovanni's first movement, on starting from sleep, was to throw open the window and gaze down into the garden which his dreams had made so fertile of mysteries. He was surprised and a little ashamed to find how real and matter-of-fact an affair it proved to be, in the first rays of the sun which gilded the dew-drops that hung upon leaf and blossom, and, while giving a brighter beauty to each rare flower, brought everything within the limits of ordinary experience. The young man rejoiced that, in the heart of the barren city, he had the privilege of overlooking this spot of lovely and luxuriant vegetation. It would serve, he said to himself, as a symbolic language to keep him in communion with Nature. Neither the sickly and thought-worn Dr. Giacomo Rappaccini, it is true, nor his brilliant daughter, were now visible; so that Giovanni could not determine how much of the singularity which he attributed to both was due to their own qualities and how much to his wonder-working fancy; but he was inclined to take a most rational view of the whole matter.

In the course of the day he paid his respects to Signor Pietro Baglioni, professor of medicine in the university, a physician of eminent repute, to whom Giovanni had brought a letter of introduction. The professor was an elderly personage, apparently of genial nature, and habits that might almost be called jovial. He kept the young man to dinner, and made himself very agreeable by the freedom and liveliness of his conversation, especially when warmed by a flask or two of Tuscan wine. Giovanni, conceiving that men of science, inhabitants of the same city, must needs be on familiar terms with one another, took an opportunity to mention the name of Dr. Rappaccini. But the professor did not respond with so much cordiality as he had anticipated.

"Ill would it become a teacher of the divine art of medicine," said Professor Pietro Baglioni, in answer to a question of Giovanni, "to withhold due and well-considered praise of a physician so eminently skilled as Rappaccini; but, on the other hand, I should answer it but scantily to my conscience were I to permit a worthy youth like yourself, Signor Giovanni, the son of an ancient friend, to imbibe erroneous ideas respecting a man who might hereafter chance to hold your life and death in his hands. The truth is, our worshipful Dr. Rappaccini has as much science as any member of the faculty—with perhaps one single exception—in Padua, or all Italy; but there are certain grave objections to his professional character."

"And what are they?" asked the young man.

"Has my friend Giovanni any disease of body or heart, that he is so inquisitive about physicians?" said the professor, with a smile. "But as for Rappaccini, it is said of him—and I, who know the man well, can answer for its truth—that he cares infinitely more for science than for mankind. His patients are interesting to him only as subjects for some new experiment. He would sacrifice human life, his own among the rest, or whatever else was dearest to him, for the sake of adding so much as a grain of mustard seed to the great heap of his accumulated knowledge."

"Methinks he is an awful man indeed," remarked Guasconti, mentally recalling the cold and purely intellectual aspect of Rappaccini. "And yet, worshipful professor, is it not a noble spirit? Are there many men capable of so spiritual a love of science?"

"God forbid," answered the professor, somewhat testily; "at least, unless they take sounder views of the healing art than those adopted by Rappaccini. It is his theory that all medicinal virtues are comprised within those substances which we term vegetable poisons. These he cultivates with his own hands, and is said even to have produced new varieties of poison, more horribly deleterious than Nature, without the assistance of this learned person, would ever have plagued the world withal. That the signor doctor does less mischief than might be expected with such dangerous substances is undeniable. Now and then, it must be owned, he has effected, or seemed to effect, a marvellous cure; but, to tell you my private mind, Signor Giovanni, he should receive little credit for such instances of success,—they being probably the work of chance,—but should be held strictly accountable for his failures, which may justly be considered his own work."

The youth might have taken Baglioni's opinions with many grains of allowance had he known that there was a professional warfare of long continuance between him and Dr. Rappaccini, in which the latter was generally thought to have gained the advantage. If the reader be inclined to judge for himself, we refer him to certain black-letter tracts on both sides, preserved in the medical department of the University of Padua.

"I know not, most learned professor," returned Giovanni, after musing on what had been said of Rappaccini's exclusive zeal for science,—"I know not how dearly this physician may love his art; but surely there is one object more dear to him. He has a daughter."

"Aha!" cried the professor, with a laugh. "So now our friend Giovanni's secret is out. You have heard of this daughter, whom all the young men in Padua are wild about, though not half a dozen have ever had the good hap to see her face. I know little of the Signora Beatrice save that Rappaccini is said to have instructed her deeply in his science, and that, young and beautiful as fame reports her, she is already qualified to fill a professor's chair. Perchance her father destines her for mine! Other absurd rumors there be, not worth talking about or listening to. So now, Signor Giovanni, drink off your glass of lachryma."

Guasconti returned to his lodgings somewhat heated with the wine he had quaffed, and which caused his brain to swim with strange fantasies in reference to Dr. Rappaccini and the beautiful Beatrice. On his way, happening to pass by a florist's, he bought a fresh bouquet of flowers.

Ascending to his chamber, he seated himself near the window, but within the shadow thrown by the depth of the wall, so that he could look down into the garden with little risk of being discovered. All beneath his eye was a solitude. The strange plants were basking in the sunshine, and now and then nodding gently to one another, as if in acknowledgment of sympathy and kindred. In the midst, by the shattered fountain, grew the magnificent shrub, with its purple gems clustering all over it; they glowed in the air, and gleamed back again out of the depths of the pool, which thus seemed to overflow with colored radiance from the rich reflection that was steeped in it. At first, as we have said, the garden was a solitude. Soon, however,—as Giovanni had half hoped, half feared, would be the case,—a figure appeared beneath the antique sculptured portal, and came down between the rows of plants, inhaling their various perfumes as if she were one of those beings of old classic fable that lived upon sweet odors. On again beholding Beatrice, the young man was even startled to perceive how much her beauty exceeded his recollection of it; so brilliant, so vivid, was its character, that she glowed amid the sunlight, and, as Giovanni whispered to himself, positively illuminated the more shadowy intervals of the garden path. Her face being now more revealed than on the former occasion, he was struck by its expression of simplicity and sweetness,—qualities that had not entered into his idea of her character, and which made him ask anew what manner of mortal she might be. Nor did he fail again to observe, or imagine, an analogy between the beautiful girl and the gorgeous shrub that hung its gemlike flowers over the fountain,—a resemblance which Beatrice seemed to have indulged a fantastic humor in heightening, both by the arrangement of her dress and the selection of its hues.

Approaching the shrub, she threw open her arms, as with a passionate ardor, and drew its branches into an intimate embrace—so intimate that her features were hidden in its leafy bosom and her glistening ringlets all intermingled with the flowers.

"Give me thy breath, my sister," exclaimed Beatrice; "for I am faint with common air. And give me this flower of thine, which I separate with gentlest fingers from the stem and place it close beside my heart."

With these words the beautiful daughter of Rappaccini plucked one of the richest blossoms of the shrub, and was about to fasten it in her bosom. But now, unless Giovanni's draughts of wine had bewildered his senses, a singular incident occurred. A small orange-colored reptile, of the lizard or chameleon species, chanced to be creeping along the path, just at the feet of Beatrice. It appeared to Giovanni,—but, at the distance from which he gazed, he could scarcely have seen anything so minute,—it appeared to him, however, that a drop or two of moisture from the broken stem of the flower descended upon the lizard's head. For an instant the reptile contorted itself violently, and then lay motionless in the sunshine. Beatrice observed this remarkable phenomenon, and crossed herself, sadly, but without surprise; nor did she therefore hesitate to arrange the fatal flower in her bosom. There it blushed, and almost glimmered with the dazzling effect of a precious stone, adding to her dress and aspect the one appropriate charm which nothing else in the world could have supplied. But Giovanni, out of the shadow of his window, bent forward and shrank back, and murmured and trembled.

"Am I awake? Have I my senses?" said he to himself. "What is this being? Beautiful shall I call her, or inexpressibly terrible?"

Beatrice now strayed carelessly through the garden, approaching closer beneath Giovanni's window, so that he was compelled to thrust his head quite out of its concealment in order to gratify the intense and painful curiosity which she excited. At this moment there came a beautiful insect over the garden wall; it had, perhaps, wandered through the city and found no flowers or verdure among those antique haunts of men until the heavy perfumes of Dr. Rappaccini's shrubs had lured it from afar. Without alighting on the flowers, this winged brightness seemed to be attracted by Beatrice, and lingered in the air and fluttered about her head. Now, here it could not be but that Giovanni Guasconti's eyes deceived him. Be that as it might, he fancied that, while Beatrice was gazing at the insect with childish delight, it grew faint and fell at her feet; its bright wings shivered; it was dead—from no cause that he could discern, unless it were the atmosphere of her breath. Again Beatrice crossed herself and sighed heavily as she bent over the dead insect.

An impulsive movement of Giovanni drew her eyes to the window. There she beheld the beautiful head of the young man—rather a Grecian than an Italian head, with fair, regular features, and a glistening of gold among his ringlets—gazing down upon her like a being that hovered in mid air. Scarcely knowing what he did, Giovanni threw down the bouquet which he had hitherto held in his hand.

"Signora," said he, "there are pure and healthful flowers. Wear them for the sake of Giovanni Guasconti."

"Thanks, signor," replied Beatrice, with her rich voice, that came forth as it were like a gush of music, and with a mirthful expression half childish and half woman-like. "I accept your gift, and would fain recompense it with this precious purple flower; but if I toss it into the air it will not reach you. So Signor Guasconti must even content himself with my thanks."

She lifted the bouquet from the ground, and then, as if inwardly ashamed at having stepped aside from her maidenly reserve to respond to a stranger's greeting, passed swiftly homeward through the garden. But few as the moments were, it seemed to Giovanni, when she was on the point of vanishing beneath the sculptured portal, that his beautiful bouquet was already beginning to wither in her grasp. It was an idle thought; there could be no possibility of distinguishing a faded flower from a fresh one at so great a distance.

For many days after this incident the young man avoided the window that looked into Dr. Rappaccini's garden, as if something ugly and monstrous would have blasted his eyesight had he been betrayed into a glance. He felt conscious of having put himself, to a certain extent, within the influence of an unintelligible power by the communication which he had opened with Beatrice. The wisest course would have been, if his heart were in any real danger, to quit his lodgings and Padua itself at once; the next wiser, to have accustomed himself, as far as possible, to the familiar and daylight view of Beatrice,—thus bringing her rigidly and systematically within the limits of ordinary experience. Least of all, while avoiding her sight, ought Giovanni to have remained so near this extraordinary being that the proximity and possibility even of intercourse should give a kind of substance and reality to the wild vagaries which his imagination ran riot continually in producing. Guasconti had not a deep heart—or, at all events, its depths were not sounded now; but he had a quick fancy, and an ardent southern temperament, which rose every instant to a higher fever pitch. Whether or no Beatrice possessed those terrible attributes, that fatal breath, the affinity with those so beautiful and deadly flowers which were indicated by what Giovanni had witnessed, she had at least instilled a fierce and subtle poison into his system. It was not love, although her rich beauty was a madness to him; nor horror, even while he fancied her spirit to be imbued with the same baneful essence that seemed to pervade her physical frame; but a wild offspring of both love and horror that had each parent in it, and burned like one and shivered like the other. Giovanni knew not what to dread; still less did he know what to hope; yet hope and dread kept a continual warfare in his breast, alternately vanquishing one another and starting up afresh to renew the contest. Blessed are all simple emotions, be they dark or bright! It is the lurid intermixture of the two that produces the illuminating blaze of the infernal regions.

Sometimes he endeavored to assuage the fever of his spirit by a rapid walk through the streets of Padua or beyond its gates: his footsteps kept time with the throbbings of his brain, so that the walk was apt to accelerate itself to a race. One day he found himself arrested;

his arm was seized by a portly personage who had turned back on recognizing the young man and expended much breath in overtaking him.

"Signor Giovanni! Stay, my young friend!" cried he. "Have you forgotten me? That might well be the case if I were as much altered as yourself."

It was Baglioni, whom Giovanni had avoided ever since their first meeting, from a doubt that the professor's sagacity would look too deeply into his secrets. Endeavoring to recover himself, he stared forth wildly from his inner world into the outer one and spoke like a man in a dream.

"Yes; I am Giovanni Guasconti. You are Professor Pietro Baglioni. Now let me pass!"

"Not yet, not yet, Signor Giovanni Guasconti," said the professor, smiling, but at the same time scrutinizing the youth with an earnest glance. "What! Did I grow up side by side with your father? and shall his son pass me like a stranger in these old streets of Padua? Stand still, Signor Giovanni; for we must have a word or two before we part."

"Speedily, then, most worshipful professor, speedily," said Giovanni, with feverish impatience. "Does not your worship see that I am in haste?"

Now, while he was speaking there came a man in black along the street, stooping and moving feebly like a person in inferior health. His face was all overspread with a most sickly and sallow hue, but yet so pervaded with an expression of piercing and active intellect that an observer might easily have overlooked the merely physical attributes and have seen only this wonderful energy. As he passed, this person exchanged a cold and distant salutation with Baglioni, but fixed his eyes upon Giovanni with an intentness that seemed to bring out whatever was within him worthy of notice. Nevertheless, there was a peculiar quietness in the look, as if taking merely a speculative, not a human, interest in the young man.

"It is Dr. Rappaccini!" whispered the professor, when the stranger had passed. "Has he ever seen your face before?"

"Not that I know," answered Giovanni, starting at the name.

"He *has* seen you! he must have seen you!" said Baglioni hastily. "For some purpose or other, this man of science is making a study of you. I know that look of his! It is the same that coldly illuminates his face as he bends over a bird, a mouse, or a butterfly, which, in pursuance of some experiment, he has killed by the perfume of a flower; a look as deep as Nature itself, but without Nature's warmth of love. Signor Giovanni, I will stake my life upon it, you are the subject of one of Rappaccini's experiments!"

"Will you make a fool of me?" cried Giovanni passionately. "*That,* signor professor, were an untoward experiment."

"Patience, patience!" replied the imperturable professor. "I tell thee, my poor Giovanni, that Rappaccini has a scientific interest in thee. Thou has fallen into fearful hands! And the Signora Beatrice,— what part does she act in this mystery?"

But Guasconti, finding Baglioni's pertinacity intolerable, here broke away, and was gone before the professor could again seize his arm. He looked after the young man intently and shook his head.

"This must not be," said Baglioni to himself. "The youth is the son of my old friend, and shall not come to any harm from which the arcana of medical science can preserve him. Besides, it is too insufferable an impertinence in Rappaccini, thus to snatch the lad out of my own hands, as I may say, and make use of him for his infernal experiments. This daughter of his! It shall be looked to. Perchance, most learned Rappaccini, I may foil you where you little dream of it!"

Meanwhile, Giovanni had pursued a circuitous route, and at length found himself at the door of his lodgings. As he crossed the threshold he was met by old Lisabetta, who smirked and smiled, and was evidently desirous to attract his attention; vainly, however, as the ebullition of his feelings had momentarily subsided into a cold and dull vacuity. He turned his eyes full upon the withered face that was puckering itself into a smile, but seemed to behold it not. The old dame, therefore, laid her grasp upon his cloak.

"Signor! signor!" whispered she, still with a smile over the whole breadth of her visage, so that it looked not unlike a grotesque carving in wood, darkened by centuries. "Listen, signor! There is a private entrance into the garden!"

"What do you say?" exclaimed Giovanni, turning quickly about, as if an inanimate thing should start into feverish life. "A private entrance into Dr. Rappaccini's garden?"

"Hush! hush! Not so loud!" whispered Lisabetta, putting her hand over his mouth. "Yes; into the worshipful doctor's garden, where you may see all his fine shrubbery. Many a young man in Padua would give gold to be admitted among those flowers."

Giovanni put a piece of gold into her hand.

"Show me the way," said he.

A surmise, probably excited by his conversation with Baglioni,

crossed his mind, that this interposition of old Lisabetta might perchance be connected with the intrigue, whatever were its nature, in
which the professor seemed to suppose that Dr. Rappaccini was involving him. But such a suspicion, though it disturbed Giovanni,
was inadequate to restrain him. The instant that he was aware of the
possibility of approaching Beatrice, it seemed an absolute necessity of
his existence to do so. It mattered not whether she were angel or
demon; he was irrevocably within her sphere, and must obey the law
that whirled him onward, in ever lessening circles, towards a result
which he did not attempt to foreshadow; and yet, strange to say, there
came across him a sudden doubt whether this intense interest on his
part were not delusory; whether it were really of so deep and positive a
nature as to justify him in now thrusting himself into an incalculable
position; whether it were not merely the fantasy of a young man's
brain, only slightly or not at all connected with his heart.

He paused, hesitated, turned half about, but again went on. His
withered guide led him along several obscure passages, and finally
undid a door, through which, as it was opened, there came the sight and
sound of rustling leaves, with the broken sunshine glimmering among
them. Giovanni stepped forth, and, forcing himself through the
entanglement of a shrub that wreathed its tendrils over the hidden
entrance, stood beneath his own window in the open area of Dr.
Rappaccini's garden.

How often is it the case that, when impossibilities have come to
pass and dreams have condensed their misty substance into tangible
realities, we find ourselves calm, and even coldly self-possessed, amid
circumstances which it would have been a delirium of joy or agony to
anticipate! Fate delights to thwart us thus. Passion will choose his own
time to rush upon the scene, and lingers sluggishly behind when an
appropriate adjustment of events would seem to summon his appearance. So was it now with Giovanni. Day after day his pulses had
throbbed with feverish blood at the improbable idea of an interview
with Beatrice, and of standing with her, face to face, in this very
garden, basking in the Oriental sunshine of her beauty, and snatching
from her full gaze the mystery which he deemed the riddle of his own
existence. But now there was a singular and untimely equanimity
within his breast. He threw a glance around the garden to discover if
Beatrice or her father were present, and, perceiving that he was alone,
began a critical observation of the plants.

The aspect of one and all of them dissatisfied him; their
gorgeousness seemed fierce, passionate, and even unnatural. There was

hardly an individual shrub which a wanderer, straying by himself through a forest, would not have been startled to find growing wild, as if an unearthly face had glared at him out of the thicket. Several also would have shocked a delicate instinct by an appearance of artificialness indicating that there had been such commixture, and, as it were, adultery, of various vegetable species, that the production was no longer of God's making, but the monstrous offspring of man's depraved fancy, glowing with only an evil mockery of beauty. They were probably the result of experiment, which in one or two cases had succeeded in mingling plants individually lovely into a compound possessing the questionable and ominous character that distinguished the whole growth of the garden. In fine, Giovanni recognized but two or three plants in the collection, and those of a kind that he well knew to be poisonous. While busy with these contemplations he heard the rustling of a silken garment, and, turning, beheld Beatrice emerging from beneath the sculptured portal.

Giovanni had not considered with himself what should be his deportment; whether he should apologize for his intrusion into the garden, or assume that he was there with the privity at least, if not by the desire, of Dr. Rappaccini or his daughter; but Beatrice's manner placed him at his ease, though leaving him still in doubt by what agency he had gained admittance. She came lightly along the path and met him near the broken fountain. There was surprise in her face, but brightened by a simple and kind expression of pleasure.

"You are a connoisseur in flowers, signor," said Beatrice, with a smile, alluding to the bouquet which he had flung her from the window. "It is no marvel, therefore, if the sight of my father's rare collection has tempted you to take a nearer view. If he were here, he could tell you many strange and interesting facts as to the nature and habits of these shrubs; for he has spent a lifetime in such studies, and this garden is his world."

"And yourself, lady," observed Giovanni, "if fame says true,—you likewise are deeply skilled in the virtues indicated by these rich blossoms and these spicy perfumes. Would you deign to be my instructress, I should prove an apter scholar than if taught by Signor Rappaccini himself."

"Are there such idle rumors?" asked Beatrice, with the music of a pleasant laugh. "Do people say that I am skilled in my father's science of plants? What a jest is there! No; though I have grown up among these flowers, I know no more of them than their hues and perfume; and sometimes methinks I would fain rid myself of even that small knowledge. There are many flowers here, and those not the least brilliant, that shock and offend me when they meet my eye. But pray, signor, do not believe these stories about my science. Believe nothing of me save what you see with your own eyes."

"And must I believe all that I have seen with my own eyes?" asked Giovanni, pointedly, while the recollection of former scenes made him shrink. "No, signora; you demand too little of me. Bid me believe nothing save what comes from your own lips."

It would appear that Beatrice understood him. There came a deep flush to her cheek, but she looked full into Giovanni's eyes and responded to his gaze of uneasy suspicion with a queenlike haughtiness.

"I do so bid you, signor," she replied. "Forget whatever you may have fancied in regard to me. If true to the outward senses, still it may be false in its essence; but the words of Beatrice Rappaccini's lips are true from the depths of the heart outward. Those you may believe."

A fervor glowed in her whole aspect and beamed upon Giovanni's consciousness like the light of truth itself; but while she spoke there was a fragrance in the atmosphere around her, rich and delightful, though evanescent, yet which the young man, from an indefinable reluctance, scarcely dared to draw into his lungs. It might be the odor of the flowers. Could it be Beatrice's breath which thus embalmed her words with a strange richness, as if by steeping them in her heart? A faintness passed like a shadow over Giovanni and flitted away; he seemed to gaze through the beautiful girl's eyes into her transparent soul, and felt no more doubt or fear.

The tinge of passion that had colored Beatrice's manner vanished; she became gay, and appeared to derive a pure delight from her communion with the youth not unlike what the maiden of a lonely island might have felt conversing with a voyager from the civilized world. Evidently her experience of life had been confined within the limits of that garden. She talked now about matters as simple as the daylight or summer clouds, and now asked questions in reference to the city, or Giovanni's distant home, his friends, his mother, and his sisters—questions indicating such seclusion, and such lack of familiarity with modes and forms, that Giovanni responded as if to an infant. Her spirit gushed out before him like a fresh rill that was just catching its first glimpse of the sunlight and wondering at the reflections of earth and sky which were flung into its bosom. There came thoughts, too, from a deep source, and fantasies of a gemlike brilliancy, as if diamonds and rubies sparkled upward among the bubbles of the fountain. Ever and anon there gleamed across the young man's mind a sense of wonder

that he should be walking side by side with the being who had so
wrought upon his imagination, whom he had idealized in such hues
of terror, in whom he had positively witnessed such manifestations of
dreadful attributes,—that he should be conversing with Beatrice like a
brother, and should find her so human and so maidenlike. But such
reflections were only momentary; the effect of her character was too real
not to make itself familiar at once.

In this free intercourse they had strayed through the garden, and
now, after many turns among its avenues, were come to the shattered
fountain, beside which grew the magnificent shrub with its treasury of
glowing blossoms. A fragrance was diffused from it which Giovanni
recognized as identical with that which he had attributed to Beatrice's
breath, but incomparably more powerful. As her eyes fell upon it,
Giovanni beheld her press her hand to her bosom, as if her heart were
throbbing suddenly and painfully.

"For the first time in my life," murmured she, addressing the
shrub, "I had forgotten thee."

"I remember, signora," said Giovanni, "that you once promised
to reward me with one of these living gems for the bouquet which I
had the happy boldness to fling to your feet. Permit me now to pluck
it as a memorial of this interview."

He made a step toward the shrub with extended hand; but
Beatrice darted forward, uttering a shriek that went through his
heart like a dagger. She caught his hand and drew it back with the
whole force of her slender figure. Giovanni felt her touch thrilling
through his fibres.

"Touch it not!" exclaimed she, in a voice of agony. "Not for thy
life! It is fatal!"

Then, hiding her face, she fled from him and vanished beneath
the sculptured portal. As Giovanni followed her with his eyes, he
beheld the emaciated figure and pale intelligence of Dr. Rappaccini,
who had been watching the scene, he knew not how long, within the
shadow of the entrance.

No sooner was Guasconti alone in his chamber than the image
of Beatrice came back to his passionate musings, invested with all the
witchery that had been gathering around it ever since his first glimpse
of her, and now likewise imbued with a tender warmth of girlish
womanhood. She was human; her nature was endowed with all gentle
and feminine qualities; she was worthiest to be worshipped; she was
capable, surely, on her part, of the height and heroism of love. Those
tokens which he had hitherto considered as proofs of a frightful

peculiarity in her physical and moral system were now either forgotten, or, by the subtle sophistry of passion transmuted into a golden crown of enchantment, rendering Beatrice the more admirable by so much as she was the more unique. Whatever had looked ugly was now beautiful; or, if incapable of such a change, it stole away and hid itself among those shapeless half ideas which throng the dim region beyond the daylight of our perfect consciousness.

Thus did he spend the night, nor fell asleep until the dawn had begun to awake the slumbering flowers in Dr. Rappaccini's garden, whither Giovanni's dreams doubtless led him. Up rose the sun in his due season, and, flinging his beams upon the young man's eyelids, awoke him to a sense of pain. When thoroughly aroused, he became sensible of a burning and tingling agony in his hand—in his right hand—the very hand which Beatrice had grasped in her own when he was on the point of plucking one of the gemlike flowers. On the back of that hand there was now a purple print like that of four small fingers, and the likeness of a slender thumb upon his wrist.

Oh, how stubbornly does love,—or even that cunning semblance of love which flourishes in the imagination, but strikes no depth of root into the heart,—how stubbornly does it hold its faith until the moment comes when it is doomed to vanish into thin mist! Giovanni wrapped a handkerchief about his hand and wondered what evil thing had stung him, and soon forgot his pain in a reverie of Beatrice.

After the first interview, a second was in the inevitable course of what we call fate. A third; a fourth; and a meeting with Beatrice in the garden was no longer an incident in Giovanni's daily life, but the whole space in which he might be said to live; for the anticipation and memory of that ecstatic hour made up the remainder. Nor was it otherwise with the daughter of Rappaccini. She watched for the youth's appearance, and flew to his side with confidence as unreserved as if they had been playmates from early infancy—as if they were such playmates still. If, by any unwonted chance, he failed to come at the appointed moment, she stood beneath the window and sent up the rich sweetness of her tones to float around him in his chamber and echo and reverberate throughout his heart: "Giovanni! Giovanni! Why tarriest thou? Come down!" And down he hastened into that Eden of poisonous flowers.

But, with all this intimate familiarity, there was still a reserve in Beatrice's demeanor, so rigidly and invariably sustained that the idea of infringing it scarcely occurred to his imagination. By all appreciable signs, they loved; they had looked love with eyes that conveyed the holy secret from the depths of one soul into the depths of the other, as if it were too sacred to be whispered by the way; they had even spoken love in those gushes of passion when their spirits darted forth in articulated breath like tongues of long-hidden flame; and yet there had been no seal of lips, no clasp of hands, nor any slightest caress such as love claims and hallows. He had never touched one of the gleaming ringlets of her hair; her garment—so marked was the physical barrier between them—had never been waved against him by a breeze. On the few occasions when Giovanni had seemed tempted to overstep the limit, Beatrice grew so sad, so stern, and withal wore such a look of desolate separation, shuddering at itself, that not a spoken word was requisite to repel him. At such times he was startled at the horrible suspicions that rose, monster-like, out of the caverns of his heart and stared him in the face; his love grew thin and faint as the morning mist; his doubts alone had substance. But, when Beatrice's face brightened again after the momentary shadow, she was transformed at once from the mysterious, questionable being whom he had watched with so much awe and horror; she was now the beautiful and unsophisticated girl whom he felt that his spirit knew with a certainty beyond all other knowledge.

A considerable time had now passed since Giovanni's last meeting with Baglioni. One morning, however, he was disagreeably surprised by a visit from the professor, whom he had scarcely thought of for whole weeks, and would willingly have forgotten still longer. Given up as he had long been to a pervading excitement, he could tolerate no companions except upon condition of their perfect sympathy with his present state of feeling. Such sympathy was not to be expected from Professor Baglioni.

The visitor chatted carelessly for a few moments about the gossip of the city and the university, and then took up another topic.

"I have been reading an old classic author lately," said he, "and met with a story that strangely interested me. Possibly you may remember it. It is of an Indian prince, who sent a beautiful woman as a present to Alexander the Great. She was as lovely as the dawn and gorgeous as the sunset; but what especially distinguished her was a certain rich perfume in her breath—richer than a garden of Persian roses. Alexander, as was natural to a youthful conqueror, fell in love at first sight with this magnificent stranger; but a certain sage physician, happening to be present, discovered a terrible secret in regard to her."

"And what was that?" asked Giovanni, turning his eyes downward to avoid those of the professor.

"That this lovely woman," continued Baglioni, with emphasis, "had been nourished with poisons from her birth upward, until her whole nature was so imbued with them that she herself had become the deadliest poison in existence. Poison was her element of life. With that rich perfume of her breath she blasted the very air. Her love would have been poison—her embrace death. Is not this a marvelous tale?"

"A childish fable," answered Giovanni, nervously starting from his chair. "I marvel how your worship finds time to read such nonsense among your graver studies."

"By the by," said the professor, looking uneasily about him, "what singular fragrance is this in your apartment? Is it the perfume of your gloves? It is faint, but delicious; and yet, after all, by no means agreeable. Were I to breathe it long, methinks it would make me ill. It is like the breath of a flower; but I see no flowers in the chamber."

"Nor are there any," replied Giovanni, who had turned pale as the professor spoke; "nor, I think, is there any fragrance except in your worship's imagination. Odors, being a sort of element combined of the sensual and the spiritual, are apt to deceive us in this manner. The recollection of a perfume, the bare idea of it, may easily be mistaken for a present reality."

"Ay; but my sober imagination does not often play such tricks," said Baglioni; "and, were I to fancy any kind of odor, it would be that of some vile apothecary drug, wherewith my fingers are likely enough to be imbued. Our worshipful friend Rappaccini, as I have heard, tinctures his medicaments with odors richer than those of Araby. Doubtless, likewise, the fair and learned Signora Beatrice would minister to her patients with draughts as sweet as a maiden's breath; but woe to him that sips them!"

Giovanni's face evinced many contending emotions. The tone in which the professor alluded to the pure and lovely daughter of Rappaccini was a torture to his soul; and yet the intimation of a view of her character, opposite to his own, gave instantaneous distinctness to a thousand dim suspicions, which now grinned at him like so many demons. But he strove hard to quell them and to respond to Baglioni with a true lover's perfect faith.

"Signor professor," said he, "you were my father's friend; perchance, too, it is your purpose to act a friendly part towards his son. I would fain feel nothing towards you save respect and deference; but I pray you to observe, signor, that there is one subject on which we must not speak. You know not the Signora Beatrice. You cannot, therefore, estimate the wrong—the blasphemy, I may even say—that is offered to her character by a light or injurious word."

63

"Giovanni! my poor Giovanni!" answered the professor, with a calm expression of pity, "I know this wretched girl far better than yourself. You shall hear the truth in respect to the poisoner Rappaccini and his poisonous daughter; yes, poisonous as she is beautiful. Listen; for, even should you do violence to my gray hairs, it shall not silence me. That old fable of the Indian woman has become a truth by the deep and deadly science of Rappaccini and in the person of the lovely Beatrice."

Giovanni groaned and hid his face.

"Her father," continued Baglioni, "was not restrained by natural affection from offering up his child in this horrible manner as the victim of his insane zeal for science; for, let us do him justice, he is as true a man of science as ever distilled his own heart in an alembic. What, then, will be your fate? Beyond a doubt you are selected as the material of some new experiment. Perhaps the result is to be death; perhaps a fate more awful still. Rappaccini, with what he calls the interest of science before his eyes, will hesitate at nothing."

"It is a dream," muttered Giovanni to himself; "surely it is a dream."

"But," resumed the professor, "be of good cheer, son of my friend. It is not yet too late for the rescue. Possibly we may even succeed in bringing back this miserable child within the limits of ordinary nature, from which her father's madness has estranged her. Behold this little silver vase! It was wrought by the hands of the renowned Benvenuto Cellini, and is well worthy to be a love gift to the fairest dame in Italy. But its contents are invaluable. One little sip of this antidote would have rendered the most virulent poisons of the Borgias innocuous. Doubt not that it will be as efficacious against those of Rappaccini. Bestow the vase, and the precious liquid within it, on your Beatrice, and hopefully await the result."

Baglioni laid a small, exquisitely wrought silver vial on the table and withdrew, leaving what he had said to produce its effect upon the young man's mind.

"We will thwart Rappaccini yet," thought he, chuckling to himself, as he descended the stairs; "but, let us confess the truth of him, he is a wonderful man—a wonderful man indeed; a vile empiric, however, in his practice, and therefore not to be tolerated by those who respect the good old rules of the medical profession."

Throughout Giovanni's whole acquaintance with Beatrice, he had occasionally, as we have said, been haunted by dark surmises as to her character; yet so thoroughly had she made herself felt by him as a simple, natural, most affectionate, and guileless creature, that the image now held up by Professor Baglioni looked as strange and incredible as if it were not in accordance with his own original conception. True, there were ugly recollections connected with his first glimpses of the beautiful girl; he could not quite forget the bouquet that withered in her grasp, and the insect that perished amid the sunny air, by no ostensible agency save the fragrance of her breath. These incidents, however, dissolving in the pure light of her character, had no longer the efficacy of facts, but were acknowledged as mistaken fantasies, by whatever testimony of the senses they might appear to be substantiated. There is something truer and more real than what we can see with the eyes and touch with the finger. On such better evidence had Giovanni founded his confidence in Beatrice, though rather by the necessary force of her high attributes than by any deep and generous faith on his part. But now his spirit was incapable of sustaining itself at the height to which the early enthusiasm of passion had exalted it; he fell down, grovelling among earthly doubts, and defiled therewith the pure whiteness of Beatrice's image. Not that he gave her up; he did but distrust. He resolved to institute some decisive test that should satisfy him, once for all, whether there were those dreadful peculiarities in her physical nature which could not be supposed to exist without some corresponding monstrosity of soul. His eyes, gazing down afar, might have deceived him as to the lizard, the insect, and the flowers; but if he could witness, at the distance of a few paces, the sudden blight of one fresh and healthful flower in Beatrice's hand, there would be room for no further question. With this idea he hastened to the florist's and purchased a bouquet that was still gemmed with the morning dew-drops.

It was now the customary hour of his daily interview with Beatrice. Before descending into the garden, Giovanni failed not to look at his figure in the mirror,—a vanity to be expected in a beautiful young man, yet, as displaying itself at that troubled and feverish moment, the token of a certain shallowness of feeling and insincerity of character. He did gaze, however, and said to himself that his features had never before possessed so rich a grace, nor his eyes such vivacity, nor his cheeks so warm a hue of superabundant life.

"At least," thought he, "her poison has not yet insinuated itself into my system. I am no flower to perish in her grasp."

With that thought he turned his eyes on the bouquet, which he had never once laid aside from his hand. A thrill of indefinable horror shot through his frame on perceiving that those dewy flowers were already beginning to droop; they wore the aspect of things that had been fresh and lovely yesterday. Giovanni grew white as marble, and stood motionless before the mirror, staring at his own reflection there as at the likeness of something frightful. He remembered Baglioni's remark about the fragrance that seemed to pervade the chamber. It must have been the poison in his breath! Then he shuddered—shuddered at himself. Recovering from his stupor, he began to watch with curious eye a spider that was busily at work hanging its web from the antique cornice of the apartment, crossing and recrossing the artful system of interwoven lines—as vigorous and active a spider as ever dangled from an old ceiling. Giovanni bent towards the insect, and emitted a deep, long breath. The spider suddenly ceased its toil; the web vibrated with a tremor originating in the body of the small artisan. Again Giovanni sent forth a breath, deeper, longer, and imbued with a venomous feeling out of his heart; he knew not whether he were wicked or only desperate. The spider made a convulsive gripe with his limbs and hung dead across the window.

"Accursed! accursed!" muttered Giovanni, addressing himself. "Hast thou grown so poisonous that this deadly insect perishes by thy breath?"

At that moment a rich, sweet voice came floating up from the garden.

"Giovanni! Giovanni! It is past the hour! Why tarriest thou? Come down!"

"Yes," muttered Giovanni again. "She is the only being whom my breath may not slay! Would that it might!"

He rushed down, and in an instant was standing before the bright and loving eyes of Beatrice. A moment ago his wrath and despair had been so fierce that he could have desired nothing so much as to wither her by a glance; but with her actual presence there came influences which had too real an existence to be at once shaken off: recollections of the delicate and benign power of her feminine nature, which had so often enveloped him in a religious calm; recollections of many a holy and passionate outgush of her heart, when the pure fountain had been unsealed from its depths and made visible in its transparency to his mental eye; recollections which, had Giovanni known how to estimate them, would have assured him that all this ugly mystery was but an earthly illusion, and that, whatever mist of evil might seem to have gathered over her, the real Beatrice was a heavenly angel. Incapable as he was of such high faith, still her presence had not utterly lost its magic. Giovanni's rage was quelled into an aspect of sullen insensibility. Beatrice, with a quick spiritual sense, immediately felt that there was a gulf of blackness between them which neither he nor she could pass. They walked on together, sad and silent, and came thus to the marble fountain and to its pool of water on the ground, in the midst of which grew the shrub that bore gemlike blossoms. Giovanni was affrighted at the eager enjoyment—the appetite, as it were—with which he found himself inhaling the fragrance of the flowers.

"Beatrice," asked he, abruptly, "whence came this shrub?"

"My father created it," answered she, with simplicity.

"Created it! created it!" repeated Giovanni. "What mean you, Beatrice?"

"He is a man fearfully acquainted with the secrets of Nature," replied Beatrice; "and at the hour when I first drew breath this plant sprang from the soil, the offspring of his science, of his intellect, while I was but his earthly child. Approach it not!" continued she, observing with terror that Giovanni was drawing nearer to the shrub. "It has qualities that you little dream of. But I, dearest Giovanni,—I grew up and blossomed with the plant and was nourished with its breath. It was my sister, and I loved it with a human affection; for, alas!—hast thou not suspected it?—there was an awful doom."

Here Giovanni frowned so darkly upon her that Beatrice paused and trembled. But her faith in his tenderness reassured her, and made her blush that she had doubted for an instant.

"There was an awful doom," she continued, "the effect of my father's fatal love of science, which estranged me from all society of my kind. Until Heaven sent thee, dearest Giovanni, oh, how lonely was thy poor Beatrice!"

"Was it a hard doom?" asked Giovanni, fixing his eyes upon her.

"Only of late have I known how hard it was," answered she, tenderly. "Oh, yes; but my heart was torpid, and therefore quiet."

Giovanni's rage broke forth from his sullen gloom like a light-ning-flash out of a dark cloud.

"Accursed one!" cried he, with venomous scorn and anger. "And, finding thy solitude wearisome, thou hast severed me likewise from all the warmth of life and enticed me into thy region of unspeak-able horror!"

"Giovanni!" exclaimed Beatrice, turning her large bright eyes upon his face. The force of his words had not found its way into her mind; she was merely thunderstruck.

"Yes, poisonous thing!" repeated Giovanni, beside himself with passion. "Thou hast done it! Thou hast blasted me! Thou hast filled my veins with poison! Thou hast made me as hateful, as ugly, as loathsome and deadly a creature as thyself—a world's wonder of hideous monstrosity! Now, if our breath be happily as fatal to ourselves as to all others, let us join our lips in one kiss of unutterable hatred, and so die!"

"What has befallen me?" murmured Beatrice, with a low moan out of her heart. "Holy Virgin, pity me, a poor heart-broken child!"

"Thou,—dost thou pray?" cried Giovanni, still with the same fiendish scorn. "Thy very prayers, as they come from thy lips, taint the atmosphere with death. Yes, yes; let us pray! Let us to church and dip our fingers in the holy water at the portal! They that come after us will perish as by a pestilence! Let us sign crosses in the air! It will be scattering curses abroad in the likeness of holy symbols!"

"Giovanni," said Beatrice calmly, for her grief was beyond passion, "why dost thou join thyself with me thus in those terrible words? I, it is true, am the horrible thing thou namest me. But thou,—what hast thou to do, save with one other shudder at my hideous misery to go forth out of the garden and mingle with thy race, and forget that there ever crawled on earth such a monster as poor Beatrice?"

"Dost thou pretend ignorance?" asked Giovanni, scowling upon her. "Behold! this power have I gained from the pure daughter of Rappaccini."

There was a swarm of summer insects flitting through the air in search of the food promised by the flower odors of the fatal garden. They circled round Giovanni's head, and were evidently attracted towards him by the same influence which had drawn them for an instant within the sphere of several of the shrubs. He sent forth a breath among them, and smiled bitterly at Beatrice as at least a score of the insects fell dead upon the ground.

"I see it! I see it!" shrieked Beatrice. "It is my father's fatal science! No, no, Giovanni; it was not I! Never, never! I dreamed only to love thee and be with thee a little time, and so to let thee pass away, leaving but thine image in mine heart. For, Giovanni, believe it, though my body be nourished with poison, my spirit is God's creature, and craves love as its daily food. But my father,—he has united us in this fearful sympathy. Yes; spurn me, tread upon me, kill me! Oh, what is death after such words as thine? But it was not I. Not for a world of bliss would I have done it."

Giovanni's passion had exhausted itself in its outburst from his lips. There now came across him a sense, mournful, and not without tenderness, of the intimate and peculiar relationship between Beatrice and himself. They stood, as it were, in an utter solitude, which would be made none the less solitary by the densest throng of human life. Ought not, then, the desert of humanity around them to press this insulated pair closer together? If they should be cruel to one another, who was there to be kind to them? Besides, thought Giovanni, might there not still be a hope of his returning within the limits of ordinary nature, and leading Beatrice, the redeemed Beatrice, by the hand? Oh, weak, and selfish, and unworthy spirit, that could dream of an earthly union and earthly happiness as possible after such deep love had been so bitterly wronged as was Beatrice's love by Giovanni's blighting words! No, no; there could be no such hope. She must pass heavily, with that broken heart, across the borders of Time—she must bathe her hurts in some fount of paradise, and forget her grief in the light of immortality, and *there* be well.

But Giovanni did not know it.

"Dear Beatrice," said he, approaching her, while she shrank away as always at his approach, but now with a different impulse, "dearest Beatrice, our fate is not yet so desperate. Behold! there is a medicine, potent, as a wise physician has assured me, and almost divine in its efficacy. It is composed of ingredients the most opposite to those by which thy awful father has brought this calamity upon thee and me. It is distilled of blessed herbs. Shall we not quaff it together, and thus be purified from evil?"

"Give it me!" said Beatrice, extending her hand to receive the little silver vial which Giovanni took from his bosom. She added, with a peculiar emphasis, "I will drink; but do thou await the result."

She put Baglioni's antidote to her lips; and, at the same moment, the figure of Rappaccini emerged from the portal and came slowly towards the marble fountain. As he drew near, the pale man of science seemed to gaze with a triumphant expression at the beautiful youth and maiden, as might an artist who should spend his life in achieving a picture or a group of statuary and finally be satisfied with his success. He paused; his bent form grew erect with conscious power; he spread out his hands over them in the attitude of a father imploring a blessing upon his children; but those were the same hands that had thrown poison into the stream of their lives. Giovanni trembled. Beatrice shuddered nervously, and pressed her hand upon her heart.

"My daughter," said Rappaccini, "thou art no longer lonely in the world. Pluck one of those precious gems from thy sister shrub and bid thy bridegroom wear it in his bosom. It will not harm him now. My science and the sympathy between thee and him have so wrought within his system that he now stands apart from common men, as thou dost, daughter of my pride and triumph, from ordinary women. Pass on, then, through the world, most dear to one another and dreadful to all besides!"

"My father," said Beatrice, feebly,—and still as she spoke she kept her hand upon her heart,—"wherefore didst thou inflict this miserable doom upon thy child?"

"Miserable!" exclaimed Rappaccini. "What mean you, foolish girl? Dost thou deem it misery to be endowed with marvelous gifts against which no power nor strength could avail an enemy—misery, to be able to quell the mightiest with a breath—misery, to be as terrible as thou art beautiful? Wouldst thou, then, have preferred the condition of a weak woman, exposed to all evil and capable of none?"

"I would fain have been loved, not feared," murmured Beatrice, sinking down upon the ground. "But now it matters not. I am going, father, where the evil which thou hast striven to mingle with my being will pass away like a dream—like the fragrance of these poisonous flowers, which will no longer taint my breath among the flowers of Eden. Farewell, Giovanni! Thy words of hatred are like lead within my heart; but they, too, will fall away as I ascend. Oh, was there not, from the first, more poison in thy nature than in mine?"

To Beatrice,—so radically had her earthly part been wrought upon by Rappaccini's skill,—as poison had been life, so the powerful antidote was death; and thus the poor victim of man's ingenuity and of thwarted nature, and of the fatality that attends all such efforts of perverted wisdom, perished there, at the feet of her father and Giovanni.

Just at that moment Professor Pietro Baglioni looked forth from the window, and called loudly, in a tone of triumph mixed with horror, to the thunderstricken man of science.

"Rappaccini! Rappaccini! And is *this* the upshot of your experiment!"

Edgar A Poe

THE CASK OF AMONTILLADO

THE PURLOINED LETTER

In part the victim of unfortunate circumstances and in part a prey to his own highly wrought sensibilities, Edgar Allan Poe lived a brief, troubled life. Born in Boston, in 1809, the son of traveling theatrical parents, he was adopted after his mother's death by John Allan of Richmond, Virginia, in 1811. After attending school in England for two years (1818-1820) and in Richmond for another six years (1820-1825), he enrolled at the University of Virginia in 1826. His foster father, however, withdrew him from the University at the end of the first term, presumably because of the debts Poe had accumulated. He served two years in the Army as an enlisted man and then entered the U. S. Military Academy at West Point, but deliberately secured his dismissal at the end of a year. Having been disowned by Allan, he was obliged to earn his own living; to do so he turned to writing as a profession, settling in Baltimore in 1831. In 1833, his "MS Found in a Bottle" won a prize, but, more important, it brought him recognition which resulted in his getting an editorial position on the *Southern Literary Messenger,* of which he became editor in 1835. In spite of the nationwide attention his reviews, poems, and stories drew to the magazine, he was dismissed as editor in 1837 because of his unstable temperament. Thereafter, while continuing to publish stories and poems, he held a succession of editorial positions on magazines in Philadelphia and New York, but the remaining years of his life were marred by his acute struggle with poverty, personal grief over the loss of his young wife, his alcoholism, and his frentic affairs with other women. He died on October 7, 1849, four days after being picked up unconscious on the streets of Baltimore.

Poe's importance in short story development depends on both the technical brilliance of his stories and on his contribution to short story theory. His concept demanded that a story be built with mathematical precision, all elements combining to produce a predetermined effect, usually horror or terror. "The Cask of Amontillado" is a nearly perfect illustration of his theory: everything falls neatly into place precisely as Poe intended. While this seemingly inflexible patterning of all elements to a single end is one source of the effectiveness of "The Cask" and similar horror tales, it appears rather less impressive a literary triumph today than do other facets of Poe's genius, specifically his management of the role of the narrator and his often brilliant manipulation of symbolic imagery to convey vividly imagined states of mind. Thus, if some critics find Poe's theory of the short story too prescriptive, others find much to admire in his craftsmanship.

In contrast to "The Cask," which is a tale of terror, "The Purloined Letter" is what Poe called a tale of "ratiocination" and what we know today as the detective story. To Poe, in fact, belongs the credit for establishing the technique of the detective story, for "The Purloined Letter" introduced for the first time most of the conventions which have since become characteristic of the modern detective story.

the cask of amontillado

The thousand injuries of Fortunato I had borne as I best could, but when he ventured upon insult I vowed revenge. You, who so well know the nature of my soul, will not suppose, however, that I gave utterance to a threat. *At length* I would be avenged; this was a point definitely settled—but the very definitiveness with which it was resolved precluded the idea of risk. I must not only punish, but punish with impunity. A wrong is unredressed when retribution overtakes its redresser. It is equally unredressed when the avenger fails to make himself felt as such to him who has done the wrong.

It must be understood that neither by word nor deed had I given Fortunato cause to doubt my good will. I continued, as was my wont, to smile in his face, and he did not perceive that my smile *now* was at the thought of his immolation.

He had a weak point—this Fortunato—although in other regards he was a man to be respected and even feared. He prided himself on his connoisseurship in wine. Few Italians have the true virtuoso spirit. For the most part their enthusiasm is adopted to suit the time and opportunity, to practise imposture upon the British and Austrian *millionnaires*. In painting and gemmary, Fortunato, like his country-men, was a quack, but in the matter of old wines he was sincere. In this respect I did not differ from him materially;—I was skilful in the Italian vintages myself, and bought largely whenever I could.

It was about dusk, one evening during the supreme madness of the carnival season, that I encountered my friend. He accosted me with excessive warmth, for he had been drinking much. The man wore motley. He had on a tight-fitting parti-striped dress, and his head was surmounted by the conical cap and bells. I was so pleased to see him that I thought I should never have done wringing his hand.

I said to him—"My dear Fortunato, you are luckily met. How remarkably well you are looking to-day. But I have received a pipe of what passes for Amontillado, and I have my doubts."

"How?" said he. "Amontillado? A pipe? Impossible! And in the middle of the carnival!"

"I have my doubts," I replied; "and I was silly enough to pay the full Amontillado price without consulting you in the matter. You were not to be found, and I was fearful of losing a bargain."

"Amontillado!"

"I have my doubts."

"Amontillado!"

"And I must satisfy them."

"Amontillado!"

"As you are engaged, I am on my way to Luchresi. If any one has a critical turn, it is he. He will tell me——"

"Luchresi cannot tell Amontillado from Sherry."

"And yet some fools will have it that his taste is a match for your own."

"Come, let us go."

"Whither?"

"To your vaults."

"My friend, no; I will not impose upon your good nature. I perceive you have an engagement. Luchresi——"

"I have no engagement;—come."

"My friend, no. It is not the engagement, but the severe cold with which I perceive you are afflicted. The vaults are insufferably damp. They are encrusted with nitre."

"Let us go, nevertheless. The cold is merely nothing. Amontillado! You have been imposed upon. And as for Luchresi, he cannot distinguish Sherry from Amontillado."

Thus speaking, Fortunato possessed himself of my arm; and putting on a mask of black silk and drawing a *roquelaire* closely about my person, I suffered him to hurry me to my palazzo.

There were no attendants at home; they had absconded to make merry in honour of the time. I had told them that I should not return until the morning, and had given them explicit orders not to stir from the house. These orders were sufficient, I well knew, to insure their immediate disappearance, one and all, as soon as my back was turned.

I took from their sconces two flambeaux, and giving one to Fortunato, bowed him through several suites of rooms to the archway that led into the vaults. I passed down a long and winding staircase, requesting him to be cautious as he followed. We came at length to the foot of the descent, and stood together on the damp ground of the catacombs of the Montresors.

The gait of my friend was unsteady, and the bells upon his cap jingled as he strode.

"The pipe?" said he.

"It is farther on," said I; "but observe the white web-work which gleams from these cavern walls."

He turned towards me, and looked into my eyes with two filmy orbs that distilled the rheum of intoxication.

"Nitre?" he asked, at length.

"Nitre," I replied. "How long have you had that cough?"

"Ugh! ugh! ugh!—ugh! ugh! ugh!—ugh! ugh! ugh!—ugh! ugh! ugh!—ugh! ugh! ugh!"

My poor friend found it impossible to reply for many minutes.

"It is nothing," he said, at last.

"Come," I said, with decision, "we will go back; your health is precious. You are rich, respected, admired, beloved; you are happy, as once I was. You are a man to be missed. For me it is no matter. We will go back; you will be ill, and I cannot be responsible. Besides, there is Luchresi——"

"Enough," he said; "the cough is a mere nothing; it will not kill me. I shall not die of a cough."

"True—true," I replied; "and, indeed, I had no intention of alarming you unnecessarily—but you should use all proper caution. A draught of this Medoc will defend us from the damps."

Here I knocked off the neck of a bottle which I drew from a long row of its fellows that lay upon the mould.

"Drink," I said, presenting him the wine.

He raised it to his lips with a leer. He paused and nodded to me familiarly, while his bells jingled.

"I drink," he said, "to the buried that repose around us."

"And I to your long life."

He again took my arm, and we proceeded.

"These vaults," he said, "are extensive."

"The Montresors," I replied, "were a great and numerous family."

"I forget your arms."

"A huge human foot d'or, in a field azure; the foot crushes a serpent rampant whose fangs are imbedded in the heel."

"And the motto?"

"*Nemo me impune lacessit.*" ~no one can harm me with impunity. (without getting back at him)~

"Good!" he said.

The wine sparkled in his eyes and the bells jingled. My own fancy grew warm with the Medoc. We had passed through long walls of piled skeletons, with casks and puncheons intermingling, into the inmost recesses of the catacombs. I paused again, and this time I made bold to seize Fortunato by an arm above the elbow.

"The nitre!" I said; "see, it increases. It hangs like moss upon the vaults. We are below the river's bed. The drops of moisture trickle among the bones. Come, we will go back ere it is too late. Your cough——"

"It is nothing," he said; "let us go on. But first, another draught of the Medoc."

I broke and reached him a flagon of De Grâve. He emptied it at a breath. His eyes flashed with a fierce light. He laughed and threw the bottle upward with a gesticulation I did not understand.

I looked at him in surprise. He repeated the movement—a grotesque one.

"You do not comprehend?" he said.

"Not I," I replied.

"Then you are not of the brotherhood."

"How?"

"You are not of the masons."

"Yes, yes," I said; "yes, yes."

"You? Impossible! A mason?"

"A mason," I replied.

"A sign," he said, "a sign."

"It is this," I answered, producing from beneath the folds of my *roquelaire* a trowel.

"You jest," he exclaimed, recoiling a few paces. "But let us proceed to the Amontillado."

"Be it so," I said, replacing the tool beneath the cloak and again offering him my arm. He leaned upon it heavily. We continued our route in search of the Amontillado. We passed through a range of low arches, descended, passed on, and descending again, arrived at a deep crypt, in which the foulness of the air caused our flambeaux rather to glow than flame.

At the most remote end of the crypt there appeared another less spacious. Its walls had been lined with human remains, piled to the vault overhead, in the fashion of the great catacombs of Paris. Three sides of this interior crypt were still ornamented in this manner. From the fourth the bones had been thrown down, and lay promiscuously upon the earth, forming at one point a mound of some size. Within the wall thus exposed by the displacing of the bones, we perceived a still interior crypt or recess, in depth about four feet, in width three, in height six or seven. It seemed to have been constructed for no especial use within itself, but formed merely the interval between two of the colossal supports of the roof of the catacombs, and was backed by one of their circumscribing walls of solid granite.

It was in vain that Fortunato, uplifting his dull torch, endeavoured to pry into the depth of the recess. Its termination the feeble light did not enable us to see.

"Proceed," I said; "herein is the Amontillado. As for Luchresi ——"

"He is an ignoramus," interrupted my friend, as he stepped unsteadily forward, while I followed immediately at his heels. In an instant he had reached the extremity of the niche, and finding his progress arrested by the rock, stood stupidly bewildered. A moment more and I had fettered him to the granite. In its surface were two iron staples, distant from each other about two feet, horizontally. From one of these depended a short chain, from the other a padlock. Throwing the links about his waist, it was but the work of a few seconds to secure it. He was too much astounded to resist. Withdrawing the key, I stepped back from the recess.

"Pass your hand," I said, "over the wall; you cannot help feeling the nitre. Indeed, it is *very* damp. Once more let me *implore* you to return. No? Then I must positively leave you. But I must first render you all the little attentions in my power."

"The Amontillado!" ejaculated my friend, not yet recovered from his astonishment.

"True," I replied; "the Amontillado."

As I said these words I busied myself among the pile of bones of which I have before spoken. Throwing them aside, I soon uncovered a quantity of building stone and mortar. With these materials and with the aid of my trowel, I began vigorously to wall up the entrance of the niche.

I had scarcely laid the first tier of the masonry when I discovered that the intoxication of Fortunato had in a great measure worn off. The earliest indication I had of this was a low moaning cry from the depth of the recess. It was *not* the cry of a drunken man. There was then a long and obstinate silence. I laid the second tier, and the third, and the fourth; and then I heard the furious vibrations of the chain. The noise lasted for several minutes, during which, that I might hearken to it with the more satisfaction, I ceased my labours and sat down upon the bones. When at last the clanking subsided, I resumed the trowel, and finished without interruption the fifth, the sixth, and the seventh tier. The wall was now nearly upon a level with my breast. I again paused, and holding the flambeaux over the mason-work, threw a few feeble rays upon the figure within.

A succession of loud and shrill screams, bursting suddenly from the throat of the chained form, seemed to thrust me violently back. For a brief moment I hesitated, I trembled. Unsheathing my rapier, I began to grope with it about the recess; but the thought of an instant reassured me. I placed my hand upon the solid fabric of the catacombs, and felt satisfied. I reapproached the wall. I replied to the yells of him who clamoured. I re-echoed, I aided, I surpassed them in volume and in strength. I did this, and the clamourer grew still.

It was now midnight, and my task was drawing to a close. I had completed the eighth, the ninth and the tenth tier. I had finished a portion of the last and the eleventh; there remained but a single stone to be fitted and plastered in. I struggled with its weight; I placed it partially in its destined position. But now there came from out the niche a low laugh that erected the hairs upon my head. It was succeeded by a sad voice, which I had difficulty in recognizing as that of the noble Fortunato. The voice said—

"Ha! ha! ha!—he! he! he!—a very good joke, indeed—an excellent jest. We will have many a rich laugh about it at the palazzo—he! he! he!—over our wine—he! he! he!"

"The Amontillado!" I said.

"He! he! he!—he! he! he!—yes, the Amontillado. But is it not getting late? Will not they be awaiting us at the palazzo, the Lady Fortunato and the rest? Let us be gone."

"Yes," I said, "let us be gone."

"For the love of God, Montresor!"

"Yes," I said, "for the love of God!"

But to these words I hearkened in vain for a reply. I grew impatient. I called aloud—

"Fortunato!"

No answer. I called again—

"Fortunato!"

No answer still. I thrust a torch through the remaining aperture and let it fall within. There came forth in return only a jingling of the bells. My heart grew sick—on account of the dampness of the catacombs. I hastened to make an end of my labour. I forced the last stone into its position; I plastered it up. Against the new masonry I re-erected the old rampart of bones. For the half of a century no mortal has disturbed them. *In pace requiescat!*

the purloined letter

Nil sapientiæ odiosius acumine nimio. *Seneca*

At Paris, just after dark one gusty evening in the autumn of
18—, I was enjoying the twofold luxury of meditation and a meerschaum, in company with my friend C. Auguste Dupin, in his little
back library, or book-closet, *au troisième, No. 33 Rue Dunôt, Faubourg
St. Germain*. For one hour at least we had maintained a profound
silence; while each, to any casual observer, might have seemed intently
and exclusively occupied with the curling eddies of smoke that oppressed
the atmosphere of the chamber. For myself, however, I was mentally
discussing certain topics which had formed matter for conversation
between us at an earlier period of the evening; I mean the affair of the
Rue Morgue, and the mystery attending the murder of Marie Rogêt.
I looked upon it, therefore, as something of a coincidence, when the
door of our apartment was thrown open and admitted our old
acquaintance, Monsieur G——, the Prefect of the Parisian police.

We gave him a hearty welcome; for there was nearly half as
much of the entertaining as of the contemptible about the man, and we
had not seen him for several years. We had been sitting in the dark,
and Dupin now arose for the purpose of lighting a lamp, but sat down
again, without doing so, upon G.'s saying that he had called to consult
us, or rather to ask the opinion of my friend, about some official business
which had occasioned a great deal of trouble.

"If it is any point requiring reflection," observed Dupin, as he
forbore to enkindle the wick, "we shall examine it to better purpose in
the dark."

"That is another of your odd notions," said the Prefect, who had
a fashion of calling every thing "odd" that was beyond his comprehension, and thus lived amid an absolute legion of "oddities."

"Very true," said Dupin, as he supplied his visitor with a pipe,
and rolled towards him a comfortable chair.

"And what is the difficulty now?" I asked. "Nothing more in
the assassination way, I hope?"

"Oh no; nothing of that nature. The fact is, the business is *very* simple indeed, and I make no doubt that we can manage it sufficiently well ourselves; but then I thought Dupin would like to hear the details of it, because it is so excessively *odd*."

"Simple and odd," said Dupin.

"Why, yes; and not exactly that either. The fact is, we have all been a good deal puzzled because the affair *is* so simple, and yet baffles us altogether."

"Perhaps it is the very simplicity of the thing which puts you at fault," said my friend.

"What nonsense you *do* talk!" replied the Prefect, laughing heartily.

"Perhaps the mystery is a little *too* plain," said Dupin.

"Oh, good heavens! who ever heard of such an idea?"

"A little *too* self-evident."

"Ha! ha! ha!—ha! ha! ha!—ho! ho! ho!"—roared our visitor, profoundly amused, "oh, Dupin, you will be the death of me yet!"

"And what, after all, *is* the matter on hand?" I asked.

"Why, I will tell you," replied the Prefect, as he gave a long, steady, and contemplative puff, and settled himself in his chair. "I will tell you in a few words; but, before I begin, let me caution you that this is an affair demanding the greatest secrecy, and that I should most probably lose the position I now hold, were it known that I confided it to any one."

"Proceed," said I.

"Or not," said Dupin.

"Well, then; I have received personal information, from a very high quarter, that a certain document of the last importance, has been purloined from the royal apartments. The individual who purloined it is known; this beyond a doubt; he was seen to take it. It is known, also, that it still remains in his possession."

"How is this known?" asked Dupin.

"It is clearly inferred," replied the Prefect, "from the nature of the document, and from the non-appearance of certain results which would at once arise from its passing *out* of the robber's possession;— that is to say, from his employing it as he must design in the end to employ it."

"Be a little more explicit," I said.

"Well, I may venture so far as to say that the paper gives its holder a certain power in a certain quarter where such power is immensely valuable." The Prefect was fond of the cant of diplomacy.

"Still I do not quite understand," said Dupin.

"No? Well; the disclosure of the document to a third person, who shall be nameless, would bring in question the honor of a personage of most exalted station; and this fact gives the holder of the document an ascendancy over the illustrious personage whose honour and peace are so jeopardized."

"But this ascendancy," I interposed, "would depend upon the robber's knowledge of the loser's knowledge of the robber. Who would dare—"

"The thief," said G., "is the Minister D——, who dares all things, those unbecoming as well as those becoming a man. The method of the theft was not less ingenious than bold. The document in question—a letter, to be frank—had been received by the personage robbed while alone in the royal *boudoir*. During its perusal she was suddenly interrupted by the entrance of the other exalted personage from whom especially it was her wish to conceal it. After a hurried and vain endeavor to thrust it in a drawer, she was forced to place it, open as it was, upon a table. The address, however, was uppermost, and, the contents thus unexposed, the letter escaped notice. At this juncture enters the Minister D——. His lynx eye immediately perceives the paper, recognizes the handwriting of the address, observes the confusion of the personage addressed, and fathoms her secret. After some business transactions, hurried through in his ordinary manner, he produces a letter somewhat similar to the one in question, opens it, pretends to read it, and then places it in close juxtaposition to the other. Again he converses, for some fifteen minutes, upon the public affairs. At length, in taking leave, he takes also from the table the letter to which he had no claim. Its rightful owner saw, but, of course, dared not call attention to the act, in the presence of the third personage who stood at her elbow. The Minister decamped; leaving his own letter—one of no importance—upon the table."

"Here, then," said Dupin to me, "you have precisely what you demand to make the ascendancy complete—the robber's knowledge of the loser's knowledge of the robber."

"Yes," replied the Prefect; "and the power thus attained has, for some months past, been wielded, for political purposes, to a very dangerous extent. The personage robbed is more thoroughly convinced, every day, of the necessity of reclaiming her letter. But this, of course, cannot be done openly. In fine, driven to despair, she has committed the matter to me."

"Than whom," said Dupin, amid a perfect whirlwind of smoke,

"no more sagacious agent could, I suppose, be desired, or even imagined."

"You flatter me," replied the Prefect; "but it is possible that some such opinion may have been entertained."

"It is clear," said I, "as you observe, that the letter is still in possession of the Minister; since it is this possession, and not any employment of the letter, which bestows the power. With the employment the power departs."

"True," said G.; "and upon this conviction I proceeded. My first care was to make thorough search of the Minister's hotel; and here my chief embarrassment lay in the necessity of searching without his knowledge. Beyond all things, I have been warned of the danger which would result from giving him reason to suspect our design."

"But," said I, "you are quite *au fait* in these investigations. The Parisian police have done this thing often before."

"Oh, yes; and for this reason I did not despair. The habits of the Minister gave me, too, a great advantage. He is frequently absent from home all night. His servants are by no means numerous. They sleep at a distance from their master's apartment, and, being chiefly Neapolitans, are readily made drunk. I have keys, as you know, with which I can open any chamber or cabinet in Paris. For three months a night has not passed, during the greater part of which I have not been engaged, personally, in ransacking the D—— Hôtel. My honour is interested, and, to mention a great secret, the reward is enormous. So I did not abandon the search until I had become fully satisfied that the thief is a more astute man than myself. I fancy that I have investigated every nook and corner of the premises in which it is possible that the paper can be concealed."

"But is it not possible," I suggested, "that although the letter may be in possession of the Minister, as it unquestionably is, he may have concealed it elsewhere than upon his own premises?"

"This is barely possible," said Dupin. "The present peculiar condition of affairs at court, and especially of those intrigues in which D—— is known to be involved, would render the instant availability of the document—its susceptibility of being produced at a moment's notice—a point of nearly equal importance with its possession."

"Its susceptibility of being produced?" said I.

"That is to say, of being *destroyed*," said Dupin.

"True," I observed; "the paper is clearly then upon the premises. As for its being upon the person of the Minister, we may consider that as out of the question."

"Entirely," said the Prefect. "He has been twice waylaid, as if by foot-pads, and his person rigorously searched under my own inspection."

"You might have spared yourself this trouble," said Dupin. "D——, I presume, is not altogether a fool, and, if not, must have anticipated these waylayings, as a matter of course."

"Not *altogether* a fool," said G., "but then he is a poet, which I take to be only one remove from a fool."

"True," said Dupin, after a long and thoughtful whiff from his meerschaum, "although I have been guilty of certain doggerel myself."

"Suppose you detail," said I, "the particulars of your search."

"Why the fact is, we took our time, and we searched *every where*. I have had long experience in these affairs. I took the entire building, room by room; devoting the nights of a whole week to each. We examined, first, the furniture of each apartment. We opened every possible drawer; and I presume you know that, to a properly trained police agent, such a thing as a *secret* drawer is impossible. Any man is a dolt who permits a 'secret' drawer to escape him in a search of this kind. The thing is *so* plain. There is a certain amount of bulk—of space—to be accounted for in every cabinet. Then we have accurate rules. The fiftieth part of a line could not escape us. After the cabinets we took the chairs. The cushions we probed with the fine long needles you have seen me employ. From the tables we removed the tops."

"Why so?"

"Sometimes the top of a table, or other similarly arranged piece of furniture, is removed by the person wishing to conceal an article; then the leg is excavated, the article deposited within the cavity, and the top replaced. The bottoms and tops of bed-posts are employed in the same way."

"But could not the cavity be detected by sounding?" I asked.

"By no means, if, when the article is deposited, a sufficient wadding of cotton be placed around it. Besides, in our case, we were obliged to proceed without noise."

"But you could not have removed—you could not have taken to pieces *all* articles of furniture in which it would have been possible to make a deposit in the manner you mention. A letter may be compressed into a thin spiral roll, not differing much in shape or bulk from a large knitting-needle, and in this form it might be inserted into the rung of a chair, for example. You did not take to pieces all the chairs?"

"Certainly not; but we did better—we examined the rungs of every chair in the hotel, and, indeed the jointings of every description of furniture, by the aid of a most powerful microscope. Had there been any traces of recent disturbance we should not have failed to detect it instantly. A single grain of gimlet-dust, for example, would have been as obvious as an apple. Any disorder in the glueing—any unusual gaping in the joints—would have sufficed to insure detection."

"I presume you looked to the mirrors, between the boards and the plates, and you probed the beds and the bed-clothes, as well as the curtains and carpets."

"That of course; and when we had absolutely completed every particle of the furniture in this way, then we examined the house itself. We divided its entire surface into compartments, which we numbered, so that none might be missed; then we scrutinized each individual square inch throughout the premises, including the two houses immediately adjoining, with the microscope as before."

"The two houses adjoining!" I exclaimed; "you must have had a great deal of trouble."

"We had; but the reward offered is prodigious."

"You include the *grounds* about the houses?"

"All the grounds are paved with brick. They gave us comparatively little trouble. We examined the moss between the bricks, and found it undisturbed."

"You looked among D——'s papers, of course, and into the books of the library?"

"Certainly; we opened every package and parcel; we not only opened every book, but we turned over every leaf in each volume, not contenting ourselves with a mere shake, according to the fashion of some of our police officers. We also measured the thickness of every book-*cover*, with the most accurate admeasurement, and applied to each the most jealous scrutiny of the microscope. Had any of the bindings been recently meddled with, it would have been utterly impossible that the fact should have escaped observation. Some five or six volumes, just from the hands of the binder, we carefully probed, longitudinally, with the needles."

"You explored the floors beneath the carpets?"

"Beyond doubt. We removed every carpet, and examined the boards with the microscope."

"And the paper on the walls?"

"Yes."

"You looked into the cellars?"

"We did."

"Then," I said; "you have been making a miscalculation, and the letter is *not* upon the premises, as you suppose."

"I fear you are right there," said the Prefect. "And now, Dupin, what would you advise me to do?"

"To make a thorough re-search of the premises."

"That is absolutely needless," replied G——. "I am not more sure that I breathe than I am that the letter is not at the hotel."

"I have no better advice to give you," said Dupin. "You have, of course, an accurate description of the letter?"

"Oh, yes!"—And here the Prefect, producing a memorandum-book, proceeded to read aloud a minute account of the internal, and especially of the external, appearance of the missing document. Soon after finishing the perusal of this description, he took his departure, more entirely depressed in spirits than I had ever known the good gentleman before.

In about a month afterward he paid us another visit, and found us occupied very nearly as before. He took a pipe and a chair and entered into some ordinary conversation. At length I said,—

"Well, but G——, what of the purloined letter? I presume you have at last made up your mind that there is no such thing as over-reaching the Minister?"

"Confound him, say I—yes; I made the re-examination, however, as Dupin suggested—but it was all labour lost, as I knew it would be."

"How much was the reward offered, did you say?" asked Dupin.

"Why, a very great deal—a *very* liberal reward—I don't like to say how much, precisely; but one thing I *will* say, that I wouldn't mind giving my individual check for fifty thousand francs to any one who could obtain me that letter. The fact is, it is becoming of more and more importance every day; and the reward has been lately doubled. If it were trebled, however, I could do no more than I have done."

"Why, yes," said Dupin, drawlingly, between the whiffs of his meerschaum, "I really—think, G——, you have not exerted yourself—to the utmost in this matter. You might—do a little more, I think, eh?"

"How?—in what way?"

"Why—puff, puff—you might—puff, puff—employ counsel in the matter, eh?—puff, puff, puff. Do you remember the story they tell of Abernethy?"

"No; hang Abernethy!"

"To be sure! hang him and welcome. But, once upon a time, a certain rich miser conceived the design of sponging upon this

Abernethy for a medical opinion. Getting up, for this purpose, an ordinary conversation in a private company, he insinuated his case to the physician, as that of an imaginary individual.

" 'We will suppose,' said the miser, 'that his symptoms are such and such; now, doctor, what would *you* have directed him to take?'

" 'Take!' said Abernethy, 'why, take *advice,* to be sure.' "

"But," said the Prefect, a little discomposed, "*I* am *perfectly* willing to take advice, and to pay for it. I would *really* give fifty thousand francs to any one who would aid me in the matter."

"In that case," replied Dupin, opening a drawer, and producing a check-book, "you may as well fill me up a check for the amount mentioned. When you have signed it, I will hand you the letter."

I was astounded. The Prefect appeared absolutely thunderstricken. For some minutes he remained speechless and motionless, looking incredulously at my friend with open mouth, and eyes that seemed starting from their sockets; then, apparently recovering himself in some measure, he seized a pen, and after several pauses and vacant stares, finally filled up and signed a check for fifty thousand francs, and handed it across the table to Dupin. The latter examined it carefully and deposited it in his pocket-book; then, unlocking an *escritoire,* took thence a letter and gave it to the Prefect. This functionary grasped it in a perfect agony of joy, opened it with a trembling hand, cast a rapid glance at its contents, and then, scrambling and struggling to the door, rushed at length unceremoniously from the room and from the house, without having uttered a syllable since Dupin had requested him to fill up the check.

When he had gone, my friend entered into some explanations.

"The Parisian police," he said, "are exceedingly able in their way. They are persevering, ingenious, cunning, and thoroughly versed in the knowledge which their duties seem chiefly to demand. Thus, when G—— detailed to us his mode of searching the premises at the Hôtel D——, I felt entire confidence in his having made a satisfactory investigation—so far as his labours extended."

"So far as his labours extended?" said I.

"Yes," said Dupin. "The measures adopted were not only the best of their kind, but carried out to absolute perfection. Had the letter been deposited within the range of their search, these fellows would, beyond a question, have found it."

I merely laughed—but he seemed quite serious in all that he said.

"The measures, then," he continued, "were good in their kind, and well executed; their defect lay in their being inapplicable to the case, and to the man. A certain set of highly ingenious resources are, with the Prefect, a sort of Procrustean bed, to which he forcibly adapts his designs. But he perpetually errs by being too deep or too shallow, for the matter in hand; and many a schoolboy is a better reasoner than he. I knew one about eight years of age, whose success at guessing in the game of 'even and odd' attracted universal admiration. This game is simple, and is played with marbles. One player holds in his hand a number of these toys, and demands of another whether that number is even or odd. If the guess is right, the guesser wins one; if wrong, he loses one. The boy to whom I allude won all the marbles of the school. Of course he had some principle of guessing; and this lay in mere observation and admeasurement of the astuteness of his opponents. For example, an arrant simpleton is his opponent, and, holding up his closed hand, asks, 'Are they even or odd?' Our schoolboy replies, 'Odd,' and loses; but upon the second trial he wins, for he then says to himself, 'The simpleton had them even upon the first trial, and his amount of cunning is just sufficient to make him have them odd upon the second; I will therefore guess odd;'—he guesses odd, and wins. Now, with a simpleton a degree above the first, he would have reasoned thus: 'This fellow finds that in the first instance I guessed odd, and, in the second, he will propose to himself upon the first impulse, a simple variation from even to odd, as did the first simpleton; but then a second thought will suggest that this is too simple a variation, and finally he will decide upon putting it even as before. I will therefore guess even;' —he guesses even, and wins. Now this mode of reasoning in the schoolboy, whom his fellows termed 'lucky,'—what, in its last analysis, is it?"

"It is merely," I said, "an identification of the reasoner's intellect with that of his opponent."

"It is," said Dupin; "and, upon inquiring of the boy by what means he effected the *thorough* identification in which his success consisted, I received answer as follows: 'When I wish to find out how wise, or how stupid, or how good, or how wicked is any one, or what are his thoughts at the moment, I fashion the expression of my face, as accurately as possible, in accordance with the expression of his, and then wait to see what thoughts or sentiments arise in my mind or heart, as if to match or correspond with the expression.' This response of the schoolboy lies at the bottom of all the spurious profundity which has been attributed to Rochefoucault, to La Bougive, to Machiavelli, and to Campanella."

"And the identification," I said, "of the reasoner's intellect with that of his opponent, depends, if I understand you aright, upon the accuracy with which the opponent's intellect is admeasured."

"For its practical value it depends upon this," replied Dupin; "and the Prefect and his cohort fail so frequently, first, by default of this identification, and, secondly, by ill-admeasurement, or rather through non-admeasurement, of the intellect with which they are engaged. They consider only their *own* ideas of ingenuity; and, in searching for anything hidden, advert only to the modes in which *they* would have hidden it. They are right in this much—that their own ingenuity is a faithful representative of that of *the mass;* but when the cunning of the individual felon is diverse in character from their own, the felon foils them, of course. This always happens when it is above their own, and very usually when it is below. They have no variation of principle in their investigations; at best, when urged by some unusual emergency—by some extraordinary reward—they extend or exaggerate their old modes of *practice,* without touching their principles. What, for example, in this case of D——, has been done to vary the principle of action? What is all this boring, and probing, and sounding, and scrutinizing with the microscope, and dividing the surface of the building into registered square inches—what is it all but an exaggeration *of the application* of the one principle or set of principles of search, which are based upon the one set of notions regarding human ingenuity, to which the Prefect, in the long routine of his duty, has been accustomed? Do you not see he has taken it for granted that *all* men proceed to conceal a letter,—not exactly in a gimlet-hole bored in a chair-leg—but, at least, in *some* out-of-the-way hole or corner suggested by the same tenor of thought which would urge a man to secrete a letter in a gimlet-hole bored in a chair-leg? And do you not see also, that such *recherchés* nooks for concealment are adapted only for ordinary occasions, and would be adopted only by ordinary intellects; for, in all cases of concealment, a disposal of the article concealed—a disposal of it in this *recherché* manner,—is, in the very first instance, presumable and presumed; and thus its discovery depends, not at all upon the acumen, but altogether upon the mere care, patience, and determination of the seekers; and where the case is of importance—or, what amounts to the same thing in the policial eyes, when the reward is of magnitude,—the qualities in question have *never* been known to fail. You will now understand what I meant in suggesting that, had the purloined letter been hidden anywhere within the limits of the Prefect's examination— in other words, had the principle of its concealment been comprehended within the principles of the Prefect—its discovery would have been a matter altogether beyond question. This functionary, however, has been thoroughly mystified; and the remote source of his defeat lies in the supposition that the Minister is a fool, because he has acquired renown as a poet. All fools are poets; this the Prefect *feels;* and he is merely guilty of a *non distributio medii* in thence inferring that all poets are fools."

"But is this really the poet?" I asked. "There are two brothers, I know; and both have attained reputation in letters. The Minister I believe has written learnedly on the Differential Calculus. He is a mathematician, and no poet."

"You are mistaken; I know him well; he is both. As poet *and* mathematician, he would reason well; as mere mathematician, he could not have reasoned at all, and thus would have been at the mercy of the Prefect."

"You surprise me," I said, "by these opinions, which have been contradicted by the voice of the world. You do not mean to set at naught the well-digested idea of centuries. The mathematical reason has long been regarded as *the* reason *par excellence.*"

"'*Il y a à parier,*'" replied Dupin, quoting from Chamfort, "'*que toute idée publique, toute convention reçue, est une sottise, car elle a convenue au plus grand nombre.*' The mathematicians, I grant you, have done their best to promulgate the popular error to which you allude, and which is none the less an error for its promulgation as truth. With an art worthy a better cause, for example, they have insinuated the term 'analysis' into application to algebra. The French are the originators of this particular deception; but if a term is of any importance—if words derive any value from applicability—then 'analysis' conveys 'algebra' about as much as, in Latin, '*ambitus*' implies 'ambition,' '*religio*' 'religion,' or '*homines honesti,*' 'a set of *honorable* men.'"

"You have a quarrel on hand, I see," said I, "with some of the algebraists of Paris; but proceed."

"I dispute the availability, and thus the value, of that reason which is cultivated in any especial form other than the abstractly logical. I dispute, in particular, the reason educed by mathematical study. The mathematics are the science of form and quantity; mathematical reasoning is merely logic applied to observation upon form and quantity. The great error lies in supposing that even the truths of what is called *pure* algebra, are abstract or general truths. And this error is so egregious that I am confounded at the universality with which it has been re-

anything the general
public believes is wrong

91

ceived. Mathematical axioms are *not* axioms of general truth. What is true of *relation*—of form and quantity—is often grossly false in regard to morals, for example. In this latter science it is very usually *un*true that the aggregated parts are equal to the whole. In chemistry also the axiom fails. In the consideration of motive it fails; for two motives, each of a given value, have not, necessarily, a value when united, equal to the sum of their values apart. There are numerous other mathematical truths which are only truths within the limits of *relation*. But the mathematician argues from his *finite truths,* through habit, as if they were of an absolutely general applicability—as the world indeed imagines them to be. Bryant, in his very learned 'Mythology,' mentions an analogous source of error, when he says that 'although the Pagan fables are not believed, yet we forget ourselves continually, and make inferences from them as existing realities.' With the algebraists, however, who are Pagans themselves, the 'Pagan fables' *are* believed, and the inferences are made, not so much through lapse of memory as through an unaccountable addling of the brains. In short, I never yet encountered the mere mathematician who could be trusted out of equal roots, or one who did not clandestinely hold it as a point of his faith that $x^2 + px$ was absolutely and unconditionally equal to q. Say to one of these gentlemen, by way of experiment, if you please, that you believe occasions may occur where $x^2 + px$ is *not* altogether equal to q, and, having made him understand what you mean, get out of his reach as speedily as convenient, for, beyond doubt, he will endeavor to knock you down.

"I mean to say," continued Dupin, while I merely laughed at his last observations, "that if the Minister had been no more than a mathematician, the Prefect would have been under no necessity of giving me this check. I knew him, however, as both mathematician and poet, and my measures were adapted to his capacity, with reference to the circumstances by which he was surrounded. I knew him as a courtier, too, and as a bold *intrigant*. Such a man, I considered, could not fail to be aware of the ordinary policial modes of action. He could not have failed to anticipate—and events have proved that he did not fail to anticipate—the waylayings to which he was subjected. He must have foreseen, I reflected, the secret investigations of his premises. His frequent absences from home at night, which were hailed by the Prefect as certain aids to his success, I regarded only as *ruses,* to afford opportunity for thorough search to the police, and thus the sooner to impress them with the conviction to which G——, in fact, did finally arrive—the conviction that the letter was not upon the premises. I felt, also, that the whole train of thought, which I was at some pains in detailing to you just now, concerning the invariable principle of policial action in searches for articles concealed—I felt that this whole train of thought would necessarily pass through the mind of the Minister. It would imperatively lead him to despise all the ordinary *nooks* of concealment. *He* could not, I reflected, be so weak as not to see that the most intricate and remote recess of his hotel would be as open as his commonest closets to the eyes, to the probes, to the gimlets, and to the microscopes of the Prefect. I saw, in fine, that he would be driven, as a matter of course, to *simplicity,* if not deliberately induced to it as a matter of choice. You will remember, perhaps, how desperately the Prefect laughed when I suggested, upon our first interview, that it was just possible this mystery troubled him so much on account of its being so *very* self-evident."

"Yes," said I, "I remember his merriment well. I really thought he would have fallen into convulsions."

"The material world," continued Dupin, "abounds with very strict analogies to the immaterial; and thus some color of truth has been given to the rhetorical dogma, that metaphor, or simile, may be made to strengthen an argument as well as to embellish a description. The principle of the *vis inertiæ,* for example, seems to be identical in physics and metaphysics. It is not more true in the former, that a large body is with more difficulty set in motion than a smaller one, and that its subsequent *momentum* is commensurate with this difficulty, than it is, in the latter, that intellects of the vaster capacity, while more forcible, more constant, and more eventful in their movements than those of inferior grade, are yet the less readily moved, and more embarrassed and full of hesitation in the first few steps of their progress. Again: have you ever noticed which of the street signs, over the shop doors, are the most attractive of attention?"

"I have never given the matter a thought," I said.

"There is a game of puzzles," he resumed, "which is played upon a map. One party playing requires another to find a given word —the name of town, river, state or empire—any word, in short, upon the motley and perplexed surface of the chart. A novice in the game generally seeks to embarrass his opponents by giving them the most minutely lettered names; but the adept selects such words as stretch, in large characters, from one end of the chart to the other. These, like the over-largely lettered signs and placards of the street, escape observation by dint of being excessively obvious; and here the physical over-sight is precisely analogous with the moral inapprehension by which the intellect suffers to pass unnoticed those considerations which are too obtrusively and too palpably self-evident. But this is a point, it appears, somewhat above or beneath the understanding of the Prefect. He never once thought it probable, or possible, that the minister had deposited the letter immediately beneath the nose of the whole world, by way of best preventing any portion of that world from perceiving it.

"But the more I reflected upon the daring, dashing, and dis-criminating ingenuity of D——; upon the fact that the document must always have been *at hand,* if he intended to use it to good purpose; and upon the decisive evidence, obtained by the Prefect, that it was not hid-den within the limits of that dignitary's ordinary search—the more satisfied I became that, to conceal this letter, the Minister had resorted to the comprehensive and sagacious expedient of not attempting to conceal it at all.

"Full of these ideas, I prepared myself with a pair of green spectacles, and called one fine morning, quite by accident, at the Ministerial hotel. I found D—— at home, yawning, lounging, and dawdling, as usual, and pretending to be in the last extremity of *ennui.* He is, perhaps, the most really energetic human being now alive—but that is only when nobody sees him.

"To be even with him, I complained of my weak eyes, and la-mented the necessity of the spectacles, under cover of which I cautiously and thoroughly surveyed the whole apartment, while seemingly intent only upon the conversation of my host.

"I paid especial attention to a large writing-table near which he sat, and upon which lay confusedly, some miscellaneous letters and other papers, with one or two musical instruments and a few books. Here, however, after a long and very deliberate scrutiny, I saw nothing to excite particular suspicion.

"At length my eyes, in going the circuit of the room, fell upon a trumpery filigree card-rack of pasteboard, that hung dangling by a dirty blue ribbon, from a little brass knob just beneath the middle of the mantel-piece. In this rack, which had three or four compartments, were five or six visiting cards and a solitary letter. This last was much soiled and crumpled. It was torn nearly in two, across the middle—as if a design, in the first instance, to tear it entirely up as worthless, had been altered, or stayed, in the second. It had a large black seal, bearing the D—— cipher *very* conspicuously, and was addressed, in a diminutive female hand, to D——, the minister, himself. It was thrust carelessly, and even, as it seemed, contemptuously, into one of the upper divisions of the rack.

"No sooner had I glanced at this letter than I concluded it to be that of which I was in search. To be sure, it was, to all appearance, radically different from the one of which the Prefect had read us so minute a description. Here the seal was large and black, with the D—— cipher; there it was small and red, with the ducal arms of the S—— family. Here, the address, to the Minister, was diminutive and feminine; there the superscription, to a certain royal personage, was markedly bold and decided; the size alone formed a point of correspondence. But, then, the *radicalness* of these differences, which was excessive; the dirt; the soiled and torn condition of the paper, so inconsistent with the *true* methodical habits of D——, and so suggestive of a design to delude the beholder into an idea of the worthlessness of the document;—these things, together with the hyperobtrusive situation of this document, full in the view of every visitor, and thus exactly in accordance with the conclusions to which I had previously arrived; these things, I say, were strongly corroborative of suspicion, in one who came with the intention to suspect.

"I protracted my visit as long as possible, and, while I maintained a most animated discussion with the Minister, upon a topic which I knew well had never failed to interest and excite him, I kept my attention really riveted upon the letter. In this examination, I committed to memory its external appearance and arrangement in the rack; and also fell, at length, upon a discovery which set at rest whatever trivial doubt I might have entertained. In scrutinizing the edges of the paper, I observed them to be more *chafed* than seemed necessary. They presented the *broken* appearance which is manifested when a stiff paper, having been once folded and pressed with a folder, is refolded in a reversed direction, in the same creases or edges which had formed the original fold. This discovery was sufficient. It was clear to me that the letter had been turned, as a glove, inside out, re-directed, and re-sealed. I bade the Minister good morning, and took my departure at once, leaving a gold snuff-box upon the table.

"The next morning I called for the snuff-box, when we resumed, quite eagerly, the conversation of the preceding day. While thus engaged, however, a loud report, as if of a pistol, was heard immediately beneath the windows of the hotel, and was succeeded by a series of fearful screams, and the shoutings of a mob. D—— rushed to a casement, threw it open, and looked out. In the meantime I stepped to the card-rack, took the letter, put it in my pocket, and replaced it by a *facsimile* (so far as regards externals), which I had carefully prepared at my lodgings; imitating the D—— cipher, very readily, by means of a seal formed of bread.

"The disturbance in the street had been occasioned by the frantic behavior of a man with a musket. He had fired it among a crowd of women and children. It proved, however, to have been without ball, and the fellow was suffered to go his way as a lunatic or a drunkard. When he had gone, D—— came from the window, whither I had followed him immediately upon securing the object in view. Soon afterward I bade him farewell. The pretended lunatic was a man in my own pay."

"But what purpose had you," I asked, "in replacing the letter by a *facsimile*? Would it not have been better, at the first visit, to have seized it openly, and departed?"

"D——," replied Dupin, "is a desperate man, and a man of nerve. His hotel, too, is not without attendants devoted to his interests. Had I made the wild attempt you suggest, I might never have left the Ministerial presence alive. The good people of Paris might have heard of me no more. But I had an object apart from these considerations. You know my political prepossessions. In this matter, I act as a partisan of the lady concerned. For eighteen months the Minister has had her in his power. She has now him in hers; since, being unaware that the letter is not in his possession, he will proceed with his exactions as if it was. Thus will he inevitably commit himself, at once, to his political destruction. His downfall, too, will not be more precipitate than awkward. It is all very well to talk about the *facilis descensus Averni;* but in all kinds of climbing, as Catalani said of singing, it is far more easy to get up than to come down. In the present instance I have no sympathy—at least no pity—for him who descends. He is that *monstrum horrendum,* an unprincipled man of genius. I confess, however, that I should like very well to know the precise character of his thoughts, when, being defied by her whom the Prefect terms 'a certain personage,' he is reduced to opening the letter which I left for him in the card-rack."

"How? Did you put any thing particular in it?"

"Why—it did not seem altogether right to leave the interior blank—that would have been insulting. D——, at Vienna once, did me an evil turn, which I told him, quite good-humoredly, that I should remember. So, as I knew he would feel some curiosity in regard to the identity of the person who had outwitted him, I thought it a pity not to give him a clew. He is well acquainted with my MS., and I just copied into the middle of the blank sheet the words—

——Un dessein si funeste,
S'il n'est digne d'Atrée, est digne de Thyeste.

They are to be found in Crébillon's 'Atrée.' "

If a fatal design is not in
the style of Atreus, it is found
in the style of Thyestes
Brothers

G. W. Harris

BART DAVIS'S DANCE

George Washington Harris is representative of the humorists—A. B. Longstreet, J. J. Hooper, T. B. Thorpe, H. C. Lewis (Madison Tensas), William T. Thompson —who flourished in the old Southwest from 1830 to the Civil War. Keenly aware of the broad comedy inherent in the life of the backwoods and frontier regions and aiming to depict authentically the people, speech, customs, and scenery peculiar to these localities, they produced tales characterized by a robust realism found in few works before or since their day. In combining "local color" with the hearty humor of the frontier, they not only influenced such post-Civil War humorists as Mark Twain and Bret Harte but also ultimately aided the development of realism.

For most of the group, writing was incidental to, or a by-product of, their active careers as lawyers, judges, soldiers, or newspaper editors. G. W. Harris is no exception to the pattern. Born in 1814, in Pennsylvania, but closely associated from early childhood with the East Tennessee region around Knoxville, he became successively a silversmith, a steamboat captain, a postmaster, a businessman, and a political writer. In the early 1840's he began contributing humorous tales and sketches to the Knoxville papers and to the New York *Spirit of the Times*. In 1867, a volume of these tales was published under the title *Sut Lovingood's Yarns*.

Sut Lovingood, the central character and narrator of the yarns, is a lanky mountaineer, who loves liquor and women but hates circuit-riding preachers and Yankees of all sorts. Because his favorite pastime is "breeding scares among darned fools," he is never happier than when a person of the type he dislikes, such as the preacher in "Bart Davis's Dance," is suffering acute physical discomfort. The tales are connected by the centralizing element of Sut's mischief-making and also by pointed references to his exploits which carry over from one tale to the next; yet each tale can be read as a separate story. In this sense the structure of the *Yarns,* on the one hand, bears a resemblance to Elizabethan picaresque fiction and, on the other, to such modern collections of stories using common characters and settings as Sherwood Anderson's *Winesburg* and Eudora Welty's *Golden Apples.* In technique, the tales are imitative of the frontier oral tales in that Sut tells the yarns in his own homely dialect and with all the hesitations, interpolations, and apparent indirections typical of unrehearsed speech. This style is markedly different from that required by Poe, yet it is probably as difficult to master as Poe's. The vigorous "matter" and heavy dialect of "Bart Davis's Dance" should not be allowed to obscure the underlying artistry of the method.

bart davis's dance

"Du yu know that bow-laiged boy on the fence thar?" said Sut.

"No; who is he?"

"That's Bart Davis's yungest son, name Obed. Jis' obsarve how his snout's skin'd an' his year slit an' so forth."

"Yes, I see; how did it happen?"

"Happen? hit didn't happen et all, hit wer dun a-pupos, permeditated a-pupos. Ther wer a dance et his dad's, las' Sat'day nite wer two weeks ago, what hed like tu bred a berryin ur two; the corpses wer mos' redy, an' nuffin but acksidint kep em frum bein finished. I wer thar mysef, an' kin say an' swar that the chances run mity even, a-tween mirth an' mournin. Fur a spell hit wer the exhitenest time I ever seed on sich a ocashun, not tu hev no more whisky nur we hed.

Thar warn't but 'bout half a barril when we begun, an' when we quit, we burnt the hoops an' staves tu dance the las' reel by.

"Everybody knows Bart is a durn'd no-count, jug-kerryin, slow-thinkin, flea-hurtin, herrin-eatin, Noth Calinian, plays a three-string fiddil wif a grasshopper jirk, while his wife totes the wood. He hes but two gifs wuf a durn: wun is, he'll vide his whisky wif yu down tu the las' half pint; thar he stops, fur that's jis' a horn yu know; an' tuther is, he ain't feard ove enything a-livin, sept ole Peg. I don't wunder et that, fur hit mus' take a man wif a onnatrally big melt, not tu be fear'd ove his wife, onless she's blind ur hes a sweethart. Peg (she's his ole quilt, yu know) is a regular steel-trap ove an 'oman; she goes wif wun side ove her frock tucked up at the hips, her har down her back, an' a roasted hickory onder her arm tu scold the brats wif, an' tu skeer Bart. They's bof great on dancin ove Sat'day nites et home, an' sum-whar else on tuther nites. Ef thar's a frolic enywhar in five mile, Bart is sure tu be thar, an' Peg, too, ef she's in travilin fix, which ain't more nur five months in the year. She goes fur two reasons: wun is, tu eat an' dance, an' tuther tu watch Bart. He hes two reasons also: wun is tu suck in all the whisky floatin roun, an' tu du a heap ove things what needs watchin. They giner'lly hes a dermestic discussun arter they gets home, in which, teeth, claws, an' beggin am the argymints, an' 'I won't du so no more,' the aind ove hit. They am a lively an' even yok'd par. Nobody else on the green yeath orter be tied tu either ove em.

"Well they mounted that par ove hames yu see on the fence thar, the boy name Obed ontu a muel, an' sent him tu the still-hous, tu narrate hit that thar wud be a dance et home the nex nite, an' fur every feller what warn't married tu fetch a gal, an' them what wer married tu fetch two. Now this rangement show'd Bart's good sence, fur he know'd that hit takes more gals tu du married fellers then single wuns. Caze people what hes but one kind ove vittils et home, hit allers takes more tu du em abroad.

"When the nite cum they wer all thar, a hous' plum full, an' amung em a lot ove counter-hoppers wif strip'd sugar candy in their pockets, an' young lawyers wif cinamint ile ontu ther har; all on em frum town, an' jis' ole enuf tu begin tu strut an' gobble. Thunder and litnin, an' sunflower pattrin calliker, mixed wif check an' stripe, hom-spun swept all about thar, wif one, jis' one black silk. They laid off two reels, wun call'd the leather shoe reel, an' tuther, the barfoot reel. I danced in the wun I nam'd las'."

"Why did they divide that way, Sut?"

"Why, durn hit, don't yu know that the dancin wud turn intu

101

fitin afore the fust set got ofen the flure, ef they mix'd em? The shoes wud scronch the bar toes in dancin, an' rite then an' thar they'd mix fur a fite. A hard-shell preacher wif his mouf mortised intu his face in shape like a muel's shoe, heels down, fotch hissef thar soon arter dark, an' made moshuns like he ment tu stay all nite. He got intu a corner, an' commenced a'tchunin up his sighin an' groanin aperatus, a-shakin ove his head, an' lookin like he hed the belly-ake. He cudn't hev look'd more solemcoly, ef his mam hed died that mornin a-owin him two dullars an' a 'alf. All these wimin an' luvely souns an' moshuns wer made on count ove the dancin, an' p'raps the cussin an' kissin. The whisky part ove that inturtainment he'd nuffin against. I *know'd* that, fur every time he roll'd his eyes to'ards the barril, he'd lick his lips sorter sloppy like, jis' es ef he'd been dippin his bill intu a crock ove chicken gravy, an' wer tryin tu save the stray draps, what hung outside his face. Oh! he wer jis' a-honin arter that ball-face whisky; he'd a jis' kiss'd hit es sweet, an' es long, es ef hit hed been a willin gal. I sorter aidged up a-side him, an' sez I—

" 'Mister, will yu hev a few draps ove camfire, ur laudamy? Yu seems tu be pow'ful ailin in yer innards. Yu hesent swallered a live rat, ur a mole, hes yu?'

"He shook his head, an' fotch a sigh, what ainded in a groan. Sez I—

" 'Rats ur moles am onhelthy things tu swaller afore they'se departed this life.'

"He blow'd out a orful sigh, part outen his nose, but mos' ove hit out whar the toe ove the muel-shoe wer, an' sez he—

" 'This am a wicked an' a parvarse generashun ove vipurs, yung man.'

" 'An' gin up tu hardness ove hart, an' deviltry, an' belevin thunderin lies,' said I; an' I puff'd out a big sigh, wif a little groan fur a tail. Sez he—

" 'Thar am no-o-o-o dancin in hell,' an sot intu shakin ove his head, till I thot he'd keep on fur everlastin, an' ever more. Sez I—

" 'Haint yu *slitely* mistaken'd in that las' re-mark ove yourn? Ef thar's es much hot truck, an' brimstone, an' cinders, an' hickory smoke, an' big hurtin, in hell es yu folks sez thar am, thar mus' be *sum* dancin, purtickelerly jigs an' quick-steps; they don't lack fur music, I reckon, fur I'se allers hearn hell wer full ove fiddlers, an' thar's Yankees enuf thar tu invent fire-proof fiddils fur em, so they don't want fur tchunes. All on yeath that bothers me is the rosim.'

" 'Ah, yung onregenerit man,' sez he, 'thar's more rosim in hell than thar's in all Noth Caliny.'

" 'But hit ain't quite hard enuf tu rub ontu fiddil bows, is hit?' sez I.

"He groan'd an' shook his head, an' sent one ove his eyes to'ards the whisky corner. I went an' fotch 'im a big slug intu a gourd. That shovel-shaped onder lip ove his'n jis' fell out'ards like ontu the fallin door ove a stone coal stove, an' he upsot the gourd inside ove his teef. I seed the mark ove the truck gwine down his froat jis' like a snake travelin thru a wet sassidge gut. He smelt intu the gourd a good long smell, turned up his eyes, an' sed 'Barlm ove life.'

"Thinks I, ole Sock, I know what fotch yu tu this frolic besides yu're hoss an' our whisky. Bart now cum up, an' Hardshell tole him he'd cum tu stay all nite, ef he suited all roun.

" 'Sartinly, oh yas, an' welcum,' sed Bart.

"The ole Sock, never alterin the shape ove the hole tore in his face, sed, mity sneerin like, 'Yu is hosspitabil.' I seed Bart sorter start, an' look at him, an' go off a-winkin at me tu foller him. We went outside the hous', intu a chimbly corner, an' thar wer two fellers, wun ove em a she, a-whisperin. We went tu tuther corner, an' thar wer two more; then we went tu the stabil, an' hearn whisperin thar; hit mout been rats a-runnin in straw. So Bart cud hold in no longer. Sez he—

" 'Never mine, I don't keer a durn who hears me. I b'leve I'se been 'sulted in my own hous'; didn't that durn'd preachin mersheen call me a hoss?'

" 'That's jis' what he sed. He call'd yu a hoss-pitabil,' sez I.

" 'Pitabil, pitabil,' sez Bart, 'dam ef I don't b'leve that's wus nur the hoss.'

" 'Sartinly,' sez I, 'pitabil is a sorter Latin tail stuck tu hit so yu moutn't onderstand; hit means pitiful hoss in Inglish, an' ef I wer yu, I'd see that his stumack wer spiled fur Peg's fried chicken an' biskit. I'd go rite in an' show him how a hoss ken kick an' sich like.' He jis' gritted his teef, like he wer a-chompin aigshells, ur paragorick phials, an' put fur the hous', a-rollin up his shut-sleeves es he went, plum up to his arm-pit.

"The durn'd, hiperkritikil, groanin ole Hardshell raskil hed dun got the dancin stop't; he'd tuck the fiddil away frum the nigger, an' wer a-holdin hit by the naik in wun han, an' a-makin gesters wif the bow in tuther. He wer mounted ontu a cheer, clost by the meal barril, an' wer exortin em orfully 'bout thar sins ove omishun an' cummishun,

103

purtickerly the cummishun wuns, wif the dancin sins at the head, warin sunflower caliker wuns nex'; an' then cum thar smaller sins, sich es ridin a-hine fellers on the same hoss, whisperin outen doors, an' a-winkin a-hine fans, tuckey-tails an' hankerchers, an' sed that black silk wer plenty in hell, that hit wer used fur mournin thar, an' not tu dance in. The *he* sins, ove the small sort, wer cumin frum town ove nites, a-warin store clothes, smellin ove cinamint ile, an' a-totin striped sugar candy in thar pockets, tu turn the minds ove the weak gals, instead ove a flask ove that good holesum ole truck, what they'se got in towns, name 'coniack.'

"The wimmen folks wer backed up in bunches, in the corners, an' agin the beds, wif thar fingers in thar moufs, an' wun ur two ove the saftest ove em wer gettin up a quiet sort ove dry cryin.

"The he fellers all looked like they'd mos' es leave fite es not, ef they knew how tu start the thing, when in bounced Bart; he looked like a catamount; wun jump an' he stood a-top ove the meal barril, squar in frunt ove Hardshell, his har a-swayin about wif pure mad, like a patch ove ripe rye in a wind, an' his eyes wer es roun an' es red as a bull's when he's a-jinin in battil wif anuther bull frum Bashan. He struck wun fistes away out a-hine, an' wif tuther reachin at arm's laingth, he cummenc'd borin, like he hed a gimblit in his shot fis', rite onder the snout ove the thunderin Hardshell, like he wer trying tu bore his mouf inter a better shape, an' a-narratin thru his teef these facs, in words what sounded like grittin hard co'n.

"'*Yu* durn'd infunel, incumpassabil warter-dorg! *yu* cuss'd hiperkritikal, ongrateful ole mus-rat! *yu* h—ll fir'd, divin, splatterin, pond-makin, iron-jacket'd ole son ove a mud-turtil, yu hes 'sulted me in my own hous', *an' in Latin et that,* an' then yu've tuck the imperdent liberty tu skare these yere children outen thar innersent mucement (still borin away frum left tu right, wif that horny fis' ove his'n, an' the Hardshell's head gwine furder back every twist.) Call'd me a hoss—Git ofen that cheer!'

"Es he sed 'git,' he loaned the passun a mos' tremenjus contushun, rite in the bull curl. I seed his shoe-soles a-gwine up each side ove Bart's fis' afore he hed time tu muve hit, arter he struck. Hit wer a lick, George, that hed hit been a kick, a four year ole muel wud hev been pow'ful proud ove. I seed ni ontu a gallon ove sparks ove fire fly outen the passun's eyes mysef (he mus hev seed a bushel) when hit reached his curl. He let the fiddil go when he wer in the highes part ove his backward summerset, an' the nigger what hed been watchin up at hit all this time, wis'ful like, es a dorg watches a meat-skin when yu holds hit too high fur him tu grab, cotch his fiddil in bof hans afore hit toch the yeath.

"'Dar by golly, you no git tu smash dis fiddil, wid yu durn fool fitin an' preachin.'

"An' holdin it wavinly abuv his head, he dodged outen the surkil ove imejut danger. The old Shell lit ontu his all fours, hit bein that much more nur a full summerset, an' *the* black silk lit a-stradil ove him. I know'd hit wer the black silk, bekase I seed the white stockins and grey garters. Hev I mention'd that thar wer one hundred an' twenty-five pouns ove live, black-eyed gal in under that black silk?"

"No, Sut."

"Well, thar wer, an' that she wer bof live an' willin, old Dipper wer soon redy tu swar. 'Black silk in hell is thar,' scream'd she, a-hissin like ontu a cat, an' cummenced a-pullin up by the roots his long har, like hit wer flax, wif bof hans, an' a-shakin the bunches ofen her fingers, an' then gwine fur more, the hissin gittin a littil louder every pull. George, that wer the fust spessamin ove a smokin mad gal I've seed in a hen's age; she kerried out my idear ove a fust-rate flax-puller, pullin agin two, fur a bet. I think she gin the ole Shell the idear that sum strong man body wer a-holden his head ni ontu the saws ove a activ cotton gin.

"Now the boy name Obed, with the hame laigs, hevin a sorter jestis' ove the peace turn ove mine, run in tu pull her off, an' cudn't du hit afore she made a rake fur his har, an' got hit. She jis' mixed the hanful wif the pile on the flure, an' gin hersef back tu the job ove preparin the passun fur a wig. A hawk-billed, weazel-eyed, rat-mouthed feller, what hed been a-struttin roun Black Silk all nite, a-trailin wun wing, an' a-lickin his lips, seed the fool boy name Obed, a-tryin tu git her tu lite ofen the old Sock, so he jis' growl'd low, an' barked once, an' kiver'd him, an' afore his mam Peg, an' me, an' five uther gals, cud git him loose, he hed made her cub the speckterkil yu sees roostin on that ar fence, an' he's hed ni ontu three weeks tu mend his looks in, by Jew David's plarster, sweet ile, an' the keer ove his mam.

"The fitin now got tu be gineral on mos' parts ove the field, an' es the cuppils cum in frum outen doors, lookin sorter sneakin, an' pale (frum the nise ove the rumpus, I speck,) wun at leas', outen every par, got jump't on by sumbody. P'raps a gal wud kiver a cumin in gal, an-uther gal wud go fur the har an' skin ove a cumin in he feller; then, agin, the fis' ove a he wud meet anuther cumin in he, right atween the eyes, an' so on till the thing got tu be durn'dably mix'd up an' lively. Peg boun up the boy name Obed's wouns, bruises, an' petrifying sores, an' then went on wif supper cookin, like all wer quiet on the Pertomack.

"Es soon es ole Shell begun to cum to, frum Bart's dubbil dis-till'd thunder-bolt, the hurtin all over his head begun tu attrack his 'tenshun, an' soaked thru his skull, an' in thar tuck the shape ove an idear; the idear shaped hitsef intu spoken wurds, an' they wer, 'Gird up yer loins an' *git.*' I seed the wurkin ove his mind, so I jis' shouted es loud es I could beller, 'The Pherlistshuns be upon yu Sampsin.' He hearn hit, an' wer struck wif the force ove the remark, an' started fur the back door, still on his all fours, in a single foot rack. Es soon es Black Silk felt him movin, she cummenced spurrin him wif her heels; while she hilt tu his har wif wun han, she tuck a pin outen her collar wif tuther, an' made a cushion fur hit in the hill, ontu the north side ove the pint ove his back-bone; he kicked up an' snorted, an' changed the single foot rack intu a tarin pace, loped outen the door intu outer darkness, an' his heel-tops wer the last I seed ove him. He stumbled an' fell down the log-steps, an' flung Black Silk like onto a full balloon over his head, (I seed a heap ove white shinin es she went). He felt his way in the dark, thru the woods, fur more pleasant places, an' she cum in larfin, 'Black silk in hell, hey?' wer every word she sed."

"Go on, Sut."

"That's all. I ain't like ole Glabbergab; when I'se spoke off what I knows, I stops talkin."

"Well, what became of Hardshell?"

"Oh! es tu that, he made his 'pearance las' Sunday, in the pulpit, es bald es a jug, wif a black spot aidged wif green an' yaller, 'bout the size ove a prickly par, on his forehead, an' preach't bout the orful kon-sekenses ove Absalom's hevin' long har, human depravity, an' the Salt Lake; sed he wer gwine thar right off, an' *he'll du hit.*"

Norman Melville

BARTLEBY

Herman Melville was born in New York City, in 1819, the son of fairly well-to-do parents. For a time he attended the Albany Academy, but in 1834, two years after his father had died bankrupt, he left school to support himself and aid the family income by working in a bank, clerking in his brother's fur and cap store, shipping as cabin boy on a merchant-man bound for Liverpool, and teaching school. In 1841, he shipped out as a seaman on the *Acushnet,* a whaler bound for the South Seas, thereby initiating a series of colorful adventures that took him into many faraway corners of the world and provided him with material he later used extensively in his works. Dissatisfied with the hardships of life aboard a whaler, Melville deserted the *Acushnet* at Nukahiva, in the Marquesas Islands, in July, 1842, and lived for a month among the cannibals in Typee Valley. After escaping from Typee on an Australian ship, which he deserted at Papeete in September, 1842, Melville worked as a field laborer in Tahiti and studied the native life of that island. He left Tahiti on a whaler, reached Honolulu, and there on August 7, 1843, enlisted as a seaman on the frigate *United States,* on which he served until he received his discharge at Boston in October, 1844.

With the enlarged knowledge of the world gained through these experiences he returned to New York and, encouraged by the Duyckincks, began his literary career. In quick succession, he published *Typee* (1846), concerned with his adventures in Typee Valley; *Omoo* (1847), based on his experiences in Tahiti; *Mardi* (1849), an allegorical novel, laid in a fictional archipelago in the South Seas; *Redburn* (1849), an account of his merchant seaman experiences; *White-Jacket* (1850), a depiction of life aboard a man-of-war; and *Moby Dick* (1851), his masterpiece, the symbolic narrative of a mad captain's pursuit of a white whale. His earlier works, particularly those dealing with exotic native life, were very successful, but his popularity began to wane after *Moby Dick*, and his next two novels, *Pierre* (1852) and *Israel Potter* (1855), added little to his contemporary fame. With the publication of *Piazza Tales* in 1856, a volume containing the finest pieces of his short fiction, and of the *Confidence Man* in 1857, he virtually stopped writing prose, turning instead to poetry. Unsuccessful in his efforts to earn a living as a lecturer, or to secure a consulship, he became an outdoor customs inspector in New York in 1863 and lived there until his death in 1891.

"Bartleby" is perhaps not only the finest but also the most complex short story Melville wrote. On the first and simplest level, the story may be interpreted as an allegory of Melville's personal situation as a writer in the early 1850's (see Hugh W. Hetherington, *Melville and His Reviewers*, pp. 265-271). On a second and more general level, it may be taken as a symbolic commentary on the plight of the artist in a democratic, materialistic society, which forces the artist to conform to (or copy) the literary fashions popular in his day or risk the possibility of his works becoming "dead letters." But the concluding words of the story, "Ah, Bartleby! Ah, humanity," suggest that on a third and still more significant level, it may be viewed as a commentary on the human predicament itself with Bartleby standing for representative man rather than for Melville in particular or for the artist in general. The specific nature of the commentary the story makes on mankind is, however, a provocative question, the answer to which must be sought in terms not only of Bartleby but also of the other characters in the story and its whole pattern of strange events.

bartleby

a story of wall street

I am a rather elderly man. The nature of my avocations, for the last thirty years, has brought me into more than ordinary contact with what would seem an interesting and somewhat singular set of men, of whom, as yet, nothing, that I know of, has ever been written—I mean, the law-copyists, or scriveners. I have known very many of them, professionally and privately, and, if I pleased, could relate divers histories, at which good-natured gentlemen might smile, and sentimental souls might weep. But I waive the biographies of all other scriveners, for a few passages in the life of Bartleby, who was a scrivener, the strangest I ever saw, or heard of. While, of other law-copyists, I might write the complete life, of Bartleby nothing of that sort can be done. I believe that no materials exist for a full and satisfactory biography of this man. It is an irreparable loss to literature. Bartleby was one of those beings of whom nothing is ascertainable, except from the original sources, and, in his case, those are very small. What my own astonished eyes saw of Bartleby, *that* is all I know of him, except, indeed, one vague report, which will appear in the sequel.

Ere introducing the scrivener, as he first appeared to me, it is fit I make some mention of myself, my *employés,* my business, my chambers, and general surroundings; because some such description is indispensable to an adequate understanding of the chief character about to be presented. Imprimis: I am a man who, from his youth upwards, has been filled with a profound conviction that the easiest way of life is the best. Hence, though I belong to a profession proverbially energetic and nervous, even to turbulence, at times, yet nothing of that sort have I ever suffered to invade my peace. I am one of those unambitious lawyers who never address a jury, or in any way draw down public applause; but, in the cool tranquillity of a snug retreat, do a snug business among rich men's bonds, and mortgages, and title-deeds. All who know me, consider me an eminently *safe* man. The late John Jacob Astor, a personage little given to poetic enthusiasm, had no hesitation in pronouncing my first grand point to be prudence; my next, method. I do not speak it in vanity, but simply record the fact, that I was not unemployed in my profession by the late John Jacob Astor; a name which, I admit, I love to repeat; for it hath a rounded and orbicular sound to it, and rings like unto bullion. I will freely add, that I was not insensible to the late John Jacob Astor's good opinion.

Some time prior to the period at which this little history begins, my avocations had been largely increased. The good old office, now extinct in the State of New York, of a Master in Chancery, had been conferred upon me. It was not a very arduous office, but very pleasantly remunerative. I seldom lose my temper; much more seldom indulge in dangerous indignation at wrongs and outrages; but I must be permitted to be rash here, and declare that I consider the sudden and violent abrogation of the office of Master in Chancery, by the new Constitution, as a —— premature act; inasmuch as I had counted upon a life-lease of the profits, whereas I only received those of a few short years. But this is by the way.

My chambers were up stairs, at No. — Wall Street. At one end, they looked upon the white wall of the interior of a spacious sky-light shaft, penetrating the building from top to bottom.

This view might have been considered rather tame than otherwise, deficient in what landscape painters call "life." But, if so, the view from the other end of my chambers offered, at least, a contrast, if nothing more. In that direction, my windows commanded an unobstructed view of a lofty brick wall, black by age and everlasting shade; which wall required no spy-glass to bring out its lurking beauties, but, for the benefit of all near-sighted spectators, was pushed up to within ten feet of my window panes. Owing to the great height of the surrounding buildings, and my chambers being on the second floor, the interval between this wall and mine not a little resembled a huge square cistern.

At the period just preceding the advent of Bartleby, I had two persons as copyists in my employment, and a promising lad as an office-boy. First, Turkey; second, Nippers; third, Ginger Nut. These may seem names, the like of which are not usually found in the Directory. In truth, they were nicknames, mutually conferred upon each other by my three clerks, and were deemed expressive of their respective persons or characters. Turkey was a short, pursy Englishman, of about my own age—that is, somewhere not far from sixty. In the morning, one might say, his face was of a fine florid hue, but after twelve o'clock, meridian—his dinner hour—it blazed like a grate full of Christmas coals; and continued blazing—but, as it were, with a gradual wane— till six o'clock, P.M., or thereabouts; after which, I saw no more of the proprietor of the face, which, gaining its meridian with the sun, seemed to set with it, to rise, culminate, and decline the following day, with the like regularity and undiminished glory. There are many singular coincidences I have known in the course of my life, not the least among which was the fact, that, exactly when Turkey displayed his fullest beams from his red and radiant countenance, just then, too, at that critical moment, began the daily period when I considered his business capacities as seriously disturbed for the remainder of the twenty-four hours. Not that he was absolutely idle, or averse to business then; far from it. The difficulty was, he was apt to be altogether too energetic. There was a strange, inflamed, flurried, flighty recklessness of activity about him. He would be incautious in dipping his pen into his inkstand. All his blots upon my documents were dropped there after twelve o'clock, meridian. Indeed, not only would he be reckless, and sadly given to making blots in the afternoon, but, some days, he went further, and was rather noisy. At such times, too, his face flamed with augmented blazonry, as if cannel coal had been heaped on anthracite. He made an unpleasant racket with his chair; spilled his sand-box; in mending his pens, impatiently split them all to pieces, and threw them on the floor in a sudden passion; stood up, and leaned over his table, boxing his papers about in a most indecorous manner, very sad to behold in an elderly man like him. Nevertheless, as he was in many ways a most valuable person to me, and all the time before twelve o'clock, meridian, was the quickest, steadiest creature, too, accomplishing a great deal of work in a style not easily to be matched—for these reasons, I was willing to overlook his eccentricities, though, indeed, occasionally, I remonstrated with him. I did this very gently, however, because, though the civilest, nay, the blandest and most reverential of men in the morning, yet, in the afternoon, he was disposed, upon provocation, to be slightly rash with his tongue—in fact, insolent. Now, valuing his morning services as I did, and resolved not to lose them—yet, at the same time, made uncomfortable by his inflamed ways after twelve o'clock—and being a man of peace, unwilling by my admonitions to call forth unseemly retorts from him, I took upon me, one Saturday noon (he was always worse on Saturdays) to hint to him, very kindly, that, perhaps, now that he was growing old, it might be well to abridge his labors; in short, he need not come to my chambers after twelve o'clock, but, dinner over, had best go home to his lodgings, and rest himself till tea-time. But no; he insisted upon his afternoon devotions. His countenance became intolerably fervid, as he oratorically assured me—gesticulating with a long ruler at the other end of the room— that if his services in the morning were useful, how indispensable, then, in the afternoon?

"With submission, sir," said Turkey, on this occasion, "I consider myself your right-hand man. In the morning I but marshal and deploy my columns; but in the afternoon I put myself at their head, and gallantly charge the foe, thus"—and he made a violent thrust with the ruler.

"But the blots, Turkey," intimated I.

"True; but, with submission, sir, behold these hairs! I am getting old. Surely, sir, a blot or two of a warm afternoon is not to be severely urged against gray hairs. Old age—even if it blot the page— is honorable. With submission, sir, we *both* are getting old."

This appeal to my fellow-feeling was hardly to be resisted. At all events, I saw that go he would not. So, I made up my mind to let him stay, resolving, nevertheless, to see to it that, during the afternoon, he had to do with my less important papers.

Nippers, the second on my list, was a whiskered, sallow, and, upon the whole, rather piratical-looking young man, of about five-and-twenty. I always deemed him the victim of two evil powers—ambition and indigestion. The ambition was evinced by a certain impatience of the duties of a mere copyist, an unwarrantable usurpation of strictly professional affairs, such as the original drawing up of legal documents. The indigestion seemed betokened in an occasional nervous testiness and grinning irritability, causing the teeth to audibly grind together over mistakes committed in copying; unnecessary maledictions, hissed, rather than spoken, in the heat of business; and especially by a continual discontent with the height of the table where he worked. Though of a very ingenious, mechanical turn, Nippers could never get this table to suit him. He put chips under it, blocks of various sorts, bits of pasteboard, and at last went so far as to attempt an exquisite adjustment, by final pieces of folded blotting-paper. But no invention would answer. If, for the sake of easing his back, he brought the table lid at a sharp angle well up towards his chin, and wrote there like a man using the steep roof of a Dutch house for his desk, then he declared that it stopped the circulation in his arms. If now he lowered the table to his waistbands, and stooped over it in writing, then there was a sore aching in his back. In short, the truth of the matter was,

Nippers knew not what he wanted. Or, if he wanted anything, it was to be rid of a scrivener's table altogether. Among the manifestations of his diseased ambition was a fondness he had for receiving visits from certain ambiguous-looking fellows in seedy coats, whom he called his clients. Indeed, I was aware that not only was he, at times, considerable of a ward-politician, but he occasionally did a little business at the Justices' courts, and was not unknown on the steps of the Tombs. I have good reason to believe, however, that one individual who called upon him at my chambers, and who, with a grand air, he insisted was his client, was no other than a dun, and the alleged title-deed, a bill. But, with all his failings, and the annoyances he caused me, Nippers, like his compatriot Turkey, was a very useful man to me; wrote a neat, swift hand; and, when he chose, was not deficient in a gentlemanly sort of deportment. Added to this, he always dressed in a gentlemanly sort of way; and so, incidentally, reflected credit upon my chambers. Whereas, with respect to Turkey, I had much ado to keep him from being a reproach to me. His clothes were apt to look oily, and smell of eating-houses. He wore his pantaloons very loose and baggy in summer. His coats were execrable; his hat not to be handled. But while the hat was a thing of indifference to me, inasmuch as his natural civility and deference, as a dependent Englishman, always led him to doff it the moment he entered the room, yet his coat was another matter. Concerning his coats, I reasoned with him; but with no effect. The truth was, I suppose, that a man with so small an income could not afford to sport such a lustrous face and a lustrous coat at one and the same time. As Nippers once observed, Turkey's money went chiefly for red ink. One winter day, I presented Turkey with a highly respectable-looking coat of my own—a padded gray coat, of a most comfortable warmth, and which buttoned straight up from the knee to the neck. I thought Turkey would appreciate the favor, and abate his rashness and obstreperousness of afternoons. But no; I verily believe that buttoning himself up in so downy and blanket-like a coat had a pernicious effect upon him—upon the same principle that too much oats are bad for horses. In fact, precisely as a rash, restive horse is said to feel his oats, so Turkey felt his coat. It made him insolent. He was a man whom prosperity harmed.

Though, concerning the self-indulgent habits of Turkey, I had my own private surmises, yet, touching Nippers, I was well persuaded that, whatever might be his faults in other respects, he was, at least, a temperate young man. But, indeed, nature herself seemed to have been his vintner, and, at his birth, charged him so thoroughly with an irritable, brandy-like disposition, that all subsequent potations were needless. When I consider how, amid the stillness of my chambers, Nippers would sometimes impatiently rise from his seat, and stooping over his table, spread his arms wide apart, seize the whole desk, and move it, and jerk it, with a grim, grinding motion on the floor, as if the table were a perverse voluntary agent, intent on thwarting and vexing him, I plainly perceive that, for Nippers, brandy-and-water were altogether superfluous.

It was fortunate for me that, owing to its peculiar cause—indigestion—the irritability and consequent nervousness of Nippers were mainly observable in the morning, while in the afternoon he was comparatively mild. So that, Turkey's paroxysms only coming on about twelve o'clock, I never had to do with their eccentricities at one time. Their fits relieved each other, like guards. When Nippers's was on, Turkey's was off; and *vice versa*. This was a good natural arrangement, under the circumstances.

Ginger Nut, the third on my list, was a lad, some twelve years old. His father was a car-man, ambitious of seeing his son on the bench instead of a cart, before he died. So he sent him to my office, as student at law, errand-boy, cleaner and sweeper, at the rate of one dollar a week. He had a little desk to himself, but he did not use it much. Upon inspection, the drawer exhibited a great array of the shells of various sorts of nuts. Indeed, to this quick-witted youth, the whole noble science of the law was contained in a nutshell. Not the least among the employments of Ginger Nut, as well as one which he discharged with the most alacrity, was his duty as cake and apple purveyor for Turkey and Nippers. Copying law-papers being proverbially a dry, husky sort of business, my two scriveners were fain to moisten their mouths very often with Spitzenbergs, to be had at the numerous stalls nigh the Custom House and Post Office. Also, they sent Ginger Nut very frequently for that peculiar cake—small, flat, round, and very spicy—after which he had been named by them. Of a cold morning, when business was but dull, Turkey would gobble up scores of these cakes, as if they were mere wafers—indeed, they sell them at the rate of six or eight for a penny—the scrape of his pen blending with the crunching of the crisp particles in his mouth. Rashest of all the fiery afternoon blunders and flurried rashnesses of Turkey, was his once moistening a ginger-cake between his lips, and clapping it on to a mortgage, for a seal. I came within an ace of dismissing him then. But he mollified me by making an oriental bow, and saying—

"With submission, sir, it was generous of me to find you in stationery on my own account."

Now my original business—that of a conveyancer and title hunter, and drawer-up of recondite documents of all sorts—was considerably increased by receiving the Master's office. There was now great work for scriveners. Not only must I push the clerks already with me, but I must have additional help.

In answer to my advertisement, a motionless young man one morning stood upon my office threshold, the door being open, for it was summer. I can see that figure now—pallidly neat, pitiably respectable, incurably forlorn! It was Bartleby.

After a few words touching his qualifications, I engaged him, glad to have among my corps of copyists a man of so singularly sedate an aspect, which I thought might operate beneficially upon the flighty temper of Turkey, and the fiery one of Nippers.

I should have stated before that ground glass folding-doors divided my premises into two parts, one of which was occupied by my scriveners, the other by myself. According to my humor, I threw open these doors, or closed them. I resolved to assign Bartleby a corner by the folding-doors, but on my side of them, so as to have this quiet man within easy call, in case any trifling thing was to be done. I placed his desk close up to a small side-window in that part of the room, a window which originally had afforded a lateral view of certain grimy backyards and bricks, but which, owing to subsequent erections, commanded at present no view at all, though it gave some light. Within three feet of the panes was a wall, and the light came down from far above, between two lofty buildings, as from a very small opening in a dome. Still further to a satisfactory arrangement, I procured a high green folding screen, which might entirely isolate Bartleby from my sight, though not remove him from my voice. And thus, in a manner, privacy and society were conjoined.

At first, Bartleby did an extraordinary quantity of writing. As if long famishing for something to copy, he seemed to gorge himself on my documents. There was no pause for digestion. He ran a day and night line, copying by sun-light and by candle-light. I should have been quite delighted with his application, had he been cheerfully industrious. But he wrote on silently, palely, mechanically.

It is, of course, an indispensable part of a scrivener's business to verify the accuracy of his copy, word by word. Where there are two or more scriveners in an office, they assist each other in this examination, one reading from the copy, the other holding the original. It is a very dull, wearisome, and lethargic affair. I can readily imagine that, to some sanguine temperaments, it would be altogether intolerable. For example, I cannot credit that the mettlesome poet, Byron, would have contentedly sat down with Bartleby to examine a law document of, say five hundred pages, closely written in a crimpy hand.

Now and then, in the haste of business, it had been my habit to assist in comparing some brief document myself, calling Turkey or Nippers for this purpose. One object I had, in placing Bartleby so handy to me behind the screen, was to avail myself of his services on such trivial occasions. It was on the third day, I think, of his being with me, and before any necessity had arisen for having his own writing examined, that, being much hurried to complete a small affair I had in hand, I abruptly called to Bartleby. In my haste and natural expectancy of instant compliance, I sat with my head bent over the original on my desk, and my right hand sideways, and somewhat nervously extended with the copy, so that, immediately upon emerging from his retreat, Bartleby might snatch it and proceed to business without the least delay.

In this very attitude did I sit when I called to him, rapidly stating what it was I wanted him to do—namely, to examine a small paper with me. Imagine my surprise, nay, my consternation, when, without moving from his privacy, Bartleby, in a singularly mild, firm voice, replied, "I would prefer not to."

I sat awhile in perfect silence, rallying my stunned faculties. Immediately it occurred to me that my ears had deceived me, or Bartleby had entirely misunderstood my meaning. I repeated my request in the clearest tone I could assume; but in quite as clear a one came the previous reply, "I would prefer not to."

"Prefer not to," echoed I, rising in high excitement, and crossing the room with a stride. "What do you mean? Are you moonstruck? I want you to help me compare this sheet here—take it," and I thrust it towards him.

"I would prefer not to," said he.

I looked at him steadfastly. His face was leanly composed; his gray eye dimly calm. Not a wrinkle of agitation rippled him. Had there been the least uneasiness, anger, impatience, or impertinence in his manner; in other words, had there been any thing ordinarily human about him, doubtless I should have violently dismissed him from the premises. But as it was, I should have as soon thought of turning my pale plaster-of-paris bust of Cicero out of doors. I stood gazing at him awhile, as he went on with his own writing, and then reseated myself at my desk. This is very strange, thought I. What had one best do? But my business hurried me. I concluded to forget the matter for the present, reserving it for my future leisure. So, calling Nippers from the other room, the paper was speedily examined.

A few days after this, Bartleby concluded four lengthy documents, being quadruplicates of a week's testimony taken before me in my High Court of Chancery. It became necessary to examine them. It was an important suit, and great accuracy was imperative. Having all things arranged, I called Turkey, Nippers, and Ginger Nut from the next room, meaning to place the four copies in the hands of my four clerks, while I should read from the original. Accordingly, Turkey, Nippers, and Ginger Nut had taken their seats in a row, each with his document in his hand, when I called to Bartleby to join this interesting group.

"Bartleby! quick, I am waiting."

I heard a slow scrape of his chair legs on the uncarpeted floor, and soon he appeared standing at the entrance of his hermitage.

"What is wanted?" said he, mildly.

"The copies, the copies," said I, hurriedly. "We are going to examine them. There—" and I held towards him the fourth quadruplicate.

"I would prefer not to," he said, and gently disappeared behind the screen.

For a few moments I was turned into a pillar of salt, standing at the head of my seated column of clerks. Recovering myself, I advanced towards the screen, and demanded the reason for such extraordinary conduct.

"*Why* do you refuse?"

"I would prefer not to."

With any other man I should have flown outright into a dreadful passion, scorned all further words, and thrust him ignominiously from my presence. But there was something about Bartleby that not only strangely disarmed me, but, in a wonderful manner, touched and disconcerted me. I began to reason with him.

"These are your own copies we are about to examine. It is labor saving to you, because one examination will answer for your four papers. It is common usage. Every copyist is bound to help examine his copy. Is it not so? Will you not speak? Answer!"

"I prefer not to," he replied in a flutelike tone. It seemed to me that, while I had been addressing him, he carefully revolved every statement that I made; fully comprehended the meaning; could not gainsay the irresistible conclusion; but, at the same time, some paramount consideration prevailed with him to reply as he did.

"You are decided, then, not to comply with my request—a request made according to common usage and common sense?"

He briefly gave me to understand, that on that point my judgment was sound. Yes: his decision was irreversible.

It is not seldom the case that, when a man is browbeaten in some unprecedented and violently unreasonable way, he begins to stagger in his own plainest faith. He begins, as it were, vaguely to surmise that, wonderful as it may be, all the justice and all the reason is on the other side. Accordingly, if any disinterested persons are present, he turns to them for some reinforcement for his own faltering mind.

"Turkey," said I, "what do you think of this? Am I not right?"

"With submission, sir," said Turkey, in his blandest tone, "I think that you are."

"Nippers," said I, "what do *you* think of it?"

"I think I should kick him out of the office."

(The reader of nice perceptions will here perceive that, it being morning, Turkey's answer is couched in polite and tranquil terms, but Nippers replies in ill-tempered ones. Or, to repeat a previous sentence, Nippers's ugly mood was on duty, and Turkey's off.)

"Ginger Nut," said I, willing to enlist the smallest suffrage in my behalf, "what do *you* think of it?"

"I think, sir, he's a little *luny*," replied Ginger Nut, with a grin.

"You hear what they say," said I, turning towards the screen, "come forth and do your duty."

But he vouchsafed no reply. I pondered a moment in sore perplexity. But once more business hurried me. I determined again to postpone the consideration of this dilemma to my future leisure. With a little trouble we made out to examine the papers without Bartleby, though at every page or two Turkey deferentially dropped his opinion, that this proceeding was quite out of the common; while Nippers, twitching in his chair with a dyspeptic nervousness, ground out, between his set teeth, occasional hissing maledictions against the stubborn oaf behind the screen. And for his (Nippers's) part, this was the first and the last time he would do another man's business without pay.

Meanwhile Bartleby sat in his hermitage, oblivious to everything but his own peculiar business there.

Some days passed, the scrivener being employed upon another lengthy work. His late remarkable conduct led me to regard his ways narrowly. I observed that he never went to dinner; indeed, that he never went anywhere. As yet I had never, of my personal knowledge, known him to be outside of my office. He was a perpetual sentry in the corner. At about eleven o'clock though, in the morning, I noticed that Ginger Nut would advance toward the opening in Bartleby's screen, as if silently beckoned thither by a gesture invisible to me where I sat. The boy would then leave the office, jingling a few pence, and reappear with a handful of ginger-nuts, which he delivered in the hermitage, receiving two of the cakes for his trouble.

He lives, then, on ginger-nuts, thought I; never eats a dinner, properly speaking; he must be a vegetarian, then; but no; he never eats even vegetables; he eats nothing but ginger-nuts. My mind then ran on in reveries concerning the probable effects upon the human constitution of living entirely on ginger-nuts. Ginger-nuts are so called, because they contain ginger as one of their peculiar constituents, and the final flavoring one. Now, what was ginger? A hot, spicy thing. Was Bartleby hot and spicy? Not at all. Ginger, then, had no effect upon Bartleby. Probably he preferred it should have none.

Nothing so aggravates an earnest person as a passive resistance. If the individual so resisted be of a not inhumane temper, and the resisting one perfectly harmless in his passivity, then, in the better moods of the former, he will endeavor charitably to construe to his imagination what proves impossible to be solved by his judgment. Even so, for the most part, I regarded Bartleby and his ways. Poor fellow! thought I, he means no mischief; it is plain he intends no insolence; his aspect sufficiently evinces that his eccentricities are involuntary. He is useful to me. I can get along with him. If I turn him away, the chances are he will fall in with some less-indulgent employer, and then he will be rudely treated, and perhaps driven forth miserably to starve. Yes. Here I can cheaply purchase a delicious self-approval. To befriend Bartleby; to humor him in his strange willfulness, will cost me little or nothing, while I lay up in my soul what will eventually prove a sweet morsel for my conscience. But this mood was not invariable with me. The passiveness of Bartleby sometimes irritated me. I felt strangely goaded on to encounter him in new opposition—to elicit some angry spark from him answerable to my own. But, indeed, I might as well have essayed to strike fire with my knuckles against a bit of Windsor soap. But one afternoon the evil

121

impulse in me mastered me, and the following little scene ensued:

"Bartleby," said I, "when those papers are all copied, I will compare them with you."

"I would prefer not to."

"How? Surely you do not mean to persist in that mulish vagary?"

No answer.

I threw open the folding-doors near by, and, turning upon Turkey and Nippers, exclaimed:

"Bartleby a second time says, he won't examine his papers. What do you think of it, Turkey?"

It was afternoon, be it remembered. Turkey sat glowing like a brass boiler; his bald head steaming; his hands reeling among his blotted papers.

"Think of it?" roared Turkey; "I think I'll just step behind his screen, and black his eyes for him!"

So saying, Turkey rose to his feet and threw his arms into a pugilistic position. He was hurrying away to make good his promise, when I detained him, alarmed at the effect of incautiously rousing Turkey's combativeness after dinner.

"Sit down, Turkey," said I, "and hear what Nippers has to say. What do you think of it, Nippers? Would I not be justified in immediately dismissing Bartleby?"

"Excuse me, that is for you to decide, sir. I think his conduct quite unusual, and, indeed, unjust, as regards Turkey and myself. But it may only be a passing whim."

"Ah," exclaimed I, "you have strangely changed your mind, then—you speak very gently of him now."

"All beer," cried Turkey; "gentleness is effects of beer—Nippers and I dined together to-day. You see how gentle *I* am, sir. Shall I go and black his eyes?"

"You refer to Bartleby, I suppose. No, not to-day, Turkey," I replied; "pray, put up your fists."

I closed the doors, and again advanced towards Bartleby. I felt additional incentives tempting me to my fate. I burned to be rebelled against again. I remembered that Bartleby never left the office.

"Bartleby," said I, "Ginger Nut is away; just step around to the Post Office, won't you?" (it was but a three minutes' walk), "and see if there is anything for me."

"I would prefer not to."

"You *will* not?"

"I *prefer* not."

I staggered to my desk, and sat there in a deep study. My blind inveteracy returned. Was there any other thing in which I could procure myself to be ignominiously repulsed by this lean, penniless wight?—my hired clerk? What added thing is there, perfectly reasonable, that he will be sure to refuse to do?

"Bartleby!"

No answer.

"Bartleby," in a louder tone.

No answer.

"Bartleby," I roared.

Like a very ghost, agreeably to the laws of magical invocation, at the third summons, he appeared at the entrance of his hermitage.

"Go to the next room, and tell Nippers to come to me."

"I prefer not to," he respectfully and slowly said, and mildly disappeared.

"Very good, Bartleby," said I, in a quiet sort of serenely-severe, self-possessed tone, intimating the unalterable purpose of some terrible retribution very close at hand. At the moment I half intended something of the kind. But upon the whole, as it was drawing towards my dinner-hour, I thought it best to put on my hat and walk home for the day, suffering much from perplexity and distress of mind.

Shall I acknowledge it? The conclusion of this whole business was, that it soon became a fixed fact of my chambers, that a pale young scrivener, by the name of Bartleby, had a desk there; that he copied for me at the usual rate of four cents a folio (one hundred words); but he was permanently exempt from examining the work done by him, that duty being transferred to Turkey and Nippers, out of compliment, doubtless, to their superior acuteness; moreover, said Bartleby was never, on any account, to be dispatched on the most trivial errand of any sort; and that even if entreated to take upon him such a matter, it was generally understood that he would "prefer not to"—in other words, that he would refuse point-blank.

As days passed on, I became considerably reconciled to Bartleby. His steadiness, his freedom from all dissipation, his incessant industry (except when he chose to throw himself into a standing revery behind his screen), his great stillness, his unalterableness of demeanor under all circumstances, made him a valuable acquisition.

123

One prime thing was this—*he was always there*—first in the morning, continually through the day, and the last at night. I had a singular confidence in his honesty. I felt my most precious papers perfectly safe in his hands. Sometimes, to be sure, I could not, for the very soul of me, avoid falling into sudden spasmodic passions with him. For it was exceeding difficult to bear in mind all the time those strange peculiarities, privileges, and unheard-of exemptions, forming the tacit stipulations on Bartleby's part under which he remained in my office. Now and then, in the eagerness of dispatching pressing business, I would inadvertently summon Bartleby, in a short, rapid tone, to put his finger, say, on the incipient tie of a bit of red tape with which I was about compressing some papers. Of course, from behind the screen the usual answer, "I prefer not to," was sure to come; and then, how could a human creature, with the common infirmities of our nature, refrain from bitterly exclaiming upon such perverseness—such unreasonableness? However, every added repulse of this sort which I received only tended to lessen the probability of my repeating the inadvertence.

Here it must be said, that according to the custom of most legal gentlemen occupying chambers in densely-populated law buildings, there were several keys to my door. One was kept by a woman residing in the attic, which person weekly scrubbed and daily swept and dusted my apartments. Another was kept by Turkey for convenience sake. The third I sometimes carried in my own pocket. The fourth I knew not who had.

Now, one Sunday morning I happened to go to Trinity Church, to hear a celebrated preacher, and finding myself rather early on the ground I thought I would walk round to my chambers for a while. Luckily I had my key with me; but upon applying it to the lock, I found it resisted by something inserted from the inside. Quite surprised, I called out; when to my consternation a key was turned from within; and thrusting his lean visage at me, and holding the door ajar, the apparition of Bartleby appeared, in his shirt sleeves, and otherwise in a strangely tattered *déshabillé,* saying quietly that he was sorry, but he was deeply engaged just then, and——preferred not admitting me at present. In a brief word or two, he moreover added, that perhaps I had better walk round the block two or three times, and by that time he would probably have concluded his affairs.

Now, the utterly unsurmised appearance of Bartleby, tenanting my law-chambers of a Sunday morning, with his cadaverously gentlemanly *nonchalance,* yet withal firm and self-possessed, had such a strange effect upon me, that incontinently I slunk away from my own door, and did as desired. But not without sundry twinges of impotent rebellion against the mild effrontery of this unaccountable scrivener. Indeed, it was his wonderful mildness chiefly, which not only disarmed me, but unmanned me, as it were. For I consider that one, for the time, is somehow unmanned when he tranquilly permits his hired clerk to dictate to him, and order him away from his own premises. Furthermore, I was full of uneasiness as to what Bartleby could possibly be doing in my office in his shirt sleeves, and in an otherwise dismantled condition of a Sunday morning. Was anything amiss going on? Nay, that was out of the question. It was not to be thought of for a moment that Bartleby was an immoral person. But what could he be doing there?—copying? Nay again, whatever might be his eccentricities, Bartleby was an eminently decorous person. He would be the last man to sit down to his desk in any state approaching to nudity. Besides, it was Sunday; and there was something about Bartleby that forbade the supposition that he would by any secular occupation violate the proprieties of the day.

Nevertheless, my mind was not pacified; and full of a restless curiosity, at last I returned to the door. Without hindrance I inserted my key, opened it, and entered. Bartleby was not to be seen. I looked round anxiously, peeped behind his screen; but it was very plain that he was gone. Upon more closely examining the place, I surmised that for an indefinite period Bartleby must have eaten, dressed, and slept in my office, and that, too, without plate, mirror, or bed. The cushioned seat of a ricketty old sofa in one corner bore the faint impress of a lean, reclining form. Rolled away under his desk, I found a blanket; under the empty grate, a blacking box and brush; on a chair, a tin basin, with soap and a ragged towel; in a newspaper a few crumbs of ginger-nuts and a morsel of cheese. Yes, thought I, it is evident enough that Bartleby has been making his home here, keeping bachelor's hall all by himself. Immediately then the thought came sweeping across me, what miserable friendlessness and loneliness are here revealed! His poverty is great; but his solitude, how horrible! Think of it. Of a Sunday, Wall Street is deserted as Petra; and every night of every day it is an emptiness. This building, too, which of weekdays hums with industry and life, at nightfall echoes with sheer vacancy, and all through Sunday is forlorn. And here Bartleby makes his home; sole spectator of a solitude which he has seen all populous—a sort of innocent and transformed Marius brooding among the ruins of Carthage!

For the first time in my life a feeling of overpowering stinging melancholy seized me. Before, I had never experienced aught but a not unpleasing sadness. The bond of a common humanity now drew me irresistibly to gloom. A fraternal melancholy! For both I and Bartleby were sons of Adam. I remembered the bright silks and sparkling faces I had seen that day, in gala trim, swan-like sailing down the Mississippi of Broadway; and I contrasted them with the pallid copyist, and thought to myself, Ah, happiness courts the light, so we deem the world is gay; but misery hides aloof, so we deem that misery there is none. These sad fancyings—chimeras, doubtless, of a sick and silly brain—led on to other and more special thoughts, concerning the eccentricities of Bartleby. Presentiments of strange discoveries hovered round me. The scrivener's pale form appeared to me laid out, among uncaring strangers, in its shivering winding sheet.

Suddenly I was attracted by Bartleby's closed desk, the key in open sight left in the lock.

I mean no mischief, seek the gratification of no heartless curiosity, thought I; besides, the desk is mine, and its contents, too, so I will make bold to look within. Everything was methodically arranged, the papers smoothly placed. The pigeon holes were deep, and removing the files of documents, I groped into their recesses. Presently I felt something there, and dragged it out. It was an old bandanna handkerchief, heavy and knotted. I opened it, and saw it was a savings' bank.

I now recalled all the quiet mysteries which I had noted in the man. I remembered that he never spoke but to answer; that, though at intervals he had considerable time to himself, yet I had never seen him reading—no, not even a newspaper; that for long periods he would stand looking out, at his pale window behind the screen, upon the dead brick wall; I was quite sure he never visited any refectory or eating house; while his pale face clearly indicated that he never drank beer like Turkey, or tea and coffee even, like other men; that he never went anywhere in particular that I could learn; never went out for a walk, unless, indeed, that was the case at present; that he had declined telling who he was, or whence he came, or whether he had any relatives in the world; that though so thin and pale, he never complained of ill health. And more than all, I remembered a certain unconscious air of pallid—how shall I call it?—of pallid haughtiness, say, or rather an austere reserve about him, which had positively awed me into my tame compliance with his eccentricities, when I had feared to ask him to do the slightest incidental thing for me, even though I might know, from his long-continued motionlessness, that behind his screen he must be standing in one of those dead-wall reveries of his.

Revolving all these things, and coupling them with the recently discovered fact, that he made my office his constant abiding place and home, and not forgetful of his morbid moodiness; revolving all these things, a prudential feeling began to steal over me. My first emotions had been those of pure melancholy and sincerest pity; but just in proportion as the forlornness of Bartleby grew and grew to my imagination, did that same melancholy merge into fear, that pity into repulsion. So true it is, and so terrible, too, that up to a certain point the thought or sight of misery enlists our best affections; but, in certain special cases, beyond that point it does not. They err who would assert that invariably this is owing to the inherent selfishness of the human heart. It rather proceeds from a certain hopelessness of remedying excessive and organic ill. To a sensitive being, pity is not seldom pain. And when at last it is perceived that such pity cannot lead to effectual succor, common sense bids the soul be rid of it. What I saw that morning persuaded me that the scrivener was the victim of innate and incurable disorder. I might give alms to his body; but his body did not pain him; it was his soul that suffered, and his soul I could not reach.

I did not accomplish the purpose of going to Trinity Church that morning. Somehow, the things I had seen disqualified me for the time from church-going. I walked homeward, thinking what I would do with Bartleby. Finally, I resolved upon this—I would put certain calm questions to him the next morning, touching his history, etc., and if he declined to answer them openly and unreservedly (and I supposed he would prefer not), then to give him a twenty dollar bill over and above whatever I might owe him, and tell him his services were no longer required; but that if in any other way I could assist him, I would be happy to do so, especially if he desired to return to his native place, wherever that might be, I would willingly help to defray the expenses. Moreover, if, after reaching home, he found himself at any time in want of aid, a letter from him would be sure of a reply.

The next morning came.

"Bartleby," said I, gently calling to him behind his screen.

No reply.

"Bartleby," said I, in a still gentler tone, "come here; I am not going to ask you to do anything you would prefer not to do—I simply wish to speak to you."

Upon this he noiselessly slid into view.

"Will you tell me, Bartleby, where you were born?"

"I would prefer not to."

"Will you tell me *anything* about yourself?"

"I would prefer not to."

"But what reasonable objection can you have to speak to me? I feel friendly towards you."

He did not look at me while I spoke, but kept his glance fixed upon my bust of Cicero, which, as I then sat, was directly behind me, some six inches above my head.

"What is your answer, Bartleby?" said I, after waiting a considerable time for a reply, during which his countenance remained immovable, only there was the faintest conceivable tremor of the white attenuated mouth.

"At present I prefer to give no answer," he said, and retired into his hermitage.

It was rather weak in me I confess, but his manner, on this occasion, nettled me. Not only did there seem to lurk in it a certain calm disdain, but his perverseness seemed ungrateful, considering the undeniable good usage and indulgence he had received from me.

Again I sat ruminating what I should do. Mortified as I was at his behavior, and resolved as I had been to dismiss him when I entered my office, nevertheless I strangely felt something superstitious knocking at my heart, and forbidding me to carry out my purpose, and denouncing me for a villain if I dared to breathe one bitter word against this forlornest of mankind. At last, familiarly drawing my chair behind his screen, I sat down and said: "Bartleby, never mind, then, about revealing your history; but let me entreat you, as a friend, to comply as far as may be with the usages of this office. Say now, you will help to examine papers to-morrow or next day: in short, say now, that in a day or two you will begin to be a little reasonable:—say so, Bartleby."

"At present I would prefer not to be a little reasonable," was his mildly cadaverous reply.

Just then the folding-doors opened, and Nippers approached. He seemed suffering from an unusually bad night's rest, induced by severer indigestion than common. He overheard those final words of Bartleby.

"*Prefer not,* eh?" gritted Nippers—"I'd *prefer* him, if I were you, sir," addressing me—"I'd *prefer* him; I'd give him preferences, the stubborn mule! What is it, sir, pray, that he *prefers* not to do now?"

Bartleby moved not a limb.

"Mr. Nippers," said I, "I'd prefer that you would withdraw for the present."

Somehow, of late, I had got into the way of involuntarily using this word "prefer" upon all sorts of not exactly suitable occasions. And I trembled to think that my contact with the scrivener had already and seriously affected me in a mental way. And what further and deeper aberration might it not yet produce? This apprehension had not been without efficacy in determining me to summary measures.

As Nippers, looking very sour and sulky, was departing, Turkey blandly and deferentially approached.

"With submission, sir," said he, "yesterday I was thinking about Bartleby here, and I think that if he would but prefer to take a quart of good ale every day, it would do much towards mending him, and enabling him to assist in examining his papers."

"So you have got the word, too," said I, slightly excited.

"With submission, what word, sir?" asked Turkey, respectfully crowding himself into the contracted space behind the screen, and by so doing, making me jostle the scrivener. "What word, sir?"

"I would prefer to be left alone here," said Bartleby, as if offended at being mobbed in his privacy.

"*That's* the word, Turkey," said I—"*that's* it."

"Oh, *prefer?* oh yes—queer word. I never use it myself. But, sir, as I was saying, if he would but prefer—"

"Turkey," interrupted I, "you will please withdraw."

"Oh certainly, sir, if you prefer that I should."

As he opened the folding-door to retire, Nippers at his desk caught a glimpse of me, and asked whether I would prefer to have a certain paper copied on blue paper or white. He did not in the least roguishly accent the word "prefer." It was plain that it involuntarily rolled from his tongue. I thought to myself, surely I must get rid of a demented man, who already has in some degree turned the tongues, if not the heads of myself and clerks. But I thought it prudent not to break the dismission at once.

The next day I noticed that Bartleby did nothing but stand at his window in his dead-wall revery. Upon asking him why he did not write, he said that he had decided upon doing no more writing.

"Why, how now? what next?" exclaimed I, "do no more writing?"

"No more."

"And what is the reason?"

"Do you not see the reason for yourself?" he indifferently replied.

I looked steadfastly at him, and perceived that his eyes looked dull and glazed. Instantly it occurred to me, that his unexampled diligence in copying by his dim window for the first few weeks of his stay with me might have temporarily impaired his vision.

I was touched. I said something in condolence with him. I hinted that of course he did wisely in abstaining from writing for a while; and urged him to embrace that opportunity of taking wholesome exercise in the open air. This, however, he did not do. A few days after this, my other clerks being absent, and being in a great hurry to dispatch certain letters by the mail, I thought that, having nothing else earthly to do, Bartleby would surely be less inflexible than usual, and carry these letters to the post-office. But he blankly declined. So, much to my inconvenience, I went myself.

Still added days went by. Whether Bartleby's eyes improved or not, I could not say. To all appearance, I thought they did. But when I asked him if they did, he vouchsafed no answer. At all events, he would do no copying. At last, in reply to my urgings, he informed me that he had permanently given up copying.

"What!" exclaimed I; "suppose your eyes should get entirely well—better than ever before—would you not copy then?"

"I have given up copying," he answered, and slid aside.

He remained as ever, a fixture in my chamber. Nay—if that were possible—he became still more of a fixture than before. What was to be done? He would do nothing in the office; why should he stay there? In plain fact, he had now become a millstone to me, not only useless as a necklace, but afflictive to bear. Yet I was sorry for him. I speak less than truth when I say that, on his own account, he occasioned me uneasiness. If he would but have named a single relative or friend, I would instantly have written, and urged their taking the poor fellow away to some convenient retreat. But he seemed alone, absolutely alone in the universe. A bit of wreck in the mid Atlantic. At length, necessities connected with my business tyrannized over all other considerations. Decently as I could, I told Bartleby that in six days' time he must unconditionally leave the office. I warned him to take measures, in the interval, for procuring some other abode. I offered to assist him in this endeavor, if he himself would but take the first step towards a removal. "And when you finally quit me, Bartleby," added I, "I shall see that you go not away entirely unprovided. Six days from this hour, remember."

At the expiration of that period, I peeped behind the screen, and lo! Bartleby was there.

I buttoned up my coat, balanced myself; advanced slowly towards him, touched his shoulder, and said, "The time has come; you must quit this place; I am sorry for you; here is money; but you must go."

"I would prefer not," he replied, with his back still towards me.

"You *must*."

He remained silent.

Now I had an unbounded confidence in this man's common honesty. He had frequently restored to me sixpences and shillings carelessly dropped upon the floor, for I am apt to be very reckless in such shirt-button affairs. The proceeding, then, which followed will not be deemed extraordinary.

"Bartleby," said I, "I owe you twelve dollars on account; here are thirty-two; the odd twenty are yours—Will you take it?" and I handed the bills towards him.

But he made no motion.

"I will leave them here, then," putting them under a weight on the table. Then taking my hat and cane and going to the door, I tranquilly turned and added—"After you have removed your things from these offices, Bartleby, you will of course lock the door—since every one is now gone for the day but you—and if you please, slip your key underneath the mat, so that I may have it in the morning. I shall not see you again; so good-by to you. If, hereafter, in your new place of abode, I can be of any service to you, do not fail to advise me by letter. Good-by, Bartleby, and fare you well."

But he answered not a word; like the last column of some ruined temple, he remained standing mute and solitary in the middle of the otherwise deserted room.

As I walked home in a pensive mood, my vanity got the better of my pity. I could not but highly plume myself on my masterly management in getting rid of Bartleby. Masterly I call it, and such it must appear to any dispassionate thinker. The beauty of my procedure seemed to consist in its perfect quietness. There was no vulgar bullying, no bravado of any sort, no choleric hectoring, and striding to and fro across the apartment, jerking out vehement commands for Bartleby to bundle himself off with his beggarly traps. Nothing of the kind. Without loudly bidding Bartleby depart—as an inferior genius might have done—I *assumed* the ground that depart he must; and upon that assumption built all I had to say. The more I thought over my procedure, the more I was charmed with it. Nevertheless, next morning, upon awakening, I had my doubts—I had somehow slept off the fumes of vanity. One of the coolest and wisest hours a man has, is just after he awakes in the morning. My procedure seemed as sagacious as ever—but only in theory. How it would prove in practice—there was the rub. It was truly a beautiful thought to have assumed Bartleby's departure; but, after all, that assumption was simply my own, and none of Bartleby's. The great point was, not whether I had assumed that he would quit me, but whether he would prefer so to do. He was more a man of preferences than assumptions.

After breakfast, I walked down town, arguing the probabilities *pro* and *con*. One moment I thought it would prove a miserable failure, and Bartleby would be found all alive at my office as usual; the next moment it seemed certain that I should find his chair empty. And so I kept veering about. At the corner of Broadway and Canal Street, I saw quite an excited group of people standing in earnest conversation.

"I'll take odds he doesn't," said a voice as I passed.

"Doesn't go?—done!" said I; "put up your money."

I was instinctively putting my hand in my pocket to produce my own, when I remembered that this was an election day. The words I had overheard bore no reference to Bartleby, but to the success or non-success of some candidate for the mayoralty. In my intent frame of mind, I had, as it were, imagined that all Broadway shared in my excitement, and were debating the same question with me. I passed on, very thankful that the uproar of the street screened my momentary absent-mindedness.

As I had intended, I was earlier than usual at my office door. I stood listening for a moment. All was still. He must be gone. I tried the knob. The door was locked. Yes, my procedure had worked to a charm; he indeed must be vanished. Yet a certain melancholy mixed with this: I was almost sorry for my brilliant success. I was fumbling under the door mat for the key, which Bartleby was to have left there for me, when accidentally my knee knocked against a panel, producing a summoning sound, and in response a voice came to me from within—"Not yet; I am occupied."

It was Bartleby.

I was thunderstruck. For an instant I stood like the man who, pipe in mouth, was killed one cloudless afternoon long ago in Virginia, by summer lightning; at his own warm open window he was killed, and remained leaning out there upon the dreamy afternoon, till some one touched him, when he fell.

"Not gone!" I murmured at last. But again obeying that wondrous ascendancy which the inscrutable scrivener had over me, and from which ascendancy, for all my chafing, I could not completely escape, I slowly went down stairs and out into the street, and while walking round the block, considered what I should next do in this unheard-of perplexity. Turn the man out by an actual thrusting I could not; to drive him away by calling him hard names would not do; calling in the police was an unpleasant idea; and yet, permit him to enjoy his cadaverous triumph over me—this, too, I could not think of. What was to be done? or, if nothing could be done, was there anything further that I could *assume* in the matter? Yes, as before I had prospectively assumed that Bartleby would depart, so now I might retrospectively assume that departed he was. In the legitimate carrying out of this assumption, I might enter my office in a great hurry, and pretending not to see Bartleby at all, walk straight against him as if he were air. Such a proceeding would in a singular degree have the appearance of a home-thrust. It was hardly possible that Bartleby could withstand such an application of the doctrine of assumptions. But upon second thoughts the success of the plan seemed rather dubious. I resolved to argue the matter over with him again.

"Bartleby," said I, entering the office, with a quietly severe expression, "I am seriously displeased. I am pained, Bartleby. I had thought better of you. I had imagined you of such a gentlemanly organization, that in any delicate dilemma a slight hint would suffice—in short, an assumption. But it appears I am deceived. Why," I added, unaffectedly starting, "you have not even touched that money yet," pointing to it, just where I had left it the evening previous.

He answered nothing.

"Will you, or will you not, quit me?" I now demanded in a sudden passion, advancing close to him.

"I would prefer *not* to quit you," he replied, gently emphasizing the *not*.

"What earthly right have you to stay here? Do you pay any rent? Do you pay my taxes? Or is this property yours?"

He answered nothing.

"Are you ready to go on and write now? Are your eyes recovered? Could you copy a small paper for me this morning? or help examine a few lines? or step round to the post-office? In a word, will you do anything at all, to give a coloring to your refusal to depart the premises?"

He silently retired into his hermitage.

I was now in such a state of nervous resentment that I thought it but prudent to check myself at present from further demonstrations. Bartleby and I were alone. I remembered the tragedy of the unfortunate Adams and the still more unfortunate Colt in the solitary office of the latter; and how poor Colt, being dreadfully incensed by Adams, and imprudently permitting himself to get wildly excited, was at unawares hurried into his fatal act—an act which certainly no man could possibly deplore more than the actor himself. Often it had occurred to me in my ponderings upon the subject that had that altercation taken place in the public street, or at a private residence, it would not have terminated as it did. It was the circumstance of being alone in a solitary office, up stairs, of a building entirely unhallowed by humanizing domestic associations—an uncarpeted office, doubtless, of a dusty, haggard sort of appearance—this it must have been, which greatly helped to enhance the irritable desperation of the hapless Colt.

But when this old Adam of resentment rose in me and tempted me concerning Bartleby, I grappled him and threw him. How? Why, simply by recalling the divine injunction: "A new commandment give I unto you, that ye love one another." Yes, this it was that saved me. Aside from higher considerations, charity often operates as a vastly wise and prudent principle—a great safeguard to its possessor. Men have committed murder for jealousy's sake, and anger's sake, and hatred's sake, and selfishness' sake, and spiritual pride's sake; but no man, that ever I heard of, ever committed a diabolical murder for sweet charity's sake. Mere self-interest, then, if no better motive can be enlisted, should, especially with high-tempered men, prompt all beings to charity and philanthropy. At any rate, upon the occasion in question, I strove to drown my exasperated feelings towards the scrivener by benevolently construing his conduct. Poor fellow, poor fellow! thought I, he don't mean anything; and besides, he has seen hard times, and ought to be indulged.

I endeavored, also, immediately to occupy myself, and at the same time to comfort my despondency. I tried to fancy, that in the course of the morning, at such time as might prove agreeable to him, Bartleby, of his own free accord, would emerge from his hermitage and take up some decided line of march in the direction of the door. But no. Half-past twelve o'clock came; Turkey began to glow in the face, overturn his inkstand, and become generally obstreperous; Nippers abated down into quietude and courtesy; Ginger Nut munched his noon apple; and Bartleby remained standing at his window in one of his profoundest dead-wall reveries. Will it be credited? Ought I to acknowledge it? That afternoon I left the office without saying one further word to him.

Some days now passed, during which, at leisure intervals I looked a little into "Edwards on the Will," and "Priestley on Necessity." Under the circumstances, those books induced a salutary feeling. Gradually I slid into the persuasion that these troubles of mine, touching the scrivener, had been all predestinated from eternity, and Bartleby was billeted upon me for some mysterious purpose of an allwise Providence, which it was not for a mere mortal like me to fathom. Yes, Bartleby, stay there behind your screen, thought I; I shall persecute you no more; you are harmless and noiseless as any of these old chairs; in short, I never feel so private as when I know you are here. At last I see it, I feel it; I penetrate to the predestinated purpose of my life. I am content. Others may have loftier parts to enact; but my mission in this world, Bartleby, is to furnish you with office-room for such period as you may see fit to remain.

I believe that this wise and blessed frame of mind would have continued with me, had it not been for the unsolicited and uncharitable remarks obtruded upon me by my professional friends who visited the rooms. But thus it often is, that the constant friction of illiberal minds wears out at last the best resolves of the more generous. Though to be sure, when I reflected upon it, it was not strange that people entering my office should be struck by the peculiar aspect of the unaccountable Bartleby, and so be tempted to throw out some sinister observations concerning him. Sometimes an attorney, having business with me, and calling at my office, and finding no one but the scrivener there, would undertake to obtain some sort of precise information from him touching my whereabouts; but without heeding his idle talk, Bartleby would remain standing immovable in the middle of the room. So after contemplating him in that position for a time, the attorney would depart, no wiser than he came.

Also, when a reference was going on, and the room full of lawyers and witnesses, and business driving fast, some deeply-occupied legal gentleman present, seeing Bartleby wholly unemployed, would request him to run round to his (the legal gentleman's) office and fetch some papers for him. Thereupon, Bartleby would tranquilly decline, and yet remain idle as before. Then the lawyer would give a great stare, and turn to me. And what could I say? At last I was made aware that all through the circle of my professional acquaintance, a whisper of wonder was running round, having reference to the strange creature I kept at my office. This worried me very much. And as the idea came upon me of his possibly turning out a long-lived man, and keep occupying my chambers, and denying my authority; and perplexing my visitors; and scandalizing my professional reputation; and casting a general gloom over the premises; keeping soul and body together to the last upon his savings (for doubtless he spent but half a dime a day), and in the end perhaps outlive me, and claim possession of my office by right of his perpetual occupancy: as all these dark anticipations crowded upon me more and more, and my friends continually intruded their relentless remarks upon the apparition in my room; a great change was wrought in me. I resolved to gather all my faculties together, and forever rid me of this intolerable incubus.

Ere revolving any complicated project, however, adapted to this end, I first simply suggested to Bartleby the propriety of his permanent departure. In a calm and serious tone, I commended the idea to his careful and mature consideration. But, having taken three days to meditate upon it, he apprised me, that his original determination remained the same; in short, that he still preferred to abide with me.

What shall I do? I now said to myself, buttoning up my coat to the last button. What shall I do? what ought I to do? what does conscience say I *should* do with this man, or, rather, ghost. Rid myself of him, I must; go, he shall. But how? You will not thrust him, the poor, pale, passive mortal—you will not thrust such a helpless creature out of your door? you will not dishonor yourself by such cruelty? No, I will not, I cannot do that. Rather would I let him live and die here, and then mason up his remains in the wall. What, then, will you do? For all your coaxing, he will not budge. Bribes he leaves under your own paper-weight on your table; in short, it is quite plain that he prefers to cling to you.

Then something severe, something unusual must be done. What! surely you will not have him collared by a constable, and commit his innocent pallor to the common jail? And upon what ground could you procure such a thing to be done?—a vagrant, is he? What! he a vagrant, a wanderer, who refuses to budge? It is because he will *not* be a vagrant, then, that you seek to count him *as* a vagrant. That is too absurd. No visible means of support: there I have him. Wrong again: for indubitably he *does* support himself, and that is the only unanswerable proof that any man can show of his possessing the means so to do. No more, then. Since he will not quit me, I must quit him. I will change my offices; I will move elsewhere, and give him fair notice, that if I find him on my new premises I will then proceed against him as a common trespasser.

Acting accordingly, next day I thus addressed him: "I find these chambers too far from the City Hall; the air is unwholesome. In a word, I propose to remove my offices next week, and shall no longer require your services. I tell you this now, in order that you may seek another place."

He made no reply; and nothing more was said.

On the appointed day I engaged carts and men, proceeded to my chambers, and, having but little furniture, everything was removed in a few hours. Throughout, the scrivener remained standing behind the screen, which I directed to be removed the last thing. It was withdrawn; and, being folded up like a huge folio, left him the motionless occupant of a naked room. I stood in the entry watching him a moment, while something from within me upbraided me.

I re-entered, with my hand in my pocket—and—and my heart in my mouth.

"Good-by, Bartleby; I am going—good-by, and God some way bless you; and take that," slipping something in his hand. But it dropped upon the floor, and then—strange to say—I tore myself from him whom I had so longed to be rid of.

Established in my new quarters, for a day or two I kept the door locked, and started at every footfall in the passages. When I returned to my rooms, after any little absence, I would pause at the threshold for an instant, and attentively listen, ere applying my key. But these fears were needless. Bartleby never came nigh me.

I thought all was going well, when a perturbed-looking stranger visited me, inquiring whether I was the person who had recently occupied rooms at No. — Wall Street.

Full of forebodings, I replied that I was.

"Then, sir," said the stranger, who proved a lawyer, "you are responsible for the man you left there. He refuses to do any copying; he refuses to do anything; he says he prefers not to; and he refuses to quit the premises."

"I am very sorry, sir," said I, with assumed tranquillity, but an inward tremor, "but, really, the man you allude to is nothing to me— he is no relation or apprentice of mine, that you should hold me responsible for him."

"In mercy's name, who is he?"

"I certainly cannot inform you. I know nothing about him. Formerly I employed him as a copyist; but he has done nothing for me now for some time past."

"I shall settle him, then—good morning, sir."

Several days passed, and I heard nothing more; and, though I often felt a charitable prompting to call at the place and see poor Bartleby, yet a certain squeamishness, of I know not what, withheld me.

All is over with him, by this time, thought I, at last, when, through another week, no further intelligence reached me. But, coming to my room the day after, I found several persons waiting at my door in a high state of nervous excitement.

"That's the man—here he comes," cried the foremost one, whom I recognized as the lawyer who had previously called upon me alone.

"You must take him away, sir, at once," cried a portly person among them, advancing upon me, and whom I knew to be the land-lord of No. — Wall Street. "These gentlemen, my tenants, cannot stand it any longer; Mr. B——," pointing to the lawyer, "has turned him out of his room, and he now persists in haunting the building generally, sitting upon the banisters of the stairs by day, and sleeping in the entry by night. Everybody is concerned; clients are leaving the offices; some fears are entertained of a mob; something you must do, and that without delay."

Aghast at this torrent, I fell back before it, and would fain have locked myself in my new quarters. In vain I persisted that Bartleby was nothing to me—no more than to any one else. In vain—I was the last person known to have anything to do with him, and they held me to the terrible account. Fearful, then, of being exposed in the papers (as one person present obscurely threatened), I considered the matter, and, at length, said, that if the lawyer would give me a confidential interview with the scrivener, in his (the lawyer's) own room, I would, that afternoon, strive my best to rid them of the nuisance they complained of.

Going up stairs to my old haunt, there was Bartleby silently sitting upon the banister at the landing.

"What are you doing here, Bartleby?" said I.

"Sitting upon the banister," he mildly replied.

I motioned him into the lawyer's room, who then left us.

"Bartleby," said I, "are you aware that you are the cause of great tribulation to me, by persisting in occupying the entry after being dismissed from the office?"

No answer.

"Now one of two things must take place. Either you must do something, or something must be done to you. Now what sort of business would you like to engage in? Would you like to re-engage in copying for some one?"

"No; I would prefer not to make any change."

"Would you like a clerkship in a dry-goods store?"

"There is too much confinement about that. No, I would not like a clerkship; but I am not particular."

"Too much confinement," I cried, "why, you keep yourself confined all the time!"

"I would prefer not to take a clerkship," he rejoined, as if to settle that little item at once.

"How would a bar-tender's business suit you? There is no trying of the eye-sight in that."

"I would not like it at all; though, as I said before, I am not particular."

His unwonted wordiness inspirited me. I returned to the charge.

"Well, then, would you like to travel through the country collecting bills for the merchants? That would improve your health."

"No, I would prefer to be doing something else."

"How, then, would going as a companion to Europe, to entertain some young gentleman with your conversation—how would that suit you?"

"Not at all. It does not strike me that there is anything definite about that. I like to be stationary. But I am not particular."

"Stationary you shall be, then," I cried, now losing all patience, and, for the first time in all my exasperating connection with him, fairly flying into a passion. "If you do not go away from these premises before night, I shall feel bound—indeed, I *am* bound—to—to—to quit the premises myself!" I rather absurdly concluded, knowing not with what possible threat to try to frighten his immobility into compliance. Despairing of all further efforts, I was precipitately leaving him, when a final thought occurred to me—one which had not been wholly unindulged before.

"Bartleby," said I, in the kindest tone I could assume under such exciting circumstances, "will you go home with me now—not to my office, but my dwelling—and remain there till we can conclude upon some convenient arrangement for you at our leisure? Come, let us start now, right away."

139

"No: at present I would prefer not to make any change at all."

I answered nothing; but, effectually dodging every one by the suddenness and rapidity of my flight, rushed from the building, ran up Wall Street towards Broadway, and, jumping into the first omnibus, was soon removed from pursuit. As soon as tranquillity returned, I distinctly perceived that I had now done all that I possibly could, both in respect to the demands of the landlord and his tenants, and with regard to my own desire and sense of duty, to benefit Bartleby, and shield him from rude persecution. I now strove to be entirely care-free and quiescent; and my conscience justified me in the attempt; though, indeed, it was not so successful as I could have wished. So fearful was I of being again hunted out by the incensed landlord and his exasperated tenants, that, surrendering my business to Nippers, for a few days, I drove about the upper part of the town and through the suburbs, in my rockaway; crossed over to Jersey City and Hoboken, and paid fugitive visits to Manhattanville and Astoria. In fact, I almost lived in my rockaway for the time.

When again I entered my office, lo, a note from the landlord lay upon the desk. I opened it with trembling hands. It informed me that the writer had sent to the police, and had Bartleby removed to the Tombs as a vagrant. Moreover, since I knew more about him than any one else, he wished me to appear at that place, and make a suitable statement of the facts. These tidings had a conflicting effect upon me. At first I was indignant; but, at last, almost approved. The landlord's energetic, summary disposition, had led him to adopt a procedure which I do not think I would have decided upon myself; and yet, as a last resort, under such peculiar circumstances, it seemed the only plan.

As I afterwards learned, the poor scrivener, when told that he must be conducted to the Tombs, offered not the slightest obstacle, but, in his pale, unmoving way, silently acquiesced.

Some of the compassionate and curious bystanders joined the party; and headed by one of the constables arm in arm with Bartleby, the silent procession filed its way through all the noise, and heat, and joy of the roaring thoroughfares at noon.

The same day I received the note, I went to the Tombs, or, to speak more properly, the Halls of Justice. Seeking the right officer, I stated the purpose of my call, and was informed that the individual I described was, indeed, within. I then assured the functionary that Bartleby was a perfectly honest man, and greatly to be compassionated, however unaccountably eccentric. I narrated all I knew, and closed by suggesting the idea of letting him remain in as indulgent confinement as possible, till something less harsh might be done—though, indeed, I hardly knew what. At all events, if nothing else could be decided upon, the alms-house must receive him. I then begged to have an interview.

Being under no disgraceful charge, and quite serene and harmless in all his ways, they had permitted him freely to wander about the prison, and, especially, in the inclosed grass-platted yards thereof. And so I found him there, standing all alone in the quietest of the yards, his face towards a high wall, while all around, from the narrow slits of the jail windows, I thought I saw peering out upon him the eyes of murderers and thieves.

"Bartleby!"

"I know you," he said, without looking round—"and I want nothing to say to you."

"It was not I that brought you here, Bartleby," said I, keenly pained at his implied suspicion. "And to you, this should not be so vile a place. Nothing reproachful attaches to you by being here. And see, it is not so sad a place as one might think. Look, there is the sky, and here is the grass."

"I know where I am," he replied, but would say nothing more, and so I left him.

As I entered the corridor again, a broad meat-like man, in an apron, accosted me, and, jerking his thumb over his shoulder, said— "Is that your friend?"

"Yes."

"Does he want to starve? If he does, let him live on the prison fare, that's all."

"Who are you?" asked I, not knowing what to make of such an unofficially speaking person in such a place.

"I am the grub-man. Such gentlemen as have friends here, hire me to provide them with something good to eat."

"Is this so?" said I, turning to the turnkey.

He said it was.

"Well, then," said I, slipping some silver into the grub-man's hands (for so they called him), "I want you to give particular attention to my friend there; let him have the best dinner you can get. And you must be as polite to him as possible."

"Introduce me, will you?" said the grub-man, looking at me with an expression which seemed to say he was all impatience for an opportunity to give a specimen of his breeding.

Thinking it would prove of benefit to the scrivener, I acquiesced; and, asking the grub-man his name, went up with him to Bartleby.

"Bartleby, this is a friend; you will find him very useful to you."

"Your sarvant, sir, your sarvant," said the grub-man, making a low salutation behind his apron. "Hope you find it pleasant here, sir; nice grounds—cool apartments—hope you'll stay with us sometime —try to make it agreeable. What will you have for dinner to-day?"

"I prefer not to dine to-day," said Bartleby, turning away. "It would disagree with me; I am unused to dinners." So saying, he slowly moved to the other side of the inclosure, and took up a position fronting the dead-wall.

"How's this?" said the grub-man, addressing me with a stare of astonishment. "He's odd, ain't he?"

"I think he is a little deranged," said I, sadly.

"Deranged? deranged is it? Well, now, upon my word, I thought that friend of yourn was a gentleman forger; they are always pale and genteel-like, them forgers. I can't help pity 'em—can't help it, sir. Did you know Monroe Edwards?" he added, touchingly, and paused. Then, laying his hand piteously on my shoulder, sighed, "he died of consumption at Sing-Sing. So you weren't acquainted with Monroe?"

"No, I was never socially acquainted with any forgers. But I cannot stop longer. Look to my friend yonder. You will not lose by it. I will see you again."

Some few days after this, I again obtained admission to the Tombs, and went through the corridors in quest of Bartleby; but without finding him.

"I saw him coming from his cell not long ago," said a turnkey, "may be he's gone to loiter in the yards."

So I went in that direction.

"Are you looking for the silent man?" said another turnkey, passing me. "Yonder he lies—sleeping in the yard there. 'Tis not twenty minutes since I saw him lie down."

The yard was entirely quiet. It was not accessible to the common prisoners. The surrounding walls, of amazing thickness, kept off all sounds behind them. The Egyptian character of the masonry weighed upon me with its gloom. But a soft imprisoned turf grew under foot. The heart of the eternal pyramids, it seemed, wherein, by some strange magic, through the clefts, grass-seed, dropped by birds, had sprung.

Strangely huddled at the base of the wall, his knees drawn up, and lying on his side, his head touching the cold stones, I saw the wasted Bartleby. But nothing stirred. I paused; then went close up to him; stooped over, and saw that his dim eyes were open; otherwise he seemed profoundly sleeping. Something prompted me to touch him. I felt his hand, when a tingling shiver ran up my arm and down my spine to my feet.

The round face of the grub-man peered upon me now. "His dinner is ready. Won't he dine to-day, either? Or does he live without dining?"

"Lives without dining," said I, and closed the eyes.

"Eh!—He's asleep, ain't he?"

"With kings and counselors," murmured I.

There would seem little need for proceeding further in this history. Imagination will readily supply the meagre recital of poor Bartleby's interment. But, ere parting with the reader, let me say, that if this little narrative has sufficiently interested him, to awaken curiosity as to who Bartleby was, and what manner of life he led prior to the present narrator's making his acquaintance, I can only reply, that in such curiosity I fully share, but am wholly unable to gratify it. Yet here I hardly know whether I should divulge one little item of rumor, which came to my ear a few months after the scrivener's decease. Upon what basis it rested, I could never ascertain; and hence, how true it is I cannot now tell. But, inasmuch as this vague report has not been without a certain suggestive interest to me, however sad, it may prove the same with some others; and so I will briefly mention it. The report was this: that Bartleby had been a subordinate clerk in the Dead Letter Office at Washington, from which he had been suddenly removed by a change in the administration. When I think over this rumor, hardly can I express the emotions which seize me. Dead letters! does it not sound like dead men? Conceive a man by nature and misfortune prone to a pallid hopelessness, can any business seem more fitted to heighten it than that of continually handling these dead letters, and assorting them for the flames? For by the cart-load they are annually burned. Sometimes from out the folded paper the pale clerk takes a ring—the finger it was meant for, perhaps, moulders in the grave; a bank-note sent in swiftest charity—he whom it would relieve, nor eats nor hungers any more; pardon for those who died despairing; hope for those who died unhoping; good tidings for those who died stifled by unrelieved calamities. On errands of life, these letters speed to death.

Ah, Bartleby! Ah, humanity!

Mark Twain

THE NOTORIOUS JUMPING FROG
OF CALAVERAS COUNTY

BAKER'S BLUE-JAY YARN

In his thoroughly American viewpoint, subject matter, and style, Mark Twain (Samuel Langhorne Clemens) reflects the influence of the frontier tradition, with which he was closely associated in his early life. Born in Florida, Missouri, in 1835, he was taken at the age of four to Hannibal, a town on the banks of the Mississippi River. There, in daily contact with the colorful life moving along the Mississippi, he attended school, learned to be a printer by serving a two-year apprenticeship in a local newspaper shop, and worked for three years on his brother Orion's newspaper, *The Western Union*. In 1853, at the age of eighteen, he left Hannibal to earn his living as a tramp printer, working on newspapers in New York, Pennsylvania, and Ohio. In 1857, lured by adventure and the possibility of a quick fortune, he set out for South America but got no farther than New Orleans. Having met Horace Bixby, a famous steamboat pilot, he served an apprenticeship under him, and eventually became a pilot on the Mississippi. When the Civil War closed the Mississippi River to traffic in 1861 and ended Twain's career as a pilot, he traveled west to Nevada, where he resumed newspaper work as a reporter, first on a Virginia City newspaper and later on one in San Francisco. Soon acquiring recognition for his humorous tales and sketches and encouraged in his literary efforts by Bret Harte, he published his first volume in 1867, *The Celebrated Jumping Frog of Calaveras County, and Other Sketches*. His second work, *Innocents Abroad* (1869), based on an excursion to Europe and the Holy Land, won him wide acclaim. He married Olivia Langdon of New York in 1870, settled in Hartford, Connecticut, and began to pursue the brilliant literary career opening to him. For the next forty years,

145

until his death in 1910, besides engaging in many side adventures—such as platform lecturing, sponsoring inventions, and owning a publishing company—Twain wrote such significant and popular works as *Roughing It* (1872), *The Gilded Age* (1873), *The Adventures of Tom Sawyer* (1876), *A Tramp Abroad* (1880), *The Adventures of Huckleberry Finn* (1884), and *A Connecticut Yankee in King Arthur's Court* (1889). Among his other important volumes of short fiction, in addition to *The Jumping Frog* collection, are *Tom Sawyer Abroad, Tom Sawyer, Detective, and Other Stories* (1896), and *The Man that Corrupted Hadleyburg and Other Stories and Essays* (1900). *The Complete Short Stories of Mark Twain,* edited by Charles Neider (1957), brings together sixty pieces which show the scope and diversity of Twain's achievement in short fiction.

In no branch of the story-telling art did Twain exhibit more skill than in his handling of the technique of the frontier oral tale, as the two stories which follow illustrate.

the notorious jumping frog of calaveras county

In compliance with the request of a friend of mine, who wrote me from the East, I called on good-natured, garrulous old Simon Wheeler, and inquired after my friend's friend, Leonidas W. Smiley, as requested to do, and I hereunto append the result. I have a lurking suspicion that *Leonidas* W. Smiley is a myth; that my friend never knew such a personage; and that he only conjectured that if I asked old Wheeler about him, it would remind him of his infamous *Jim* Smiley, and he would go to work and bore me to death with some exasperating reminiscence of him as long and as tedious as it should be useless to me. If that was the design, it succeeded.

I found Simon Wheeler dozing comfortably by the bar-room stove of the dilapidated tavern in the decayed mining camp of Angel's, and I noticed that he was fat and bald-headed, and had an expression of winning gentleness and simplicity upon his tranquil countenance. He roused up, and gave me good day. I told him that a friend of mine had commissioned me to make some inquiries about a cherished companion of his boyhood named *Leonidas* W. Smiley—*Rev. Leonidas* W. Smiley, a young minister of the Gospel, who he had heard was at one time a resident of Angel's Camp. I added that if Mr. Wheeler could tell me anything about this Rev. Leonidas W. Smiley, I would feel under many obligations to him.

Simon Wheeler backed me into a corner and blockaded me there with his chair, and then sat down and reeled off the monotonous narrative which follows this paragraph. He never smiled, he never frowned, he never changed his voice from the gentle-flowing key to which he tuned his initial sentence, he never betrayed the slightest suspicion of enthusiasm; but all through the interminable narrative there ran a vein of impressive earnestness and sincerity, which showed me plainly that, so far from his imagining that there was anything ridiculous or funny about his story, he regarded it as a really important matter, and admired its two heroes as men of transcendent genius in *finesse.* I let him go on in his own way, and never interrupted him once.

"Rev. Leonidas W. H'm, Reverend Le—well, there was a feller here once by the name of *Jim* Smiley, in the winter of '49—or maybe it was the spring of '50—I don't recollect exactly, somehow, though what makes me think it was one or the other is because I remember the big flume warn't finished when he first come to the camp; but anyway, he was the curiousest man about always betting on anything that turned up you ever see, if he could get anybody to bet on the other side; and if he couldn't he'd change sides. Any way that suited the other man would suit *him*—any way just so's he got a bet, *he* was satisfied. But still he was lucky, uncommon lucky; he most always come out winner. He was always ready and laying for a chance; there couldn't be no solit'ry thing mentioned but that feller'd offer to bet on it, and take ary side you please, as I was just telling you. If there was a horse-race, you'd find him flush or you'd find him busted at the end of it; if there was a dog-fight, he'd bet on it; if there was a cat-fight, he'd bet on it; if there was a chicken-fight, he'd bet on it; why, if there was two birds setting on a fence, he would bet you which one would fly first; or if there was a camp-meeting, he would be there reg'lar to bet on Parson Walker, which he judged to be the best exhorter about here, and so he was too, and a good man. If he even see a straddle-bug start to go anywheres, he would bet you how long it would take him to get to—to wherever he was going to, and if you took him up, he would foller that straddle-bug to Mexico but what he would find out where he was bound for and how long he was on the road. Lots of the boys here has seen that Smiley, and can tell you about him. Why, it never made no difference to *him*—he'd bet on *any* thing—the dangdest feller. Parson Walker's wife laid very sick once, for a good while, and it seemed as if they warn't going to save her; but one morning he come in, and Smiley up and asked him how she was, and he said she was considerable better—thank the Lord for his inf'nite mercy—and coming on so smart that with the blessing of Prov'dence she'd get well yet; and Smiley, before he thought, says, 'Well, I'll resk two-and-a-half she don't anyway.'

"Thish-yer Smiley had a mare—the boys called her the fifteen-minute nag, but that was only in fun, you know, because of course she was faster than that—and he used to win money on that horse, for all she was so slow and always had the asthma, or the distemper, or the consumption, or something of that kind. They used to give her two or three hundred yards' start, and then pass her under way; but always at the fag end of the race she'd get excited and desperate like, and come cavorting and straddling up, and scattering her legs around limber, sometimes in the air, and sometimes out to one side among the fences, and kicking up m-o-r-e dust and raising m-o-r-e racket with her coughing and sneezing and blowing her nose—and *always* fetch up at the stand just about a neck ahead, as near as you could cipher it down.

"And he had a little small bull-pup, that to look at him you'd think he warn't worth a cent but to set around and look ornery and lay for a chance to steal something. But as soon as money was up on him he was a different dog; his under-jaw'd begin to stick out like the fo'castle of a steamboat, and his teeth would uncover and shine like the furnaces. And a dog might tackle him and bully-rag him, and bite him, and throw him over his shoulder two or three times, and Andrew Jackson—which was the name of the pup—Andrew Jackson would never let on but what *he* was satisfied, and hadn't expected nothing else—and the bets being doubled and doubled on the other side all the time, till the money was all up; and then all of a sudden he would grab that other dog jest by the j'int of his hind leg and freeze to it—not chaw, you understand, but only just grip and hang on till they throwed up the sponge, if it was a year. Smiley always come out winner on that pup, till

148   clemens

he harnessed a dog once that didn't have no hind legs, because they'd been sawed off in a circular saw, and when the thing had gone along far enough, and the money was all up, and he come to make a snatch for his pet holt, he see in a minute how he'd been imposed on, and how the other dog had him in the door, so to speak, and he 'peared surprised, and then he looked sorter discouraged-like, and didn't try no more to win the fight, and so he got shucked out bad. He give Smiley a look, as much as to say his heart was broke, and it was *his* fault, for putting up a dog that hadn't no hind legs for him to take holt of, which was his main dependence in a fight, and then he limped off a piece and laid down and died. It was a good pup, was that Andrew Jackson, and would have made a name for hisself if he'd lived, for the stuff was in him and he had genius—I know it, because he hadn't no opportunities to speak of, and it don't stand to reason that a dog could make such a fight as he could under them circumstances if he hadn't no talent. It always makes me feel sorry when I think of that last fight of his'n, and the way it turned out.

"Well, thish-yer Smiley had rat-tarriers, and chicken cocks, and tom-cats and all them kind of things, till you couldn't rest, and you couldn't fetch nothing for him to bet on but he'd match you. He ketched a frog one day, and took him home, and said he cal'lated to educate him; and so he never done nothing for three months but set in his back yard and learn that frog to jump. And you bet you he *did* learn him, too. He'd give him a little punch behind, and the next minute you'd see that frog whirling in the air like a doughnut—see him turn one summerset, or maybe a couple, if he got a good start, and come down flat-footed and all right, like a cat. He got him up so in the matter of ketching flies, and kep' him in practice so constant, that he'd nail a fly every time as fur as he could see him. Smiley said all a frog wanted was education, and he could do 'most anything—and I believe him. Why, I've seen him set Dan'l Webster down here on this floor—Dan'l Webster was the name of the frog—and sing out, 'Flies, Dan'l, flies!' and quicker'n you could wink he'd spring straight up and snake a fly off'n the counter there, and flop down on the floor ag'in as solid as a gob of mud, and fall to scratching the side of his head with his hind foot as indifferent as if he hadn't no idea he'd been doin' any more'n any frog might do. You never see a frog so modest and straightfor'ard as he was, for all he was so gifted. And when it come to fair and square jumping on a dead level, he could get over more ground at one straddle than any animal of his breed you ever see. Jumping on a dead level was his strong suit, you understand; and when it come to that, Smiley would ante up money on him as long as he had a red. Smiley was monstrous proud of his frog, and well he might be, for fellers that had traveled and been everywheres, all said he laid over any frog that ever *they* see.

"Well, Smiley kep' the beast in a little lattice box, and he used to fetch him down-town sometimes and lay for a bet. One day a feller—a stranger in the camp, he was—come acrost him with his box, and says:

" 'What might it be that you've got in the box?'

"And Smiley says, sorter indifferent-like, 'It might be a parrot, or it might be a canary, maybe, but it ain't—it's only just a frog.'

"And the feller took it, and looked at it careful, and turned it round this way and that, and says, 'H'm—so 'tis. Well, what's *he* good for?'

" 'Well,' Smiley says, easy and careless, 'he's good enough for *one* thing, I should judge—he can outjump any frog in Calaveras County.'

"The feller took the box again, and took another long, particular look, and give it back to Smiley, and says, very deliberate, 'Well,' he says, 'I don't see no p'ints about that frog that's any better'n any other frog.'

" 'Maybe you don't,' Smiley says. 'Maybe you understand frogs and maybe you don't understand 'em; maybe you've had experience, and maybe you ain't only a amature, as it were. Anyways, I've got *my* opinion, and I'll resk forty dollars that he can outjump any frog in Calaveras County.'

"And the feller studied a minute, and then says, kinder sad-like 'Well, I'm only a stranger here, and I ain't got no frog; but if I had a frog, I'd bet you.'

"And then Smiley says, 'That's all right—that's all right—if you'll hold my box a minute, I'll go and get you a frog.' And so the feller took the box, and put up his forty dollars along with Smiley's, and set down to wait.

"So he set there a good while thinking and thinking to himself, and then he got the frog out and prized his mouth open and took a teaspoon and filled him full of quail-shot—filled him pretty near up to his chin—and set him on the floor. Smiley he went to the swamp and slopped around in the mud for a long time, and finally he ketched a frog, and fetched him in, and give him to this feller, and says:

" 'Now, if you're ready, set him alongside of Dan'l, with his fore paws just even with Dan'l's, and I'll give the word.' Then he says, 'One—two—three—*git!*' and him and the feller touched up the frogs from behind, and the new frog hopped off lively, but Dan'l give a heave, and hysted up his shoulders—so—like a Frenchman, but it warn't no use—he couldn't budge; he was planted as solid as a church, and he couldn't no more stir than if he was anchored out. Smiley was a good deal surprised, and he was disgusted too, but he didn't have no idea what the matter was, of course.

"The feller took the money and started away; and when he was going out at the door, he sorter jerked his thumb over his shoulder—so—at Dan'l, and says again, very deliberate, 'Well,' he says, 'I don't see no p'ints about that frog that's any better'n any other frog.'

"Smiley he stood scratching his head and looking down at Dan'l a long time, and at last he says, 'I do wonder what in the nation that frog throw'd off for—I wonder if there ain't something the matter with him—he 'pears to look mighty baggy, somehow.' And he ketched Dan'l by the nap of the neck, and hefted him, and says, 'Why blame my cats if he don't weigh five pound!' and turned him upside down and he belched out a double handful of shot. And then he see how it was, and he was the maddest man—he set the frog down and took out after that feller, but he never ketched him. And—"

[Here Simon Wheeler heard his name called from the front yard, and got up to see what was wanted.] And turning to me as he moved away, he said: "Just set where you are, stranger, and rest easy—I ain't going to be gone a second."

But, by your leave, I did not think that a continuation of the history of the enterprising vagabond *Jim* Smiley would be likely to afford me much information concerning the Rev. *Leonidas* W. Smiley, and so I started away.

At the door I met the sociable Wheeler returning, and he button-holed me and recommenced:

"Well, thish-yer Smiley had a yaller one-eyed cow that didn't have no tail, only just a short stump like a bannanner, and—"

However, lacking both time and inclination, I did not wait to hear about the afflicted cow, but took my leave.

baker's blue-jay yarn

Animals talk to each other, of course. There can be no question about that; but I suppose there are very few people who can understand them. I never knew but one man who could. I knew he could, however, because he told me so himself. He was a middle-aged, simple-hearted miner who had lived in a lonely corner of California, among the woods and mountains, a good many years, and had studied the ways of his only neighbors, the beasts and the birds, until he believed he could accurately translate any remark which they made. This was Jim Baker. According to Jim Baker, some animals have only a limited education, and use only very simple words, and scarcely ever a comparison or a flowery figure; whereas, certain other animals have a large vocabulary, a fine command of language and a ready and fluent delivery; consequently these latter talk a great deal; they like it; they are conscious of their talent, and they enjoy "showing off." Baker said, that after long and careful observation, he had come to the conclusion that the blue-jays were the best talkers he had found among birds and beasts. Said he:—

"There more *to* a blue-jay than any other creature. He has got more moods, and more different kinds of feelings than other creatures and mind you, whatever a blue-jay feels, he can put into language. And no mere commonplace language, either, but rattling, out-and-out book-talk—and bristling with metaphor, too—just bristling! And as for command of language—why *you* never see a blue-jay get stuck for a word. No man ever did. They just boil out of him! And another thing: I've noticed a good deal, and there's no bird, or cow, or anything that uses as good grammar as a blue-jay. You may say a cat uses good grammar. Well, a cat does—but you let a cat get excited, once; you let a cat get to pulling fur with another cat on a shed, nights, and you'll hear grammar that will give you the lockjaw. Ignorant people think it's the *noise* which fighting cats make that is so aggravating, but it ain't so; it's the sickening grammar they use. Now I've never heard a jay use bad grammar but very seldom; and when they do, they are as ashamed as a human; they shut right down and leave.

"You may call a jay a bird. Well, so he is, in a measure—because he's got feathers on him, and don't belong to no church, perhaps; but otherwise he is just as much a human as you be. And I'll tell you for why. A jay's gifts, and instincts, and feelings, and interests, cover the whole ground. A jay hasn't got any more principle than a Congressman. A jay will lie, a jay will steal, a jay will deceive, a jay will betray; and four times out of five, a jay will go back on his solemnest promise. The sacredness of an obligation is a thing which you can't cram into no blue-jay's head. Now on top of all this, there's another thing: a jay can outswear any gentleman in the mines. You think a cat can swear. Well, a cat can; but you give a blue-jay a subject that calls for his reserve powers, and where is your cat? Don't talk to *me*—I know too much about this thing. And there's yet another thing: in the one little particular of scolding—just good, clean, out-and-out scolding—a blue-jay can lay over anything, human or divine. Yes, sir, a jay is everything that a man is. A jay can cry, a jay can laugh, a jay can feel shame, a jay can reason and plan and discuss, a jay likes gossip and scandal, a jay has got a sense of humor, a jay knows when he is an ass as well as you do—maybe better. If a jay ain't human, he better take in his sign, that's all. Now I'm going to tell you a perfectly true fact about some blue-jays.

"When I first begun to understand jay language correctly, there was a little incident happened here. Seven years ago, the last man in this region but me, moved away. There stands his house,—been empty ever since; a log house, with a plank roof—just one big room, and no more; no ceiling—nothing between the rafters and the floor. Well, one Sunday morning I was sitting out here in front of my cabin, with my cat, taking the sun, and looking at the blue hills, and listening to the leaves rustling so lonely in the trees, and thinking of the home away yonder in the States, that I hadn't heard from in thirteen years, when a jay lit on that house, with an acorn in his mouth, and says, 'Hello, I reckon I've struck something.' When he spoke, the acorn dropped out of his mouth and rolled down the roof, of course, but he didn't care; his mind was all on the thing he had struck. It was a knot-hole in the roof. He cocked his head to one side, shut one eye and put the other one to the hole, like a 'possum looking down a jug; then he glanced up with his bright eyes, gave a wink or two with his wings—which signifies gratification, you understand,—and says, 'It looks like a hole, it's located like a hole,—blamed if I don't believe it *is* a hole!'

"Then he cocked his head down and took another look; he glances up perfectly joyful, this time; winks his wings and his tail both, and says, 'O, no, this ain't no fat thing, I reckon! If I ain't in luck!—why it's a perfectly elegant hole!' So he flew down and got that acorn, and fetched it up and dropped it in, and was just tilting his head back, with the heavenliest smile on his face, when all of a sudden he was paralyzed into a listening attitude and that smile faded gradually out of his countenance like breath off'n a razor, and the queerest look of surprise took its place. Then he says, 'Why I didn't hear it fall!' He cocked his eye at the hole again, and took a long look; raised up and shook his head; stepped around to the other side of the hole and took another look from that side; shook his head again. He studied a while, then he just went into the *de*tails—walked round and round the hole and spied into it from every point of the compass. No use. Now he took a thinking attitude on the comb of the roof and scratched the back of his head with his right foot a minute, and finally says, 'Well, it's too many for *me,* that's certain; must be a mighty long hole; however, I ain't got no time to fool around here, I got to 'tend to business; I reckon it's all right—chance it, anyway.'

"So he flew off and fetched another acorn and dropped it in, and tried to flirt his eye to the hole quick enough to see what become of it, but he was too late. He held his eye there as much as a minute; then he raised up and sighed, and says, 'Consound it, I don't seem to understand this thing, no way; however, I'll tackle her again.' He fetched another acorn, and done his level best to see what become of it, but he couldn't. He says, 'Well, *I* never struck no such a hole as this, before; I'm of the opinion it's a totally new kind of a hole.' Then he begun to get mad. He held in for a spell, walking up and down the comb of the roof and shaking his head and muttering to himself; but his feelings got the upper hand of him, presently, and he broke loose and cussed himself black in the face. I never see a bird take on so about a little thing. When he got through he walks to the hole and looks in again for half a minute; then he says, 'Well, you're a long hole, and a deep hole, and a mighty singular hole altogether—but I've started in to fill you, and I'm d——d if I don't fill you, if it takes a hundred years!'

"And with that, away he went. You never see a bird work so since you was born. He laid into his work like a nigger, and the way he hove acorns into that hole for about two hours and a half was one of the most exciting and astonishing spectacles I ever struck. He never stopped to take a look any more—he just hove 'em in and went for more. Well at last he could hardly flop his wings, he was so tuckered out. He comes a-drooping down, once more, sweating like an ice-pitcher, drops his acorn in and says, '*Now* I guess I've got the bulge on you by this time!' So he bent down for a look. If you'll believe me, when his head come up again he was just pale with rage. He says, 'I've shoveled acorns enough in there to keep the family thirty years, and if I can see a sign of one of 'em I wish I may land in a museum with a belly full of sawdust in two minutes!'

"He just had strength enough to crawl up on to the comb and lean his back agin the chimbly, and then he collected his impressions and begun to free his mind. I see in a second that what I had mistook for profanity in the mines was only just the rudiments, as you may say.

"Another jay was going by, and heard him doing his devotions, and stops to inquire what was up. The sufferer told him the whole circumstance, and says, 'Now yonder's the hole, and if you don't believe me, go and look for yourself.' So this fellow went and looked, and comes back and says, 'How many did you say you put in there?' 'Not any less than two tons,' says the sufferer. The other jay went and looked again. He couldn't seem to make it out, so he raised a yell, and three more jays come. They all examined the hole, they all made the sufferer tell it over again, then they all discussed it, and got off as many leather-headed opinions about it as an average crowd of humans could have done.

"They called in more jays; then more and more, till pretty soon this whole region 'peared to have a blue flush about it. There must have been five thousand of them; and such another jawing and dis-puting and ripping and cussing, you never heard. Every jay in the whole lot put his eye to the hole and delivered a more chuckle-headed opinion about the mystery than the jay that went there before him. They examined the house all over, too. The door was standing half open, and at last one old jay happened to go and light on it and look in. Of course that knocked the mystery galley-west in a second. There lay the acorns, scattered all over the floor. He flopped his wings and raised a whoop. 'Come here!' he says, 'Come here, everybody; hang'd if this fool hasn't been trying to fill up a house with acorns!' They all came a-swooping down like a blue cloud, and as each fellow lit on the door and took a glance, the whole absurdity of the contract that the first jay had tackled hit him home and he fell over backwards suffocating with laughter, and the next jay took his place and done the same.

"Well, sir, they roosted around here on the house-top and the trees for an hour, and guffawed over that thing like human beings. It ain't any use to tell me a blue-jay hasn't got a sense of humor, because I know better. And memory, too. They brought jays here from all over the United States to look down that hole, every summer for three years. Other birds too. And they could all see the point, except an owl that come from Nova Scotia to visit the Yo Semite, and he took this thing in on his way back. He said he couldn't see anything funny in it. But then he was a good deal disappointed about Yo Semite, too."

TENNESSEE'S PARTNER

Local color, perennially popular with story writers from Irving on, became such a vogue after the Civil War that it almost dominated the short story of the 1870's and 1880's. Perhaps no writer of the period had more to do with starting the vogue than Bret Harte. To readers in other sections of the country, his stories introduced new and unusual character types peculiar to California of the post gold-rush era and pictured the exotic scenery of the West, a colorful backdrop for the action of these characters, with their distinctive speech, dress, and moral codes. Despite the fact that he was more concerned with creating effects than with presenting his materials realistically, Harte inspired other writers to duplicate his success by depicting the life peculiar to their regions. Although the earlier local colorists had generally flourished only in New England and the old Southwest, very soon every section of the United States had its local colorists.

Bret Harte was not native to the region he portrayed so successfully. Born in 1836, in New York, he did not, in fact, see the West until 1854, when he joined his mother and foster father in California. For a time after his arrival there, he held a succession of jobs—as school teacher, tutor, Wells Fargo express messenger—but he was soon contributing verse and prose to various local newspapers and magazines. In 1868, shortly after becoming editor of the *Overland Monthly,* he published in its second issue (August, 1868) "The Luck of Roaring Camp," a story which brought him national fame. Two years later the immediate success of his first volume of stories, *The Luck of Roaring Camp and Other Sketches* (1870), secured for him a highly lucrative contract with the *Atlantic Monthly* in 1871. His arrangement with the *Atlantic* did not work out satisfactorily, however,

159

and was not renewed after the first year. After trying unsuccessfully for a number of years to earn his livelihood as a public lecturer, Harte went abroad in 1878, first to Germany as a commercial agent and later to Glasgow, Scotland, as consul. In 1885, he gave up his consulship but continued to live abroad, writing for British magazines until his death in 1902.

Although Harte's other volumes of stories were extravagantly praised during his lifetime, he tended to repeat his earliest successes and never surpassed the merit of those in his first volume. And even the earlier stories were marred by his overemphasis of sentimental themes and theatrical devices, his posturing, and his striving for sharp effects. His literary position is thus dependent not so much upon the esthetic as upon the historical worth of his work in giving impetus to local color fiction. But whatever his limitations as a creative writer, Harte was a keen critic of literature and the art of writing. In an essay published in *Cornhill's Magazine* in 1899, he contended that the humorous anecdote of the Southwestern yarnspinner was the forebear of the distinctly "American" story. Thoroughly acquainted with the tradition of native humor, Harte made it an integral part of his method, even weaving humor into incidents as grimly pathetic as those depicted in "Tennessee's Partner."

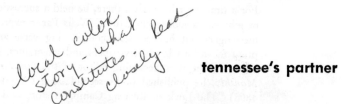

local color story - what read constitutes closely

tennessee's partner

I do not think that we ever knew his real name. Our ignorance of it certainly never gave us any social inconvenience, for at Sandy Bar in 1854 most men were christened anew. Sometimes these appellatives were derived from some distinctiveness of dress, as in the case of "Dungaree Jack"; or from some peculiarity of habit, as shown in "Saleratus Bill," so called from an undue proportion of that chemical in his daily bread; or from some unlucky slip, as exhibited in "The Iron Pirate," a mild, inoffensive man, who earned that baleful title by his unfortunate mispronunciation of the term "iron pyrites." Perhaps this may have been the beginning of a rude heraldry; but I am constrained to think that it was because a man's real name in that day rested solely upon his own unsupported statement. "Call yourself Clifford, do you?" said Boston, addressing a timid newcomer with infinite scorn; "hell is full of such Cliffords!" He then introduced the unfortunate man, whose name happened to be really Clifford, as "Jay-bird Charley"—an unhallowed inspiration of the moment that clung to him ever after.

But to return to Tennessee's Partner, whom we never knew by any other than this relative title. That he had ever existed as a separate and distinct individuality we only learned later. It seems that in 1853 he left Poker Flat to go to San Francisco, ostensibly to procure a wife. He never got any farther than Stockton. At that place he was attracted by a young person who waited upon the table at the hotel where he took his meals. One morning he said something to her which caused her to smile not unkindly, to somewhat coquettishly break a plate of toast over his upturned, serious, simple face, and to retreat to the kitchen. He followed her, and emerged a few moments later, covered with more toast and victory. That day week they were married by a justice of the peace, and returned to Poker Flat. I am aware that something more might be made of this episode, but I prefer to tell it as it was current at Sandy Bar—in the gulches and barrooms—where all sentiment was modified by a strong sense of humor.

Of their married felicity but little is known, perhaps for the reason that Tennessee, then living with his partner, one day took occasion to say something to the bride on his own account, at which, it is said, she smiled not unkindly and chastely retreated—this time as far as Marysville, where Tennessee followed her, and where they went to housekeeping without the aid of a justice of the peace. Tennessee's Partner took the loss of his wife simply and seriously, as was his fashion. But to everybody's surprise, when Tennessee one day returned from Marysville, without his partner's wife—she having smiled and retreated with somebody else—Tennessee's Partner was the first man to shake his hand and greet him with affection. The boys who had gathered in the cañon to see the shooting were naturally indignant. Their indignation might have found vent in sarcasm but for a certain look in Tennessee's Partner's eye, that indicated a lack of humorous appreciation. In fact, he was a grave man, with a steady application to practical detail which was unpleasant in a difficulty.

Meanwhile a popular feeling against Tennessee had grown up on the Bar. He was known to be a gambler; he was suspected to be a thief. In these suspicions Tennessee's Partner was equally compromised; his continued intimacy with Tennessee after the affair above quoted could only be accounted for on the hypothesis of a copartnership of crime. At last Tennessee's guilt became flagrant. One day he overtook a stranger on his way to Red Dog. The stranger afterward related that Tennessee beguiled the time with interesting anecdote and reminiscence, but illogically concluded the interview in the following words: "And now, young man, I'll trouble you for your knife, your pistols, and your money. You see your weppings might get you into trouble at Red Dog, and your money's a temptation to the evilly disposed. I think you said your address was San Francisco. I shall endeavor to call." It may be stated here that Tennessee had a fine flow of humor, which no business preoccupation could wholly subdue.

This exploit was his last. Red Dog and Sandy Bar made common cause against the highwayman. Tennessee was hunted in very much the same fashion as his prototype, the grizzly. As the toils closed around him, he made a desperate dash through the Bar, emptying his revolver at the crowd before the Arcade Saloon, and so on up Grizzly Cañon; but at its farther extremity he was stopped by a small man on a gray horse. The men looked at each other a moment in silence. Both were fearless, both self-possessed and independent; and both types of a civilization that in the seventeenth century would have been called heroic, but in the nineteenth simply "reckless."

"What have you got there?—I call," said Tennessee, quietly.

"Two bowers and an ace," said the stranger, as quietly, showing two revolvers and a bowie knife.

"That takes me," returned Tennessee; and, with this gambler's epigram, he threw away his useless pistol, and rode back with his captor.

It was a warm night. The cool breeze which usually sprang up with the going down of the sun behind the chaparral-crested mountain was that evening withheld from Sandy Bar. The little cañon was stifling with heated resinous odors, and the decaying driftwood on the Bar sent forth faint, sickening exhalations. The feverishness of day and its fierce passions still filled the camp. Lights moved restlessly along the bank of the river, striking no answering reflection from its tawny current. Against the blackness of the pines the windows of the old loft above the express office stood out staringly bright; and through their curtainless panes the loungers below could see the forms of those who were even then deciding the fate of Tennessee. And above all this, etched on the dark firmament, rose the Sierra, remote and passionless, crowned with remoter passionless stars.

The trial of Tennessee was conducted as fairly as was consistent with a judge and jury who felt themselves to some extent obliged to justify, in their verdict, the previous irregularities of arrest and indictment. The law of Sandy Bar was implacable, but not vengeful. The excitement and personal feeling of the chase were over; with Tennessee safe in their hands, they were ready to listen patiently to any defense, which they were already satisfied was insufficient. There being no doubt in their own minds, they were willing to give the prisoner the benefit of any that might exist. Secure in the hypothesis that he ought to be hanged on general principles, they indulged him with more latitude of defense than his reckless hardihood seemed to ask. The judge appeared to be more anxious than the prisoner, who, otherwise unconcerned, evidently took a grim pleasure in the responsibility he had created. "I don't take any hand in this yer game," had been his invariable, but good-humored reply to all questions. The judge—who was also his captor—for a moment vaguely regretted that he had not shot him "on sight" that morning, but presently dismissed this human weakness as unworthy of the judicial mind. Nevertheless, when there was a tap at the door, and it was said that Tennessee's Partner was there on behalf of the prisoner, he was admitted at once without question. Perhaps the younger members of the jury, to whom the proceedings were becoming irksomely thoughtful, hailed him as a relief.

For he was not, certainly, an imposing figure. Short and stout, with a square face, sunburned into a preternatural redness, clad in a loose duck "jumper" and trousers streaked and splashed with red soil, his aspect under any circumstances would have been quaint, and was now even ridiculous. As he stooped to deposit at his feet a heavy carpetbag he was carrying, it became obvious, from partially developed legends and inscriptions, that the material with which his trousers had been patched had been originally intended for a less ambitious covering. Yet he advanced with great gravity, and after having shaken the hand of each person in the room with labored cordiality, he wiped his serious perplexed face on a red bandana handkerchief, a shade lighter than his complexion, laid his powerful hand upon the table to steady himself, and thus addressed the judge:

"I was passin' by," he began, by way of apology, "and I thought

I'd just step in and see how things was gittin' on with Tennessee thar— my pardner. It's a hot night. I disremember any sich weather before on the Bar."

He paused a moment, but nobody volunteering any other meteorological recollection, he again had recourse to his pocket handkerchief, and for some moments mopped his face diligently.

"Have you anything to say in behalf of the prisoner?" said the judge finally.

"Thet's it," said Tennessee's Partner, in a tone of relief. "I come yar as Tennessee's pardner—knowing him nigh on four year, off and on, wet and dry, in luck and out o' luck. His ways ain't aller my ways, but thar ain't any p'ints in that young man, thar ain't any liveliness as he's been up to, as I don't know. And you sez to me, sez you— confidential-like, and between man and man—sez you, 'Do you know anything in his behalf?' and I sez to you, sez I—confidential-like, as between man and man—'What should a man know of his pardner?' "

"Is this all you have to say?" asked the judge impatiently, feeling, perhaps, that a dangerous sympathy of humor was beginning to humanize the court.

"Thet's so," continued Tennessee's Partner. "It ain't for me to say anything agin' him. And now, what's the case? Here's Tennessee wants money, wants it bad, and doesn't like to ask it of his old pardner. Well, what does Tennessee do? He lays for a stranger, and he fetches that stranger; and you lays for *him,* and you fetches *him;* and the honors is easy. And I put it to you, bein' a fa'r-minded man, and to you, gentlemen all, as fa'r-minded men, ef this isn't so."

"Prisoner," said the judge, interrupting, "have you any questions to ask this man?"

"No! no!" continued Tennessee's Partner, hastily. "I play this yer hand alone. To come down to the bedrock, it's just this: Tennessee, thar, has played it pretty rough and expensive-like on a stranger, and on this yer camp. And now, what's the fair thing? Some would say more, some would say less. Here's seventeen hundred dollars in coarse gold and a watch,—it's about all my pile,—and call it square!" And before a hand could be raised to prevent him, he had emptied the contents of the carpetbag upon the table.

For a moment his life was in jeopardy. One or two men sprang to their feet, several hands groped for hidden weapons, and a suggestion to "throw him from the window" was only overridden by a gesture from the judge. Tennessee laughed. And apparently oblivious of the excitement, Tennessee's Partner improved the opportunity to mop his face again with his handkerchief.

When order was restored, and the man was made to understand, by the use of forcible figures and rhetoric, that Tennessee's offense could not be condoned by money, his face took a more serious and sanguinary hue, and those who were nearest to him noticed that his rough hand trembled slightly on the table. He hesitated a moment as he slowly returned the gold to the carpetbag, as if he had not yet entirely caught the elevated sense of justice which swayed the tribunal, and was perplexed with the belief that he had not offered enough. Then he turned to the judge, and saying, "This yer is a lone hand, played alone, and without my pardner," he bowed to the jury and was about to withdraw, when the judge called him back:

"If you have anything to say to Tennessee, you had better say it now."

For the first time that evening the eyes of the prisoner and his strange advocate met. Tennessee smiled, showed his white teeth, and saying, "Euchred, old man!" held out his hand. Tennessee's Partner took it in his own, and saying, "I just dropped in as I was passin' to see how things was gettin' on," let the hand passively fall, and adding that "it was a warm night," again mopped his face with his handkerchief, and without another word withdrew.

The two men never again met each other alive. For the unparalleled insult of a bribe offered to Judge Lynch—who, whether bigoted, weak, or narrow, was at least incorruptible—firmly fixed in the mind of that mythical personage any wavering determination of Tennessee's fate; and at the break of day he was marched, closely guarded, to meet it at the top of Marley's Hill.

How he met it, how cool he was, how he refused to say anything, how perfect were the arrangements of the committee, were all duly reported, with the addition of a warning moral and example to all future evil-doers, in the *Red Dog Clarion,* by its editor, who was present, and to whose vigorous English I cheerfully refer the reader. But the beauty of that midsummer morning, the blessed amity of earth and air and sky, the awakened life of the free woods and hills, the joyous renewal and promise of Nature, and above all, the infinite serenity that thrilled through each, was not reported, as not being a part of the social lesson. And yet, when the weak and foolish deed was done, and a life, with its possibilities and responsibilities, had passed out of the misshapen thing that dangled between earth and sky, the birds sang, the flowers bloomed, the sun shone, as cheerily as before; and possibly the *Red Dog Clarion* was right.

Tennessee's Partner was not in the group that surrounded the ominous tree. But as they turned to disperse, attention was drawn to the singular appearance of a motionless donkey cart halted at the side of the road. As they approached, they at once recognized the venerable Jenny and the two-wheeled cart as the property of Tennessee's Partner, used by him in carrying dirt from his claim; and a few paces distant the owner of the equipage himself, sitting under a buckeye tree, wiping the perspiration from his glowing face. In answer to an inquiry, he said he had come for the body of the "diseased," "if it was all the same to the committee." He didn't wish to "hurry anything"; he could "wait." He was not working that day; and when the gentlemen were done with the "diseased," he would take him. "Ef thar is any present," he added, in his simple, serious way, "as would care to jine in the fun'l, they kin come." Perhaps it was from a sense of humor, which I have already intimated was a feature of Sandy Bar—perhaps it was from something even better than that, but two thirds of the loungers accepted the invitation at once.

It was noon when the body of Tennessee was delivered into the hands of his partner. As the cart drew up to the fatal tree, we noticed that it contained a rough oblong box,—apparently made from a section of sluicing,—and half filled with bark and the tassels of pine. The cart was further decorated with slips of willow, and made fragrant with buckeye blossoms. When the body was deposited in the box, Tennessee's Partner drew over it a piece of tarred canvas, and gravely mounting the narrow seat in front, with his feet upon the shafts, urged the little donkey forward. The equipage moved slowly on, at that decorous pace which was habitual with Jenny even under less solemn circumstances. The men—half curiously, half jestingly, but all good-humoredly—strolled along beside the cart, some in advance, some a little in the rear of the homely catafalque. But whether from the narrowing of the road or some present sense of decorum, as the cart passed on, the company fell to the rear in couples, keeping step, and otherwise assuming the external show of a formal procession. Jack Folinsbee, who had at the outset played a funeral march in dumb show upon an imaginary trombone, desisted from a lack of sympathy and appreciation—not having, perhaps, your true humorist's capacity to be content with the enjoyment of his own fun.

The way led through Grizzly Cañon, by this time clothed in funereal drapery and shadows. The redwoods, burying their moccasined feet in the red soil, stood in Indian file along the track, trailing an uncouth benediction from their bending boughs upon the passing bier. A hare, surprised into helpless inactivity, sat upright and pulsating in the ferns by the roadside, as the cortège went by. Squirrels hastened to gain a secure outlook from higher boughs; and the bluejays, spreading their wings, fluttered before them like outriders, until the outskirts of Sandy Bar were reached, and the solitary cabin of Tennessee's Partner.

Viewed under more favorable circumstances, it would not have been a cheerful place. The unpicturesque site, the rude and unlovely outlines, the unsavory details, which distinguish the nest-building of the California miner, were all here, with the dreariness of decay superadded. A few paces from the cabin there was a rough enclosure, which, in the brief days of Tennessee's Partner's matrimonial felicity, had been used as a garden, but was now overgrown with fern. As we approached it, we were surprised to find that what we had taken for a recent attempt at cultivation was the broken soil about an open grave.

The cart was halted before the enclosure, and rejecting the offers of assistance with the same air of simple self-reliance he had displayed throughout, Tennessee's Partner lifted the rough coffin on his back, and deposited it unaided within the shallow grave. He then nailed down the board which served as a lid, and mounting the little mound of earth beside it, took off his hat and slowly mopped his face with his handkerchief. This the crowd felt was a preliminary to speech, and they disposed themselves variously on stumps and boulders, and sat expectant.

"When a man," began Tennessee's Partner slowly, "has been running free all day, what's the natural thing for him to do? Why, to come home. And if he ain't in a condition to go home, what can his best friend do? Why, bring him home. And here's Tennessee has been running free, and we brings him home from his wandering." He paused and picked up a fragment of quartz, rubbed it thoughtfully on his sleeve and went on: "It ain't the first time that I've packed him on my back, as you see'd me now. It ain't the first time that I brought him to this yer cabin when he couldn't help himself; it ain't the first time that I and Jinny have waited for him on yon hill, and picked him up and so fetched him home, when he couldn't speak and didn't know me. And now that it's the last time, why"—he paused, and rubbed the quartz gently on his sleeve—"you see it's sort of rough on his pardner. And now, gentlemen," he added abruptly, picking up his long-handled shovel, "the fun'l's over; and my thanks, and Tennessee's thanks, to you for your trouble."

Resisting any proffers of assistance, he began to fill in the grave, turning his back upon the crowd, that after a few moments' hesitation gradually withdrew. As they crossed the little ridge that hid Sandy Bar from view, some, looking back, thought they could see Tennessee's Partner, his work done, sitting upon the grave, his shovel between his knees, and his face buried in his red bandana handkerchief. But it was argued by others that you couldn't tell his face from his handkerchief at that distance, and this point remained undecided.

In the reaction that followed the feverish excitement of that day, Tennessee's Partner was not forgotten. A secret investigation had cleared him of any complicity in Tennessee's guilt, and left only a suspicion of his general sanity. Sandy Bar made a point of calling on him, and proffering various uncouth but well-meant kindnesses. But from that day his rude health and great strength seemed visibly to decline; and when the rainy season fairly set in, and the tiny grass blades were beginning to peep from the rocky mound above Tennessee's grave, he took to his bed.

One night, when the pines beside the cabin were swaying in the storm and trailing their slender fingers over the roof, and the roar and rush of the swollen river were heard below, Tennessee's Partner lifted his head from the pillow, saying, "It is time to go for Tennessee; I must put Jinny in the cart"; and would have risen from his bed but for the restraint of his attendant. Struggling, he still pursued his singular fancy: "There, now, steady, Jinny—steady, old girl. How dark it is! Look out for the ruts—and look out for him, too, old gal. Sometimes, you know, when he's blind drunk, he drops down right in the trail. Keep on straight up to the pine on the top of the hill. Thar! I told you so!—thar he is—coming this way, too—all by himself, sober, and his face a-shining. Tennessee! Pardner!"

And so they met.

W. D. Howells.

EDITHA

The life of William Dean Howells exemplifies the American success story, for with native ability and hard work he rose from a modest provincial background to become one of the nation's foremost men of letters. Born in 1837, in Martin's Ferry, Ohio, where his father was a struggling newspaper publisher, Howells was intimately associated with journalistic work from childhood, progressing naturally from setting type on his father's newspaper to reporting, serving as correspondent, and working as a free-lance writer. By 1860, he had already gained some national prominence; he was commissioned to write a campaign biography of Abraham Lincoln, and the following year he was appointed to a four-year term as American consul in Venice. After his return to the United States in 1865, he wrote for various papers, including the New York *Times,* served as assistant editor of the *Atlantic Monthly,* and lectured at Harvard from 1869 to 1871. As editor-in-chief of the *Atlantic Monthly* from 1871 to 1881, he exerted great influence on the literature of the day through both his extensive literary criticism and his whole-hearted encouragement of younger writers— even such well-established and diverse writers as Harte, Twain, and James profited from his counsels. In his later years, his most important journalistic work appeared in "The Editor's Easy Chair" of *Harper's.* During his long literary career, which ended in 1920, his service to literature brought him many honors— honorary degrees from Harvard, Yale, Columbia, and Oxford, and the presidency of the American Academy of Arts and Letters.

Howells' prolific publications fill more than a hundred volumes and include nearly every type of literature: autobiography, criticism, poetry, plays, novels, and short stories. His most enduring literary efforts, however, are in the fields of criticism and fiction. As a critic he not only stood for high artistic standards but also—and even more important—championed realism in fiction, holding the view that the writer should depict the commonplace rather than the exceptional because Howells believed ordinary individuals and events to be more truly representative of American life. "Realism," he said, "is nothing more and nothing less than the truthful treatment of material." Since a representative, truthful treatment did not, in his opinion, warrant the splashing of sex and crime in the pages of fiction, Howells was ridiculed as a "genteel realist" by later critics, who noted that his brand of realism did indeed look pale and wan beside that of Norris, Crane, and Dreiser. Now, however, Howells' significance as both a pioneer realist and a distinguished literary craftsman is once again being recognized in the upgrading of his reputation.

A close student of the social precepts and conditions affecting human behavior, he frequently concerned himself with social problems in his novels and short stories. In his most successful work the problem is kept in the background so that it does not overshadow the characters as real people going about the day-by-day business of living. Thus war-hysteria in "Editha" is completely secondary to the relationship involving Editha, her fiancé, and his mother. But the story is likewise a dramatic attack upon what Howells regarded as the viciousness of romantic folly. Editha's lack of depth, her inability to face the hard facts of life with sober, common-sense realism, symbolizes much of the evil that he had come to associate with romantic attitudes and posturings in the popular fiction of the 1880's.

editha

The air was thick with the war feeling, like the electricity of a storm which has not yet burst. Editha sat looking out into the hot spring afternoon, with her lips parted, and panting with the intensity of the question whether she could let him go. She had decided that she could not let him stay, when she saw him at the end of the still leafless avenue, making slowly up towards the house, with his head down and his figure relaxed. She ran impatiently out on the veranda, to the edge of the steps, and imperatively demanded greater haste of him with her will before she called aloud to him: "George!"

He had quickened his pace in mystical response to her mystical urgence, before he could have heard her; now he looked up and answered, "Well?"

"Oh, how united we are!" she exulted, and then she swooped down the steps to him. "What is it?" she cried.

"It's war," he said, and he pulled her up to him and kissed her. She kissed him back intensely, but irrelevantly, as to their passion, and uttered from deep in her throat, "How glorious!"

"It's war," he repeated, without consenting to her sense of it; and she did not know just what to think at first. She never knew what to think of him; that made his mystery, his charm. All through their courtship, which was contemporaneous with the growth of the war feeling, she had been puzzled by his want of seriousness about it. He seemed to despise it even more than he abhorred it. She could have understood his abhorring any sort of bloodshed; that would have been a survival of his old life when he thought he would be a minister, and before he changed and took up the law. But making light of a cause so high and noble seemed to show a want of earnestness at the core of his being. Not but that she felt herself able to cope with a congenital defect of that sort, and make his love for her save him from himself. Now perhaps the miracle was already wrought in him. In the presence

From *Between the Dark and the Daylight* by William Dean Howells, Harper & Brothers, 1907. Copyright 1907 by Harper & Brothers. Copyright 1935 by Mildred Howells and John Mead Howells.

173

of the tremendous fact that he announced, all triviality seemed to have gone out of him; she began to feel that. He sank down on the top step, and wiped his forehead with his handkerchief, while she poured out upon him her question of the origin and authenticity of his news.

All the while, in her duplex emotioning, she was aware that now at the very beginning she must put a guard upon herself against urging him, by any word or act, to take the part that her whole soul willed him to take, for the completion of her ideal of him. He was very nearly perfect as he was, and he must be allowed to perfect himself. But he was peculiar, and he might very well be reasoned out of his peculiarity. Before her reasoning went her emotioning: her nature pulling upon his nature, her womanhood upon his manhood, without her knowing the means she was using to the end she was willing. She had always supposed that the man who won her would have done something to win her; she did not know what, but something. George Gearson had simply asked her for her love, on the way home from a concert, and she gave her love to him, without, as it were, thinking. But now, it flashed upon her, if he could do something worthy to *have* won her—be a hero, *her* hero—it would be even better than if he had done it before asking her; it would be grander. Besides, she had believed in the war from the beginning.

"But don't you see, dearest," she said, "that it wouldn't have come to this if it hadn't been in the order of Providence? And I call any war glorious that is for the liberation of people who have been struggling for years against the cruelest oppression. Don't you think so, too?"

"I suppose so," he returned, languidly. "But war! Is it glorious to break the peace of the world?"

"That ignoble peace! It was no peace at all, with that crime and shame at our very gates." She was conscious of parroting the current phrases of the newspapers, but it was no time to pick and choose her words. She must sacrifice anything to the high ideal she had for him, and after a good deal of rapid argument she ended with the climax: "But now it doesn't matter about the how or why. Since the war has come, all that is gone. There are no two sides any more. There is nothing now but our country."

He sat with his eyes closed and his head leant back against the veranda, and he remarked, with a vague smile, as if musing aloud, "Our country—right or wrong."

"Yes, right or wrong!" she returned, fervidly. "I'll go and get you some lemonade." She rose rustling, and whisked away; when she came back with two tall glasses of clouded liquid on a tray, and the ice clucking in them, he still sat as she had left him, and she said, as if there had been no interruption: "But there is no question of wrong in this case. I call it a sacred war. A war for liberty and humanity, if ever there was one. And I know you will see it just as I do, yet."

He took half the lemonade at a gulp, and he answered as he set the glass down: "I know you always have the highest ideal. When I differ from you I ought to doubt myself."

A generous sob rose in Editha's throat for the humility of a man, so very nearly perfect, who was willing to put himself below her.

Besides, she felt, more subliminally, that he was never so near slipping through her fingers as when he took that meek way.

"You shall not say that! Only, for once I happen to be right." She seized his hand in her two hands, and poured her soul from her eyes into his. "Don't you think so?" she entreated him.

He released his hand and drank the rest of his lemonade, and she added, "Have mine, too," but he shook his head in answering, "I've no business to think so, unless I act so, too."

Her heart stopped a beat before it pulsed on with leaps that she felt in her neck. She had noticed that strange thing in men: they seemed to feel bound to do what they believed, and not think a thing was finished when they said it, as girls did. She knew what was in his mind, but she pretended not, and she said, "Oh, I am not sure," and then faltered.

He went on as if to himself, without apparently heeding her: "There's only one way of proving one's faith in a thing like this."

She could not say that she understood, but she did understand.

He went on again. "If I believed—if I felt as you do about the war—Do you wish me to feel as you do?"

Now she was really not sure; so she said: "George, I don't know what you mean."

He seemed to muse away from her as before. "There is a sort of fascination in it. I suppose that at the bottom of his heart every man would like at times to have his courage tested, to see how he would act."

"How can you talk in that ghastly way?"

"It *is* rather morbid. Still, that's what it comes to, unless you're swept away by ambition or driven by conviction. I haven't the conviction or the ambition, and the other thing is what it comes to with me. I ought to have been a preacher, after all; then I couldn't have asked it of myself, as I must, now I'm a lawyer. And you believe it's a holy war, Editha?" he suddenly addressed her. "Oh, I know you do! But *you* wish me to believe so, too?"

She hardly knew whether he was mocking or not, in the ironical way he always had with her plainer mind. But the only thing was to be outspoken with him.

"George, I wish you to believe whatever you think is true, at any and every cost. If I've tried to talk you into anything, I take it all back."

"Oh, I know that, Editha. I know how sincere you are, and how—I wish I had your undoubting spirit! I'll think it over; I'd like to believe as you do. But I don't, now; I don't, indeed. It isn't this war alone; though this seems peculiarly wanton and needless; but it's every war—so stupid; it makes me sick. Why shouldn't this thing have been settled reasonably?"

"Because," she said, very throatily again, "God meant it to be war."

"You think it was God? Yes, I suppose that is what people will say."

"Do you suppose it would have been war if God hadn't meant it?"

"I don't know. Sometimes it seems as if God had put this world into men's keeping to work it as they pleased."

"Now, George, that is blasphemy."

"Well, I won't blaspheme. I'll try to believe in your pocket Providence," he said, and then he rose to go.

"Why don't you stay to dinner?" Dinner at Balcom's Works was at one o'clock.

"I'll come back to supper, if you'll let me. Perhaps I shall bring you a convert."

"Well, you may come back, on that condition."

"All right. If I don't come, you'll understand."

He went away without kissing her, and she felt it a suspension of their engagement. It all interested her intensely; she was undergoing a tremendous experience, and she was being equal to it. While she stood looking after him, her mother came out through one of the long windows onto the veranda, with a catlike softness and vagueness.

"Why didn't he stay to dinner?"

"Because—because—war has been declared," Editha pronounced, without turning.

Her mother said, "Oh, my!" and then said nothing more until

she had sat down in one of the large Shaker chairs and rocked herself for some time. Then she closed whatever tacit passage of thought there had been in her mind with the spoken words: "Well, I hope *he* won't go."

"And *I* hope he *will*," the girl said, and confronted her mother with a stormy exaltation that would have frightened any creature less unimpressionable than a cat.

Her mother rocked herself again for an interval of cogitation. What she arrived at in speech was: "Well, I guess you've done a wicked thing, Editha Balcom."

The girl said, as she passed indoors through the same window her mother had come out by: "I haven't done anything—yet."

In her room, she put together all her letters and gifts from Gearson, down to the withered petals of the first flower he had offered, with that timidity of his veiled in that irony of his. In the heart of the packet she enshrined her engagement ring which she had restored to the pretty box he had brought it her in. Then she sat down, if not calmly yet strongly, and wrote:

> *George:—I understood when you left me. But I think we had better emphasize your meaning that if we cannot be one in everything we had better be one in nothing. So I am sending these things for your keeping till you have made up your mind.*
>
> *I shall always love you, and therefore I shall never marry anyone else. But the man I marry must love his country first of all, and be able to say to me,*
> > *"I could not love thee, dear, so much,*
> > *Loved I not honor more."*
>
> *There is no honor above America with me. In this great hour there is no other honor.*
>
> *Your heart will make my words clear to you. I had never expected to say so much, but it has come upon me that I must say the utmost.*
>
> *Editha.*

She thought she had worded her letter well, worded it in a way that could not be bettered; all had been implied and nothing expressed.

She had it ready to send with the packet she had tied with red, white, and blue ribbon, when it occurred to her that she was not just to him, that she was not giving him a fair chance. He said he would go and think it over, and she was not waiting. She was pushing, threatening, compelling. That was not a woman's part. She must leave him free, free, free. She could not accept for her country or herself a forced sacrifice.

In writing her letter she had satisfied the impulse from which it sprang; she could well afford to wait till he had thought it over. She put the packet and the letter by, and rested serene in the consciousness of having done what was laid upon her by her love itself to do, and yet used patience, mercy, justice.

She had her reward. Gearson did not come to tea, but she had given him till morning, when, late at night there came up from the village the sound of a fife and drum, with a tumult of voices, in shouting, singing, and laughing. The noise drew nearer and nearer; it reached the street end of the avenue; there it silenced itself, and one voice, the voice she knew best, rose over the silence. It fell; the air was filled with cheers; the fife and drum struck up, with the shouting, singing, and laughing again, but now retreating; and a single figure came hurrying up the avenue.

She ran down to meet her lover and clung to him. He was very gay, and he put his arm round her with a boisterous laugh. "Well, you must call me Captain now; or Cap, if you prefer; that's what the boys call me. Yes, we've had a meeting at the town hall, and everybody has volunteered; and they selected me for captain, and I'm going to the war, the big war, the glorious war, the holy war ordained by the pocket Providence that blesses butchery. Come along: let's tell the whole family about it. Call them from their downy beds, father, mother, Aunt Hitty, and all the folks!"

But when they mounted the veranda steps he did not wait for a larger audience; he poured the story out upon Editha alone.

"There was a lot of speaking, and then some of the fools set up a shout for me. It was all going one way, and I thought it would be a good joke to sprinkle a little cold water on them. But you can't do that with a crowd that adores you. The first thing I knew I was sprinkling hell-fire on them. 'Cry havoc, and let slip the dogs of war.' That was the style. Now that it had come to the fight, there were no two parties; there was one country, and the thing was to fight to a finish as quick as possible. I suggested volunteering then and there, and I wrote my name first of all on the roster. Then they elected me—that's all. I wish I had some ice-water."

She left him walking up and down the veranda, while she ran for the ice-pitcher and a goblet, and when she came back he was still walking up and down, shouting the story he had told her to her father and mother, who had come out more sketchily dressed than they commonly were by day. He drank goblet after goblet of the ice-water without noticing who was giving it, and kept on talking, and laughing through his talk wildly. "It's astonishing," he said, "how well the worse reason looks when you try to make it appear the better. Why, I believe I was the first convert to the war in that crowd tonight! I never thought I should like to kill a man; but now I shouldn't care; and the smokeless powder lets you see the man drop that you kill. It's all for the country! What a thing it is to have a country that *can't* be wrong, but if it is, is right, anyway."

Editha had a great, vital thought, an inspiration. She set down the ice-pitcher on the veranda floor, and ran upstairs and got the letter she had written him. When at last he noisily bade her father and mother, "Well, good-night. I forgot I woke you up: I shan't want any sleep myself," she followed him down the avenue to the gate. There, after the whirling words that seemed to fly away from her thoughts and refuse to serve them, she made a last effort to solemnize the moment that seemed so crazy, and pressed the letter she had written upon him.

"What's this?" he said. "Want me to mail it?"

"No, no. It's for you. I wrote it after you went this morning. Keep it—keep it—and read it sometime—" She thought, and then her inspiration came: "Read it if ever you doubt what you've done, or fear that I regret your having done it. Read it after you've started."

They strained each other in embraces that seemed as ineffective as their words, and he kissed her face with quick, hot breaths that were so unlike him, that made her feel as if she had lost her old lover and found a stranger in his place. The stranger said: "What a gorgeous flower you are, with your red hair, and your blue eyes that look black now, and your face with the color painted out by the white moonshine! Let me hold you under the chin, to see whether I love blood, you tiger-lily!" Then he laughed Gearson's laugh, and released her, scared and giddy. Within her willfulness she had been frightened by a sense of subtler force in him, and mystically mastered as she had never been before.

She ran all the way back to the house, and mounted the steps panting. Her mother and father were talking of the great affair. Her mother said: "Wa'n't Mr. Gearson in rather of an excited state of mind?

179

Didn't you think he acted curious?"

"Well, not for a man who'd just been elected captain and had set 'em up for the whole of Company A," her father chuckled back.

"What in the world do you mean, Mr. Balcom? Oh! There's Editha!" She offered to follow the girl indoors.

"Don't come, mother!" Editha called, vanishing.

Mrs. Balcom remained to reproach her husband. "I don't see much of anything to laugh at."

"Well, it's catching. Caught it from Gearson. I guess it won't be much of a war, and I guess Gearson don't think so, either. The other fellows will back down as soon as they see we mean it. I wouldn't lose any sleep over it. I'm going back to bed, myself."

Gearson came again next afternoon, looking pale and rather sick, but quite himself, even to his languid irony. "I guess I'd better tell you, Editha, that I consecrated myself to your god of battles last night by pouring too many libations to him down my own throat. But I'm all right now. One has to carry off the excitement, somehow."

"Promise me," she commanded, "that you'll never touch it again!"

"What! Not let the cannikin clink? Not let the soldier drink? Well, I promise."

"You don't belong to yourself now; you don't even belong to *me*. You belong to your country, and you have a sacred charge to keep yourself strong and well for your country's sake. I have been thinking, thinking all night and all day long."

"You look as if you had been crying a little, too," he said, with his queer smile.

"That's all past. I've been thinking, and worshipping *you*. Don't you suppose I know all that you've been through, to come to this? I've followed you every step from your old theories and opinions."

"Well, you've had a long row to hoe."

"And I know you've done this from the highest motives—"

"Oh, there won't be much pettifogging to do till this cruel war is—"

"And you haven't simply done it for my sake. I couldn't respect you if you had."

"Well, then we'll say I haven't. A man that hasn't got his own respect intact wants the respect of all the other people he can corner. But we won't go into that. I'm in for the thing now, and we've got to face our future. My idea is that this isn't going to be a very protracted struggle; we shall just scare the enemy to death before it comes to a fight at all. But we must provide for contingencies, Editha. If anything happens to me—"

"Oh, George!" She clung to him, sobbing.

"I don't want you to feel foolishly bound to my memory. I should hate that, wherever I happen to be."

"I am yours, for time and eternity—time and eternity." She liked the words; they satisfied her famine for phrases.

"Well, say eternity; that's all right; but time's another thing; and I'm talking about time. But there is something! My mother! If anything happens—"

She winced, and he laughed. "You're not the bold soldier-girl of yesterday!" Then he sobered. "If anything happens, I want you to help my mother out. She won't like my doing this thing. She brought me up to think war a fool thing as well as a bad thing. My father was in the Civil War; all through it; lost his arm in it." She thrilled with the sense of the arm round her; what if that should be lost? He laughed as if divining her: "Oh, it doesn't run in the family, as far as I know!" Then he added, gravely: "He came home with misgivings about war, and they grew on him. I guess he and mother agreed between them that I was to be brought up in his final mind about it; but that was before my time. I only knew him from my mother's report of him and his opinions; I don't know whether they were hers first; but they were hers last. This will be a blow to her. I shall have to write and tell her—"

He stopped, and she asked: "Would you like me to write, too, George?"

"I don't believe that would do. No, I'll do the writing. She'll understand a little if I say that I thought the way to minimize it was to make war on the largest possible scale at once—that I felt I must have been helping on the war somehow if I hadn't helped keep it from coming, and I knew I hadn't; when it came, I had no right to stay out of it."

Whether his sophistries satisfied him or not, they satisfied her. She clung to his breast, and whispered, with closed eyes and quivering lips: "Yes, yes, yes!"

"But if anything should happen, you might go to her and see what you could do for her. You know? It's rather far off; she can't leave her chair—"

"Oh, I'll go, if it's the ends of the earth! But nothing will happen! Nothing can! I—"

She felt herself lifted with his rising, and Gearson was saying, with his arm still round her, to her father: "Well, we're off at once, Mr. Balcom. We're to be formally accepted at the capital, and then bunched up with the rest somehow, and sent into camp somewhere, and go to the front as soon as possible. We all want to be in the van, of course; we're the first company to report to the Governor. I came to tell Editha, but I hadn't got round to it."

She saw him again for a moment at the capital, in the station, just before the train started southward with his regiment. He looked well, in his uniform, and very soldierly, but somehow girlish, too, with his clean-shaven face and slim figure. The manly eyes and the strong voice satisfied her, and his preoccupation with some unexpected details of duty flattered her. Other girls were weeping and bemoaning themselves, but she felt a sort of noble distinction in the abstraction, the almost unconsciousness, with which they parted. Only at the last moment he said: "Don't forget my mother. It mayn't be such a walkover as I supposed," and he laughed at the notion.

He waved his hand to her as the train moved off—she knew it among a score of hands that were waved to other girls from the platform of the car, for it held a letter which she knew was hers. Then he went inside the car to read it, doubtless, and she did not see him again. But she felt safe for him through the strength of what she called her love. What she called her God, always speaking the name in a deep voice and with the implication of a mutual understanding, would watch over him and keep him and bring him back to her. If with an empty sleeve, then he should have three arms instead of two, for both of hers should be his for life. She did not see, though, why she should always be thinking of the arm his father had lost.

There were not many letters from him, but they were such as she could have wished, and she put her whole strength into making hers such as she imagined he could have wished, glorifying and supporting him. She wrote to his mother glorifying him as their hero, but the brief answer she got was merely to the effect that Mrs. Gearson was not well enough to write herself, and thanking her for her letter by the hand of someone who called herself "Yrs truly, Mrs. W. J. Andrews."

Editha determined not to be hurt, but to write again quite as if the answer had been all she expected. Before it seemed as if she could have written, there came news of the first skirmish, and in the list of the killed, which was telegraphed as a trifling loss on our side, was Gearson's name. There was a frantic time of trying to make out that it might be, must be, some other Gearson; but the name and the company and the regiment and the State were too definitely given.

Then there was a lapse into depths out of which it seemed as if she never could rise again; then a lift into clouds far above all grief, black clouds, that blotted out the sun, but where she soared with him, with George—George! She had the fever that she expected of herself, but she did not die in it; she was not even delirious, and it did not last long. When she was well enough to leave her bed, her one thought was of George's mother, of his strangely worded wish that she should go to her and see what she could do for her. In the exaltation of the duty laid upon her—it buoyed her up instead of burdening her—she rapidly recovered.

Her father went with her on the long railroad journey from Northern New York to Western Iowa; he had business out at Davenport, and he said he could just as well go then as any other time; and he went with her to the little country town where George's mother lived in a little house on the edge of the illimitable cornfields, under trees pushed to a top of the rolling prairie. George's father had settled there after the Civil War, as so many other old soldiers had done; but they were Eastern people, and Editha fancied touches of the East in the June rose overhanging the front door, and the garden with early summer flowers stretching from the gate of the paling fence.

It was very low inside the house, and so dim, with the closed blinds, that they could scarcely see one another: Editha tall and black in her crapes which filled the air with the smell of their dyes; her father standing decorously apart with his hat on his forearm, as at funerals; a woman rested in a deep armchair, and the woman who had let the strangers in stood behind the chair.

The seated woman turned her head round and up, and asked the woman behind her chair: *"Who* did you say?"

Editha, if she had done what she expected of herself, would have gone down on her knees at the feet of the seated figure and said, "I am George's Editha," for answer.

But instead of her own voice she heard that other woman's voice, saying: "Well, I don't know as I *did* get the name just right. I guess I'll have to make a little more light in here," and she went and pushed two of the shutters ajar.

Then Editha's father said, in his public will-now-address-a-few-remarks tone: "My name is Balcom, ma'am—Junius H. Balcom, of Balcom's Works, New York; my daughter—"

"Oh!" the seated woman broke in, with a powerful voice, the voice that always surprised Editha from Gearson's slender frame. "Let me see you. Stand round where the light can strike on your face," and Editha dumbly obeyed. "So, you're Editha Balcom," she sighed.

"Yes," Editha said, more like a culprit than a comforter.

"What did you come for?" Mrs. Gearson asked.

Editha's face quivered and her knees shook. "I came—because—because George—" She could go no further.

"Yes," the mother said, "he told me he had asked you to come if he got killed. You didn't expect that, I suppose, when you sent him."

"I would rather have died myself than done it!" Editha said, with more truth in her deep voice than she ordinarily found in it. "I tried to leave him free—"

"Yes, that letter of yours, that came back with his other things, left him free."

Editha saw now where George's irony came from.

"It was not to be read before—unless—until—I told him so," she faltered.

"Of course, he wouldn't read a letter of yours, under the circumstances, till he thought you wanted him to. Been sick?" the woman abruptly demanded.

"Very sick," Editha said, with self-pity.

"Daughter's life," her father interposed, "was almost despaired of, at one time."

Mrs. Gearson gave him no heed. "I suppose you would have been glad to die, such a brave person as you! I don't believe *he* was glad to die. He was always a timid boy, that way; he was afraid of a good many things; but if he was afraid he did what he made up his mind to. I suppose he made up his mind to go, but I knew what it cost him by what it cost me when I heard of it. I had been through *one* war before. When you sent him you didn't expect he would get killed."

The voice seemed to compassionate Editha, and it was time. "No," she huskily murmured.

"No, girls don't; women don't, when they give their men up to their country. They think they'll come marching back, somehow, just as gay as they went, or if it's an empty sleeve, or even an empty pantaloon it's all the more glory, and they're so much the prouder of them, poor things!"

The tears began to run down Editha's face; she had not wept till then; but it was now such a relief to be understood that the tears came.

"No, you didn't expect him to get killed," Mrs. Gearson repeated, in a voice which was startlingly like George's again. "You just expected him to kill someone else, some of those foreigners, that weren't there because they had any say about it, but because they had to be there, poor wretches—conscripts, or whatever they call 'em. You thought it would be all right for my George, *your* George, to kill the sons of those miserable mothers and the husbands of those girls that you would never see the faces of." The woman lifted her powerful voice in a psalmlike note. "I thank my God he didn't live to do it! I thank my God they killed him first, and that he ain't livin' with their blood on his hands!" She dropped her eyes, which she had raised with her voice, and glared at Editha. "What you got that black on for?" She lifted herself by her powerful arms so high that her helpless body seemed to hang limp its full length. "Take it off, take it off, before I tear it from your back!"

playing part. heroine.

The lady who was passing the summer near Balcom's Works was sketching Editha's beauty, which lent itself wonderfully to the effects of a colorist. It had come to that confidence which is rather apt to grow between artist and sitter, and Editha had told her everything.

"To think of your having such a tragedy in your life!" the lady said. She added: "I suppose there are people who feel that way about war. But when you consider the good this war has done—how much it has done for the country! I can't understand such people, for my part. And when you had come all the way out there to console her—got up out of a sickbed! Well!"

"I think," Editha said, magnanimously, "she wasn't quite in her right mind; and so did papa."

"Yes," the lady said, looking at Editha's lips in nature and then at her lips in art, and giving an empirical touch to them in the picture. "But how dreadful of her! How perfectly—excuse me—how *vulgar!*"

A light broke upon Editha in the darkness which she felt had been without a gleam of brightness for weeks and months. The mystery that had bewildered her was solved by the word; and from that moment she rose from groveling in shame and self-pity, and began to live again in the ideal.

Class snobbery. E. is better than a mother.

Ambrose Bierce

THE COUP de GRÂCE

Born in Ohio, in 1842, the son of a poor farmer and the youngest in a family of nine children, Ambrose Bierce grew up with little formal schooling. He enlisted in the Ninth Indiana Volunteers in 1861, and, during his four-year period of service, took part in some of the bloodiest campaigns of the Civil War, an experience which provided him with material he later used in his stories and probably was responsible for his bitter outlook on life. After the war, Bierce, like Twain and Harte, served for a time as a newspaperman in San Francisco. In 1871, he married Mary Ellen Day and the following year took up residence in England, where he joined the staff of *Fun*, contributed to *Hood's Comic Almanac*, and published three volumes of sketches, *The Fiend's Delight* (1872), *Nuggets and Dust Panned Out in California* (1872), and *Cobwebs from an Empty Skull* (1874), works so biting and sardonic in tone that critics called him "Bitter Bierce." Returning to California in 1876 because of poor health, he contributed a column entitled "Prattle" to the San Francisco *Examiner* and, by virtue of his acid wit, soon gained an important place among the writers of the Pacific Coast. In 1891, he published a volume of short stories, *Tales of Soldiers and Civilians* (retitled *In the Midst of Life*), and in 1893, a second volume, *Can Such Things Be?* His best stories are included among the fifty pieces in these two volumes.

Continuing in journalistic work as a Washington correspondent for Hearst's New York *American* (1897) and as a contributor to Hearst's *Cosmopolitan Magazine* (1905-1909), he also published a number of books of a miscellaneous nature, such as *Fantastic Fables* (1899), *The Cynic's Word Book* (1906), and *Antepenultimata* (1909). Personal suffering caused by the death of one son in 1899, of the second in 1901, and by divorce from his wife in 1904 deepened his long-evident pessimism and resulted ultimately in his settling his affairs in 1913 and disappearing into Mexico. Although there is no authentic information concerning his fate, it is presumed that he died in Mexico in 1914.

In his use of horror and the supernatural, as well as in his finished technique, Bierce resembles Poe; there, however, the resemblance stops, for Poe is a romantic and Bierce not merely a realist but a sardonic pessimist, who seems to delight in showing what a sorry, terror-ridden creature man is and in how many ways he can be dismembered by fate. Writing to create a powerful effect, Bierce uses such devices as the surprise ending, the double reversal of the situation, and coincidence. Even though Bierce's extensive use of these devices results in artificiality, he is often able to construct a story that "explodes" in the last several lines and stuns the reader with a sudden, horrible revelation. "The Coup de Grâce" illustrates this feature of Bierce's technique.

the coup de grâce

The fighting had been hard and continuous; that was attested by all the senses. The very taste of battle was in the air. All was now over; it remained only to succor the wounded and bury the dead—to "tidy up a bit," as the humorist of a burial squad put it. A good deal of "tidying up" was required. As far as one could see through the forests, among the splintered trees, lay wrecks of men and horses. Among them moved the stretcher-bearers, gathering and carrying away the few who showed signs of life. Most of the wounded had died of neglect while the right to minister to their wants was in dispute. It is an army regulation that the wounded must wait; the best way to care for them is to win the battle. It must be confessed that victory is a distinct advantage to a man requiring attention, but many do not live to avail themselves of it.

The dead were collected in groups of a dozen or a score and laid side by side in rows while the trenches were dug to receive them. Some, found at too great a distance from these rallying points, were buried where they lay. There was little attempt at identification, though in most cases, the burial parties being detailed to glean the same ground which they had assisted to reap, the names of the victorious dead were known and listed. The enemy's fallen had to be content with counting. But of that they got enough: many of them were counted several times, and the total, as given afterward in the official report of the victorious commander, denoted rather a hope than a result.

At some little distance from the spot where one of the burial parties had established its "bivouac of the dead," a man in the uniform of a Federal officer stood leaning against a tree. From his feet upward to his neck his attitude was that of weariness reposing; but he turned his head uneasily from side to side; his mind was apparently not at rest. He was perhaps uncertain in which direction to go; he was not likely to remain long where he was, for already the level rays of the setting sun straggled redly through the open spaces of the wood and the weary soldiers were quitting their task for the day. He would hardly make a night of it alone there among the dead. Nine men in ten whom you meet after a battle inquire the way to some fraction of the army—as if any one could know. Doubtless this officer was lost. After resting himself a moment he would presumably follow one of the retiring burial squads.

When all were gone he walked straight away into the forest toward the red west, its light staining his face like blood. The air of confidence with which he now strode along showed that he was on familiar ground; he had recovered his bearings. The dead on his right and on his left were unregarded as he passed. An occasional low moan from some sorely-stricken wretch whom the relief-parties had not reached, and who would have to pass a comfortless night beneath the stars with his thirst to keep him company, was equally unheeded. What, indeed, could the officer have done, being no surgeon and having no water?

At the head of a shallow ravine, a mere depression of the ground, lay a small group of bodies. He saw, and swerving suddenly from his course walked rapidly toward them. Scanning each one sharply as he passed, he stopped at last above one which lay at a slight remove from the others, near a clump of small trees. He looked at it narrowly. It seemed to stir. He stooped and laid his hand upon its face. It screamed.

The officer was Captain Downing Madwell, of a Massachusetts regiment of infantry, a daring and intelligent soldier, an honorable man.

In the regiment were two brothers named Halcrow—Caffal and Creede Halcrow. Caffal Halcrow was a sergeant in Captain Madwell's company, and these two men, the sergeant and the captain, were devoted friends. In so far as disparity of rank, differences in duties and considerations of military discipline would permit they were commonly together. They had, indeed, grown up together from childhood. A habit of the heart is not easily broken off. Caffal Halcrow had nothing military in his taste nor disposition, but the thought of separation from his friend was disagreeable; he enlisted in the company in which Madwell was second-lieutenant. Each had taken two steps upward in rank, but between the highest non-commissioned and the lowest commissioned officer the gulf is deep and wide and the old relation was maintained with difficulty and a difference.

Creede Halcrow, the brother of Caffal, was the major of the regiment—a cynical, saturnine man, between whom and Captain Madwell there was a natural antipathy which circumstances had nourished and strengthened to an active animosity. But for the restraining influence of their mutual relation to Caffal these two patriots would doubtless have endeavored to deprive their country of each other's services.

At the opening of the battle that morning the regiment was performing outpost duty a mile away from the main army. It was attacked and nearly surrounded in the forest, but stubbornly held its ground. During a lull in the fighting, Major Halcrow came to Captain Madwell. The two exchanged formal salutes, and the major said: "Captain, the colonel directs that you push your company to the head of this ravine and hold your place there until recalled. I need hardly apprise you of the dangerous character of the movement, but if you wish, you can, I suppose, turn over the command to your first-lieutenant. I was not, however, directed to authorize the substitution; it is merely a suggestion of my own, unofficially made."

To this deadly insult Captain Madwell coolly replied:

"Sir, I invite you to accompany the movement. A mounted officer would be a conspicuous mark, and I have long held the opinion that it would be better if you were dead."

The art of repartee was cultivated in military circles as early as 1862.

A half-hour later Captain Madwell's company was driven from its position at the head of the ravine, with a loss of one-third its number. Among the fallen was Sergeant Halcrow. The regiment was soon afterward forced back to the main line, and at the close of the battle was miles away. The captain was now standing at the side of his subordinate and friend.

Sergeant Halcrow was mortally hurt. His clothing was deranged; it seemed to have been violently torn apart, exposing the abdomen. Some of the buttons of his jacket had been pulled off and lay on the ground beside him and fragments of his other garments were strewn about. His leather belt was parted and had apparently been dragged from beneath him as he lay. There had been no great effusion of blood. The only visible wound was a wide, ragged opening in the abdomen. It was defiled with earth and dead leaves. Protruding from it was a loop of small intestine. In all his experience Captain Madwell had not seen a wound like this. He could neither conjecture how it was made nor explain the attendant circumstances—the strangely torn clothing, the parted belt, the besmirching of the white skin. He knelt and made a closer examination. When he rose to his feet, he turned his eyes in different directions as if looking for an enemy. Fifty yards away, on the crest of a low, thinly wooded hill, he saw several dark objects moving about among the fallen men—a herd of swine. One stood with its back to him, its shoulders sharply elevated. Its forefeet were upon a human body, its head was depressed and invisible. The bristly ridge of its chine showed black against the red west. Captain Madwell drew away his eyes and fixed them again upon the thing which had been his friend.

The man who had suffered these monstrous mutilations was alive. At intervals he moved his limbs; he moaned at every breath. He stared blankly into the face of his friend and if touched screamed. In his giant agony he had torn up the ground on which he lay; his clenched hands were full of leaves and twigs and earth. Articulate speech was beyond his power; it was impossible to know if he were sensible to anything but pain. The expression of his face was an appeal; his eyes were full of prayer. For what?

There was no misreading that look; the captain had too frequently seen it in eyes of those whose lips had still the power to formulate it by an entreaty for death. Consciously or unconsciously,

191

this writhing fragment of humanity, this type and example of acute sensation, this handiwork of man and beast, this humble, unheroic Prometheus, was imploring everything, all, the whole non-ego, for the boon of oblivion. To the earth and the sky alike, to the trees, to the man, to whatever took form in sense or consciousness, this incarnate suffering addressed that silent plea.

For what, indeed? For that which we accord to even the meanest creature without sense to demand it, denying it only to the wretched of our own race: for the blessed release, the rite of uttermost compassion, the *coup de grâce*.

Captain Madwell spoke the name of his friend. He repeated it over and over without effect until emotion choked his utterance. His tears plashed upon the livid face beneath his own and blinded himself. He saw nothing but a blurred and moving object, but the moans were more distinct than ever, interrupted at briefer intervals by sharper shrieks. He turned away, struck his hand upon his forehead, and strode from the spot. The swine, catching sight of him, threw up their crimson muzzles, regarding him suspiciously a second, and then with a gruff, concerted grunt, raced away out of sight. A horse, its foreleg splintered by a cannon-shot, lifted its head sidewise from the ground and neighed piteously. Madwell stepped forward, drew his revolver and shot the poor beast between the eyes, narrowly observing its death-struggle, which, contrary to his expectation, was violent and long; but at last it lay still. The tense muscles of its lips, which had uncovered the teeth in a horrible grin, relaxed; the sharp, clean-cut profile took on a look of profound peace and rest.

Along the distant, thinly wooded crest to westward the fringe of sunset fire had now nearly burned itself out. The light upon the trunks of the trees had faded to a tender gray; shadows were in their tops, like great dark birds aperch. Night was coming and there were miles of haunted forest between Captain Madwell and camp. Yet he stood there at the side of the dead animal, apparently lost to all sense of his surroundings. His eyes were bent upon the earth at his feet; his left hand hung loosely at his side, his right still held the pistol. Presently he lifted his face, turned it toward his dying friend and walked rapidly back to his side. He knelt upon one knee, cocked the weapon, placed the muzzle against the man's forehead, and turning away his eyes pulled the trigger. There was no report. He had used his last cartridge for the horse.

The sufferer moaned and his lips moved convulsively. The froth that ran from them had a tinge of blood.

Captain Madwell rose to his feet and drew his sword from the scabbard. He passed the fingers of his left hand along the edge from hilt to point. He held it out straight before him, as if to test his nerves. There was no visible tremor of the blade; the ray of bleak skylight that it reflected was steady and true. He stooped and with his left hand tore away the dying man's shirt, rose and placed the point of the sword just over the heart. This time he did not withdraw his eyes. Grasping the hilt with both hands, he thrust downward with all his strength and weight. The blade sank into the man's body—through his body into the earth; Captain Madwell came near falling forward upon his work. The dying man drew up his knees and at the same time threw his right arm across his breast and grasped the steel so tightly that the knuckles of the hand visibly whitened. By a violent but vain effort to withdraw the blade the wound was enlarged; a rill of blood escaped, running sinuously down into the deranged clothing. At that moment three men stepped silently forward from behind the clump of young trees which had concealed their approach. Two were hospital attendants and carried a stretcher.

The third was Major Creede Halcrow.

Henry James

"EUROPE"

THE JOLLY CORNER

Believing as Howells did that fiction should present a serious, truthful, but dramatically interesting view of life, Henry James dedicated a lifetime of theory and practice toward showing how this aim might best be fulfilled. If his critical theories and his successful embodiment of them in his fiction were less widely appreciated in his own day than Howells' were, they have nevertheless so pervaded the method of twentieth-century fiction that few writers have failed to profit directly or indirectly from them.

Unlike Howells, James enjoyed from early childhood the advantages of wealth, leisure, extensive travel, and freedom to cultivate the arts. Born in New York City in 1843, James from childhood on enjoyed a vigorously intellectual family atmosphere, stimulated by the interests and friends of his father, Henry, Sr., and his elder brother, William, the psychologist and philosopher. To cultivate his children as future citizens of the world possessing a thoroughly cosmopolitan outlook, the father took his family abroad in 1855, where for the next three years young James continued his eclectic education and began his long study of European culture. From 1862 to 1864 he attended Harvard Law School but with little aim of entering law as a profession, for already literature was becoming his consuming passion. Encouraged by Howells and others, he began contributing critical reviews and short stories to the *Nation,* the *North American Review,* and the *Atlantic Monthly,* and by 1871, with the publication of *A Passionate Pilgrim* and *Watch and Ward,* was well embarked on his professional career. Feeling that America was too young and raw to provide the fiction writer with proper materials, in 1876 he took up residence in England, where he continued to live, with only occasional visits to America, until his death in 1916. An astute student of Hawthorne and Balzac and of his great European contemporaries, Turgenev, De Maupassant, Flaubert, Daudet, and Zola, he sought to achieve perfection in his own work with the result that throughout his long writing career he steadily grew in power and skill. In addition to his volumes of criticism, his plays, and his many novels, he wrote numerous short stories, some of the most significant collections of which are *The Lesson of the Master* (1892), *The Real Thing and Other Tales* (1893), *The Soft Side* (1900), and *The Better Sort* (1903).

In his most important statement of theory, *The Art of Fiction* (1884), James identified a successful work of fiction as a living organism: "in proportion as it lives it will be found . . . that in each of the parts there is something of each of the other parts." This principle, he made clear, applies just as surely to the short story as to the novel; and the fact that character, incident, setting, plot, and point of view must all be inseparably articulated in a successful short piece of fiction may be illustrated in any of his stories, for instance, "Europe" and "The Jolly Corner." To approach the stories through theme only and say they are merely different treatments of the influence on Americans of European culture would be misleading. To consider them, on the other hand, only as character studies would be equally misleading. In both, James has so closely woven together theme, character, plot, and setting that no one element can be isolated from the others without damage to the whole fabric of the story. A further noteworthy fact is that despite the similarity of James' method in the two stories, they are quite unlike each other in tone, atmosphere, effect, and the point of view from which they are narrated.

"europe"

"Our feeling is, you know, that Becky *should* go." That earnest little remark comes back to me, even after long years, as the first note of something that began, for my observation, the day I went with my sister-in-law to take leave of her good friends. It's a memory of the American time, which revives so at present—under some touch that doesn't signify—that it rounds itself off as an anecdote. That walk to say good-bye was the beginning; and the end, so far as I enjoyed a view of it, was not till long after; yet even the end also appears to me now as of the old days. I went, in those days, on occasion, to see my sister-in-law, in whose affairs, on my brother's death, I had had to take a helpful hand. I continued to go indeed after these little matters were straightened out, for the pleasure, periodically, of the impression—the change to the almost pastoral sweetness of the good Boston suburb from the loud longitudinal New York. It was another world, with other manners, a different tone, a different taste; a savour nowhere so mild, yet so distinct, as in the square white house—with the pair of elms, like gigantic wheat-sheaves, in front, the rustic orchard not far behind, the old-fashioned door-lights, the big blue-and-white jars on the porch, the straight bricked walk from the high gate—that enshrined the extraordinary merit of Mrs. Rimmle and her three daughters.

These ladies were so much of the place and the place so much of themselves that from the first of their being revealed to me I felt that nothing else at Brookbridge much mattered. They were what, for me, at any rate, Brookbridge had most to give: I mean in the way of what it was naturally strongest in, the thing we called in New York the New England expression, the air of Puritanism reclaimed and refined. The Rimmles had brought this down to a wonderful delicacy. They struck me even then—all four almost equally—as very ancient and very earnest, and I think theirs must have been the house in all the world in which "culture" first came to the aid of morning calls. The head of the family was the widow of a great public character—as public characters were understood at Brookbridge—whose speeches on anniversaries formed a part of the body of national eloquence spouted in the New England schools by little boys covetous of the most marked, though perhaps the easiest, distinction. He was reported to have been celebrated, and in such fine declamatory connexions that he seemed to gesticulate even from the tomb. He was understood to have made, in his wife's company, the tour of Europe at a date not immensely removed from that of the battle of Waterloo. What was the age then of the bland firm antique Mrs. Rimmle at the period of her being first revealed to me? That's a point I'm not in a position to determine—I remember mainly that I was young enough to regard her as having reached the limit. And yet the limit for Mrs. Rimmle must have been prodigiously extended; the scale of its extension is in fact the very moral of this reminiscence. She was old, and her daughters were old, but I was destined to know them all as older. It was only by comparison and habit that—however much I recede—Rebecca, Maria and Jane were the "young ladies."

I think it was felt that, though their mother's life, after thirty years of widowhood, had had a grand backward stretch, her blandness and firmness—and this in spite of her extreme physical frailty—would be proof against any surrender not overwhelmingly justified by time. It had appeared, years before, at a crisis of which the waves had not even yet quite subsided, a surrender not justified by anything nameable, that she should go to Europe with her daughters and for her health. Her health was supposed to require constant support; but when it had at that period tried conclusions with the idea of Europe it was not the idea of Europe that had been insidious enough to prevail. She hadn't gone, and Becky, Maria and Jane hadn't gone, and this was long ago. They still merely floated in the air of the visit achieved, with such introductions and such acclamations, in the early part of the century; they still, with fond glances at the sunny parlour-walls, only referred, in conversation, to divers pictorial and other reminders of it. The Miss Rimmles had quite been brought up on it, but Becky, as the most literary, had most mastered the subject. There were framed letters—tributes to their eminent father—suspended among the mementoes, and of two or three of these, the most foreign and complimentary, Becky had executed translations that figured beside the text. She knew already, through this and other illumination, so much about Europe that it was hard to believe for her in that limit of adventure which consisted only of her having been twice to Philadelphia. The others hadn't been to Philadelphia, but there was a legend that Jane had been to Saratoga. Becky was a short stout fair person with round serious eyes, a high forehead, the sweetest neatest enunciation, and a miniature of her father—"done in Rome"—worn as a breastpin. She had written the life, she had edited the speeches, of the original of this ornament, and now at last, beyond the seas, she was really to tread in his footsteps.

Fine old Mrs. Rimmle, in the sunny parlour and with a certain austerity of cap and chair—though with a gay new "front" that looked like rusty brown plush—had had so unusually good a winter that the question of her sparing two members of her family for an absence had been threshed as fine, I could feel, as even under that Puritan roof, any case of conscience had ever been threshed. They were to make their dash while the coast, as it were, was clear, and each of the daughters had tried—heroically, angelically and for the sake of each of her sisters —not to be one of the two. What I encountered that first time was an opportunity to concur with enthusiasm in the general idea that Becky's wonderful preparation would be wasted if she were the one to stay with their mother. Their talk of Becky's preparation (they had a sly old-maidish humour that was as mild as milk) might have been of some mixture, for application somewhere, that she kept in a precious bottle. It had been settled at all events that, armed with this concoction and borne aloft by their introductions, she and Jane were to start. They were wonderful on their introductions, which proceeded naturally from their mother and were addressed to the charming families that in vague generations had so admired vague Mr. Rimmle. Jane, I found at Brookbridge, had to be described, for want of other description, as the pretty one, but it wouldn't have served to identify her unless you had seen the others. *Her* preparation was only this figment of her prettiness—only, that is, unless one took into account something that, on the spot, I silently divined: the lifelong secret passionate ache of her little rebellious desire. They were all growing old in the yearning to go, but Jane's yearning was the sharpest. She struggled with it as people at Brookbridge mostly struggled with what they liked, but fate, by threatening to prevent what she *dis*liked and what was therefore duty—which was to stay at home instead of Maria—had bewildered her, I judged, not a little. It was she who, in the words I have quoted, mentioned to me Becky's case and Becky's affinity as the clearest of all. Her mother moreover had on the general subject still more to say.

"I positively desire, I really quite insist that they shall go," the old lady explained to us from her stiff chair. "We've talked about it so often, and they've had from me so clear an account—I've amused them again and again with it—of what's to be seen and enjoyed. If they've had hitherto too many duties to leave, the time seems to have come to recognise that there are also many duties to *seek*. Wherever we go we find them—I always remind the girls of that. There's a duty that calls them to those wonderful countries, just as it called, at the right time, their father and myself—if it be only that of laying-up for the years to come the same store of remarkable impressions, the same wealth of knowledge and food for conversation as, since my return, I've found myself so happy to possess." Mrs. Rimmle spoke of her return as of something of the year before last, but the future of her daughters was somehow, by a different law, to be on the scale of great vistas, of endless after-tastes. I think that, without my being quite ready to say it, even this first impression of her was somewhat upsetting; there was a large placid perversity, a grim secrecy of intention, in her estimate of the ages.

"Well, I'm so glad you don't delay it longer," I said to Miss Becky before we withdrew. "And whoever should go," I continued in the spirit of the sympathy with which the good sisters had already inspired me, "I quite feel, with your family, you know, that *you* should. But of course I hold that every one should." I suppose I wished to attenuate my solemnity; there was, however, something in it I couldn't help. It must have been a faint foreknowledge.

"Have you been a great deal yourself?" Miss Jane, I remembered, enquired.

"Not so much but that I hope to go a good deal more. So perhaps we shall meet," I encouragingly suggested.

I recall something—something in the nature of susceptibility to encouragement—that this brought into the more expressive brown eyes to which Miss Jane mainly owed it that she was the pretty one. "Where, do you think?"

I tried to think. "Well, on the Italian lakes—Como, Bellaggio, Lugano." I liked to say the names to them.

" 'Sublime, but neither bleak nor bare—nor misty are the mountains there!' " Miss Jane softly breathed, while her sister looked at her as if her acquaintance with the poetry of the subject made her the most interesting feature of the scene she evoked.

But Miss Becky presently turned to me. "Do you know everything—?"

"Everything?"

"In Europe."

"Oh yes," I laughed, "and one or two things even in America."

The sisters seemed to me furtively to look at each other. "Well, you'll have to be quick—to meet *us,*" Miss Jane resumed.

"But surely when you're once there you'll stay on."

"Stay on?"—they murmured it simultaneously and with the oddest vibration of dread as well as of desire. It was as if they had been in presence of a danger and yet wished me, who "knew everything," to torment them with still more of it.

Well, I did my best. "I mean it will never do to cut it short."

"No, that's just what I keep saying," said brilliant Jane. "It would be better in that case not to go."

"Oh don't talk about not going—at this time!" It was none of my business, but I felt shocked and impatient.

"No, not at *this* time!" broke in Miss Maria, who, very red in the face, had joined us. Poor Miss Maria was known as the flushed one; but she was not flushed—she only had an unfortunate surface. The third day after this was to see them embark.

Miss Becky, however, desired as little as any one to be in any way extravagant. "It's only the thought of our mother," she explained.

I looked a moment at the old lady, with whom my sister-in-law was engaged. "Well—your mother's magnificent."

"*Isn't* she magnificent?"—they eagerly took it up.

She *was*—I could reiterate it with sincerity, though I perhaps mentally drew the line when Miss Maria again risked, as a fresh ejaculation: "I think she's better than Europe!"

"Maria!" they both, at this, exclaimed with a strange emphasis: it was as if they feared she had suddenly turned cynical over the deep domestic drama of their casting of lots. The innocent laugh with which she answered them gave the measure of her cynicism.

We separated at last, and my eyes met Mrs. Rimmle's as I held for an instant her aged hand. It was doubtless only my fancy that her calm cold look quietly accused me of something. Of what *could* it accuse me? Only, I thought, of thinking.

2

I left Brookbridge the next day, and for some time after that had no occasion to hear from my kinswoman; but when she finally wrote there was a passage in her letter that affected me more than all the rest. "Do you know the poor Rimmles never, after all, 'went'? The old lady, at the eleventh hour, broke down; everything broke down, and all of *them* on top of it, so that the dear things are with us still. Mrs. Rimmle, the night after our call, had, in the most unexpected manner, a turn for the worse—something in the nature (though they're rather mysterious about it) of a seizure; Becky and Jane felt it—dear devoted stupid angels that they are—heartless to leave her at such a moment, and Europe's indefinitely postponed. However, they think they're still going—or *think* they think it—when she's better. They also think—or think they think—that she *will* be better. I certainly pray she may." So did I—quite fervently. I was conscious of a real pang—I didn't know how much they had made me care.

Late that winter my sister-in-law spent a week in New York; when almost my first enquiry on meeting her was about the health of Mrs. Rimmle.

"Oh she's rather bad—she really is, you know. It's not surprising that at her age she should be infirm."

"Then what the deuce *is* her age?"

"I can't tell you to a year—but she's immensely old."

"That of course I saw," I replied—"unless you literally mean so old that the records have been lost."

My sister-in-law thought. "Well, I believe she wasn't positively young when she married. She lost three or four children before these women were born."

We surveyed together a little, on this, the "dark backward." "And they were born, I gather, *after* the famous tour? Well then, as the famous tour was in a manner to celebrate—wasn't it?—the restoration of the Bourbons—" I considered, I gasped. "My dear child, what on earth do you make her out?"

My relative, with her Brookbridge habit, transferred her share of the question to the moral plane—turned it forth to wander, by implication at least, in the sandy desert of responsibility. "Well, you know, we all immensely admire her."

"You can't admire her more than I do. She's awful."

My converser looked at me with a certain fear. "She's *really* ill."

"Too ill to get better?"

"Oh no—we hope not. Because then they'll be able to go."

"And *will* they go if she should?"

"Oh the moment they should be quite satisfied. I mean *really*," she added.

I'm afraid I laughed at her—the Brookbridge "really" was a thing so by itself. "But if she shouldn't get better?" I went on.

"Oh don't speak of it! They want so to go."

"It's a pity they're so infernally good," I mused.

"No—don't say that. It's what keeps them up."

"Yes, but isn't it what keeps *her* up too?"

My visitor looked grave. "Would you like them to kill her?"

I don't know that I was then prepared to say I should—though I believe I came very near it. But later on I burst all bounds, for the subject grew and grew. I went again before the good sisters ever did— I mean I went to Europe. I think I went twice, with a brief interval, before my fate again brought round for me a couple of days at Brook-bridge. I had been there repeatedly, in the previous time, without making the acquaintance of the Rimmles; but now that I had had the revelation I couldn't have it too much, and the first request I preferred was to be taken again to see them. I remember well indeed the scruple I felt—the real delicacy—about betraying that *I* had, in the pride of my power, since our other meeting, stood, as their phrase went, among romantic scenes; but they were themselves the first to speak of it, and what moreover came home to me was that the coming and going of their friends in general—Brookbridge itself having even at that period one foot in Europe—was such as to place constantly before them the pleasure that was only postponed. They were thrown back after all on what the situation, under a final analysis, had most to give—the sense that, as every one kindly said to them and they kindly said to every one, Europe would keep. Every one felt for them so deeply that their own kindness in alleviating every one's feelings was really what came out most. Mrs. Rimmle was still in her stiff chair and in the sunny parlour, but if *she* made no scruple of introducing the Italian lakes my heart sank to observe that she dealt with them, as a topic, not in the least in the leave-taking manner in which Falstaff babbled of green fields.

I'm not sure that after this my pretexts for a day or two with my sister-in-law weren't apt to be a mere cover for another glimpse of these particulars: I at any rate never went to Brookbridge without an irrepressible eagerness for our customary call. A long time seems to me thus to have passed, with glimpses and lapses, considerable impatience and still more pity. Our visits indeed grew shorter, for, as my companion said, they were more and more of a strain. It finally struck me that the good sisters even shrank from me a little as from one who penetrated their consciousness in spite of himself. It was as if they knew where I thought they ought to be, and were moved to deprecate at last, by a systematic silence on the subject of that hemisphere, the criminality I fain would fix on them. They were full instead—as with the instinct of throwing dust in my eyes—of little pathetic hypocrisies about Brookbridge interests and delights. I dare say that as time went on my deeper sense of their situation came practically to rest on my

203

companion's report of it. I certainly think I recollect every word we ever exchanged about them, even if I've lost the thread of the special occasions. The impression they made on me after each interval always broke out with extravagance as I walked away with her.

"*She* may be as old as she likes—I don't care. It's the fearful age the 'girls' are reaching that constitutes the scandal. One shouldn't pry into such matters, I know; but the years and the chances are really going. They're all growing old together—it will presently be too late; and their mother meanwhile perches over them like a vulture—what shall I call it?—calculating. Is she waiting for them successively to drop off? She'll survive them each and all. There's something too remorseless in it."

"Yes, but what do you want her to do? If the poor thing *can't* die she can't. Do you want her to take poison or to open a blood-vessel? I dare say she'd prefer to go."

"I beg your pardon," I must have replied; "you daren't say anything of the sort. If she'd prefer to go she *would* go. She'd feel the propriety, the decency, the necessity of going. She just prefers *not* to go. She prefers to stay and keep up the tension, and her calling them 'girls' and talking of the good time they'll still have is the mere conscious mischief of a subtle old witch. They won't have *any* time—there isn't any time to have! I mean there's, on her own part, no real loss of measure or of perspective in it. She *knows* she's a hundred and ten, and she takes a cruel pride in it."

My sister-in-law differed with me about this; she held that the old woman's attitude was an honest one and that her magnificent vitality, so great in spite of her infirmities, made it inevitable she should attribute youth to persons who had come into the world so much later. "Then suppose she should die?"—so my fellow student of the case always put it to me.

"Do you mean while her daughters are away? There's not the least fear of that—not even if at the very moment of their departure she should be *in extremis*. They'd find her all right on their return."

"But think how they'd feel not to have been with her!"

"That's only, I repeat, on the unsound assumption. If they'd only go to-morrow—literally make a good rush for it—they'll be with her when they come back. That will give them plenty of time." I'm afraid I even heartlessly added that if she *should*, against every probability, pass away in their absence they wouldn't have to come back at all—which would be just the compensation proper to their long privation. And then Maria would come out to join the two others, and they would be—though but for the too scanty remnant of their career—as merry as the day is long.

I remained ready, somehow, pending the fulfilment of that vision, to sacrifice Maria; it was only over the urgency of the case for the others respectively that I found myself balancing. Sometimes it was for Becky I thought the tragedy deepest—sometimes, and in quite a different manner, I thought it most dire for Jane. It was Jane after all who had most sense of life. I seemed in fact dimly to descry in Jane a sense—as yet undescribed by herself or by any one—of all sorts of queer things. Why didn't *she* go? I used desperately to ask; why didn't she make a bold personal dash for it, strike up a partnership with some one or other of the travelling spinsters in whom Brookbridge more and more abounded? Well, there came a flash for me at a particular point of the grey middle desert: my correspondent was able to let me know that poor Jane at last *had* sailed. She had gone of a sudden—I liked my sister-in-law's view of suddenness—with the kind Hathaways, who had made an irresistible grab at her and lifted her off her feet. They were going for the summer and for Mr. Hathaway's health, so that the opportunity was perfect and it was impossible not to be glad that something very like physical force had finally prevailed. This was the general feeling at Brookbridge, and I might imagine what Brookbridge had been brought to from the fact that, at the very moment she was hustled off, the doctor, called to her mother at the peep of dawn, had considered that *he* at least must stay. There had been real alarm—greater than ever before; it actually did seem as if this time the end had come. But it was Becky, strange to say, who, though fully recognising the nature of the crisis, had kept the situation in hand and insisted upon action. This, I remember, brought back to me a discomfort with which I had been familiar from the first. One of the two had sailed, and I was sorry it wasn't the other. But if it had been the other I should have been equally sorry.

I saw with my eyes that very autumn what a fool Jane would have been if she had again backed out. Her mother had of course survived the peril of which I had heard, profiting by it indeed as she had profited by every other; she was sufficiently better again to have come downstairs. It was there that, as usual, I found her, but with a difference of effect produced somehow by the absence of one of the girls. It was as if, for the others, though they hadn't gone to Europe, Europe had come to them: Jane's letters had been so frequent and so beyond even what could have been hoped. It was the first time, however, that I perceived on the old woman's part a certain failure of lucidity. Jane's flight was clearly the great fact with her, but she spoke of it as if the fruit had now been plucked and the parenthesis closed. I don't know what sinking sense of still further physical duration I gathered, as a menace, from this first hint of her confusion of mind.

"My daughter has been; my daughter has been—" She kept saying it, but didn't say where; that seemed unnecessary, and she only repeated the words to her visitors with a face that was all puckers and yet now, save in so far as it expressed an ineffaceable complacency, all blankness. I think she rather wanted us to know how little she had stood in the way. It added to something—I scarce knew what—that I found myself desiring to extract privately from Becky. As our visit was to be of the shortest my opportunity—for one of the young ladies always came to the door with us—was at hand. Mrs. Rimmle, as we took leave, again sounded her phrase, but she added this time: "I'm so glad she's going to have always—"

I knew so well what she meant that, as she again dropped, looking at me queerly and becoming momentarily dim, I could help her out. "Going to have what *you* have?"

"Yes, yes—my privilege. Wonderful experience," she mumbled. She bowed to me a little as if I would understand. "She has things to tell."

I turned, slightly at a loss, to Becky. "She has then already arrived?"

Becky was at that moment looking a little strangely at her mother, who answered my question. "She reached New York this morning—she comes on to-day."

"Oh then—!" But I let the matter pass as I met Becky's eye—I saw there was a hitch somewhere. It was not she but Maria who came out with us; on which I cleared up the question of their sister's reappearance.

"Oh no, not to-night," Maria smiled; "that's only the way mother puts it. We shall see her about the end of November—the Hathaways are so indulgent. They kindly extend their tour."

"For *her* sake? How sweet of them!" my sister-in-law exclaimed.

I can see our friend's plain mild old face take on a deeper mildness, even though a higher colour, in the light of the open door. "Yes, it's for Jane they prolong it. And do you know what they write?" She gave us time, but it was too great a responsibility to guess. "Why that it has brought her out."

"Oh, I knew it *would!*" my companion sympathetically sighed. Maria put it more strongly still. "They say we wouldn't know her."

This sounded a little awful, but it was after all what I had expected.

3

My correspondent in Brookbridge came to me that Christmas, with my niece, to spend a week; and the arrangement had of course been prefaced by an exchange of letters, the first of which from my sister-in-law scarce took space for acceptance of my invitation before going on to say: "The Hathaways are back—but without Miss Jane!" She presented in a few words the situation thus created at Brookbridge, but was not yet, I gathered, fully in possession of the other one—the situation created in "Europe" by the presence there of that lady. The two together, however that might be, demanded, I quickly felt, all my attention, and perhaps my impatience to receive my relative was a little sharpened by my desire for the whole story. I had it at last, by the Christmas fire, and I may say without reserve that it gave me all I could have hoped for. I listened eagerly, after which I produced the comment: "Then she simply refused—"

"To budge from Florence? Simply. She had it out there with the poor Hathaways, who felt responsible for her safety, pledged to restore her to her mother's, to her sisters' hands, and showed herself in a light, they mention under their breath, that made their dear old hair stand on end. Do you know what, when they first got back, they said of her—at least it was *his* phrase—to two or three people?"

I thought a moment. "That she had 'tasted blood'?"

My visitor fairly admired me. "How clever of you to guess! It's exactly what he did say. She appeared—she continues to appear, it seems—in a new character."

I wondered a little. "But that's exactly—don't you remember?— what Miss Maria reported to us from them; that we 'wouldn't know her.'"

My sister-in-law perfectly remembered. "Oh yes—she broke out from the first. But when they left her she was worse."

"Worse?"

"Well, different—different from anything she ever *had* been or— for that matter—had had a chance to be." My reporter hung fire a moment, but presently faced me. "Rather strange and free and obstreperous."

"Obstreperous?" I wondered again.

"Peculiarly so, I inferred, on the question of not coming away. She wouldn't hear of it and, when they spoke of her mother, said she had given her mother up. She had thought she should like Europe, but didn't know she should like it so much. They had been fools to bring her if they expected to take her away. She was going to see what she could—she hadn't yet seen half. The end of it at any rate was that they had to leave her alone."

I seemed to see it all—to see even the scared Hathaways. "So she *is* alone?"

"She told them, poor thing, it appears, and in a tone they'll never forget, that she was in any case quite old enough to be. She cried—she quite went on—over not having come sooner. That's why the only way for her," my companion mused, *"is,* I suppose, to stay. They wanted to put her with some people or other—to find some American family. But she says she's on her own feet."

"And she's still in Florence?"

"No—I believe she was to travel. She's bent on the East."

I burst out laughing. "Magnificent Jane! It's most interesting. Only I feel that I distinctly *should* 'know' her. To my sense, always, I must tell you, she had it in her."

My relative was silent a little. "So it now appears Becky always felt."

"And yet pushed her off? Magnificent Becky!"

My companion met my eyes a moment. "You don't know the queerest part. I mean the way it has *most* brought her out."

I turned it over; I felt I should like to know—to that degree indeed that, oddly enough, I jocosely disguised my eagerness. "You don't mean she has taken to drink?"

My visitor had a dignity—and yet had to have a freedom. "She has taken to flirting."

I expressed disappointment. "Oh she took to *that* long ago. Yes," I declared at my kinswoman's stare, "she positively flirted—with *me!*"

The stare perhaps sharpened. "Then you flirted with *her?*"

"How else could I have been as sure as I wanted to be? But has she means?"

"Means to flirt?"—my friend looked an instant as if she spoke literally. "I don't understand about the means—though of course they have something. But I have my impression," she went on. "I think that Becky—" It seemed almost too grave to say.

But *I* had no doubts. "That Becky's backing her?"

She brought it out. "Financing her."

"Stupendous Becky! So that morally then—"

"Becky's quite in sympathy. But isn't it too odd?" my sister-in-law asked.

"Not in the least. Didn't we know, as regards Jane, that Europe was to bring her out? Well, it has also brought out Rebecca."

"It has indeed!" my companion indulgently sighed. "So what would it do if she were there?"

"I should like immensely to see. And we *shall* see."

"Do you believe then she'll still go?"

"Certainly. She *must.*"

But my friend shook it off. "She won't."

"She shall!" I retorted with a laugh. But the next moment I said: "And what does the old woman say?"

"To Jane's behaviour? Not a word—never speaks of it. She talks now much less than she used—only seems to wait. But it's my belief she thinks."

"And—do you mean—knows?"

"Yes, knows she's abandoned. In her silence there she takes it in."

"It's her way of making Jane pay?" At this, somehow, I felt more serious. "Oh dear, dear—she'll disinherit her!"

When in the following June I went on to return my sister-in-law's visit the first object that met my eyes in her little white parlour was a figure that, to my stupefaction, presented itself for the moment as that of Mrs. Rimmle. I had gone to my room after arriving and had come down when dressed; the apparition I speak of had arisen in the interval. Its ambiguous character lasted, however, but a second or two —I had taken Becky for her mother because I knew no one but her mother of that extreme age. Becky's age was quite startling; it had made a great stride, though, strangely enough, irrecoverably seated as she now was in it, she had a wizened brightness that I had scarcely yet seen in her. I remember indulging on this occasion in two silent observations: one on the article of my not having hitherto been conscious of her full resemblance to the old lady, and the other to the effect that, as I had said to my sister-in-law at Christmas, "Europe," even as reaching her only through Jane's sensibilities, had really at last brought her out. She was in fact "out" in a manner of which this encounter offered to my eyes a unique example: it was the single hour, often as I had been at Brookbridge, of my meeting her elsewhere than in her mother's drawing-room. I surmise that, besides being adjusted to her more marked time of life, the garments she wore abroad, and in particular her little plain bonnet, presented points of resemblance to the close sable sheath and the quaint old head-gear that, in the white house behind the elms, I had from far back associated with the eternal image in the stiff chair. Of course I immediately spoke of Jane, showing an interest and asking for news; on which she answered me with a smile, but not at all as I had expected.

"*Those* are not really the things you want to know—where she is, whom she's with, how she manages and where she's going next—oh no!" And the admirable woman gave a laugh that was somehow both light and sad—sad, in particular, with a strange long weariness. "What you do want to know is when she's coming back."

I shook my head very kindly, but out of a wealth of experience that, I flattered myself, was equal to Miss Becky's. "I do know it. Never."

Miss Becky exchanged with me at this a long deep look. "Never."

We had, in silence, a little luminous talk about it, at the end of which she seemed to have told me the most interesting things. "And how's your mother?" I then enquired.

She hesitated, but finally spoke with the same serenity. "My mother's all right. You see she's not alive."

"Oh Becky!" my sister-in-law pleadingly interjected.

But Becky only addressed herself to me. "Come and see if she is. *I* think she isn't—but Maria perhaps isn't so clear. Come at all events and judge and tell me."

It was a new note, and I was a little bewildered. "Ah but I'm not a doctor!"

"No, thank God—you're not. That's why I ask you." And now she said good-bye.

I kept her hand a moment. "*You're* more alive than ever!"

"I'm very tired." She took it with the same smile, but for Becky it was much to say.

4

"Not alive," the next day, was certainly what Mrs. Rimmle looked when, arriving in pursuit of my promise, I found her, with Miss Maria, in her usual place. Though wasted and shrunken she still occupied her high-backed chair with a visible theory of erectness, and her intensely aged face—combined with something dauntless that belonged to her very presence and that was effective even in this extremity—might have been that of some immemorial sovereign, of indistinguishable sex, brought forth to be shown to the people in disproof of the rumour of extinction. Mummified and open-eyed she looked at me, but I had no impression that she made me out. I had come this time without my sister-in-law, who had frankly pleaded to me—which also, for a daughter of Brookbridge, was saying much—that the house had grown too painful. Poor Miss Maria excused Miss Becky on the score of her not being well—and that, it struck me, was saying most of all. The absence of the others gave the occasion a different note; but I talked with Miss Maria for five minutes and recognised that—save for her saying, of her own movement, anything about Jane—she now spoke as if her mother had lost hearing or sense, in fact both, alluding freely and distinctly, though indeed favourably, to her condition. "She has expected your visit and much enjoys it," my entertainer said, while the old woman, soundless and motionless, simply fixed me without expression. Of course there was little to keep me; but I became aware as I rose to go that there was more than I had supposed.

On my approaching her to take leave Mrs. Rimmle gave signs of consciousness. "Have you heard about Jane?"

I hesitated, feeling a responsibility, and appealed for direction to Maria's face. But Maria's face was troubled, was turned altogether to her mother's. "About her life in Europe?" I then rather helplessly asked.

The old lady fronted me on this in a manner that made me feel silly. "Her life?"—and her voice, with this second effort, came out stronger. "Her death, if you please."

"Her death?" I echoed, before I could stop myself, with the accent of deprecation.

Miss Maria uttered a vague sound of pain, and I felt her turn away, but the marvel of her mother's little unquenched spark still held me. "Jane's dead. We've heard," said Mrs. Rimmle. "We've heard from—where is it we've heard from?" She had quite revived—she appealed to her daughter.

The poor old girl, crimson, rallied to her duty. "From Europe."

Mrs. Rimmle made at us both a little grim inclination of the head. "From Europe." I responded, in silence, by a deflexion from every rigour, and, still holding me, she went on: "And now Rebecca's going."

She had gathered by this time such emphasis to say it that again, before I could help myself, I vibrated in reply. "To Europe—now?" It was as if for an instant she had made me believe it.

She only stared at me, however, from her wizened mask; then her eyes followed my companion. "Has she gone?"

"Not yet, mother." Maria tried to treat it as a joke, but her smile was embarrassed and dim.

"Then where is she?"

"She's lying down."

The old woman kept up her hard queer gaze, but directing it after a minute to me. "She's going."

"Oh some day!" I foolishly laughed; and on this I got to the door, where I separated from my younger hostess, who came no further.

Only, as I held the door open, she said to me under cover of it and very quietly: "It's poor mother's idea."

I saw—it was her idea. Mine was—for some time after this, even after I had returned to New York and to my usual occupations—that I should never again see Becky. I had seen her for the last time, I believed, under my sister-in-law's roof, and in the autumn it was given to me to hear from that fellow admirer that she had succumbed at last to the situation. The day of the call I have just described had been a date in the process of her slow shrinkage—it was literally the first time she had, as they said at Brookbridge, given up. She had been ill for years, but the other state of health in the contemplation of which she had spent so much of her life had left her till too late no margin for heeding it. The power of attention came at last simply in the form of the discovery that it *was* too late; on which, naturally, she had given up more and more. I had heard indeed, for weeks before, by letter, how Brookbridge had watched her do so; in consequence of which the end found me in a manner prepared. Yet in spite of my preparation there remained with me a soreness, and when I was next—it was some six months later—on the scene of her martyrdom I fear I replied with an almost rabid negative to the question put to me in due course by my kinswoman. "Call on them? Never again!"

I went none the less the very next day. Everything was the same in the sunny parlour—everything that most mattered, I mean: the centenarian mummy in the high chair and the tributes, in the little frames on the walls, to the celebrity of its late husband. Only Maria Rimmle was different: if Becky, on my last seeing her, had looked as old as her mother, Maria—save that she moved about—looked older. I remember she moved about, but I scarce remember what she said; and indeed what was there to say? When I risked a question, however, she found a reply.

"But *now* at least—?" I tried to put it to her suggestively.

At first she was vague. " 'Now'?"

"Won't Miss Jane come back?"

Oh the headshake she gave me! "Never." It positively pictured to me, for the instant, a well-preserved woman, a rich ripe *seconde jeunesse* by the Arno.

"Then that's only to make more sure of your finally joining her."

Maria Rimmle repeated her headshake. "Never."

We stood so a moment bleakly face to face; I could think of no attenuation that would be particularly happy. But while I tried I heard a hoarse gasp that fortunately relieved me—a signal strange and at first formless from the occupant of the high-backed chair. "Mother wants to speak to you," Maria then said.

So it appeared from the drop of the old woman's jaw, the expression of her mouth opened as if for the emission of sound. It was somehow difficult to me to seem to sympathise without hypocrisy, but, so far as a step nearer could do that, I invited communication. "Have you heard where Becky's gone?" the wonderful witch's white lips then extraordinarily asked.

It drew from Maria, as on my previous visits, an uncontrollable groan, and this in turn made me take time to consider. As I considered, however, I had an inspiration. "To Europe?"

I must have adorned it with a strange grimace, but my inspiration had been right. "To Europe," said Mrs. Rimmle.

the jolly corner

"Every one asks me what I 'think' of everything," said Spencer Brydon; "and I make answer as I can—begging or dodging the question, putting them off with any nonsense. It wouldn't matter to any of them really," he went on, "for, even were it possible to meet in that stand-and-deliver way so silly a demand on so big a subject, my 'thoughts' would still be almost altogether about something that concerns only myself." He was talking to Miss Staverton, with whom for a couple of months now he had availed himself of every possible occasion to talk; this disposition and this resource, this comfort and support, as the situation in fact presented itself, having promptly enough taken the first place in the considerable array of rather unattenuated surprises attending his so strangely belated return to America. Everything was somehow a surprise; and that might be natural when one had so long and so consistently neglected everything, taken pains to give surprises so much margin for play. He had given them more than thirty years—thirty-three, to be exact; and they now seemed to him to have organised their performance quite on the scale of that licence. He had been twenty-three on leaving New York—he was fifty-six today: unless indeed he were to reckon as he had sometimes, since his repatriation, found himself feeling; in which case he would have lived longer than is often allotted to man. It would have taken a century, he repeatedly said to himself, and said also to Alice Staverton, it would have taken a longer absence and a more averted mind than those even of which he had been guilty, to pile up the differences, the newnesses, the queernesses, above all the bignesses, for the better or the worse, that at present assaulted his vision wherever he looked.

The great fact all the while however had been the incalculability;

Reprinted from Volume XVII of *The Novels and Tales of Henry James;* copyright 1909 by Charles Scribner's Sons, 1937 by Henry James; used by permission of the publishers.

since he *had* supposed himself, from decade to decade, to be allowing, and in the most liberal and intelligent manner, for brilliancy of change. He actually saw that he had allowed for nothing; he missed what he would have been sure of finding, he found what he would never have imagined. Proportions and values were upside-down; the ugly things he had expected, the ugly things of his far-away youth, when he had too promptly waked up to a sense of the ugly—these uncanny phenomena placed him rather, as it happened, under the charm; whereas the "swagger" things, the modern, the monstrous, the famous things, those he had more particularly, like thousands of ingenuous enquirers every year, come over to see, were exactly his sources of dismay. They were as so many set traps for displeasure, above all for reaction, of which his restless tread was constantly pressing the spring. It was interesting, doubtless, the whole show, but it would have been too disconcerting hadn't a certain finer truth saved the situation. He had distinctly not, in this steadier light, come over *all* for the monstrosities; he had come, not only in the last analysis but quite on the face of the act, under an impulse with which they had nothing to do. He had come—putting the thing pompously—to look at his "property," which he had thus for a third of a century not been within four thousand miles of; or, expressing it less sordidly, he had yielded to the humour of seeing again his house on the jolly corner, as he usually, and quite fondly, described it—the one in which he had first seen the light, in which various members of his family had lived and had died, in which the holidays of his overschooled boyhood had been passed and the few social flowers of his chilled adolescence gathered, and which, alienated then for so long a period, had, through the successive deaths of his two brothers and the termination of old arrangements, come wholly into his hands. He was the owner of another, not quite so "good"—the jolly corner having been, from far back, superlatively extended and consecrated; and the value of the pair represented his main capital, with an income consisting, in these later years, of their respective rents which (thanks precisely to their original excellent type) had never been depressingly low. He could live in "Europe," as he had been in the habit of living, on the product of these flourishing New York leases, and all the better since, that of the second structure, the mere number in its long row, having within a twelvemonth fallen in, renovation at a high advance had proved beautifully possible.

These were items of property indeed, but he had found himself since his arrival distinguishing more than ever between them. The house within the street, two bristling blocks westward, was already in course of reconstruction as a tall mass of flats; he had acceded, some time before, to overtures for this conversion—in which, now that it was going forward, it had been not the least of his astonishments to find himself able, on the spot, and though without a previous ounce of such experience, to participate with a certain intelligence, almost with a certain authority. He had lived his life with his back so turned to such concerns and his face addressed to those of so different an order that he scarce knew what to make of this lively stir, in a compartment of his mind never yet penetrated, of a capacity for business and a sense for construction. These virtues, so common all round him now, had been dormant in his own organism—where it might be said of them perhaps that they had slept the sleep of the just. At present, in the splendid autumn weather—the autumn at least was a pure boon in the terrible place—he loafed about his "work" undeterred, secretly agitated; not in the least "minding" that the whole proposition, as they said, was vulgar and sordid, and ready to climb ladders, to walk the plank, to handle materials and look wise about them, to ask questions, in fine, and challenge explanations and really "go into" figures.

It amused, it verily quite charmed him; and, by the same stroke, it amused, and even more, Alice Staverton, though perhaps charming her perceptibly less. She wasn't however going to be better off for it, as *he* was—and so astonishingly much: nothing was now likely, he knew, ever to make her better off than she found herself, in the afternoon of life, as the delicately frugal possessor and tenant of the small house in Irving Place to which she had subtly managed to cling through her almost unbroken New York career. If he knew the way to it now better than to any other address among the dreadful multiplied numberings which seemed to him to reduce the whole place to some vast ledger-page, overgrown, fantastic, of ruled and criss-crossed lines and figures—if he had formed, for his consolation, that habit, it was really not a little because of the charm of his having encountered and recognised, in the vast wilderness of the wholesale, breaking through the mere gross generalisation of wealth and force and success, a small still scene where items and shades, all delicate things, kept the sharpness of the notes of a high voice perfectly trained, and where economy hung about like the scent of a garden. His old friend lived with one maid and herself, dusted her relics and trimmed her lamps and polished her silver; she stood off, in the awful modern crush, when she could, but she sallied forth and did battle when the challenge was really to "spirit," the spirit she after all confessed to, proudly and a little shyly, as to that of the better time, that of *their* common, their quite far-away and antediluvian social period and order. She made use of the street-cars when need be, the terrible things that people scrambled for as the panic-stricken at sea scramble for the boats; she affronted, inscrutably, under stress, all the public concussions and ordeals; and yet, with that slim mystifying grace of her appearance, which defied you to say if she were a fair young woman who looked older through trouble, or a fine smooth older one who looked young through successful indifference; with her precious reference, above all, to memories and histories into which he could enter, she was as exquisite for him as some pale pressed flower (a rarity to begin with), and, failing other sweetnesses, she was a sufficient reward of his effort. They had communities of knowledge, "their" knowledge (this discriminating possessive was always on her lips) of presences of the other age, presences all overlaid, in his case, by the experience of a man and the freedom of a wanderer, overlaid by pleasure, by infidelity, by passages of life that were strange and dim to her, just by "Europe" in short, but still unobscured, still exposed and cherished, under that pious visitation of the spirit from which she had never been diverted.

She had come with him one day to see how his "apartment-house" was rising; he had helped her over gaps and explained to her plans, and while they were there had happened to have, before her, a brief but lively discussion with the man in charge, the representative of the building-firm that had undertaken his work. He had found him-self quite "standing-up" to this personage over a failure on the latter's part to observe some detail of one of their noted conditions, and had so lucidly argued his case that, besides ever so prettily flushing, at the time, for sympathy in his triumph, she had afterwards said to him (though to a slightly greater effect of irony) that he had clearly for too many years neglected a real gift. If he had but stayed at home he would have anticipated the inventor of the sky-scraper. If he had but stayed at home he would have discovered his genius in time really to start some new variety of awful architectural hare and run it till it burrowed in a gold-mine. He was to remember these words, while the weeks elapsed, for the small silver ring they had sounded over the queerest and deepest of his own lately most disguised and most muffled vibrations.

It had begun to be present to him after the first fortnight, it had broken out with the oddest abruptness, this particular wanton wonder-ment: it met him there—and this was the image under which he himself judged the matter, or at least, not a little, thrilled and flushed with it—very much as he might have been met by some strange figure, some unexpected occupant, at a turn of one of the dim passages of an empty house. The quaint analogy quite hauntingly remained with him, when he didn't indeed rather improve it by a still intenser form: that of his opening a door behind which he would have made sure of finding nothing, a door into a room shuttered and void, and yet so coming, with a great suppressed start, on some quite erect confronting presence, something planted in the middle of the place and facing him through the dusk. After that visit to the house in construction he walked with his companion to see the other and always so much the better one, which in the eastward direction formed one of the corners, the "jolly" one precisely, of the street now so generally dishonoured and disfigured in its westward reaches, and of the comparatively conservative Avenue. The Avenue still had pretensions, as Miss Staverton said, to decency; the old people had mostly gone, the old names were unknown, and here and there an old association seemed to stray, all vaguely, like some very aged person, out too late, whom you might meet and feel the impulse to watch or follow, in kindness, for safe restoration to shelter.

They went in together, our friends; he admitted himself with his key, as he kept no one there, he explained, preferring, for his reasons, to leave the place empty, under a simple arrangement with a good woman living in the neighbourhood and who came for a daily hour to open windows and dust and sweep. Spencer Brydon had his reasons and was growingly aware of them; they seemed to him better each time he was there, though he didn't name them all to his companion, any more than he told her, as yet how often, how quite absurdly often, he himself came. He only let her see for the present, while they walked through the great blank rooms, that absolute vacancy reigned and that, from top to bottom, there was nothing but Mrs. Muldoon's broomstick, in a corner, to tempt the burglar. Mrs. Muldoon was then on the premises, and she loquaciously attended the visitors, preceding them from room to room and pushing back shutters and throwing up sashes —all to show them, as she remarked, how little there was to see. There was little indeed to see in the great gaunt shell where the main dispositions and the general apportionment of space, the style of an age of ampler allowances, had nevertheless for its master their honest pleading message, affecting him as some good old servant's, some lifelong retainer's appeal for a character, or even for a retiring-pension; yet it was also a remark of Mrs. Muldoon's that, glad as she was to oblige him by her noonday round, there was a request she greatly hoped he would never make of her. If he should wish her for any reason to come in after dark she would just tell him, if he "plased," that he must ask it of somebody else.

The fact that there was nothing to see didn't militate for the worthy woman against what one *might* see, and she put it frankly to Miss Staverton that no lady could be expected to like, could she? "craping up to thim top storeys in the ayvil hours." The gas and the electric light were off the house, and she fairly evoked a gruesome vision of her march through the great grey rooms—so many of them as there were too!—with her glimmering taper. Miss Staverton met her honest glare with a smile and the profession that she herself certainly would recoil from such an adventure. Spencer Brydon meanwhile held his peace—for the moment; the question of the "evil" hours in his old home had already become too grave for him. He had begun some time since to "crape," and he knew just why a packet of candles addressed to that pursuit had been stowed by his own hand, three weeks before, at the back of the drawer of the fine old sideboard that occupied, as a "fixture," the deep recess in the dining-room. Just now he laughed at his companions—quickly however changing the subject; for the reason that, in the first place, his laugh struck him even at that moment as starting the odd echo, the conscious human resonance (he scarce knew how to qualify it) that sounds made while he was there alone sent back to his ear or his fancy; and that, in the second, he imagined Alice Staverton for the instant on the point of asking him, with a divination, if he ever so prowled. There were divinations he was unprepared for, and he had at all events averted enquiry by the time Mrs. Muldoon had left them, passing on to other parts.

There was happily enough to say, on so consecrated a spot, that could be said freely and fairly; so that a whole train of declarations was precipitated by his friend's having herself broken out, after a yearning look round: "But I hope you don't mean they want you to pull *this* to pieces!" His answer came, promptly, with his re-awakened wrath: it was of course exactly what they wanted, and what they were "at" him for, daily, with the iteration of people who couldn't for their life understand a man's liability to decent feelings. He had found the place, just as it stood and beyond what he could express, an interest and a joy. There were values other than the beastly rent-values, and in short, in short—! But it was thus Miss Staverton took him up. "In short you're to make so good a thing of your sky-scraper that, living in luxury on *those* ill-gotten gains, you can afford for a while to be sentimental here!" Her smile had for him, with the words, the particular mild irony with which he found half her talk suffused; an irony without bitterness and that came, exactly, from her having so much imagination—not, like the cheap sarcasms with which one heard most people, about the world of "society," bid for the reputation of cleverness, from nobody's really having any. It was agreeable to him at this very moment to be sure that when he had answered, after a brief demur, "Well yes: so, precisely, you may put it!" her imagination would still do him justice. He explained that even if never a dollar were to come to him from the other house he would nevertheless cherish this one; and he dwelt, further, while they lingered and wandered, on the fact of the stupefaction he was already exciting, the positive mystification he felt himself create.

He spoke of the value of all he read into it, into the mere sight of the walls, mere shapes of the rooms, mere sound of the floors, mere feel, in his hand, of the old silver-plated knobs of the several mahogany doors, which suggested the pressure of the palms of the dead; the seventy years of the past in fine that these things represented, the annals of nearly three generations, counting his grandfather's, the one that had ended there, and the impalpable ashes of his long-extinct youth, afloat in the very air like microscopic motes. She listened to everything; she was a woman who answered intimately but who utterly didn't chatter. She scattered abroad therefore no cloud of words; she could assent, she could agree, above all she could encourage, without doing that. Only at the last she went a little further than he had done himself. "And then how do you know? You may still, after all, want to live here." It rather indeed pulled him up, for it wasn't what he had been thinking, at least in her sense of the words. "You mean I may decide to stay on for the sake of it?"

"Well, *with* such a home—!" But, quite beautifully, she had too much tact to dot so monstrous an *i,* and it was precisely an illustration of the way she didn't rattle. How could any one—of any wit—insist on any one else's "wanting" to live in New York?

"Oh," he said, "I *might* have lived here (since I had my opportunity early in life); I might have put in here all these years. Then everything would have been different enough—and, I dare say, 'funny' enough. But that's another matter. And then the beauty of it—I mean of my perversity, of my refusal to agree to a 'deal'—is just in the total absence of a reason. Don't you see that if I had a reason about the matter at all it would *have* to be the other way, and would then be inevitably a reason of dollars? There are no reasons here *but* of dollars. Let us therefore have none whatever—not the ghost of one."

They were back in the hall then for departure, but from where they stood the vista was large, through an open door, into the great square main saloon, with its almost antique felicity of brave spaces between windows. Her eyes came back from that reach and met his own a moment. "Are you very sure the 'ghost' of one doesn't, much rather, serve—?"

He had a positive sense of turning pale. But it was as near as they were then to come. For he made answer, he believed, between a glare and a grin: "Oh ghosts—of course the place must swarm with them! I should be ashamed of it if it didn't. Poor Mrs. Muldoon's right, and it's why I haven't asked her to do more than look in."

Miss Staverton's gaze again lost itself, and things she didn't utter, it was clear, came and went in her mind. She might even for the minute, off there in the fine room, have imagined some element dimly gathering. Simplified like the death-mask of a handsome face, it perhaps produced for her just then an effect akin to the stir of an expression in the "set" commemorative plaster. Yet whatever her impression may have been she produced instead a vague platitude. "Well, if it were only furnished and lived in—!"

She appeared to imply that in case of its being still furnished he might have been a little less opposed to the idea of a return. But she passed straight into the vestibule, as if to leave her words behind her, and the next moment he had opened the house-door and was standing with her on the steps. He closed the door and, while he re-pocketed his key, looking up and down, they took in the comparatively harsh actuality of the Avenue, which reminded him of the assault of the outer light of the Desert on the traveller emerging from an Egyptian tomb. But he risked before they stepped into the street his gathered answer to her speech. "For me it *is* lived in. For me it *is* furnished." At which it was easy for her to sigh "Ah yes—!" all vaguely and discreetly; since his parents and his favourite sister, to say nothing of other kin, in numbers, had run their course and met their end there. That represented, within the walls, ineffaceable life.

It was a few days after this that, during an hour passed with her again, he had expressed his impatience of the too flattering curiosity—among the people he met—about his appreciation of New York. He had arrived at none at all that was socially producible, and as for that matter of his "thinking" (thinking the better or the worse of anything there) he was wholly taken up with one subject of thought. It was mere vain egoism, and it was moreover, if she liked, a morbid obsession. He found all things come back to the question of what he personally might have been, how he might have led his life and "turned out," if he had not so, at the outset, given it up. And confessing for the first time to the intensity within him of this absurd speculation—which but proved also, no doubt, the habit of too selfishly thinking—he affirmed

221

the impotence there of any other source of interest, any other native appeal. "What would it have made of me, what would it have made of me? I keep for ever wondering, all idiotically; as if I could possibly know! I see what it has made of dozens of others, those I meet, and it positively aches within me, to the point of exasperation, that it would have made something of me as well. Only I can't make out *what,* and the worry of it, the small rage of curiosity never to be satisfied, brings back what I remember to have felt, once or twice, after judging best, for reasons, to burn some important letter unopened. I've been sorry, I've hated it—I've never known what was in the letter. You may of course say it's a trifle—!"

"I don't say it's a trifle," Miss Staverton gravely interrupted.

She was seated by her fire, and before her, on his feet and rest-less, he turned to and fro between this intensity of his idea and a fitful and unseeing inspection, through his single eyeglass, of the dear little old objects on her chimney-piece. Her interruption made him for an instant look at her harder. "I shouldn't care if you did!" he laughed, however; "and it's only a figure, at any rate, for the way I now feel. *Not* to have followed my perverse young course—and almost in the teeth of my father's curse, as I may say; not to have kept it up, so, 'over there,' from that day to this, without a doubt or a pang; not, above all, to have liked it, to have loved it, so much, loved it, no doubt, with such an abysmal conceit of my own preference: some variation from *that,* I say, must have produced some different effect for my life and for my 'form.' I should have stuck here—if it had been possible; and I was too young, at twenty-three, to judge, *pour deux sous,* whether it *were* possible. If I had waited I might have seen it was, and then I might have been, by staying here, something nearer to one of these types who have been hammered so hard and made so keen by their conditions. It isn't that I admire them so much—the question of any charm in them, or of any charm, beyond that of the rank money-passion, exerted by their conditions *for* them, has nothing to do with the matter: it's only a question of what fantastic, yet perfectly possible, development of my own nature I mayn't have missed. It comes over me that I had then a strange *alter ego* deep down somewhere within me, as the full-blown flower is in the small tight bud, and that I just took the course, I just transferred him to the climate, that blighted him for once and for ever."

"And you wonder about the flower," Miss Staverton said. "So do I, if you want to know; and so I've been wondering these several weeks. I believe in the flower," she continued, "I feel it would have been quite splendid, quite huge and monstrous."

"Monstrous above all!" her visitor echoed; "and I imagine, by the same stroke, quite hideous and offensive."

"You don't believe that," she returned; "if you did you wouldn't wonder. You'd know, and that would be enough for you. What you feel—and what I feel *for* you—is that you'd have had power."

"You'd have liked me that way?" he asked.

She barely hung fire. "How should I not have liked you?"

"I see. You'd have liked me, have preferred me, a billionaire!"

"How should I not have liked you?" she simply again asked.

He stood before her still—her question kept him motionless. He took it in, so much there was of it; and indeed his not otherwise meeting it testified to that. "I know at least what I am," he simply went on; "the other side of the medal's clear enough. I've not been edifying—I believe I'm thought in a hundred quarters to have been barely decent. I've followed strange paths and worshipped strange gods; it must have come to you again and again—in fact you've admitted to me as much—that I was leading, at any time these thirty years, a selfish frivolous scandalous life. And you see what it has made of me."

She just waited, smiling at him. "You see what it has made of *me.*"

"Oh you're a person whom nothing can have altered. You were born to be what you are, anywhere, anyway: you've the perfection nothing else could have blighted. And don't you see how, without my exile, I shouldn't have been waiting till now—?" But he pulled up for the strange pang.

"The great thing to see," she presently said, "seems to me to be that it has spoiled nothing. It hasn't spoiled your being here at last. It hasn't spoiled this. It hasn't spoiled your speaking—" She also however faltered.

He wondered at everything her controlled emotion might mean. "Do you believe then—too dreadfully!—that I *am* as good as I might ever have been?"

"Oh no! Far from it!" With which she got up from her chair and was nearer to him. "But I don't care," she smiled.

"You mean I'm good enough?"

She considered a little. "Will you believe it if I say so? I mean will you let that settle your question for you?" And then as if making out in his face that he drew back from this, that he had some idea which, however absurd, he couldn't yet bargain away: "Oh you don't care either—but very differently: you don't care for anything but yourself."

223

Spencer Brydon recognised it—it was in fact what he had absolutely professed. Yet he importantly qualified. *"He* isn't myself. He's
the just so totally other person. But I do want to see him," he added.
"And I can. And I shall."

Their eyes met for a minute while he guessed from something
in hers that she divined his strange sense. But neither of them otherwise expressed it, and her apparent understanding, with no protesting
shock, no easy derision, touched him more deeply than anything yet,
constituting for his stifled perversity, on the spot, an element that was
like breathable air. What she said however was unexpected. "Well,
I've seen him."

"You—?"

"I've seen him in a dream."

"Oh a 'dream'—!" It let him down.

"But twice over," she continued. "I saw him as I see you now."

"You've dreamed the same dream—?"

"Twice over," she repeated. "The very same."

This did somehow a little speak to him, as it also gratified him.
"You dream about me at that rate?"

"Ah about *him!*" she smiled.

His eyes again sounded her. "Then you know all about him."
And as she said nothing more: "What's the wretch like?"

She hesitated, and it was as if he were pressing her so hard that,
resisting for reasons of her own, she had to turn away. "I'll tell you
some other time!"

2

It was after this that there was most of a virtue for him, most
of a cultivated charm, most of a preposterous secret thrill, in the
particular form of surrender to his obsession and of address to what
he more and more believed to be his privilege. It was what in these
weeks he was living for—since he really felt life to begin but after
Mrs. Muldoon had retired from the scene and, visiting the ample house
from attic to cellar, making sure he was alone, he knew himself in safe
possession and, as he tacitly expressed it, let himself go. He sometimes
came twice in the twenty-four hours; the moments he liked best were
those of gathering dusk, of the short autumn twilight; this was the
time of which, again and again, he found himself hoping most. Then
he could, as seemed to him, most intimately wander and wait, linger
and listen, feel his fine attention, never in his life before so fine, on

the pulse of the great vague place: he preferred the lampless hour and only wished he might have prolonged each day the deep crepuscular spell. Later—rarely much before midnight, but then for a considerable vigil—he watched with his glimmering light; moving slowly, holding it high, playing it far, rejoicing above all, as much as he might, in open vistas, reaches of communication between rooms and by passages; the long straight chance or show, as he would have called it, for the revelation he pretended to invite. It was a practice he found he could perfectly "work" without exciting remark; no one was in the least the wiser for it; even Alice Staverton, who was moreover a well of discretion, didn't quite fully imagine.

He let himself in and let himself out with the assurance of calm proprietorship; and accident so far favoured him that, if a fat Avenue "officer" had happened on occasion to see him entering at eleven-thirty, he had never yet, to the best of his belief, been noticed as emerging at two. He walked there on the crisp November nights, arrived regularly at the evening's end; it was as easy to do this after dining out as to take his way to a club or to his hotel. When he left his club, if he hadn't been dining out, it was ostensibly to go to his hotel; and when he left his hotel, if he had spent a part of the evening there, it was ostensibly to go to his club. Everything was easy in fine; everything conspired and promoted: there was truly even in the strain of his experience something that glossed over, something that salved and simplified, all the rest of consciousness. He circulated, talked, renewed, loosely and pleasantly, old relations—met indeed, so far as he could, new expectations and seemed to make out on the whole that in spite of the career, of such different contacts, which he had spoken of to Miss Staverton as ministering so little, for those who might have watched it, to edification, he was positively rather liked than not. He was a dim secondary social success—and all with people who had truly not an idea of him. It was all mere surface sound, this murmur of their welcome, this popping of their corks—just as his gestures of response were the extravagant shadows, emphatic in proportion as they meant little, of some game of *ombres chinoises*. He projected himself all day, in thought, straight over the bristling line of hard unconscious heads and into the other, the real, the waiting life; the life that, as soon as he had heard behind him the click of his great house-door, began for him, on the jolly corner, as beguilingly as the slow opening bars of some rich music follows the tap of the conductor's wand.

He always caught the first effect of the steel point of his stick on the old marble of the hall pavement, large black-and-white squares

225

that he remembered as the admiration of his childhood and that had then made in him, as he now saw, for the growth of an early conception of style. This effect was the dim reverberating tinkle as of some far-off bell hung who should say where?—in the depths of the house, of the past, of that mystical other world that might have flourished for him had he not, for weal or woe, abandoned it. On this impression he did ever the same thing; he put his stick noiselessly away in a corner—feeling the place once more in the likeness of some great glass bowl, all precious concave crystal, set delicately humming by the play of a moist finger round its edge. The concave crystal held, as it were, this mystical other world, and the indescribably fine murmur of its rim was the sigh there, the scarce audible pathetic wail to his strained ear, of all the old baffled forsworn possibilities. What he did therefore by this appeal of his hushed presence was to wake them into such measure of ghostly life as they might still enjoy. They were shy, all but unappeasably shy, but they weren't really sinister; at least they weren't as he had hitherto felt them—before they had taken the Form he so yearned to make them take, the Form he at moments saw himself in the light of fairly hunting on tiptoe, the points of his evening-shoes, from room to room and from storey to storey.

That was the essence of his vision—which was all rank folly, if one would, while he was out of the house and otherwise occupied, but which took on the last verisimilitude as soon as he was placed and posted. He knew what he meant and what he wanted; it was as clear as the figure on a cheque presented in demand for cash. His *alter ego* "walked"—that was the note of his image of him, while his image of his motive for his own odd pastime was the desire to waylay him and meet him. He roamed, slowly, warily, but all restlessly, he himself did —Mrs. Muldoon had been right, absolutely, with her figure of their "craping"; and the presence he watched for would roam restlessly too. But it would be as cautious and as shifty; the conviction of its probable, in fact its already quite sensible, quite audible evasion of pursuit grew for him from night to night, laying on him finally a rigour to which nothing in his life had been comparable. It had been the theory of many superficially-judging persons, he knew, that he was wasting that life in a surrender to sensations, but he had tasted of no pleasure so fine as his actual tension, had been introduced to no sport that demanded at once the patience and the nerve of this stalking of a creature more subtle, yet at bay perhaps more formidable, than any beast of the forest. The terms, the comparisons, the very practices of the chase positively came again into play; there were even moments when passages of his occasional experience as a sportsman, stirred memories, from his younger time, of moor and mountain and desert, revived for him—and to the increase of his keenness—by the tremendous force of analogy. He found himself at moments—once he had placed his single light on some mantel-shelf or in some recess—stepping back into shelter or shade, effacing himself behind a door or in an embrasure, as he had sought of old the vantage of rock and tree; he found himself holding his breath and living in the joy of the instant, the supreme suspense created by big game alone.

He wasn't afraid (though putting himself the question as he believed gentlemen on Bengal tiger-shoots or in close quarters with the great bear of the Rockies had been known to confess to having put it); and this indeed—since here at least he might be frank!—because of the impression, so intimate and so strange, that he himself produced as yet a dread, produced certainly a strain, beyond the liveliest he was likely to feel. They fell for him into categories, they fairly became familiar, the signs, for his own perception, of the alarm his presence and his vigilance created; though leaving him always to remark, portentously, on his probably having formed a relation, his probably enjoying a consciousness, unique in the experience of man. People enough, first and last, had been in terror of apparitions, but who had ever before so turned the tables and become himself, in the apparitional world, an incalculable terror? He might have found this sublime had he quite dared to think of it; but he didn't too much insist, truly, on that side of his privilege. With habit and repetition he gained to an extraordinary degree the power to penetrate the dusk of distances and the darkness of corners, to resolve back into their innocence the treacheries of uncertain light, the evil-looking forms taken in the gloom by mere shadows, by accidents of the air, by shifting effects of perspective; putting down his dim luminary he could still wander on without it, pass into other rooms and, only knowing it was there behind him in case of need, see his way about, visually project for his purpose a comparative clearness. It made him feel, this acquired faculty, like some monstrous stealthy cat; he wondered if he would have glared at these moments with large shining yellow eyes, and what it mightn't verily be, for the poor hard-pressed *alter ego,* to be confronted with such a type.

He liked however the open shutters; he opened everywhere those Mrs. Muldoon had closed, closing them as carefully afterwards, so that she shouldn't notice: he liked—oh this he did like, and above all in the upper rooms!—the sense of the hard silver of the autumn stars through the window-panes, and scarcely less the flare of the street-lamps below, the white electric lustre which it would have taken curtains to keep out. This was human actual social; this was of the world he had lived in, and he was more at his ease certainly for the countenance, coldly general and impersonal, that all the while and in spite of his detachment it seemed to give him. He had support of course mostly in the rooms at the wide front and the prolonged side; it failed him considerably in the central shades and the parts at the back. But if he sometimes, on his rounds, was glad of his optical reach, so none the less often the rear of the house affected him as the very jungle of his prey. The place was there more subdivided; a large "extension" in particular, where small rooms for servants had been multiplied, abounded in nooks and corners, in closets and passages, in the ramifications especially of an ample back staircase over which he leaned, many a time, to look far down—not deterred from his gravity even while aware that he might, for a spectator, have figured some solemn simpleton playing at hide-and-seek. Outside in fact he might himself make that ironic *rapprochement,* but within the walls, and in spite of the clear windows, his consistency was proof against the cynical light of New York.

It had belonged to that idea of the exasperated consciousness of his victim to become a real test for him; since he had quite put it to himself from the first that, oh distinctly! he could "cultivate" his whole perception. He had felt it as above all open to cultivation—which indeed was but another name for his manner of spending his time. He was bringing it on, bringing it to perfection, by practice; in consequence of which it had grown so fine that he was now aware of impressions, attestations of his general postulate, that couldn't have broken upon him at once. This was the case more specifically with a phenomenon at last quite frequent for him in the upper rooms, the recognition—absolutely unmistakeable, and by a turn dating from a particular hour, his resumption of his campaign after a diplomatic drop, a calculated absence of three nights—of his being definitely followed, tracked at a distance carefully taken and to the express end that he should the less confidently, less arrogantly, appear to himself merely to pursue. It worried, it finally quite broke him up, for it proved, of all the conceivable impressions, the one least suited to his book. He was kept in sight while remaining himself—as regards the essence of his position—sightless, and his only recourse then was in abrupt turns, rapid recoveries of ground. He wheeled about, retracing his steps, as if he might so catch in his face at least the stirred air of some other quick revolution. It was indeed true that his fully dislocalised thought of these manœuvres recalled to him Pantaloon, at the Christmas farce, buffeted and tricked from behind by ubiquitous Harlequin; but it left intact the influence of the conditions themselves each time he was re-exposed to them, so that in fact this association, had he suffered it to become constant, would on a certain side have but ministered to his intenser gravity. He had made, as I have said, to create on the premises the baseless sense of a reprieve, his three absences; and the result of the third was to confirm the after-effect of the second.

On his return, that night—the night succeeding his last inter-mission—he stood in the hall and looked up the staircase with a certainty more intimate than any he had yet known. "He's *there,* at the top, and waiting—not, as in general, falling back for disappearance. He's holding his ground, and it's the first time—which is a proof, isn't it? that something has happened for him." So Brydon argued with his hand on the banister and his foot on the lowest stair; in which position he felt as never before the air chilled by his logic. He himself turned cold in it, for he seemed of a sudden to know what now was involved. "Harder pressed?—yes, he takes it in, with its thus making clear to him that I've come, as they say, 'to stay.' He finally doesn't like and can't bear it, in the sense, I mean, that his wrath, his menaced interest, now balances with his dread. I've hunted him till he has 'turned': that, up there, is what has happened—he's the fanged or the antlered animal brought at last to bay." There came to him, as I say—but determined by an influence beyond my notation!—the acuteness of this certainty; under which however the next moment he had broken into a sweat that he would as little have consented to attribute to fear as he would have dared immediately to act upon it for enterprise. It marked none the less a prodigious thrill, a thrill that represented sudden dismay, no doubt, but also represented, and with the selfsame throb, the strangest, the most joyous, possibly the next minute almost the proudest, duplication of consciousness.

"He has been dodging, retreating, hiding, but now, worked up to anger, he'll fight!"—this intense impression made a single mouthful, as it were, of terror and applause. But what was wondrous was that the applause, for the felt fact, was so eager, since, if it was his other self he was running to earth, this ineffable identity was thus in the last resort not unworthy of him. It bristled there—somewhere near at hand, however unseen still—as the hunted thing, even as the trodden worm of the adage *must* at last bristle; and Brydon at this instant tasted probably of a sensation more complex than had ever before found itself consistent with sanity. It was as if it would have shamed him that a

229

character so associated with his own should triumphantly succeed in just skulking, should to the end not risk the open, so that the drop of this danger was, on the spot, a great lift of the whole situation. Yet with another rare shift of the same subtlety he was already trying to measure by how much more he himself might now be in peril of fear; so rejoicing that he could, in another form, actively inspire that fear, and simultaneously quaking for the form in which he might passively know it.

The apprehension of knowing it must after a little have grown in him, and the strangest moment of his adventure perhaps, the most memorable or really most interesting, afterwards, of his crisis, was the lapse of certain instants of concentrated conscious *combat,* the sense of a need to hold on to something, even after the manner of a man slipping and slipping on some awful incline; the vivid impulse, above all, to move, to act, to charge, somehow and upon something—to show himself, in a word, that he wasn't afraid. The state of "holding-on" was thus the state to which he was momentarily reduced; if there had been anything, in the great vacancy, to seize, he would presently have been aware of having clutched it as he might under a shock at home have clutched the nearest chair-back. He had been surprised at any rate—of this he *was* aware—into something unprecedented since his original appropriation of the place; he had closed his eyes, held them tight, for a long minute, as with that instinct of dismay and that terror of vision. When he opened them the room, the other contiguous rooms, extraordinarily, seemed lighter—so light, almost, that at first, he took the change for day. He stood firm, however that might be, just where he had paused; his resistance had helped him—it was as if there were something he had tided over. He knew after a little what this was—it had been in the imminent danger of flight. He had stiffened his will against going; without this he would have made for the stairs, and it seemed to him that, still with his eyes closed, he would have descended them, would have known how, straight and swiftly, to the bottom.

Well, as he had held out, here he was—still at the top, among the more intricate upper rooms and with the gauntlet of the others, of all the rest of the house, still to run when it should be his time to go. He would go at his time—only at his time: didn't he go every night very much at the same hour? He took out his watch—there was light for that: it was scarcely a quarter past one, and he had never withdrawn so soon. He reached his lodgings for the most part at two—with his walk of a quarter of an hour. He would wait for the last quarter—he wouldn't stir till then; and he kept his watch there with his eyes on it, reflecting while he held it that this deliberate wait, a wait with an effort, which he recognised, would serve perfectly for the attestation he desired to make. It would prove his courage—unless indeed the latter might most be proved by his budging at last from his place. What he mainly felt now was that, since he hadn't originally scuttled, he had his dignities—which had never in his life seemed so many—all to preserve and to carry aloft. This was before him in truth as a physical image, an image almost worthy of an age of greater romance. That remark indeed glimmered for him only to glow the next instant with a finer light; since what age of romance, after all, could have matched either the state of his mind or, "objectively," as they said, the wonder of his situation? The only difference would have been that, brandishing his dignities over his head as in a parchment scroll, he might then—that is in the heroic time—have proceeded downstairs with a drawn sword in his other grasp.

At present, really, the light he had set down on the mantel of the next room would have to figure his sword; which utensil, in the course of a minute, he had taken the requisite number of steps to possess himself of. The door between the rooms was open, and from the second another door opened to a third. These rooms, as he remembered, gave all three upon a common corridor as well, but there was a fourth, beyond them, without issue save through the preceding. To have moved, to have heard his step again, was appreciably a help; though even in recognising this he lingered once more a little by the chimney-piece on which his light had rested. When he next moved, just hesitating where to turn, he found himself considering a circumstance that, after his first and comparatively vague apprehension of it, produced in him the start that often attends some pang of recollection, the violent shock of having ceased happily to forget. He had come into sight of the door in which the brief chain of communication ended and which he now surveyed from the nearer threshold, the one not directly facing it. Placed at some distance to the left of this point, it would have admitted him to the last room of the four, the room without other approach or egress, had it not, to his intimate conviction, been closed *since* his former visitation, the matter probably of a quarter of an hour before. He stared with all his eyes at the wonder of the fact, arrested again where he stood and again holding his breath while he sounded its sense. Surely it had been *subsequently* closed—that is, it had been on his previous passage indubitably open!

He took it full in the face that something had happened between —that he couldn't not have noticed before (by which he meant on his original tour of all the rooms that evening) that such a barrier had exceptionally presented itself. He had indeed since that moment undergone an agitation so extraordinary that it might have muddled for him any earlier view; and he tried to convince himself that he might perhaps then have gone into the room and, inadvertently, automatically, on coming out, have drawn the door after him. The difficulty was that this exactly was what he never did; it was against his whole policy, as he might have said, the essence of which was to keep vistas clear. He had them from the first, as he was well aware, quite on the brain: the strange apparition, at the far end of one of them, of his baffled "prey" (which had become by so sharp an irony so little the term now to apply!) was the form of success his imagination had most cherished, projecting into it always a refinement of beauty. He had known fifty times the start of perception that had afterwards dropped; had fifty times gasped to himself "There" under some fond brief hallucination. The house, as the case stood, admirably lent itself; he might wonder at the taste, the native architecture of the particular time, which could rejoice so in the multiplication of doors—the opposite extreme to the modern, the actual almost complete proscription of them; but it had fairly contributed to provoke this obsession of the presence encountered telescopically, as he might say, focussed and studied in diminishing perspective and as by a rest for the elbow.

It was with these considerations that his present attention was charged—they perfectly availed to make what he saw portentous. He *couldn't,* by any lapse, have blocked that aperture; and if he hadn't, if it was unthinkable, why what else was clear but that there had been another agent? Another agent?—he had been catching, as he felt, a moment back, the very breath of him; but when had he been so close as in this simple, this logical, this completely personal act? It was so logical, that is, that one might have *taken* it for personal; yet for what did Brydon take it, he asked himself, while, softly panting, he felt his eyes almost leave their sockets. Ah this time at last they *were,* the two, the opposed projections of him, in presence; and this time, as much as one would, the question of danger loomed. With it rose, as not before, the question of courage—for what he knew the blank face of the door to say to him was "Show us how much you have!" It stared, it glared back at him with that challenge; it put to him the two alternatives: should he just push it open or not? Oh to have this consciousness was to *think*—and to think, Brydon knew, as he stood there, was with the lapsing moments, not to have acted! Not to have acted—that was the misery and the pang—was even still not to act; was in fact *all* to feel the thing in another, in a new and terrible way. How long did he pause and how long did he debate? There was presently nothing to measure it; for his vibration had already changed—as just by the effect of its intensity. Shut up there, at bay, defiant, and with the prodigy of the thing palpably proveably *done,* thus giving notice like some stark signboard—under that accession of accent the situation itself had turned; and Brydon at last remarkably made up his mind on what it had turned to.

It had turned altogether to a different admonition; to a supreme hint, for him, of the value of Discretion! This slowly dawned, no doubt —for it could take its time; so perfectly, on his threshold, had he been stayed, so little as yet had he either advanced or retreated. It was the strangest of all things that now when, by his taking ten steps and applying his hand to a latch, or even his shoulder and his knee, if necessary, to a panel, all the hunger of his prime need might have been met, his high curiosity crowned, his unrest assuaged—it was amazing, but it was also exquisite and rare, that insistence should have, at a touch, quite dropped from him. Discretion—he jumped at that; and yet not, verily, at such a pitch, because it saved his nerves or his skin, but because, much more valuably, it saved the situation. When I say he "jumped" at it I feel the consonance of this term with the fact that—at the end indeed of I know not how long—he did move again, he crossed straight to the door. He wouldn't touch it—it seemed now that he might *if* he would: he would only just wait there a little, to show, to prove, that he wouldn't. He had thus another station, close to the thin partition by which revelation was denied him; but with his eyes bent and his hands held off in a mere intensity of stillness. He listened as if there had been something to hear, but this attitude, while it lasted, was his own communication. "If you won't then—good: I spare you and I give up. You affect me as by the appeal positively for pity: you convince me that for reasons rigid and sublime—what do I know?—we both of us should have suffered. I respect them then, and, though moved and privileged as, I believe, it has never been given to man, I retire, I renounce—never, on my honour, to try again. So rest for ever—and let *me!*"

That, for Brydon, was the deep sense of this last demonstration—solemn, measured, directed, as he felt it to be. He brought it to a close, he turned away; and now verily he knew how deeply he had been stirred. He retraced his steps, taking up his candle, burnt, he observed,

233

well-nigh to the socket, and marking again, lighten it as he would, the distinctness of his footfall; after which, in a moment, he knew himself at the other side of the house. He did here what he had not yet done at these hours—he opened half a casement, one of those in the front, and let in the air of the night; a thing he would have taken at any time previous for a sharp rupture of his spell. His spell was broken now, and it didn't matter—broken by his concession and his surrender, which made it idle henceforth that he should ever come back. The empty street—its other life so marked even by the great lamplit vacancy —was within call, within touch; he stayed there as to be in it again, high above it though he was still perched; he watched as for some comforting common fact, some vulgar human note, the passage of a scavenger or a thief, some night-bird however base. He would have blessed that sign of life; he would have welcomed positively the slow approach of his friend the policeman, whom he had hitherto only sought to avoid, and was not sure that if the patrol had come into sight he mightn't have felt the impulse to get into relation with it, to hail it, on some pretext, from his fourth floor.

The pretext that wouldn't have been too silly or too compromising, the explanation that would have saved his dignity and kept his name, in such a case, out of the papers, was not definite to him: he was so occupied with the thought of recording his Discretion—as an effect of the vow he had just uttered to his intimate adversary—that the importance of this loomed large and something had overtaken all ironically his sense of proportion. If there had been a ladder applied to the front of the house, even one of the vertiginous perpendiculars employed by painters and roofers and sometimes left standing overnight, he would have managed somehow, astride of the window-sill, to compass by outstretched leg and arm that mode of descent. If there had been some such uncanny thing as he had found in his room at hotels, a workable fire-escape in the form of notched cable or a canvas shoot, he would have availed himself of it as a proof—well, of his present delicacy. He nursed that sentiment, as the question stood, a little in vain, and even—at the end of he scarce knew, once more, how long—found it, as by the action on his mind of the failure of response of the outer world, sinking back to vague anguish. It seemed to him he had waited an age for some stir of the great grim hush; the life of the town was itself under a spell—so unnaturally, up and down the whole prospect of known and rather ugly objects, the blankness and the silence lasted. Had they ever, he asked himself, the hard-faced houses, which had begun to look livid in the dim dawn, had they ever spoken so little to any need of his spirit? Great builded voids, great crowded stillnesses put on, often, in the heart of cities, for the small hours, a sort of sinister mask, and it was of this large collective negation that Brydon presently became conscious—all the more that the break of day was, almost incredibly, now at hand, proving to him what a night he had made of it.

He looked again at his watch, saw what had become of his time-values (he had taken hours for minutes—not, as in other tense situations, minutes for hours) and the strange air of the streets was but the weak, the sullen flush of a dawn in which everything was still locked up. His choked appeal from his own open window had been the sole note of life, and he could but break off at last as for a worse despair. Yet while so deeply demoralised he was capable again of an impulse denoting—at least by his present measure—extraordinary resolution; of retracing his steps to the spot where he had turned cold with the extinction of his last pulse of doubt as to there being in the place another presence than his own. This required an effort strong enough to sicken him; but he had his reason, which overmastered for the moment everything else. There was the whole of the rest of the house to traverse, and how should he screw himself to that if the door he had seen closed were at present open? He could hold to the idea that the closing had practically been for him an act of mercy, a chance offered him to descend, depart, get off the ground and never again profane it. This conception held together, it worked; but what it meant for him depended now clearly on the amount of forbearance his recent action, or rather his recent inaction, had engendered. The image of the "presence," whatever it was, waiting there for him to go—this image had not yet been so concrete for his nerves as when he stopped short of the point at which certainty would have come to him. For, with all his resolution, or more exactly with all his dread, he did stop short—he hung back from really seeing. The risk was too great and his fear too definite: it took at this moment an awful specific form.

He knew—yes, as he had never known anything—that, *should* he see the door open, it would all too abjectly be the end of him. It would mean that the agent of his shame—for his shame was the deep abjection—was once more at large and in general possession; and what glared him thus in the face was the act that this would determine for him. It would send him straight about to the window he had left open, and by that window, be long ladder and dangling rope as absent as they would, he saw himself uncontrollably insanely fatally take his way

235

to the street. The hideous chance of this he at least could avert; but he could only avert it by recoiling in time from assurance. He had the whole house to deal with, this fact was still there; only he now knew that uncertainty alone could start him. He stole back from where he had checked himself—merely to do so was suddenly like safety—and, making blindly for the greater staircase, left gaping rooms and sounding passages behind. Here was the top of the stairs, with a fine large dim descent and three spacious landings to mark off. His instinct was all for mildness, but his feet were harsh on the floors, and, strangely, when he had in a couple of minutes become aware of this, it counted somehow for help. He couldn't have spoken, the tone of his voice would have scared him, and the common conceit or resource of "whistling in the dark" (whether literally or figuratively) have appeared basely vulgar; yet he liked none the less to hear himself go, and when he had reached his first landing—taking it all with no rush, but quite steadily —that stage of success drew from him a gasp of relief.

The house, withal, seemed immense, the scale of space again inordinate; the open rooms, to no one of which his eyes deflected, gloomed in their shuttered state like mouths of caverns; only the high skylight that formed the crown of the deep well created for him a medium in which he could advance, but which might have been, for queerness of colour, some watery under-world. He tried to think of something noble, as that his property was really grand, a splendid possession; but this nobleness took the form too of the clear delight with which he was finally to sacrifice it. They might come in now, the builders, the destroyers—they might come as soon as they would. At the end of two flights he had dropped to another zone, and from the middle of the third, with only one more left, he recognised the influence of the lower windows, of half-drawn blinds, of the occasional gleam of street-lamps, of the glazed spaces of the vestibule. This was the bottom of the sea, which showed an illumination of its own and which he even saw paved—when at a given moment he drew up to sink a long look over the banisters—with the marble squares of his childhood. By that time indubitably he felt, as he might have said in a commoner cause, better; it had allowed him to stop and draw breath, and the ease increased with the sight of the old black-and-white slabs. But what he most felt was that now surely, with the element of impunity pulling him as by hard firm hands, the case was settled for what he might have seen above had he dared that last look. The closed door, blessedly remote now, was still closed—and he had only in short to reach that of the house.

He came down further, he crossed the passage forming the access to the last flight; and if here again he stopped an instant it was almost for the sharpness of the thrill of assured escape. It made him shut his eyes—which opened again to the straight slope of the remainder of the stairs. Here was impunity still, but impunity almost excessive; inasmuch as the sidelights and the high fan-tracery of the entrance were glimmering straight into the hall; an appearance produced, he the next instant saw, by the fact that the vestibule gaped wide, that the hinged halves of the inner door had been thrown far back. Out of that again the *question* sprang at him, making his eyes, as he felt, half-start from his head, as they had done, at the top of the house, before the sign of the other door. If he had left that one open, hadn't he left this one closed, and wasn't he now in *most* immediate presence of some inconceivable occult activity? It was as sharp, the question, as a knife in his side, but the answer hung fire still and seemed to lose itself in the vague darkness to which the thin admitted dawn, glimmering archwise over the whole outer door, made a semi-circular margin, a cold silvery nimbus that seemed to play a little as he looked—to shift and expand and contract.

It was as if there had been something within it, protected by indistinctness and corresponding in extent with the opaque surface behind, the painted panels of the last barrier to his escape, of which the key was in his pocket. The indistinctness mocked him even while he stared, affected him as somehow shrouding or challenging certitude, so that after faltering an instant on his step he let himself go with the sense that here *was* at last something to meet, to touch, to take, to know —something all unnatural and dreadful, but to advance upon which was the condition for him either of liberation or of supreme defeat. The penumbra, dense and dark, was the virtual screen of a figure which stood in it as still as some image erect in a niche or as some black-vizored sentinel guarding a treasure. Brydon was to know afterwards, was to recall and make out, the particular thing he had believed during the rest of his descent. He saw, in its great grey glimmering margin, the central vagueness diminish, and he felt it to be taking the very form toward which, for so many days, the passion of his curiosity had yearned. It gloomed, it loomed, it was something, it was somebody, the prodigy of a personal presence.

Rigid and conscious, spectral yet human, a man of his own substance and stature waited there to measure himself with his power to dismay. This only could it be—this only till he recognised, with his advance, that what made the face dim was the pair of raised hands that covered it and in which, so far from being offered in defiance, it was buried as for dark deprecation. So Brydon, before him, took him in; with every fact of him now, in the higher light, hard and acute—his planted stillness, his vivid truth, his grizzled bent head and white masking hands, his queer actuality of evening-dress, of dangling double eyeglass, of gleaming silk lappet and white linen, of pearl button and gold watch-guard and polished shoe. No portrait by a great modern master could have presented him with more intensity, thrust him out of his frame with more art, as if there had been "treatment," of the consummate sort, in his every shade and salience. The revulsion, for our friend, had become, before he knew it, immense—this drop, in the act of apprehension, to the sense of his adversary's inscrutable manœuvre. That meaning at least, while he gaped, it offered him; for he could but gape at his other self in this other anguish, gape as a proof that *he,* standing there for the achieved, the enjoyed, the triumphant life, couldn't be faced in his triumph. Wasn't the proof in the splendid covering hands, strong and completely spread?—so spread and so intentional that, in spite of a special verity that surpassed every other, the fact that one of these hands had lost two fingers, which were reduced to stumps, as if accidentally shot away, the face was effectually guarded and saved.

"Saved," though, *would* it be?—Brydon breathed his wonder till the very impunity of his attitude and the very insistence of his eyes produced, as he felt, a sudden stir which showed the next instant as a deeper portent, while the head raised itself, the betrayal of a braver purpose. The hands, as he looked, began to move, to open; then, as if deciding in a flash, dropped from the face and left it uncovered and presented. Horror, with the sight, had leaped into Brydon's throat, gasping there in a sound he couldn't utter; for the bared identity was too hideous as *his,* and his glare was the passion of his protest. The face, *that* face, Spencer Brydon's?—he searched it still, but looking away from it in dismay and denial, falling straight from his height of sublimity. It was unknown, inconceivable, awful, disconnected from any possibility—! He had been "sold," he inwardly moaned, stalking such game as this: the presence before him was a presence, the horror within him a horror, but the waste of his nights had been only grotesque and the success of his adventure an irony. Such an identity fitted his at *no* point, made its alternative monstrous. A thousand times yes, as it came upon him nearer now—the face was the face of a stranger. It came upon him nearer now, quite as one of those expanding fantastic images projected by the magic lantern of childhood; for the stranger, whoever he might be, evil, odious, blatant, vulgar, had advanced as for aggression, and he knew himself give ground. Then harder pressed still, sick with the force of his shock, and falling back as under the hot breath and the roused passion of a life larger than his own, a rage of personality before which his own collapsed, he felt the whole vision turn to darkness and his very feet give way. His head went round; he was going; he had gone.

3

What had next brought him back, clearly—though after how long?—was Mrs. Muldoon's voice, coming to him from quite near, from so near that he seemed presently to see her as kneeling on the ground before him while he lay looking up at her; himself not wholly on the ground, but half-raised and upheld—conscious, yes, of tenderness of support and, more particularly, of a head pillowed in extraordinary softness and faintly refreshing fragrance. He considered, he wondered, his wit but half at his service; then another face intervened, bending more directly over him, and he finally knew that Alice Staverton had made her lap an ample and perfect cushion to him, and that she had to this end seated herself on the lowest degree of the staircase, the rest of his long person remaining stretched on his old black-and-white slabs. They were cold, these marble squares of his youth; but *he* somehow was not, in this rich return of consciousness—the most wonderful hour, little by little, that he had ever known, leaving him, as it did, so gratefully, so abysmally passive, and yet as with a treasure of intelligence waiting all round him for quiet appropriation; dissolved, he might call it, in the air of the place and producing the golden glow of a late autumn afternoon. He had come back, yes—come back from further away than any man but himself had ever travelled; but it was strange how with this sense what he had come back *to* seemed really the great thing, and as if his prodigious journey had been all for the sake of it. Slowly but surely his consciousness grew, his vision of his state thus completing itself: he had been miraculously *carried* back—lifted and carefully borne as from where he had been picked up, the uttermost end of an interminable grey passage. Even with this he was suffered to rest, and what had now brought him to knowledge was the break in the long mild motion.

It had brought him to knowledge, to knowledge—yes, this was

the beauty of his state; which came to resemble more and more that of a man who has gone to sleep on some news of a great inheritance, and then, after dreaming it away, after profaning it with matters strange to it, has waked up again to serenity of certitude and has only to lie and watch it grow. This was the drift of his patience—that he had only to let it shine on him. He must moreover, with intermissions, still have been lifted and borne; since why and how else should he have known himself, later on, with the afternoon glow intenser, no longer at the foot of his stairs—situated as these now seemed at that dark other end of his tunnel—but on a deep window-bench of his high saloon, over which had been spread, couch-fashion, a mantle of soft stuff lined with grey fur that was familiar to his eyes and that one of his hands kept fondly feeling as for its pledge of truth. Mrs. Muldoon's face had gone, but the other, the second he had recognised, hung over him in a way that showed how he was still propped and pillowed. He took it all in, and the more he took it the more it seemed to suffice: he was as much at peace as if he had had food and drink. It was the two women who had found him, on Mrs. Muldoon's having plied, at her usual hour, her latch-key—and on her having above all arrived while Miss Staverton still lingered near the house. She had been turning away, all anxiety, from worrying the vain bell-handle—her calculation having been of the hour of the good woman's visit; but the latter, blessedly, had come up while she was still there, and they had entered together. He had then lain, beyond the vestibule, very much as he was lying now—quite, that is, as he appeared to have fallen, but all so wondrously without bruise or gash; only in a depth of stupor. What he most took in, however, at present, with the steadier clearance, was that Alice Staverton had for a long unspeakable moment not doubted he was dead.

"It must have been that I *was*." He made it out as she held him. "Yes—I can only have died. You brought me literally to life. Only," he wondered, his eyes rising to her, "only, in the name of all the benedictions, how?"

It took her but an instant to bend her face and kiss him, and something in the manner of it, and in the way her hands clasped and locked his head while he felt the cool charity and virtue of her lips, something in all this beatitude somehow answered everything. "And now I keep you," she said.

"Oh keep me, keep me!" he pleaded while her face still hung over him: in response to which it dropped again and stayed close, clingingly close. It was the seal of their situation—of which he tasted the impress for a long blissful moment in silence. But he came back. "Yet how did you know—?"

"I was uneasy. You were to have come, you remember—and you had sent no word."

"Yes, I remember—I was to have gone to you at one today." It caught on to their "old" life and relation—which were so near and so far. "I was still out there in my strange darkness—where was it, what was it? I must have stayed there so long." He could but wonder at the depth and the duration of his swoon.

"Since last night?" she asked with a shade of fear for her possible indiscretion.

"Since this morning—it must have been: the cold dim dawn of today. Where have I been," he vaguely wailed, "where have I been?" He felt her hold him close, and it was as if this helped him now to make in all security his mild moan. "What a long dark day!"

All in her tenderness she had waited a moment. "In the cold dim dawn?" she quavered.

But he had already gone on piecing together the parts of the whole prodigy. "As I didn't turn up you came straight—?"

She barely cast about. "I went first to your hotel—where they told me of your absence. You had dined out last evening and hadn't been back since. But they appeared to know you had been at your club."

"So you had the idea of *this*—?"

"Of what?" she asked in a moment.

"Well—of what has happened."

"I believed at least you'd have been here. I've known, all along," she said, "that you've been coming."

" 'Known' it—?"

"Well, I've believed it. I said nothing to you after that talk we had a month ago—but I felt sure. I knew you *would*," she declared.

"That I'd persist, you mean?"

"That you'd see him."

"Ah but I didn't!" cried Brydon with his long wail. "There's somebody—an awful beast; whom I brought, too horribly, to bay. But it's not me."

At this she bent over him again, and her eyes were in his eyes. "No—it's not you." And it was as if, while her face hovered, he might have made out in it, hadn't it been so near, some particular meaning

241

blurred by a smile. "No, thank heaven," she repeated—"it's not you! Of course it wasn't to have been."

"Ah but it *was*," he gently insisted. And he stared before him now as he had been staring for so many weeks. "I was to have known myself."

"You couldn't!" she returned consolingly. And then reverting, and as if to account further for what she had herself done, "But it wasn't only *that*, that you hadn't been at home," she went on. "I waited till the hour at which we had found Mrs. Muldoon that day of my going with you; and she arrived, as I've told you, while, failing to bring any one to the door, I lingered in my despair on the steps. After a little, if she hadn't come, by such a mercy, I should have found means to hunt her up. But it wasn't," said Alice Staverton, as if once more with her fine intention—"it wasn't only that."

His eyes, as he lay, turned back to her. "What more then?"

She met it, the wonder she had stirred. "In the cold dim dawn, you say? Well, in the cold dim dawn of this morning I too saw you."

"Saw *me*—?"

"Saw *him*," said Alice Staverton. "It must have been at the same moment."

He lay an instant taking it in—as if he wished to be quite reasonable. "At the same moment?"

"Yes—in my dream again, the same one I've named to you. He came back to me. Then I knew it for a sign. He had come to you."

At this Brydon raised himself; he had to see her better. She helped him when she understood his movement, and he sat up, steadying himself beside her there on the window-bench and with his right hand grasping her left. "*He* didn't come to me."

"You came to yourself," she beautifully smiled.

"Ah I've come to myself now—thanks to you, dearest. But this brute, with his awful face—this brute's a black stranger. He's none of *me*, even as I *might* have been," Brydon sturdily declared.

But she kept the clearness that was like the breath of infallibility. "Isn't the whole point that you'd have been different?"

He almost scowled for it. "As different as *that*—?"

Her look again was more beautiful to him than the things of this world. "Haven't you exactly wanted to know *how* different? So this morning," she said, "you appeared to me."

"Like *him*?"

"A black stranger!"

"Then how did you know it was I?"

"Because, as I told you weeks ago, my mind, my imagination, had worked so over what you might, what you mightn't have been— to show you, you see, how I've thought of you. In the midst of that you came to me—that my wonder might be answered. So I knew," she went on; "and believed that, since the question held you too so fast, as you told me that day, you too would see for yourself. And when this morning I again saw I knew it would be because you had—and also then, from the first moment, because you somehow wanted me. *He* seemed to tell me of that. So why," she strangely smiled, "shouldn't I like him?"

It brought Spencer Brydon to his feet. "You 'like' that horror—?"

"I *could* have liked him. And to me," she said, "he was no horror. I had accepted him."

" 'Accepted'—?" Brydon oddly sounded.

"Before, for the interest of his difference—yes. And as *I* didn't disown him, as *I* knew him—which you at last, confronted with him in his difference, so cruelly didn't, my dear—well, he must have been, you see, less dreadful to me. And it may have pleased him that I pitied him."

She was beside him on her feet, but still holding his hand—still with her arm supporting him. But though it all brought for him thus a dim light, "You 'pitied' him?" he grudgingly, resentfully asked.

"He has been unhappy; he has been ravaged," she said.

"And haven't I been unhappy? Am not I—you've only to look at me!—ravaged?"

"Ah I don't say I like him *better*," she granted after a thought. "But he's grim, he's worn—and things have happened to him. He doesn't make shift, for sight, with your charming monocle."

"No"—it struck Brydon: "I couldn't have sported mine 'downtown.' They'd have guyed me there."

"His great convex pince-nez—I saw it, I recognised the kind—is for his poor ruined sight. And his poor right hand—!"

"Ah!" Brydon winced—whether for his proved identity or for his lost fingers. Then, "He has a million a year," he lucidly added. "But he hasn't you."

"And he isn't—no, he isn't—*you!*" she murmured as he drew her to his breast.

Joel Chandler Harris

FREE JOE AND THE REST OF THE WORLD

Joel Chandler Harris was born near Eatonton, Georgia, in 1848, and at thirteen was already working on *The Countryman,* a small weekly newspaper published on a neighboring plantation. The editor of the newspaper, Joseph Addison Turner, had a well-stocked library, where the boy indulged fully the taste for good reading instilled in him by his mother, Mary Harris. While he was learning to set type and continuing his education by wide reading, he was also, through his association with the slaves on the Turner plantation, becoming intimately acquainted with the speech and folklore of the Negro. He was later able to say, perhaps with complete truthfulness, that not a single Uncle Remus story had been fabricated entirely from his own imagination, and clearly this association accounts in large part for his unexcelled accuracy as a writer of Negro dialect.

A precocious youth, he was soon contributing articles to *The Countryman,* and when this paper ceased publication after the war, Harris worked on newspapers in Macon, New Orleans, and Savannah before he joined the staff of the Atlanta *Constitution* in 1876, a paper with which he remained associated until 1906, two years prior to his death. His Uncle Remus stories began to appear in the *Constitution* in 1878-1879. They proved to be so popular both in the South and in the North that the first collection in book form, *Uncle Remus: His Songs and His Sayings,* became a classic almost immediately after its publication in 1880. Thereafter, for the remainder of Harris' life, additional Uncle Remus volumes appeared at frequent intervals, some of which are *Nights with Uncle Remus* (1883), *Uncle Remus and His Friends* (1892), *Mr. Rabbit at Home* (1895), *The Tar-Baby and Other Rhymes of Uncle Remus* (1904), and *Uncle*

245

Remus and Br'er Rabbit (1906). A masterly presentation of the dialect, folk wisdom, and character of the Old South Negro, the Uncle Remus stories are the greatest achievement of Harris. Their popularity, however, tends to obscure the variety and excellence of his stories using different materials and characters— the poor white, the moonshiner mountaineer at war with the ineffectual revenue agent, the aristocratic plantation owner, and, above all, numerous other types and varieties of the Negro character. Among the volumes in which such stories appear are *Mingo, and Other Sketches in Black and White* (1884), *Free Joe, and Other Georgian Sketches* (1887), *Daddy Jake the Runaway, and Other Stories Told After Dark* (1889), and *The Chronicles of Aunt Minervy Ann* (1899).

"Free Joe and the Rest of the World" depicts the situation of a freed slave in the ante-bellum South. Without means of a livelihood, persecuted by the slave owner, cut off from association with slaves, and otherwise isolated from society except for the casual relationship with the poor whites, Joe ironically carries a heavy burden in being "free." In this story, as in all his others, the vividly drawn characters and the accurate dialect, whether of Negro or white, illustrate Harris' belief that "the very marrow and essence of all literary art is its localism." Nevertheless, he opposed narrow sectionalism, holding that "literature that is Georgian or Southern is necessarily American, and in the broadest sense."

free joe and the rest of the world

The name of Free Joe strikes humorously upon the ear of memory. It is impossible to say why, for he was the humblest, the simplest, and the most serious of all God's living creatures, sadly lacking in all those elements that suggest the humorous. It is certain, moreover, that in 1850 the sober-minded citizens of the little Georgian village of Hillsborough were not inclined to take a humorous view of Free Joe, and neither his name nor his presence provoked a smile. He was a black atom, drifting hither and thither without an owner, blown about by all the winds of circumstances and given over to shiftlessness.

The problems of one generation are the paradoxes of a succeeding one, particularly if war, or some such incident, intervenes to clarify the atmosphere and strengthen the understanding. Thus, in 1850, Free Joe represented not only a problem of large concern, but, in the watchful eyes of Hillsborough, he was the embodiment of that vague and mysterious danger that seemed to be forever lurking on the outskirts of slavery, ready to sound a shrill and ghostly signal in the impenetrable swamps, and steal forth under the midnight stars to murder, rapine, and pillage,—a danger always threatening, and yet never assuming shape; intangible, and yet real; impossible, and yet not improbable. Across the serene and smiling front of safety, the pale outlines of the awful shadow of insurrection sometimes fell. With this invisible panorama as background, it was natural that the figure of Free Joe, simple and humble as it was, should assume undue proportions. Go where he would, do what he might, he could not escape the finger of observation and the kindling eye of suspicion. His lightest words were noted, his slightest actions marked.

Under all the circumstances it was natural that his peculiar condition should reflect itself in his habits and manners. The slaves laughed loudly day by day, but Free Joe rarely laughed. The slaves sang at their work and danced at their frolics, but no one ever heard Free Joe sing or saw him dance. There was something painfully plaintive and appealing in his attitude, something touching in his anxiety to please. He was of the friendliest nature, and seemed to be delighted when he could amuse the little children who had made a play-ground of the public square. At times he would please them by making his little dog Dan perform all sorts of curious tricks, or he would tell them quaint stories of the beasts of the field and birds of the air; and frequently he was coaxed into relating the story of his own freedom. The story was brief, but tragical.

In the year of our Lord 1840, when a negro-speculator of a sportive turn of mind reached the little village of Hillsborough on his way to the Mississippi region, with a caravan of likely negroes of both sexes, he found much to interest him. In that day and at that time there were a number of young men in the village who had not bound themselves over to repentance for the various misdeeds of the flesh. To these young men the negro-speculator (Major Frampton was his name) proceeded to address himself. He was a Virginian, he declared; and, to prove the statement, he referred all the festively inclined young men of Hillsborough to a barrel of peach-brandy in one of his covered wagons. In the minds of these young men there was less doubt in regard to the age and quality of the brandy than there was in regard to the negro-trader's birthplace. Major Frampton might or might not have been born in the Old Dominion—that was a matter for consideration and inquiry—but there could be no question as to the mellow pungency of the peach-brandy.

In his own estimation, Major Frampton was one of the most accomplished of men. He had summered at the Virginia Springs; he had been to Philadelphia, to Washington, to Richmond, to Lynchburg, and to Charleston, and had accumulated a great deal of experience which he found useful. Hillsborough was hid in the woods of middle Georgia, and its general aspect of innocence impressed him. He looked on the young men who had shown their readiness to test his peach-brandy, as overgrown country boys who needed to be introduced to some of the arts and sciences he had at his command. Thereupon the major pitched his tents, figuratively speaking, and became, for the time being, a part and parcel of the innocence that characterized Hillsborough. A wiser man would doubtless have made the same mistake.

The little village possessed advantages and seemed to be providentially arranged to fit the various enterprises that Major Frampton had in view. There was the auction-block in front of the stuccoed court-house, if he desired to dispose of a few of his negroes; there was a quarter-track, laid out to his hand and in excellent order, if he chose to enjoy the pleasures of horse-racing; there were secluded pine thickets within easy reach, if he desired to indulge in the exciting pastime of cock-fighting; and various lonely and unoccupied rooms in the second story of the tavern, if he cared to challenge the chances of dice or cards.

Major Frampton tried them all with varying luck, until he began his famous game of poker with Judge Alfred Wellington, a stately gentleman with a flowing white beard and mild blue eyes that gave him the appearance of a benevolent patriarch. The history of the game in which Major Frampton and Judge Alfred Wellington took part is something more than a tradition in Hillsborough, for there are still living three or four who sat around the table and watched its progress. It is said that at various stages of the game Major Frampton would destroy the cards with which they were playing, and send for a new pack, but the result was always the same. The mild blue eyes of Judge Wellington, with few exceptions, continued to overlook "hands" that were invincible—a habit they had acquired during a long and arduous course of training from Saratoga to New Orleans. Major Frampton lost his money, his horses, his wagons, and all his negroes but one, his body-servant. When his misfortune had reached this limit, the major adjourned the game. The sun was shining brightly, and all nature was cheerful. It is said that the major also seemed to be cheerful. However this may be, he visited the court-house and executed the papers that gave his body-servant his freedom. This being done, Major Frampton sauntered into a convenient pine thicket, and blew out his brains.

The negro thus freed came to be known as Free Joe. Compelled, under the law, to choose a guardian, he chose Judge Wellington, chiefly because his wife Lucinda was among the negroes won from Major Frampton. For several years Free Joe had what may be called a jovial time. His wife Lucinda was well provided for, and he found it a comparatively easy matter to provide for himself; so that, taking all the circumstances into consideration, it is not matter for astonishment that he became somewhat shiftless.

When Judge Wellington died, Free Joe's troubles began. The judge's negroes, including Lucinda, went to his half-brother, a man named Calderwood, who was a hard master and a rough customer generally—a man of many eccentricities of mind and character. His neighbors had a habit of alluding to him as "Old Spite"; and the name seemed to fit him so completely that he was known far and near as "Spite" Calderwood. He probably enjoyed the distinction the name gave him, at any rate he never resented it, and it was not often that he missed an opportunity to show that he deserved it. Calderwood's place was two or three miles from the village of Hillsborough, and Free Joe visited his wife twice a week, Wednesday and Saturday nights.

One Sunday morning he was sitting in front of Lucinda's cabin, when Calderwood happened to pass that way.

"Howdy, marster?" said Free Joe, taking off his hat.

"Who are you?" exclaimed Calderwood abruptly, halting and staring at the negro.

"I'm name' Joe, marster, I'm Lucindy's ole man."

"Who do you belong to?"

"Marse John Evans is my gyardeen, marster."

"Big name—gyardeen. Show your pass."

Free Joe produced the document, and Calderwood read it aloud slowly, as if he found it difficult to get at the meaning:

"To whom it may concern: This is to certify that the boy Joe Frampton has my permission to visit his wife Lucinda."

This was dated at Hillsborough, and signed *"John W. Evans."*

Calderwood read it twice, and then looked at Free Joe, elevating his eyebrows, and showing his discolored teeth.

"Some mighty big words in that there. Evans owns this place, I reckon. When's he comin' down to take hold?"

Free Joe fumbled with his hat. He was badly frightened.

"Lucindy say she speck you wouldn't min' my comin', long ez I behave, marster."

Calderwood tore the pass in pieces and flung it away.

"Don't want no free niggers 'round here," he exclaimed. "There's the big road. It'll carry you to town. Don't let me catch you here no more. Now, mind what I tell you."

Free Joe presented a shabby spectacle as he moved off with his little dog Dan slinking at his heels. It should be said in behalf of Dan, however, that his bristles were up, and that he looked back and growled. It may be that the dog had the advantage of insignificance, but it is difficult to conceive how a dog bold enough to raise his bristles under Calderwood's very eyes could be as insignificant as Free Joe. But both the negro and his little dog seemed to give a new and more dismal aspect to forlornness as they turned into the road and went towards Hillsborough.

After this incident Free Joe seemed to have clear ideas concerning his peculiar condition. He realized the fact that though he was free he was more helpless than any slave. Having no owner, every man was his master. He knew that he was the object of suspicion, and therefore all his slender resources (ah! how pitifully slender they were!) were devoted to winning, not kindness and appreciation, but toleration; all his efforts were in the direction of mitigating the circumstances that tended to make his condition so much worse than that of the negroes around him—negroes who had friends because they had masters.

So far as his own race was concerned, Free Joe was an exile. If the slaves secretly envied him his freedom (which is to be doubted, considering his miserable condition), they openly despised him, and lost no opportunity to treat him with contumely. Perhaps this was in some measure the result of the attitude which Free Joe chose to maintain toward them. No doubt his instinct taught him that to hold himself aloof from the slaves would be to invite from the whites the toleration which he coveted, and without which even his miserable condition would be rendered more miserable still.

His greatest trouble was the fact that he was not allowed to visit his wife; but he soon found a way out of this difficulty. After he had been ordered away from the Calderwood place, he was in the habit of wandering as far in that direction as prudence would permit. Near the Calderwood place, but not on Calderwood's land, lived an old man named Micajah Staley and his sister Becky Staley. These people were old and very poor. Old Micajah had a palsied arm and hand; but, in spite of this, he managed to earn a precarious living with his turning-lathe.

When he was a slave Free Joe would have scorned these representatives of a class known as poor white trash, but now he found them sympathetic and helpful in various ways. From the back door of the cabin he could hear the Calderwood negroes singing at night, and he fancied he could distinguish Lucinda's shrill treble rising above the other voices. A large poplar grew in the woods some distance from the Staley cabin, and at the foot of this tree Free Joe would sit for hours with his face turned towards Calderwood's. His little dog Dan would curl up in the leaves near by, and the two seemed to be as comfortable as possible.

One Saturday afternoon Free Joe, sitting at the foot of this friendly poplar, fell asleep. How long he slept he could not tell; but when he awoke little Dan was licking his face, the moon was shining brightly, and Lucinda his wife stood before him laughing. The dog, seeing that Free Joe was asleep, had grown somewhat impatient, and he concluded to make an excursion to the Calderwood place on his own account. Lucinda was inclined to give the incident a twist in the direction of superstition.

"I'z settin' down front er de fireplace," she said, "cookin' me some meat, w'en all of a sudden I year sumpin at de do'—scratch, scratch. I tuck'n tu'n de meat over, en make out I aint year it. Bimeby it come dar 'gin—scratch, scratch. I up en open de do', I did, en, bless de Lord! dar wuz little Dan, en it look like ter me dat his ribs done grow tergeer. I gin 'im some bread, en den, w'en he start out, I tuck'n foller 'im, kaze I say ter myse'f, maybe my nigger man mought be some'rs 'roun'. Dat ar little dog got sense, mon."

Free Joe laughed and dropped his hand lightly on Dan's head. For a long time after that, he had no difficulty in seeing his wife. He had only to sit by the poplar tree until little Dan could run and fetch her. But after a while the other negroes discovered that Lucinda was meeting Free Joe in the woods, and information of the fact soon reached Calderwood's ears. He said nothing; but one day he put Lucinda in his buggy, and carried her to Macon, sixty miles away. He carried her to Macon, and came back without her; and nobody in or around Hillsborough, or in that section, ever saw her again.

For many a night after that Free Joe sat in the woods and waited. Little Dan would run merrily off and be gone a long time, but he always came back without Lucinda. This happened over and over again. The "willis-whistlers" would call and call, like phantom huntsmen wandering on a far-off shore; the screech-owl would shake and shiver in the depths of the woods; the night-hawks, sweeping by on noiseless wings, would snap their beaks as though they enjoyed the huge joke of which Free Joe and little Dan were the victims; and the whip-poor-wills would cry to each other through the gloom. Each night seemed to be lonelier than the preceding, but Free Joe's patience was proof against loneliness. There came a time, however, when little Dan refused to go after Lucinda. When Free Joe motioned him in the direction of the Calderwood place, he would simply move about uneasily and whine; then he would curl up in the leaves and make himself comfortable.

One night, instead of going to the poplar-tree to wait for Lucinda, Free Joe went to the Staley cabin, and, in order to make his welcome good, as he expressed it, he carried with him an armful of fat-pine splinters. Miss Becky Staley had a great reputation in those parts as a fortune-teller, and the school-girls, as well as older people, often tested her powers in that direction, some in jest and some in earnest. Free Joe placed his humble offering of light-wood in the chimney-corner, and then seated himself on the steps, dropping his hat on the ground outside.

"Miss Becky," he said presently, "whar in de name er gracious you reckon Lucindy is?"

"Well, the Lord he'p the nigger!" exclaimed Miss Becky, in a tone that seemed to reproduce, by some curious agreement of sight with sound, her general aspect of peakedness. "Well, the Lord he'p the nigger! haint you been a-seein' her all this blessed time? She's over at old Spite Calderwood's, if she's anywhere, I reckon."

"No'm, dat I aint, Miss Becky. I aint seen Lucindy in now gwine on mighty nigh a mont'."

"Well, it haint a-gwine to hurt you," said Miss Becky, somewhat sharply. "In my day an' time it wuz allers took to be a bad sign when niggers got to honeyin' 'roun' an' gwine on."

"Yessum," said Free Joe, cheerfully assenting to the proposition—"yessum, dat's so, but me an' my ole 'oman, we 'uz raise tergeer, en dey aint bin many days w'en we 'uz 'way fum one 'n'er like we is now."

"Maybe she's up an' took up wi' some un else," said Micajah Staley from the corner. "You know what the sayin' is, 'New master, new nigger.'"

"Dat's so, dat's de sayin', but taint wid my ole 'oman like 'tis wid yuther niggers. Me en her wuz des natally raise up tergeer. Dey's lots likelier niggers dan w'at I is," said Free Joe, viewing his shabbiness with a critical eye, "but I know Lucindy mos' good ez I does little Dan dar—dat I does."

There was no reply to this, and Free Joe continued—

"Miss Becky, I wish you please, ma'am, take en run yo' kyards en see sump'n n'er 'bout Lucindy; kaze ef she sick, I'm gwine dar. Dey ken take en take me up en gimme a stroppin', but I'm gwine dar."

Miss Becky got her cards, but first she picked up a cup, in the bottom of which were some coffee grounds. These she whirled slowly round and round, ending finally by turning the cup upside down on the hearth and allowing it to remain in that position.

"I'll turn the cup first," said Miss Becky, "and then I'll run the cards and see what they say."

As she shuffled the cards the fire on the hearth burned slow, and in its fitful light the gray-haired, thin-featured woman seemed to deserve the weird reputation which rumor and gossip had given her. She shuffled the cards for some moments, gazing intently in the dying fire; then, throwing a piece of pine on the coals, she made three divisions of the pack, disposing them about in her lap. Then she took the first pile, ran the cards slowly through her fingers, and studied them carefully. To the first she added the second pile. The study of these was evidently not satisfactory. She said nothing, but frowned heavily; and the frown deepened as she added the rest of the cards until the entire fifty-two had passed in review before her. Though she frowned, she seemed to be deeply interested. Without changing the relative position of the cards, she ran them over again. Then she threw a larger piece of pine on the fire, shuffled the cards afresh, divided them into three piles, and subjected them to the same careful and critical examination.

"I can't tell the day when I've seed the cards run this a-way," she said after a while. "What is an' what aint, I'll never tell you; but I know what the cards sez."

"W'at does dey say, Miss Becky?" the negro inquired, in a tone the solemnity of which was heightened by its eagerness.

"They er runnin' quare. These here that I'm a lookin' at," said Miss Becky, "they stan' for the past. Them there, they er the present; and the t'others, they er the future. Here's a bundle"—tapping the ace of clubs with her thumb—"an' here's a journey as plain as the nose on a man's face. Here's Lucinda"—

"Whar she, Miss Becky?"

"Here she is—the queen of spades."

Free Joe grinned. The idea seemed to please him immensely.

"Well, well, well!" he exclaimed. "Ef dat don't beat my time! De queen er spades! W'en Lucindy year dat hit'll tickle 'er, sho'!"

Miss Becky continued to run the cards back and forth through her fingers.

"Here's a bundle an' a journey, and here's Lucinda. An' here's ole Spite Calderwood."

She held the cards toward the negro and touched the king of clubs.

"De Lord he'p my soul!" exclaimed Free Joe with a chuckle. "De faver's dar. Yesser, dat's him! W'at de matter 'long wid all un um, Miss Becky?"

The old woman added the second pile of cards to the first, and then the third, still running them through her fingers slowly and critically. By this time the piece of pine in the fireplace had wrapped itself in a mantle of flame, illuminating the cabin and throwing into strange relief the figure of Miss Becky as she sat studying the cards.

She frowned ominously at the cards and mumbled a few words to herself. Then she dropped her hands in her lap and gazed once more into the fire. Her shadow danced and capered on the wall and floor behind her, as if, looking over her shoulder into the future, it could behold a rare spectacle. After a while she picked up the cup that had been turned on the hearth. The coffee grounds, shaken around, presented what seemed to be a most intricate map.

"Here's the journey," said Miss Becky, presently; "here's the big road, here's rivers to cross, here's the bundle to tote." She paused and sighed. "They haint no names writ here, an' what it all means I'll never tell you. Cajy, I wish you'd be so good as to han' me my pipe."

"I haint no hand wi' the kyards," said Cajy, and he handed the pipe, "but I reckon I can patch out your misinformation, Becky, bekaze the other day, whiles I was a-fishin' up Mizzer Perdue's rolling-pin, I hearn a rattlin' in the road. I looked out, an' Spite Calderwood was a-drivin' by in his buggy, an' thar sot Lucinda by him. It'd in-about drapt out er my min'."

Free Joe sat on the door-sill and fumbled at his hat, flinging it from one hand to the other.

"You haint see um gwine back, is you, Marse Cajy?" he asked after a while.

"Ef they went back by this road," said Mr. Staley, with the air of one who is accustomed to weigh well his words, "it must 'a' bin endurin' of the time whiles I was asleep, bekase I haint bin no furder from my shop than to yon bed."

"Well, sir!" exclaimed Free Joe in an awed tone, which Mr. Staley seemed to regard as a tribute to his extraordinary power of statement.

"Ef it's my beliefs you want," continued the old man, "I'll pitch 'em at you fair and free. My beliefs is that Spite Calderwood is gone an' took Lucindy outen the county. Bless your heart and soul! when Spite Calderwood meets the Old Boy in the road they'll be a turrible scuffle. You mark what I tell you."

Free Joe, still fumbling with his hat, rose and leaned against the door-facing. He seemed to be embarrassed. Presently he said:

"I speck I better be gittin' 'long. Nex' time I see Lucindy, I'm gwine tell 'er w'at Miss Becky say 'bout de queen er spades—dat I is. If dat don't tickle 'er, dey aint no nigger 'oman never bin tickle'."

He paused a moment, as though waiting for some remark or comment, some confirmation of misfortune, or, at the very least, some endorsement of his suggestion that Lucinda would be greatly pleased to know that she had figured as the queen of spades; but neither Miss Becky nor her brother said anything.

"One minnit ridin' in the buggy, 'longside er Mars Spite, en de nex' highfalutin' 'roun' playin' de queen er spades. Mon, deze yer nigger gals gittin' up in de pictur's; dey sholy is."

With a brief "Good-night, Miss Becky, Mars Cajy," Free Joe went out into the darkness, followed by little Dan. He made his way to the poplar, where Lucinda had been in the habit of meeting him, and sat down. He sat there a long time; he sat there until little Dan, growing restless, trotted off in the direction of the Calderwood place. Dozing against the poplar in the gray dawn of the morning, Free Joe heard Spite Calderwood's fox-hounds in full cry a mile away.

"Shoo!" he exclaimed, scratching his head, and laughing to himself, "dem ar dogs is des a-warmin' dat old fox up."

But it was Dan the hounds were after, and the little dog came back no more. Free Joe waited and waited, until he grew tired of waiting. He went back the next night and waited, and for many nights thereafter. His waiting was in vain, and yet he never regarded it as in vain. Careless and shabby as he was, Free Joe was thoughtful enough to have his theory. He was convinced that little Dan had found Lucinda, and that some night when the moon was shining brightly through the trees, the dog would rouse him from his dreams as he sat sleeping at the foot of the poplar-tree, and he would open his eyes and behold Lucinda standing over him, laughing merrily as of old; and then he thought what fun they would have about the queen of spades.

How many long nights Free Joe waited at the foot of the poplar-tree for Lucinda and little Dan no one can ever know. He kept no account of them and they were not recorded by Micajah Staley or by Miss Becky. The season ran into summer and then into fall. One night he went to the Staley cabin, cut the two old people an armful of wood, and seated himself on the door-steps, where he rested. He was always thankful—and proud, as it seemed—when Miss Becky gave him a cup of coffee, which she was sometimes thoughtful enough to do. He was especially thankful on this particular night.

"You er still layin' off for to strike up wi' Lucindy out thar in the woods, I reckon," said Micajah Staley, smiling grimly. The situation was not without its humorous aspects.

"Oh, dey er comin', Mars Cajy, dey er comin', sho," Free Joe replied, "I boun' you dey'll come; en w'en dey does come, I'll des take en fetch um yer, whar you kin see um wid you own eyes, you en Miss Becky."

"No," said Mr. Staley, with a quick and emphatic gesture of disapproval. "Don't! don't fetch 'em anywheres. Stay right wi' 'em as long as may be."

Free Joe chuckled, and slipped away into the night, while the two old people sat gazing in the fire. Finally Micajah spoke:

"Look at that nigger; look at 'im. He's pine-blank as happy now as a killdee by a mill-race. You can't 'feze 'em. I'd in-about give up my t'other hand ef I could stan' flat-footed, an' grin at trouble like that there nigger."

"Niggers is niggers," said Miss Becky, smiling grimly, "an' you can't rub it out; yet I lay I've seed a heap of white people lots meaner'n Free Joe. He grins,—an' that's nigger,—but I've ketched his under jaw a-trimblin' when Lucindy's name uz brung up. An' I tell you," she went on bridling up a little, and speaking with almost fierce emphasis, "the Old Boy's done sharpened his claws for Spite Calderwood. You'll see it."

"Me, Rebecca?" said Mr. Staley, hugging his palsied arm; "me? I hope not."

"Well, you'll know it then," said Miss Becky, laughing heartily at her brother's look of alarm.

The next morning Micajah Staley had occasion to go into the woods after a piece of timber. He saw Free Joe sitting at the foot of the poplar, and the sight vexed him somewhat.

"Git up from there," he cried, "an' go an' arn your livin'. A mighty purty pass it's come to, when great big buck niggers can lie a-snorin' in the woods all day, when t'other folks is got to be up an' a-gwine. Git up from there!"

Receiving no response, Mr. Staley went to Free Joe, and shook him by the shoulder; but the negro made no response. He was dead. His hat was off, his head was bent, and a smile was on his face. It was as if he had bowed and smiled when death stood before him, humble to the last. His clothes were ragged; his hands were rough and callous; his shoes were literally tied together with strings; he was shabby in the extreme. A passer-by, glancing at him, could have no idea that such a humble creature had been summoned as a witness before the Lord God of Hosts.

THE DULHAM LADIES

Sarah Orne Jewett, the daughter of a country doctor, was born in 1849 in South Berwick, Maine, where she spent nearly the whole sixty years of her life. Largely educated at home, she was the frequent companion of her father as he made professional calls in rural homes, and she soon became intimately acquainted with the desiccated farming and seaport life of the countryside around South Berwick. Inspired by Harriet Beecher Stowe's local color stories of Maine country folk, she determined to record the life of the Maine region she knew, and as early as 1869, when she was only nineteen, a story of hers entitled "Mr. Bruce" was accepted for publication in the *Atlantic Monthly*. Working slowly and carefully, she continued to publish in the *Atlantic Monthly,* and by the 1880's her work had won the acclaim of such important literary critics as Lowell, James, and Howells. During her lifetime, she published in all approximately fifteen volumes of stories, novels, and sketches, as well as numerous children's books. Her most important short story collections are *Deephaven* (1877), *Old Friends and New* (1879), *The Mate of the Daylight and Friends Ashore* (1883), *A White Heron and Other Stories* (1886), *A Native of Winby and Other Tales* (1893), *The Country of the Pointed Firs* (1896), *The Queen's Twin and Other Stories* (1899). *The Best Stories of Sarah Orne Jewett,* edited by Willa Cather (1925) contains her finest stories.

By focusing on a decaying past, emphasizing the picturesque, and avoiding the coarse and unpleasant, Miss Jewett is more closely allied to the tradition of local color fiction represented by Washington Irving than to the robust one represented by George Washington Harris, Bret Harte, and Mark Twain. However, in her depiction of simple, earthy people, grappling with the fundamental problems of life, her realistic if sometimes oversympathetic character portrayals, her accurate use of dialect, and her close-to-nature settings, she anticipates Willa Cather, on whom in fact she exerted a direct and profound influence. Her work thus marks a transitional stage between romanticism and realism.

Compared to other local colorists, Miss Jewett handles plot development rather casually in her stories; instead, she focuses attention upon a character or group of characters, and what little action or plot movement she engages them in serves primarily as a means of revealing their minds and personalities against their localized background. Gripping suspense and sharp dramatic effects of the Poe-Bierce type are, as a result, missing from her stories. Offsetting the customary means of provoking suspense is the interest she arouses by character contrasts, economical detail, and a graceful, sustained style. If her stories are the less dramatic thereby, they nevertheless sometimes produce a more complex and durable effect than showier stories. The effect of "The Dulham Ladies," for example, is remarkable in being at one and the same time ironic and sympathetic.

the dulham ladies

To be leaders of society in the town of Dulham was as satisfactory to Miss Dobin and Miss Lucinda Dobin as if Dulham were London itself. Of late years, though they would not allow themselves to suspect such treason the most ill-bred of the younger people in the village made fun of them behind their backs, and laughed at their treasured summer mantillas, their mincing steps, and the shape of their parasols.

They were always conscious of the fact that they were the daughters of a once eminent Dulham minister; but beside this unanswerable claim to the respect of the First Parish, they were aware that their mother's social position was one of superior altitude. Madam Dobin's grandmother was a Greenaple, of Boston. In her younger days she had often visited her relatives, the Greenaples and Hightrees, and in seasons of festivity she could relate to a select and properly excited audience her delightful experiences of town life. Nothing could be finer than her account of having taken tea at Governor Clovenfoot's on Beacon Street in company with an English Lord, who was indulging himself in a brief vacation from his arduous duties at the Court of St. James.

"He exclaimed that he had seldom seen in England so beautiful and intelligent a company of ladies," Madam Dobin would always say in conclusion. "He was decorated with the blue ribbon of the Knights of the Garter." Miss Dobin and Miss Lucinda thought for many years that this famous blue ribbon was tied about the noble gentleman's leg. One day they even discussed the question openly; Miss Dobin placing the decoration at his knee, and Miss Lucinda locating it much lower down, according to the length of the short gray socks with which she was familiar.

"You have no imagination, Lucinda," the elder sister replied impatiently. "Of course, those were the days of small-clothes and long silk stockings!"—whereat Miss Lucinda was rebuked, but not persuaded.

"I wish that my dear girls could have the outlook upon society which fell to my portion," Madam Dobin sighed, after she had set these ignorant minds to rights, and enriched them by communicating the final truth about the blue ribbon. "I must not chide you for the absence of opportunities, but if our cousin Harriet Greenaple were only living you would not lack enjoyment or social education."

Madam Dobin had now been dead a great many years. She seemed an elderly woman to her daughters some time before she left them; later they thought that she had really died comparatively young, since their own years had come to equal the record of hers. When they visited her tall white tombstone in the orderly Dulham burying-ground, it was a strange thought to both the daughters that they were older women than their mother had been when she died. To be sure, it was the fashion to appear older in her day,—they could remember the sober effect of really youthful married persons in cap and frisette;

261

but, whether they owed it to the changed times or to their own qualities, they felt no older themselves than they ever had. Beside upholding the ministerial dignity of their father, they were obliged to give a lenient sanction to the ways of the world for their mother's sake; and they combined the two duties with reverence and impartiality.

Madam Dobin was, in her prime, a walking example of refinements and courtesies. If she erred in any way, it was by keeping too strict watch and rule over her small kingdom. She acted with great dignity in all matters of social administration and etiquette, but, while it must be owned that the parishioners felt a sense of freedom for a time after her death, in their later years they praised and valued her more and more, and often lamented her generously and sincerely.

Several of her distinguished relatives attended Madam Dobin's funeral, which was long considered the most dignified and elegant pageant of that sort which ever had taken place in Dulham. It seemed to mark the close of a famous epoch in Dulham history, and it was increasingly difficult forever afterward to keep the tone of society up to the old standard. Somehow, the distinguished relatives had one by one disappeared, though they all had excellent reasons for the discontinuance of their visits. A few had left this world altogether, and the family circle of the Greenaples and Hightrees was greatly reduced in circumference. Sometimes, in summer, a stray connection drifted Dulham-ward, and was displayed to the townspeople (not to say paraded) by the gratified hostesses. It was a disappointment if the guest could not be persuaded to remain over Sunday and appear at church. When household antiquities became fashionable, the ladies remarked a surprising interest in their corner cupboard and best chairs, and some distant relatives revived their almost forgotten custom of paying a summer visit to Dulham. They were not long in finding out with what desperate affection Miss Dobin and Miss Lucinda clung to their mother's wedding china and other inheritances, and were allowed to depart without a single teacup. One graceless descendant of the Hightrees prowled from garret to cellar, and admired the household belongings diligently, but she was not asked to accept even the dislocated cherry-wood footstool that she had discovered in the far corner of the parsonage pew.

Some of the Dulham friends had long suspected that Madam Dobin made a social misstep when she chose the Reverend Edward Dobin for her husband. She was no longer young when she married, and though she had gone through the wood and picked up a crooked stick at last, it made a great difference that her stick possessed an ecclesiastical bark. The Reverend Edward was, moreover, a respectable graduate of Harvard College, and to a woman of her standards a clergyman was by no means insignificant. It was impossible not to respect his office, at any rate, and she must have treated him with proper veneration for the sake of that, if for no other reason, though his early advantages had been insufficient, and he was quite insensible to the claims of the Greenaple pedigree, and preferred an Indian pudding to pie crust that was, without exaggeration, half a quarter high. The delicacy of Madam Dobin's touch and preference in everything, from hymns to cookery, was quite lost upon this respected preacher, yet he was not without pride or complete confidence in his own decisions.

The Reverend Mr. Dobin was never very enlightening in his discourses, and was providentially stopped short by a stroke of paralysis in the middle of his clerical career. He lived on and on through many dreary years, but his children never accepted the fact that he was a tyrant, and served him humbly and patiently. He fell at last into a condition of great incapacity and chronic trembling, but was able for nearly a quarter of a century to be carried to the meeting-house from time to time to pronounce farewell discourses. On high days of the church he was always placed in the pulpit, and held up his shaking hands when the benediction was pronounced, as if the divine gift were exclusively his own, and the other minister did but say empty words. Afterward, he was usually tired and displeased and hard to cope with, but there was always a proper notice taken of these too often recurring events. For old times' and for pity's sake and from natural goodness of heart, the elder parishioners rallied manfully about the Reverend Mr. Dobin; and whoever his successor or colleague might be, the Dobins were always called the minister's folks, while the active laborer in that vineyard was only Mr. Smith or Mr. Jones, as the case might be. At last the poor old man died, to everybody's relief and astonishment; and after he was properly preached about and lamented, his daughters, Miss Dobin and Miss Lucinda, took a good look at life from a new standpoint, and decided that now they were no longer constrained by home duties they must make themselves a great deal more used to the town.

Sometimes there is such a household as this (which has been perhaps too minutely described), where the parents linger until their children are far past middle age, and always keep them in a too childish and unworthy state of subjection. The Misses Dobins' characters were much influenced by such an unnatural prolongation of the filial relationship, and they were amazingly slow to suspect that they were not so young as they used to be. There was nothing to measure themselves by but Dulham people and things. The elm-trees were growing yet, and many of the ladies of the First Parish were older than they, and called them, with pleasant familiarity, the Dobin girls. These elderly persons seemed really to be growing old, and Miss Lucinda frequently lamented the change in society; she thought it a freak of nature and too sudden blighting of earthly hopes that several charming old friends of her mother's were no longer living. They were advanced in age when Miss Lucinda was a young girl, though time and space are but relative, after all.

Their influence upon society would have made a great difference in many ways. Certainly, the new parishioners, who had often enough been instructed to pronounce their pastor's name as if it were spelled with one "b," would not have boldly returned again and again to their obnoxious habit of saying Dobbin. Miss Lucinda might carefully speak to the neighbor and newcomers of "my sister, Miss Do-bin;" only the select company of intimates followed her lead, and at last there was something humiliating about it, even though many persons spoke of them only as "the ladies."

"The name was originally *D'Aubigne,* we think," Miss Lucinda would say coldly and patiently, as if she had already explained this foolish mistake a thousand times too often. It was like the sorrows in many a provincial château in the Reign of Terror. The ladies looked on with increasing dismay at the retrogression in society. They felt as if they were a feeble garrison, to whose lot it had fallen to repulse a noisy, irreverent mob, an increasing band of marauders who would overthrow all land-marks of the past, all etiquette and social rank. The new minister himself was a round-faced, unspiritual-looking young man, whom they would have instinctively ignored if he had not been a minister. The new people who came to Dulham were not like the older residents, and they had no desire to be taught better. Little they cared about the Greenaples or the Hightrees; and once, when Miss Dobin essayed to speak of some detail of her mother's brilliant opportunities in Boston high life, she was interrupted, and the newcomer who sat next her at the parish sewing society began to talk about something else. We cannot believe that it could have been the tea-party at Governor Clovenfoot's which the rude creature so disrespectfully ignored, but some persons are capable of showing any lack of good taste.

The ladies had an unusual and most painful sense of failure, as they went home together that evening. "I have always made it my object to improve and interest the people at such times; it would seem so possible to elevate their thoughts and direct them into higher channels," said Miss Dobin sadly. "But as for that Woolden woman, there is no use in casting pearls before swine!"

Miss Lucinda murmured an indignant assent. She had a secret suspicion that the Woolden woman had heard the story in question oftener than had pleased her. She was but an ignorant creature; though she had lived in Dulham twelve or thirteen years, she was no better than when she came. The mistake was in treating sister Harriet as if she were on a level with the rest of the company. Miss Lucinda had observed more than once, lately, that her sister sometimes repeated herself, unconsciously, a little oftener than was agreeable. Perhaps they were getting a trifle dull; toward spring it might be well to pass a few days with some of their friends, and have a change.

"If I have tried to do anything," said Miss Dobin in an icy tone, "it has been to stand firm in my lot and place, and to hold the standard of cultivated mind and elegant manners as high as possible. You would think it had been a hundred years since our mother's death, so completely has the effect of her good breeding and exquisite hospitality been lost sight of, here in Dulham. I could wish that our father had chosen to settle in a larger and more appreciative place. They would like to put us on the shelf, too. I can see that plainly."

"I am sure we have our friends," said Miss Lucinda anxiously, but with a choking voice. "We must not let them think we do not mean to keep up with the times, as we always have. I do feel as if perhaps—our hair"—

And the sad secret was out at last. Each of the sisters drew a long breath of relief at this beginning of a confession.

It was certain that they must take some steps to retrieve their lost ascendency. Public attention had that evening been called to their fast-disappearing locks, poor ladies; and Miss Lucinda felt the discomfort most, for she had been the inheritor of the Hightree hair, long and curly, and chestnut in color. There used to be a waviness about it, and sometimes pretty escaping curls, but these were gone long ago. Miss Dobin resembled her father, and her hair had not been luxuriant, so that she was less changed by its absence than one might suppose. The straightness and thinness had increased so gradually that neither sister had quite accepted the thought that other persons would particularly notice their altered appearance.

They had shrunk, with the reticence born of close family association, from speaking of the cause even to each other, when they made themselves pretty little lace and dotted muslin caps. Breakfast caps, they called them, and explained that these were universally worn in town; the young Princess of Wales originated them, or at any rate adopted them. The ladies offered no apology for keeping the breakfast caps on until bedtime, and in spite of them a forward child had just spoken, loud and shrill, an untimely question in the ears of the for once silent sewing society. "Do Miss Dobbinses wear them great caps because their bare heads is cold?" the little beast had said; and everybody was startled and dismayed.

Miss Dobin had never shown better her good breeding and valor, the younger sister thought.

"No, little girl," replied the stately Harriet, with a chilly smile. "I believe that our head-dresses are quite in the fashion for ladies of all ages. And you must remember that it is never polite to make such personal remarks." It was after this that Miss Dobin had been reminded of Madam Somebody's unusual headgear at the evening entertainment in Boston. Nobody but the Woolden woman could have interrupted her under such trying circumstances.

Miss Lucinda, however, was certain that the time had come for making some effort to replace her lost adornment. The child had told an unwelcome truth, but had paved the way for further action, and now was the time to suggest something that had slowly been taking shape in Miss Lucinda's mind. A young grand-nephew of their mother and his bride had passed a few days with them, two or three summers before, and the sisters had been quite shocked to find that the pretty young woman wore a row of frizzes, not originally her own, over her smooth forehead. At the time, Miss Dobin and Miss Lucinda had spoken severely with each other of such bad taste, but now it made a great difference that the wearer of the frizzes was not only a relative by marriage and used to good society, but also that she came from town, and might be supposed to know what was proper in the way of toilet.

"I really think, sister, that we had better see about having some—arrangements, next time we go anywhere," Miss Dobin said unexpectedly, with a slight tremble in her voice, just as they reached their own door. "There seems to be quite a fashion for them nowadays. For the parish's sake we ought to recognize"—and Miss Lucinda responded with instant satisfaction. She did not like to complain, but she had been troubled with neuralgic pains in her forehead on suddenly meeting the cold air. The sisters felt a new bond of sympathy in keeping this secret with and for each other; they took pains to say to several acquaintances that they were thinking of going to the next large town to do a few errands for Christmas.

A bright, sunny morning seemed to wish the ladies good-fortune. Old Hetty Downs, their faithful maid-servant and protector, looked after them in affectionate foreboding. "Dear sakes, what devil's wiles may be played on them blessed innocents afore they're safe home again!" she murmured, as they vanished round the corner of the street that led to the railway station.

Miss Dobin and Miss Lucinda paced discreetly side by side down the main street of Westbury. It was nothing like Boston, of course, but the noise was slightly confusing, and the passers-by sometimes roughly pushed against them. Westbury was a consequential manufacturing town, but a great convenience at times like this. The trifling Christmas gifts for their old neighbors and Sunday-school scholars were purchased and stowed away in their neat Fayal basket before the serious commission of the day was attended to. Here and there, in the shops, disreputable frizzes were displayed in unblushing effrontery, but no such vulgar shopkeeper merited the patronage of the Misses Dobin. They pretended not to observe the unattractive goods, and went their way to a low, one-storied building on a side street, where an old tradesman lived. He had been useful to the minister while he still remained upon the earth and had need of a wig, sandy in hue and increasingly sprinkled with gray, as if it kept pace with other changes of existence. But old Paley's shutters were up, and a bar of rough wood was nailed firmly across the one that had lost its fastening and would rack its feeble hinges in the wind. Old Paley had always been polite and bland, they really had looked forward to a little chat with him; they had heard a year or two before of his wife's death, and meant to offer sympathy. His business of hair-dressing had been carried on with that of parasol and umbrella mending, and the condemned umbrella which was his sign cracked and swung in the rising wind, a tattered skeleton before the closed door. The ladies sighed and turned away; they were beginning to feel tired; the day was long, and they had not met with any pleasures yet. "We might walk up the street a little farther," suggested Miss Lucinda; "that is, if you are not tired," as they stood hesitating on the corner after they had finished a short discussion of Mr. Paley's disappearance. Happily it was only a few minutes before they came to a stop together in front of a new, shining shop, where smirking waxen heads all in a row were decked with the latest fashions of wigs and frizzes. One smiling fragment of a gentleman stared so straight at Miss Lucinda with his black eyes that she felt quite coy and embarrassed, and was obliged to feign not to be conscious of his admiration. But Miss Dobin, after a brief delay, boldly opened the door and entered; it was better to be sheltered in the shop than exposed to public remark as they gazed in at the windows. Miss Lucinda felt her heart beat and her courage give out; she, coward like, left the transaction of their business to her sister, and turned to contemplate the back of the handsome model. It was a slight shock to find that he was not so attractive from this point of view. The wig he wore was well made all round, but his shoulders were roughly finished in a substance that looked like plain plaster of Paris.

"What can I have ze pleasure of showing you, young ladees?" asked a person who advanced; and Miss Lucinda faced about to discover a smiling, middle-aged Frenchman, who rubbed his hands together and looked at his customers, first one and then the other, with delightful deference. He seemed a very civil, nice person, the young ladies thought.

"My sister and I were thinking of buying some little arrangements to wear above the forehead," Miss Dobin explained, with pathetic dignity; but the Frenchman spared her any further words. He looked with eager interest at the bonnets, as if no lack had attracted his notice before. "Ah, yes, *Je comprends;* ze high foreheads are not now ze mode. Je prefer them, moi, yes, yes, but ze ladies must accept ze fashion; zay must now cover ze forehead with ze frizzes, ze bangs, you say. As you wis', as you wis'!" and the tactful little man, with many shrugs and merry gestures at such girlish fancies, pulled down one box after another.

It was a great relief to find that this was no worse, to say the least, than any other shopping, though the solemnity and secrecy of the occasion were infringed upon by the great supply of "arrangements" and the loud discussion of the color of some crimps a noisy girl was buying from a young saleswoman the other side of the shop.

Miss Dobin waved aside the wares which were being displayed for her approval. "Something—more simple, if you please,"—she did not like to say "older."

"But these are *très simple,*" protested the Frenchman. "We have nothing younger;" and Miss Dobin and Miss Lucinda blushed, and said no more. The Frenchman had his own way; he persuaded them that nothing was so suitable as some conspicuous forelocks that matched their hair as it used to be. They would have given anything rather than leave their breakfast caps at home, if they had known that their proper winter bonnets must come off. They hardly listened to the wig merchant's glib voice as Miss Dobin stood revealed before the merciless mirror at the back of the shop.

He made everything as easy as possible, the friendly creature, and the ladies were grateful to him. Beside, now that the bonnet was on again there was a great improvement in Miss Dobin's appearance. She turned to Miss Lucinda, and saw a gleam of delight in her eager countenance. "It really is very becoming. I like the way it parts over your forehead," said the younger sister, "but if it were long enough to go behind the ears"—"*Non, non,*" entreated the Frenchman. "To make her the old woman at once would be cruelty!" And Lucinda, who was wondering how well she would look in her turn, succumbed promptly to such protestations. Yes, there was no use in being old before their time. Dulham was not quite keeping pace with the rest of the world in these days, but they need not drag behind everybody else, just because they lived there.

The price of the little arrangements was much less than the sisters expected, and the uncomfortable expense of their reverend father's wigs had been, it was proved, a thing of the past. Miss Dobin treated her polite Frenchman with great courtesy; indeed, Miss Lucinda had more than once whispered to her to talk French, and as they were bowed out of the shop the gracious *Bong-sure* of the elder lady seemed to act like the string of a shower-bath, and bring down an awesome torrent of foreign words upon the two guileless heads. It was impossible to reply; the ladies bowed again, however, and Miss Lucinda caught a last smile from the handsome wax countenance in the window. He appeared to regard her with fresh approval, and she departed down the street with mincing steps.

"I feel as if anybody might look at me now, sister," said gentle Miss Lucinda. "I confess, I have really suffered sometimes, since I knew I looked so distressed."

"Yours is lighter than I thought it was in the shop," remarked Miss Dobin, doubtfully, but she quickly added that perhaps it would change a little. She was so perfectly satisfied with her own appearance that she could not bear to dim the pleasure of any one else. The truth remained that she never would have let Lucinda choose that particular arrangement if she had seen it first in a good light. And Lucinda was thinking exactly the same of her companion.

"I am sure we shall have no more neuralgia," said Miss Dobin. "I am sorry we waited so long, dear," and they tripped down the main street of Westbury, confident that nobody would suspect them of being over thirty. Indeed, they felt quite girlish, and unconsciously looked sideways as they went along, to see their satisfying reflections in the windows. The great panes made excellent mirrors, with not too clear or lasting pictures of these comforted passers-by.

The Frenchman in the shop was making merry with his assistants. The two great frisettes had long been out of fashion; he had been lying in wait with them for two unsuspecting country ladies, who could be cajoled into such a purchase.

"Sister," Miss Lucinda was saying, "you know there is still an hour to wait before our train goes. Suppose we take a little longer walk down the other side of the way"; and they strolled slowly back again. In fact, they nearly missed the train, naughty girls! Hetty would have been so worried, they assured each other, but they reached the station just in time.

"Lutie," said Miss Dobin, "put up your hand and part it from your forehead; it seems to be getting out of place a little," and Miss Lucinda, who had just got breath enough to speak, returned the information that Miss Dobin's was almost covering her eyebrows. They might have to trim them a little shorter; of course it could be done. The darkness was falling; they had taken an early dinner before they started, and now they were tired and hungry after the exertion of the afternoon, but the spirit of youth flamed afresh in their hearts, and they were very happy. If one's heart remains young, it is a sore trial to have the outward appearance entirely at variance. It was the ladies' nature to be girlish, and they found it impossible not to be grateful to the flimsy, ineffectual disguise which seemed to set them right with the world. The old conductor, who had known them for many years, looked hard at them as he took their tickets, and, being a man of humor and compassion, affected not to notice anything remarkable in their appearance. "You ladies never mean to grow old, like the rest of us," he said gallantly, and the sisters fairly quaked with joy.

"Bless us!" the obnoxious Mrs. Woolden was saying, at the other end of the car. "There's the old maid Dobbinses, and they've bought 'em some bangs. I expect they wanted to get thatched-in a little before real cold weather; but don't they look just like a pair o' poodle dogs."

The little ladies descended wearily from the train. Somehow they did not enjoy a day's shopping as much as they used. They were certainly much obliged to Hetty for sending her niece's boy to meet them, with a lantern; also for having a good warm supper ready when they came in. Hetty took a quick look at her mistresses, and returned to the kitchen. "I knew somebody would be foolin' of 'em," she assured herself angrily, but she had to laugh. Their dear, kind faces were wrinkled and pale, and the great frizzes had lost their pretty curliness, and were hanging down, almost straight and very ugly, into the ladies' eyes. They could not tuck them up under their caps, as they were sure might be done.

Then came a succession of rainy days, and nobody visited the rejuvenated household. The frisettes looked very bright chestnut by the light of day, and it must be confessed that Miss Dobin took the scissors and shortened Miss Lucinda's half an inch, and Miss Lucinda returned the compliment quite secretly, because each thought her sister's forehead lower than her own. Their dear gray eyebrows were honestly displayed, as if it were the fashion not to have them match with wigs. Hetty at last spoke out, and begged her mistresses, as they sat at breakfast, to let her take the frizzes back and change them. Her sister's daughter worked in that very shop, and, though in the work-room, would be able to oblige them, Hetty was sure.

But the ladies looked at each other in pleased assurance, and then turned together to look at Hetty, who stood already a little apprehensive near the table, where she had just put down a plateful of smoking dropcakes. The good creature really began to look old.

"They are worn very much in town," said Miss Dobin. "We think it was quite fortunate that the fashion came in just as our hair was growing a trifle thin. I dare say we may choose those that are a shade duller in color when these are a little past. Oh, we shall not want tea this evening, you remember, Hetty. I am glad there is likely to be such a good night for the sewing circle." And Miss Dobin and Miss Lucinda nodded and smiled.

"Oh, my sakes alive!" the troubled handmaiden groaned. "Going to the circle, be they, to be snickered at! Well, the Dobbin girls they was born, and the Dobbin girls they will remain till they die; but if they ain't innocent Christian babes to those that knows 'em well, mark me down for an idjit myself! They believe them frontpieces has set the clock back forty year or more, but if they're pleased to think so, let 'em!"

Away paced the Dulham ladies, late in the afternoon, to grace the parish occasion, and face the amused scrutiny of their neighbors. "I think we owe it to society to observe the fashions of the day," said Miss Lucinda. "A lady cannot afford to be unattractive. I feel now as if we were prepared for anything!"

Kate Chopin

DÉSIRÉE'S BABY

Kate O'Flaherty Chopin began writing only in her thirties and died in her early fifties. As a result, by comparison with such contemporaries as Joel Chandler Harris, Sarah Orne Jewett, and Mary E. Wilkins Freeman, she produced but a small body of fiction—only two volumes of short stories and two novels. Slender as her contribution to short fiction is, it nevertheless illustrates the progressive development of the post-war local color movement into nearly every distinctive phase of American life, including the problem of miscegenation which earlier local colorists were loath to touch. In their best vein, her stories show that the technique of the "well-made" story could be used in depicting materials as peculiar to a specific locality as the bayou country of Louisiana.

Of French and Irish ancestry, Kate O'Flaherty was born in 1851 in St. Louis, Missouri. A wide reader from early youth, she received her educational training at the Sacred Heart Convent, from which she graduated in 1868. Two years later she married Oscar Chopin, a native of Louisiana, who took her to live in New Orleans, where he was a cotton broker. She and her husband participated in the social life of that exotic city, despite the responsibilities of a steadily growing family, which ultimately numbered six children—five boys and a girl. When her husband gave up his cotton brokerage business to manage a large plantation he owned on the Red River in central Louisiana, the family relocated there, and the writer was thus brought to the section of the country which was to provide her with the distinctive settings and characters of her stories. Her husband died in 1882, and feeling herself unable to assume the responsibilities of operating the plantation, she sold it and returned to St. Louis, where her mother still lived.

Encouraged to write by friends who had admired her letters, she first produced an amateurish novel, *At Fault* (1890). Then she began publishing skillfully written stories in *Century* and *Harper's* magazines. Two collections soon appeared: *Bayou Folk* (1894) and *Night in Acadie* (1897). Her final work, *The Awakening* (1899), a novel, received unfavorable critical notices because of its treatment of mixed marriage and adultery. She died suddenly in 1904.

Without question, "Désirée's Baby" is Kate Chopin's most famous story. In its compactness and structural finesse, it suggests De Maupassant, a writer she greatly admired.

désirée's baby

As the day was pleasant, Madame Valmondé drove over to L'Abri to see Désirée and the baby.

It made her laugh to think of Désirée with a baby. Why, it seemed but yesterday that Désirée was little more than a baby herself, when Monsieur in riding through the gateway of Valmondé had found her lying asleep in the shadow of the big stone pillar.

The little one awoke in his arms and began to cry for "Dada." That was as much as she could do or say. Some people thought she might have strayed there of her own accord, for she was of the toddling age. The prevailing belief was that she had been purposely left by a party of Texans, whose canvas-covered wagon, late in the day, had crossed the ferry that Coton Maïs kept, just below the plantation. In time Madame Valmondé abandoned every speculation but the one that Désirée had been sent to her by a beneficent Providence to be the child of her affection, seeing that she was without child of the flesh. For the girl grew to be beautiful and gentle, affectionate and sincere—the idol of Valmondé.

It was no wonder, when she stood one day against the stone pillar in whose shadow she had lain asleep, eighteen years before, that

Armand Aubigny riding by and seeing her there, had fallen in love with her. That was the way all the Aubignys fell in love, as if struck by a pistol shot. The wonder was that he had not loved her before; for he had known her since his father brought him home from Paris, a boy of eight, after his mother died there. The passion that awoke in him that day, when he saw her at the gate, swept along like an avalanche, or like a prairie fire, or like anything that drives headlong over all obstacles.

Monsieur Valmondé grew practical and wanted things well considered: that is, the girl's obscure origin. Armand looked into her eyes and did not care. He was reminded that she was nameless. What did it matter about a name when he could give her one of the oldest and proudest in Louisiana? He ordered the *corbeille* from Paris, and contained himself with what patience he could until it arrived; then they were married.

Madame Valmondé had not seen Désirée and the baby for four weeks. When she reached L'Abri she shuddered at the first sight of it, as she always did. It was a sad-looking place, which for many years had not known the gentle presence of a mistress, old Monsieur Aubigny having married and buried his wife in France, and she having loved her own land too well ever to leave it. The roof came down steep and black like a cowl, reaching out beyond the wide galleries that encircled the yellow stuccoed house. Big, solemn oaks grew close to it, and their thick-leaved, far-reaching branches shadowed it like a pall. Young Aubigny's rule was a strict one, too, and under it his negroes had forgotten how to be gay, as they had been during the old master's easy-going and indulgent lifetime.

The young mother was recovering slowly, and lay full length, in her soft white muslins and laces, upon a couch. The baby was beside her, upon her arm, where he had fallen asleep, at her breast. The yellow nurse woman sat beside a window fanning herself.

Madame Valmondé bent her portly figure over Désirée and kissed her, holding her an instant tenderly in her arms. Then she turned to the child.

"This is not the baby!" she exclaimed, in startled tones. French was the language spoken at Valmondé in those days.

"I knew you would be astonished!" laughed Désirée, "at the way he has grown. The little *cochon de lait!* Look at his legs, mamma, and his hands and finger-nails—real finger-nails. Zandrine had to cut them this morning. Isn't it true, Zandrine?"

The woman bowed her turbaned head majestically, *"Mais si, Madame."*

"And the way he cries," went on Désirée, "is deafening. Armand heard him the other day as far away as La Blanche's cabin."

Madame Valmondé had never removed her eyes from the child. She lifted it and walked with it over to the window that was lightest. She scanned the baby narrowly, then looked as searchingly at Zandrine, whose face was turned to gaze across the fields.

"Yes, the child has grown, has changed," said Madame Valmondé, slowly, as she replaced it beside its mother. "What does Armand say?"

Désirée's face became suffused with a glow that was happiness itself.

"Oh, Armand is the proudest father in the parish, I believe, chiefly because it is a boy, to bear his name; though he says not—that he would have loved a girl as well. But I know it isn't true. I know he says that to please me. And mamma," she added, drawing Madame Valmondé's head down to her, and speaking in a whisper, "he hasn't punished one of them—not one of them—since baby is born. Even Négrillon, who pretended to have burnt his leg that he might rest from work—he only laughed, and said Négrillon was a great scamp. Oh, mamma, I'm so happy; it frightens me."

What Désirée said was true. Marriage, and later the birth of his son, had softened Armand Aubigny's imperious and exacting nature greatly. This was what made the gentle Désirée so happy, for she loved him desperately. When he frowned she trembled, but loved him. When he smiled, she asked no greater blessing of God. But Armand's dark, handsome face had not often been disfigured by frowns since the day he fell in love with her.

When the baby was about three months old, Désirée awoke one day to the conviction that there was something in the air menacing her peace. It was at first too subtle to grasp. It had only been a disquieting suggestion; an air of mystery among the blacks; unexpected visits from far-off neighbors who could hardly account for their coming. Then a strange, an awful change in her husband's manner, which she dared not ask him to explain. When he spoke to her, it was with averted eyes, from which the old love-light seemed to have gone out. He absented himself from home; and when there, avoided her presence and that of her child, without excuse. And the very spirit of Satan seemed suddenly to take hold of him in his dealings with the slaves. Désirée was miserable enough to die.

She sat in her room, one hot afternoon, in her *peignoir,* listlessly drawing through her fingers the strands of her long, silky brown hair that hung about her shoulders. The baby, half naked, lay asleep upon her own great mahogany bed, that was like a sumptuous throne, with its satin-lined half-canopy. One of La Blanche's little quadroon boys— half naked too—stood fanning the child slowly with a fan of peacock feathers. Désirée's eyes had been fixed absently and sadly upon the baby, while she was striving to penetrate the threatening mist that she felt closing about her. She looked from her child to the boy who stood beside him, and back again; over and over. "Ah!" It was a cry that she could not help; which she was not conscious of having uttered. The blood turned like ice in her veins, and a clammy moisture gathered upon her face.

She tried to speak to the little quadroon boy; but no sound would come, at first. When he heard his name uttered, he looked up, and his mistress was pointing to the door. He laid aside the great, soft fan, and obediently stole away, over the polished floor, on his bare tiptoes.

She stayed motionless, with gaze riveted upon her child, and her face the picture of fright.

Presently her husband entered the room, and without noticing her, went to a table and began to search among some papers which covered it.

"Armand," she called to him, in a voice which must have stabbed him, if he was human. But he did not notice. "Armand," she said again. Then she rose and tottered towards him. "Armand," she panted once more, clutching his arm, "look at our child. What does it mean? tell me."

He coldly but gently loosened her fingers from about his arm and thrust the hand away from him. "Tell me what it means!" she cried despairingly.

"It means," he answered lightly, "that the child is not white; it means that you are not white."

A quick conception of all that this accusation meant for her nerved her with unwonted courage to deny it. "It is a lie; it is not true, I am white! Look at my hair, it is brown; and my eyes are gray, Armand, you know they are gray. And my skin is fair," seizing his wrist. "Look at my hand; whiter than yours, Armand," she laughed hysterically.

"As white as La Blanche's," he returned cruelly; and went away leaving her alone with their child.

When she could hold a pen in her hand, she sent a despairing letter to Madame Valmondé.

"My mother, they tell me I am not white. Armand has told me I am not white. For God's sake tell them it is not true. You must know it is not true. I shall die. I must die. I cannot be so unhappy, and live."

The answer that came was as brief:

"My own Désirée: Come home to Valmondé; back to your mother who loves you. Come with your child."

When the letter reached Désirée she went with it to her husband's study, and laid it open upon the desk before which he sat. She was like a stone image: silent, white, motionless after she placed it there.

In silence he ran his cold eyes over the written words. He said nothing. "Shall I go, Armand?" she asked in tones sharp with agonized suspense.

"Yes, go."

"Do you want me to go?"

"Yes, I want you to go."

He thought Almighty God had dealt cruelly and unjustly with him; and felt, somehow, that he was paying Him back in kind when he stabbed thus into his wife's soul. Moreover he no longer loved her, because of the unconscious injury she had brought upon his home and his name.

She turned away like one stunned by a blow, and walked slowly towards the door, hoping he would call her back.

"Good-by, Armand," she moaned.

He did not answer her. That was his last blow at fate.

Désirée went in search of her child. Zandrine was pacing the sombre gallery with it. She took the little one from the nurse's arms with no word of explanation, and descending the steps, walked away, under the live-oak branches.

It was an October afternoon; the sun was just sinking. Out in the still fields the negroes were picking cotton.

Désirée had not changed the thin white garment nor the slippers which she wore. Her hair was uncovered and the sun's rays brought a golden gleam from its brown meshes. She did not take the broad, beaten road which led to the far-off plantation of Valmondé. She walked across a deserted field, where the stubble bruised her tender feet, so delicately shod, and tore her thin gown to shreds.

She disappeared among the reeds and willows that grew thick along the banks of the deep, sluggish bayou; and she did not come back again.

Some weeks later there was a curious scene enacted at L'Abri. In the centre of the smoothly swept back yard was a great bonfire. Armand Aubigny sat in the wide hallway that commanded a view of the spectacle; and it was he who dealt out to a half dozen negroes the material which kept this fire ablaze.

A graceful cradle of willow, with all its dainty furbishings, was laid upon the pyre, which had already been fed with the richness of a priceless *layette*. Then there were silk gowns, and velvet and satin ones added to these; laces, too, and embroideries; bonnets and gloves; for the *corbeille* had been of rare quality.

The last thing to go was a tiny bundle of letters; innocent little scribblings that Désirée had sent to him during the days of their espousal. There was the remnant of one back in the drawer from which he took them. But it was not Désirée's; it was part of an old letter from his mother to his father. He read it. She was thanking God for the blessing of her husband's love:

"But, above all," she wrote, "night and day, I thank the good God for having so arranged our lives that our dear Armand will never know that his mother, who adores him, belongs to the race that is cursed with the brand of slavery."

A NEW ENGLAND NUN

Mary E. Wilkins Freeman, like her contemporary,
Sarah Orne Jewett, won distinction for her portrayal
of simple New England folk. However, beyond re-
stricting her characters primarily to one region, she
has little in common with Jewett and other local colorists of her period. Although meticulous in her use of
dialect and localized mannerisms, she is less concerned
in her stories with these character externals than with
the internal ones of mind, heart, and conscience. Further, she stresses the pinched souls, and the drabness
of the lives of her people. As a result, the local color
element in her work, so far as it may be considered
present at all, exists not for its own sake but rather as
an organic part of her materials. Finally, she seldom
gives way to the temptation besetting some local
colorists to substitute the appeal of subject matter for
sound workmanship: the finished artistry of her best
stories compares favorably with that of such masters
as Hawthorne and Poe.

Miss Wilkins was born in 1852, in Randolph,
Massachusetts, a town near Boston, and spent much of
her life there among people still touched by the length-
ening shadow of Puritanism. A frail child, she received
most of her education at home, isolating herself among
her books for many formative years, in somewhat the
fashion of Hawthorne. Her first published work, light
poems in the *vers de société* vein, appeared in the
Century Magazine in 1881; but in 1883, when her
father's death confronted her with the necessity of
earning a livelihood, she began to write short stories.
Within four years she demonstrated her competency in
this field by writing thirty stories for leading magazines and by publishing her first volume, *A Humble
Romance and Other Stories* (1887); but it was not
until the appearance of her second volume, *A New*

281

England Nun and Other Stories, in 1891, that her stories won wide critical recognition. Shortly before her marriage in 1902 to Dr. C. M. Freeman and their removal to Metuchen, New Jersey, she turned her attention to other types of literature, and, during the latter part of her writing career, published twelve novels, in addition to one play and two volumes of poetry. That she never lost interest in the short story—clearly the field for which her talent was best fitted—is apparent from the fact that during her lifetime (1852-1930) she published the amazing total of nearly two hundred and fifty stories. It is further remarkable that a collection appearing as late in her career as 1918, *Edgewater People,* has in it stories fully as good as those in earlier volumes.

Characteristically, as in "The New England Nun," her stories center on one dominant character facing a major crisis in life, and they are told with a minimum of exposition and description but in such a manner as to reveal the character's personality. The detached objectivity, compression, and irony of her method are suggestive of the French master, Guy de Maupassant.

a new england nun

It was late in the afternoon, and the light was waning. There was a difference in the look of the tree shadows out in the yard. Somewhere in the distance cows were lowing and a little bell was tinkling; now and then a farm-wagon tilted by, and the dust flew; some blue-shirted laborers with shovels over their shoulders plodded past; little swarms of flies were dancing up and down before the people's faces in the soft air. There seemed to be a gentle stir arising over everything for the mere sake of subsidence—a very premonition of rest and hush and night.

This soft diurnal commotion was over Louisa Ellis also. She had been peacefully sewing at her sitting-room window all the afternoon. Now she quilted her needle carefully into her work, which she folded precisely, and laid in a basket with her thimble and thread and scissors. Louisa Ellis could not remember that ever in her life she had mislaid one of these little feminine appurtenances, which had become, from long use and constant association, a very part of her personality.

Louisa tied a green apron round her waist, and got out a flat straw hat with a green ribbon. Then she went into the garden with a little blue crockery bowl, to pick some currants for her tea. After the currants were picked she sat on the back door-step and stemmed them, collecting the stems carefully in her apron, and afterward throwing them into the hen-coop. She looked sharply at the grass beside the step to see if any had fallen there.

Louisa was slow and still in her movements; it took her a long time to prepare her tea; but when ready it was set forth with as much grace as if she had been a veritable guest to her own self. The little square table stood exactly in the centre of the kitchen, and was covered with a starched linen cloth whose border pattern of flowers glistened. Louisa had a damask napkin on her tea-tray, where were arranged a cut-glass tumbler full of teaspoons, a silver cream-pitcher, a china sugar-bowl, and one pink china cup and saucer. Louisa used china every day—something which none of her neighbors did. They whispered about it among themselves. Their daily tables were laid with common crockery, their sets of best china stayed in the parlor closet, and Louisa Ellis was no richer nor better bred than they. Still she would use the china. She had for her supper a glass dish full of sugared currants, a plate of little cakes, and one of light white biscuits. Also a leaf or two of lettuce, which she cut up daintily. Louisa was very fond of lettuce, which she raised to perfection in her little garden. She ate quite heartily, though in a delicate, pecking way; it seemed almost surprising that any considerable bulk of the food should vanish.

After tea she filled a plate with nicely baked thin corn-cakes, and carried them out into the back-yard.

"Cæsar!" she called. "Cæsar! Cæsar!"

There was a little rush, and the clank of a chain, and a large yellow-and-white dog appeared at the door of his tiny hut, which was half hidden among the tall grasses and flowers. Louisa patted him and gave him the corn-cakes. Then she returned to the house and washed the tea-things, polishing the china carefully. The twilight had deepened; the chorus of the frogs floated in at the open window wonderfully loud and shrill, and once in a while a long sharp drone from a tree-toad pierced it. Louisa took off her green gingham apron, disclosing a shorter one of pink-and-white print. She lighted her lamp, and sat down again with her sewing.

In about half an hour Joe Dagget came. She heard his heavy step on the walk, and rose and took off her pink-and-white apron. Under that was still another—white linen with a little cambric edging on the bottom; that was Louisa's company apron. She never wore it without her calico sewing apron over it unless she had a guest. She had barely folded the pink and white one with methodical haste and laid it in a table-drawer when the door opened and Joe Dagget entered.

He seemed to fill up the whole room. A little yellow canary that had been asleep in his green cage at the south window woke up and fluttered wildly, beating his little yellow wings against the wires. He always did so when Joe Dagget came into the room.

"Good-evening," said Louisa. She extended her hand with a kind of solemn cordiality.

"Good-evening, Louisa," returned the man, in a loud voice.

She placed a chair for him, and they sat facing each other, with the table between them. He sat bolt-upright, toeing out his heavy feet squarely, glancing with a good-humored uneasiness around the room. She sat gently erect, folding her slender hands in her white-linen lap.

"Been a pleasant day," remarked Dagget.

"Real pleasant," Louisa assented softly. "Have you been haying?" she asked, after a little while.

"Yes, I've been haying all day, down in the ten-acre lot. Pretty hot work."

"It must be."

"Yes, it's pretty hot work in the sun."

"Is your mother well to-day?"

"Yes, mother's pretty well."

"I suppose Lily Dyer's with her now?"

Dagget colored. "Yes, she's with her," he answered, slowly.

He was not very young, but there was a boyish look about his large face. Louisa was not quite as old as he, her face was fairer and smoother, but she gave people the impression of being older.

"I suppose she's a good deal of help to your mother," she said, further.

"I guess she is; I don't know how mother'd get along without her," said Dagget, with a sort of embarrassed warmth.

"She looks like a real capable girl. She's pretty-looking too," remarked Louisa.

"Yes, she is pretty fair looking."

Presently Dagget began fingering the books on the table. There was a square red autograph album, and a Young Lady's Gift-Book which had belonged to Louisa's mother. He took them up one after the other and opened them; then laid them down again, the album on the Gift-Book.

Louisa kept eying them with mild uneasiness. Finally she rose and changed the position of the books, putting the album underneath. That was the way they had been arranged in the first place.

Dagget gave an awkward little laugh. "Now what difference did it make which book was on top?" said he.

Louisa looked at him with a deprecating smile. "I always keep them that way," murmured she.

"You do beat everything," said Dagget, trying to laugh again. His large face was flushed.

He remained about an hour longer, then rose to take leave. Going out, he stumbled over a rug, and trying to recover himself, hit Louisa's work-basket on the table, and knocked it on the floor.

He looked at Louisa, then at the rolling spools; he ducked himself awkwardly toward them, but she stopped him. "Never mind," said she; "I'll pick them up after you're gone."

She spoke with a mild stiffness. Either she was a little disturbed, or his nervousness affected her, and made her seem constrained in her effort to reassure him.

When Joe Dagget was outside he drew in the sweet evening air with a sigh, and felt much as an innocent and perfectly well-intentioned bear might after his exit from a china shop.

Louisa, on her part, felt much as the kind-hearted, long-suffering owner of the china shop might have done after the exit of the bear.

She tied on the pink, then the green apron, picked up all the scattered treasures and replaced them in her work-basket, and straightened the rug. Then she set the lamp on the floor, and began sharply examining the carpet. She even rubbed her fingers over it, and looked at them.

"He's tracked in a good deal of dust," she murmured. "I thought he must have."

Louisa got a dust-pan and brush, and swept Joe Dagget's track carefully.

If he could have known it, it would have increased his perplexity and uneasiness, although it would not have disturbed his loyalty in the least. He came twice a week to see Louisa Ellis, and every time, sitting there in her delicately sweet room, he felt as if surrounded by a hedge of lace. He was afraid to stir lest he should put a clumsy foot or hand through the fairy web, and he had always the consciousness that Louisa was watching fearfully lest he should.

Still the lace and Louisa commanded perforce his perfect respect and patience and loyalty. They were to be married in a month, after a singular courtship which had lasted for a matter of fifteen years. For fourteen out of the fifteen years the two had not once seen each other, and they had seldom exchanged letters. Joe had been all those years in Australia, where he had gone to make his fortune, and where he had stayed until he made it. He would have stayed fifty years if it had taken so long, and come home feeble and tottering, or never come home at all, to marry Louisa.

But the fortune had been made in the fourteen years, and he had come home now to marry the woman who had been patiently and unquestioningly waiting for him all that time.

Shortly after they were engaged he had announced to Louisa his determination to strike out into new fields, and secure a competency before they should be married. She had listened and assented with the sweet serenity which never failed her, not even when her lover set forth on that long and uncertain journey. Joe, buoyed up as he was by his sturdy determination, broke down a little at the last, but Louisa kissed him with a mild blush, and said good-by.

"It won't be for long," poor Joe had said, huskily; but it was for fourteen years.

In that length of time much had happened. Louisa's mother and brother had died, and she was all alone in the world. But greatest happening of all—a subtle happening which both were too simple to understand—Louisa's feet had turned into a path, smooth maybe under a calm, serene sky, but so straight and unswerving that it could only meet a check at the grave, and so narrow that there was no room for any one at her side.

Louisa's first emotion when Joe Dagget came home (he had not apprised her of his coming) was consternation, although she would not admit it to herself, and he never dreamed of it. Fifteen years ago she had been in love with him—at least she considered herself to be. Just at that time, gently acquiescing with and falling into the natural drift of girlhood, she had seen marriage ahead as a reasonable feature and a probable desirability of life. She had listened with calm docility to her mother's views upon the subject. Her mother was remarkable for her cool sense and sweet, even temperament. She talked wisely to her daughter when Joe Dagget presented himself, and Louisa accepted him with no hesitation. He was the first lover she had ever had.

She had been faithful to him all these years. She had never dreamed of the possibility of marrying any one else. Her life, especially for the last seven years, had been full of a pleasant peace, she had never felt discontented nor impatient over her lover's absence; still she had always looked forward to his return and their marriage as the inevitable conclusion of things. However, she had fallen into a way of placing it so far in the future that it was almost equal to placing it over the boundaries of another life.

When Joe came she had been expecting him, and expecting to be married for fourteen years, but she was as much surprised and taken aback as if she had never thought of it.

Joe's consternation came later. He eyed Louisa with an instant confirmation of his old admiration. She had changed but little. She still kept her pretty manner and soft grace, and was, he considered, every whit as attractive as ever. As for himself, his stent was done; he had his face turned away from fortune-seeking, and the old winds of romance whistled as loud and sweet as ever through his ears. All the song which he had been wont to hear in them was Louisa; he had for a long time a loyal belief that he heard it still, but finally it seemed to him that although the winds sang always that one song, it had another name. But for Louisa the wind had never more than murmured; now it had gone down, and everything was still. She listened for a little while with half-wistful attention; then she turned quietly away and went to work on her wedding clothes.

Joe had made some extensive and quite magnificent alterations in his house. It was the old homestead; the newly-married couple would live there, for Joe could not desert his mother, who refused to leave her old home. So Louisa must leave hers. Every morning, rising and going about among her neat maidenly possessions, she felt as one looking her last upon the faces of dear friends. It was true that in a measure she could take them with her, but, robbed of their old environments, they would appear in such new guises that they would almost cease to be themselves. Then there were some peculiar features of her happy solitary life which she would probably be obliged to relinquish altogether. Sterner tasks than these graceful but half-needless ones would probably devolve upon her. There would be a large house to care for; there would be company to entertain; there would be Joe's rigorous and feeble old mother to wait upon; and it would be contrary to all thrifty village traditions for her to keep more than one servant. Louisa had a little still, and she used to occupy herself pleasantly in summer weather with distilling the sweet aromatic essences from roses and peppermint and spearmint. By-and-by her still must be laid away. Her store of essences was already considerable, and there would be no time for her to distil for the mere pleasure of it. Then Joe's mother would think it foolishness; she had already hinted her opinion in the matter. Louisa dearly loved to sew a linen seam, not always for use, but for the simple, mild pleasure which she took in it. She would have been loath to confess how more than once she had ripped a seam for the mere delight of sewing it together again. Sitting at her window during long sweet afternoons, drawing her needle gently through the dainty fabric, she was peace itself. But there was small chance of such foolish comfort in the future. Joe's mother, domineering, shrewd old matron that she was even in her old age, and very likely even Joe himself, with his honest masculine rudeness, would laugh and frown down all these pretty but senseless old maiden ways.

Louisa had almost the enthusiasm of an artist over the mere order and cleanliness of her solitary home. She had throbs of genuine triumph at the sight of the window-panes which she had polished until they shone like jewels. She gloated gently over her orderly bureau-drawers, with their exquisitely folded contents redolent with lavender and sweet clover and very purity. Could she be sure of the endurance of even this? She had visions, so startling that she half repudiated them as indelicate, of coarse masculine belongings strewn about in endless litter; of dust and disorder arising necessarily from a coarse masculine presence in the midst of all this delicate harmony.

Among her forebodings of disturbance, not the least was with regard to Cæsar. Cæsar was a veritable hermit of a dog. For the greater part of his life he had dwelt in his secluded hut, shut out from the society of his kind and all innocent canine joys. Never had Cæsar since his early youth watched at a woodchuck's hole; never had he known the delights of a stray bone at a neighbor's kitchen door. And it was all on account of a sin committed when hardly out of his puppyhood. No one knew the possible depth of remorse of which this mild-visaged, altogether innocent-looking old dog might be capable; but whether or not he had encountered remorse, he had encountered a full measure of righteous retribution. Old Cæsar seldom lifted up his voice in a growl or a bark; he was fat and sleepy; there were yellow rings which looked like spectacles around his dim old eyes; but there was a neighbor who bore on his hand the imprint of several of Cæsar's sharp white youthful teeth, and for that he had lived at the end of a chain, all alone in a little hut, for fourteen years. The neighbor, who was choleric and smarting with the pain of his wound, had demanded either Cæsar's death or complete ostracism. So Louisa's brother, to whom the dog had belonged, had built him his little kennel and tied him up. It was now fourteen years since, in a flood of youthful spirits, he had inflicted that memorable bite, and with the exception of short excursions, always at the end of the chain, under the strict guardianship of his master or Louisa, the old dog had remained a close prisoner. It is doubtful if, with his limited ambition, he took much pride in the fact, but it is certain that he was possessed of considerable cheap fame. He was regarded by all the children in the village and by many adults as a very monster of ferocity. St. George's dragon could hardly have surpassed in evil repute Louisa Ellis's old yellow dog. Mothers charged their children with solemn emphasis not to go too near to him, and the children listened and believed greedily, with a fascinated appetite for terror, and ran by Louisa's house stealthily, with many sidelong glances at the terrible dog. If perchance he sounded a hoarse bark, there was a panic. Wayfarers chancing into Louisa's yard eyed him with respect, and inquired if the chain were stout. Cæsar at large might have seemed a very ordinary dog, and excited no comment whatever; chained, his reputation overshadowed him, so that he lost his own proper outlines and looked darkly vague and enormous. Joe Dagget, however, with his good-humored sense and shrewdness, saw him as he was. He strode valiantly up to him and patted him on the head, in spite of Louisa's soft clamor of warning, and even attempted to set him loose. Louisa grew so alarmed that he desisted, but kept announcing his opinion in the matter quite forcibly at intervals. "There ain't a better-natured dog in town," he would say, "and it's downright cruel to keep him tied up there. Some day I'm going to take him out."

Louisa had very little hope that he would not, one of these days, when their interests and possessions should be more completely fused in one. She pictured to herself Cæsar on the rampage through the quiet and unguarded village. She saw innocent children bleeding in his path. She was herself very fond of the old dog, because he had belonged to her dead brother, and he was always very gentle with her; still she had great faith in his ferocity. She always warned people not to go too near him. She fed him on ascetic fare of corn-mush and cakes, and never fired his dangerous temper with heating and sanguinary diet of flesh and bones. Louisa looked at the old dog munching his simple fare, and thought ot her approaching marriage and trembled. Still no anticipation of disorder and confusion in lieu of sweet peace and harmony, no forebodings of Cæsar on the rampage, no wild fluttering of her little yellow canary, were sufficient to turn her a hair's breadth. Joe Dagget had been fond of her and working for her all these years. It was not for her, whatever came to pass, to prove untrue and break his heart. She put the exquisite little stitches into her wedding-garments, and the time went on till it was only a week before her wedding-day. It was a Tuesday evening, and the wedding was to be a week from Wednesday.

There was a full moon that night. About nine o'clock Louisa strolled down the road a little way. There were harvest-fields on either hand, bordered by low stone walls. Luxuriant clumps of bushes grew beside the wall, and trees—wild cherry and old apple trees—at intervals. Presently Louisa sat down on the wall and looked about her with mildly sorrowful reflectiveness. Tall shrubs of blueberry and meadowsweet, all woven together and tangled with blackberry vines and horsebriers, shut her in on either side. She had a little clear space between them. Opposite her, on the other side of the road, was a spreading tree; the moon shone between its boughs, and the leaves twinkled like silver. The road was bespread with a beautiful shifting dapple of silver and shadow; the air was full of a mysterious sweetness. "I wonder if it's wild grapes?" murmured Louisa. She sat there some time. She was just thinking of rising, when she heard footsteps and low voices, and remained quiet. It was a lonely place, and she felt a little timid. She thought she would keep still in the shadow and let the persons, whoever they might be, pass her.

But just before they reached her the voices ceased, and the footsteps. She understood that their owners had also found seats upon the stone wall. She was wondering if she could not steal away unobserved, when the voice broke the stillness. It was Joe Dagget's. She sat still and listened.

The voice was announced by a loud sigh, which was as familiar as itself. "Well," said Dagget, "you've made up your mind, then, I suppose?"

"Yes," returned another voice; "I'm going day after to-morrow."

"That's Lily Dyer," thought Louisa to herself. The voice embodied itself in her mind. She saw a girl tall and full-figured, with a firm, fair face, looking fairer and firmer in the moonlight, her strong yellow hair braided in a close knot. A girl full of a calm rustic strength and bloom, with a masterful way which might have beseemed a princess. Lily Dyer was a favorite with the village folk; she had just the qualities to arouse the admiration. She was good and handsome and smart. Louisa had often heard her praises sounded.

"Well," said Joe Dagget, "I ain't got a word to say."

"I don't know what you could say," returned Lily Dyer.

"Not a word to say," repeated Joe, drawing out the words heavily. Then there was a silence. "I ain't sorry," he began at last, "that that happened yesterday—that we kind of let on how we felt to each other. I guess it's just as well we knew. Of course I can't do anything any different. I'm going right on an' get married next week. I ain't going back on a woman that's waited for me fourteen years, an' break her heart."

"If you should jilt her to-morrow, I wouldn't have you," spoke up the girl, with sudden vehemence.

"Well, I ain't going to give you the chance," said he; "but I don't believe you would, either."

"You'd see I wouldn't. Honor's honor, an' right's right. An' I'd never think anything of any man that went against 'em for me or any other girl; you'd find that out, Joe Dagget."

"Well, you'll find out fast enough that I ain't going against 'em for you or any other girl," returned he. Their voices sounded almost as if they were angry with each other. Louisa was listening eagerly.

"I'm sorry you feel as if you must go away," said Joe, "but I don't know but it's best."

"Of course it's best. I hope you and I have got common-sense."

"Well, I suppose you're right." Suddenly Joe's voice got an undertone of tenderness. "Say, Lily," he said, "I'll get along well enough myself, but I can't bear to think— You don't suppose you're going to fret much about it?"

"I guess you'll find out I sha'n't fret much over a married man."

"Well, I hope you won't—I hope you won't, Lily. God knows I do. And—I hope—one of these days—you'll—come across somebody else—"

"I don't see any reason why I shouldn't." Suddenly her tone changed. She spoke in a sweet, clear voice, so loud that she could have been heard across the street. "No, Joe Dagget," said she, "I'll never marry any other man as long as I live. I've got good sense, an' I ain't going to break my heart nor make a fool of myself; but I'm never going to be married, you can be sure of that. I ain't that sort of a girl to feel this way twice."

Louisa heard an exclamation and a soft commotion behind the bushes; then Lily spoke again—the voice sounded as if she had risen. "This must be put a stop to," said she. "We've stayed here long enough. I'm going home."

Louisa sat there in a daze, listening to their retreating steps. After a while she got up and slunk softly home herself. The next day she did her housework methodically; that was as much a matter of course as breathing; but she did not sew on her wedding-clothes. She sat at her window and meditated. In the evening Joe came. Louisa Ellis had never known that she had any diplomacy in her, but when she came to look for it that night she found it, although meek of its kind, among her little feminine weapons. Even now she could hardly believe that she had heard aright, and that she would not do Joe a terrible injury should she break her troth-plight. She wanted to sound him without betraying too soon her own inclinations in the matter. She did it successfully, and they finally came to an understanding; but it was a difficult thing, for he was as afraid of betraying himself as she.

She never mentioned Lily Dyer. She simply said that while she had no cause of complaint against him, she had lived so long in one way that she shrank from making a change.

"Well, I never shrank, Louisa," said Dagget. "I'm going to be honest enough to say that I think maybe it's better this way; but if you'd wanted to keep on, I'd have stuck to you till my dying day. I hope you know that."

"Yes, I do," said she.

That night she and Joe parted more tenderly than they had done for a long time. Standing in the door, holding each other's hands, a last great wave of regretful memory swept over them.

"Well, this ain't the way we've thought it was all going to end, is it, Louisa?" said Joe.

She shook her head. There was a little quiver on her placid face.

"You let me know if there's ever anything I can do for you," said he. "I ain't ever going to forget you, Louisa." Then he kissed her, and went down the path.

Louisa, all alone by herself that night, wept a little, she hardly knew why; but the next morning, on waking, she felt like a queen who, after fearing lest her domain be wrested away from her, sees it firmly insured in her possession.

Now the tall weeds and grasses might cluster around Cæsar's little hermit hut, the snow might fall on its roof year in and year out, but he never would go on a rampage through the unguarded village. Now the little canary might turn itself into a peaceful yellow ball night after night, and have no need to wake and flutter with wild terror against its bars. Louisa could sew linen seams, and distil roses, and dust and polish and fold away in lavender, as long as she listed. That afternoon she sat with her needle-work at the window, and felt fairly steeped in peace. Lily Dyer, tall and erect and blooming, went past; but she felt no qualm. If Louisa Ellis had sold her birthright she did not know it, the taste of the pottage was so delicious, and had been her sole satisfaction for so long. Serenity and placid narrowness had become to her as the birthright itself. She gazed ahead through a long reach of future days strung together like pearls in a rosary, every one like the others, and all smooth and flawless and innocent, and her heart went up in thankfulness. Outside was the fervid summer afternoon; the air was filled with the sounds of the busy harvest of men and birds and bees; there were halloos, metallic clatterings, sweet calls, and long hummings. Louisa sat, prayerfully numbering her days, like an uncloistered nun.

Hamlin Garland

UNDER THE LION'S PAW

Hamlin Garland's belief in a harsher realism than Howells' sprang directly from the austerity of his early life on the prairies. He was born in 1860, on a farm near West Salem, Wisconsin, of pioneer parents who subsequently moved farther west, first to Iowa and later to North Dakota. He attended the Cedar Valley Seminary at Osage, Iowa, from 1876 to 1881, getting in that brief period nearly all the formal education he was ever to receive. After tramping through the Eastern states and working as a carpenter in Illinois and Massachusetts, he returned west to establish himself on a farm in North Dakota. He soon resolved, however, to escape from the deadly routine of farm life and went to Boston in 1884, where, subsisting on meager funds, he continued his education by independent reading in the Boston Public Library and by attending the Boston School of Oratory. After a time, he secured employment as a teacher and lecturer, forming friendships with artists and writers who encouraged his growing awareness of literary currents and social problems.

Visits back to the Middle West, with the enlarged perspective afforded by his Boston life, so confirmed Garland's impression of the misery and ugliness of farm life that he determined to depict that life in all its harshness. Already a contributor to the Boston *Transcript*, he now began to write stories so realistic that some were refused by magazine editors, even though public acceptance of realistic fiction was increasing in the 1890's. His first collection of stories, *Main-Travelled Roads* (1891), however, won critical acclaim and established him on the literary scene. As his reputation grew, he published two other volumes of stories, *Prairie Folks* (1893) and *Wayside Courtships* (1897), which were reprinted in one volume, *Other Main-Travelled Roads,* in 1910; but thereafter, until his death in 1940, he devoted his chief energies to novels and autobiographical works. His later and longer fiction never again reached the artistic level of his earliest work because he failed to live up to his own standard. To maintain a comfortable income he compromised his definition of *veritism* either by transforming his material into sheer romanticism or by subverting it to propaganda.

Veritism, as Garland described it in *Crumbling Idols* (1894), is truth-telling, and though the writer may state—in fact, must state—the truth in an individual way, he is yet obliged to depict the ugly and vulgar in life along with the beautiful and good. The same viewpoint carries over to his concept of local color, which he thought should avoid the picturesque and be "a statement of life as indigenous as plant growth." By truthfully portraying life and living conditions, Garland believed that the writer without overt preachments might implicitly suggest needed social changes. "Under the Lion's Paw" is an effective, though not a flawlessly artistic, application of these principles. The story is narrated simply and, on the whole, objectively; but its tone of urgent protest, conveyed through editorialized descriptive touches, produces the inescapable impression that a land system which gives the rewards of back-breaking farm labor to a person who has not earned them needs reform.

under the lion's paw

It was the last of autumn and first day of winter coming together. All day long the plowmen on their prairie farms had moved to and fro in their wide level fields through the falling snow, which melted as it fell, wetting them to the skin—all day, notwithstanding the frequent squalls of snow, the dripping, desolate clouds, and the muck of the furrows, black and tenacious as tar.

Under their dripping harness the horses swung to and fro silently, with that marvelous uncomplaining patience which marks the horse. All day the wild geese, honking wildly, as they sprawled sidewise down the wind, seemed to be fleeing from an enemy behind, and with neck outthrust and wings extended, sailed down the wind, soon lost to sight.

Yet the plowman behind his plow, though the snow lay on his ragged great-coat, and the cold clinging mud rose on his heavy boots, fettering him like gyves, whistled in the very beard of the gale. As day passed, the snow, ceasing to melt, lay along the plowed land, and lodged in the depth of the stubble, till on each slow round the last furrow stood out black and shining as jet between the plowed land and the gray stubble.

When night began to fall, and the geese, flying low, began to alight invisibly in the near corn-field, Stephen Council was still at work "finishing a land." He rode on his sulky plow when going with the wind, but walked when facing it. Sitting bent and cold but cheery under his slouch hat, he talked encouragingly to his four-in-hand.

"Come round there, boys!—Round agin! We got t' finish this land. Come in there, Dan! *Stiddy,* Kate,—stiddy! None o' y'r tantrums, Kittie. It's purty tuff, but got a be did. *Tchk! tchk!* Step along, Pete! Don't let Kate git y'r single-tree on the wheel. *Once* more!"

They seemed to know what he meant, and that this was the last round, for they worked with greater vigor than before.

"Once more, boys, an' then, sez I, oats an' a nice warm stall, an' sleep f'r all."

By the time the last furrow was turned on the land it was too dark to see the house, and the snow was changing to rain again. The tired and hungry man could see the light from the kitchen shining through the leafless hedge, and he lifted a great shout, "Supper f'r a half a dozen!"

It was nearly eight o'clock by the time he had finished his chores and started for supper. He was picking his way carefully through the mud, when the tall form of a man loomed up before him with a premonitory cough.

"Waddy ye want?" was the rather startled question of the farmer.

"Well, ye see," began the stranger, in a deprecating tone, "we'd like t' git in f'r the night. We've tried every house f'r the last two miles, but they hadn't any room f'r us. My wife's jest about sick, 'n' the children are cold and hungry——"

"Oh, y' want 'o stay all night, eh?"

"Yes, sir; it 'ud be a great accom——"

"Wall, I don't make it a practice t' turn anybuddy way hungry, not on sech nights as this. Drive right in. We ain't got much, but sech as it is——"

But the stranger had disappeared. And soon his steaming, weary team, with drooping heads and swinging single-trees, moved past the well to the block beside the path. Council stood at the side of the "schooner" and helped the children out—two little half-sleeping children—and then a small woman with a babe in her arms.

"There ye go!" he shouted jovially, to the children. "*Now* we're all right! Run right along to the house there, an' tell Mam' Council you wants sumpthin' t' eat. Right this way, Mis'—keep right off t' the right there. I'll go an' git a lantern. Come," he said to the dazed and silent group at his side.

"Mother," he shouted, as he neared the fragrant and warmly lighted kitchen, "here are some wayfarers an' folks who need sumpthin' t' eat an' a place t' snooze." He ended by pushing them all in.

Mrs. Council, a large, jolly, rather coarse-looking woman, took the children in her arms. "Come right in, you little rabbits. Most asleep, hey? Now here's a drink o' milk f'r each o' ye. I'll have s'm tea in a minute. Take off y'r things and set up t' the fire."

While she set the children to drinking milk, Council got out his lantern and went out to the barn to help the stranger about his team, where his loud, hearty voice could be heard as it came and went between the haymow and the stalls.

The woman came to light as a small, timid, and discouraged-looking woman, but still pretty, in a thin and sorrowful way.

"Land sakes! An' you've traveled all the way from Clear Lake t'-day in this mud! Waal! waal! No wonder you're all tired out. Don't wait f'r the men, Mis'——" She hesitated, waiting for the name.

"Haskins."

"Mis' Haskins, set right up to the table an' take a good swig o' tea whilst I make y' s'm toast. It's green tea, an' it's good. I tell Council as I git older I don't seem to enjoy Young Hyson n'r Gunpowder. I want the reel green tea, jest as it comes off'n the vines. Seems t'have more heart in it, some way. Don't s'pose it has. Council says it's all in m' eye." Going on in this easy way, she soon had the children filled with bread and milk and the woman thoroughly at home, eating some toast and sweet-melon pickles, and sipping the tea.

"See the little rats!" she laughed at the children. "They're full as they can stick now, and they want to go to bed. Now, don't git up, Mis' Haskins; set right where you are an' let me look after 'em. I know all about young ones, though I'm all alone now. Jane went an' married last fall. But, as I tell Council, it's lucky we keep our health. Set right there, Mis' Haskins; I won't have you stir a finger."

It was an unmeasured pleasure to sit there in the warm, homely kitchen, the jovial chatter of the housewife driving out and holding at bay the growl of the impotent, cheated wind.

The little woman's eyes filled with tears which fell down upon the sleeping baby in her arms. The world was not so desolate and cold and hopeless, after all.

"Now I hope Council won't stop out there and talk politics all night. He's the greatest man to talk politics an' read the *Tribune*— How old is it?"

She broke off and peered down at the face of the babe.

"Two months 'n' five days," said the mother, with a mother's exactness.

"Ye don't say! I want 'o know! The dear little pudzy-wudzy!" she went on, stirring it up in the neighborhood of the ribs with her fat forefinger. "Pooty tough on 'oo to go galivant'n' 'cross lots this way——"

"Yes, that's so; a man can't lift a mountain," said Council, entering the door. "Mother, this is Mr. Haskins, from Kansas. He's been eat up 'n' drove out by grasshoppers."

"Glad t' see yeh!—Pa, empty that washbasin 'n' give him a chance t' wash."

Haskins was a tall man, with a thin, gloomy face. His hair was a reddish brown, like his coat, and seemed equally faded by the wind and sun, and his sallow face, though hard and set, was pathetic somehow. You would have felt that he had suffered much by the line of his mouth showing under his thin, yellow mustache.

"Hain't Ike got home yet, Sairy?"

"Hain't seen 'im."

"W-a-a-l, set right up, Mr. Haskins; wade right into what we've got; 'tain't much; but we manage to live on it—she gits fat on it," laughed Council, pointing his thumb at his wife.

After supper, while the women put the children to bed, Haskins and Council talked on, seated near the huge cooking-stove, the steam rising from their wet clothing. In the Western fashion Council told as much of his own life as he drew from his guest. He asked but few questions, but by and by the story of Haskins' struggles and defeat came out. The story was a terrible one, but he told it quietly, seated with his elbows on his knees, gazing most of the time at the hearth.

"I didn't like the looks of the country, anyhow," Haskins said, partly rising and glancing at his wife. "I was ust t' northern Ingyannie, where we have lots o' timber 'n' lots o' rain, 'n' I didn't like the looks o' that dry prairie. What galled me the worst was goin' s' far away acrosst so much fine land layin' all through here vacant."

"And the 'hoppers eat ye four years, hand runnin', did they?"

"Eat! They wiped us out. They chawed everything that was green. They jest set around waitin' f'r us to die t' eat us, too. My God! I ust t' dream of 'em sittin' 'round on the bedpost, six feet long, workin' their jaws. They eet the fork-handles. They got worse 'n' worse till they jest rolled on one another, piled up like snow in winter. Well, it ain't no use. If I was t' talk all winter I couldn't tell nawthin'. But all the while I couldn't help thinkin' of all that land back here that nobuddy was usin' that I ought 'o had 'stead o' bein' out there in that cussed country."

"Waal, why didn't ye stop an' settle here?" asked Ike, who had come in and was eating his supper.

"Fer the simple reason that you fellers wantid ten 'r fifteen dollars an acre fer the bare land, and I hadn't no money fer that kind o' thing."

"Yes, I do my own work," Mrs. Council was heard to say in the pause which followed. "I'm a-gettin' purty heavy t' be on m' laigs all day, but we can't afford t' hire, so I keep rackin' around somehow, like a foundered horse. S' lame—I tell Council he can't tell how lame I am, f'r I'm jest as lame in one laig as t' other." And the good soul laughed at the joke on herself as she took a handful of flour and dusted the biscuit-board to keep the dough from sticking.

"Well, I hain't *never* been very strong," said Mrs. Haskins. "Our folks was Canadians an' small-boned, and then since my last child I hain't got up again fairly. I don't like t' complain. Tim has about all he can bear now—but they was days this week when I jes wanted to lay right down an' die."

"Waal, now, I'll tell ye," said Council, from his side of the stove, silencing everybody with his good-natured roar, "I'd go down and *see* Butler, *anyway,* if I was you. I guess he'd let you have his place purty cheap; the farm's all run down. He's ben anxious t' let t' somebuddy next year. It 'ud be a good chance fer you. Anyhow, you go to bed and sleep like a babe. I've got some plowin' t' do, anyhow, an' we'll see if somethin' can't be done about your case. Ike, you go out an' see if the horses is all right, an' I'll show the folks t' bed."

When the tired husband and wife were lying under the generous quilts of the spare bed, Haskins listened a moment to the wind in the eaves, and then said, with a slow and solemn tone, "There are people in this world who are good enough t' be angels, an' only haff t' die to *be* angels."

2

Jim Butler was one of those men called in the West "land poor." Early in the history of Rock River he had come into the town and started in the grocery business in a small way, occupying a small building in a mean part of the town. At this period of his life he earned all he got, and was up early and late sorting beans, working over butter, and carting his goods to and from the station. But a change came over him at the end of the second year, when he sold a lot of land for four times what he paid for it. From that time forward he believed in land speculation as the surest way of getting rich. Every cent he could save or spare from his trade he put into land at forced sale, or mortgages on land, which were "just as good as the wheat," he was accustomed to say.

Farm after farm fell into his hands, until he was recognized as one of the leading landowners of the county. His mortgages were scattered all over Cedar County, and as they slowly but surely fell in he sought usually to retain the former owner as tenant.

He was not ready to foreclose; indeed, he had the name of being one of the "easiest" men in the town. He let the debtor off again and again, extending the time whenever possible.

"I don't want y'r land," he said. "All I'm after is the int'rest on my money—that's all. Now, if y' want 'o stay on the farm, why, I'll give y' a good chance. I can't have the land layin' vacant." And in many cases the owner remained as tenant.

In the meantime he had sold his store; he couldn't spend time in it; he was mainly occupied now with sitting around town on rainy days smoking and "gassin' with the boys," or in riding to and from his farms. In fishing-time he fished a good deal. Doc Grimes, Ben Ashley, and Cal Cheatham were his cronies on these fishing excursions or hunting trips in the time of chickens or partridges. In winter they went to Northern Wisconsin to shoot deer.

In spite of all these signs of easy life Butler persisted in saying he "hadn't enough money to pay taxes on his land," and was careful to convey the impression that he was poor in spite of his twenty farms. At one time he was said to be worth fifty thousand dollars, but land had been a little slow of sale of late, so that he was not worth so much.

A fine farm, known as the Higley place, had fallen into his hands in the usual way the previous year, and he had not been able to find a tenant for it. Poor Higley, after working himself nearly to death on it in the attempt to lift the mortgage, had gone off to Dakota, leaving the farm and his curse to Butler. This was the farm which Council advised Haskins to apply for; and the next day Council hitched up his team and drove down town to see Butler.

"You jest let *me* do the talkin'," he said. "We'll find him wearin' out his pants on some salt barrel somew'ers; and if he thought you *wanted* a place he'd sock it to you hot and heavy. You jest keep quiet; I'll fix 'im."

Butler was seated in Ben Ashley's store telling fish yarns when Council sauntered in casually.

"Hello, But; lyin' agin, hey!"

"Hello, Steve! how goes it?"

"Oh, so-so. Too dang much rain these days. I thought it was goin' t' freeze up f'r good last night. Tight squeak if I get m' plowin' done. How's farmin' with *you* these days?"

"Bad. Plowin' ain't half done."

"It 'ud be a religious idee f'r you t' go out an' take a hand y'rself."

"I don't haff to," said Butler, with a wink.

"Got anybody on the Higley place?"

"No. Know of anybody?"

"Waal, no; not eggsackly. I've got a relation back t' Michigan who's ben hot an' cold on the idee o' comin' West f'r some time. *Might* come if he could get a good layout. What do you talk on the farm?"

"Well, I d'know. I'll rent it on shares or I'll rent it money rent."

"Wall, how much money, say?"

"Well, say ten per cent, on the price—two-fifty."

"Wall, that ain't bad. Wait on 'im till 'e thrashes?"

Haskins listened eagerly to his important question, but Council was coolly eating a dried apple which he had speared out of a barrel with his knife. Butler studied him carefully.

"Well, knocks me out of twenty-five dollars interest."

"My relation'll need all he's got t' git his crops in," said Council, in the same, indifferent way.

"Well, all right; say wait," concluded Butler.

"All right; this is the man. Haskins, this is Mr. Butler—no relation to Ben—the hardest-working man in Cedar County."

On the way home Haskins said: "I ain't much better off. I'd like that farm; it's a good farm, but it's all run down, an' so 'm I. I could make a good farm of it if I had half a show. But I can't stock it n'r seed it."

"Wall, now, don't you worry," roared Council in his ear. "We'll pull y' through somehow till next harvest. He's agreed t' hire it plowed, an' you can earn a hundred dollars plowin' an' y' c'n git the seed o' me, an' pay me back when y' can."

Haskins was silent with emotion, but at last he said, "I ain't got nothin' t' live on."

"Now, don't you worry 'bout that. You jest make your head-quarters at ol' Steve Council's. Mother'll take a pile o' comfort in havin' y'r wife an' children 'round. Y' see, Jane's married off lately, an' Ike's away a good 'eal, so we'll be darn glad t' have y' stop with us this winter. Nex' spring we'll see if y' can't git a start agin." And he chirruped to the team, which sprang forward with the rumbling, clattering wagon.

"Say, looky here, Council, you can't do this. I never saw—" shouted Haskins in his neighbor's ear.

Council moved about uneasily in his seat and stopped his stammering gratitude by saying: "Hold on, now: don't make such a fuss over a little thing. When I see a man down, an' things all on top of 'm, I jest like t' kick 'em off an' help 'm up. That's the kind of religion I got, an' it's about the *only* kind."

They rode the rest of the way home in silence. And when the red light of the lamp shone out into the darkness of the cold and windy night, and he thought of this refuge for his children and wife, Haskins could have put his arm around the neck of his burly companion and squeezed him like a lover. But he contented himself with saying, "Steve Council, you'll git y'r pay f'r this some day."

"Don't want any pay. My religion ain't run on such business principles."

The wind was growing colder, and the ground was covered with a white frost, as they turned into the gate of the Council farm, and the children came rushing out, shouting, "Papa's come!" They hardly looked like the same children who had sat at the table the night before. Their torpidity, under the influence of sunshine and Mother Council, had given way to a sort of spasmodic cheerfulness, as insects in winter revive when laid on the hearth.

3

Haskins worked like a fiend, and his wife, like the heroic woman that she was, bore also uncomplainingly the most terrible burdens. They rose early and toiled without intermission till the darkness fell on the plain, then tumbled into bed, every bone and muscle aching with fatigue, to rise with the sun next morning to the same round of the same ferocity of labor.

The eldest boy drove a team all through the spring, plowing and seeding, milked the cows, and did chores innumerable, in most ways taking the place of a man.

An infinitely pathetic but common figure, this boy on the American farm, where there is no law against child labor. To see him in his coarse clothing, his huge boots, and his ragged cap, as he staggered with a pail of water from the well, or trudged in the cold and cheerless dawn out into the frosty field behind his team, gave the city-bred visitor a sharp pang of sympathetic pain. Yet Haskins loved his boy, and would have saved him from this if he could, but he could not.

By June the first year the result of such Herculean toil began to show on the farm. The yard was cleaned up and sown to grass, the garden plowed and planted, and the house mended.

Council had given them four of his cows.

"Take 'em an' run 'em on shares. I don't want 'o milk s' many. Ike's away s' much now, Sat'd'ys an' Sund'ys, I can't stand the bother anyhow."

Other men, seeing the confidence of Council in the newcomer, had sold him tools on time; and as he was really an able farmer, he soon had round him many evidences of his care and thrift. At the advice of Council he had taken the farm for three years, with the privilege of re-renting or buying at the end of the term.

"It's a good bargain, an' y' want 'o nail it," said Council. "If you have any kind ov a crop, you c'n pay y'r debts, an' keep seed an' bread."

The new hope which now sprang up in the heart of Haskins and his wife grew great almost as a pain by the time the wide field of wheat began to wave and swirl in the winds of July. Day after day he would snatch a few moments after supper to go and look at it.

"Have ye seen the wheat t'-day, Nettie?" he asked one night as he rose from supper.

"No, Tim, I ain't had time."

"Well, take time now. Le's go look at it."

She threw an old hat on her head—Tommy's hat—and looking almost pretty in her thin, sad way, went out with her husband to the hedge.

"Ain't it grand, Nettie? Just look at it."

It was grand. Level, russet here and there, heavy-headed, wide as a lake, and full of multitudinous whispers and gleams of wealth, it stretched away before the gazers like the fabled field of the cloth of gold.

"Oh, I think—I *hope* we'll have a good crop, Tim; and oh, how good the people have been to us!"

"Yes; I don't know where we'd be t'-day if it hadn't ben f'r Council and his wife."

"They're the best people in the world," said the little woman, with a great sob of gratitude.

"We'll be in the field on Monday, sure," said Haskins, gripping the rail on the fence as if already at the work of the harvest.

The harvest came, bounteous, glorious, but the winds came and blew it into tangles, and the rain matted it here and there close to the ground, increasing the work of gathering it threefold.

Oh, how they toiled in those glorious days! Clothing dripping with sweat, arms aching, filled with briers, fingers raw and bleeding, backs broken with the weight of heavy bundles, Haskins and his man toiled on. Tommy drove the harvester, while his father and a hired man bound on the machine. In this way they cut ten acres every day, and almost every night after supper, when the hand went to bed, Haskins returned to the field shocking the bound grain in the light of the moon. Many a night he worked till his anxious wife came out at ten o'clock to call him in to rest and lunch.

At the same time she cooked for the men, took care of the children, washed and ironed, milked the cows at night, made the butter, and sometimes fed the horses and watered them while her husband kept at the shocking.

No slave in the Roman galleys could have toiled so frightfully and lived, for this man thought himself a free man, and that he was working for his wife and babes.

When he sank into his bed with a deep groan of relief, too tired to change his grimy, dripping clothing, he felt that he was getting nearer and nearer to a home of his own, and pushing the wolf of want a little farther from his door.

There is no despair so deep as the despair of a homeless man or woman. To roam the roads of the country or the streets of the city, to feel there is no rood of ground on which the feet can rest, to halt weary and hungry outside lighted windows and hear laughter and song within,—these are the hungers and rebellions that drive men to crime and women to shame.

It was the memory of this homelessness, and the fear of its coming again, that spurred Timothy Haskins and Nettie, his wife, to such ferocious labor during that first year.

4

"'M, yes; 'm, yes; first-rate," said Butler, as his eye took in the neat garden, the pigpen, and the well-filled barnyard. "You're gitt'n' quite a stock around yeh. Done well, eh?"

Haskins was showing Butler around the place. He had not seen it for a year, having spent the year in Washington and Boston with Ashley, his brother-in-law, who had been elected to Congress.

"Yes, I've laid out a good deal of money durin' the last three years. I've paid out three hundred dollars f'r fencin'."

"Um—h'm! I see, I see," said Butler while Haskins went on:

"The kitchen there cost two hundred; the barn ain't cost much in money, but I've put a lot o' time on it. I've dug a new well, and I—"

"Yes, yes, I see. You've done well. Stock worth a thousand dollars," said Butler, picking his teeth with a straw.

"About that," said Haskins, modestly. "We begin to feel 's if we was gitt'n a home f'r ourselves; but we've worked hard. I tell you we begin to feel it, Mr. Butler, and we're goin' t' begin to ease up purty soon. We've been kind o' plannin' a trip back t' *her* folks after the fall plowin's done."

"*Eggs*-actly!' said Butler, who was evidently thinking of something else. "I suppose you've kind o' calc'lated on stayin' here three years more?"

"Well, yes. Fact is, I think I c'n buy the farm this fall, if you'll give me a reasonable show."

"Um—m! What do you call a reasonable show?"

"Well, say a quarter down and three years' time."

Butler looked at the huge stacks of wheat, which filled the yard, over which the chickens were fluttering and crawling, catching grasshoppers, and out of which the crickets were singing innumerably. He smiled in a peculiar way as he said, "Oh, I won't be hard on yeh. But what did you expect to pay f'r the place?"

"Why, about what you offered it for before, two thousand five hundred, or *possibly* three thousand dollars," he added quickly as he saw the owner shake his head.

"This farm is worth five thousand and five hundred dollars," said Butler, in a careless and decided voice.

"*What!*" almost shrieked the astounded Haskins. "What's that? Five thousand? Why, that's double what you offered it for three years ago."

"Of course, and it's worth it. It was all run down then; now it's in good shape. You've laid out fifteen hundred dollars in improvements, according to your own story."

"But *you* had nothin' t' do about that. It's my work an' my money."

"You bet it was; but it's my land."

"But what's to pay me for all my——"

"Ain't you had the use of 'em?" replied Butler, smiling calmly into his face.

Haskins was like a man struck on the head with a sandbag; he couldn't think; he stammered as he tried to say: "But—I never'd git the use— You'd rob me! More'n that: you agreed—you promised that I could buy or rent at the end of three years at——"

"That's all right. But I didn't say I'd let you carry off the improvements, nor that I'd go on renting the farm at two-fifty. The land is doubled in value, it don't matter how; it don't enter into the question; an' now you can pay me five hundred dollars a year rent, or take it on your own terms at fifty-five hundred, or—git out."

He was turning away when Haskins, the sweat pouring from his face, fronted him, saying again:

"But *you've* done nothing to make it so. You hain't added a cent. I put it all there myself, expectin' to buy. I worked an' sweat to improve it. I was workin' for my self an' babes——"

"Well, why didn't you buy when I offered to sell? What y' kickin' about?"

"I'm kickin' about payin' you twice f'r my own things,—my own fences, my own kitchen, my own garden."

Butler laughed. "You're too green t'eat, young feller. *Your* improvements! The law will sing another tune."

"But I trusted your word."

"Never trust anybody, my friend. Besides, I didn't promise not to do this thing. Why, man, don't look at me like that. Don't take me for a thief. It's the law. The reg'lar thing. Everybody does it."

"I don't care if they do. It's stealin' jest the same. You take three thousand dollars of my money—the work o' my hands and my wife's." He broke down at this point. He was not a strong man mentally. He could face hardship, ceaseless toil, but he could not face the cold and sneering face of Butler.

"But I don't take it," said Butler, coolly. "All you've got to do is to go on jest as you've been a-doin', or give me a thousand dollars down, and a mortgage at ten per cent on the rest."

Haskins sat down blindly on a bundle of oats near by, and with staring eyes and drooping head went over the situation. He was under the lion's paw. He felt a horrible numbness in his heart and limbs. He was hid in a mist, and there was no path out.

Butler walked about, looking at the huge stacks of grain, and pulling now and again a few handfuls out, shelling the heads in his hands and blowing the chaff away. He hummed a little tune as he did so. He had an accommodating air of waiting.

Haskins was in the midst of the terrible toil of the last year. He was walking again in the rain and the mud behind his plow; he felt the dust and dirt of the threshing. The ferocious husking-time, with its cutting wind and biting, clinging snows, lay hard upon him. Then he thought of his wife, how she had cheerfully cooked and baked, without holiday and without rest.

"Well, what do you think of it?" inquired the cool, mocking, insinuating voice of Butler.

"I think you're a thief and a liar!" shouted Haskins, leaping up. "A blackhearted houn'!" Butler's smile maddened him; with a sudden leap he caught a fork in his hands, and whirled it in the air. "You'll never rob another man, damn ye!" he grated through his teeth, a look of pitiless ferocity in his accusing eyes.

Butler shrank and quivered, expecting the blow; stood, held hypnotized by the eyes of the man he had a moment before despised— a man transformed into an avenging demon. But in the deadly hush between the lift of the weapon and its fall there came a gush of faint, childish laughter and then across the range of his vision, far away and dim, he saw the sun-bright head of his baby girl, as, with the pretty, tottering run of a two-year-old, she moved across the grass of the dooryard. His hands relaxed; the fork fell to the ground; his head lowered.

"Make out y'r deed an' mor'gage, an' git off'n my land, an' don't ye never cross my line again; if y' do, I'll kill ye."

Butler backed away from the man in wild haste, and climbing into his buggy with trembling limbs drove off down the road, leaving Haskins seated dumbly on the sunny piles of sheaves, his head sunk into his hands.

Sydney Porter

MAMMON AND THE ARCHER

William Sydney Porter, better known as O. Henry, was born in Greensboro, North Carolina, in 1862. Virtually orphaned at three, he was reared and educated by a maiden aunt who encouraged his bent toward literature and drawing. At fifteen he began working as an apprentice in his uncle's drug store and became a licensed pharmacist in 1881. The following year he went to Texas, where he remained for fourteen years, drifting through a variety of experiences in both the cattle country and the booming towns of Austin, Houston, and San Antonio. After his marriage in 1886 he held a number of jobs—draftsman, bank teller, newspaper columnist—but in 1894 he began publishing sketches and tales in his own comic weekly, *The Rolling Stone,* and later in his column for the *Houston Daily Post.*

Indicted for the embezzlement of bank funds, Porter fled to Central America in 1896. The next year he was tried and sentenced to imprisonment in the federal penitentiary at Columbus, Ohio. During his term there his fabulous career as O. Henry, the unknown author of popular magazine fiction, began. Upon his release from prison in 1901 he went to New York City and soon became the most famous short story writer of his day. Writing with amazing speed, he produced about 250 stories for the New York *Sunday World* and other magazines between 1902 and his death in 1910. All but a handful of these appeared in collections bearing such familiar titles as *Cabbages and Kings* (1904), *The Four Million* (1906), *The Trimmed Lamp* (1907), *The Voice of the City* (1908), *Roads of Destiny* (1909). Most of them have been translated into many languages and reprinted in hundreds of editions.

Writing frankly to make money, O. Henry shaped his stories to meet the ephemeral demands of mass-circulation periodicals, his purpose being, as he put it, to please "Mr. Everybody." But the enormous

311

popularity of his method has been due to something more than its mere formula, which substituted technical tricks for the more demanding task of revealing character in conflict and action. In this sense O. Henry's work marks the culmination of the story-of-effect tradition begun by Poe and refined by many other writers, notably De Maupassant. Sleight-of-hand plot jugglery; a crackling style with a punch in nearly every line; humor and wit combined with sentimentality; a racing, breathless narrative tempo; and, of course, the surprising reversal or twist at the climax—all such devices, used to the fullest by O. Henry, are plainly visible in a typical story like "Mammon and the Archer." Yet, however impalpable his plots or transparent his formulae, there is a pervasive quality in O. Henry's best stories that stamps him as an original, a minor classic whom the literate masses of the world have taken to heart and refuse to outgrow.

mammon and the archer

Old Anthony Rockwall, retired manufacturer and proprietor of Rockwall's Eureka Soap, looked out the library window of his Fifth Avenue mansion and grinned. His neighbour to the right—the aristocratic clubman, G. Van Schuylight Suffolk-Jones—came out to his waiting motor-car, wrinkling a contumelious nostril, as usual, at the Italian renaissance sculpture of the soap palace's front elevation.

"Stuck-up old statuette of nothing doing!" commented the ex-Soap King. "The Eden Musée'll get that old frozen Nesselrode yet if he don't watch out. I'll have this house painted red, white, and blue next summer and see if that'll make his Dutch nose turn up any higher."

And then Anthony Rockwall, who never cared for bells, went to the door of his library and shouted "Mike!" in the same voice that had once chipped off pieces of the welkin on the Kansas prairies.

"Tell my son," said Anthony to the answering menial, "to come in here before he leaves the house."

When young Rockwall entered the library the old man laid aside his newspaper, looked at him with a kindly grimness on his big, smooth, ruddy countenance, rumpled his mop of white hair with one hand and rattled the keys in his pocket with the other.

"Richard," said Anthony Rockwall, "what do you pay for the soap that you use?"

Richard, only six months home from college, was startled a little. He had not yet taken the measure of this sire of his, who was as full of unexpectednesses as a girl at her first party.

"Six dollars a dozen, I think, dad."

"And your clothes?"

"I suppose about sixty dollars, as a rule."

"You're a gentleman," said Anthony, decidedly. "I've heard of these young bloods spending $24 a dozen for soap, and going over the hundred mark for clothes. You've got as much money to waste as any of 'em, and yet you stick to what's decent and moderate. Now I use the old Eureka—not only for sentiment, but it's the purest soap made. Whenever you pay more than 10 cents a cake for soap you buy bad perfumes and labels. But 50 cents is doing very well for a young man in your generation, position and condition. As I said, you're a gentleman. They say it takes three generations to make one. They're off. Money'll do it as slick as soap grease. It's made you one. By hokey! it's almost made one of me. I'm nearly as impolite and disagreeable and ill-mannered as these two old knickerbocker gents on each side of me that can't sleep of nights because I bought in between 'em."

"There are some things that money can't accomplish," remarked young Rockwall, rather gloomily.

"Now, don't say that," said old Anthony, shocked. "I bet my money on money every time. I've been through the encyclopaedia down to Y looking for something you can't buy with it; and I expect to have to take up the appendix next week. I'm for money against the field. Tell me something money won't buy."

"For one thing," answered Richard, rankling a little, "it won't buy one into the exclusive circles of society."

"Oho! won't it?" thundered the champion of the root of evil. "You tell me where your exclusive circles would be if the first Astor hadn't had the money to pay for his steerage passage over?"

Richard sighed.

"And that's what I was coming to," said the old man, less boisterously. "That's why I asked you to come in. There's something going wrong with you, boy. I've been noticing it for two weeks. Out with it. I guess I could lay my hands on eleven millions within twenty-four hours, besides the real estate. If it's your liver, there's the *Rambler* down in the bay, coaled, and ready to steam down to the Bahamas in two days."

"Not a bad guess, dad; you haven't missed it far."

"Ah," said Anthony, keenly; "what's her name?"

Richard began to walk up and down the library floor. There was enough comradeship and sympathy in this crude old father of his to draw his confidence.

"Why don't you ask her?" demanded old Anthony. "She'll jump at you. You've got the money and the looks, and you're a decent boy. Your hands are clean. You've got no Eureka soap on 'em. You've been to college, but she'll overlook that."

"I haven't had a chance," said Richard.

"Make one," said Anthony. "Take her for a walk in the park, or a straw ride, or walk home with her from church. Chance! Pshaw!"

"You don't know the social mill, dad. She's part of the stream that turns it. Every hour and minute of her time is arranged for days in advance. I must have that girl, dad, or this town is a blackjack swamp forevermore. And I can't write it—I can't do that."

"Tut!" said the old man. "Do you mean to tell me that with all the money I've got you can't get an hour or two of a girl's time for yourself?"

"I've put it off too late. She's going to sail for Europe at noon day after to-morrow for a two years' stay. I'm to see her alone to-morrow evening for a few minutes. She's at Larchmont now at her aunt's. I can't go there. But I'm allowed to meet her with a cab at the Grand Central Station to-morrow evening at the 8:30 train. We drive down Broadway to Wallack's at a gallop, where her mother and a box party will be waiting for us in the lobby. Do you think she would listen to a declaration from me during that six or eight minutes under those circumstances? No. And what chance would I have in the theatre or afterward? None. No, dad, this is one tangle that your money can't unravel. We can't buy one minute of time with cash; if we could, rich people would live longer. There's no hope of getting a talk with Miss Lantry before she sails."

"All right, Richard, my boy," said old Anthony, cheerfully. "You may run along down to your club now. I'm glad it ain't your liver. But don't forget to burn a few punk sticks in the joss house to the great god Mazuma from time to time. You say money won't buy time? Well, of course, you can't order eternity wrapped up and delivered at your residence for a price, but I've seen Father Time get pretty bad stone bruises on his heels when he walked through the gold diggings."

That night came Aunt Ellen, gentle, sentimental, wrinkled, sighing, oppressed by wealth, in to Brother Anthony at his evening paper, and began discourse on the subject of lovers' woes.

"He told me all about it," said Brother Anthony, yawning. "I told him my bank account was at his service. And then he began to knock money. Said money couldn't help. Said the rules of society couldn't be bucked for a yard by a team of ten-millionaires."

"Oh, Anthony," sighed Aunt Ellen, "I wish you would not think so much of money. Wealth is nothing where a true affection is concerned. Love is all-powerful. If he only had spoken earlier! She could not have refused our Richard. But now I fear it is too late. He will have no opportunity to address her. All your gold cannot bring happiness to your son."

At eight o'clock the next evening Aunt Ellen took a quaint old gold ring from a moth-eaten case and gave it to Richard.

"Wear it to-night, nephew," she begged. "Your mother gave it to me. Good luck in love she said it brought. She asked me to give it to you when you had found the one you loved."

Young Rockwall took the ring reverently and tried it on his smallest finger. It slipped as far as the second joint and stopped. He took it off and stuffed it into his vest pocket, after the manner of man. And then he 'phoned for his cab.

At the station he captured Miss Lantry out of the gabbing mob at eight thirty-two.

"We mustn't keep mamma and the others waiting," said she.

"To Wallack's Theatre as fast as you can drive!" said Richard loyally.

They whirled up Forty-second to Broadway, and then down the white-starred lane that leads from the soft meadows of sunset to the rocky hills of morning.

At Thirty-fourth Street young Richard quickly thrust up the trap and ordered the cabman to stop.

"I've dropped a ring," he apologized, as he climbed out. "It was my mother's, and I'd hate to lose it. I won't detain you a minute—I saw where it fell."

In less than a minute he was back in the cab with the ring.

But within that minute a crosstown car had stopped directly in front of the cab. The cab-man tried to pass to the left, but a heavy express wagon cut him off. He tried the right and had to back away from a furniture van that had no business to be there. He tried to back out, but dropped his reins and swore dutifully. He was blockaded in a tangled mess of vehicles and horses.

One of those street blockades had occurred that sometimes tie up commerce and movement quite suddenly in the big city.

"Why don't you drive on?" said Miss Lantry, impatiently. "We'll be late."

Richard stood up in the cab and looked around. He saw a congested flood of wagons, trucks, cabs, vans and street cars filling the vast space where Broadway, Sixth Avenue, and Thirty-fourth Street cross one another as a twenty-six inch maiden fills her twenty-two inch girdle. And still from all the cross streets they were hurrying and rattling toward the converging point at full speed, and hurling themselves into the straggling mass, locking wheels and adding their drivers' imprecations to the clamor. The entire traffic of Manhattan seemed to have jammed itself around them. The oldest New Yorker among the thousands of spectators that lined the sidewalks had not witnessed a street blockade of the proportions of this one.

"I'm very sorry," said Richard, as he resumed his seat, "but it looks as if we are stuck. They won't get this jumble loosened up in an hour. It was my fault. If I hadn't dropped the ring we—"

"Let me see the ring," said Miss Lantry. "Now that it can't be helped, I don't care. I think theatres are stupid, anyway."

At 11 o'clock that night somebody tapped lightly on Anthony Rockwall's door.

"Come in," shouted Anthony, who was in a red dressing-gown, reading a book of piratical adventures.

Somebody was Aunt Ellen, looking like a gray-haired angel that had been left on earth by mistake.

"They're engaged, Anthony," she said, softly. "She has promised to marry our Richard. On their way to the theatre there was a street blockade, and it was two hours before their cab could get out of it.

"And oh, Brother Anthony, don't ever boast of the power of money again. A little emblem of true love—a little ring that symbolized unending and unmercenary affection—was the cause of our Richard finding his happiness. He dropped it in the street, and got out to recover it. And before they could continue the blockade occurred. He spoke to his love and won her there while the cab was hemmed in. Money is dross compared with true love, Anthony."

"All right," said old Anthony. "I'm glad the boy has got what he wanted. I told him I wouldn't spare any expense in the matter if—"

"But, Brother Anthony, what good could your money have done?"

"Sister," said Anthony Rockwall. "I've got my pirate in a devil of a scrape. His ship has just been scuttled, and he's too good a judge of the value of money to let drown. I wish you would let me go on with this chapter."

The story should end here. I wish it would as heartily as you who read it wish it did. But we must go to the bottom of the well for truth.

The next day a person with red hands and a blue polka-dot necktie, who called himself Kelly, called at Anthony Rockwall's house, and was at once received in the library.

"Well," said Anthony, reaching for his check-book, "it was a good bilin' of soap. Let's see—you had $5,000 in cash."

"I paid out $300 more of my own," said Kelly. "I had to go a little above the estimate. I got the express wagons and cabs mostly for $5; but the trucks and two-horse teams mostly raised me to $10. The motorman wanted $10, and some of the loaded teams $20. The cops struck me hardest—$50 I paid two, and the rest $20 and $25. But didn't it work beautiful, Mr. Rockwall? I'm glad William A. Brady wasn't onto that little outdoor vehicle mob scene. I wouldn't want William to break his heart with jealousy. And never a rehearsal, either! The boys was on time to the fraction of a second. It was two hours before a snake could get below Greeley's statue."

"Thirteen hundred—there you are, Kelly," said Anthony, tearing off a check. "Your thousand, and the $300 you were out. You don't despise money, do you, Kelly?"

"Me?" said Kelly. "I can lick the man that invented poverty."

Anthony called Kelly when he was at the door.

"You didn't notice," said he, "anywhere in the tie-up, a kind of a fat boy without any clothes on shooting arrows around with a bow, did you?"

"Why, no," said Kelly, mystified. "I didn't. If he was like you say, maybe the cops pinched him before I got there."

"I thought the little rascal wouldn't be on hand," chuckled Anthony. "Good-by, Kelly."

Stephen Crane

A MYSTERY OF HEROISM

THE BRIDE COMES TO YELLOW SKY

Stephen Crane, despite a small body of fiction, is a pivotal figure in the history of the short story. In both his detached vision of life and his individualized technique, he anticipates a major phase of the twentieth-century short story. His importance, however, depends not merely on his being the herald of future literary modes; in their own right his stories have intrinsic merit and daring originality.

Within a lifetime briefer than Poe's—twenty-nine years from his birth in Newark, New Jersey, in 1871 to his death from tuberculosis in Badenweiler, Germany, in 1900—Crane pursued an equally intensive literary career, remarkable for its varied achievements. After three years of preparatory school at Claverack College, near Hudson, New York, a year of college training at Lafayette College, and a second year at Syracuse University, he went to New York, where he became a reporter. Soon, his literary aims having transcended journalism, he wrote a short novel, *Maggie: A Girl of the Streets,* which was so frankly naturalistic in viewpoint, language, and treatment of sex that it failed to sell even after Crane published it at his own expense in 1893 and reputedly employed persons to flourish it on streetcars. His next novel, however, *The Red Badge of Courage* (1895), a vividly impressionistic study of battle psychology which artfully concealed his lack of wartime experience, not only found a publisher but also established his reputation. During his last five years, Crane's activities included writing for a syndicate and reporting the Greco-Turkish and Spanish-American Wars. Added to these experiences were his marriage to Cora Taylor, residence in England, and the frequent publication of new novels, poems, and stories. His most important short stories appear in *The Little Regiment and Other Episodes of the American War* (1896),

The Open Boat and Other Tales (1898), *The Monster and Other Stories* (1899), and *Whilomville Stories* (1900).

Crane's stories, as illustrated in "A Mystery of Heroism" and "The Bride Comes to Yellow Sky," reveal his flair for bold metaphors and vivid, precise phrasing. The imagery thus created is often so striking that it calls attention to itself; but, at the same time, it is one of the means by which Crane achieves startlingly original effects, as well as an excellent vehicle for conveying his ironic viewpoint. Irony, in fact, is at the basis of Crane's art whether he writes about war or about less sensational human experiences; for his purpose is to reveal with cool detachment the incongruity between appearance and reality, the contrast between man's expectations and achievements, in a world where at any moment chance may turn the tables on him.

a mystery of heroism

The dark uniforms of the men were so coated with dust from the incessant wrestling of the two armies that the regiment almost seemed a part of the clay bank which shielded them from the shells. On the top of the hill a battery was arguing in tremendous roars with some other guns, and to the eye of the infantry, the artillerymen, the guns, the caissons, the horses, were distinctly outlined upon the blue sky. When a piece was fired, a red streak as round as a log flashed low in the heavens, like a monstrous bolt of lightning. The men of the battery wore white duck trousers, which somehow emphasized their legs; and when they ran and crowded in little groups at the bidding of the shouting officers, it was more impressive than usual to the infantry.

Fred Collins, of A Company, was saying: "Thunder! I wisht I had a drink. Ain't there any water round here?" Then somebody yelled, "There goes th' bugler!"

As the eyes of half the regiment swept in one machinelike

movement there was an instant's picture of a horse in a great convulsive leap of a death wound and a rider leaning back with a crooked arm and spread fingers before his face. On the ground was the crimson terror of an exploding shell, with fibres of flame that seemed like lances. A glittering bugle swung clear of the rider's back as fell headlong the horse and the man. In the air was an odour as from a conflagration.

Sometimes they of the infantry looked down at a fair little meadow which spread at their feet. Its long, green grass was rippling gently in a breeze. Beyond it was the gray form of a house half torn to pieces by shells and by the busy axes of soldiers who had pursued firewood. The line of an old fence was now dimly marked by long weeds and by an occasional post. A shell had blown the well-house to fragments. Little lines of gray smoke ribboning upward from some embers indicated the place where had stood the barn.

From beyond a curtain of green woods there came the sound of some stupendous scuffle, as if two animals of the size of islands were fighting. At a distance there were occasional appearances of swift-moving men, horses, batteries, flags, and, with the crashing of infantry volleys were heard, often, wild and frenzied cheers. In the midst of it all Smith and Ferguson, two privates of A Company, were engaged in a heated discussion, which involved the greatest questions of the national existence.

The battery on the hill presently engaged in a frightful duel. The white legs of the gunners scampered this way and that way, and the officers redoubled their shouts. The guns, with their demeanours of stolidity and courage, were typical of something infinitely self-possessed in this clamour of death that swirled around the hill.

One of a "swing" team was suddenly smitten quivering to the ground, and his maddened brethren dragged his torn body in their struggle to escape from this turmoil and danger. A young soldier astride one of the leaders swore and fumed in his saddle, and furiously jerked at the bridle. An officer screamed out an order so violently that his voice broke and ended the sentence in a falsetto shriek.

The leading company of the infantry regiment was somewhat exposed, and the colonel ordered it moved more fully under the shelter of the hill. There was the clank of steel against steel.

A lieutenant of the battery rode down and passed them, holding his right arm carefully in his left hand. And it was as if this arm was not at all a part of him, but belonged to another man. His sober and reflective charger went slowly. The officer's face was grimy and perspiring, and his uniform was tousled as if he had been in direct grapple with an enemy. He smiled grimly when the men stared at him. He turned his horse toward the meadow.

Collins, of A Company, said: "I wisht I had a drink. I bet there's water in that there ol' well yonder!"

"Yes; but how you goin' to git it?"

For the little meadow which intervened was now suffering a terrible onslaught of shells. Its green and beautiful calm had vanished utterly. Brown earth was being flung in monstrous handfuls. And there was a massacre of the young blades of grass. They were being torn, burned, obliterated. Some curious fortune of the battle had made this gentle little meadow the object of the red hate of the shells, and each one as it exploded seemed like an imprecation in the face of a maiden.

The wounded officer who was riding across this expanse said to himself, "Why, they couldn't shoot any harder if the whole army was massed here!"

A shell struck the gray ruins of the house, and as, after the roar, the shattered wall fell in fragments, there was a noise which resembled the flapping of shutters during a wild gale of winter. Indeed, the infantry paused in the shelter of the bank appeared as men standing upon a shore contemplating a madness of the sea. The angel of calamity had under its glance the battery upon the hill. Fewer white-legged men laboured about the guns. A shell had smitten one of the pieces, and after the flare, the smoke, the dust, the wrath of this blow were gone, it was possible to see white legs stretched horizontally upon the ground. And at that interval to the rear, where it is the business of battery horses to stand with their noses to the fight awaiting the command to drag their guns out of the destruction or into it or wheresoever these incomprehensible humans demanded with whip and spur—in this line of passive and dumb spectators, whose fluttering hearts yet would not let them forget the iron laws of man's control of them—in this rank of brute-soldiers there had been relentless and hideous carnage. From the ruck of bleeding and prostrate horses, the men of the infantry could see one animal raising its stricken body with its fore legs, and turning its nose with mystic and profound eloquence toward the sky.

Some comrades joked Collins about his thirst. "Well, if yeh want a drink so bad, why don't yeh go git it!"

"Well, I will in a minnet, if yeh don't shut up!"

A lieutenant of artillery floundered his horse straight down the hill with as great concern as if it were level ground. As he galloped past the colonel of the infantry, he threw up his hand in swift salute. "We've got to get out of that," he roared angrily. He was a black-bearded officer, and his eyes, which resembled beads, sparkled like those of an insane man. His jumping horse sped along the column of infantry.

The fat major, standing carelessly with his sword held horizontally behind him and with his legs far apart, looked after the receding horseman and laughed. "He wants to get back with orders pretty quick, or there'll be no batt'ry left," he observed.

The wise young captain of the second company hazarded to the lieutenant colonel that the enemy's infantry would probably soon attack the hill, and the lieutenant colonel snubbed him.

A private in one of the rear companies looked out over the meadow, and then turned to a companion and said, "Look there, Jim!" It was the wounded officer from the battery, who some time before had started to ride across the meadow, supporting his right arm carefully with his left hand. This man had encountered a shell apparently at a time when no one perceived him, and he could now be seen lying face downward with a stirruped foot stretched across the body of his dead horse. A leg of the charger extended slantingly upward precisely as stiff as a stake. Around this motionless pair the shells still howled.

There was a quarrel in A Company. Collins was shaking his fist in the faces of some laughing comrades. "Dern yeh! I ain't afraid t' go. If yeh say much, I will go!"

"Of course, yeh will! You'll run through that there medder, won't yeh?"

Collins said, in a terrible voice, "You see now!" At this ominous threat his comrades broke into renewed jeers.

Collins gave them a dark scowl and went to find his captain. The latter was conversing with the colonel of the regiment.

"Captain," said Collins, saluting and standing at attention—in those days all trousers bagged at the knees—"captain, I want t' get permission to go git some water from that there well over yonder!"

The colonel and the captain swung about simultaneously and stared across the meadow. The captain laughed. "You must be pretty thirsty, Collins?"

"Yes sir, I am."

"Well—ah," said the captain. After a moment he asked, "Can't you wait?"

"No, sir."

The colonel was watching Collins's face. "Look here, my lad," he said, in a pious sort of a voice—"look here, my lad"—Collins was not a lad—"don't you think that's taking pretty big risks for a little drink of water?"

"I dunno," said Collins uncomfortably. Some of the resentment toward his companions, which perhaps had forced him into this affair, was beginning to fade. "I dunno wether 'tis."

The colonel and the captain contemplated him for a time.

"Well," said the captain finally.

"Well," said the colonel, "if you want to go, why, go."

Collins saluted. "Much obliged t' yeh."

As he moved away the colonel called after him. "Take some of the other boys' canteens with you an' hurry back now."

"Yes, sir, I will."

The colonel and the captain looked at each other then, for it had suddenly occurred that they could not for the life of them tell whether Collins wanted to go or whether he did not.

They turned to regard Collins, and as they perceived him surrounded by gesticulating comrades, the colonel said: "Well, by thunder! I guess he's going."

Collins appeared as a man dreaming. In the midst of the questions, the advice, the warnings, all the excited talk of his company mates, he maintained a curious silence.

They were very busy in preparing him for his ordeal. When they inspected him carefully it was somewhat like the examination that grooms give a horse before a race; and they were amazed, staggered by the whole affair. Their astonishment found vent in strange repetitions.

"Are yeh sure a-goin'?" they demanded again and again.

"Certainly I am," cried Collins, at last furiously.

He strode sullenly away from them. He was swinging five or six canteens by their cords. It seemed that his cap would not remain firmly on his head, and often he reached and pulled it down over his brow.

There was a general movement in the compact column. The long animal-like thing moved slightly. Its four hundred eyes were turned upon the figure of Collins.

"Well, sir, if that ain't th' derndest thing! I never thought Fred Collins had the blood in him for that kind of business."

"What's he goin' to do, anyhow?"

"He's goin' to that well there after water."

"We ain't dyin' of thirst, are we? That's foolishness."

"Well, somebody put him up to it, an' he's doin' it."

"Say, he must be a desperate cuss."

When Collins faced the meadow and walked away from the regiment, he was vaguely conscious that a chasm, the deep valley of all prides, was suddenly between him and his comrades. It was provisional, but the provision was that he return as a victor. He had blindly been led by quaint emotions, and laid himself under an obligation to walk squarely up to the face of death.

But he was not sure that he wished to make a retraction, even if he could do so without shame. As a matter of truth, he was sure of very little. He was mainly surprised.

It seemed to him supernaturally strange that he had allowed his mind to manœuver his body into such a situation. He understood that it might be called dramatically great.

However, he had no full appreciation of anything, excepting that he was actually conscious of being dazed. He could feel his dulled mind groping after the form and colour of this incident. He wondered why he did not feel some keen agony of fear cutting his sense like a knife. He wondered at this, because human expression had said loudly for centuries that men should feel afraid of certain things, and that all men who did not feel this fear were phenomena—heroes.

He was, then, a hero. He suffered that disappointment which we would all have if we discovered that we were ourselves capable of those deeds which we most admire in history and legend. This, then, was a hero. After all, heroes were not much.

No, it could not be true. He was not a hero. Heroes had no shames in their lives, and, as for him, he remembered borrowing fifteen dollars from a friend and promising to pay it back the next day, and then avoiding that friend for ten months. When at home his mother had aroused him for the early labour of his life on the farm, it had often been his fashion to be irritable, childish, diabolical; and his mother had died since he had come to the war.

He saw that, in this matter of the well, the canteens, the shells, he was an intruder in the land of fine deeds.

He was now about thirty paces from his comrades. The regiment had just turned its many faces toward him.

From the forest of terrific noises there suddenly emerged a little uneven line of men. They fired fiercely and rapidly at distant foliage on which appeared little puffs of white smoke. The spatter of skirmish firing was added to the thunder of the guns on the hill. The little line of men ran forward. A colour sergeant fell flat with his flag as if he had slipped on ice. There was hoarse cheering from this distant field.

Collins suddenly felt that two demon fingers were pressed into his ears. He could see nothing but flying arrows, flaming red. He lurched from the shock of this explosion, but he made a mad rush for the house, which he viewed as a man submerged to the neck in a boiling surf might view the shore. In the air, little pieces of shell howled and the earthquake explosions drove him insane with the menace of their roar. As he ran the canteens knocked together with a rhythmical tinkling.

As he neared the house, each detail of the scene became vivid to him. He was aware of some bricks of the vanished chimney lying on the sod. There was a door which hung by one hinge.

Rifle bullets called forth by the insistent skirmishers came from the far-off bank of foliage. They mingled with the shells and the pieces of shells until the air was torn in all directions by hootings, yells, howls. The sky was full of fiends who directed all their wild rage at his head.

When he came to the well, he flung himself face downward and peered into its darkness. There were furtive silver glintings some feet from the surface. He grabbed one of the canteens and, unfastening its cap, swung it down by the cord. The water flowed slowly in with an indolent gurgle.

And now as he lay with his face turned away he was suddenly smitten with the terror. It came upon his heart like the grasp of claws. All the power faded from his muscles. For an instant he was no more than a dead man.

The canteen filled with a maddening slowness, in the manner of all bottles. Presently he recovered his strength and addressed a screaming oath to it. He leaned over until it seemed as if he intended to try to push water into it with his hands. His eyes as he gazed down into the well shone like two pieces of metal and in their expression was a great appeal and a great curse. The stupid water derided him.

There was the blaring thunder of a shell. Crimson light shone through the swift-boiling smoke and made a pink reflection on part of the wall of the well. Collins jerked out his arm and canteen with the same motion that a man would use in withdrawing his head from a furnace.

He scrambled erect and glared and hesitated. On the ground near him lay the old well bucket, with a length of rusty chain. He lowered it swiftly into the well. The bucket struck the water and then, turning lazily over, sank. When, with hand reaching tremblingly over hand, he hauled it out, it knocked often against the walls of the well and spilled some of its contents.

In running with a filled bucket, a man can adopt but one kind of gait. So through this terrible field over which screamed practical angels of death Collins ran in the manner of a farmer chased out of a dairy by a bull.

His face went staring white with anticipation—anticipation of a blow that would whirl him around and down. He would fall as he had seen other men fall, the life knocked out of them so suddenly that their knees were no more quick to touch the ground than their heads. He saw the long blue line of the regiment, but his comrades were standing looking at him from the edge of an impossible star. He was aware of some deep wheel ruts and hoofprints in the sod beneath his feet.

The artillery officer who had fallen in this meadow had been making groans in the teeth of the tempest of sound. These futile cries, wrenched from him by his agony, were heard only by shells, bullets. When wild-eyed Collins came running, this officer raised himself. His face contorted and blanched from pain, he was about to utter some great beseeching cry. But suddenly his face straightened and he called: "Say, young man, give me a drink of water, will you?"

Collins had no room amid his emotions for surprise. He was mad from the threats of destruction.

"I can't!" he screamed, and in his reply was a full description of his quaking apprehension. His cap was gone and his hair was riotous. His clothes made it appear that he had been dragged over the ground by the heels. He ran on.

The officer's head sank down and one elbow crooked. His foot in its brass-bound stirrup still stretched over the body of his horse and the other leg was under the steed.

But Collins turned. He came dashing back. His face had now turned gray and in his eyes was all terror. "Here it is! here it is!"

The officer was as a man gone in drink. His arm bent like a twig. His head drooped as if his neck were of willow. He was sinking to the ground, to lie face downward.

Collins grabbed him by the shoulder. "Here it is. Here's your drink. Turn over. Turn over, man, for God's sake!"

With Collins hauling at his shoulder, the officer twisted his body and fell with his face turned toward that region where lived the unspeakable noises of the swirling missiles. There was the faintest shadow of a smile on his lips as he looked at Collins. He gave a sigh, a little primitive breath like that from a child.

Collins tried to hold the bucket steadily, but his shaking hands caused the water to splash all over the face of the dying man. Then he jerked it away and ran on.

The regiment gave him a welcoming roar. The grimed faces were wrinkled in laughter.

His captain waved the bucket away. "Give it to the men!"

327

The two genial, skylarking young lieutenants were the first to gain possession of it. They played over it in their fashion.

When one tried to drink the other teasingly knocked his elbow. "Don't, Billie! You'll make me spill it," said the one. The other laughed.

Suddenly there was an oath, the thud of wood on the ground, and a swift murmur of astonishment among the ranks. The two lieutenants glared at each other. The bucket lay on the ground empty.

the bride comes to yellow sky

The great Pullman was whirling onward with such dignity of motion that a glance from the window seemed simply to prove that the plains of Texas were pouring eastward. Vast flats of green grass, dull-hued spaces of mesquit and cactus, little groups of frame houses, woods of light and tender trees, all were sweeping into the east, sweeping over the horizon, a precipice.

A newly married pair had boarded this coach at San Antonio. The man's face was reddened from many days in the wind and sun, and a direct result of his new black clothes was that his brick-colored hands were constantly performing in a most conscious fashion. From time to time he looked down respectfully at his attire. He sat with a hand on each knee, like a man waiting in a barber's shop. The glances he devoted to other passengers were furtive and shy.

The bride was not pretty, nor was she very young. She wore a dress of blue cashmere, with small reservations of velvet here and there, and with steel buttons abounding. She continually twisted her head to regard her puff sleeves, very stiff, straight, and high. They embarrassed her. It was quite apparent that she had cooked, and that she expected to cook, dutifully. The blushes caused by the careless scrutiny of some passengers as she had entered the car were strange to see upon this plain, under-class countenance, which was drawn in placid, almost emotionless lines.

Reprinted from *Twenty Stories* by Stephen Crane, by permission of Alfred A. Knopf, Inc. Copyright 1925 by William H. Crane.

They were evidently very happy. "Ever been in a parlor-car before?" he asked, smiling with delight.

"No," she answered; "I never was. It's fine, ain't it?"

"Great! And then after a while we'll go forward to the diner, and get a big lay-out. Finest meal in the world. Charge a dollar."

"Oh, do they?" cried the bride. "Charge a dollar? Why, that's too much—for us—ain't it, Jack?"

"Not this trip, anyhow," he answered bravely. "We're going to go the whole thing."

Later he explained to her about the trains. "You see, it's a thousand miles from one end of Texas to the other; and this train runs right across it, and never stops but four times." He had the pride of an owner. He pointed out to her the dazzling fittings of the coach; and in truth her eyes opened wider as she contemplated the sea-green figured velvet, the shining brass, silver, and glass, the wood that gleamed as darkly brilliant as the surface of a pool of oil. At one end a bronze figure sturdily held a support for a separated chamber, and at convenient places on the ceiling were frescos in olive and silver.

To the minds of the pair, their surroundings reflected the glory of their marriage that morning in San Antonio; this was the environment of their new estate; and the man's face in particular beamed with an elation that made him appear ridiculous to the negro porter. This individual at times surveyed them from afar with an amused and superior grin. On other occasions he bullied them with skill in ways that did not make it exactly plain to them that they were being bullied. He subtly used all the manners of the most unconquerable kind of snobbery. He oppressed them; but of this oppression they had small knowledge, and they speedily forgot that infrequently a number of travellers covered them with stares of derisive enjoyment. Historically there was supposed to be something infinitely humorous in their situation.

"We are due in Yellow Sky at 3:42," he said, looking tenderly into her eyes.

"Oh, are we?" she said, as if she had not been aware of it. To evince surprise at her husband's statement was part of her wifely amiability. She took from a pocket a little silver watch; and as she held it before her, and stared at it with a frown of attention, the new husband's face shone.

"I bought it in San Anton' from a friend of mine," he told her gleefully.

"It's seventeen minutes past twelve," she said, looking up at him with a kind of shy and clumsy coquetry. A passenger, noting this play, grew excessively sardonic, and winked at himself in one of the numerous mirrors.

At last they went to the dining-car. Two rows of negro waiters, in glowing white suits, surveyed their entrance with the interest, and also the equanimity, of men who had been forewarned. The pair fell to the lot of a waiter who happened to feel pleasure in steering them through their meal. He viewed them with the manner of a fatherly pilot, his countenance radiant with benevolence. The patronage, entwined with the ordinary deference, was not plain to them. And yet, as they returned to their coach, they showed in their faces a sense of escape.

To the left, miles down a long purple slope, was a little ribbon of mist where moved the keening Rio Grande. The train was approaching it at an angle, and the apex was Yellow Sky. Presently it was apparent that, as the distance from Yellow Sky grew shorter, the husband became commensurately restless. His brick-red hands were more insistent in their prominence. Occasionally he was even rather absent-minded and far-away when the bride leaned forward and addressed him.

As a matter of truth, Jack Potter was beginning to find the shadow of a deed weigh upon him like a leaden slab. He, the town marshal of Yellow Sky, a man known, liked, and feared in his corner, a prominent person, had gone to San Antonio to meet a girl he believed he loved, and there, after the usual prayers, had actually induced her to marry him, without consulting Yellow Sky for any part of the transaction. He was now bringing his bride before an innocent and unsuspecting community.

Of course people in Yellow Sky married as it pleased them, in accordance with a general custom; but such was Potter's thought of his duty to his friends, or of their idea of his duty, or of an unspoken form which does not control men in these matters, that he felt he was heinous. He had committed an extraordinary crime. Face to face with this girl in San Antonio, and spurred by his sharp impulse, he had gone headlong over all the social hedges. At San Antonio he was like a man hidden in the dark. A knife to sever any friendly duty, any form, was easy to his hand in that remote city. But the hour of Yellow Sky—the hour of daylight—was approaching.

He knew full well that his marriage was an important thing to his town. It could only be exceeded by the burning of the new hotel. His friends could not forgive him. Frequently he had reflected on the advisability of telling them by telegraph, but a new cowardice had been upon him. He feared to do it. And now the train was hurrying him toward a scene of amazement, glee, and reproach. He glanced out of the window at the line of haze swinging slowly in toward the train.

Yellow Sky had a kind of brass band, which played painfully, to the delight of the populace. He laughed without heart as he thought of it. If the citizens could dream of his prospective arrival with his bride, they would parade the band at the station and escort them, amid cheers and laughing congratulations, to his adobe home.

He resolved that he would use all the devices of speed and plains-craft in making the journey from the station to his house. Once within that safe citadel, he could issue some sort of vocal bulletin, and then not go among the citizens until they had time to wear off a little of their enthusiasm.

The bride looked anxiously at him. "What's worrying you, Jack?"

He laughed again. "I'm not worrying, girl; I'm only thinking of Yellow Sky."

She flushed in comprehension.

A sense of mutual guilt invaded their minds and developed a finer tenderness. They looked at each other with eyes softly aglow. But Potter often laughed the same nervous laugh; the flush upon the bride's face seemed quite permanent.

The traitor to the feelings of Yellow Sky narrowly watched the speeding landscape. "We're nearly there," he said.

Presently the porter came and announced the proximity of Potter's home. He held a brush in his hand, and, with all his airy superiority gone, he brushed Potter's new clothes as the latter slowly turned this way and that way. Potter fumbled out a coin and gave it to the porter, as he had seen others do. It was a heavy and muscle-bound business, as that of a man shoeing his first horse.

The porter took their bag, and as the train began to slow they moved forward to the hooded platform of the car. Presently the two engines and their long string of coaches rushed into the station of Yellow Sky.

"They have to take water here," said Potter, from a constricted throat and in mournful cadence, as one announcing death. Before the train stopped his eye had swept the length of the platform, and he was glad and astonished to see there was none upon it but the station-agent, who, with a slightly hurried and anxious air, was walking toward the water-tanks. When the train had halted, the porter alighted first, and placed in position a little temporary step. "Come on, girl," said Potter, hoarsely. As he helped her down they each laughed on a false note. He took the bag from the negro, and bade his wife cling to his arm. As they slunk rapidly away, his hang-dog glance perceived that they were unloading the two trunks, and also that the station-agent, far ahead near the baggage-car, had turned and was running toward him, making gestures. He laughed, and groaned as he laughed, when he noted the first effect of his marital bliss upon Yellow Sky. He gripped his wife's arm firmly to his side, and they fled. Behind them the porter stood, chuckling fatuously.

2

The California express on the Southern Railway was due at Yellow Sky in twenty-one minutes. There were six men at the bar of the Weary Gentleman saloon. One was a drummer who talked a great deal and rapidly; three were Texans who did not care to talk at that time; and two were Mexican sheep-herders, who did not talk as a general practice in the Weary Gentleman saloon. The barkeeper's dog lay on the board walk that crossed in front of the door. His head was on his paws, and he glanced drowsily here and there with the constant vigilance of a dog that is kicked on occasion. Across the sandy street were some vivid green grass-plots, so wonderful in appearance, amid the sands that burned near them in a blazing sun, that they caused a doubt in the mind. They exactly resembled the grass mats used to represent lawns on the stage. At the cooler end of the railway station, a man without a coat sat in a tilted chair and smoked his pipe. The fresh-cut bank of the Rio Grande circled near the town, and there could be seen beyond it a great plum-colored plain of mesquit.

Save for the busy drummer and his companions in the saloon, Yellow Sky was dozing. The new-comer leaned gracefully upon the bar, and recited many tales with the confidence of a bard who has come upon a new field.

"—and at the moment that the old man fell downstairs with the bureau in his arms, the old woman was coming up with two scuttles of coal, and of course—"

The drummer's tale was interrupted by a young man who suddenly appeared in the open door. He cried: "Scratchy Wilson's drunk, and has turned loose with both hands." The two Mexicans at once set down their glasses and faded out of the rear entrance of the saloon.

The drummer, innocent and jocular, answered: "All right, old man. S'pose he has? Come in and have a drink, anyhow."

But the information had made such an obvious cleft in every skull in the room that the drummer was obliged to see its importance. All had become instantly solemn. "Say," said he, mystified, "what is this?" His three companions made the introductory gesture of eloquent speech; but the young man at the door forestalled them.

"It means, my friend," he answered, as he came into the saloon, "that for the next two hours this town won't be a health resort."

The barkeeper went to the door, and locked and barred it; reaching out of the window, he pulled in heavy wooden shutters, and barred them. Immediately a solemn, chapel-like gloom was upon the place. The drummer was looking from one to another.

"But say," he cried, "what is this, anyhow? You don't mean there is going to be a gun-fight?"

"Don't know whether there'll be a fight or not," answered one man, grimly; "but there'll be some shootin'—some good shootin'."

The young man who had warned them waved his hand. "Oh, there'll be a fight fast enough, if any one wants it. Anybody can get a fight out there in the street. There's a fight just waiting."

The drummer seemed to be swayed between the interest of a foreigner and a perception of personal danger.

"What did you say his name was?" he asked.

"Scratchy Wilson," they answered in chorus.

"And will he kill anybody? What are you going to do? Does this happen often? Does he rampage around like this once a week or so? Can he break in that door?"

"No; he can't break down that door," replied the barkeeper. "He's tried it three times. But when he comes you'd better lay down on the floor, stranger. He's dead sure to shoot at it, and a bullet may come through."

Thereafter the drummer kept a strict eye upon the door. The time had not yet been called for him to hug the floor, but, as a minor precaution, he sidled near to the wall. "Will he kill anybody?" he said again.

The men laughed low and scornfully at the question.

"He's out to shoot, and he's out for trouble. Don't see any good in experimentin' with him."

"But what do you do in a case like this? What do you do?"

A man responded: "Why, he and Jack Potter—"

"But," in chorus the other men interrupted, "Jack Potter's in San Anton'."

"Well, who is he? What's he got to do with it?"

"Oh, he's the town marshal. He goes out and fights Scratchy when he gets on one of these tears."

"Wow!" said the drummer, mopping his brow. "Nice job he's got."

The voices had toned away to mere whisperings. The drummer wished to ask further questions, which were born of an increasing anxiety and bewilderment; but when he attempted them, the men merely looked at him in irritation and motioned him to remain silent. A tense waiting hush was upon them. In the deep shadows of the room their eyes shone as they listened for sounds from the street. One man made three gestures at the barkeeper; and the latter, moving like a ghost, handed him a glass and a bottle. The man poured a full glass of whisky, and set down the bottle noiselessly. He gulped the whisky in a swallow, and turned again toward the door in immovable silence. The drummer saw that the barkeeper, without a sound, had taken a Winchester from beneath the bar. Later he saw this individual beckoning to him, so he tiptoed across the room.

"You better come with me back of the bar."

"No, thanks," said the drummer, perspiring; "I'd rather be where I can make a break for the back door."

Whereupon the man of bottles made a kindly but peremptory gesture. The drummer obeyed it, and, finding himself seated on a box with his head below the level of the bar, balm was laid upon his soul at sight of various zinc and copper fittings that bore a resemblance to armor-plate. The barkeeper took a seat comfortably upon an adjacent box.

"You see," he whispered, "this here Scratchy Wilson is a wonder with a gun—a perfect wonder; and when he goes on the war-trail, we hunt our holes—naturally. He's about the last one of the old gang that used to hang out along the river here. He's a terror when he's drunk. When he's sober he's all right—kind of simple—wouldn't hurt a fly—nicest fellow in town. But when he's drunk—whoo!"

There were periods of stillness. "I wish Jack Potter was back from San Anton'," said the barkeeper. "He shot Wilson up once—in the leg—and he would sail in and pull out the kinks in this thing."

Presently they heard from a distance the sound of a shot,

followed by three wild yowls. It instantly removed a bond from the men in the darkened saloon. There was a shuffling of feet. They looked at each other. "Here he comes," they said.

3

A man in a maroon-colored flannel shirt, which had been purchased for purposes of decoration, and made principally by some Jewish women on the East Side of New York, rounded a corner and walked into the middle of the main street of Yellow Sky. In either hand the man held a long, heavy, blue-black revolver. Often he yelled, and these cries rang through a semblance of a deserted village, shrilly flying over the roofs in a volume that seemed to have no relation to the ordinary vocal strength of a man. It was as if the surrounding stillness formed the arch of a tomb over him. These cries of ferocious challenge rang against walls of silence. And his boots had red tops with gilded imprints, of the kind beloved in winter by little sledding boys on the hillsides of New England.

The man's face flamed in a rage begot of whiskey. His eyes, rolling, and yet keen for ambush, hunted the still doorways and windows. He walked with the creeping movement of the midnight cat. As it occurred to him, he roared menacing information. The long revolvers in his hands were as easy as straws; they were moved with an electric swiftness. The little fingers of each hand played sometimes in a musician's way. Plain from the low collar of the shirt, the cords of his neck straightened and sank, straightened and sank, as passion moved him. The only sounds were his terrible invitations. The calm adobes preserved their demeanor at the passing of this small thing in the middle of the street.

There was no offer of fight—no offer of fight. The man called to the sky. There were no attractions. He bellowed and fumed and swayed his revolvers here and everywhere.

The dog of the barkeeper of the Weary Gentleman saloon had not appreciated the advance of events. He yet lay dozing in front of his master's door. At sight of the dog, the man paused and raised his revolver humorously. At sight of the man, the dog sprang up and walked diagonally away, with a sullen head, and growling. The man yelled, and the dog broke into a gallop. As it was about to enter an alley, there was a loud noise, a whistling, and something spat the ground directly before it. The dog screamed, and, wheeling in terror, galloped headlong in a new direction. Again there was a noise, a whistling, and sand was kicked viciously before it. Fear-stricken, the dog turned and flurried like an animal in a pen. The man stood laughing, his weapons at his hips.

Ultimately the man was attracted by the closed door of the Weary Gentleman saloon. He went to it and, hammering with a revolver, demanded drink.

The door remaining imperturbable, he picked a bit of paper from the walk, and nailed it to the framework with a knife. He then turned his back contemptuously upon this popular resort and, walking to the opposite side of the street and spinning there on his heel quickly and lithely, fired at the bit of paper. He missed it by a half-inch. He swore at himself, and went away. Later he comfortably fusilladed the windows of his most intimate friend. The man was playing with this town; it was a toy for him.

But still there was no offer of fight. The name of Jack Potter, his ancient antagonist, entered his mind, and he concluded that it would be a glad thing if he should go to Potter's house, and by bombardment induce him to come out and fight. He moved in the direction of his desire, chanting Apache scalp-music.

When he arrived at it, Potter's house presented the same still front as had the other adobes. Taking up a strategic position, the man howled a challenge. But this house regarded him as might a great stone god. It gave no sign. After a decent wait, the man howled further challenges, mingling with them wonderful epithets.

Presently there came the spectacle of a man churning himself into deepest rage over the immobility of a house. He fumed at it as the winter wind attacks a prairie cabin in the North. To the distance there should have gone the sound of a tumult like the fighting of two hundred Mexicans. As necessity bade him, he paused for breath or to reload his revolvers.

4

Potter and his bride walked sheepishly and with speed. Sometimes they laughed together shamefacedly and low.

"Next corner, dear," he said finally.

They put forth the efforts of a pair walking bowed against a strong wind. Potter was about to raise a finger to point the first appearance of the new home when, as they circled the corner, they came face to face with a man in a maroon-colored shirt, who was feverishly pushing cartridges into a large revolver. Upon the instant the man dropped his revolver to the ground and, like lightning, whipped another from its holster. The second weapon was aimed at the bridegroom's chest.

There was a silence. Potter's mouth seemed to be merely a grave for his tongue. He exhibited an instinct to at once loosen his arm from the woman's grip, and he dropped the bag to the sand. As for the bride, her face had gone as yellow as old cloth. She was a slave to hideous rites, gazing at the apparitional snake.

The two men faced each other at a distance of three paces. He of the revolver smiled with a new and quiet ferocity.

"Tried to sneak up on me," he said. "Tried to sneak up on me!" His eyes grew more baleful. As Potter made a slight movement, the man thrust his revolver venomously forward. "No; don't you do it, Jack Potter. Don't you move a finger toward a gun just yet. Don't you move an eyelash. The time has come for me to settle with you, and I'm goin' to do it my own way, and loaf along with no interferin'. So if you don't want a gun bent on you, just mind what I tell you."

Potter looked at his enemy. "I ain't got a gun on me, Scratchy," he said. "Honest, I ain't." He was stiffening and steadying, but yet somewhere at the back of his mind a vision of the Pullman floated: the sea-green figured velvet, the shining brass, silver, and glass, the wood that gleamed as darkly brilliant as the surface of a pool of oil—all the glory of the marriage, the environment of the new estate. "You know I fight when it comes to fighting, Scratchy Wilson; but I ain't got a gun on me. You'll have to do all the shootin' yourself."

His enemy's face went livid. He stepped forward, and lashed his weapon to and fro before Potter's chest. "Don't you tell me you ain't got no gun on you, you whelp. Don't tell me no lie like that. There ain't a man in Texas ever seen you without no gun. Don't take me for no kid." His eyes blazed with light, and his throat worked like a pump.

"I ain't takin' you for no kid," answered Potter. His heels had not moved an inch backward. "I'm takin' you for a damn fool. I tell you I ain't got a gun, and I ain't. If you're goin' to shoot me up, you better begin now; you'll never get a chance like this again."

So much enforced reasoning had told on Wilson's rage; he was calmer. "If you ain't got a gun, why ain't you got a gun?" he sneered. "Been to Sunday-school?"

"I ain't got a gun because I've just come from San Anton' with my wife. I'm married," said Potter. "And if I'd thought there was going to be any galoots like you prowling around when I brought my wife home, I'd had a gun, and don't you forget it."

"Married!" said Scratchy, not at all comprehending.

"Yes, married. I'm married," said Potter, distinctly.

"Married?" said Scratchy. Seemingly for the first time, he saw the drooping, drowning woman at the other man's side. "No!" he said. He was like a creature allowed a glimpse of another world. He moved a pace backward, and his arm, with the revolver, dropped to his side. "Is this the lady?" he asked.

"Yes; this is the lady," answered Potter.

There was another period of silence.

"Well," said Wilson at last, slowly, "I s'pose it's all off now."

"It's all off if you say so, Scratchy. You know I didn't make the trouble." Potter lifted his valise.

"Well, I 'low it's off, Jack," said Wilson. He was looking at the ground. "Married!" He was not a student of chivalry; it was merely that in the presence of this foreign condition he was a simple child of the earlier plains. He picked up his starboard revolver, and, placing both weapons in their holsters, he went away. His feet made funnel-shaped tracks in the heavy sand.

Theodore Dreiser

FREE

It is significant that Theodore Dreiser's first novel was published through the influence of Frank Norris in 1900, the year of Stephen Crane's death: for Dreiser, with greater emphasis, continued in the twentieth century the revolt against genteel realism begun by Norris, Crane, and Garland during the 1890's. In his undeviating honesty of purpose and his refusal to bow to accepted notions of literary morality, he set the example for numerous younger writers and aided the short story, as well as the novel, to reach new levels of freedom and originality.

Dreiser was born in Terre Haute, Indiana, in 1871, the twelfth of thirteen children of poor parents. He attended Roman Catholic schools in Terre Haute, Sullivan, and Evansville, and public school in Warsaw, and spent one year at the University of Indiana on funds supplied by a former teacher. He then worked at various jobs, including driving a laundry wagon in Chicago, and in 1892 became a reporter on the Chicago *Globe*. His work on the *Globe* led to better positions, first as a reporter on newspapers in St. Louis and Pittsburgh, and then as an editor of magazines in New York. He began to publish short stories in the 1890's, but since neither these nor the novel *Sister Carrie* (1900) brought him financial security, he was forced to continue for a while longer his editorial work, finally becoming editor-in-chief of the Butterick publications. His second novel, *Jennie Gerhardt* (1911), was successful enough to permit him to give up editorial work and devote himself to writing. Other novels appeared at intervals—*The Financier* (1912), *The Titan* (1914), *The Genius* (1915), and his masterpiece, *An American Tragedy* (1925). His most important short stories appear in *Free and Other Stories* (1918), *Chains, Lesser Novels and Stories* (1927), and *A Gallery of Women* (2 vols., 1929). In addition to novels

341

and short stories, Dreiser also wrote poems, plays, essays, and several autobiographical works. His last two novels, *The Bulwark* and *The Stoic,* were completed shortly before his death in 1945.

Because Dreiser's style seems lumbering, colorless, and cliché-ridden, critics have understandably approved his content and themes while apologizing for his manner and technique. Yet the fact should be noted that Dreiser's style, even with its defects, is appropriate to his method, the cardinal feature of which is the page by page amassing of detail to the end of at length exposing every facet of his story idea. This approach necessarily foregoes the appeal to reader interest that arises from the brilliant turn of phrase, as well as the appeal of the fast-paced narrative and the provocation of the imagination by what is left unsaid. Nevertheless, the best of his stories, like "Free," make such a massive, powerful impact on the reader's mind that they are remembered long after more cleverly written stories are forgotten.

free

The large and rather comfortable apartment of Rufus Haymaker, architect, in Central Park West, was very silent. It was scarcely dawn yet, and at the edge of the park, over the way, looking out from the front windows which graced this abode and gave it its charm, a stately line of poplars was still shrouded in a gray morning mist. From his bedroom at one end of the hall, where, also, a glimpse of the park was to be had, came Mr. Haymaker at this early hour to sit by one of these broader windows and contemplate these trees and

From *Free and Other Stories* by Theodore Dreiser, by permission of a special arrangement with Mrs. Theodore Dreiser. Copyright 1918, by Boni and Liveright, Inc.

a small lake beyond. He was very fond of Nature in its manifold art forms—quite poetic, in fact.

He was a tall and spare man of about sixty, not ungraceful, though slightly stoop-shouldered, with heavy overhanging eyebrows and hair, and a short, professionally cut gray mustache and beard, which gave him a severe and yet agreeable presence. For the present he was clad in a light-blue dressing gown with silver cords, which enveloped him completely. He had thin, pale, long-fingered hands, wrinkled at the back and slightly knotted at the joints, which bespoke the artist, in mood at least, and his eyes had a weary and yet restless look in them.

For only yesterday Doctor Storm, the family physician, who was in attendance on his wife, ill now for these three weeks past with a combination of heart lesion, kidney poisoning and neuritis, had taken him aside and said very softly and affectionately, as though he were trying to spare his feelings: "To-morrow, Mr. Haymaker, if your wife is no better I will call in my friend, Doctor Grainger, whom you know, for a consultation. He is more of an expert in these matters of the heart"—the heart, Mr. Haymaker had time to note ironically—"than I am. Together we will make a thorough examination, and then I hope we will be better able to say what the possibilities of her recovery really are. It's been a very trying case, a very stubborn one, I might say. Still, she has a great deal of vitality and is doing as well as could be expected, all things considered. At the same time, though I don't wish to alarm you unnecessarily—and there is no occasion for great alarm yet—still I feel it my duty to warn you that her condition is very serious indeed. Not that I wish you to feel that she is certain to die. I don't think she is. Not at all. Just the contrary. She may get well, and probably will, and live all of twenty years more." (Mentally Mr. Haymaker sighed a purely spiritual sigh.) "She has fine recuperative powers, so far as I can judge, but she has a bad heart, and this kidney trouble has not helped it any. Just now, when her heart should have the least strain, it has the most.

"She is just at that point where, as I may say, things are in the balance. A day or two, or three or four at the most, ought to show which way things will go. But, as I have said before, I do not wish to alarm you unnecessarily. We are not nearly at the end of our tether. We haven't tried blood transfusion yet, and there are several arrows to that bow. Besides, at any moment she may respond more vigorously to medication than she has heretofore—especially in connection with her kidneys. In that case the situation would be greatly relieved at once.

"However, as I say, I feel it my duty to speak to you in this way in order that you may be mentally prepared for any event, because in such an odd combination as this the worst may happen at any time. We never can tell. As an old friend of yours and Mrs. Haymaker's, and knowing how much you two mean to each other"—Mr. Haymaker merely stared at him vacantly—"I feel it my duty to prepare you in this way. We all of us have to face these things. Only last year I lost my dear Matilda, my youngest child, as you know. Just the same, as I say, I have the feeling that Mrs. Haymaker is not really likely to die soon, and that we—Doctor Grainger and myself—will still be able to pull her through. I really do."

Doctor Storm looked at Mr. Haymaker as though he were very sorry for him—an old man long accustomed to his wife's ways and likely to be made very unhappy by her untimely end; whereas Mr. Haymaker, though staring in an almost sculptural way, was really thinking what a farce it all was, what a dull mixture of error and illusion on the part of all. Here he was, sixty years of age, weary of all this, of life really—a man who had never been really happy in all the time that he had been married; and yet here was his wife, who from conventional reasons believed that he was or should be, and who on account of this was serenely happy herself, or nearly so. And this doctor, who imagined that he was old and weak and therefore in need of this loving woman's care and sympathy and understanding! Unconsciously he raised a deprecating hand.

Also his children, who thought him dependent on her and happy with her; his servants and her and his friends thinking the same thing, and yet he really was not. It was all a lie. He was unhappy. Always he had been unhappy, it seemed, ever since he had been married—for over thirty-one years now. Never in all that time, for even so much as a single day, had he ever done anything but long, long, long, in a pale, constrained way—for what, he scarcely dared think—not to be married any more—to be free—to be as he was before ever he saw Mrs. Haymaker.

And yet being conventional in mood and training and utterly domesticated by time and conditions over which he seemed not to have much control—nature, custom, public opinion, and the like, coming into play as forces—he had drifted, had not taken any drastic action. No, he had merely drifted, wondering if time, accident or something might not interfere and straighten out his life for him, but it never had. Now weary, old, or rapidly becoming so, he condemned himself for his inaction. Why hadn't he done something about it years before? Why hadn't he broken it up before it was too late, and saved his own soul, his longing for life, color? But no, he had not. Why complain so bitterly now?

All the time the doctor had talked this day before he had wanted to smile a wry, dry, cynical smile, for in reality he did not want Mrs. Haymaker to live—or at least at the moment he thought so. He was too miserably tired of it all. And so now, after nearly twenty-four hours of the same unhappy thought, sitting by this window looking at a not distant building which shone faintly in the haze, he ran his fingers through his hair as he gazed, and sighed.

How often in these weary months, and even years, past—ever since he and his wife had been living here, and before—had he come to these or similar windows while she was still asleep, to sit and dream! For some years now they had not even roomed together, so indifferent had the whole state become; though she did not seem to consider that significant, either. Life had become more or less of a practical problem to her, one of position, place, prestige. And yet how often, viewing his life in retrospect, had he wished that his life had been as sweet as his dreams—that his dreams had come true.

After a time on this early morning, for it was still gray, with the faintest touch of pink in the east, he shook his head solemnly and sadly, then rose and returned along the hall to his wife's bedroom, at the door of which he paused to look where she lay seriously ill, and beside her in an armchair, fast asleep, a trained nurse who was supposedly keeping the night vigil ordered by the doctor, but who no doubt was now very weary. His wife was sleeping also—very pale, very thin now, and very weak. He felt sorry for her at times, in spite of his own weariness; now, for instance. Why need he have made so great a mistake so long ago? Perhaps it was his own fault for not having been wiser in his youth. Then he went quietly on to his own room, to lie down and think.

Always these days, now that she was so very ill and the problem of her living was so very acute, the creeping dawn thus roused him—to think. It seemed as though he could not really sleep soundly any more, so stirred and distrait was he. He was not so much tired or physically worn as mentally bored or disappointed. Life had treated him so badly, he kept thinking to himself over and over. He had never had the woman he really wanted, though he had been married so long, had been faithful, respectable and loved by her, in her way. "In her way," he half quoted to himself as he lay there.

Presently he would get up, dress and go down to his office as usual if his wife were not worse. But—but, he asked himself—would she be? Would that slim and yet so durable organism of hers—quite as old as his own, or nearly so—break under the strain of this really severe illness? That would set him free again, and nicely, without blame or comment on him. He could then go where he chose once more, do as he pleased—think of that—without let or hindrance. For she was ill at last, so very ill, the first and really great illness she had endured since their marriage. For weeks now she had been lying so, hovering, as it were, between life and death, one day better, the next day worse, and yet not dying, and with no certainty that she would, and yet not getting better either. Doctor Storm insisted that it was a leak in her heart which had suddenly manifested itself which was causing all the real trouble. He was apparently greatly troubled as to how to control it.

During all this period Mr. Haymaker had been, as usual, most sympathetic. His manner toward her was always soft, kindly, apparently tender. He had never really begrudged her anything—nothing certainly that he could afford. He was always glad to see her and the children humanly happy—though they, too, largely on account of her, he thought, had proved a disappointment to him—because he had always sympathized with her somewhat unhappy youth, narrow and stinted; and yet he had never been happy himself, either, never in all the time that he had been married. If she had endured much, he kept telling himself when he was most unhappy, so had he, only it was harder perhaps for women to endure things than men—he was always willing to admit that—only also she had had his love, or thought she had, an actual spiritual peace, which he had never had. She knew she had a faithful husband. He felt that he had never really had a wife at all, not one that he could love as he knew a wife should be loved. His dreams as to that!

Going to his office later this same day—it was in one of those tall buildings that face Madison Square—he had looked first, in passing, at the trees that line Central Park West, and then at the bright wall of apartment houses facing it, and meditated sadly, heavily. Here the sidewalks were crowded with nursemaids and children at play, and in between them, of course, the occasional citizen loitering or going about his errands. The day was so fine, so youthful, as spring days will seem at times. As he looked, especially at the children, and the young men bustling office-ward, mostly in new spring suits, he sighed and wished that he were young once more. Think how brisk and hopeful they were! Everything was before them. They could still pick and choose—

no age or established conditions to stay them. Were any of them, he asked himself for the thousandth time, it seemed to him, as wearily connected as he had been at their age? Did they each have a charming young wife to love—one of whom they were passionately fond—such a one as he had never had; or did they not?

Wondering, he reached his office on one of the topmost floors of one of those highest buildings commanding a wide view of the city, and surveyed it wearily. Here were visible the two great rivers of the city, its towers and spires and far-flung walls. From these sometimes, even yet, he seemed to gain a patience to live, to hope. How in his youth all this had inspired him—or that other city that was then. Even now he was always at peace here, so much more so than in his own home, pleasant as it was. Here he could look out over this great scene and dream or he could lose the memory in his work that his love-life had been a failure. The great city, the buildings he could plan or supervise, the efficient help that always surrounded him—his help, not hers—aided to take his mind off himself and that deep-seated inner ache or loss.

The care of Mr. Haymaker's apartment during his wife's illness and his present absence throughout the day, devolved upon a middle-aged woman of great seriousness, Mrs. Elfridge by name, whom Mrs. Haymaker had employed years before; and under her a maid of all work, Hester, who waited on table, opened the door, and the like; and also at present two trained nurses, one for night and one for day service, who were in charge of Mrs. Haymaker. The nurses were both bright, healthy, blue-eyed girls, who attracted Mr. Haymaker and suggested all the youth he had never had—without really disturbing his poise. It would seem as though that could never be any more.

In addition, of course, there was the loving interest of his son Wesley and his daughter Ethelberta—whom his wife had named so in spite of him—both of whom had long since married and had children of their own and were living in different parts of the great city. In this crisis both of them came daily to learn how things were, and occasionally to stay for the entire afternoon or evening, or both. Ethelberta had wanted to come and take charge of the apartment entirely during her mother's illness, only Mrs. Haymaker, who was still able to direct, and fond of doing so, would not hear of it. She was not so ill but that she could still speak, and in this way could inquire and direct. Besides, Mrs. Elfridge was as good as Mrs. Haymaker in all things that related to Mr. Haymaker's physical comfort, or so she thought.

If the truth will come out—as it will in so many pathetic cases—

347

it was never his physical so much as his spiritual or affectional comfort that Mr. Haymaker craved. As said before, he had never loved Mrs. Haymaker, or certainly not since that now long-distant period back in Muskegon, Michigan, where both had been born and where they had lived and met at the ages, she of fifteen, he of seventeen. It had been, strange as it might seem now, a love match at first sight with them. She had seemed so sweet, a girl of his own age or a little younger, the daughter of a local chemist. Later, when he had been forced by poverty to go out into the world to make his own way, he had written her much, and imagined her to be all that she had seemed at fifteen, and more—a dream among fair women. But Fortune, slow in coming to his aid and fickle in fulfilling his dreams, had brought it about that for several years more he had been compelled to stay away nearly all of the time, unable to marry her; during which period, unknown to himself really, his own point of view had altered. How it had happened he could never tell really, but so it was. The great city, larger experiences—while she was still enduring the smaller ones—other faces, dreams of larger things, had all combined to destroy it or her, only he had not quite realized it then. He was always so slow in realizing the full import of the immediate thing, he thought.

That was the time, as he had afterward told himself—how often!—that he should have discovered his mistake and stopped. Later it always seemed to become more and more impossible. Then, in spite of some heartache to her and some distress to himself, no doubt, all would be well for him now. But no; he had been too inexperienced, too ignorant, too bound by all the conventions and punctilio of his simple Western world. He thought an engagement, however unsatisfactory it might come to seem afterward, was an engagement, and binding. An honorable man would not break one—or so his country moralists argued.

Yes, at that time he might have written her, he might have told her, then. But he had been too sensitive and kindly to speak of it. Afterward it was too late. He feared to wound her, to undo her, to undo her life. But now—now—look at his! He had gone back on several occasions before marriage, and might have seen and done and been free if he had had but courage and wisdom—but no; duty, order, the beliefs of the region in which he had been reared, and of America— what it expected and what she expected and was entitled to—had done for him completely. He had not spoken. Instead, he had gone on and married her without speaking of the change in himself, without letting her know how worse than ashes it had all become. God, what a fool he had been! how often since he had told himself over and over.

Well, having made a mistake it was his duty perhaps, at least according to current beliefs, to stick by it and make the best of it;—a bargain was a bargain in marriage, if no where else—but still that had never prevented him from being unhappy. He could not prevent that himself. During all these long years, therefore, owing to these same conventions—what people would think and say—he had been compelled to live with her, to cherish her, to pretend to be happy with her—"another perfect union," as he sometimes said to himself. In reality he had been unhappy, horribly so. Even her face wearied him at times, and her presence, her mannerisms. Only this other morning Doctor Storm, by his manner indicating that he thought him lonely, in danger of being left all alone and desperately sad and neglected in case she died, had irritated him greatly. Who would take care of him? his eyes had seemed to say—and yet he himself wanted nothing so much as to be alone for a time, at least, in this life, to think for himself, to do for himself, to forget this long, dreary period in which he had pretended to be something that he was not.

Was he never to be rid of the dull round of it, he asked himself now, never before he himself died? And yet shortly afterward he would reproach himself for these very thoughts, as being wrong, hard, unkind—thoughts that would certainly condemn him in the eyes of the general public, that public which made reputations and one's general standing before the world.

During all this time he had never even let her know—no, not once—of the tremendous and soul-crushing sacrifice he had made. Like the Spartan boy, he had concealed the fox gnawing at his vitals. He had not complained. He had been, indeed, the model husband, as such things go in conventional walks. If you doubted it look at his position, or that of his children; or his wife—her mental and physical comfort, even in her illness, her unfailing belief that he was all he should be! Never once apparently, during all these years, had she doubted his love or felt him to be unduly unhappy—or, if not that exactly, if not fully accepting his love as something that was still at a fever heat, the thing it once was—still believing that he found pleasure and happiness in being with her, a part of the home which together they had built up, these children they had reared, comfort in knowing that it would endure to the end! To the end! During all these years she had gone on molding his and her lives—as much as that was possible in his case—and those of their children, to suit herself; and thinking all the time that she was doing what he wanted or at least what was best for him and them.

How she adored convention! What did she not think she knew in regard to how things ought to be—mainly what her old home surroundings had taught her, the American idea of this, that and the other. Her theories in regard to friends, education of the children, and so on, had in the main prevailed, even when he did not quite agree with her; her desires for certain types of pleasure and amusement, of companionship, and so on, were conventional types always and had also prevailed. There had been little quarrels, of course, always had been—what happy home is free of them?—but still he had always given in, or nearly always, and had acted as though he were satisfied in so doing.

But why, therefore, should he complain now, or she ever imagine, or ever have imagined, that he was unhappy? She did not, had not. Like all their relatives and friends of the region from which they sprang, and here also—and she had been most careful to regulate that, courting whom she pleased and ignoring all others—she still believed most firmly, more so than ever, that she knew what was best for him, what he really thought and wanted. It made him smile most wearily at times.

For in her eyes—in regard to him, at least, not always so with others, he had found—marriage was a sacrament, sacrosanct, never to be dissolved. One life, one love. Once a man had accepted the yoke or even asked a girl to marry him it was his duty to abide by it. To break an engagement, to be unfaithful to a wife, even unkind to her—what a crime, in her eyes! Such people ought to be drummed out of the world. They were really not fit to live—dogs, brutes!

And yet, look at himself—what of him? What of one who had made a mistake in regard to all this? Where was his compensation to come from, his peace and happiness? Here on earth or only in some mythical heaven—that odd, angelic heaven that she still believed in? What a farce! And all her friends and his would think he would be so miserable now if she died, or at least ought to be. So far had asinine convention and belief in custom carried the world. Think of it!

But even that was not the worst. No; that was not the worst, either. It had been the gradual realization coming along through the years that he had married an essentially small, narrow woman who could never really grasp his point of view—or, rather, the significance of his dreams or emotions—and yet with whom, nevertheless, because of this original promise or mistake, he was compelled to live. Grant her every quality of goodness, energy, industry, intent—as he did freely—still there was this; and it could never be adjusted, never. Essentially, as he had long since discovered, she was narrow, ultra-conventional, whereas he was an artist by nature, brooding and dreaming strange dreams and thinking of far-off things which she did not or could not understand or did not sympathize with, save in a general and very remote way. The nuances of his craft, the wonders and subtleties of forms and angles—had she ever realized how significant these were to him, let alone to herself? No, never. She had not the least true appreciation of them—never had had. Architecture? Art? What could they really mean to her, desire as she might to appreciate them? And he could not now go elsewhere to discover that sympathy. No. He had never really wanted to, since the public and she would object, and he thinking it half evil himself.

Still, how was it, he often asked himself, that Nature could thus allow one conditioned or equipped with emotions and seekings such as his, not of an utterly conventional order, to seek out and pursue one like Ernestine, who was not fitted to understand him or to care what his personal moods might be? Was love truly blind, as the old saw insisted, or did Nature really plan, and cleverly, to torture the artist mind—as it did the pearl-bearing oyster with a grain of sand—with something seemingly inimical, in order that it might produce beauty? Sometimes he thought so. Perhaps the many interesting and beautiful buildings he had planned—the world called them so, at least—had been due to the loving care he lavished on them, being shut out from love and beauty elsewhere. Cruel Nature, that cared so little for the dreams of man—the individual man or woman!

At the time he had married Ernestine he was really too young to know exactly what it was he wanted to do or how it was he was going to feel in the years to come; and yet there was no one to guide him, to stop him. The custom of the time was all in favor of this dread disaster. Nature herself seemed to desire it—mere children being the be-all and end-all of everything everywhere. Think of that as a theory! Later, when it became so clear to him what he had done, and in spite of all the conventional thoughts and conditions that seemed to bind him to this fixed condition, he had grown restless and weary, but never really irritable. No, he had never become that.

Instead he had concealed it all from her, persistently, in all kindness; only this hankering after beauty of mind and body in ways not·represented by her had hurt so—grown finally almost too painful to bear. He had dreamed and dreamed of something different until it had become almost an obsession. Was it never to be, that something different, never, anywhere, in all time? What a tragedy! Soon he would be dead and then it would never be anywhere—anymore! Ernestine was charming, he would admit, or had been at first, though time had proved that she was not charming to him either mentally or physically in any compelling way; but how did that help him now? How could it? He had actually found himself bored by her for more than twenty-seven years now, and this other dream growing, growing, growing—until—

By now he was old, and she was dying, or might be, and it could not make so much difference what happened to him or to her; only it could, too, because he wanted to be free for a little while, just for a little while, before he died.

To be free! free!

One of the things that had always irritated him about Mrs. Haymaker was this, that in spite of his determination never to offend the social code in any way—he had felt for so many reasons, emotional as well as practical, that he could not afford so to do—and also in spite of the fact that he had been tortured by this show of beauty in the eyes and bodies of others, his wife, fearing perhaps in some strange psychic way that he might change, had always tried to make him feel or believe—premeditatedly and of a purpose, he thought—that he was not the kind of man who would be attractive to women; that he lacked some physical fitness, some charm that other men had, which would cause all young and really charming women to turn away from him. Think of it! He to whom so many women had turned with questioning eyes!

Also that she had married him largely because she had felt sorry for him! He chose to let her believe that, because he was sorry for her. Because other women had seemed to draw near to him at times in some appealing or seductive way she had insisted that he was not even a cavalier, let alone a Lothario; that he was ungainly, slow, uninteresting—to all women but her!

Persistently, he thought, and without any real need, she had harped on this, fighting chimeras, a chance danger in the future; though he had never given her any real reason, and had never even planned to sin against her in any way—never. She had thus tried to poison his own mind in regard to himself and his art—and yet—and yet——Ah, those eyes of other women, their haunting beauty, the flitting something they said to him of infinite, inexpressible delight. Why had his life been so very hard?

One of the disturbing things about all this was the iron truth which it had driven home, namely, that Nature, unless it were expressed or represented by some fierce determination within, which drove one to do, be, cared no whit for him or any other man or woman. Unless one acted for oneself, upon some stern conclusion nurtured within, one might rot and die spiritually. Nature did not care. "Blessed be the meek"—yes. Blessed be the strong, rather, for they made their own happiness. All these years in which he had dwelt and worked in this knowledge, hoping for something but not acting, nothing had happened, except to him, and that in an unsatisfactory way. All along he had seen what was happening to him; and yet held by convention he had refused to act always, because somehow he was not hard enough to act. He was not strong enough, that was the real truth—had not been. Almost like a bird in a cage, an animal peeping out from behind bars, he had viewed the world of free thought and freer action. In many a drawing-room, on the street, or in his own home even, had he not looked into an eye, the face of someone who seemed to offer understanding, to know, to sympathize, though she might not have, of course; and yet religiously and moralistically, like an anchorite, because of duty and current belief and what people would say and think, Ernestine's position and faith in him, her comfort, his career and that of the children—he had put them all aside, out of his mind, forgotten them almost, as best he might. It had been hard at times, and sad, but so it had been.

And look at him now, old, not exactly feeble yet—no, not that yet, not quite!—but life weary and almost indifferent. All these years he had wanted, wanted—wanted—an understanding mind, a tender heart, the some one woman—she must exist somewhere—who would have sympathized with all the delicate shades and meanings of his own character, his art, his spiritual as well as his material dreams——And yet look at him! Mrs. Haymaker had always been with him, present in the flesh or the spirit, and—so——

Though he could not ever say that she was disagreeable to him in a material way—he could not say that she had ever been that exactly—still she did not correspond to his idea of what he needed, and so——Form had meant so much to him, color; the glorious perfectness of a glorious woman's body, for instance, the color of her thoughts, moods—exquisite they must be, like his own at times; but no, he had never had the opportunity to know one intimately. No, not one, though he had dreamed of her so long. He had never even dared whisper this to any one, scarcely to himself. It was not wise, not socially fit. Thoughts like this would tend to social ostracism in his circle, or rather hers—for had she not made the circle?

And here was the rub with Mr. Haymaker, at least, that he could not make up his mind whether in his restlessness and private mental complaints he were not even now guilty of a great moral crime in so thinking. Was it not true that men and women should be faithful in marriage whether they were happy or not? Was there not some psychic law governing this matter of union—one life, one love—which made the thoughts and pains and the subsequent sufferings and hardships of the individual, whatever they might be, seem unimportant? The churches said so. Public opinion and the law seemed to accept this. There were so many problems, so much order to be disrupted, so much pain caused, many insoluble problems where children were concerned—if people did not stick. Was it not best, more blessed— socially, morally, and in every other way important—for him to stand by a bad bargain rather than to cause so much disorder and pain, even though he lost his own soul emotionally? He had thought so— or at least he had acted as though he thought so—and yet——How often had he wondered over this!

Take, now, some other phases. Granting first that Mrs. Haymaker had, according to the current code, measured up to the requirements of a wife, good and true, and that at first after marriage there had been just enough of physical and social charm about her to keep his state from becoming intolerable, still there was this old ache; and then newer things which came with the birth of the several children: First Elwell—named after a cousin of hers, not his—who had died only two years after he was born; and then Wesley; and then Ethelberta. How he had always disliked that name!—largely because he had hoped to call her Ottilie, a favorite name of his; or Janet, after his mother.

Curiously the arrival of these children and the death of poor little Elwell at two had somehow, in spite of his unrest, bound him to this matrimonial state and filled him with a sense of duty, and pleasure even—almost entirely apart from her, he was sorry to say—in these young lives; though if there had not been children, as he sometimes told himself, he surely would have broken away from her; he could not have stood it. They were so odd in their infancy, those little ones, so troublesome and yet so amusing—little Elwell, for instance, whose nose used to crinkle with delight when he would pretend to bite his neck, and whose gurgle of pleasure was so sweet and heart-filling that it positively thrilled and lured him. In spite of his thoughts concerning Ernestine—and always in those days they were rigidly put down as unmoral and even evil, a certain unsocial streak in him perhaps which was against law and order and social well-being—he came to have a deep and abiding feeling for Elwell. The latter, in some chemic, almost unconscious way, seemed to have arrived as a balm to his misery, a bandage for his growing wound—sent by whom, by what, how? Elwell had seized upon his imagination, and so his heartstrings—had come, indeed, to make him feel understanding and sympathy there in that little child; to supply, or seem to at least, what he lacked in the way of love and affection from one whom he could truly love. Elwell was never so happy apparently as when snuggling in his arms, not Ernestine's, or lying against his neck. And when he went for a walk or elsewhere there was Elwell always ready, arms up, to cling to his neck. He seemed, strangely enough, inordinately fond of his father, rather than his mother, and never happy without him. On his part, Haymaker came to be wildly fond of him—that queer little lump of a face, suggesting a little of himself and of his own mother, not so much of Ernestine, or so he thought, though he would not have objected to that. Not at all. He was not so small as that. Toward the end of the second year, when Elwell was just beginning to be able to utter a word or two, he had taught him that silly old rhyme which ran "There were three kittens," and when it came to "and they shall have no——" he would stop and say to Elwell, "What now?" and the latter would gurgle "puh!"— meaning, of course, pie.

Ah, those happy days with little Elwell, those walks with him over his shoulder or on his arm, those hours in which of an evening he would rock him to sleep in his arms! Always Ernestine was there, and happy in the thought of his love for little Elwell and her, her more than anything else perhaps; but it was an illusion—that latter part. He did not care for her even then as she thought he did. All his fondness was for Elwell, only she took it as evidence of his growing or enduring affection for her—another evidence of the peculiar working of her mind. Women were like that, he supposed— some women.

And then came that dreadful fever, due to some invading microbe which the doctors could not diagnose or isolate, infantile paralysis perhaps; and little Elwell had finally ceased to be as flesh and was eventually carried forth to the lorn, disagreeable graveyard near Woodlawn. How he had groaned internally, indulged in sad, despondent thoughts concerning the futility of all things human, when this had happened! It seemed for the time being as if all color and beauty had really gone out of his life for good.

"Man born of woman is of few days and full of troubles," the preacher whom Mrs. Haymaker had insisted upon having into the house at the time of the funeral had read. "He fleeth also as a shadow and continueth not."

Yes; so little Elwell had fled, as a shadow, and in his own deep sorrow at the time he had come to feel the first and only sad, deep sympathy for Ernestine that he had ever felt since marriage; and that because she had suffered so much—had lain in his arms after the funeral and cried so bitterly. It was terrible, her sorrow. Terrible— a mother grieving for her first-born! Why was it, he had thought at the time, that he had never been able to think or make her all she ought to be to him? Ernestine at this time had seemed better, softer, kinder, wiser, sweeter than she had ever seemed; more worthy, more interesting than ever he had thought her before. She had slaved so during the child's illness, stayed awake night after night, watched over him with such loving care—done everything, in short, that a loving human heart could do to rescue her young from the depths; and yet even then he had not really been able to love her. No, sad and unkind as it might seem, he had not. He had just pitied her and thought her better, worthier! What cursed stars disordered the minds and moods of people so? Why was it that these virtues of people, their good qualities, did not make you love them, did not really bind them to you, as against the things you could not like? Why? He had resolved to do better in his thoughts, but somehow, in spite of himself, he had never been able so to do.

Nevertheless, at that time he seemed to realize more keenly than ever her order, industry, frugality, a sense of beauty within limits, a certain laudable ambition to do something and be somebody—only, only he could not sympathize with her ambitions, could not see that she had anything but a hopelessly common-place and always unimportant point of view. There was never any flare to her, never any true distinction of mind or soul. She seemed always, in spite of anything he might say or do, hopelessly to identify doing and being with money and current opinion—neighborhood public opinion, almost— and local social position, whereas he knew that distinguished doing might as well be connected with poverty and shame and disgrace as with these other things—wealth and station, for instance; a thing which she could never quite understand apparently, though he often tried to tell her, much against her mood always.

Look at the cases of the great artists! Some of the greatest architects right here in the city, or in history, were of peculiar, almost disagreeable, history. But no, Mrs. Haymaker could not understand anything like that, anything connected with history, indeed—she hardly believed in history, its dark, sad pages, and would never read it, or at least did not care to. And as for art and artists—she would never have believed that wisdom and art understanding and true distinction might take their rise out of things necessarily low and evil—never.

Take now, the case of young Zingara. Zingara was an architect like himself, whom he had met more than thirty years before, here in New York, when he had first arrived, a young man struggling to become an architect of significance, only he was very poor and rather unkempt and disreputable-looking. Haymaker had found him several years before his marriage to Ernestine in the dark offices of Pyne & Starboard, Architects, and had been drawn to him definitely; but because he smoked all the time and was shabby as to his clothes and had no money—why, Mrs. Haymaker, after he had married her, and though he had known Zingara nearly four years, would have none of him. To her he was low, and a failure, one who would never succeed. Once she had seen him in some cheap restaurant that she chanced to be passing, in company with a drabby-looking maid, and that was the end.

"I wish you wouldn't bring him here any more, dear," she had insisted; and to have peace he had complied—only, now look. Zingara had since become a great architect, but now of course, owing to Mrs. Haymaker, he was definitely alienated. He was the man who had since designed the Aesculapian Club; and Symphony Hall with its delicate façade; as well as the tower of the Wells Building, sending its sweet lines so high, like a poetic thought or dream. But Zingara was now a dreamy recluse like himself, very exclusive, as Haymaker had long since come to know, and indifferent as to what people thought or said.

But perhaps it was not just obtuseness to certain of the finer shades and meanings of life, but an irritating aggressiveness at times, backed only by her limited understanding, which caused her to seek and wish to be here, there and the other place; wherever, in her mind, the truly successful—which meant nearly always the materially successful of a second or third rate character—were, which irritated him

357

most of all. How often had he tried to point out the difference between true and shoddy distinction—the former rarely connected with great wealth.

But no. So often she seemed to imagine such queer people to be truly successful, when they were really not—usually people with just money, or a very little more.

And in the matter of rearing and educating and marrying their two children, Wesley and Ethelberta, who had come after Elwell— what peculiar pains and feelings had not been involved in all this for him. In infancy both of these had seemed sweet enough, and so close to him, though never quite so wonderful as Elwell. But, as they grew, it seemed somehow as though Ernestine had come between him and them. First, it was the way she had raised them, the very stiff and formal manner in which they were supposed to move and be, copied from the few new-rich whom she had chanced to meet through him— and admired in spite of his warnings. That was the irony of architecture as a profession—it was always bringing such queer people close to one, and for the sake of one's profession, sometimes, particularly in the case of the young architect, one had to be nice to them. Later, it was the kind of school they should attend. He had half imagined at first that it would be the public school, because they both had begun as simple people; but no, since they were prospering it had to be a private school for each, and not one of his selection, either—or hers, really—but one to which the Barlows and the Westervelts, two families of means with whom Ernestine had become intimate, sent their children and therefore thought excellent!

The Barlows! Wealthy, but, to him, gross and mediocre people who had made a great deal of money in the manufacture of patent medicines out West, and who had then come to New York to splurge, and had been attracted to Ernestine—not him particularly, he imagined—because Haymaker had built a town house for them, and also because he was gaining a fine reputation. They were dreadful really, so *gauche,* so truly dull; and yet somehow they seemed to suit Ernestine's sense of fitness and worth at the time, because, as she said, they were good and kind—like her Western home folks; only they were not really. She just imagined so. They were worthy enough people in their way, though with no taste. Young Fred Barlow had been sent to the expensive Gaillard School for Boys, near Morristown, where they were taught manners and airs, and little else, as Haymaker always thought, though Ernestine insisted that they were given a religious training as well. And so Wesley had to go there—for a time, anyhow. It was the best school.

And similarly, because Mercedes Westervelt, senseless, vain little thing, was sent to Briarcliff School, near White Plains, Ethelberta had to go there. Think of it! It was all so silly, so pushing. How well he remembered the long, delicate campaign which preceded this, the logic and tactics employed, the importance of it socially to Ethelberta, the tears and cajolery. Mrs. Haymaker could always cry so easily, or seem to be on the verge of it, when she wanted anything; and somehow, in spite of the fact that he knew her tears were unimportant, or timed and for a purpose, he could never stand out against them, and she knew it. Always he felt moved or weakened in spite of himself. He had no weapon wherewith to fight them, though he resented them as a part of the argument. Positively Mrs. Haymaker could be as sly and as ruthless as Machiavelli himself at times, and yet believe all the while that she was tender, loving, self-sacrificing, generous, moral and a dozen other things, all of which led to the final achievement of her own aims. Perhaps this was admirable from one point of view, but it irritated him always. But if one were unable to see him- or herself, their actual disturbing inconsistencies, what were you to do?

And again, he had by then been married so long that it was almost impossible to think of throwing her over, or so it seemed at the time. They had reached the place then where they had supposedly achieved position together, though in reality it was all his—and not such position as he was entitled to, at that. Ernestine—and he was thinking this in all kindness—could never attract the ideal sort. And anyhow, the mere breath of a scandal between them, separation or unfaithfulness, which he never really contemplated, would have led to endless bickering and social and commercial injury, or so he thought. All her strong friends—and his, in a way—those who had originally been his clients, would have deserted him. Their wives, their own social fears, would have compelled them to ostracize him! He would have been a scandal-marked architect, a brute for objecting to so kind and faithful and loving a wife. And perhaps he would have been, at that. He could never quite tell, it was all so mixed and tangled.

Take, again, the marriage of his son Wesley into the De Gaud family—George de Gaud *père* being nothing more than a retired real-estate speculator and promoter who had money, but nothing more; and Irma de Gaud, the daughter, being a gross, coarse, sensuous girl, physically attractive no doubt, and financially reasonably secure, or so

359

she had seemed; but what else? Nothing, literally nothing; and his son had seemed to have at least some spiritual ideals at first. Ernestine had taken up with Mrs. George de Gaud—a miserable, narrow creature, so Haymaker thought—largely for Wesley's sake, he presumed. Anyhow, everything had been done to encourage Wesley in his suit and Irma in her toleration, and now look at them! De Gaud *père* had since failed and left his daughter practically nothing. Irma had been interested in anything but Wesley's career, had followed what she considered the smart among the new-rich—a smarter, wilder, newer new-rich than ever Ernestine had fancied, or could. To-day she was without a thought for anything besides teas and country clubs and theaters—and what else?

And long since Wesley had begun to realize it himself. He was an engineer now, in the employ of one of the great construction companies, a moderately successful man. But even Ernestine, who had engineered the match and thought it wonderful, was now down on her. She had begun to see through her some years ago, when Irma had begun to ignore her; only before it was always the De Gauds here, and the De Gauds there. Good gracious, what more could any one want than the De Gauds—Irma de Gaud, for instance? Then came the concealed dissension between Irma and Wesley, and now Mrs. Haymaker insisted that Irma had held, and was holding Wesley back. She was not the right woman for him. Almost—against all her prejudices—she was willing that he should leave her. Only, if Haymaker had broached anything like that in connection with himself!

And yet Mrs. Haymaker had been determined, because of what she considered the position of the De Gauds at that time, that Wesley should marry Irma. Wesley now had to slave at mediocre tasks in order to have enough to allow Irma to run in so-called fast society of a second or third rate. And even at that she was not faithful to him—or so Haymaker believed. There were so many strange evidences. And yet Haymaker felt that he did not care to interfere now. How could he? Irma was tired of Wesley, and that was all there was to it. She was looking elsewhere, he was sure.

Take but one more case, that of Ethelberta. What a name! In spite of all Ernestine's determination to make her so successful and thereby reflect some credit on her had she really succeeded in so doing? To be sure, Ethelberta's marriage was somewhat more successful financially than Wesley's had proved to be, but was she any better placed in other ways? John Kelso—"Jack," as she always called him—with his light ways and lighter mind, was he really any one!—anything more than a waster? His parents stood by him no doubt, but that was all; and so much the worse for him. According to Mrs. Haymaker at the time, he, too, was an ideal boy, admirable, just the man for Ethelberta, because the Kelsos, *père* and *mère,* had money. Horner Kelso had made a kind of fortune in Chicago in the banknote business, and had settled in New York, about the time that Ethelberta was fifteen, to spend it. Ethelberta had met Grace Kelso at school.

And now see! She was not unattractive, and had some pleasant, albeit highly affected, social ways; she had money, and a comfortable apartment in Park Avenue; but what had it all come to? John Kelso had never done anything really, nothing. His parents' money and indulgence and his early training for a better social state had ruined him if he had ever had a mind that amounted to anything. He was idle, pleasure-loving, mentally indolent, like Irma de Gaud. Those two should have met and married, only they could never have endured each other. But how Mrs. Haymaker had courted the Kelsos in her eager and yet diplomatic way, giving teas and receptions and theater parties; and yet he had never been able to exchange ten significant words with either of them, or the younger Kelsos either. Think of it!

And somehow in the process Ethelberta, for all his early affection and tenderness and his still kindly feeling for her, had been weaned away from him and had proved a limited and conventional girl, somewhat like her mother, and more inclined to listen to her than to him—though he had not minded that really. It had been the same with Wesley before her. Perhaps, however, a child was entitled to its likes and dislikes, regardless.

But why had he stood for it all, he now kept asking himself. Why? What grand results, if any, had been achieved? Were their children so wonderful?—their lives? Would he not have been better off without her—his children better, even, by a different woman?—hers by a different man? Wouldn't it have been better if he had destroyed it all, broken away? There would have been pain, of course, terrible consequences, but even so he would have been free to go, to do, to reorganize his life on another basis. Zingara had avoided marriage entirely—wise man. But no, no; always convention, that long list of reasons and terrors he was always reciting to himself. He had allowed himself to be pulled round by the nose, God only knows why, and that was all there was to it. Weakness, if you will, perhaps; fear of convention; fear of what people would think and say.

Always now he found himself brooding over the dire results to him of all this respect on his part for convention, moral order, the duty of keeping society on an even keel, of not bringing disgrace to his children and himself and her, and yet ruining his own life emotionally by so doing. To be respectable had been so important that it had resulted in spiritual failure for him. But now all that was over with him, and Mrs. Haymaker was ill, near to death, and he was expected to wish her to get well, and be happy with her for a long time yet! Be happy! In spite of anything he might wish or think he ought to do, he couldn't. He couldn't even wish her to get well.

It was too much to ask. There was actually a haunting satisfaction in the thought that she might die now. It wouldn't be much, but it would be something—a few years of freedom. That was something. He was not utterly old yet, and he might have a few years of peace and comfort to himself still—and—and——That dream—that dream—though it might never come true now—it couldn't really—still—still——He wanted to be free to go his own way once more, to do as he pleased, to walk, to think, to brood over what he had not had—to brood over what he had not had! Only, only, whenever he looked into her pale sick face and felt her damp limp hands he could not quite wish that, either; not quite, not even now. It seemed too hard, too brutal—only—only——So he wavered.

No; in spite of her long-past struggle over foolish things and in spite of himself and all he had endured or thought he had, he was still willing that she should live; only he couldn't wish it exactly. Yes, let her live if she could. What matter to him now whether she lived or died? Whenever he looked at her he could not help thinking how helpless she would be without him, what a failure at her age, and so on. And all along, as he wryly repeated to himself, she had been thinking and feeling that she was doing the very best for him and her and the children!—that she was really the ideal wife for him, making every dollar go as far as it would, every enjoyment yield the last drop for them all, every move seeming to have been made to their general advantage! Yes, that was true. There was a pathos about it, wasn't there? But as for the actual results——!

The next morning, the second after his talk with Doctor Storm, found him sitting once more beside his front window in the early dawn, and so much of all this, and much more, was coming back to him, as before. For the thousandth or the ten-thousandth time, as it seemed to him, in all the years that had gone, he was concluding again that his life was a failure. If only he were free for a little while just to be alone and think, perhaps to discover what life might bring him yet; only on this occasion his thoughts were colored by a new turn in the situation. Yesterday afternoon, because Mrs. Haymaker's condition had grown worse, the consultation between Grainger and Storm was held, and to-day sometime transfusion was to be tried, that last grim stand taken by physicians in distress over a case; blood taken from a strong ex-cavalryman out of a position, in this case, and the best to be hoped for, but not assured. In this instance his thoughts were as before wavering. Now supposing she really died, in spite of this? What would he think of himself then? He went back after a time and looked in on her where she was still sleeping. Now she was not so strong as before, or so she seemed; her pulse was not so good, the nurse said. And now as before his mood changed in her favor, but only for a little while. For later, waking, she seemed to look and feel better.

Later he came up to the dining room, where the nurse was taking her breakfast, and seating himself beside her, as was his custom these days, asked: "How do you think she is to-day?"

He and the night nurse had thus had their breakfasts together for days. This nurse, Miss Filson, was such a smooth, pink, graceful creature, with light hair and blue eyes, the kind of eyes and color that of late, and in earlier years, had suggested to him the love time or youth that he had missed.

The latter looked grave, as though she really feared the worse but was concealing it.

"No worse, I think, and possibly a little better," she replied, eyeing him sympathetically. He could see that she too felt that he was old and in danger of being neglected. "Her pulse is a little stronger, nearly normal now, and she is resting easily. Doctor Storm and Doctor Grainger are coming, though, at ten. Then they'll decide what's to be done. I think if she's worse that they are going to try transfusion. The man has been engaged. Doctor Storm said that when she woke to-day she was to be given strong beef tea. Mrs. Elfridge is making it now. The fact that she is not much worse, though, is a good sign in itself, I think."

Haymaker merely stared at her from under his heavy gray eyebrows. He was so tired and gloomy, not only because he had not slept much of late himself but because of this sawing to and fro between his varying moods. Was he never to be able to decide for himself what he really wished? Was he never to be done with this interminable moral or spiritual problem? Why could he not make up his mind on the side of moral order, sympathy, and be at peace? Miss

Filson pattered on about other heart cases, how so many people lived years and years after they were supposed to die of heart lesion; and he meditated as to the grayness and strangeness of it all, the worthlessness of his own life, the variability of his own moods. Why was he so? How queer—how almost evil, sinister—he had become at times; how weak at others. Last night as he had looked at Ernestine lying in bed, and this morning before he had seen her, he had thought if she only would die—if he were only really free once more, even at this late date. But then when he had seen her again this morning and now when Miss Filson spoke of transfusion, he felt sorry again. What good would it do him now? Why should he want to kill her? Could such evil ideas go unpunished either in this world or the next? Supposing his children could guess! Supposing she did die now—and he wished it so fervently only this morning—how would he feel? After all, Ernestine had not been so bad. She had tried, hadn't she?—only she had not been able to make a success of things, as he saw it, and he had not been able to love her, that was all. He reproached himself once more now with the hardness and the cruelty of his thoughts.

The opinion of the two physicians was that Mrs. Haymaker was not much better and that this first form of blood transfusion must be resorted to—injected straight via a pump—which should restore her greatly provided her heart did not bleed it out too freely. Before doing so, however, both men once more spoke to Haymaker, who in an excess of self-condemnation insisted that no expense must be spared. If her life was in danger, save it by any means—all. It was precious to her, to him and to her children. So he spoke. Thus he felt that he was lending every force which could be expected of him, aside from fervently wishing for her recovery, which even now, in spite of himself, he could not do. He was too weary of it all, the conventional round of duties and obligations. But if she recovered, as her physicians seemed to think she might if transfusion were tried, if she gained even, it would mean that he would have to take her away for the summer to some quiet mountain resort—to be with her hourly during the long period in which she would be recovering. Well, he would not complain now. That was all right. He would do it. He would be bored of course, as usual, but it would be too bad to have her die when she could be saved. Yes, that was true. And yet——

He went down to his office again and in the meantime this first form of transfusion was tried, and proved a great success, apparently. She was much better, so the day nurse phoned at three; very much better. At five-thirty Mr. Haymaker returned, no unsatisfactory word having come in the interim, and there she was, resting on a raised pillow, if you please, and looking so cheerful, more like her old self than he had seen her in some time.

At once then his mood changed again. They were amazing, these variations in his own thoughts, almost chemic, not volitional, decidedly peculiar for a man who was supposed to know his own mind—only did one, ever? Now she would not die. Now the whole thing would go on as before. He was sure of it. Well, he might as well resign himself to the old sense of failure. He would never be free now. Everything would go on as before, the next and the next day the same. Terrible! Though he seemed glad—really grateful, in a way, seeing her cheerful and hopeful once more—still the obsession of failure and being once more bound forever returned now. In his own bed at midnight he said to himself: "Now she will really get well. All will be as before. I will never be free. I will never have a day—a day! Never!"

But the next morning, to his surprise and fear or comfort, as his moods varied, she was worse again; and then once more he reproached himself for his black thoughts. Was he not really killing her by what he thought? he asked himself—these constant changes in his mood? Did not his dark wishes have power? Was he not as good as a murderer in his way? Think, if he had always to feel from now on that he had killed her by wishing so! Would not that be dreadful—an awful thing really? Why was he this way? Could he not be human, kind?

When Doctor Storm came at nine-thirty, after a telephone call from the nurse, and looked grave and spoke of horses' blood as being better, thicker than human blood—not so easily bled out of the heart when injected as a serum—Haymaker was beside himself with self-reproaches and sad, disturbing fear. His dark, evil thoughts of last night and all these days had done this, he was sure. Was he really a murderer at heart, a dark criminal, plotting her death?—and for what? Why had he wished last night that she would die? Her case must be very desperate.

"You must do your best," he now said to Doctor Storm. "Whatever is needful—she must not die if you can help it."

"No, Mr. Haymaker," returned the latter sympathetically. "All that can be done will be done. You need not fear. I have an idea that we didn't inject enough yesterday, and anyhow human blood is not thick enough in this case. She responded, but not enough. We will see what we can do to-day."

Haymaker, pressed with duties, went away, subdued and sad. Now once more he decided that he must not tolerate these dark ideas any more, must rid himself of these black wishes, whatever he might feel. It was evil. They would eventually come back to him in some dark way, he might be sure. They might be influencing her. She must be allowed to recover if she could without any opposition on his part. He must now make a further sacrifice of his own life, whatever it cost. It was only decent, only human. Why should he complain now, anyhow, after all these years! What difference would a few more years make? He returned at evening, consoled by his own good thoughts and a telephone message at three to the effect that his wife was much better. This second injection had proved much more effective. Horses' blood was plainly better for her. She was stronger, and sitting up again. He entered at five, and found her lying there pale and weak, but still with a better light in her eye, a touch of color in her cheeks—or so he thought—more force, and a very faint smile for him, so marked had been the change. How great and kind Doctor Storm really was! How resourceful! If she would only get well now! If this dread siege would only abate! Doctor Storm was coming again at eight.

"Well, how are you, dear?" she asked, looking at him sweetly and lovingly, and taking his hand in hers.

He bent and kissed her forehead—a Judas kiss, he had thought up to now, but not so to-night. To-night he was kind, generous—anxious, even, for her to live.

"All right, dearest; very good indeed. And how are you? It's such a fine evening out. You ought to get well soon so as to enjoy these spring days."

"I'm going to," she replied softly. "I feel so much better. And how have you been? Has your work gone all right?"

He nodded and smiled and told her bits of news. Ethelberta had phoned that she was coming, bringing violets. Wesley had said he would be here at six, with Irma! Such-and-such people had asked after her. How could he have been so evil, he now asked himself, as to wish her to die? She was not so bad—really quite charming in her way, an ideal wife for some one, if not him. She was as much entitled to live and enjoy her life as he was to enjoy his; and after all she was the mother of his children, had been with him all these years. Besides, the day had been so fine—it was now—a wondrous May evening. The air and sky were simply delicious. A lavender haze was in the air. The telephone bell now ringing brought still another of a long series of inquiries as to her condition. There had been so many of these during the last few days, the maid said, and especially to-day—and she gave Mr. Haymaker a list of names. See, he thought, she had even more friends than he, being so good, faithful, worthy. Why should he wish her ill?

He sat down to dinner with Ethelberta and Wesley when they arrived, and chatted quite gayly—more hopefully than he had in weeks. His own varying thoughts no longer depressing him, for the moment he was happy. How were they? What were the children all doing? At eight-thirty Doctor Storm came again, and announced that he thought Mrs. Haymaker was doing very well indeed, all things considered.

"Her condition is fairly promising, I must say," he said. "If she gets through another night or two comfortably without falling back I think she'll do very well from now on. Her strength seems to be increasing a fraction. However, we must not be too optimistic. Cases of this kind are very treacherous. To-morrow we'll see how she feels, whether she needs any more blood."

He went away, and at ten Ethelberta and Wesley left for the night, asking to be called if she grew worse, thus leaving him alone once more. He sat and meditated. At eleven, after a few moments at his wife's bedside—absolute quiet had been the doctor's instructions these many days—he himself went to bed. He was very tired. His varying thoughts had afflicted him so much that he was always tired, it seemed—his evil conscience, he called it—but to-night he was sure he would sleep. He felt better about himself, about life. He had done better, to-day. He should never have tolerated such dark thoughts. And yet—and yet—and yet——

He lay on his bed near a window which commanded a view of a small angle of the park, and looked out. There were the spring trees, as usual, silvered now by the light, a bit of lake showing at one end. Here in the city a bit of sylvan scenery such as this was so rare and so expensive. In his youth he had been so fond of water, any small lake or stream or pond. In his youth, also, he had loved the moon, and to walk in the dark. It had all, always, been so suggestive of love and happiness, and he had so craved love and happiness and never had it. Once he had designed a yacht club, the base of which suggested waves. Once, years ago, he had thought of designing a lovely cottage or country house for himself and some new love—that wonderful one— if ever she came and he were free. How wonderful it would all have been. Now—now—the thought at such an hour and especially when it was too late, seemed sacrilegious, hard, cold, unmoral, evil. He turned his face away from the moonlight and sighed, deciding to sleep and shut out these older and darker and sweeter thoughts if he could, and did.

Presently he dreamed, and it was as if some lovely spirit of beauty—that wondrous thing he had always been seeking—came and took him by the hand and led him out, out by dimpling streams and clear rippling lakes and a great, noble highway where were temples and towers and figures in white marble. And it seemed as he walked as if something had been, or were, promised him—a lovely fruition to something which he craved—only the world toward which he walked was still dark or shadowy, with something sad and repressing about it, a haunting sense of a still darker distance. He was going toward beauty apparently, but he was still seeking, seeking, and it was dark there when——

"Mr. Haymaker! Mr. Haymaker!" came a voice—soft, almost mystical at first, and then clearer and more disturbing, as a hand was laid on him. "Will you come at once? It's Mrs. Haymaker!"

On the instant he was on his feet seizing the blue silk dressing gown hanging at his bed's head, and adjusting it as he hurried. Mrs. Elfridge and the nurse were behind him, very pale and distrait, wringing their hands. He could tell by that that the worst was at hand. When he reached the bedroom—her bedroom—there she lay as in life—still, peaceful, already limp, as though she were sleeping. Her thin, and as he sometimes thought, cold, lips were now parted in a faint, gracious smile, or trace of one. He had seen her look that way, too, at times; a really gracious smile, and wise, wiser than she was. The long, thin, graceful hands were open, the fingers spread slightly apart as though she were tired, very tired. The eyelids, too, rested wearily on tired eyes. Her form, spare as always, was outlined clearly under the thin coverlets. Miss Filson, the night nurse, was saying something about having fallen asleep for a moment, and waking only to find her so. She was terribly depressed and disturbed, possibly because of Doctor Storm.

Haymaker paused, greatly shocked and moved by the sight—more so than by anything since the death of little Elwell. After all, she had tried, according to her light. But now she was dead—and they had been together so long! He came forward, tears of sympathy springing to his eyes, then sank down beside the bed on his knees so as not to disturb her right hand where it lay.

"Ernie, dear," he said gently, "Ernie—are you really gone?" His voice was full of sorrow; but to himself it sounded false, traitorous.

He lifted the hand and put it to his lips sadly, then leaned his head against her, thinking of his long, mixed thoughts these many days, while both Mrs. Elfridge and the nurse began wiping their eyes. They were so sorry for him, he was so old now!

After a while he got up—they came forward to persuade him at last—looking tremendously sad and distrait, and asked Mrs. Elfridge and the nurse not to disturb his children. They could not aid her now. Let them rest until morning. Then he went back to his own room and sat down on the bed for a moment, gazing out on the same silvery scene that had attracted him before. It was dreadful. So then his dark wishing had come true at last? Possibly his black thoughts had killed her after all. Was that possible? Had his voiceless prayers been answered in this grim way? And did she know now what he had really thought? Dark thought. Where was she now? What was she thinking now if she knew? Would she hate him—haunt him? It was not dawn yet, only two or three in the morning, and the moon was still bright. And in the next room she was lying, pale and cool, gone forever now out of his life.

He got up after a time and went forward into that pleasant front room where he had so often loved to sit, then back into her room to view the body again. Now that she was gone, here more than elsewhere, in her dead presence, he seemed better able to collect his scattered thoughts. She might see or she might not—might know or not. It was all over now. Only he could not help but feel a little evil. She had been so faithful, if nothing more, so earnest in behalf of him and of his children. He might have spared her these last dark thoughts of these last few days. His feelings were so jumbled that he could not place them half the time. But at the same time the ethics of the past, of his own irritated feelings and moods in regard to her, had to be adjusted somehow before he could have peace. They must be adjusted, only how—how? He and Mrs. Elfridge had agreed not to disturb Doctor Storm any more to-night. They were all agreed to get what rest they could against the morning.

After a time he came forward once more to the front room to sit and gaze at the park. Here, perhaps, he could solve these mysteries for himself, think them out, find out what he did feel. He was evil for having wished all he had, that he knew and felt. And yet there was his own story, too—his life. The dawn was breaking by now; a faint grayness shaded the east and dimly lightened this room. A tall pier mirror between two windows now revealed him to himself—spare, angular, disheveled, his beard and hair astray and his eyes weary. The figure he made here as against his dreams of a happier life, once he were free, now struck him forcibly. What a farce! What a failure! Why should he, of all people, think of further happiness in love, even if he were free? Look at his reflection here in this mirror. What a picture—old, grizzled, done for! Had he not known that for so long? Was it not too ridiculous? Why should he have tolerated such vain thoughts? What could he of all people hope for now? No thing of beauty would have him now. Of course not. That glorious dream of his youth was gone forever. It was a mirage, an ignis fatuus. His wife might just as well have lived as died, for all the difference it would or could make to him. Only, he was really free just the same, almost as it were in spite of his varying moods. But he was old, weary, done for, a recluse and ungainly.

Now the innate cruelty of life, its blazing ironic indifference to him and so many grew rapidly upon him. What had he had? What all had he not missed? Dismally he stared first at his dark wrinkled skin; the crow's-feet at the sides of his eyes; the wrinkles across his forehead and between the eyes; his long, dark, wrinkled hands—handsome hands they once were, he thought; his angular, stiff body. Once he had been very much of a personage, he thought, striking, forceful, dynamic—but now! He turned and looked out over the park where the young trees were, and the lake, to the pinking dawn—just a trace now—a significant thing in itself at this hour surely—the new dawn, so wondrously new for younger people—then back at himself. What could he wish for now—what hope for?

As he did so his dream came back to him—that strange dream of seeking and being led and promised and yet always being led forward into a dimmer, darker land. What did that mean? Had it any real significance? Was it all to be dimmer, darker still? Was it typical of his life? He pondered.

"Free!" he said after a time. "Free! I know now how that is. I am free now, at last! Free! . . . Free . . . Yes—free . . . to die!"

So he stood there ruminating and smoothing his hair and his beard.

Willa Cather

THE SCULPTOR'S FUNERAL

Willa Cather's fiction embraces the literary aims of both the past and the emerging twentieth century. In her use of local color and her concern with life on the frontier, she continued the development of two major phases of nineteenth-century fiction; in her approach to the interpretation of character through heredity and environment and the avoidance in her best stories of technical clichés, she adopted the new modes of the twentieth century. To this fusion of the old and new, she brought a sincerity and clarity of artistic vision which raised her work to a level of major importance.

Willa Cather (1874?-1947) was born near Winchester, Virginia, but in 1882, her father, Charles Cather, moved the family to a farm near Red Cloud, Nebraska, where she grew to be closely identified with the immigrant homesteaders struggling to establish themselves in a new way of life on the bleak prairies. After attending the preparatory school of the University of Nebraska, she entered the University, concentrating on English and classical literature and vigorously committing herself to writing for the student newspaper, editing the senior yearbook, and submitting articles to the Nebraska *State Journal.* After her graduation in 1895, she spent one year as associate editor of the Lincoln *Courier* and then went to Pittsburgh, first to write for the *Leader* and later to teach English in the Allegheny High School. She was soon contributing stories and poems to *Cosmopolitan, McClure's Magazine, Lippincott's Magazine,* and other periodicals. In 1903, she published a volume of verse, *April Twilights,* and two years later, her first collection of stories, *The Troll Garden.* From 1906 to 1912, she was on the staff of *McClure's Magazine,* and while serving for several years as managing editor traveled widely in Europe and the Southwestern states.

With the publication of her first and not too

373

praiseworthy novel, *Alexander's Bridge,* in 1912, she retired from editorial work to devote her full energies to writing. In her next novel, *O Pioneers!* (1913), she—to use her own words—"hit the home pasture" by turning back to the Nebraska farm-immigrant life she had known in her youth. The heroic toil of these western pioneers and the equally heroic earlier struggles of frontier priests in the Southwest provided the inspiration for most of her later fiction. Among the best of her other novels are *My Ántonia* (1918), *A Lost Lady* (1923), *The Professor's House* (1925), and *Death Comes for the Archbishop* (1927). In addition to *The Troll Garden,* she published only two other collections of short stories, *Youth and the Bright Medusa* (1920) and *Obscure Destinies* (1932). In all her novels and stories, no other themes so consistently drew from her such sympathetic treatment as those underlying "The Sculptor's Funeral": the conflict between the cultural values inherited from an old established civilization and those of a newer, vulgarized, commercial civilization springing up in America; the contrast between crass philistinism and the durable claims of art; and the mingled suffering and triumph of the sensitive artist who, caught in the crosscurrents of these forces, yet manages through his craftsmanship to pull free of them. In this story, though the lawyer's harangue that focuses these themes may seem too obviously contrived, they are given added intensity by being set against the drab, cheerless background of a prairie town.

the sculptor's funeral

A group of the townspeople stood on the station siding of a little Kansas town, awaiting the coming of the night train, which was already twenty minutes overdue. The snow had fallen thick over everything; in the pale starlight the line of bluffs across the wide, white meadows south of the town made soft, smoke-coloured curves against the clear sky. The men on the siding stood first on one foot and then on the other, their hands thrust deep into their trousers pockets, their overcoats open, their shoulders screwed up with the cold; and they glanced from time to time toward the southeast, where the railroad track wound along the river shore. They conversed in low tones and moved about restlessly, seeming uncertain as to what was expected of them. There was but one of the company who looked as though he knew exactly why he was there; and he kept conspicuously apart; walking to the far end of the platform, returning to the station door, then pacing up the track again, his chin sunk in the high collar of his overcoat, his burly shoulders drooping forward, his gait heavy and dogged. Presently he was approached by a tall, spare, grizzled man clad in a faded Grand Army suit, who shuffled out from the group and advanced with a certain deference, craning his neck forward until his back made the angle of a jack-knife three-quarters open.

"I reckon she's a-goin' to be pretty late again to-night, Jim," he remarked in a squeaky falsetto. "S'pose it's the snow?"

"I don't know," responded the other man with a shade of annoyance, speaking from out an astonishing cataract of red beard that grew fiercely and thickly in all directions.

The spare man shifted the quill toothpick he was chewing to the other side of his mouth. "It ain't likely that anybody from the East will come with the corpse, I s'pose," he went on reflectively.

"I don't know," responded the other, more curtly than before.

"It's too bad he didn't belong to some lodge or other. I like an order funeral myself. They seem more appropriate for people of some reputation," the spare man continued, with an ingratiating concession in his shrill voice, as he carefully placed his toothpick in his vest pocket. He always carried the flag at the G. A. R. funerals in the town.

The heavy man turned on his heel, without replying, and walked up the siding. The spare man shuffled back to the uneasy group. "Jim's ez full ez a tick, ez ushel," he commented commiseratingly.

Just then a distant whistle sounded, and there was a shuffling of feet on the platform. A number of lanky boys of all ages appeared as suddenly and slimily as eels wakened by the crack of thunder; some came from the waiting-room, where they had been warming themselves by the red stove, or half asleep on the slat benches; others uncoiled themselves from baggage trucks or slid out of express wagons. Two clambered down from the driver's seat of a hearse that stood backed up against the siding. They straightened their stooping shoulders and lifted their heads, and a flash of momentary animation kindled their dull eyes at that cold, vibrant scream, the world-wide call for men. It stirred them like the note of a trumpet; just as it had often stirred the man who was coming home to-night, in his boyhood.

The night express shot, red as a rocket, from out the eastward marsh lands and wound along the river shore under the long lines of shivering poplars that sentinelled the meadows, the escaping steam hanging in grey masses against the pale sky and blotting out the Milky Way. In a moment the red glare from the headlight streamed up the snow-covered track before the siding and glittered on the wet, black rails. The burly man with the dishevelled red beard walked swiftly up the platform toward the approaching train, uncovering his head as he went. The group of men behind him hesitated, glanced questioningly at one another, and awkwardly followed his example. The train stopped, and the crowd shuffled up to the express car just as the door was thrown open, the spare man in the G. A. R. suit thrusting his head forward with curiosity. The express messenger appeared in the doorway, accompanied by a young man in a long ulster and travelling cap.

"Are Mr. Merrick's friends here?" inquired the young man.

The group on the platform swayed and shuffled uneasily. Philip Phelps, the banker, responded with dignity: "We have come to take charge of the body. Mr. Merrick's father is very feeble and can't be about."

"Send the agent out here," growled the express messenger, "and tell the operator to lend a hand."

The coffin was got out of its rough box and down on the snowy platform. The townspeople drew back enough to make room for it and then formed a close semicircle about it, looking curiously at the palm leaf which lay across the black cover. No one said anything. The baggage man stood by his truck, waiting to get at the trunks. The engine panted heavily, and the fireman dodged in and out among the wheels with his yellow torch and long oil-can, snapping the spindle boxes. The young Bostonian, one of the dead sculptor's pupils who had come with the body, looked about him helplessly. He turned to the banker, the only one of that black, uneasy, stoop-shouldered group who seemed enough of an individual to be addressed.

"None of Mr. Merrick's brothers are here?" he asked uncertainly.

The man with the red beard for the first time stepped up and joined the group. "No, they have not come yet; the family is scattered. The body will be taken directly to the house." He stooped and took hold of one of the handles of the coffin.

"Take the long hill road up, Thompson, it will be easier on the horses," called the liveryman as the undertaker snapped the door of the hearse and prepared to mount to the driver's seat.

Laird, the red-bearded lawyer, turned again to the stranger: "We didn't know whether there would be any one with him or not," he explained. "It's a long walk, so you'd better go up in the hack." He pointed to a single battered conveyance, but the young man replied stiffly: "Thank you, but I think I will go up with the hearse. If you don't object," turning to the undertaker, "I'll ride with you."

They clambered up over the wheels and drove off in the starlight up the long, white hill toward the town. The lamps in the still village were shining from under the low, snow-burdened roofs; and beyond, on every side, the plains reached out into emptiness, peaceful and wide as the soft sky itself, and wrapped in a tangible, white silence.

When the hearse backed up to a wooden sidewalk before a naked, weather-beaten frame house, the same composite, ill-defined group that had stood upon the station siding was huddled about the gate. The front yard was an icy swamp, and a couple of warped planks, extending from the sidewalk to the door, made a sort of rickety footbridge. The gate hung on one hinge, and was opened wide with difficulty. Steavens, the young stranger, noticed that something black was tied to the knob of the front door.

The grating sound made by the casket, as it was drawn from the hearse, was answered by a scream from the house; the front door was wrenched open, and a tall, corpulent woman rushed out bareheaded into the snow and flung herself upon the coffin, shrieking: "My boy, my boy! And this is how you've come home to me!"

As Steavens turned away and closed his eyes with a shudder of unutterable repulsion, another woman, also tall, but flat and angular, dressed entirely in black, darted out of the house and caught Mrs. Merrick by the shoulders, crying sharply: "Come, come, mother; you musn't go on like this!" Her tone changed to one of obsequious solemnity as she turned to the banker: "The parlour is ready, Mr. Phelps."

The bearers carried the coffin along the narrow boards, while the undertaker ran ahead with the coffin-rests. They bore it into a large, unheated room that smelled of dampness and disuse and furniture polish, and set it down under a hanging lamp ornamented with jingling glass prisms and before a "Rogers group" of John Alden and Priscilla, wreathed with smilax. Henry Steavens stared about him with the sickening conviction that there had been some horrible mistake, and that he had somehow arrived at the wrong destination. He looked painfully about over the clover-green Brussels, the fat plush upholstery; among the hand-painted china placques and panels, and vases, for some mark of identification, for something that might once conceivably have belonged to Harvey Merrick. It was not until he recognized his friend in the crayon portrait of a little boy in kilts and curls hanging above the piano, that he felt willing to let any of these people approach the coffin.

"Take the lid off, Mr. Thompson; let me see my boy's face," wailed the elder woman between her sobs. This time Steavens looked fearfully, almost beseechingly into her face, red and swollen under its masses of strong, black, shiny hair. He flushed, dropped his eyes, and then, almost incredulously, looked again. There was a kind of power about her face—a kind of brutal handsomeness, even, but it was scarred and furrowed by violence, and so coloured and coarsened by fiercer passions that grief seemed never to have laid a gentle finger there. The long nose was distended and knobbed at the end, and there were deep lines on either side of it; her heavy, black brows almost met across her forehead, her teeth were large and square, and set far apart—teeth that could tear. She filled the room; the men were obliterated, seemed tossed about like twigs in an angry water, and even Steavens felt himself being drawn into the whirlpool.

The daughter—the tall, raw-boned woman in crêpe, with a mourning comb in her hair which curiously lengthened her long face— sat stiffly upon the sofa, her hands, conspicuous for their large knuckles, folded in her lap, her mouth and eyes drawn down, solemnly awaiting the opening of the coffin. Near the door stood a mulatto woman, evidently a servant in the house, with a timid bearing and an emaciated face pitifully sad and gentle. She was weeping silently, the corner of her calico apron lifted to her eyes, occasionally suppressing a long, quivering sob. Steavens walked over and stood beside her.

Feeble steps were heard on the stairs, and an old man, tall and frail, odorous of pipe smoke, with shaggy, unkept grey hair and a dingy beard, tobacco stained about the mouth, entered uncertainly. He went slowly up to the coffin and stood rolling a blue cotton handkerchief between his hands, seeming so pained and embarrassed by his wife's orgy of grief that he had no consciousness of anything else.

"There, there, Annie, dear, don't take on so," he quavered timidly, putting out a shaking hand and awkwardly patting her elbow. She turned with a cry, and sank upon his shoulder with such violence that he tottered a little. He did not even glance toward the coffin, but continued to look at her with a dull, frightened, appealing expression, as a spaniel looks at the whip. His sunken cheeks slowly reddened and burned with miserable shame. When his wife rushed from the room, her daughter strode after her with set lips. The servant stole up to the coffin, bent over it for a moment, and then slipped away to the kitchen, leaving Steavens, the lawyer and the father to themselves. The old man stood trembling and looking down at his dead son's face. The sculptor's splendid head seemed even more noble in its rigid stillness than in life. The dark hair had crept down upon the wide forehead; the face seemed strangely long, but in it there was not that beautiful and chaste repose which we expect to find in the faces of the dead. The brows were so drawn that there were two deep lines above the beaked nose, and the chin was thrust forward defiantly. It was as though the strain of life had been so sharp and bitter that death could not at once wholly relax the tension and smooth the countenance into perfect peace—as though he were still guarding something precious and holy, which might even yet be wrested from him.

The old man's lips were working under his stained beard. He turned to the lawyer with timid deference: "Phelps and the rest are comin' back to set up with Harve, ain't they?" he asked. "Thank 'ee, Jim, thank 'ee." He brushed the hair back gently from his son's forehead. "He was a good boy, Jim; always a good boy. He was ez gentle ez a child and the kindest of 'em all—only we didn't none of us ever onderstand him." The tears trickled slowly down his beard and dropped upon the sculptor's coat.

"Martin, Martin. Oh, Martin! come here," his wife wailed from the top of the stairs. The old man started timorously: "Yes, Annie, I'm coming." He turned away, hesitated, stood for a moment in miserable indecision; then reached back and patted the dead man's hair softly, and stumbled from the room.

"Poor old man, I didn't think he had any tears left. Seems as if his eyes would have gone dry long ago. At his age nothing cuts very deep," remarked the lawyer.

Something in his tone made Steavens glance up. While the mother had been in the room, the young man had scarcely seen any one else; but now, from the moment he first glanced into Jim Laird's florid face and blood-shot eyes, he knew that he had found what he had been heartsick at not finding before—the feeling, the understanding, that must exist in some one, even here.

The man was red as his beard, with features swollen and blurred by dissipation, and a hot, blazing blue eye. His face was strained—that of a man who is controlling himself with difficulty—and he kept plucking at his beard with a sort of fierce resentment. Steavens, sitting by the window, watched him turn down the glaring lamp, still its jangling pendants with an angry gesture, and then stand with his hands locked behind him, staring down into the master's face. He could not help wondering what link there could have been between the porcelain vessel and so sooty a lump of potter's clay.

From the kitchen an uproar was sounding; when the dining-room door opened, the import of it was clear. The mother was abusing the maid for having forgotten to make the dressing for the chicken salad which had been prepared for the watchers. Steavens had never heard anything in the least like it; it was injured, emotional, dramatic abuse, unique and masterly in its excruciating cruelty, as violent and unrestrained as had been her grief of twenty minutes before. With a shudder of disgust the lawyer went into the dining-room and closed the door into the kitchen.

"Poor Roxy's getting it now," he remarked when he came back. "The Merricks took her out of the poor-house years ago; and if her loyalty would let her, I guess the poor old thing could tell tales that would curdle your blood. She's the mulatto woman who was standing in here a while ago, with her apron to her eyes. The old woman is a fury; there never was anybody like her for demonstrative piety and ingenious cruelty. She made Harvey's life a hell for him when he lived at home; he was so sick ashamed of it. I never could see how he kept himself so sweet."

"He was wonderful," said Steavens slowly, "wonderful; but until to-night I have never known how wonderful."

"That is the true and eternal wonder of it, anyway; that it can come even from such a dung heap as this," the lawyer cried, with a sweeping gesture which seemed to indicate much more than the four walls within which they stood.

"I think I'll see whether I can get a little air. The room is so close I am beginning to feel rather faint," murmured Steavens, struggling with one of the windows. The sash was stuck, however, and would not yield, so he sat down dejectedly and began pulling at his collar. The lawyer came over, loosened the sash with one blow of his red fist and sent the window up a few inches. Steavens thanked him, but the nausea which had been gradually climbing into his throat for the last half hour left him with but one desire—a desperate feeling that he must get away from this place with what was left of Harvey Merrick. Oh, he comprehended well enough now the quiet bitterness of the smile that he had seen so often on his master's lips!

He remembered that once, when Merrick returned from a visit home, he brought with him a singularly feeling and suggestive bas-relief of a thin, faded old woman, sitting and sewing something pinned to her knee; while a full-lipped, full-blooded little urchin, his trousers held up by a single gallows, stood beside her, impatiently twitching her gown to call her attention to a butterfly he had caught. Steavens, impressed by the tender and delicate modelling of the thin, tired face, had asked him if it were his mother. He remembered the dull flush that had burned up in the sculptor's face.

The lawyer was sitting in a rocking-chair beside the coffin, his head thrown back and his eyes closed. Steavens looked at him earnestly, puzzled at the line of the chin, and wondering why a man should conceal a feature of such distinction under that disfiguring shock of beard. Suddenly, as though he felt the young sculptor's keen glance, he opened his eyes.

"Was he always a good deal of an oyster?" he asked abruptly. "He was terribly shy as a boy."

"Yes, he was an oyster, since you put it so," rejoined Steavens. "Although he could be very fond of people, he always gave one the impression of being detached. He disliked violent emotion; he was reflective, and rather distrustful of himself—except, of course, as regarded his work. He was sure-footed enough there. He distrusted men pretty thoroughly and women even more, yet somehow without believing ill of them. He was determined, indeed, to believe the best, but he seemed afraid to investigate."

"A burnt dog dreads the fire," said the lawyer grimly, and closed his eyes.

Steavens went on and on, reconstructing that whole miserable boyhood. All this raw, biting ugliness had been the portion of the man whose tastes were refined beyond the limits of the reasonable—whose mind was an exhaustless gallery of beautiful impressions, and so sensitive that the mere shadow of a poplar leaf flickering against a sunny wall would be etched and held there forever. Surely, if ever a man had the magic word in his finger tips, it was Merrick. Whatever he touched, he revealed its holiest secret; liberated it from enchantment and restored it to its pristine loveliness, like the Arabian prince who fought the enchantress spell for spell. Upon whatever he had come in contact with, he had left a beautiful record of the experience—a sort of ethereal signature; a scent, a sound, a colour that was his own.

Steavens understood now the real tragedy of his master's life; neither love nor wine, as many had conjectured; but a blow which had fallen earlier and cut deeper than these could have done—a shame not his, and yet so unescapably his, to hide in his heart from his very boyhood. And without—the frontier warfare; the yearning of a boy, cast ashore upon a desert of newness and ugliness and sordidness, for all that is chastened and old, and noble with traditions.

At eleven o'clock the tall, flat woman in black crêpe entered and announced that the watchers were arriving, and asked them "to step into the dining-room." As Steavens rose, the lawyer said dryly: "You go on—it'll be a good experience for you, doubtless; as for me, I'm not equal to that crowd to-night; I've had twenty years of them."

As Steavens closed the door after him he glanced back at the lawyer, sitting by the coffin in the dim light, with his chin resting on his hand.

The same misty group that had stood before the door of the express car shuffled into the dining-room. In the light of the kerosene lamp they separated and became individuals. The minister, a pale, feeble-looking man with white hair and blond chin-whiskers, took his seat beside a small side table and placed his Bible upon it. The Grand Army man sat down behind the stove and tilted his chair back comfortably against the wall, fishing his quill toothpick from his waistcoat pocket. The two bankers, Phelps and Elder, sat off in a corner behind the dinner-table, where they could finish their discussion of the new usury law and its effect on chattel security loans. The real estate agent, an old man with a smiling, hypocritical face, soon joined them. The coal and lumber dealer and the cattle shipper sat on opposite sides of the hard coal-burner, their feet on the nickel-work. Steavens took a book from his pocket and began to read. The talk around him ranged through various topics of local interest while the house was quieting down. When it was clear that the members of the family were in bed, the Grand Army man hitched his shoulders and, untangling his long legs, caught his heels on the rounds of his chair.

"S'pose there'll be a will, Phelps?" he queried in his weak falsetto.

The banker laughed disagreeably, and began trimming his nails with a pearl-handled pocket-knife.

"There'll scarcely be any need for one, will there?" he queried in his turn.

The restless Grand Army man shifted his position again, getting his knees still nearer his chin. "Why, the ole man says Harve's done right well lately," he chirped.

The other banker spoke up. "I reckon he means by that Harve ain't asked him to mortgage any more farms lately, so as he could go on with his education."

"Seems like my mind don't reach back to a time when Harve wasn't bein' edycated," tittered the Grand Army man.

There was a general chuckle. The minister took out his handkerchief and blew his nose sonorously. Banker Phelps closed his knife with a snap. "It's too bad the old man's sons didn't turn out better," he remarked with reflective authority. "They never hung together. He spent money enough on Harve to stock a dozen cattle-farms and he might as well have poured it into Sand Creek. If Harve had stayed at home and helped nurse what little they had, and gone into stock on the old man's bottom farm, they might all have been well fixed. But the old man had to trust everything to tenants and was cheated right and left."

"Harve never could have handled stock none," interposed the cattleman. "He hadn't it in him to be sharp. Do you remember when he bought Sander's mules for eight-year olds, when everybody in town knew that Sander's father-in-law give 'em to his wife for a wedding present eighteen years before, an' they was full-grown mules then."

Every one chuckled, and the Grand Army man rubbed his knees with a spasm of childish delight.

"Harve never was much account for anything practical, and he shore was never fond of work," began the coal and lumber dealer. "I mind the last time he was home; the day he left, when the old man was out to the barn helpin' his hand hitch up to take Harve to the train, and

Cal Moots was patchin' up the fence, Harve, he come out on the step and sings out, in his lady-like voice: "Cal Moots, Cal Moots! please come cord my trunk."

"That's Harve for you," approved the Grand Army man gleefully. "I kin hear him howlin' yet when he was a big feller in long pants and his mother used to whale him with a rawhide in the barn for lettin' the cows git foundered in the cornfield when he was drivin' 'em home from pasture. He killed a cow of mine that-a-way onct—a pure Jersey and the best milker I had, an' the ole man had to put up for her. Harve, he was watchin' the sun set acrost the marshes when the anamile got away; he argued that sunset was oncommon fine."

"Where the old man made his mistake was in sending the boy East to school," said Phelps, stroking his goatee and speaking in a deliberate, judicial tone. "There was where he got his head full of trapseing to Paris and all such folly. What Harve needed, of all people, was a course in some first-class Kansas City business college."

The letters were swimming before Steavens's eyes. Was it possible that these men did not understand, that the palm on the coffin meant nothing to them? The very name of their town would have remained forever buried in the postal guide had it not been now and again mentioned in the world in connection with Harvey Merrick's. He remembered what his master had said to him on the day of his death, after the congestion of both lungs had shut off any probability of recovery, and the sculptor had asked his pupil to send his body home. "It's not a pleasant place to be lying while the world is moving and doing and bettering," he had said with a feeble smile, "but it rather seems as though we ought to go back to the place we came from in the end. The townspeople will come in for a look at me; and after they have had their say I shan't have much to fear from the judgment of God. The wings of the Victory, in there"—with a weak gesture toward his studio—"will not shelter me."

The cattleman took up the comment. "Forty's young for a Merrick to cash in; they usually hang on pretty well. Probably he helped it along with whisky."

"His mother's people were not long lived, and Harvey never had a robust constitution," said the minister mildly. He would have liked to say more. He had been the boy's Sunday-school teacher, and had been fond of him; but he felt that he was not in a position to speak. His own sons had turned out badly, and it was not a year since one of them had made his last trip home in the express car, shot in a gambling-house in the Black Hills.

"Nevertheless, there is no disputin' that Harve frequently looked upon the wine when it was red, also variegated, and it shore made an oncommon fool of him," moralized the cattleman.

Just then the door leading into the parlour rattled loudly and every one started involuntarily, looking relieved when only Jim Laird came out. His red face was convulsed with anger, and the Grand Army man ducked his head when he saw the spark in his blue, blood-shot eye. They were all afraid of Jim; he was a drunkard, but he could twist the law to suit his client's needs as no other man in all western Kansas could do; and there were many who tried. The lawyer closed the door gently behind him, leaned back against it and folded his arms, cocking his head a little to one side. When he assumed this attitude in the court-room, ears were always pricked up, as it usually foretold a flood of withering sarcasm.

"I've been with you gentlemen before," he began in a dry, even tone, "when you've sat by the coffins of boys born and raised in this town; and, if I remember rightly, you were never any too well satisfied when you checked them up. What's the matter, anyhow? Why is it that reputable young men are as scarce as millionaires in Sand City? It might almost seem to a stranger that there was some way something the matter with your progressive town. Why did Ruben Sayer, the brightest young lawyer you ever turned out, after he had come home from the university as straight as a die, take to drinking and forge a check and shoot himself? Why did Bill Merrit's son die of the shakes in a saloon in Omaha? Why was Mr. Thomas's son, here, shot in a gambling-house? Why did young Adams burn his mill to beat the insurance companies and go to the pen?"

The lawyer paused and unfolded his arms, laying one clenched fist quietly on the table. "I'll tell you why. Because you drummed nothing but money and knavery into their ears from the time they wore knickerbockers; because you carped away at them as you've been carping here to-night, holding our friends Phelps and Elder up to them for their models, as our grandfathers held up George Washington and John Adams. But the boys, worse luck, were young, and raw at the business you put them to; and how could they match coppers with such artists as Phelps and Elder? You wanted them to be successful rascals; they were only unsuccessful ones—that's all the difference. There was only one boy ever raised in this borderland between ruffianism and civilization, who didn't come to grief, and you hated Harvey Merrick more for winning out than you hated all the other boys who got under the wheels. Lord, Lord, how you did hate him! Phelps, here, is fond of saying that he could buy and sell us all out any time he's a mind to; but he knew Harve wouldn't have given a tinker's damn for his bank and all his cattle-farms put together; and a lack of appreciation, that way, goes hard with Phelps.

"Old Nimrod, here, thinks Harve drank too much; and this from such as Nimrod and me!

"Brother Elder says Harve was too free with the old man's money—fell short in filial consideration, maybe. Well, we can all remember the very tone in which brother Elder swore his own father was a liar, in the county court; and we all know that the old man came out of that partnership with his son as bare as a sheared lamb. But maybe I'm getting personal, and I'd better be driving ahead at what I want to say."

The lawyer paused a moment, squared his heavy shoulders, and went on: "Harvey Merrick and I went to school together, back East. We were dead in earnest, and we wanted you all to be proud of us some day. We meant to be great men. Even I, and I haven't lost my sense of humour, gentlemen, I meant to be a great man. I came back here to practise, and I found you didn't in the least want me to be a great man. You wanted me to be a shrewd lawyer—oh, yes! Our veteran here wanted me to get him an increase of pension, because he had dyspepsia; Phelps wanted a new county survey that would put the widow Wilson's little bottom farm inside his south line; Elder wanted to lend money at 5 per cent a month, and get it collected; old Stark here wanted to wheedle old women up in Vermont into investing their annuities in real-estate mortgages that are not worth the paper they are written on. Oh, you needed me hard enough, and you'll go on needing me; and that's why I'm not afraid to plug the truth home to you this once.

"Well, I came back here and became the damned shyster you wanted me to be. You pretend to have some sort of respect for me; and yet you'll stand up and throw mud at Harvey Merrick, whose soul you couldn't dirty and whose hands you couldn't tie. Oh, you're a discriminating lot of Christians! There have been times when the sight of Harvey's name in some Eastern paper has made me hang my head like a whipped dog; and, again, times when I liked to think of him off there in the world, away from all this hog-wallow, doing his great work and climbing the big, clean up-grade he'd set for himself.

"And we? Now that we've fought and lied and sweated and stolen, and hated as only the disappointed strugglers in a bitter, dead little Western town know how to do, what have we got to show for it? Harvey Merrick wouldn't have given one sunset over your marshes for all you've got put together, and you know it. It's not for me to say why, in the inscrutable wisdom of God, a genius should ever have been called from his place of hatred and bitter waters; but I want this Boston man to know that the drivel he's been hearing here to-night is the only tribute any truly great man could ever have from such a lot of sick, side-tracked, burnt-dog, land-poor sharks as the here-present financiers of Sand City—upon which town may God have mercy!"

The lawyer thrust out his hand to Steavens as he passed him, caught up his overcoat in the hall, and had left the house before the Grand Army man had had time to lift his ducked head and crane his long neck about at his fellows.

Next day Jim Laird was drunk and unable to attend the funeral services. Steavens called twice at his office, but was compelled to start East without seeing him. He had a presentiment that he would hear from him again, and left his address on the lawyer's table; but if Laird found it, he never acknowledged it. The thing in him that Harvey Merrick had loved must have gone under ground with Harvey Merrick's coffin; for it never spoke again, and Jim got the cold he died of driving across the Colorado mountains to defend one of Phelps's sons who had got into trouble out there by cutting government timber.

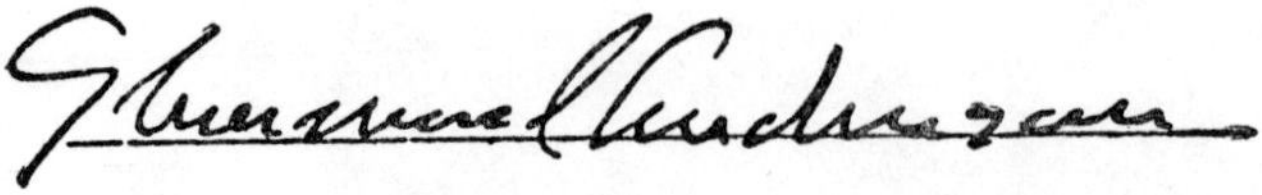

DEATH IN THE WOODS

Sherwood Anderson shared with other writers of the
early twentieth century a conviction that the short
story, under the aegis of the popular magazine, had
become standardized in technique, a "plot" story, written by formula. Objecting to the "plot notion" and to
arbitrary rules of any kind, Anderson cultivated
artistic freedom in his method of writing. As a result
of its unconventionality in technique and subject matter, his first collection, *Winesburg, Ohio,* was roundly criticized on its appearance in 1919 but now stands
as a landmark in the short story's development.

Although Anderson became a professional
writer relatively late in life, after a career in business,
his predisposition for storytelling probably dated from
his early childhood in Camden, Ohio, his birthplace
(1876), where he heard his imaginative, jack-of-all-
trades father enthrall country listeners with tall tales.
Compelled to earn his own way without the benefit of
much schooling, he successively worked as newsboy,
farm laborer, stable boy, factory hand, and copywriter
in an advertising office. Service as a soldier during the
Spanish-American War stimulated him to enlarge his
horizons, and he enrolled in the Wittenberg Academy
in Springfield, Ohio. Through the acquaintanceship
he formed in his one term there with a friendly editor,
he secured a position as copywriter and solicitor in a
Chicago advertising agency. From copywriting, he
soon branched out into articles and attempts at fiction,
but he was yet far from being a professional writer.
Resigning from the agency in 1906, he entered business
for himself, first as president of a mail-order store
in Cleveland and next as part owner and manager
of a paint factory in Elyria, Ohio. In 1912, unable
longer to continue business in the daytime and writing
at night, he left his factory, returned to Chicago, and
supported himself by advertising work again while he

389

entered seriously into his writing career. His first novels, *Windy McPherson's Son* (1916) and *Marching Men* (1917), and a volume of poetry, *Mid-American Chants* (1918), brought him some attention, but wide recognition came only with *Winesburg, Ohio* (1919) and such later works as *Poor White* (1920) and, particularly, *Dark Laughter* (1925). In addition to *Winesburg,* his most important story collections are *Triumph of the Egg* (1921), *Horses and Men* (1923), and *Death in the Woods and Other Stories* (1933). He published various other works before his death in 1941.

Anderson's chief objection to the "plot notion" was that the compulsion on the writer to make his characters fit a mechanical scheme of action inevitably resulted in a false, distorted presentation of life. Rather than plot, the writer should concentrate on *form*—"an altogether more elusive and difficult thing to come at." "Form," he said, "grew out of the materials of the tale and the teller's reaction to them," by which he meant that each story is a highly individualistic problem incapable of being solved by any set technical formula. His way of attempting to realize the elusiveness of form may be profitably studied in "Death in the Woods," which he considered his best story.

death in the woods

She was an old woman and lived on a farm near the town in which I lived. All country and small-town people have seen such old women, but no one knows much about them. Such an old woman comes into town driving an old worn-out horse or she comes afoot carrying a basket. She may own a few hens and have eggs to sell. She brings them in a basket and takes them to a grocer. There she trades

From *Death in the Woods and Other Stories* by Sherwood Anderson. Published by Liveright Publishing Corporation, N. Y. C. Copyright: Sherwood Anderson, 1933.

them in. She gets some salt pork and some beans. Then she gets a pound or two of sugar and some flour.

Afterwards she goes to the butcher's and asks for some dog-meat. She may spend ten or fifteen cents, but when she does she asks for something. Formerly the butchers gave liver to any one who wanted to carry it away. In our family we were always having it. Once one of my brothers got a whole cow's liver at the slaughter-house near the fairgrounds in our town. We had it until we were sick of it. It never cost a cent. I have hated the thought of it ever since.

The old farm woman got some liver and a soup-bone. She never visited with any one, and as soon as she got what she wanted she lit out for home. It made quite a load for such an old body. No one gave her a lift. People drive right down a road and never notice an old woman like that.

There was such an old woman who used to come into town past our house one Summer and Fall when I was a young boy and was sick with what was called inflammatory rheumatism. She went home later carrying a heavy pack on her back. Two or three large gaunt-looking dogs followed at her heels.

The old woman was nothing special. She was one of the nameless ones that hardly any one knows, but she got into my thoughts. I have just suddenly now, after all these years, remembered her and what happened. It is a story. Her name was Grimes, and she lived with her husband and son in a small unpainted house on the bank of a small creek four miles from town.

The husband and son were a tough lot. Although the son was but twenty-one, he had already served a term in jail. It was whispered about that the woman's husband stole horses and ran them off to some other county. Now and then, when a horse turned up missing, the man had also disappeared. No one ever caught him. Once, when I was loafing at Tom Whitehead's livery-barn, the man came there and sat on the bench in front. Two or three other men were there, but no one spoke to him. He sat for a few minutes and then got up and went away. When he was leaving he turned around and stared at the men. There was a look of defiance in his eyes. "Well, I have tried to be friendly. You don't want to talk to me. It has been so wherever I have gone in this town. If, some day, one of your fine horses turns up missing, well, then what?" He did not say anything actually. "I'd like to bust one of you on the jaw," was about what his eyes said. I remember how the look in his eyes made me shiver.

The old man belonged to a family that had had money once.

His name was Jake Grimes. It all comes back clearly now. His father, John Grimes, had owned a sawmill when the country was new, and had made money. Then he got to drinking and running after women. When he died there wasn't much left.

Jake blew in the rest. Pretty soon there wasn't any more lumber to cut and his land was nearly all gone.

He got his wife off a German farmer, for whom he went to work one June day in the wheat harvest. She was a young thing then and scared to death. You see, the farmer was up to something with the girl—she was, I think, a bound girl and his wife had her suspicions. She took it out on the girl when the man wasn't around. Then, when the wife had to go off to town for supplies, the farmer got after her. She told young Jake that nothing really ever happened, but he didn't know whether to believe it or not.

He got her pretty easy himself, the first time he was out with her. He wouldn't have married her if the German farmer hadn't tried to tell him where to get off. He got her to go riding with him in his buggy one night when he was threshing on the place, and then he came for her the next Sunday night.

She managed to get out of the house without her employer's seeing, but when she was getting into the buggy he showed up. It was almost dark, and he just popped up suddenly at the horse's head. He grabbed the horse by the bridle and Jake got out his buggy-whip.

They had it out all right! The German was a tough one. Maybe he didn't care whether his wife knew or not. Jake hit him over the face and shoulders with the buggy-whip, but the horse got to acting up and he had to get out.

Then the two men went for it. The girl didn't see it. The horse started to run away and went nearly a mile down the road before the girl got him stopped. Then she managed to tie him to a tree beside the road. (I wonder how I know all this. It must have stuck in my mind from small-town tales when I was a boy.) Jake found her there after he got through with the German. She was huddled up in the buggy seat, crying, scared to death. She told Jake a lot of stuff, how the German had tried to get her, how he chased her once into the barn, how another time, when they happened to be alone in the house together, he tore her dress open clear down the front. The German, she said, might have got her that time if he hadn't heard his old woman drive in at the gate. She had been off to town for supplies. Well, she would be putting the horse in the barn. The German managed to sneak off to the fields without his wife seeing. He told the girl he would kill her if she told. What could she do? She told a lie about ripping her dress in the barn when she was feeding the stock. I remember now that she was a bound girl and did not know where her father and mother were. Maybe she did not have any father. You know what I mean.

Such bound children were often enough cruelly treated. They were children who had no parents, slaves really. There were very few orphan homes then. They were legally bound into some home. It was a matter of pure luck how it came out.

2

She married Jake and had a son and daughter, but the daughter died.

Then she settled down to feed stock. That was her job. At the German's place she had cooked the food for the German and his wife. The wife was a strong woman with big hips and worked most of the time in the fields with her husband. She fed them and fed the cows in the barn, fed the pigs, the horses and the chickens. Every moment of every day, as a young girl, was spent feeding something.

Then she married Jake Grimes and he had to be fed. She was a slight thing, and when she had been married for three or four years, and after the two children were born, her slender shoulders became stooped.

Jake always had a lot of big dogs around the house, that stood near the unused sawmill near the creek. He was always trading horses when he wasn't stealing something and had a lot of poor bony ones about. Also he kept three or four pigs and a cow. They were all pastured in the few acres left of the Grimes place and Jake did little enough work.

He went into debt for a threshing outfit and ran it for several years, but it did not pay. People did not trust him. They were afraid he would steal the grain at night. He had to go a long way off to get work and it cost too much to get there. In the Winter he hunted and cut a little firewood, to be sold in some nearby town. When the son grew up he was just like the father. They got drunk together. If there wasn't anything to eat in the house when they came home the old man gave his old woman a cut over the head. She had a few chickens of her own and had to kill one of them in a hurry. When they were all killed she wouldn't have any eggs to sell when she went to town, and then what would she do?

393

She had to scheme all her life about getting things fed, getting the pigs fed so they would grow fat and could be butchered in the Fall. When they were butchered her husband took most of the meat off to town and sold it. If he did not do it first the boy did. They fought sometimes and when they fought the old woman stood aside trembling.

She had got the habit of silence anyway—that was fixed. Sometimes, when she began to look old—she wasn't forty yet—and when the husband and son were both off, trading horses or drinking or hunting or stealing, she went around the house and the barnyard muttering to herself.

How was she going to get everything fed?—that was her problem. The dogs had to be fed. There wasn't enough hay in the barn for the horses and the cow. If she didn't feed the chickens how could they lay eggs? Without eggs to sell how could she get things in town, things she had to have to keep the life of the farm going? Thank heaven, she did not have to feed her husband—in a certain way. That hadn't lasted long after their marriage and after the babies came. Where he went on his long trips she did not know. Sometimes he was gone from home for weeks, and after the boy grew up they went off together.

They left everything at home for her to manage and she had no money. She knew no one. No one ever talked to her in town. When it was Winter she had to gather sticks of wood for her fire, had to try to keep the stock fed with very little grain.

The stock in the barn cried to her hungrily, the dogs followed her about. In the Winter the hens laid few enough eggs. They huddled in the corners of the barn and she kept watching them. If a hen lays an egg in the barn in the Winter and you do not find it, it freezes and breaks.

One day in Winter the old woman went off to town with a few eggs and the dogs followed her. She did not get started until nearly three o'clock and the snow was heavy. She hadn't been feeling very well for several days and so she went muttering along, scantily clad, her shoulders stooped. She had an old grain bag in which she carried her eggs, tucked away down in the bottom. There weren't many of them, but in Winter the price of eggs is up. She would get a little meat in exchange for the eggs, some salt pork, a little sugar, and some coffee perhaps. It might be the butcher would give her a piece of liver.

When she had got to town and was trading in her eggs the dogs lay by the door outside. She did pretty well, got the things she needed, more than she had hoped. Then she went to the butcher and he gave her some liver and some dog-meat.

It was the first time any one had spoken to her in a friendly way for a long time. The butcher was alone in his shop when she came in and was annoyed by the thought of such a sick-looking old woman out on such a day. It was bitter cold and the snow, that had let up during the afternoon, was falling again. The butcher said something about her husband and her son, swore at them, and the old woman stared at him, a look of mild surprise in her eyes as he talked. He said that if either the husband or the son were going to get any of the liver or the heavy bones with scraps of meat hanging to them that he had put into the grain bag, he'd see him starve first.

Starve, eh? Well, things had to be fed. Men had to be fed, and horses that weren't any good but maybe could be traded off, and the poor thin cow that hadn't given any milk for three months.

Horses, cows, pigs, dogs, men.

3

The old woman had to get back before darkness came if she could. The dogs followed at her heels, sniffing at the heavy grain bag she had fastened on her back. When she got to the edge of town she stopped by a fence and tied the bag on her back with a piece of rope she had carried in her dress-pocket for just that purpose. It was hard when she had to crawl over fences and once she fell over and landed in the snow. The dogs went frisking about. She had to struggle to get to her feet again, but she made it. The point of climbing over the fences was that there was a short cut over a hill and through a woods. She might have gone around by the road, but it was a mile farther that way. She was afraid she couldn't make it. And then, besides, the stock had to be fed. There was a little hay left and a little corn. Perhaps her husband and son would bring some home when they came. They had driven off in the only buggy the Grimes family had, a rickety thing, a rickety horse hitched to the buggy, two other rickety horses led by halters. They were going to trade horses, get a little money if they could. They might come home drunk. It would be well to have something in the house when they came back.

The son had an affair on with a woman at the county seat, fifteen miles away. She was a rough enough woman, a tough one. Once, in the Summer, the son had brought her to the house. Both she and the son had been drinking. Jake Grimes was away and the son and his woman ordered the old woman about like a servant. She didn't mind much; she was used to it. Whatever happened she never said anything. That was her way of getting along. She had managed that way when she was a young girl at the German's and ever since she had married Jake. That time her son brought his woman to the house they stayed all night, sleeping together just as though they were married. It hadn't shocked the old woman, not much. She had got past being shocked early in life.

With the pack on her back she went painfully along across an open field, wading in the deep snow, and got into the woods.

There was a path, but it was hard to follow. Just beyond the top of the hill, where the woods was thickest, there was a small clearing. Had some one once thought of building a house there? The clearing was as large as a building lot in town, large enough for a house and a garden. The path ran along the side of the clearing, and when she got there the old woman sat down to rest at the foot of a tree.

It was a foolish thing to do. When she got herself placed, the pack against the tree's trunk, it was nice, but what about getting up again? She worried about that for a moment and then quietly closed her eyes.

She must have slept for a time. When you are about so cold you can't get any colder. The afternoon grew a little warmer and the snow came thicker than ever. Then after a time the weather cleared. The moon even came out.

There were four Grimes dogs that had followed Mrs. Grimes into town, all tall gaunt fellows. Such men as Jake Grimes and his son always keep just such dogs. They kick and abuse them, but they stay. The Grimes dogs, in order to keep from starving, had to do a lot of foraging for themselves, and they had been at it while the old woman slept with her back to the tree at the side of the clearing. They had been chasing rabbits in the woods and in adjoining fields and in their ranging had picked up three other farm dogs.

After a time all the dogs came back to the clearing. They were excited about something. Such nights, cold and clear and with a moon, do things to dogs. It may be that some old instinct, come down from the time when they were wolves and ranged the woods in packs on Winter nights, comes back into them.

The dogs in the clearing, before the old woman, had caught two or three rabbits and their immediate hunger had been satisfied.

They began to play, running in circles in the clearing. Round and round they ran, each dog's nose at the tail of the next dog. In the clearing, under the snow-laden trees and under the wintry moon they made a strange picture, running thus silently, in a circle their running had beaten in the soft snow. The dogs made no sound. They ran around and around in the circle.

It may have been that the old woman saw them doing that before she died. She may have awakened once or twice and looked at the strange sight with dim old eyes.

She wouldn't be very cold now, just drowsy. Life hangs on a long time. Perhaps the old woman was out of her head. She may have dreamed of her girlhood at the German's, and before that, when she was a child and before her mother lit out and left her.

Her dreams couldn't have been very pleasant. Not many pleasant things had happened to her. Now and then one of the Grimes dogs left the running circle and came to stand before her. The dog thrust his face to her face. His red tongue was hanging out.

The running of the dogs may have been a kind of death ceremony. It may have been that the primitive instinct of the wolf, having been aroused in the dogs by the night and the running, made them somehow, afraid.

"Now we are no longer wolves. We are dogs, the servants of men. Keep alive, man! When man dies we become wolves again." When one of the dogs came to where the old woman sat with her back against the tree and thrust his nose close to her face he seemed satisfied and went back to run with the pack. All the Grimes dogs did it at some time during the evening, before she died. I knew all about it afterward, when I grew to be a man, because once in a woods in Illinois, on another Winter night, I saw a pack of dogs act just like that. The dogs were waiting for me to die as they had waited for the old woman that night when I was a child, but when it happened to me I was a young man and had no intention whatever of dying.

The old woman died softly and quietly. When she was dead and when one of the Grimes dogs had come to her and had found her dead all the dogs stopped running.

They gathered about her.

Well, she was dead now. She had fed the Grimes dogs when she was alive, what about now?

There was the pack on her back, the grain bag containing the piece of salt pork, the liver the butcher had given her, the dog-meat,

397

the soup bones. The butcher in town, having been suddenly overcome with a feeling of pity, had loaded her grain bag heavily. It had been a big haul for the old woman.

It was a big haul for the dogs now.

4

One of the Grimes dogs sprang suddenly out from among the others and began worrying the pack on the old woman's back. Had the dogs really been wolves that one would have been the leader of the pack. What he did, all the others did.

All of them sank their teeth into the grain bag the old woman had fastened with ropes to her back.

They dragged the old woman's body out into the open clearing. The worn-out dress was quickly torn from her shoulders. When she was found, a day or two later, the dress had been torn from her body clear to the hips, but the dogs had not touched her body. They had got the meat out of the grain bag, that was all. Her body was frozen stiff when it was found, and the shoulders were so narrow and the body so slight that in death it looked like the body of some charming young girl.

Such things happened in towns of the Middle West, on farms near town, when I was a boy. A hunter out after rabbits found the old woman's body and did not touch it. Something, the beaten round path in the little snow-covered clearing, the silence of the place, the place where the dogs had worried the body trying to pull the grain bag away or tear it open—something startled the man and he hurried off to town.

I was in Main Street with one of my brothers who was town newsboy and who was taking the afternoon papers to the stores. It was almost night.

The hunter came into a grocery and told his story. Then he went into a hardware-shop and into a drugstore. Men began to gather on the sidewalks. Then they started out along the road to the place in the woods.

My brother should have gone on about his business of distributing papers but he didn't. Every one was going to the woods. The undertaker went and the town marshal. Several men got on a dray and rode out to where the path left the road and went into the woods, but the horses weren't very sharply shod and slid about on the slippery roads. They made no better time than those of us who walked.

The town marshal was a large man whose leg had been injured in the Civil War. He carried a heavy cane and limped rapidly along the road. My brother and I followed at his heels, and as we went other men and boys joined the crowd.

It had grown dark by the time we got to where the old woman had left the road but the moon had come out. The marshal was thinking there might have been a murder. He kept asking the hunter questions. The hunter went along with his gun across his shoulders, a dog following at his heels. It isn't often a rabbit hunter has a chance to be so conspicuous. He was taking full advantage of it, leading the procession with the town marshal. "I didn't see any wounds. She was a beautiful young girl. Her face was buried in the snow. No, I didn't know her." As a matter of fact, the hunter had not looked closely at the body. He had been frightened. She might have been murdered and some one might spring out from behind a tree and murder him. In a woods, in the late afternoon, when the trees are all bare and there is white snow on the ground, when all is silent, something creepy steals over the mind and body. If something strange or uncanny has happened in the neighborhood all you think about is getting away from there as fast as you can.

The crowd of men and boys had got to where the old woman had crossed the field and went, following the marshal and the hunter, up the slight incline and into the woods.

My brother and I were silent. He had his bundle of papers in a bag slung across his shoulder. When he got back to town he would have to go on distributing his papers before he went home to supper. If I went along, as he had no doubt already determined I should, we would both be late. Either mother or our older sister would have to warm our supper.

Well, we would have something to tell. A boy did not get such a chance very often. It was lucky we just happened to go into the grocery when the hunter came in. The hunter was a country fellow. Neither of us had ever seen him before.

Now the crowd of men and boys had got to the clearing. Darkness comes quickly on such Winter nights, but the full moon made everything clear. My brother and I stood near the tree, beneath which the old woman had died.

She did not look old, lying there in that light, frozen and still. One of the men turned her over in the snow and I saw everything. My body trembled with some strange mystical feeling and so did my brother's. It might have been the cold.

Neither of us had ever seen a woman's body before. It may have been the snow, clinging to the frozen flesh, that made it look so white and lovely, so like marble. No woman had come with the party from town; but one of the men, he was the town blacksmith, took off his overcoat and spread it over her. Then he gathered her into his arms and started off to town, all the others following silently. At that time no one knew who she was.

5

I had seen everything, had seen the oval in the snow, like a miniature race-track, where the dogs had run, had seen how the men were mystified, had seen the white bare young-looking shoulders, had heard the whispered comments of the men.

The men were simply mystified. They took the body to the undertaker's, and when the blacksmith, the hunter, the marshal and several others had got inside they closed the door. If father had been there perhaps he could have got in, but we boys couldn't.

I went with my brother to distribute the rest of his papers and when we got home it was my brother who told the story.

I kept silent and went to bed early. It may have been I was not satisfied with the way he told it.

Later, in the town, I must have heard other fragments of the old woman's story. She was recognized the next day and there was an investigation.

The husband and son were found somewhere and brought to town and there was an attempt to connect them with the woman's death, but it did not work. They had perfect enough alibis.

However, the town was against them. They had to get out. Where they went I never heard.

I remember only the picture there in the forest, the men standing about, the naked girlish-looking figure, face down in the snow, the tracks made by the running dogs and the clear cold Winter sky above. White fragments of clouds were drifting across the sky. They went racing across the little open space among the trees.

The scene in the forest had become for me, without my knowing it, the foundation for the real story I am now trying to tell. The fragments, you see, had to be picked up slowly, long afterwards.

Things happened. When I was a young man I worked on the farm of a German. The hired-girl was afraid of her employer. The farmer's wife hated her.

I saw things at that place. Once later, I had a half-uncanny, mystical adventure with dogs in an Illinois forest on a clear, moon-lit Winter night. When I was a schoolboy, and on a Summer day, I went with a boy friend out along a creek some miles from town and came to the house where the old woman had lived. No one had lived in the house since her death. The doors were broken from the hinges; the window lights were all broken. As the boy and I stood in the road outside, two dogs, just roving farm dogs no doubt, came running around the corner of the house. The dogs were tall, gaunt fellows and came down to the fence and glared through at us, standing in the road.

The whole thing, the story of the old woman's death, was to me as I grew older like music heard from far off. The notes had to be picked up slowly one at a time. Something had to be understood.

The woman who died was one destined to feed animal life. Anyway, that is all she ever did. She was feeding animal life before she was born, as a child, as a young woman working on the farm of the German, after she married, when she grew old and when she died. She fed animal life in cows, in chickens, in pigs, in horses, in dogs, in men. Her daughter had died in childhood and with her one son she had no articulate relations. On the night when she died she was hurrying homeward, bearing on her body food for animal life.

She died in the clearing in the woods and even after her death continued feeding animal life.

You see it is likely that, when my brother told the story, that night when we got home and my mother and sister sat listening, I did not think he got the point. He was too young and so was I. A thing so complete has its own beauty.

I shall not try to emphasize the point. I am only explaining why I was dissatisfied then and have been ever since. I speak of that only that you may understand why I have been impelled to try to tell the simple story over again.

William Carlos Williams

THE USE OF FORCE

William Carlos Williams was born in Rutherford, New Jersey, in 1883. He attended the public schools there and in New York City, but continued his preparatory schooling in Geneva, Switzerland, and in Paris. He next enrolled as a medical student at the University of Pennsylvania, where he became an intimate friend of Ezra Pound, a fellow student, and Marianne Moore, then a student at Bryn Mawr. Upon receiving his M.D. in 1906, he served his internship in New York, studied pediatrics in Leipzig for a year, and then returned to Rutherford, where he spent the remainder of his life, quietly pursuing his twofold profession as pediatrician and literary artist. Widely honored, admired, and loved, he died there on March 5, 1963.

For the first fifteen years of his literary career, which opened in 1909 with the publication of *Poems,* he devoted his creative efforts almost entirely to poetry and achieved recognition as an important member of the Imagist-Objectivist group. In 1926, he won an award of $2,000 from *Dial* for "distinguished service to American literature," and in 1931, he was given the Guarantors Prize by *Poetry.* Among his many volumes of poetry are *Tempers* (1913), *Al Que Quiere!* (1917), *Kora in Hell* (1920), *Sour Grapes* (1921), *Spring and All* (1922), *Adam and Eve and the City* (1936), *The Broken Span* (1941), *Paterson* (1946-1958), and *The Collected Poems* (1950, 1951). Though his interest in poetry never flagged, during the last forty years of his life Williams devoted much of his time to prose, publishing numerous volumes of critical essays, novels, and short stories. Some of his best stories are included in *The Knife of the Times and Other Stories* (1932) and *Life Along the Passaic River* (1938).

In his stories Williams displays many of the same noteworthy qualities found in his poetry: for example, the avoidance of formal structural patterns,

403

the emphasis on sensory experience, the bare directness of his language, and the objective presentation of situations. "In my own work it has always sufficed that the object of my attention be presented without further comment," he remarked in "A Note on Poetry." "All art is necessarily objective. It doesn't declaim or explain; it presents." Although "The Use of Force" is narrated from the first-person viewpoint, it illustrates the working out of this objective method. The story may be interpreted in a broad or symbolic sense as offering a commentary on the use of force generally with which the modern world is all too familiar. Such an idea, however, arises only from the implications of the concrete events of the story rather than from explanation or author comment. Thus the story merely "presents" the objective facts through which terrifying emotional truths are revealed.

the use of force

They were new patients to me, all I had was the name, Olson. Please come down as soon as you can, my daughter is very sick.

When I arrived I was met by the mother, a big startled looking woman, very clean and apologetic who merely said, Is this the doctor? and let me in. In the back, she added, You must excuse us, doctor, we have her in the kitchen where it is warm. It is very damp here sometimes.

The child was fully dressed and sitting on her father's lap near the kitchen table. He tried to get up, but I motioned for him not to bother, took off my overcoat and started to look things over. I could see that they were all very nervous, eyeing me up and down distrustfully. As often, in such cases, they weren't telling me more than they had to, it was up to me to tell them; that's why they were spending three dollars on me.

The child was fairly eating me up with her cold, steady eyes, and no expression to her face whatever. She did not move and seemed, inwardly, quiet; an unusually attractive little thing, and as strong as a heifer in appearance. But her face was flushed, she was breathing rapidly, and I realized that she had a high fever. She had magnificent blonde hair, in profusion. One of those picture children often reproduced in advertising leaflets and the photogravure sections of the Sunday papers.

She's had a fever for three days, began the father and we don't know what it comes from. My wife has given her things, you know, like people do, but it don't do no good. And there's been a lot of sickness around. So we tho't you'd better look her over and tell us what is the matter.

As doctors often do I took a trial shot at it as a point of departure. Had she had a sore throat?

Both parents answered me together, No . . . No, she says her throat don't hurt her.

Does your throat hurt you? added the mother to the child. But the little girl's expression didn't change nor did she move her eyes from my face.

Have you looked?

I tried to, said the mother, but I couldn't see.

As it happens we had been having a number of cases of diphtheria in the school to which this child went during that month and we were all, quite apparently, thinking of that, though no one had as yet spoken of the thing.

Well, I said, suppose we take a look at the throat first. I smiled in my best professional manner and asking for the child's first name I said, come on, Mathilda, open your mouth and let's take a look at your throat.

Nothing doing.

Aw, come on, I coaxed, just open your mouth wide and let me take a look. Look, I said opening both hands wide, I haven't anything in my hands. Just open up and let me see.

Such a nice man, put in the mother. Look how kind he is to you. Come on, do what he tells you to. He won't hurt you.

At that I ground my teeth in disgust. If only they wouldn't use the word "hurt" I might be able to get somewhere. But I did not allow myself to be hurried or disturbed but speaking quietly and slowly I approached the child again.

As I moved my chair a little nearer suddenly with one cat-like movement both her hands clawed instinctively for my eyes and she almost reached them too. In fact she knocked my glasses flying and they fell, though unbroken, several feet away from me on the kitchen floor.

Both the mother and father almost turned themselves inside out in embarrassment and apology. You bad girl, said the mother, taking her and shaking her by one arm. Look what you've done. The nice man . . .

For heaven's sake, I broke in. Don't call me a nice man to her. I'm here to look at her throat on the chance that she might have diphtheria and possibly die of it. But that's nothing to her. Look here, I said to the child, we're going to look at your throat. You're old enough to understand what I'm saying. Will you open it now by yourself or shall we have to open it for you? *Threatening force.*

Not a move. Even her expression hadn't changed. Her breaths however were coming faster and faster. Then the battle began. I had to do it. I had to have a throat culture for her own protection. But first I told the parents that it was entirely up to them. I explained the danger but said that I would not insist on a throat examination so long as they would take the responsibility. *Almost unprofession*

If you don't do what the doctor says you'll have to go to the hospital, the mother admonished her severely.

Oh yeah? I had to smile to myself. After all, I had already fallen in love with the savage brat, the parents were contemptible to me. In the ensuing struggle they grew more and more abject, crushed, exhausted while she surely rose to magnificent heights of insane fury of effort bred of her terror of me.

The father tried his best, and he was a big man but the fact that she was his daughter, his shame at her behavior and his dread of hurting her made him release her just at the critical moment several times when I had almost achieved success, till I wanted to kill him. But his dread also that she might have diphtheria made him tell me to go on, go on though he himself was almost fainting, while the mother moved back and forth behind us raising and lowering her hands in an agony of apprehension.

Put her in front of you on your lap, I ordered, and held both her wrists.

But as soon as he did the child let out a scream. Don't, you're hurting me. Let go of my hands. Let them go I tell you. Then she shrieked terrifyingly, hysterically. Stop it! Stop it! You're killing me!

Do you think she can stand it, doctor! said the mother.

You get out, said the husband to his wife. Do you want her to die of diphtheria?

Come on now, hold her, I said.

Then I grasped the child's head with my left hand and tried to get the wooden tongue depressor between her teeth. She fought, with clenched teeth, desperately! But now I also had grown furious—at a child. I tried to hold myself down but I couldn't. I know how to expose a throat for inspection. And I did my best. When finally I got the wooden spatula behind the last teeth and just the point of it into the mouth cavity, she opened up for an instant but before I could see anything she came down again and gripping the wooden blade between her molars she reduced it to splinters before I could get it out again.

Aren't you ashamed, the mother yelled at her. Aren't you ashamed to act like that in front of the doctor?

Get me a smooth-handled spoon of some sort, I told the mother. We're going through with this. The child's mouth was already bleeding. Her tongue was cut and she was screaming in wild hysterical shrieks. Perhaps I should have desisted and come back in an hour or more. No doubt it would have been better. But I have seen at least two children lying dead in bed of neglect in such cases, and feeling that I must get a diagnosis now or never I went at it again. But the worst of it was that I too had got beyond reason. I could have torn the child apart in my own fury and enjoyed it. It was a pleasure to attack her. My face was burning with it.

The damned little brat must be protected against her own idiocy, one says to one's self at such times. Others must be protected against her. It is a social necessity. And all these things are true. But a blind fury, a feeling of adult shame, bred of a longing for muscular release are the operatives. One goes on to the end.

In a final unreasoning assault I overpowered the child's neck and jaws. I forced the heavy silver spoon back of her teeth and down her throat till she gagged. And there it was—both tonsils covered with membrane. She had fought valiantly to keep me from knowing her secret. She had been hiding that sore throat for three days at least and lying to her parents in order to escape just such an outcome as this.

Now truly she *was* furious. She had been on the defensive before but now she attacked. Tried to get off her father's lap and fly at me while tears of defeat blinded her eyes.

407

Symbolic
Rape of
little girl.

Ring W. Lardner

THE LOVE NEST

While critics in the early decades of the twentieth century were indicting mass-circulation periodicals for exerting a damaging influence on the serious short story, Ring Lardner was quietly winning fame from the stories he published in the very periodicals under attack. This fact would hardly be noteworthy had he written the kind of fiction typically associated with the popular magazine; instead, his fiction includes some of the most harshly realistic stories to be found in American literature, and he was as much the practitioner of an individual approach to writing as Sherwood Anderson was. Lardner thus presents the unusual example of a writer whose work appealed to a wide popular audience at the same time that it won the respect of the most discriminating literary critics. His best stories entitle him to a rank among the foremost masters of the short story.

Lardner was born in Niles, Michigan, in 1885; he finished high school there and spent a semester at the Armour Institute in Chicago studying engineering. After working at odd jobs, he became a newspaperman, first on a South Bend paper and later on papers in Chicago, where he established a reputation as a sports writer specializing in baseball stories. In 1913, the Chicago *Tribune* engaged him to write a daily variety column, "In the Wake of the News," and shortly thereafter he launched a career as a fiction writer. Despite the considerable number of stories he published—over 120—he continued his career as a journalist and a columnist almost to the end of his life. He died in 1933, at the age of 48.

Early in his career as a fiction writer, Lardner wrote many stories about athletes, most notably five sequence groups, centering on a comical rookie baseball pitcher, Jack Keefe, some of which were republished in *You Know Me Al* (1916), *Treat 'Em Rough*

(1918), and *The Real Dope* (1919). Soon, however,
Lardner extended the scope of his fiction to other types
of characters and other phases of American life: to a
stupid police detective in *Own Your Own Home*
(1919), to white-collar "wise-boobs" in *Gullible's
Travels, Etc.* (1917) and *The Big Town* (1921), and
finally, at the peak of his career in the 1920's, to all
main phases of American life from the small town to
the big city. His best separate stories are collected in
How to Write Short Stories (1924), *The Love Nest
and Other Stories* (1926), and *The Round Up* (1929).

An acutely sensitive idealist, Lardner ruthlessly
satirized the dullness, hypocrisy, meanness, and false
values he found in all types of people from the gum-
chewing stenographer to the pompous millionaire of
the sort portrayed in "The Love Nest." Characteristically, he achieved his highly ironic interpretations objectively by withholding authorial comment and making his characters reveal themselves through their own
words and actions.

the love nest

"I'll tell you what I'm going to do with you, Mr. Bartlett," said
the great man. "I'm going to take you right out to my home and have
you meet the wife and family; stay to dinner and all night. We've got
plenty of room and extra pajamas, if you don't mind them silk. I
mean that'll give you a chance to see us just as we are. I mean you can
get more that way than if you sat here a whole week, asking me
questions."

"But I don't want to put you to a lot of trouble," said Bartlett.

"Trouble!" The great man laughed. "There's no trouble about
it. I've got a house that's like a hotel. I mean a big house with lots of
servants. But anyway I'm always glad to do anything I can for a

writing man, especially a man that works for Ralph Doane. I'm very fond of Ralph. I mean I like him personally besides being a great editor. I mean I've known him for years and when there's anything I can do for him, I'm glad to do it. I mean it'll be a pleasure to have you. So if you want to notify your family——"

"I haven't any family," said Bartlett.

"Well, I'm sorry for you! And I bet when you see mine, you'll wish you had one of your own. But I'm glad you can come and we'll start now so as to get there before the kiddies are put away for the night. I mean I want you to be sure and see the kiddies. I've got three."

"I've seen their pictures," said Bartlett. "You must be very proud of them. They're all girls, aren't they?"

"Yes, sir; three girls. I wouldn't have a boy. I mean I always wanted girls. I mean girls have got a lot more zip to them. I mean they're a lot zippier. But let's go! The Rolls is downstairs and if we start now we'll get there before dark. I mean I want you to see the place while it's still daylight."

The great man—Lou Gregg, president of Modern Pictures, Inc.—escorted his visitor from the magnificent office by a private door and down a private stairway to the avenue, where the glittering car with its glittering chauffeur waited.

"My wife was in town today," said Gregg as they glided northward, "and I hoped we could ride out together, but she called up about two and asked would I mind if she went on home in the Pierce. She was through with her shopping and she hates to be away from the house and the kiddies any longer than she can help. Celia's a great home girl. You'd never know she was the same girl now as the girl I married seven years ago. I mean she's different. I mean she's not the same. I mean her marriage and being a mother has developed her. Did you ever see her? I mean in pictures?"

"I think I did once," replied Bartlett. "Didn't she play the young sister in 'The Cad'?"

"Yes, with Harold Hodgson and Marie Blythe."

"I thought I'd seen her. I remember her as very pretty and vivacious."

"She certainly was! And she is yet! I mean she's even prettier, but of course she ain't a kid, though she looks it. I mean she was only seventeen in that picture and that was ten years ago. I mean she's twenty-seven years old now. But I never met a girl with as much zip as she had in those days. It's remarkable how marriage changes them. I mean nobody would ever thought Celia Sayles would turn out to be a sit-by-the-fire. I mean she still likes a good time, but her home and kiddies come first. I mean her home and kiddies come first."

"I see what you mean," said Bartlett.

An hour's drive brought them to Ardsley-on-Hudson and the great man's home.

"A wonderful place!" Bartlett exclaimed with a heroic semblance of enthusiasm as the car turned in at an *arc de triomphe* of a gateway and approached a white house that might have been mistaken for the Yale Bowl.

"It ought to be!" said Gregg, "I mean I've spent enough on it. I mean these things cost money."

He indicated with a gesture the huge house and Urbanesque landscaping.

"But no amount of money is too much to spend on home. I mean it's a good investment if it tends to make your family proud and satisfied with their home. I mean every nickel I've spent here is like so much insurance; it insures me of a happy wife and family. And what more can a man ask!"

Bartlett didn't know, but the topic was forgotten in the business of leaving the resplendent Rolls and entering the even more resplendent reception hall.

"Forbes will take your things," said Gregg. "And, Forbes, you may tell Dennis that Mr. Bartlett will spend the night." He faced the wide stairway and raised his voice. "Sweetheart!" he called.

From above came the reply in contralto: "Hello, sweetheart!"

"Come down, sweetheart. I've brought you a visitor."

"All right, sweetheart, in just a minute."

Gregg led Bartlett into a living-room that was five laps to the mile and suggestive of an Atlantic City auction sale.

"Sit there," said the host, pointing to a balloon-stuffed easy chair, "and I'll see if we can get a drink. I've got some real old Bourbon that I'd like you to try. You know I come from Chicago and I always liked Bourbon better than Scotch. I mean I always preferred it to Scotch. Forbes," he addressed the servant, "we want a drink. You'll find a full bottle of that Bourbon in the cupboard."

"It's only half full, sir," said Forbes.

"Half full! That's funny! I mean I opened it last night and just took one drink. I mean it ought to be full."

"It's only half full," repeated Forbes, and went to fetch it.

"I'll have to investigate," Gregg told his guest. "I mean this ain't the first time lately that some of my good stuff has disappeared.

When you keep so many servants, it's hard to get all honest ones. But here's Celia!"

Bartlett rose to greet the striking brunette who at this moment made an entrance so Delsarte as to be almost painful. With never a glance at him, she minced across the room to her husband and took a half interest in a convincing kiss.

"Well, sweetheart," she said when it was at last over.

"This is Mr. Bartlett, sweetheart," said her husband. "Mr. Bartlett, meet Mrs. Gregg."

Bartlett shook his hostess's proffered two fingers.

"I'm so pleased!" said Celia in a voice reminiscent of Miss Claire's imitation of Miss Barrymore.

"Mr. Bartlett," Gregg went on, "is with Mankind, Ralph Doane's magazine. He is going to write me up; I mean us."

"No, you mean you," said Celia. "I'm sure the public is not interested in great men's wives."

"I am sure you are mistaken, Mrs. Gregg," said Bartlett politely. "In this case at least. You are worth writing up aside from being a great man's wife."

"I'm afraid you're a flatterer, Mr. Bartlett," she returned. "I have been out of the limelight so long that I doubt if anybody remembers me. I'm no longer an artist; merely a happy wife and mother."

"And I claim, sweetheart," said Gregg, "that it takes an artist to be that."

"Oh, no, sweetheart!" said Celia. "Not when they have you for a husband!"

The exchange of hosannahs was interrupted by the arrival of Forbes with the tray.

"Will you take yours straight or in a high-ball?" Gregg inquired of his guest. "Personally I like good whisky straight. I mean mixing it with water spoils the flavor. I mean whisky like this, it seems like a crime to mix it with water."

"I'll have mine straight," said Bartlett, who would have preferred a high-ball.

While the drinks were being prepared, he observed his hostess more closely and thought how much more charming she would be if she had used finesse in improving on nature. Her cheeks, her mouth, her eyes, and lashes had been, he guessed, far above the average in beauty before she had begun experimenting with them. And her experiments had been clumsy. She was handsome in spite of her efforts to be handsomer.

"Listen, sweetheart," said her husband. "One of the servants has been helping himself to this Bourbon. I mean it was a full bottle last night and I only had one little drink out of it. And now it's less than half full. Who do you suppose has been at it?"

"How do I know, sweetheart? Maybe the groceryman or the iceman or somebody."

"But you and I and Forbes are the only ones that have a key. I mean it was locked up."

"Maybe you forgot to lock it."

"I never do. Well, anyway, Bartlett, here's a go!"

"Doesn't Mrs. Gregg indulge?" asked Bartlett.

"Only a cocktail before dinner," said Celia. "Lou objects to me drinking whisky, and I don't like it much anyway."

"I don't object to you drinking whisky, sweetheart. I just object to you drinking to excess. I mean I think it coarsens a woman to drink. I mean it makes them coarse."

"Well, there's no argument, sweetheart. As I say, I don't care whether I have it or not."

"It certainly is great Bourbon!" said Bartlett, smacking his lips and putting his glass back on the tray.

"You bet it is!" Gregg agreed. "I mean you can't buy that kind of stuff any more. I mean it's real stuff. You help yourself when you want another. Mr. Bartlett is going to stay all night, sweetheart. I told him he could get a whole lot more of a line on us that way than just interviewing me in the office. I mean I'm tongue-tied when it comes to talking about my work and my success. I mean it's better to see me out here as I am, in my home, with my family. I mean my home life speaks for itself without me saying a word."

"But, sweetheart," said his wife, "what about Mr. Latham?"

"Gosh! I forgot all about him! I must phone and see if I can call it off. That's terrible! You see," he explained to Bartlett, "I made a date to go up to Tarrytown tonight, to K. L. Latham's, the sugar people. We're going to talk over the new club. We're going to have a golf club that will make the rest of them look like a toy. I mean a real golf club! They want me to kind of run it. And I was to go up there tonight and talk it over. I'll phone and see if I can postpone it."

"Oh, don't postpone it on my account!" urged Bartlett. "I can come out again some other time, or I can see you in town."

"I don't see how you *can* postpone it, sweetheart," said Celia. "Didn't he say old Mr. King was coming over from White Plains? They'll be mad at you if you don't go."

"I'm afraid they would resent it, sweetheart. Well, I'll tell you. You can entertain Mr. Bartlett and I'll go up there right after dinner and come back as soon as I can. And Bartlett and I can talk when I get back. I mean we can talk when I get back. How is that?"

"That suits me," said Bartlett.

"I'll be as entertaining as I can," said Celia, "but I'm afraid that isn't very entertaining. However, if I'm too much of a bore, there's plenty to read."

"No danger of my being bored," said Bartlett.

"Well, that's all fixed then," said the relieved host. "I hope you'll excuse me running away. But I don't see how I can get out of it. I mean with old King coming over from White Plains. I mean he's an old man. But listen, sweetheart—where are the kiddies? Mr. Bartlett wants to see them."

"Yes, indeed!" agreed the visitor.

"Of course you'd say so!" Celia said. "But we *are* proud of them! I suppose all parents are the same. They all think their own children are the only children in the world. Isn't that so, Mr. Bartlett? Or haven't you any children?"

"I'm sorry to say I'm not married."

"Oh, you poor thing! We pity him, don't we, sweetheart? But why aren't you, Mr. Bartlett? Don't tell me you're a woman hater!"

"Not now, anyway," said the gallant Bartlett.

"Do you get that, sweetheart? He's paying you a pretty compliment."

"I heard it, sweetheart. And now I'm sure he's a flatterer. But I must hurry and get the children before Hortense puts them to bed."

"Well," said Gregg when his wife had left the room, "would you say she's changed?"

"A little, and for the better. She's more than fulfilled her early promise."

"I think so," said Gregg. "I mean I think she was a beautiful girl and now she's an even more beautiful woman. I mean wifehood and maternity have given her a kind of a—well, you know—I mean a kind of a pose. I mean a pose. How about another drink?"

They were emptying their glasses when Celia returned with two of her little girls.

"The baby's in bed and I was afraid to ask Hortense to get her up again. But you'll see her in the morning. This is Norma and this is Grace. Girls, this is Mr. Bartlett."

The girls received this news calmly.

"Well, girls," said Bartlett.

"What do you think of them, Bartlett?" demanded their father. "I mean what do you think of them?"

"They're great!" replied the guest with creditable warmth.

"I mean aren't they pretty?"

"I should say they are!"

"There, girls! Why don't you thank Mr. Bartlett?"

"Thanks," murmured Norma.

"How old are you, Norma?" asked Bartlett.

"Six," said Norma.

"Well," said Bartlett. "And how old is Grace?"

"Four," replied Norma.

"Well," said Bartlett. "And how old is baby sister?"

"One and a half," answered Norma.

"Well," said Bartlett.

As this seemed to be final, "Come, girls," said their mother. "Kiss daddy good night and I'll take you back to Hortense."

"I'll take them," said Gregg. "I'm going up-stairs anyway. And you can show Bartlett around. I mean before it gets any darker."

"Good night, girls," said Bartlett, and the children murmured a good night.

"I'll come and see you before you're asleep," Celia told them. And after Gregg had led them out, "Do you really think they're pretty?" she asked Bartlett.

"I certainly do. Especially Norma. She's the image of you," said Bartlett.

"She looks a little like I used to," Celia admitted. "But I hope she doesn't look like me now. I'm too old looking."

"You look remarkably young!" said Bartlett. "No one would believe you were the mother of three children."

"Oh, Mr. Bartlett! But I mustn't forget I'm to 'show you around.' Lou is so proud of our home!"

"And with reason," said Bartlett.

"It *is* wonderful! I call it our love nest. Quite a big nest, don't you think? Mother says it's too big to be cozy; she says she can't think of it as a home. But I always say a place is whatever one makes of it. A woman can be happy in a tent if they love each other. And miserable in a royal palace without love. Don't you think so, Mr. Bartlett?"

"Yes, indeed."

"Is this really such wonderful Bourbon? I think I'll just take a sip of it and see what it's like. It can't hurt me if it's so good. Do you think so, Mr. Bartlett?"

"I don't believe so."

"Well then, I'm going to taste it and if it hurts me it's your fault."

Celia poured a whisky glass two-thirds full and drained it at a gulp.

"It *is* good, isn't it?" she said. "Of course I'm not much of a judge as I don't care for whisky and Lou won't let me drink it. But he's raved so about this Bourbon that I did want to see what it was like. You won't tell on me, will you, Mr. Bartlett?"

"Not I!"

"I wonder how it would be in a high-ball. Let's you and I have just one. But I'm forgetting I'm supposed to show you the place. We won't have time to drink a high-ball and see the place too before Lou comes down. Are you so crazy to see the place?"

"Not very."

"Well, then, what do you say if we have a high-ball? And it'll be a secret between you and I."

They drank in silence and Celia pressed a button by the door.

"You may take the bottle and tray," she told Forbes. "And now," she said to Bartlett, "we'll go out on the porch and see as much as we can see. You'll have to guess the rest."

Gregg, having changed his shirt and collar, joined them.

"Well," he said to Bartlett, "have you seen everything?"

"I guess I have, Mr. Gregg," lied the guest readily. "It's a wonderful place!"

"We like it. I mean it suits us. I mean it's my idear of a real home. And Celia calls it her love nest."

"So she told me," said Bartlett.

"She'll always be sentimental," said her husband.

He put his hand on her shoulder, but she drew away.

"I must run up and dress," she said.

"Dress!" exclaimed Bartlett, who had been dazzled by her flowered green chiffon.

"Oh, I'm not going to really dress," she said. "But I couldn't wear this thing for dinner!"

"Perhaps you'd like to clean up a little, Bartlett," said Gregg. "I mean Forbes will show you your room if you want to go up."

"It might be best," said Bartlett.

Celia, in a black lace dinner gown, was rather quiet during the

417

elaborate meal. Three or four times when Gregg addressed her, she seemed to be thinking of something else and had to ask, "What did you say, sweetheart?" Her face was red and Bartlett imagined that she had "sneaked" a drink or two besides the two helpings of Bourbon and the cocktail that had preceded dinner.

"Well, I'll leave you," said Gregg when they were in the living-room once more. "I mean the sooner I get started, the sooner I'll be back. Sweetheart, try and keep your guest awake and don't let him die of thirst. *Au revoir,* Bartlett. I'm sorry, but it can't be helped. There's a fresh bottle of the Bourbon, so go to it. I mean help yourself. It's too bad you have to drink alone."

"It *is* too bad, Mr. Bartlett," said Celia when Gregg had gone.

"What's too bad?" asked Bartlett.

"That you have to drink alone. I feel like I wasn't being a good hostess to let you do it. In fact, I refuse to let you do it. I'll join you in just a little wee sip."

"But it's so soon after dinner!"

"It's never too soon! I'm going to have a drink myself and if you don't join me, you're a quitter."

She mixed two life-sized high-balls and handed one to her guest.

"Now we'll turn on the radio and see if we can't stir things up. There! No, no! Who cares about the old baseball! Now! This is better! Let's dance."

"I'm sorry, Mrs. Gregg, but I don't dance."

"Well, you're an old cheese! To make me dance alone! 'All alone, yes, I'm all alone.'"

There was no affectation in her voice now and Bartlett was amazed at her unlabored grace as she glided around the big room.

"But it's no fun alone," she complained. "Let's shut the damn thing off and talk."

"I love to watch you dance," said Bartlett.

"Yes, but I'm no Pavlowa," said Celia as she silenced the radio. "And besides, it's time for a drink."

"I've still got more than half of mine."

"Well, you had that wine at dinner, so I'll have to catch up with you."

She poured herself another high-ball and went at the task of "catching up."

"The trouble with you, Mr.——now isn't that a scream! I can't think of your name."

"Bartlett."

"The trouble with you, Barker—do you know what's the trouble with you? You're too sober. See? You're too damn sober! That's the whole trouble, see? If you weren't so sober, we'd be better off. See? What I can't understand is how you can be so sober and me so high."

"You're not used to it."

"Not used to it! That's the cat's pajamas! Say, I'm like this half the time, see? If I wasn't, I'd die!"

"What does your husband say?"

"He don't say because he don't know. See, Barker? There's nights when he's out and there's a few nights when I'm out myself. And there's other nights when we're both in and I pretend I'm sleepy and I go upstairs. See? But I don't go to bed. See? I have a little party all by myself. See? If I didn't, I'd die!"

"What do you mean, you'd die?"

"You're dumb, Barker! You may be sober, but you're dumb! Did you fall for all that applesauce about the happy home and the contented wife? Listen, Barker—I'd give anything in the world to be out of this mess. I'd give anything to never see him again."

"Don't you love him any more? Doesn't he love you? Or what?"

"Love! I never did love him! I didn't know what love was! And all his love is for himself!"

"How did you happen to get married?"

"I was a kid; that's the answer. A kid and ambitious. See? He was a director then and he got stuck on me and I thought he'd make me a star. See, Barker? I married him to get myself a chance. And now look at me!"

"I'd say you were fairly well off."

"Well off, am I? I'd change places with the scum of the earth just to be free! See, Barker? And I could have been a star without any help if I'd only realized it. I had the looks and I had the talent. I've got it yet. I could be a Swanson and get myself a marquis; maybe a prince! And look what I did get! A self-satisfied, self-centered——! I thought he'd *make* me! See, Barker? Well, he's made me all right; he's made me a chronic mother and it's a wonder I've got any looks left.

"I fought at first. I told him marriage didn't mean giving up my art, my life work. But it was no use. He wanted a beautiful wife and beautiful children for his beautiful home. Just to show us off. See? I'm part of his chattels. See, Barker? I'm just like his big diamond or his cars or his horses. And he wouldn't stand for his wife 'lowering' herself to act in pictures. Just as if pictures hadn't made him!

"You go back to your magazine tomorrow and write about our

419

love nest. See, Barker? And be sure and don't get mixed and call it a baby ranch. Babies! You thought little Norma was pretty. Well, she is. And what is it going to get her? A rich —— of a husband that treats her like a ——! That's what it'll get her if I don't interfere. I hope I don't last long enough to see her grow up, but if I do, I'm going to advise her to run away from home and live her own life. And *be* somebody! Not a *thing* like I am! See, Barker?"

"Did you ever think of a divorce?"

"Did I ever think of one! Listen—but there's no chance. I've got nothing on him, and no matter what he had on me, he'd never let the world know it. He'd keep me here and torture me like he does now, only worse. But I haven't done anything wrong, see? The men I might care for, they're all scared of him and his money and power. See, Barker? And the others are just as bad as him. Like fat old Morris, the hotel man, that everybody thinks he's a model husband. The reason he don't step out more is because he's too stingy. But I could have him if I wanted him. Every time he gets near enough to me, he squeezes my hand. I guess he thinks it's a nickel, the tight old——! But come on, Barker. Let's have a drink. I'm running down."

"I think it's about time you were running up——up-stairs," said Bartlett. "If I were you, I'd try to be in bed and asleep when Gregg gets home."

"You're all right, Barker. And after this drink I'm going to do just as you say. Only I thought of it before you did, see? I think of it lots of nights. And tonight you can help me out by telling him I had a bad headache."

Left alone, Bartlett thought a while, then read, and finally dozed off. He was dozing when Gregg returned.

"Well, well, Bartlett," said the great man, "did Celia desert you?"

"It was perfectly all right, Mr. Gregg. She had a headache and I told her to go to bed."

"She's had a lot of headaches lately; reads too much, I guess. Well, I'm sorry I had this date. It was about a new golf club and I had to be there. I mean I'm going to be president of it. I see you consoled yourself with some of the Bourbon. I mean the bottle doesn't look as full as it did."

"I hope you'll forgive me for helping myself so generously," said Bartlett. "I don't get stuff like that every day!"

"Well, what do you say if we turn in? We can talk on the way to town tomorrow. Though I guess you won't have much to ask me. I guess you know all about us. I mean you know all about us now."

"Yes, indeed, Mr. Gregg. I've got plenty of material if I can just handle it."

Celia had not put in an appearance when Gregg and his guest were ready to leave the house next day.

"She always sleeps late," said Gregg. "I mean she never wakes up very early. But she's later than usual this morning. Sweetheart!" he called up the stairs.

"Yes, sweetheart," came the reply.

"Mr. Bartlett's leaving now. I mean he's going."

"Oh, good-by, Mr. Bartlett. Please forgive me for not being down to see you off."

"You're forgiven, Mrs. Gregg. And thanks for your hospitality."

"Good-by, sweetheart!"

"Good-by, sweetheart!"

Katherine Anne Porter

FLOWERING JUDAS

It seems contradictory that a great-great-great grand-daughter of Daniel Boone, the robust frontiersman, should win the reputation of being one of literature's most élite, finished prose stylists. Yet that distinction belongs to Katherine Anne Porter, who has been described as moving in the "illustrious company, headed by Hawthorne, Flaubert, and Henry James." It is even more noteworthy that she has established this reputation on a relatively slender volume of creative work, a fact which bespeaks the quality of her writing.

Miss Porter was born in 1894, in Indian Creek, Texas, near San Antonio, the daughter of Harrison Boone and Mary Alice Porter. She received her education in small southern schools for girls, supplementing her formal training by extensive reading. Although from her earliest youth she wanted to write fiction, she entered her professional career by the way of journalism and miscellaneous writing. For a time she was a news reporter in Dallas and later in Denver, but after an illness interrupted her newspaper work, she traveled in the United States and many foreign countries, supporting herself by book reviewing, articles, and hack writing of various kinds. She first began publishing stories in *Century, Transition, New Masses, Scribner's,* and *Hound and Horn,* and her first collection, *Flowering Judas* (1930), reissued in 1935 with four additional stories, was of such merit that critics acclaimed her as one of the most talented short story writers of the day. She has continued to hold this position on the basis of the equally high merit of other collections which have appeared at intervals: *Hacienda* (1934), *Pale Horse, Pale Rider* (1939), and *The Leaning Tower and Other Stories* (1944). Periodically she has continued to travel and has lived in different parts of the United States, Europe, and Mexico; her

423

cosmopolitanism is reflected in her acute understanding of the varied groups portrayed in her fiction, notably in her novel *The Ship of Fools* (1962).

Among the special qualities of Miss Porter's writing, displayed at their best in "Flowering Judas," are her prose style, which has the precision and metaphorical richness of poetry, and her use of symbolism which, if subtle and complex, is yet clear. The two are closely interrelated, for the metaphorical language gives rise to symbolism: for example, such phrases as "hungry world saviours," "immaculate voices," "sour gloom," and "holy talismanic word" both vivify the style and function symbolically to communicate the story idea. The symbolism also arises from other sources—from the action, such as the footwashing scene; from the names of the characters, such as Eugenio; and from references to objects such as the Judas tree and automobiles. The full meaning of the story, however, is conveyed not alone through style or symbol but through the organic relationship of all the story elements. In fact, the story illustrates not only Anderson's theory of dependence on form rather than plot, but also James' ideal of a story in which "in each of the parts there is something of each of the other parts."

flowering judas

Braggioni sits heaped upon the edge of a straightbacked chair much too small for him, and sings to Laura in a furry, mournful voice. Laura has begun to find reasons for avoiding her own house until the latest possible moment, for Braggioni is there almost every night. No matter how late she is, he will be sitting there with a surly, waiting expression, pulling at his kinky yellow hair, thumbing the strings of his guitar, snarling a tune under his breath. Lupe the Indian maid meets Laura at the door, and says with a flicker of a glance toward the upper room, "He waits."

Laura wishes to lie down, she is tired of her hairpins and the feel of her long tight sleeves, but she says to him, "Have you a new song for me this evening?" If he says yes, she asks him to sing it. If he says no, she remembers his favorite one, and asks him to sing it again. Lupe brings her a cup of chocolate and a plate of rice, and Laura eats at the small table under the lamp, first inviting Braggioni, whose answer is always the same: "I have eaten, and besides, chocolate thickens the voice."

Laura says, "Sing, then," and Braggioni heaves himself into song. He scratches the guitar familiarly as though it were a pet animal, and sings passionately off key, taking the high notes in a prolonged painful squeal. Laura, who haunts the markets listening to the ballad singers, and stops every day to hear the blind boy playing his reed-flute in Sixteenth of September Street, listens to Braggioni with pitiless courtesy, because she dares not smile at his miserable performance. Nobody dares to smile at him. Braggioni is cruel to every-one, with a kind of specialized insolence, but he is so vain of his talents, and so sensitive to slights, it would require a cruelty and vanity greater than his own to lay a finger on the vast cureless wound of his self-esteem. It would require courage, too, for it is dangerous to offend him, and nobody has this courage.

Braggioni loves himself with such tenderness and amplitude and eternal charity that his followers—for he is a leader of men, a skilled revolutionist, and his skin has been punctured in honorable warfare—warm themselves in the reflected glow, and say to each other: "He has a real nobility, a love of humanity raised above mere personal affections." The excess of this self-love has flowed out, inconveniently for her, over Laura, who, with so many others, owes her comfortable situation and her salary to him. When he is in a very good humor, he tells her, "I am tempted to forgive you for being a *gringa. Gringita!*" and Laura, burning, imagines herself leaning forward suddenly, and with a sound back-handed slap wiping the suety smile from his face. If he notices her eyes at these moments he gives no sign.

She knows what Braggioni would offer her, and she must re-sist tenaciously without appearing to resist, and if she could avoid it she would not admit even to herself the slow drift of his intention. During these long evenings which have spoiled a long month for her, she sits in her deep chair with an open book on her knees, resting her eyes on the consoling rigidity of the printed page when the sight and sound of Braggioni singing threaten to identify themselves with all her remembered afflictions and to add their weight to her uneasy premonitions of the future. The gluttonous bulk of Braggioni has become a symbol of her many disillusions, for a revolutionist should be lean, animated by heroic faith, a vessel of abstract virtues. This is nonsense, she knows it now and is ashamed of it. Revolution must have leaders, and leadership is a career for energetic men. She is, her comrades tell her, full of romantic error, for what she defines as cynicism in them is merely "a developed sense of reality." She is almost too willing to say, "I am wrong, I suppose I don't really understand the principles," and afterward she makes a secret truce with herself, determined not to surrender her will to such expedient logic. But she cannot help feeling that she has been betrayed irreparably by the disunion between her way of living and her feeling of what life should be, and at times she is almost contented to rest in this sense of grievance as a private store of consolation. Sometimes she wishes to run away, but she stays. Now she longs to fly out of this room, down the narrow stairs, and into the street where the houses lean together like conspirators under a single mottled lamp, and leave Braggioni singing to himself.

Instead she looks at Braggioni, frankly and clearly, like a good child who understands the rules of behavior. Her knees cling together under sound blue serge, and her round white collar is not purposely nunlike. She wears the uniform of an idea, and has renounced vanities. She was born Roman Catholic, and in spite of her fear of being seen by someone who might make a scandal of it, she slips now and again into some crumbling little church, kneels on the chilly stone, and says a Hail Mary on the gold rosary she bought in Tehuantepec. It is no good and she ends by examining the altar with its tinsel flowers and ragged brocades, and feels tender about the battered doll-shape of some male saint whose white, lace-trimmed drawers hang limply around his ankles below the hieratic dignity of his velvet robe. She had encased herself in a set of principles derived from her early training, leaving no detail of gesture or of personal taste untouched, and for this reason she will not wear lace made on machines. This is her private heresy, for in her special group the machine is sacred, and will be the salvation of the workers. She loves fine lace, and there is a tiny edge of fluted cobweb on this collar, which is one of twenty precisely alike, folded in blue tissue paper in the upper drawer of her clothes chest.

Braggioni catches her glance solidly as if he had been waiting for it, leans forward, balancing his paunch between his spread knees, and sings with tremendous emphasis, weighing his words. He has, the song relates, no father and no mother, nor even a friend to console him; lonely as a wave of the sea he comes and goes, lonely as a wave. His mouth opens round and yearns sideways, his balloon cheeks grow oily with the labor of song. He bulges marvelously in his expensive garments. Over his lavender collar, crushed upon a purple necktie, held by a diamond hoop: over his ammunition belt of tooled leather worked in silver, buckled cruelly around his gasping middle: over the tops of his glossy yellow shoes Braggioni swells with ominous ripeness, his mauve silk hose stretched taut, his ankles bound with the stout leather thongs of his shoes.

When he stretches his eyelids at Laura she notes again that his eyes are the true tawny yellow cat's eyes. He is rich, not in money, he tells her, but in power, and this power brings with it the blameless ownership of things, and the right to indulge his love of small luxuries. "I have a taste for the elegant refinements," he said once, flourishing a yellow silk handkerchief before her nose. "Smell that? It is Jockey Club, imported from New York." Nonetheless he is wounded by life. He will say so presently. "It is true everything turns to dust in the hand, to gall on the tongue." He sighs and his leather belt creaks like a saddle girth. "I am disappointed in everything as it comes. Everything." He shakes his head. "You, poor thing, you will be disappointed too. You are born for it. We are more alike than you realize in some things. Wait and see. Some day you will remember what I have told you, you will know that Braggioni was your friend."

Laura feels a slow chill, a purely physical sense of danger, a warning in her blood that violence, mutilation, a shocking death, wait for her with lessening patience. She has translated this fear into something homely, immediate, and sometimes hesitates before crossing the street. "My personal fate is nothing, except as the testimony of a mental attitude," she reminds herself, quoting from some forgotten philosophic primer, and is sensible enough to add, "Anyhow, I shall not be killed by an automobile if I can help it."

"It may be true I am as corrupt, in another way, as Braggioni," she thinks in spite of herself, "as callous, as incomplete," and if this is so, any kind of death seems preferable. Still she sits quietly, she does

427

not run. Where could she go? Uninvited she has promised herself to this place; she can no longer imagine herself as living in another country, and there is no pleasure in remembering her life before she came here.

Precisely what is the nature of this devotion, its true motives, and what are its obligations? Laura cannot say. She spends part of her days in Xochimilco, near by, teaching Indian children to say in English, "The cat is on the mat." When she appears in the classroom they crowd about her with smiles on their wise, innocent, clay-colored faces, crying, "Good morning, my ticher!" in immaculate voices, and they make of her desk a fresh garden of flowers every day.

During her leisure she goes to union meetings and listens to busy important voices quarreling over tactics, methods, internal politics. She visits the prisoners of her own political faith in their cells, where they entertain themselves with counting cockroaches, repenting on their indiscretions, composing their memoirs, writing out manifestoes and plans for their comrades who are still walking about free, hands in pockets, sniffing fresh air. Laura brings them food and cigarettes and a little money, and she brings messages disguised in equivocal phrases from the men outside who dare not set foot in the prison for fear of disappearing into the cells kept empty for them. If the prisoners confuse night and day, and complain, "Dear little Laura, time doesn't pass in this infernal hole, and I won't know when it is time to sleep unless I have a reminder," she brings them their favorite narcotics, and says in a tone that does not wound them with pity, "Tonight will really be night for you," and though her Spanish amuses them, they find her comforting, useful. If they lose patience and all faith, and curse the slowness of their friends in coming to their rescue with money and influence, they trust her not to repeat everything, and if she inquires, "Where do you think we can find money, or influence?" they are certain to answer, "Well, there is Braggioni, why doesn't he do something?"

She smuggles letters from headquarters to men hiding from firing squads in back streets in mildewed houses, where they sit in tumbled beds and talk bitterly as if all Mexico were at their heels, when Laura knows positively they might appear at the band concert in the Alameda on Sunday morning, and no one would notice them. But Braggioni says, "Let them sweat a little. The next time they may be careful. It is very restful to have them out of the way for a while." She is not afraid to knock on any door in any street after midnight, and enter in the darkness, and say to one of these men who is really in danger: "They will be looking for you—seriously—tomorrow morning after six. Here is some money from Vicente. Go to Vera Cruz and wait."

She borrows money from the Roumanian agitator to give to his bitter enemy the Polish agitator. The favor of Braggioni is their disputed territory, and Braggioni holds the balance nicely, for he can use them both. The Polish agitator talks love to her over café tables, hoping to exploit what he believes is her secret sentimental preference for him, and he gives her misinformation which he begs her to repeat as the solemn truth to certain persons. The Roumanian is more adroit. He is generous with his money in all good causes, and lies to her with an air of ingenuous candor, as if he were her good friend and confidant. She never repeats anything they may say. Braggioni never asks questions. He has other ways to discover all that he wishes to know about them.

Nobody touches her, but all praise her gray eyes, and the soft, round under lip which promises gayety, yet is always grave, nearly always firmly closed: and they cannot understand why she is in Mexico. She walks back and forth on her errands, with puzzled eyebrows, carrying her little folder of drawings and music and school papers. No dancer dances more beautifully than Laura walks, and she inspires some amusing, unexpected ardors, which cause little gossip, because nothing comes of them. A young captain who had been a soldier in Zapata's army attempted, during a horseback ride near Cuernavaca, to express his desire for her with the noble simplicity befitting a rude folk-hero: but gently, because he was gentle. This gentleness was his defeat, for when he alighted, and removed her foot from the stirrup, and essayed to draw her down into his arms, her horse, ordinarily a tame one, shied fiercely, reared and plunged away. The young hero's horse careered blindly after his stable-mate, and the hero did not return to the hotel until rather late that evening. At breakfast he came to her table in full charro dress, gray buckskin jacket and trousers with strings of silver buttons down the leg, and he was in a humorous, careless mood. "May I sit with you?" and "You are a wonderful rider. I was terrified that you might be thrown and dragged. I should never have forgiven myself. But I cannot admire you enough for your riding!"

"I learned to ride in Arizona," said Laura.

"If you will ride with me again this morning, I promise you a horse that will not shy with you," he said. But Laura remembered that she must return to Mexico City at noon.

Next morning the children made a celebration and spent their playtime writing on the blackboard, "We lov ar ticher," and with tinted chalks they drew wreaths of flowers around the words. The young hero wrote her a letter: "I am a very foolish, wasteful, impulsive man. I should have first said I love you, and then you would not have run away. But you shall see me again." Laura thought, "I must send him a box of colored crayons," but she was trying to forgive herself for having spurred her horse at the wrong moment.

A brown, shock-haired youth came and stood in her patio one night and sang like a lost soul for two hours, but Laura could think of nothing to do about it. The moonlight spread a wash of gauzy silver over the clear spaces of the garden, and the shadows were cobalt blue. The scarlet blossoms of the Judas tree were dull purple, and the names of the colors repeated themselves automatically in her mind, while she watched not the boy, but his shadow, fallen like a dark garment across the fountain rim, trailing in the water. Lupe came silently and whispered expert counsel in her ear: "If you will throw him one little flower, he will sing another song or two and go away." Laura threw the flower, and he sang a last song and went away with the flower tucked in the band of his hat. Lupe said, "He is one of the organizers of the Typographers Union, and before that he sold corridos in the Merced market, and before that, he came from Guanajuato, where I was born. I would not trust any man, but I trust least those from Guanajuato."

She did not tell Laura that he would be back again the next night, and the next, nor that he would follow her at a certain fixed distance around the Merced market, through the Zócolo, up Francisco I. Madero Avenue, and so along the Paseo de la Reforma to Chapultepec Park, and into the Philosopher's Footpath, still with that flower withering in his hat, and an indivisible attention in his eyes.

Now Laura is accustomed to him, it means nothing except that he is nineteen years old and is observing a convention with all propriety, as though it were founded on a law of nature, which in the end it might well prove to be. He is beginning to write poems which he prints on a wooden press, and he leaves them stuck like handbills in her door. She is pleasantly disturbed by the abstract, unhurried watchfulness of his black eyes which will in time turn easily towards another object. She tells herself that throwing the flower was a mistake, for she is twenty-two years old and knows better; but she refuses to regret it, and persuades herself that her negation of all external events as they occur is a sign that she is gradually perfecting herself in the stoicism she strives to cultivate against that disaster she fears, though she cannot name it.

She is not at home in the world. Every day she teaches children who remain strangers to her, though she loves their tender round hands and their charming opportunist savagery. She knocks at unfamiliar doors not knowing whether a friend or a stranger shall answer, and even if a known face emerges from the sour gloom of that unknown interior, still it is the face of a stranger. No matter what this stranger says to her, nor what her message to him, the very cells of her flesh reject knowledge and kinship in one monotonous word. No. No. No. She draws her strength from this one holy talismanic word no. which does not suffer her to be led into evil. Denying everything, she may walk anywhere in safety, she looks at everything without amazement.

No, repeats this firm unchanging voice of her blood; and she looks at Braggioni without amazement. He is a great man, he wishes to impress this simple girl who covers her great round breasts with thick dark cloth, and who hides long, invaluably beautiful legs under a heavy skirt. She is almost thin except for the incomprehensible fullness of her breasts, like a nursing mother's, and Braggioni, who considers himself a judge of women, speculates again on the puzzle of her notorious virginity, and takes the liberty of speech which she permits without a sign of modesty, indeed, without any sort of sign, which is disconcerting.

"You think you are so cold, gringita! Wait and see. You will surprise yourself some day! May I be there to advise you!" He stretches his eyelids at her, and his ill-humored cat's eyes waver in a separate glance for the two points of light marking the opposite ends of a smoothly drawn path between the swollen curve of her breasts. He is not put off by that blue serge, nor by her resolutely fixed gaze. There is all the time in the world. His cheeks are bellying with the wind of song. "O girl with the dark eyes," he sings, and reconsiders. "But yours are not dark. I can change all that. O girl with the green eyes, you have stolen my heart away!" then his mind wanders to the song, and Laura feels the weight of his attention being shifted elsewhere. Singing thus, he seems harmless, he is quite harmless, there is nothing to do but sit patiently and say "No," when the moment comes. She draws a full breath, and her mind wanders also, but not far. She dares not wander too far.

Not for nothing has Braggioni taken pains to be a good revolutionist and a professional lover of humanity. He will never die of it.

He has the malice, the cleverness, the wickedness, the sharpness of wit, the hardness of heart, stipulated for loving the world profitably. *He will never die of it*. He will live to see himself kicked out from his feeding trough by other hungry world-saviours. Traditionally he must sing in spite of his life which drives him to bloodshed, he tells Laura, for his father was a Tuscany peasant who drifted to Yucatan and married a Maya woman: a woman of race, an aristocrat. They gave him the love and knowledge of music, thus: and under the rip of his thumbnail, the strings of the instrument complain like exposed nerves.

Once he was called Delgadito by all the girls and married women who ran after him; he was so scrawny all his bones showed under his thin cotton clothing, and he could squeeze his emptiness to the very backbone with his two hands. He was a poet and the revolution was only a dream then; too many women loved him and sapped away his youth, and he could never find enough to eat anywhere, anywhere! Now he is a leader of men, crafty men who whisper in his ear, hungry men who wait for hours outside his office for a word with him, emaciated men with wild faces who waylay him at the street gate with a timid, "Comrade, let me tell you . . ." and they blow the foul breath from their empty stomachs in his face.

He is always sympathetic. He gives them handfuls of small coins from his own pocket, he promises them work, there will be demonstrations, they must join the unions and attend the meetings, above all they must be on the watch for spies. They are closer to him than his own brothers, without them he can do nothing—until tomorrow, comrade!

Until tomorrow. "They are stupid, they are lazy, they are treacherous, they would cut my throat for nothing," he says to Laura. He has good food and abundant drink, he hires an automobile and drives in the Paseo on Sunday morning, and enjoys plenty of sleep in a soft bed beside a wife who dares not disturb him, and he sits pampering his bones in easy billows of fat, singing to Laura, who knows and thinks these things about him. When he was fifteen, he tried to drown himself because he loved a girl, his first love, and she laughed at him. "A thousand women have paid for that," and his tight little mouth turns down at the corners. Now he perfumes his hair with Jockey Club, and confides to Laura: "One woman is really as good as another for me, in the dark. I prefer them all."

His wife organizes unions among the girls in the cigarette factories, and walks in picket lines, and even speaks at meetings in the evening. But she cannot be brought to acknowledge the benefits of true liberty. "I tell her I must have my freedom, net. She does not understand my point of view." Laura has heard this many times. Braggioni scratches the guitar and meditates. "She is an instinctively virtuous woman, pure gold, no doubt of that. If she were not, I should lock her up, and she knows it."

His wife, who works so hard for the good of the factory girls, employs part of her leisure lying on the floor weeping because there are so many women in the world, and only one husband for her, and she never knows where nor when to look for him. He told her: "Unless you can learn to cry when I am not here, I must go away for good." That day he went away and took a room at the Hotel Madrid.

It is this month of separation for the sake of higher principles that has been spoiled not only for Mrs. Braggioni, whose sense of reality is beyond criticism, but for Laura, who feels herself bogged in a nightmare. Tonight Laura envies Mrs. Braggioni, who is alone, and free to weep as much as she pleases about a concrete wrong. Laura has just come from a visit to the prison, and she is waiting for tomorrow with a bitter anxiety as if tomorrow may not come, but time may be caught immovably in this hour, with herself transfixed, Braggioni singing on forever, and Eugenio's body not yet discovered by the guard.

Braggioni says: "Are you going to sleep?" Almost before she can shake her head, he begins telling her about the May-day disturbances coming on in Morelia, for the Catholics hold a festival in honor of the Blessed Virgin, and the Socialists celebrate their martyrs on that day. "There will be two independent processions, starting from either end of town, and they will march until they meet, and the rest depends . . ." He asks her to oil and load his pistols. Standing up, he unbuckles his ammunition belt, and spreads it laden across her knees. Laura sits with the shells slipping through the cleaning cloth dipped in oil, and he says again he cannot understand why she works so hard for the revolutionary idea unless she loves some man who is in it. "Are you not in love with someone?" "No," says Laura. "And no one is in love with you?" "No." "Then it is your own fault. No woman need go begging. Why, what is the matter with you? The legless beggar woman in the Alameda has a perfectly faithful lover. Did you know that?"

Laura peers down the pistol barrel and says nothing, but a long, slow faintness rises and subsides in her; Braggioni curves his swollen fingers around the throat of the guitar and softly smothers the music out of it, and when she hears him again he seems to have forgotten her, and is speaking in the hypnotic voice he uses when talking in small rooms to a listening, close-gathered crowd. Some day this world, now seemingly so composed and eternal to the edges of every sea shall be merely a tangle of gaping trenches, of crashing walls and broken bodies. Everything must be torn from its accustomed place where it has rotted for centuries, hurled skyward and distributed, cast down again clean as rain, without separate identity. Nothing shall survive that the stiffened hands of poverty have created for the rich and no one shall be left alive except the elect spirits destined to procreate a new world cleansed of cruelty and injustice, ruled by benevolent anarchy: "Pistols are good, I love them, cannon are even better, but in the end I pin my faith to good dynamite," he concludes, and strokes the pistol lying in her hands. "Once I dreamed of destroying this city, in case it offered resistance to General Ortíz, but it fell into his hands like an overripe pear."

He is made restless by his own words, rises and stands waiting. Laura holds up the belt to him: "Put that on, and go kill somebody in Morelia, and you will be happier," she says softly. The presence of death in the room makes her bold. "Today, I found Eugenio going into a stupor. He refused to allow me to call the prison doctor. He had taken all the tablets I brought him yesterday. He said he took them because he was bored."

"He is a fool, and his death is his own business," says Braggioni, fastening his belt carefully.

"I told him if he had waited only a little while longer, you would have got him set free," says Laura. "He said he did not want to wait."

"He is a fool and we are well rid of him," says Braggioni, reaching for his hat.

He goes away. Laura knows his mood has changed, she will not see him any more for a while. He will send word when he needs her to go on errands into strange streets, to speak to the strange faces that will appear, like clay masks with the power of human speech, to mutter their thanks to Braggioni for his help. Now she is free, and she thinks, I must run while there is time. But she does not go.

Braggioni enters his own house where for a month his wife has spent many hours every night weeping and tangling her hair upon her pillow. She is weeping now, and she weeps more at the sight of him, the cause of all her sorrows. He looks about the room. Nothing is changed, the smells are good and familiar, he is well acquainted with the woman who comes toward him with no reproach except grief on her face. He says to her tenderly: "You are so good, please don't cry any more, you dear good creature." She says, "Are you tired, my angel? Sit here and I will wash your feet." She brings a bowl of water, and kneeling, unlaces his shoes, and when from her knees she raises her sad eyes under her blackened lids, he is sorry for everything, and bursts into tears. "Ah, yes, I am hungry, I am tired, let us eat something together," he says, between sobs. His wife leans her head on his arm and says, "Forgive me!" and this time he is refreshed by the solemn, endless rain of her tears.

Laura takes off her serge dress and puts on a white linen nightgown and goes to bed. She turns her head a little to one side, and lying still, reminds herself that it is time to sleep. Numbers tick in her brain like little clocks, soundless doors close of themselves around her. If you would sleep, you must not remember anything, the children will say tomorrow, good morning, my teacher, the poor prisoners who come every day bringing flowers to their jailor. 1-2-3-4-5 it is monstrous to confuse love with revolution, night with day, life with death—ah, Eugenio!

The tolling of the midnight bell is a signal, but what does it mean? Get up, Laura, and follow me: come out of your sleep, out of your bed, out of this strange house. What are you doing in this house? Without a word, without fear she rose and reached for Eugenio's hand, but he eluded her with a sharp, sly smile and drifted away. This is not all, you shall see—Murderer, he said, follow me, I will show you a new country, but it is far away and we must hurry. No, said Laura, not unless you take my hand, no; and she clung first to the stair rail, and then to the topmost branch of the Judas tree that bent down slowly and set her upon the earth, and then to the rocky ledge of a cliff, and then to the jagged wave of a sea that was not water but a desert of crumbling stone. Where are you taking me, she asked in wonder but without fear. To death, and it is a long way off, and we must hurry, said Eugenio. No, said Laura, not unless you take my hand. Then eat these flowers, poor prisoner, said Eugenio in a voice of pity, take and eat: and from the Judas tree he stripped the warm bleeding flowers, and held them to her lips. She saw that his hand was fleshless, a cluster of small white petrified branches, and his eye sockets were without light, but she ate the flowers greedily for they satisfied both hunger and thirst. Murderer! said Eugenio, and Cannibal! This is my body and my blood. Laura cried No! and at the sound of her own voice, she awoke trembling, and was afraid to sleep again.

James Thurber

THE CATBIRD SEAT

During the heyday of his career James Thurber was noted for a particularly original brand of humor, not only in the essays, fables, and stories he wrote, but also in the cartoons he drew to illustrate them. Because this humor was firmly rooted in a sensitive awareness of the lunacies of human behavior rather than in a mere impulse to be the jester, Thurber won high regard as a serious critic of mankind.

Born in Columbus, Ohio, in 1894, he attended public school there and then entered Ohio State University, where he edited a humorous undergraduate magazine. In his senior year he left college for war service as a code clerk in the State Department in Washington and later (1918-1920) in the American Embassy in Paris. After the war, he made journalism his profession, working successively as a reporter on the Columbus *Dispatch,* the Paris edition of the Chicago *Tribune,* and the New York *Evening Post.* After contributing some pieces to *The New Yorker,* he joined its staff in 1927 and remained closely associated with that magazine either in an editorial capacity or as a frequent contributor until his death in 1961. His first book, *Is Sex Necessary?* (1929), a parody of sex books, was written in collaboration with E. B. White. His next two books, *The Owl in the Attic and Other Perplexities* (1931) and *The Seal in the Bedroom and Other Predicaments* (1932), both collections of nonsense essays, enhanced his reputation as a humorist. Subsequently, he maintained his position as one of America's most original and talented writers with such other volumes as *My Life and Hard Times* (1933), *The Middle Aged Man on the Flying Trapeze* (1935), *Let Your Mind Alone* (1937), *Fables for Our Time and Famous Poems Illustrated* (1946), and *The 13 Clocks* (1950). He also collaborated with Elliot Nugent on the successful play, *The Male Animal* (1940). Primarily regarded as a humorous essayist, he also wrote a number of short stories of distinguished excellence.

With its tight plotting, neat reversal of situation, and surprise ending, "The Catbird Seat" would have delighted both Poe and O. Henry. The effectiveness of the story, however, depends not so much on these mechanical features as on the sharply drawn characterization and humorous tone—both of which are the result of precision, balance, and control in the use of language.

the catbird seat

Mr. Martin bought the pack of Camels on Monday night in the most crowded cigar store on Broadway. It was theatre time and seven or eight men were buying cigarettes. The clerk didn't even glance at Mr. Martin, who put the pack in his overcoat pocket and went out. If any of the staff at F & S had seen him buy the cigarettes, they would have been astonished, for it was generally known that Mr. Martin did not smoke, and never had. No one saw him.

It was just a week to the day since Mr. Martin had decided to rub out Mrs. Ulgine Barrows. The term "rub out" pleased him because it suggested nothing more than the correction of an error— in this case an error of Mr. Fitweiler. Mr. Martin had spent each night of the past week working out his plan and examining it. As he walked home now he went over it again. For the hundredth time he resented the element of imprecision, the margin of guesswork that entered into the business. The project as he had worked it out was casual and bold, the risks were considerable. Something might go wrong anywhere along the line. And therein lay the cunning of his scheme. No one would ever see in it the cautious, painstaking hand of Erwin Martin, head of the filing department at F & S, of whom Mr. Fitweiler had once said, "Man is fallible but Martin isn't." No one would see his hand, that is, unless it were caught in the act.

Reprinted by permission; Copr. © 1942 The New Yorker Magazine, Inc.

Sitting in his apartment, drinking a glass of milk, Mr. Martin reviewed his case against Mrs. Ulgine Barrows, as he had every night for seven nights. He began at the beginning. Her quacking voice and braying laugh had first profaned the halls of F & S on March 7, 1941 (Mr. Martin had a head for dates). Old Roberts, the personnel chief, had introduced her as the newly appointed special adviser to the president of the firm, Mr. Fitweiler. The woman had appalled Mr. Martin instantly, but he hadn't shown it. He had given her his dry hand, a look of studious concentration, and a faint smile. "Well," she had said, looking at the papers on his desk, "are you lifting the oxcart out of the ditch?" As Mr. Martin recalled that moment, over his milk, he squirmed slightly. He must keep his mind on her crimes as a special adviser, not on her peccadillos as a personality. This he found difficult to do, in spite of entering an objection and sustaining it. The faults of the woman as a woman kept chattering on in his mind like an unruly witness. She had, for almost two years now, baited him. In the halls, in the elevator, even in his own office, into which she romped now and then like a circus horse, she was constantly shouting these silly questions at him. "Are you lifting the oxcart out of the ditch? Are you tearing up the pea patch? Are you hollering down the rain barrel? Are you scraping around the bottom of the pickle barrel? Are you sitting in the catbird seat?"

It was Joey Hart, one of Mr. Martin's two assistants, who had explained what the gibberish meant. "She must be a Dodger fan," he had said. "Red Barber announces the Dodger games over the radio and he uses those expressions—picked 'em up down South." Joey had gone on to explain one or two. "Tearing up the pea patch" meant going on a rampage; "sitting in the catbird seat" meant sitting pretty, like a batter with three balls and no strikes on him. Mr. Martin dismissed all this with an effort. It had been annoying, it had driven him near to distraction, but he was too solid a man to be moved to murder by anything so childish. It was fortunate, he reflected as he passed on to the important charges against Mrs. Barrows, that he had stood up under it so well. He had maintained always an outward appearance of polite tolerance. "Why, I even believe you like the woman," Miss Paird, his other assistant, had once said to him. He had simply smiled.

A gavel rapped in Mr. Martin's mind and the case proper was resumed. Mrs. Ulgine Barrows stood charged with willful, blatant, and persistent attempts to destroy the efficiency and system of F & S. It was competent, material, and relevant to review her advent and rise to power. Mr. Martin had got the story from Miss Paird, who seemed always able to find things out. According to her, Mrs. Barrows had met Mr. Fitweiler at a party, where she had rescued him from the embraces of a powerfully built drunken man who had mistaken the president of F & S for a famous retired Middle Western football coach. She had led him to a sofa and somehow worked upon him a monstrous magic. The aging gentleman had jumped to the conclusion there and then that this was a woman of singular attainments, equipped to bring out the best in him and in the firm. A week later he had introduced her into F & S as his special adviser. On that day confusion got its foot in the door. After Miss Tyson, Mr. Brundage, and Mr. Bartlett had been fired and Mr. Munson had taken his hat and stalked out, mailing in his resignation later, old Roberts had been emboldened to speak to Mr. Fitweiler. He mentioned that Mr. Munson's department had been "a little disrupted" and hadn't they perhaps better resume the old system there? Mr. Fitweiler had said certainly not. He had the greatest faith in Mrs. Barrows' ideas. "They require a little seasoning, a little seasoning, is all," he had added. Mr. Roberts had given it up. Mr. Martin reviewed in detail all the changes wrought by Mrs. Barrows. She had begun chipping at the cornices of the firm's edifice and now she was swinging at the foundation stones with a pickaxe.

Mr. Martin came now, in his summing up, to the afternoon of Monday, November 2, 1942—just one week ago. On that day, at 3 P.M., Mrs. Barrows had bounced into his office. "Boo!" she had yelled. "Are you scraping around the bottom of the pickle barrel?" Mr. Martin had looked at her from under his green eyeshade, saying nothing. She had begun to wander about the office, taking it in with her great, popping eyes. "Do you really need *all* these filing cabinets?" she had demanded suddenly. Mr. Martin's heart had jumped. "Each of these files," he had said, keeping his voice even, "plays an indispensable part in the system of F & S." She had brayed at him, "Well, don't tear up the pea patch!" and gone to the door. From there she had bawled, "But you sure have got a lot of fine scrap in here!" Mr. Martin could no longer doubt that the finger was on his beloved department. Her pickaxe was on the upswing, poised for the first blow. It had not come yet; he had received no blue memo from the enchanted Mr. Fitweiler bearing nonsensical instructions deriving from the obscene woman. But there was no doubt in Mr. Martin's mind that one would be forthcoming. He must act quickly. Already a precious week had gone by. Mr. Martin stood up in his living room, still holding his milk glass. "Gentlemen of the jury," he said to himself, "I demand the death penalty for this horrible person."

The next day Mr. Martin followed his routine, as usual. He polished his glasses more often and once sharpened an already sharp pencil, but not even Miss Paird noticed. Only once did he catch sight of his victim; she swept past him in the hall with a patronizing "Hi!" At five-thirty he walked home, as usual, and had a glass of milk, as usual. He had never drunk anything stronger in his life—unless you could count ginger ale. The late Sam Schlosser, the S of F & S, had praised Mr. Martin at a staff meeting several years before for his temperate habits. "Our most efficient worker neither drinks nor smokes," he had said. "The results speak for themselves." Mr. Fitweiler had sat by, nodding approval.

Mr. Martin was still thinking about that red-letter day as he walked over to the Schrafft's on Fifth Avenue near Forty-sixth Street. He got there, as he always did, at eight o'clock. He finished his dinner and the financial page of the *Sun* at a quarter to nine, as he always did. It was his custom after dinner to take a walk. This time he walked down Fifth Avenue at a casual pace. His gloved hands felt moist and warm, his forehead cold. He transferred the Camels from his overcoat to a jacket pocket. He wondered, as he did so, if they did not represent an unnecessary note of strain. Mrs. Barrows smoked only Luckies. It was his idea to puff a few puffs on a Camel (after the rubbing-out), stub it out in the ashtray holding her lipstick-stained Luckies, and thus drag a small red herring across the trail. Perhaps it was not a good idea. It would take time. He might even choke, too loudly.

Mr. Martin had never seen the house on West Twelfth Street where Mrs. Barrows lived, but he had a clear enough picture of it. Fortunately, she had bragged to everybody about her ducky first-floor apartment in the perfectly darling three-story red-brick. There would be no doorman or other attendants; just the tenants of the second and third floors. As he walked along, Mr. Martin realized that he would get there before nine-thirty. He had considered walking north on Fifth Avenue from Schrafft's to a point from which it would take him until ten o'clock to reach the house. At that hour people were less likely to be coming in or going out. But the procedure would have made an awkward loop in the straight thread of his casualness, and he had abandoned it. It was impossible to figure when people would be entering or leaving the house, anyway. There was a great risk at any hour. If he ran into anybody, he would simply have to place the rubbing-out of Ulgine Barrows in the inactive file forever. The same thing would hold true if there were someone in her apartment. In that case he would just say that he had been passing by, recognized her charming house, and thought to drop in.

It was eighteen minutes after nine when Mr. Martin turned into Twelfth Street. A man passed him, and a man and a woman, talking. There was no one within fifty paces when he came to the house, halfway down the block. He was up the steps and in the small vestibule in no time, pressing the bell under the card that said "Mrs. Ulgine Barrows." When the clicking in the lock started, he jumped forward against the door. He got inside fast, closing the door behind him. A bulb in a lantern hung from the hall ceiling on a chain seemed to give a monstrously bright light. There was nobody on the stair, which went up ahead of him along the left wall. A door opened down the hall in the wall on the right. He went toward it swiftly, on tiptoe.

"Well, for God's sake, look who's here!" bawled Mrs. Barrows, and her braying laugh rang out like the report of a shotgun. He rushed past her like a football tackle, bumping her. "Hey, quit shoving!" she said, closing the door behind them. They were in her living room, which seemed to Mr. Martin to be lighted by a hundred lamps. "What's after you?" she said. "You're as jumpy as a goat." He found he was unable to speak. His heart was wheezing in his throat. "I—yes," he finally brought out. She was jabbering and laughing as she started to help him off with his coat. "No, no," he said. "I'll put it here." He took it off and put it on a chair near the door. "Your hat and gloves, too," she said. "You're in a lady's house." He put his hat on top of the coat. Mrs. Barrows seemed larger than he had thought. He kept his gloves on. "I was passing by," he said. "I recognized—is there anyone here?" She laughed louder than ever. "No," she said, "we're all alone. You're as white as a sheet, you funny man. Whatever *has* come over you? I'll mix you a toddy." She started toward a door across the room. "Scotch-and-soda be all right? But say, you don't drink, do you?" She turned and gave him her amused look. Mr. Martin pulled himself together. "Scotch-and-soda will be all right," he heard himself say. He could hear her laughing in the kitchen.

Mr. Martin looked quickly around the living room for the weapon. He had counted on finding one there. There were andirons and a poker and something in a corner that looked like an Indian club. None of them would do. It couldn't be that way. He began to pace around. He came to a desk. On it lay a metal paper knife with an ornate handle. Would it be sharp enough? He reached for it and knocked over a small brass jar. Stamps spilled out of it and it fell to the floor with a clatter. "Hey," Mrs. Barrows yelled from the kitchen, "are you tearing up the pea patch?" Mr. Martin gave a strange laugh. Picking up the knife, he tried its point against his left wrist. It was blunt. It wouldn't do.

When Mrs. Barrows reappeared, carrying two highballs, Mr. Martin, standing there with his gloves on, became acutely conscious of the fantasy he had wrought. Cigarettes in his pocket, a drink prepared for him—it was all too grossly improbable. It was more than that; it was impossible. Somewhere in the back of his mind a vague idea stirred, sprouted. "For heaven's sake, take off those gloves," said Mrs. Barrows. "I always wear them in the house," said Mr. Martin. The idea began to bloom, strange and wonderful. She put the glasses on a coffee table in front of a sofa and sat on the sofa. "Come over here, you odd little man," she said. Mr. Martin went over and sat beside her. It was difficult getting a cigarette out of the pack of Camels, but he managed it. She held a match for him, laughing. "Well," she said, handing him his drink, "this is perfectly marvellous. You with a drink and a cigarette."

Mr. Martin puffed, not too awkwardly, and took a gulp of the highball. "I drink and smoke all the time," he said. He clinked his glass against hers. "Here's nuts to that old windbag, Fitweiler," he said, and gulped again. The stuff tasted awful, but he made no grimace. "Really, Mr. Martin," she said, her voice and posture changing, "you are insulting our employer." Mrs. Barrows was now all special adviser to the president. "I am preparing a bomb," said Mr. Martin, "which will blow the old goat higher than hell." He had only had a little of the drink, which was not strong. It couldn't be that. "Do you take dope or something?" Mrs. Barrows asked coldly. "Heroin," said Mr. Martin. "I'll be coked to the gills when I bump that old buzzard off." "Mr. Martin!" she shouted, getting to her feet. "That will be all of that. You must go at once." Mr. Martin took another swallow of his drink. He tapped his cigarette out in the ashtray and put the pack of Camels on the coffee table. Then he got up. She stood glaring at him. He walked over and put on his hat and coat. "Not a word about this," he said, and laid an index finger against his lips. All Mrs. Barrows could bring out was "Really!" Mr. Martin put his hand on the doorknob. "I'm sitting in the catbird seat," he said. He stuck his tongue out at her and left. Nobody saw him go.

Mr. Martin got to his apartment, walking, well before eleven. No one saw him go in. He had two glasses of milk after brushing his teeth, and he felt elated. It wasn't tipsiness, because he hadn't been tipsy. Anyway, the walk had worn off all effects of the whiskey. He got in bed and read a magazine for a while. He was asleep before midnight.

Mr. Martin got to the office at eight-thirty the next morning, as usual. At a quarter to nine, Ulgine Barrows, who had never before arrived at work before ten, swept into his office. "I'm reporting to Mr. Fitweiler now!" she shouted. "If he turns you over to the police, it's no more than you deserve!" Mr. Martin gave her a look of shocked surprise. "I beg your pardon?" he said. Mrs. Barrows snorted and bounced out of the room, leaving Miss Paird and Joey Hart staring after her. "What's the matter with that old devil now?" asked Miss Paird. "I have no idea," said Mr. Martin, resuming his work. The other two looked at him and then at each other. Miss Paird got up and went out. She walked slowly past the closed door of Mr. Fitweiler's office. Mrs. Barrows was yelling inside, but she was not braying. Miss Paird could not hear what the woman was saying. She went back to her desk.

Forty-five minutes later, Mrs. Barrows left the president's office and went into her own, shutting the door. It wasn't until half an hour later that Mr. Fitweiler sent for Mr. Martin. The head of the filing department, neat, quiet, attentive, stood in front of the old man's desk. Mr. Fitweiler was pale and nervous. He took his glasses off and twiddled them. He made a small, bruffing sound in his throat. "Martin," he said, "you have been with us more than twenty years." "Twenty-two, sir," said Mr. Martin. "In that time," pursued the president, "your work and your—uh—manner have been exemplary." "I trust so, sir," said Mr. Martin. "I have understood, Martin," said Mr. Fitweiler, "that you have never taken a drink or smoked." "That is correct, sir," said Mr. Martin. "Ah, yes." Mr. Fitweiler polished his glasses. "You may describe what you did after leaving the office yesterday, Martin," he said. Mr. Martin allowed less than a second for his bewildered pause. "Certainly, sir," he said. "I walked home. Then I went to Schrafft's for dinner. Afterward I walked home again. I went to bed early, sir, and read a magazine for a while. I was asleep before eleven." "Ah, yes," said Mr. Fitweiler again. He was silent for a moment, searching for the proper words to say to the head of the filing department. "Mrs. Barrows," he said finally, "Mrs. Barrows has worked hard, Martin, very hard. It grieves me to report that she has suffered a severe breakdown. It has taken the form of a persecution complex accompanied by distressing hallucinations." "I am very sorry, sir," said Mr. Martin. "Mrs. Barrows is under the delusion," continued Mr. Fitweiler, "that you visited her last evening and behaved yourself in an—uh—unseemly manner." He raised his hand to silence Mr. Martin's little pained outcry. "It is the nature of these psychological diseases," Mr. Fitweiler said, "to fix upon the least likely and most innocent party as the—uh—source of persecution. These matters are not for the lay mind to grasp, Martin. I've just had my psychiatrist, Dr. Fitch, on the phone. He would not, of course, commit himself, but he made enough generalizations to substantiate my suspicions. I suggested to Mrs. Barrows, when she had completed her—uh—story to me this morning, that she visit Dr. Fitch, for I suspected a condition at once. She flew, I regret to say, into a rage, and demanded—uh—requested that I call you on the carpet. You may not know, Martin, but Mrs. Barrows had planned a reorganization of your department —subject to my approval, of course, subject to my approval. This brought you, rather than anyone else, to her mind—but again that is a phenomenon for Dr. Fitch and not for us. So, Martin, I am afraid Mrs. Barrows' usefulness here is at an end." "I am dreadfully sorry, sir," said Mr. Martin.

It was at this point that the door to the office blew open with the suddenness of a gas-main explosion and Mrs. Barrows catapulted through it. "Is the little rat denying it?" she screamed. "He can't get away with that!" Mr. Martin got up and moved discreetly to a point beside Mr. Fitweiler's chair. "You drank and smoked at my apartment," she bawled at Mr. Martin, "and you know it! You called Mr. Fitweiler an old windbag and said you were going to blow him up when you got coked to the gills on your heroin!" She stopped yelling to catch her breath and a new glint came into her popping eyes. "If you weren't such a drab, ordinary little man," she said, "I'd think you'd planned it all. Sticking your tongue out, saying you were sitting in the catbird seat, because you thought no one would believe me when I told it! My God, it's really too perfect!" She brayed loudly and hysterically, and the fury was on her again. She glared at Mr. Fitweiler. "Can't you see how he has tricked us, you old fool? Can't you see his little game?" But Mr. Fitweiler had been surreptitiously pressing all the buttons under the top of his desk and employees of F & S began pouring into the room. "Stockton," said Mr. Fitweiler, "you and Fishbein will take Mrs. Barrows to her home. Mrs. Powell, you will go with them." Stockton, who had played a little football in high school, blocked Mrs. Barrows as she made for Mr. Martin. It took him and Fishbein together to force her out of the door into the hall, crowded with stenographers and office boys. She was still screaming imprecations at Mr. Martin, tangled and contradictory imprecations. The hubbub finally died out down the corridor.

"I regret that this has happened," said Mr. Fitweiler. "I shall ask you to dismiss it from your mind, Martin." "Yes, sir," said Mr. Martin, anticipating his chief's "That will be all" by moving to the door. "I will dismiss it." He went out and shut the door, and his step was light and quick in the hall. When he entered his department he had slowed down to his customary gait, and he walked quietly across the room to the W20 file, wearing a look of studious concentration.

F Scott Fitzgerald

THE BABY PARTY

Closely associated in the public mind with the Jazz Age, of which he was the chief literary spokesman, F. Scott Fitzgerald suffered a decline in popularity with the passing of that era around 1930. The recent revival of interest in him reflects in part a renewed interest in the glittering, feverish life of the 1920's that he so accurately mirrored in his novels and stories, but it indicates also that the perspective of time has brought an increased appreciation of his contribution to American literature.

Fitzgerald's own life exemplifies the frenetic living of the age he recorded. He was born in St. Paul, Minnesota, in 1896, of a father who had descended from an old Maryland family and a mother who was "straight 1850 potato-famine Irish," a combination which may have contributed to his temperamental instability. After spending two years in an eastern preparatory school, he enrolled in 1913 at Princeton University. Driven by the desire to be socially prominent among his fellow students, he devoted his energies to such extracurricular activities as writing for the *Nassau Lit,* the campus literary magazine, and *The Tiger,* a humorous publication, working on musical comedies for the Triangle Club, and attending the theater in New York. His course work suffered to the extent that during his junior year he was dropped from Princeton for low grades. He then served in the Army, and after the Armistice worked in a New York advertising agency. He soon quit this job to write his first novel, *This Side of Paradise,* which was immediately successful on its publication in 1920. Flushed with triumph, he married the socially prominent Zelda Sayre, whom he had met while stationed at an Army camp near her home town, Montgomery, Alabama, and plunged into a gay whirl of New York café-society life.

449

As subsequent novels and stories brought additional
fame and income, the Fitzgeralds continued their
reckless, glittering social life in New York and Europe
as members of the Paris-Riviera international set. But
personal suffering and economic trouble of a sort suggestive of Fitzgerald's own stories, in time disrupted
this mode of living. In 1930 Zelda became mentally
ill, and Fitzgerald thereafter fought a losing battle
against his own irregular habits and a declining income
resulting from his waning literary popularity. In his
last years, however, he wrote but left unfinished at his
death in 1940, a novel about Hollywood life entitled
The Last Tycoon, which many critics regard as his
most mature effort. Among his novels, *The Great
Gatsby* (1925) is his masterpiece. His short story
collections are *Flappers and Philosophers* (1920), *Tales
of the Jazz Age* (1922), *All the Sad Young Men*
(1926), and *Taps at Reveille* (1935).

In Fitzgerald's stories, the characters are frequently the victims of a false or insecure sense of
values: a real or imagined injury, sometimes quite
trivial, often motivates them to desperate, even ridiculous, action. In "The Baby Party," for example, the
violent conflict between the two couples is completely
out of proportion to the incident that generates it.

the baby party

When John Andros felt old he found solace in the thought of
life continuing through his child. The dark trumpets of oblivion were
less loud at the patter of his child's feet or at the sound of his
child's voice babbling mad non sequiturs to him over the telephone.
The latter incident occurred every afternoon at three when his wife

called the office from the country, and he came to look forward to it as one of the vivid minutes of his day.

He was not physically old, but his life had been a series of struggles up a series of rugged hills, and here at thirty-eight having won his battles against ill-health and poverty he cherished less than the usual number of illusions. Even his feeling about his little girl was qualified. She had interrupted his rather intense love-affair with his wife, and she was the reason for their living in a suburban town, where they paid for country air with endless servant troubles and the weary merry-go-round of the commuting train.

It was little Ede as a definite piece of youth that chiefly interested him. He liked to take her on his lap and examine minutely her fragrant, downy scalp and her eyes with their irises of morning blue. Having paid this homage John was content that the nurse should take her away. After ten minutes the very vitality of the child irritated him; he was inclined to lose his temper when things were broken, and one Sunday afternoon when she had disrupted a bridge game by permanently hiding up the ace of spades, he had made a scene that had reduced his wife to tears.

This was absurd and John was ashamed of himself. It was inevitable that such things would happen, and it was impossible that little Ede should spend all her indoor hours in the nursery upstairs when she was becoming, as her mother said, more nearly a "real person" every day.

She was two and a half, and this afternoon, for instance, she was going to a baby party. Grown up Edith, her mother, had telephoned the information to the office, and little Ede had confirmed the business by shouting "I yam going to a *pantry!*" into John's unsuspecting left ear.

"Drop in at the Markeys' when you get home, won't you, dear?" resumed her mother. "It'll be funny. Ede's going to be all dressed up in her new pink dress——"

The conversation terminated abruptly with a squawk which indicated that the telephone had been pulled violently to the floor. John laughed and decided to get an early train out; the prospect of a baby party in some one else's house amused him.

"What a peach of a mess!" he thought humorously. "A dozen mothers, and each one looking at nothing but her own child. All the babies breaking things and grabbing at the cake, and each mamma going home thinking about the subtle superiority of her own child to every other child there."

He was in a good humor today—all the things in his life were going better than they had ever gone before. When he got off the train at his station he shook his head at an importunate taxi man, and began to walk up the long hill toward his house through the crisp December twilight. It was only six o'clock but the moon was out, shining with proud brilliance on the thin sugary snow that lay over the lawns.

As he walked along drawing his lungs full of cold air his happiness increased, and the idea of a baby party appealed to him more and more. He began to wonder how Ede compared to other children of her own age, and if the pink dress she was to wear was something radical and mature. Increasing his gait he came in sight of his own house, where the lights of a defunct Christmas tree still blossomed in the window, but he continued on past the walk. The party was at the Markeys' next door.

As he mounted the brick step and rang the bell he became aware of voices inside, and he was glad he was not too late. Then he raised his head and listened—the voices were not children's voices, but they were loud and pitched high with anger; there were at least three of them and one, which rose as he listened to a hysterical sob, he recognized immediately as his wife's.

"There's been some trouble," he thought quickly.

Trying the door, he found it unlocked and pushed it open.

The baby party began at half past four, but Edith Andros, calculating shrewdly that the new dress would stand out more sensationally against vestments already rumpled, planned the arrival of herself and little Ede for five. When they appeared it was already a flourishing affair. Four baby girls and nine baby boys, each one curled and washed and dressed with all the care of a proud and jealous heart, were dancing to the music of a phonograph. Never more than two or three were dancing at once, but as all were continually in motion running to and from their mothers for encouragement, the general effect was the same.

As Edith and her daughter entered, the music was temporarily drowned out by a sustained chorus, consisting largely of the word *cute* and directed toward little Ede, who stood looking timidly about and fingering the edges of her pink dress. She was not kissed—this is the sanitary age—but she was passed along a row of mammas each one of whom said "cu-u-ute" to her and held her pink little hand before passing her on to the next. After some encouragement and a few mild pushes she was absorbed into the dance, and became an active member of the party.

Edith stood near the door talking to Mrs. Markey, and keeping one eye on the tiny figure in the pink dress. She did not care for Mrs. Markey; she considered her both snippy and common, but John and Joe Markey were congenial and went in together on the commuting train every morning, so the two women kept up an elaborate pretense of warm amity. They were always reproaching each other for "not coming to see me," and they were always planning the kind of parties that began with "You'll have to come to dinner with us soon, and we'll go in to the theatre," but never matured further.

"Little Ede looks perfectly darling," said Mrs. Markey, smiling and moistening her lips in a way that Edith found particularly repulsive. "So *grown-up*—I can't *believe* it!"

Edith wondered if "little Ede" referred to the fact that Billy Markey, though several months younger, weighed almost five pounds more. Accepting a cup of tea she took a seat with two other ladies on a divan and launched into the real business of the afternoon, which of course lay in relating the recent accomplishments and insouciances of her child.

An hour passed. Dancing palled and the babies took to sterner sport. They ran into the dining-room, rounded the big table, and essayed the kitchen door, from which they were rescued by an expeditionary force of mothers. Having been rounded up they immediately broke loose, and rushing back to the dining-room tried the familiar swinging door again. The word "overheated" began to be used, and small white brows were dried with small white handkerchiefs. A general attempt to make the babies sit down began, but the babies squirmed off laps with peremptory cries of "Down! Down!" And the rush into the fascinating dining-room began anew.

This phase of the party came to an end with the arrival of refreshments, a large cake with two candles, and saucers of vanilla ice cream. Billy Markey, a stout laughing baby with red hair and legs somewhat bowed, blew out the candles, and placed an experimental thumb on the white frosting. The refreshments were distributed, and the children ate, greedily but without confusion—they had behaved remarkably well all afternoon. They were modern babies who ate and slept at regular hours, so their dispositions were good, and their faces healthy and pink—such a peaceful party would not have been possible thirty years ago.

After the refreshments a gradual exodus began. Edith glanced anxiously at her watch—it was almost six, and John had not arrived. She wanted him to see Ede with the other children—to see how dignified and polite and intelligent she was, and how the only ice-cream spot on her dress was some that had dropped from her chin when she was joggled from behind.

"You're a darling," she whispered to her child, drawing her suddenly against her knee. "Do you know you're a darling? Do you *know* you're a darling?"

Ede laughed. "Bow-wow," she said suddenly.

"Bow-wow?" Edith looked around. "There isn't any bow-wow."

"Bow-wow," repeated Ede. "I want a bow-wow."

Edith followed the small pointing finger.

"That isn't a bow-wow, dearest, that's a teddy-bear."

"Bear?"

"Yes, that's a teddy-bear, and it belongs to Billy Markey. You don't want Billy Markey's teddy-bear, do you?"

Ede did want it.

She broke away from her mother and approached Billy Markey, who held the toy closely in his arms. Ede stood regarding him with inscrutable eyes, and Billy laughed.

Grown-up Edith looked at her watch again, this time impatiently.

The party had dwindled until, besides Ede and Billy, there were only two babies remaining—and one of the two remained only by virtue of having hidden himself under the dining-room table. It was selfish of John not to come. It showed so little pride in the child. Other fathers had come, half a dozen of them, to call for their wives, and they had stayed for a while and looked on.

There was a sudden wail. Ede had obtained Billy's teddy-bear by pulling it forcibly from his arms, and on Billy's attempt to recover it, she had pushed him casually to the floor.

"Why, Ede!" cried her mother, repressing an inclination to laugh.

Joe Markey, a handsome, broad-shouldered man of thirty-five, picked up his son and set him on his feet. "You're a fine fellow," he said jovially. "Let a girl knock you over! You're a fine fellow."

"Did he bump his head?" Mrs. Markey returned anxiously from bowing the next to last remaining mother out the door.

"No-o-o-o," exclaimed Markey. "He bumped something else, didn't you, Billy? He bumped something else."

Billy had so far forgotten the bump that he was already making an attempt to recover his property. He seized a leg of the bear which projected from Ede's enveloping arms and tugged at it but without success.

"No," said Ede emphatically.

Suddenly, encouraged by the success of her former half-accidental manœuvre, Ede dropped the teddy-bear, placed her hands on Billy's shoulders and pushed him backward off his feet.

This time he landed less harmlessly; his head hit the bare floor just off the rug with a dull hollow sound, whereupon he drew in his breath and delivered an agonized yell.

Immediately the room was in confusion. With an exclamation Markey hurried to his son, but his wife was first to reach the injured baby and catch him up into her arms.

"Oh, *Billy,*" she cried, "what a terrible bump! She ought to be spanked."

Edith, who had rushed immediately to her daughter, heard this remark, and her lips came sharply together.

"Why, Ede," she whispered perfunctorily, "you bad girl!"

Ede put back her little head suddenly and laughed. It was a loud laugh, a triumphant laugh with victory in it and challenge and contempt. Unfortunately it was also an infectious laugh. Before her mother realized the delicacy of the situation, she too had laughed, an audible, distinct laugh not unlike the baby's, and partaking of the same overtones.

Then, as suddenly, she stopped.

Mrs. Markey's face had grown red with anger, and Markey, who had been feeling the back of the baby's head with one finger, looked at her, frowning.

"It's swollen already," he said with a note of reproof in his voice. "I'll get some witch-hazel."

But Mrs. Markey had lost her temper. "I don't see anything funny about a child being hurt!" she said in a trembling voice.

Little Ede meanwhile had been looking at her mother curiously. She noted that her own laugh had produced her mother's, and she wondered if the same cause would always produce the same effect. So she chose this moment to throw back her head and laugh again.

To her mother the additional mirth added the final touch of hysteria to the situation. Pressing her handkerchief to her mouth she giggled irrepressibly. It was more than nervousness—she felt that in a peculiar way she was laughing with her child—they were laughing together.

It was in a way a defiance—those two against the world.

While Markey rushed upstairs to the bathroom for ointment, his wife was walking up and down rocking the yelling boy in her arms.

"Please go home!" she broke out suddenly. "The child's badly hurt, and if you haven't the decency to be quiet, you'd better go home."

"Very well," said Edith, her own temper rising. "I've never seen any one make such a mountain out of ——"

"Get out!" cried Mrs. Markey frantically. "There's the door, get out—I never want to see you in our house again. You or your brat either!"

Edith had taken her daughter's hand and was moving quickly toward the door, but at this remark she stopped and turned around, her face contracting with indignation.

"Don't you dare call her that!"

Mrs. Markey did not answer but continued walking up and down, muttering to herself and to Billy in an inaudible voice.

Edith began to cry.

"I will get out!" she sobbed, "I've never heard anybody so rude and c-common in my life. I'm glad your baby did get pushed down—he's nothing but a f-fat little fool anyhow."

Joe Markey reached the foot of the stairs just in time to hear this remark.

"Why, Mrs. Andros," he said sharply, "can't you see the child's hurt? You really ought to control yourself."

"Control m-myself!" exclaimed Edith brokenly. "You better ask her to c-control herself. I've never heard anybody so c-common in my life."

"She's insulting me!" Mrs. Markey was now livid with rage. "Did you hear what she said, Joe? I wish you'd put her out. If she won't go, just take her by the shoulders and put her out!"

"Don't you dare touch me!" cried Edith. "I'm going just as quick as I can find my c-coat!"

Blind with tears she took a step toward the hall. It was just at this moment that the door opened and John Andros walked anxiously in.

"John!" cried Edith, and fled to him wildly.

"What's the matter? Why, what's the matter?"

"They're—they're putting me out!" she wailed, collapsing against him. "He'd just started to take me by the shoulders and put me out. I want my coat!"

"That's not true," objected Markey hurriedly. "Nobody's going to put you out." He turned to John. "Nobody's going to put her out," he repeated. "She's——"

"What do you mean 'put her out'?" demanded John abruptly. "What's all this talk, anyhow?"

"Oh, let's go!" cried Edith. "I want to go. They're so *common*, John!"

"Look here!" Markey's face darkened. "You've said that about enough. You're acting sort of crazy."

"They called Ede a brat!"

For the second time that afternoon little Ede expressed emotion at an inopportune moment. Confused and frightened at the shouting voices, she began to cry, and her tears had the effect of conveying that she felt the insult in her heart.

"What's the idea of this?" broke out John. "Do you insult your guests in your own house?"

"It seems to me it's your wife that's done the insulting!" answered Markey crisply. "In fact, your baby there started all the trouble."

John gave a contemptuous snort. "Are you calling names at a little baby?" he inquired. "That's a fine manly business!"

"Don't talk to him, John," insisted Edith. "Find my coat!"

"You must be in a bad way," went on John angrily, "if you have to take out your temper on a helpless little baby."

"I never heard anything so damn twisted in my life," shouted Markey. "If that wife of yours would shut her mouth for a minute——"

"Wait a minute! You're not talking to a woman and child now——"

There was an incidental interruption. Edith had been fumbling on a chair for her coat, and Mrs. Markey had been watching her with hot, angry eyes. Suddenly she laid Billy down on the sofa, where he immediately stopped crying and pulled himself upright, and coming into the hall she quickly found Edith's coat and handed it to her without a word. Then she went back to the sofa, picked up Billy, and rocking him in her arms looked again at Edith with hot, angry eyes. The interruption had taken less than half a minute.

"Your wife comes in here and begins shouting around about how common we are!" burst out Markey violently. "Well, if we're so damn common, you'd better stay away! And, what's more, you'd better get out now!"

Again John gave a short, contemptuous laugh.

"You're not only common," he returned, "you're evidently an awful bully—when there's any helpless women and children around." He felt for the knob and swung the door open. "Come on, Edith."

Taking up her daughter in her arms, his wife stepped outside and John, still looking contemptuously at Markey, started to follow.

"Wait a minute!" Markey took a step forward; he was trembling slightly, and two large veins on his temple were suddenly full of blood. "You don't think you can get away with that, do you? With me?"

Without a word, John walked out the door, leaving it open.

Edith, still weeping, had started for home. After following her with his eyes until she reached her own walk, John turned back toward the lighted doorway where Markey was slowly coming down the slippery steps. He took off his overcoat and hat, tossed them off the path onto the snow. Then, sliding a little on the iced walk, he took a step forward.

At the first blow, they both slipped and fell heavily to the sidewalk, half rising then, and again pulling each other to the ground. They found a better foothold in the thin snow to the side of the walk and rushed at each other, both swinging wildly and pressing out the snow into a pasty mud underfoot.

The street was deserted, and except for their short tired gasps and the padded sound as one or the other slipped down into the slushy mud, they fought in silence, clearly defined to each other by the full moonlight as well as by the amber glow that shone out of the open door. Several times they both slipped down together, and then for a while the conflict threshed about wildly on the lawn.

For ten, fifteen, twenty minutes they fought there senselessly in the moonlight. They had both taken off coats and vests at some silently agreed upon interval and now their shirts dripped from their backs in wet pulpy shreds. Both were torn and bleeding and so exhausted that they could stand only when by their position they mutually supported each other—the impact, the mere effort of a blow, would send them both to their hands and knees.

But it was not weariness that ended the business, and the very meaninglessness of the fight was a reason for not stopping. They stopped because once when they were straining at each other on the ground, they heard a man's footsteps coming along the sidewalk. They had rolled somehow into the shadow, and when they heard these footsteps they stopped fighting, stopped moving, stopped breathing, lay huddled together like two boys playing Indian until the footsteps had passed. Then, staggering to their feet, they looked at each other like two drunken men.

"I'll be damned if I'm going on with this thing any more," cried Markey thickly.

"I'm not going on any more either," said John Andros. "I've had enough of this thing."

Again they looked at each other, sulkily this time, as if each suspected the other of urging him to a renewal of the fight. Markey spat out a mouthful of blood from a cut lip; then he cursed softly, and picking up his coat and vest, shook off the snow from them in a surprised way, as if their comparative dampness was his only worry in the world.

"Want to come in and wash up?" he asked suddenly.

"No, thanks," said John. "I ought to be going home—my wife'll be worried."

He too picked up his coat and vest and then his overcoat and hat. Soaking wet and dripping with perspiration, it seemed absurd that less than half an hour ago he had been wearing all these clothes.

"Well—good night," he said hesitantly.

Suddenly they both walked toward each other and shook hands. It was no perfunctory hand-shake: John Andros's arm went around Markey's shoulder, and he patted him softly on the back for a little while.

"No harm done," he said brokenly.

"No—you?"

"No, no harm done."

"Well," said John Andros after a minute, "I guess I'll say good night."

"Good night."

Limping slightly and with his clothes over his arm, John Andros turned away. The moonlight was still bright as he left the dark patch of trampled ground and walked over the intervening lawn. Down at the station, half a mile away, he could hear the rumble of the seven o'clock train.

"But you must have been crazy," cried Edith brokenly. "I thought you were going to fix it all up there and shake hands. That's why I went away."

459

"Did you want us to fix it up?"

"Of course not, I never want to see them again. But I thought of course that was what you were going to do." She was touching the bruises on his neck and back with iodine as he sat placidly in a hot bath. "I'm going to get the doctor," she said insistently. "You may be hurt internally."

He shook his head. "Not a chance," he answered. "I don't want this to get all over town."

"I don't understand yet how it all happened."

"Neither do I." He smiled grimly. "I guess these baby parties are pretty rough affairs."

"Well, one thing—" suggested Edith hopefully, "I'm certainly glad we have beefsteak in the house for tomorrow's dinner."

"Why?"

"For your eye, of course. Do you know I came within an ace of ordering veal? Wasn't that the luckiest thing?"

Half an hour later, dressed except that his neck would accommodate no collar, John moved his limbs experimentally before the glass. "I believe I'll get myself in better shape," he said thoughtfully. "I must be getting old."

"You mean so that next time you can beat him?"

"I did beat him," he announced. "At least, I beat him as much as he beat me. And there isn't going to be any next time. Don't you go calling people common any more. If you get in any trouble, you just take your coat and go home. Understand?"

"Yes, dear," she said meekly. "I was very foolish and now I understand."

Out in the hall, he paused abruptly by the baby's door.

"Is she asleep?"

"Sound asleep. But you can go in and peek at her—just to say good night."

They tiptoed in and bent together over the bed. Little Ede, her cheeks flushed with health, her pink hands clasped tight together, was sleeping soundly in the cool, dark room. John reached over the railing of the bed and passed his hand lightly over the silken hair.

"She's asleep," he murmured in a puzzled way.

"Naturally, after such an afternoon."

"Miz Andros," the colored maid's stage whisper floated in from the hall, "Mr. and Miz Markey downstairs an' want to see you. Mr. Markey he's all cut up in pieces, ma'am. His face look like a roast beef. An' Miz Markey she 'pear mighty mad."

"Why, what incomparable nerve!" exclaimed Edith. "Just tell them we're not home. I wouldn't go down for anything in the world."

"You most certainly will." John's voice was hard and set.

"What?"

"You'll go down right now, and, what's more, whatever that other woman does, you'll apologize for what you said this afternoon. After that you don't ever have to see her again."

"Why—John, I can't."

"You've got to. And just remember that she probably hated to come over here just twice as much as you hate to go downstairs."

"Aren't you coming? Do I have to go alone?"

"I'll be down—in just a minute."

John Andros waited until she had closed the door behind her; then he reached over into the bed, and picking up his daughter, blankets and all, sat down in the rocking-chair holding her tightly in his arms. She moved a little, and he held his breath, but she was sleeping soundly, and in a moment she was resting quietly in the hollow of his elbow. Slowly he bent his head until his cheek was against her bright hair. "Dear little girl," he whispered. "Dear little girl, dear little girl."

John Andros knew at length what it was he had fought for so savagely that evening. He had it now, he possessed it forever, and for some time he sat there rocking very slowly to and fro in the darkness.

William Faulkner (signature)

A ROSE FOR EMILY

Since the death of William Faulkner in 1962 at the age
of 64, the critical assessment of his literary achievement
has continued, and there seems little doubt that his
ranking as one of the truly great masters of twentieth-
century fiction will in the least diminish. Perhaps the
single most impressive quality of his fiction is its
creative range—in subject matter from hilarious comedy to violent tragedy, in technique from the straight-
forward and traditional to the most complex and
unconventional, and in character types from the most
common and lifelike to the weirdest and most grotesque distortions. Despite the fact that his work is uneven in quality or that even his best may have its defects, the fictional world he creates is one of limitless
variety and richness. It is thus hardly surprising that his
fiction won for him not only all the significant literary
awards, including the Nobel Prize in 1950, but also an
international, as well as national, audience.

Probably few writers in modern times so completely isolated themselves from metropolitan literary
centers or stuck so closely to the locale of their materials as Faulkner did. He was born in 1897, in New
Albany, Mississippi, but at an early age moved to the
nearby university and county-seat town of Oxford,
where, except for brief periods, he spent his entire
life. He attended public school in Oxford but never
graduated, served during World War I in the British
Royal Air Force, and spent some time after his return
to Oxford as a student at the University of Mississippi.
After working at a succession of odd jobs in Oxford, he
lived for a while in New Orleans, forming there short-
lived acquaintances with Sherwood Anderson and
other writers then residing in the Old French Quarter.
He next worked in a New York bookstore for three

months, took a long walking tour of Europe, and returned to Oxford to settle down to his writing career. As early as 1924, he published a collection of poems, *The Marble Faun,* and in 1926 his novels began to appear at regular intervals. The first five—*Soldiers' Pay* (1926), *Mosquitoes* (1927), *Sartoris* (1929), *The Sound and the Fury* (1929), and *As I Lay Dying* (1930)—brought him considerable recognition, but it was only after he published the deliberately shocking *Sanctuary* (1931) that he won fame. Other important novels include: *Light in August* (1932), *Absalom, Absalom!* (1936), *The Wild Palms* (1939), *The Hamlet* (1940), *Intruder in the Dust* (1948), and *Requiem for a Nun* (1951), *The Fable* (1954), *The Town* (1957), *The Mansion* (1959), and *The Reivers* (1962). He wrote a large number of short stories, some of which were published separately and later rewoven into the fabric of his novels. Among his short story volumes are *These Thirteen* (1931), *Doctor Martino* (1934), *Go Down, Moses* (1942), and *Collected Stories* (1950).

In the horror of the shocking climax to which it builds, "A Rose for Emily" illustrates the macabre, Poe-like side of Faulkner's genius. Two features of the fictional technique of the story are particularly interesting: the presentation of the action in a logical instead of a chronological time sequence order and the narration of the story from the plural first point of view. The first device permitted the author to arrange the events in the manner best suited for staging the sensational climax. The "we" narrative point of view not only gave him greater freedom in moving back and forth in time but also enabled him to present Miss Emily through a narrator who represents the collected viewpoint of the community.

a rose for emily

When Miss Emily Grierson died, our whole town went to her funeral: the men through a sort of respectful affection for a fallen monument, the women mostly out of curiosity to see the inside of her house, which no one save an old manservant—a combined gardener and cook—had seen in at least ten years.

It was a big, squarish frame house that had once been white, decorated with cupolas and spires and scrolled balconies in the heavily lightsome style of the seventies, set on what had once been our most select street. But garages and cotton gins had encroached and obliterated even the august names of that neighborhood; only Miss Emily's house was left, lifting its stubborn and coquettish decay above the cotton wagons and the gasoline pumps—an eyesore among eyesores. And now Miss Emily had gone to join the representatives of those august names where they lay in the cedar-bemused cemetery among the ranked and anonymous graves of Union and Confederate soldiers who fell at the battle of Jefferson. *no battle, no Jefferson. Created a world.*

Alive, Miss Emily had been a tradition, a duty, and a care; a sort of hereditary obligation upon the town, dating from that day in 1894 when Colonel Sartoris, the mayor—he who fathered the edict that no Negro woman should appear on the streets without an apron—remitted her taxes, the dispensation dating from the death of her father on into perpetuity. Not that Miss Emily would have accepted charity. Colonel Sartoris invented an involved tale to the effect that Miss Emily's father had loaned money to the town, which the town, as a matter of business, preferred this way of repaying. Only a man of Colonel Sartoris' generation and thought could have invented it, and only a woman could have believed it.

When the next generation, with its more modern ideas, became mayors and aldermen, this arrangement created some little dissatisfaction. On the first of the year they mailed her a tax notice. February came, and there was no reply. They wrote her a formal letter, asking her to call at the sheriff's office at her convenience. A week later the mayor wrote her himself, offering to call or to send his car for her, and received in reply a note on paper of an archaic shape, in a thin flowing calligraphy in faded ink, to the effect that she no longer went out at all. The tax notice was also enclosed, without comment.

They called a special meeting of the Board of Aldermen. A deputation waited upon her, knocked at the door through which no visitor had passed since she ceased giving china-painting lessons eight or ten years earlier. They were admitted by the old Negro into a dim hall from which a stairway mounted into still more shadow. It smelled of dust and disuse—a close, dank smell. The Negro led them into the parlor. It was furnished in heavy, leather-covered furniture. When the Negro opened the blinds of one window, they could see that the leather was cracked; and when they sat down, a faint dust rose sluggishly about their thighs, spinning with slow motes in the single sun-ray. On a tarnished gilt easel before the fireplace stood a crayon portrait of Miss Emily's father.

They rose when she entered—a small, fat woman in black, with a thin gold chain descending to her waist and vanishing into her belt, leaning on an ebony cane with a tarnished gold head. Her skeleton was small and spare; perhaps that was why what would have been merely plumpness in another was obesity in her. She looked bloated, like a body long submerged in motionless water, and of that pallid hue. Her eyes, lost in the fatty ridges of her face, looked like two small pieces of coal pressed into a lump of dough as they moved from one face to another while the visitors stated their errand.

She did not ask them to sit. She just stood in the door and listened quietly until the spokesman came to a stumbling halt. Then they could hear the invisible watch ticking at the end of the gold chain.

Her voice was dry and cold. "I have no taxes in Jefferson. Colonel Sartoris explained it to me. Perhaps one of you can gain access to the city records and satisfy yourselves."

"But we have. We are the city authorities, Miss Emily. Didn't you get a notice from the sheriff, signed by him?"

"I received a paper, yes," Miss Emily said. "Perhaps he considers himself the sheriff . . . I have no taxes in Jefferson."

"But there is nothing on the books to show that, you see. We must go by the—"

"See Colonel Sartoris. I have no taxes in Jefferson."

"But, Miss Emily—"

"See Colonel Sartoris." (Colonel Sartoris had been dead almost ten years.) "I have no taxes in Jefferson. Tobe!" The Negro appeared. "Show these gentlemen out."

2

So she vanquished them, horse and foot, just as she had vanquished their fathers thirty years before about the smell. That was two years after her father's death and a short time after her sweetheart—the one we believed would marry her—had deserted her. After her father's death she went out very little; after her sweetheart went away, people hardly saw her at all. A few of the ladies had the temerity to call, but were not received, and the only sign of life about the place was the Negro man—a young man then—going in and out with a market basket.

"Just as if a man—any man—could keep a kitchen properly," the ladies said; so they were not surprised when the smell developed. It was another link between the gross, teeming world and the high and mighty Griersons.

A neighbor, a woman, complained to the mayor, Judge Stevens, eighty years old.

"But what will you have me do about it, madam?" he said.

"Why, send her word to stop it," the woman said. "Isn't there a law?"

"I'm sure that won't be necessary," Judge Stevens said. "It's probably just a snake or a rat that nigger of hers killed in the yard. I'll speak to him about it."

The next day he received two more complaints, one from a man who came in diffident deprecation. "We really must do something about it, Judge. I'd be the last one in the world to bother Miss Emily, but we've got to do something." That night the Board of Aldermen met— three graybeards and one younger man, a member of the rising generation.

"It's simple enough," he said. "Send her word to have her place cleaned up. Give her a certain time to do it in, and if she don't . . ."

"Dammit, sir," Judge Stevens said, "will you accuse a lady to her face of smelling bad?"

So the next night, after midnight, four men crossed Miss Emily's lawn and slunk about the house like burglars, sniffing along the base of the brickwork and at the cellar openings while one of them performed a regular sowing motion with his hand out of a sack slung from his shoulder. They broke open the cellar door and sprinkled lime there, and in all the outbuildings. As they recrossed the lawn, a window that had been dark was lighted and Miss Emily sat in it, the light behind her, and her upright torso motionless as that of an idol. They crept quietly across the lawn and into the shadow of the locusts that lined the street. After a week or two the smell went away.

That was when people had begun to feel really sorry for her. People in our town, remembering how old lady Wyatt, her great-aunt, had gone completely crazy at last, believed that the Griersons held themselves a little too high for what they really were. None of the young men were quite good enough to Miss Emily and such. We had long thought of them as a tableau; Miss Emily a slender figure in white in the background, her father a spraddled silhouette in the foreground, his back to her and clutching a horse-whip, the two of them framed by the back-flung front door. So when she got to be thirty and was still single, we were not pleased exactly, but vindicated; even with insanity in the family she wouldn't have turned down all of her chances if they had really materialized.

When her father died, it got about that the house was all that was left to her; and in a way, people were glad. At last they could pity Miss Emily. Being left alone, and a pauper, she had become humanized. Now she too would know the old thrill and the old despair of a penny more or less.

The day after his death all the ladies prepared to call at the house and offer condolence and aid, as is our custom. Miss Emily met them at the door, dressed as usual and with no trace of grief on her face. She told them that her father was not dead. She did that for three days, with the ministers calling on her, and the doctors, trying to persuade her to let them dispose of the body. Just as they were about to resort to law and force, she broke down, and they buried her father quickly.

We did not say she was crazy then. We believed she had to do that. We remembered all the young men her father had driven away, and we knew that with nothing left, she would have to cling to that which had robbed her, as people will.

3

She was sick for a long time. When we saw her again, her hair was cut short, making her look like a girl, with a vague resemblance to those angels in colored church windows—sort of tragic and serene.

The town had just let the contracts for paving the sidewalks, and in the summer after her father's death they began the work. The construction company came with niggers and mules and machinery, and a foreman named Homer Barron, a Yankee—a big, dark, ready man, with a big voice and eyes lighter than his face. The little boys would follow in groups to hear him cuss the niggers, and the niggers singing in time to the rise and fall of picks. Pretty soon he knew everybody in town. Whenever you heard a lot of laughing anywhere about the square, Homer Barron would be in the center of the group. Presently we began to see him and Miss Emily on Sunday afternoons driving in the yellow-wheeled buggy and the matched team of bays from the livery stable.

At first we were glad that Miss Emily would have an interest, because the ladies all said, "Of course a Grierson would not think seriously of a Northerner, a day laborer." But there were still others, older people, who said that even grief could not cause a real lady to forget *noblesse oblige*—without calling it *noblesse oblige*. They just said, "Poor Emily. Her kinsfolk should come to her." She had some kin in Alabama; but years ago her father had fallen out with them over the estate of old lady Wyatt, the crazy woman, and there was no communication between the two families. They had not even been represented at the funeral.

And as soon as the old people said, "Poor Emily," the whispering began. "Do you suppose it's really so?" they said to one another. "Of course it is. What else could . . ." This behind their hands; rustling of craned silk and satin behind jalousies closed upon the sun of Sunday afternoon as the thin, swift clop-clop-clop of the matched team passed: "Poor Emily."

She carried her head high enough—even when we believed that she was fallen. It was as if she demanded more than ever the recognition of her dignity as the last Grierson; as if it had wanted that touch of earthiness to reaffirm her imperviousness. Like when she bought the rat poison, the arsenic. That was over a year after they had begun to say "Poor Emily," and while the two female cousins were visiting her.

"I want some poison," she said to the druggist. She was over thirty then, still a slight woman, though thinner than usual, with cold, haughty black eyes in a face the flesh of which was strained across the temples and about the eye-sockets as you imagine a lighthouse keeper's face ought to look. "I want some poison," she said.

"Yes, Miss Emily. What kind? For rats and such? I'd recom—"

"I want the best you have. I don't care what kind."

The druggist named several. "They'll kill anything up to an elephant. But what you want is—"

"Arsenic," Miss Emily said. "Is that a good one?"

"Is . . . arsenic? Yes, ma'am. But what you want—"

"I want arsenic."

The druggist looked down at her. She looked back at him, erect, her face like a strained flag. "Why, of course," the druggist said. "If that's what you want. But the law requires you to tell what you are going to use it for."

Miss Emily just stared at him, her head tilted back in order to look him eye for eye, until he looked away and went and got the arsenic and wrapped it up. The Negro delivery boy brought her the package; the druggist didn't come back. When she opened the package at home there was written on the box, under the skull and bones: "For rats."

4

So the next day we all said, "She will kill herself"; and we said it would be the best thing. When she had first begun to be seen with Homer Barron, we had said, "She will marry him." Then we said, "She will persuade him yet," because Homer himself had remarked—he liked men, and it was known that he drank with the younger men in the Elks' Club—that he was not a marrying man. Later we said, "Poor Emily" behind the jalousies as they passed on Sunday afternoon in the glittering buggy, Miss Emily with her head high and Homer Barron with his hat cocked and a cigar in his teeth, reins and whip in a yellow glove.

Then some of the ladies began to say that it was a disgrace to the town and a bad example to the young people. The men did not want to interfere, but at last the ladies forced the Baptist minister—Miss Emily's people were Episcopal—to call upon her. He would never divulge what happened during that interview, but he refused to go back again. The next Sunday they again drove about the streets, and the following day the minister's wife wrote to Miss Emily's relations in Alabama.

So she had blood-kin under her roof again and we sat back to watch developments. At first nothing happened. Then we were sure that they were to be married. We learned that Miss Emily had been to the jeweler's and ordered a man's toilet set in silver, with the letters H.B. on each piece. Two days later we learned that she had bought a complete outfit of men's clothing, including a nightshirt, and we said, "They are married." We were really glad. We were glad because the two female cousins were even more Grierson than Miss Emily had ever been.

So we were not surprised when Homer Barron—the streets had been finished some time since—was gone. We were a little disappointed that there was not a public blowing-off, but we believed that he had gone on to prepare for Miss Emily's coming, or to give her a chance to get rid of the cousins. (By that time it was a cabal, and we were all Miss Emily's allies to help circumvent the cousins.) Sure enough, after another week they departed. And, as we had expected all along, within three days Homer Barron was back in town. A neighbor saw the Negro man admit him at the kitchen door at dusk one evening.

And that was the last we saw of Homer Barron. And of Miss Emily for some time. The Negro man went in and out with the market basket, but the front door remained closed. Now and then we would see her at a window for a moment, as the men did that night when they sprinkled the lime, but for almost six months she did not appear on the streets. Then we knew that this was to be expected too; as if that quality of her father which had thwarted her woman's life so many times had been too virulent and too furious to die.

When we next saw Miss Emily, she had grown fat and her hair was turning gray. During the next few years it grew grayer and grayer until it attained an even pepper-and-salt iron-gray, when it ceased turning. Up to the day of her death at seventy-four it was still that vigorous iron-gray, like the hair of an active man.

From that time on her front door remained closed, save for a period of six or seven years, when she was about forty, during which she gave lessons in china-painting. She fitted up a studio in one of the downstairs rooms, where the daughters and granddaughters of Colonel Sartoris' contemporaries were sent to her with the same regularity and in the same spirit that they were sent to church on Sundays with a twenty-five cent piece for the collection plate. Meanwhile her taxes had been remitted.

Then the newer generation became the backbone and the spirit of the town, and the painting pupils grew up and fell away and did not send their children to her with boxes of color and tedious brushes and pictures cut from the ladies' magazines. The front door closed upon the last one and remained closed for good. When the town got free postal delivery, Miss Emily alone refused to let them fasten the metal numbers above her door and attach a mailbox to it. She would not listen to them.

Daily, monthly, yearly we watched the Negro grow grayer and more stooped, going in and out with the market basket. Each December we sent her a tax notice, which would be returned by the post office a week later, unclaimed. Now and then we would see her in one of the downstairs windows—she had evidently shut up the top floor of the house—like the carven torso of an idol in a niche, looking or not looking at us, we could never tell which. Thus she passed from generation to generation—dear, inescapable, impervious, tranquil, and perverse.

And so she died. Fell ill in the house filled with dust and shadows, with only a doddering Negro man to wait on her. We did not even know she was sick; we had long since given up trying to get any information from the Negro. He talked to no one, probably not even to her, for his voice had grown harsh and rusty, as if from disuse.

She died in one of the downstairs rooms, in a heavy walnut bed with a curtain, her gray head propped on a pillow yellow and moldy with age and lack of sunlight.

5

The Negro met the first of the ladies at the front door and let them in, with their hushed, sibilant voices and their quick, curious glances, and then he disappeared. He walked right through the house and out the back and was not seen again.

The two female cousins came at once. They held the funeral on the second day, with the town coming to look at Miss Emily beneath a mass of bought flowers, with the crayon face of her father musing profoundly above the bier and the ladies sibilant and macabre; and the very old men—some in their brushed Confederate uniforms—on the porch and the lawn, talking of Miss Emily as if she had been a contemporary of theirs, believing that they had danced with her and courted her perhaps, confusing time with its mathematical progression, as the old do, to whom all the past is not a diminishing road but, instead, a huge meadow which no winter ever quite touches, divided from them now by the narrow bottle-neck of the most recent decade of years.

Already we knew that there was one room in that region above stairs which no one had seen in forty years, and which would have to be forced. They waited until Miss Emily was decently in the ground before they opened it.

The violence of breaking down the door seemed to fill this room with pervading dust. A thin, acrid pall as of the tomb seemed to lie everywhere upon this room decked and furnished as for a bridal: upon the valence curtains of faded rose color, upon the rose-shaded lights, upon the dressing table, upon the delicate array of crystal and the man's toilet things backed with tarnished silver, silver so tarnished that the monogram was obscured. Among them lay a collar and tie, as if they had just been removed, which, lifted, left upon the surface a pale crescent in the dust. Upon a chair hung the suit, carefully folded; beneath it the two mute shoes and the discarded socks.

The man himself lay in the bed.

For a long while we just stood there, looking down at the profound and fleshless grin. The body had apparently once lain in the attitude of an embrace, but now the long sleep that outlasts love, that conquers even the grimace of love, had cuckolded him. What was left of him, rotted beneath what was left of the nightshirt, had become inextricable from the bed in which he lay; and upon him and upon the pillow beside him lay that even coating of the patient and biding dust.

Then we noticed that in the second pillow was the indentation of a head. One of us lifted something from it, and leaning forward, that faint and invisible dust dry and acrid in the nostrils, we saw a long strand of iron-gray hair.

Ernest Hemingway.

A CLEAN, WELL-LIGHTED PLACE

Ernest Hemingway was the leading exponent of the "hard-boiled" school of fiction. Throughout the post-war decades his name in fact became identified with a distinctly individualized prose style, crisp, unadorned, staccato, which revealed a world of toughness and violence with an underlying attitude of cynicism and despair. His approach was so widely, if often poorly, imitated that he thereby exerted a major influence on both the content and technique of contemporary fiction.

Hemingway's entire career matched, in muscular activity, the sinewy quality of his prose. He was born in Oak Park, Illinois, in 1898, the son of a doctor who developed in him a fondness for the out-of-doors life by taking him on frequent boating and fishing trips to northern Michigan. He attended public school in Oak Park, where he played football and boxed and worked at various odd jobs in his free time. After graduating from high school, he became a reporter for the Kansas City *Star,* but gave up this position after a few months to go to France as a volunteer ambulance driver before the United States entered World War I. He later transferred to the Italian infantry, and was wounded severely in action. After the war, he returned to newspaper work as a reporter and European correspondent for the Toronto *Star.* In Paris, he met Ezra Pound and Gertrude Stein, who offered him encouragement in his literary career. His first volume of short stories, *In Our Time* (1925), drew favorable attention, and his reputation increased as other works appeared: *The Sun Also Rises* (1926); *Men Without Women* (1927), a collection of stories; *A Farewell to Arms* (1929); *To Have and Have Not* (1937); *The Fifth Column* [a play] *and the First Forty-nine Stories* (1938); *For Whom the Bell Tolls* (1940); *Across the*

River and Into the Trees (1950), and *The Old Man and the Sea* (1953). After World War II Hemingway kept on projecting his favorite image as a pugilistic literary champion by recording his activities as both spectator and participant at prize fights, bullfights, deep-sea fishing, and big-game hunting safaris. In 1962, like one of his own characters, he met death violently with a shotgun in his own hands.

A seemingly casual structure and apparent naïvete make the best of Hemingway's stories appear artless, almost childishly simple. "A Clean, Well-lighted Place," for example, is almost barren in its simplicity: two waiters in a cafe engage in conversation while an old man drinks brandy; they close the cafe and go home, one waiter stopping on his way to drink a cup of coffee. Yet, within the framework of these events, Hemingway dramatizes a highly complex philosophical question, that of the preservation of one's dignity and integrity in the midst of chaos, after coming to recognize life as *Nada*. The effect of the story is heightened by the restrained, austere style in which it is narrated.

a clean, well-lighted place

It was late and every one had left the café except an old man who sat in the shadow the leaves of the tree made against the electric light. In the day time the street was dusty, but at night the dew settled the dust and the old man liked to sit late because he was deaf and now at night it was quiet and he felt the difference. The two waiters inside the café knew that the old man was a little drunk, and while he was a good client they knew that if he became too drunk he would leave without paying, so they kept watch on him.

"Last week he tried to commit suicide," one waiter said.

"Why?"

"He was in despair."

"What about?"

"Nothing."

"How do you know it was nothing?"

"He has plenty of money."

They sat together at a table that was close against the wall near the door of the café and looked at the terrace where the tables were all empty except where the old man sat in the shadow of the leaves of the tree that moved slightly in the wind. A girl and a soldier went by in the street. The street light shone on the brass number on his collar. The girl wore no head covering and hurried beside him.

"The guard will pick him up," one waiter said.

"What does it matter if he gets what he's after?"

"He had better get off the street now. The guard will get him. They went by five minutes ago."

The old man sitting in the shadow rapped on his saucer with his glass. The younger waiter went over to him.

"What do you want?"

The old man looked at him. "Another brandy," he said.

"You'll be drunk," the waiter said. The old man looked at him. The waiter went away.

"He'll stay all night," he said to his colleague. "I'm sleepy now. I never get into bed before three o'clock. He should have killed himself last week."

The waiter took the brandy bottle and another saucer from the counter inside the café and marched out to the old man's table. He put down the saucer and poured the glass full of brandy.

"You should have killed yourself last week," he said to the deaf man. The old man motioned with his finger. "A little more," he said. The waiter poured on into the glass so that the brandy slopped over and ran down the stem into the top saucer of the pile. "Thank you," the old man said. The waiter took the bottle back inside the café. He sat down at the table with his colleague again.

"He's drunk now," he said.

"He's drunk every night."

"What did he want to kill himself for?"

"How should I know."

"How did he do it?"

"He hung himself with a rope."

"Who cut him down?"

"His niece."

"Why did they do it?"

"Fear for his soul."

"How much money has he got?"

"He's got plenty."

"He must be eighty years old."

"Anyway I should say he was eighty."

"I wish he would go home. I never get to bed before three o'clock. What kind of hour is that to go to bed?"

"He stays up because he likes it."

"He's lonely. I'm not lonely. I have a wife waiting in bed for me."

"He had a wife once too."

"A wife would be no good to him now."

"You can't tell. He might be better with a wife."

"His niece looks after him."

"I know. You said she cut him down."*

"I wouldn't want to be that old. An old man is a nasty thing."

"Not always. This old man is clean. He drinks without spilling. Even now, drunk. Look at him."

"I don't want to look at him. I wish he would go home. He has no regard for those who must work."

The old man looked from his glass across the square, then over at the waiters.

"Another brandy," he said, pointing to his glass. The waiter who was in a hurry came over.

"Finished," he said, speaking with that omission of syntax stupid people employ when talking to drunken people or foreigners. "No more tonight. Close now."

"Another," said the old man.

"No. Finished." The waiter wiped the edge of the table with a towel and shook his head.

The old man stood up, slowly counted the saucers, took a leather coin purse from his pocket and paid for the drinks, leaving half a peseta tip.

* There has been much discussion regarding the confused dialogue in this story. Very likely, "You said she cut him down" belongs on the line above, making the passage read as follows:

Young waiter: "His niece looks after him. You said she cut him down."
Old waiter: "I know."

See John V. Hagopian, "Tidying Up Hemingway's Clean, Well-lighted Place." *Studies in Short Fiction*, I (Winter 1964), p. 146.

The waiter watched him go down the street, a very old man walking unsteadily but with dignity.

"Why didn't you let him stay and drink?" the unhurried waiter asked. They were putting up the shutters. "It is not half-past two."

"I want to go home to bed."

"What is an hour?"

"More to me than to him."

"An hour is the same."

"You talk like an old man yourself. He can buy a bottle and drink at home."

"It's not the same."

"No, it is not," agreed the waiter with a wife. He did not wish to be unjust. He was only in a hurry.

"And you? You have no fear of going home before your usual hour?"

"Are you trying to insult me?"

"No, hombre, only to make a joke."

"No," the waiter who was in a hurry said, rising from pulling down the metal shutters. "I have confidence. I am all confidence."

"You have youth, confidence, and a job," the older waiter said. "You have everything."

"And what do you lack?"

"Everything but work."

"You have everything I have."

"No. I have never had confidence and I am not young."

"Come on. Stop talking nonsense and lock up."

"I am of those who like to stay late at the café," the older waiter said. "With all those who do not want to go to bed. With all those who need a light for the night."

"I want to go home and into bed."

"We are of two different kinds," the older waiter said. He was now dressed to go home. "It is not only a question of youth and confidence although those things are very beautiful. Each night I am reluctant to close up because there may be some one who needs the café."

"Hombre, there are bodegas open all night long."

"You do not understand. This is a clean and pleasant café. It is well lighted. The light is very good and also, now, there are shadows of the leaves."

"Good night," said the younger waiter.

"Good night," the other said. Turning off the electric light

479

he continued the conversation with himself. It is the light of course but it is necessary that the place be clean and pleasant. You do not want music. Certainly you do not want music. Nor can you stand before a bar with dignity although that is all that is provided for these hours. What did he fear? It was not fear or dread. It was a nothing that he knew too well. It was all a nothing and a man was nothing too. It was only that and light was all it needed and a certain cleanness and order. Some lived in it and never felt it but he knew it all was nada y pues nada y nada y pues nada. Our nada who art in nada, nada be thy name thy kingdom nada thy will be nada in nada as it is in nada. Give us this nada our daily nada and nada us our nada as we nada our nadas and nada us not into nada but deliver us from nada; pues nada. Hail nothing full of nothing, nothing is with thee. He smiled and stood before a bar with a shining steam pressure coffee machine.

"What's yours?" asked the barman.

"Nada."

"Otro loco mas," said the barman and turned away.

"A little cup," said the waiter.

The barman poured it for him.

"The light is very bright and pleasant but the bar is unpolished," the waiter said.

The barman looked at him but did not answer. It was too late at night for conversation.

"You want another copita?" the barman asked.

"No, thank you," said the waiter and went out. He disliked bars and bodegas. A clean, well-lighted café was a very different thing. Now, without thinking further, he would go home to his room. He would lie in the bed and finally, with daylight, he would go to sleep. After all, he said to himself, it is probably only insomnia. Many must have it.

John Steinbeck

THE WHITE QUAIL

Since John Steinbeck often depicts simple, rudimentary folk in his fiction, he, like Hemingway, is sometimes described as a primitivist. From another view, his involvement in sociological problems and his obvious sympathy for the underdog place him among the proletarian writers. Neither primitivism nor proletarianism, however, makes allowance for yet a third and perhaps more durable quality in his work: a concern with abstract philosophical values which often leads him into symbolism and near-mysticism. His desire that no "tag" of any kind be "pinned" on him has been realized, for his work transcends narrow classification. He is simply a thoughtful, sincere writer who sees mankind in the grip of hard and confusing battles; yet he can be strongly affirmative in his attitude toward life.

   Steinbeck was born in Salinas, California, in 1902, and, during his high school years there, worked on nearby farms and in local laboratories. At Stanford University, which he attended intermittently from 1919 through 1925, he took the courses which interested him rather than those which would lead to a degree. Having already decided on writing as a career, he supported himself and enlarged his experience by working for several years at a variety of jobs: as bricklayer, ranch hand, carpenter, fruit picker, newspaper reporter in New York, and caretaker of a Lake Tahoe estate. A conscientious worker, he reputedly wrote three or four novels before his first, *Cup of Gold,* based on the life of the pirate Henry Morgan, was published in 1929; but neither this one nor his next two, *The Pastures of Heaven* (1932) and *To a God Unknown* (1933), brought him critical or financial success. *Tortilla Flat* (1935), however, was highly successful. With the publication of *In Dubious Battle*

483

(1936), *Of Mice and Men* (1937), and especially of *The Grapes of Wrath* (1939)—for which he was awarded the Pulitzer Prize in 1940—he established himself securely in the front rank of contemporary writers. His later activities have included leading a research expedition to the Galapagos Islands, serving for a period during World War II as a foreign correspondent, and taking a journey through the Soviet Union with the photographer Robert Capa. His most recent works—among which are *The Pearl* (1947), *The Wayward Bus* (1947), *Burning Bright* (1950), *Sweet Thursday* (1954), and *East of Eden* (1955)—have not added substantially to his artistic stature; yet on the strength of his literary achievement as a whole, he was awarded the Nobel Prize in 1962.

In his short stories—*The Long Valley* (1938) is his only collected volume—Steinbeck often infuses realistic, matter-of-fact objects or events with a symbolic meaning. By this means, he better dramatizes a character relationship or a psychological situation. Through the symbolic use of the garden and the quail in "The White Quail," the husband's act in killing the quail assumes the significance of being the spiritual murder of his dominating wife.

the white quail

The wall opposite the fireplace in the living-room was a big dormer window stretching from the cushioned window seats almost to the ceiling—small diamond panes set in lead. From the window, preferably if you were sitting on the window seat, you could look across the garden and up the hill. There was a stretch of shady lawn under the garden oaks—around each oak there was a circle of carefully tended earth in which grew cinerarias, big ones with loads of flowers so heavy they bent the stems over, and ranging in color from scarlet to ultramarine. At the edge of the lawn, a line of fuchsias grew like little symbolic trees. In front of the fuchsias lay a shallow garden pool, the coping flush with the lawn for a very good reason.

Right at the edge of the garden, the hill started up, wild with cascara bushes and poison oak, with dry grass and live oak, very wild. If you didn't go around to the front of the house you couldn't tell it was on the very edge of the town.

Mary Teller, Mrs. Harry E. Teller, that is, knew the window and the garden were Right and she had a very good reason for knowing. Hadn't she picked out the place where the house and the garden would be years ago? Hadn't she seen the house and the garden a thousand times while the place was still a dry flat against the shoulder of a hill? For that matter, hadn't she, during five years, looked at every attentive man and wondered whether he and that garden would go together? She didn't think so much, "Would this man like such a garden?" but, "Would the garden like such a man?" For the garden was herself, and after all she had to marry some one she liked.

When she met Harry Teller, the garden seemed to like him. It may have surprised him a little when, after he had proposed and was waiting sulkily for his answer, as men do, Mary broke into a description of a big dormer window and a garden with a lawn and oak trees and cinerarias and then a wild hill.

He said, "Of course," rather perfunctorily.

Mary asked, "Do you think it's silly?"

He was waiting a little sullenly. "Of course not."

And then she remembered that he had proposed to her, and she accepted him, and let him kiss her. She said, "There will be a little cement pool flush with the lawn. Do you know why? Well, there are more birds on that hill than you'd ever think, yellowhammers and wild canaries and red-wing blackbirds, and of course sparrows and linnets, and lots of quail. Of course they'll be coming down to drink there, won't they?"

She was very pretty. He wanted to kiss her over and over, and she let him. "And fuchsias," she said. "Don't forget fuchsias. They're like little tropical Christmas trees. We'll have to have the lawn raked every day to keep the oak leaves clear."

He laughed at her. "You're a funny little bug. The lot isn't bought, and the house isn't built, and the garden isn't planted; and already you're worrying about oak leaves on the lawn. You're so pretty. You make me kind of—hungry."

That startled her a little. A little expression of annoyance crossed her face. But nevertheless she let him kiss her again, and then sent him home and went to her room, where she had a little blue writing desk and on it a copy-book to write things in. She took up a pen, of which the handle was a peacock feather, and she wrote, "Mary Teller" over and over again. Once or twice she wrote, "Mrs. Harry E. Teller."

2

The lot was bought and the house was built, and they were married. Mary drew a careful plan of the garden, and when the workmen were putting it in she didn't leave them alone for a moment. She knew to an inch where everything should be. And she drew the shape of the shallow pool for the cement workers, a kind of heart-shaped pool with no point at the bottom, with gradually sloping edges so the birds could drink easily.

Harry watched her with admiration. "Who could tell that such a pretty girl could have so much efficiency," he said.

That pleased her, too; and she was very happy, so that she said, "You can plant some of the things you like in the garden, if you want."

"No, Mary, I like too much to see your own mind coming out in the garden. You do it all your own way."

She loved him for that; but after all, it was her garden. She had invented it, and willed it, and she had worked out the colors too, so carefully. It really wouldn't have been nice, if for instance, Harry had wanted some flowers that didn't go with the garden.

At last the green lawn was up, and the cinerarias around the oak trees bloomed in sunken pots. The little fuchsia trees had been moved in so carefully that not a leaf wilted.

The window seats behind the dormer windows were piled with cushions covered with bright, fadeless fabrics, for the sun shone in that window a good part of the day.

Mary waited until it was all done, all finished exactly as her mind had seen it; and then one evening when Harry came home from the office, she led him to the window seat. "You see," she said softly. "There it is, just the way I wanted it."

"It's beautiful," said Harry, "very beautiful."

"In a way I'm sad that it's done," she said. "But mostly I'm glad. We won't ever change it, will we, Harry? If a bush dies, we'll put another one just like it in the same place."

"Curious little bug," he said.

"Well, you see I've thought about it so long that it's part of me. If anything should be changed it would be like part of me being torn out."

He put out his hand to touch her, and then withdrew it. "I love you so much," he said, and then paused. "But I'm afraid of you, too."

She smiled quietly. "You? Afraid of me? What's there about me you can be afraid of?"

"Well, you're kind of untouchable. There's an inscrutability about you. Probably you don't even know it yourself. You're kind of like your own garden—fixed, and just so. I'm afraid to move around. I might disturb some of your plants."

Mary was pleased. "Dear," she said. "You let me do it. You made it my garden. Yes, you are dear." And she let him kiss her.

3

He was proud of her when people came in to dinner. She was so pretty, so cool and perfect. Her bowls of flowers were exquisite, and she talked about the garden modestly, hesitantly, almost as though she were talking about herself. Sometimes she took her guests into the garden. She pointed to a fuchsia tree. "I didn't know whether he would succeed," she said, just as though the plant were a person. "He ate a lot of plant food before he decided to come around." She smiled quietly to herself.

She was delightful when she worked in the garden. She wore a bright print dress, quite long in the skirt, and sleeveless. Somewhere she had found an old-fashioned sunbonnet. She wore good sturdy gloves to protect her hands. Harry liked to watch her going about with a bag and a big spoon, putting plant food about the roots of her flowers. He liked it, too, when they went out at night to kill slugs and snails. Mary held the flashlight while Harry did the actual killing, crushing the slugs and snails into oozy, bubbling masses. He knew it must be a disgusting business to her, but the light never wavered. "Brave girl," he thought. "She has a sturdiness in back of that fragile beauty." She made the hunts exciting too. "There's a big one, creep-

487

ing and creeping," she would say. "He's after that big bloom. Kill him! Kill him quickly!" They came into the house after the hunts laughing happily.

Mary was worried about the birds. "They don't come down to drink," she complained. "Not many of them. I wonder what's keeping them away."

"Maybe they aren't used to it yet. They'll come later. Maybe there's a cat around."

Her face flushed and she breathed deeply. Her pretty lips tightened away from her teeth. "If there's a cat, I'll put out poisoned fish," she cried. "I won't have a cat after my birds!"

Harry had to soothe her. "I'll tell you what I'll do. I'll buy an air gun. Then if a cat comes, we can shoot it, and it won't kill the cat, but it'll hurt, and the cat won't come back."

"Yes," she said more calmly. "That might be better."

The living-room was very pleasant at night. The fire burned up in a sheet of flame. If there was a moon, Mary turned off the lights and then they sat looking through the window at the cool blue garden and the dark oak trees. It was utterly calm and eternal out there. And then the garden ended and the dark thickets of the hill began.

"That's the enemy," Mary said one time. "That's the world that wants to get in, all rough and tangled and unkempt. But it can't get in because the fuchsias won't let it. That's what the fuchsias are there for, and they know it. The birds can get in. They live out in the wild, but they come to my garden for peace and for water." She laughed softly. "There's something profound in all that, Harry. I don't know quite what it is. The quail are beginning to come down now. At least a dozen were at the pool this evening."

He said, "I wish I could see the inside of your mind. It seems to flutter around, but it's a cool, collected mind. It's so—sure of itself."

Mary went to sit on his lap for a moment. "Not so awfully sure. You don't know, and I'm glad you don't."

4

One night when Harry was reading his paper under the lamp, Mary jumped up. "I left my garden scissors outside," she said. "The dew will rust them."

Harry looked over his paper. "Can't I get them for you?"

"No, I'll go. You couldn't find them." She went out into the garden and found the shears, and then she looked in the window, into the living-room. Harry was still reading his paper. The room was clear, like a picture, like the set of a play that was about to start. A curtain of fire waved up in the fireplace. Mary stood still and looked. There was the big, deep chair she had been sitting in a minute ago. What would she be doing if she hadn't come outside? Suppose only essence, only mind and sight had come, leaving Mary in the chair? She could almost see herself sitting there. Her round arms and long fingers were resting on the chair. Her delicate, sensitive face was in profile, looking reflectively into the firelight. "What is she thinking about?" Mary whispered. "I wonder what's going on in her mind. Will she get up? No, she's just sitting there. The neck of that dress is too wide, see how it slips sideways over the shoulder. But that's rather pretty. It looks careless, but neat and pretty. Now—she's smiling. She must be thinking something nice."

Suddenly Mary came to herself and realized what she had been doing. She was delighted. "There were two me's," she thought. "It was like having two lives, being able to see myself. That's wonderful. I wonder whether I can see it whenever I want to. I saw just what other people see when they look at me. I must tell Harry about that." But then a new picture formed; she saw herself explaining, trying to describe what had happened. She saw him looking over his paper with an intent, puzzled, almost pained look in his eyes. He tried so hard to understand when she told him things. He wanted to understand, and he never quite succeeded. If she told him about this vision tonight, he would ask questions. He would turn the thing over and over, trying to understand it, until finally he ruined it. He didn't want to spoil the things she told him, but he just couldn't help it. He needed too much light on things that light shriveled. No, she wouldn't tell him. She would want to come out and do it again, and she couldn't if he spoiled it for her.

Through the window she saw Harry put his paper down on his knee and look up at the door. She hurried in, showing him the shears to prove what she had gone for. "See, the rust was forming already. They'd've been all brown and nasty by morning."

He nodded and smiled at her. "It says in the paper we're going to have more trouble with that new loan bill. They put a lot of difficulties in our way. Somebody has to loan money when people want to borrow."

"I don't understand loans," she said. "Somebody told me your company had title to nearly every automobile in town."

He laughed. "Well, not all, but a good many of them, anyway. When times are a little bit hard, we make money."

"It sounds terrible," she observed. "It sounds like taking unfair advantage."

He folded the paper and put it on the table beside his chair. "No, I don't think it's unfair," he said. "The people must have the money, and we supply it. The law regulates the interest rate. We haven't anything to do with that."

She stretched her pretty arms and fingers on the chair, as she had seen them through the window. "I suppose it really isn't unfair," she said. "It just sounds as though you took advantage of people when they were down."

Harry looked seriously into the fire for a long time. Mary could see him, and she knew he was worrying about what she said. Well, it would do him no harm to see what business really was like. Things seemed righter when you did them than when you thought about them. A little mental house-cleaning mightn't be a bad thing for Harry.

After a little, he looked over at her. "Dear, you don't think it's unfair practice, do you?"

"Why, I don't know anything about loans. How can I tell what is fair?"

Harry insisted, "But do you feel it's unfair? Are you ashamed of my business? I wouldn't like it if you were."

Suddenly Mary felt very glad and pleased. "I'm not ashamed, silly. Everyone has a right to make a living. You do what you do well."

"You're sure, now?"

"Of course I'm sure, silly."

After she was in bed in her own little bedroom she heard a faint click and saw the door knob turn, and then turn slowly back. The door was locked. It was a signal; there were things Mary didn't like to talk about. The lock was an answer to a question, a clean, quick, decisive answer. It was peculiar about Harry, though. He always tried the door silently. It seemed as though he didn't want her to know he had tried it. But she always did know. He was sweet and gentle. It seemed to make him ashamed when he turned the knob and found the door locked.

Mary pulled the light chain, and when her eyes had become accustomed to the dark, she looked out the window at her garden in the half moonlight. Harry was sweet, and understanding, too. That time about the dog. He had come running into the house, really running. His face was so red and excited that Mary had a nasty shock. She thought there had been an accident. Later in the evening she had a headache from the shock. Harry had shouted, "Joe Adams—his Irish Terrier bitch had puppies. He's going to give me one! Thorough-bred stock, red as strawberries!" He had really wanted one of the pups. It hurt Mary that he couldn't have one. But she was proud of his quick understanding of the situation. When she explained how a dog would—do things on the plants of her garden, or even dig in her flower beds, how, worst of all, a dog would keep the birds away from the pool, Harry understood. He might have trouble with complicated things, like that vision from the garden, but he understood about the dog. Later in the evening, when her head ached, he soothed her and patted Florida Water on her head. That was the curse of imagination. Mary had seen, actually seen the dog in her garden, and the dug holes, and ruined plants. It was almost as bad as though it actually happened. Harry was ashamed, but really he couldn't help it if she had such an imagination. Mary couldn't blame him, how could he have known?

5

Late in the afternoon, when the sun had gone behind the hill, there was a time Mary called the really-garden-time. Then the high school girl was in from school and had taken charge of the kitchen. It was almost a sacred time. Mary walked out into the garden and across the lawn to a folding chair half behind one of the lawn oaks. She could watch the birds drinking in the pool from there. She could really feel the garden. When Harry came home from the office, he stayed in the house and read his paper until she came in from the garden, star-eyed. It made her unhappy to be disturbed.

The summer was just breaking. Mary looked into the kitchen and saw that everything was all right there. She went through the living-room and lighted the laid fire, and then she was ready for the garden. The sun had just dropped behind the hill, and the blue gauze of the evening had settled among the oaks.

Mary thought, "It's like millions of not quite invisible fairies coming into my garden. You can't see one of them, but the millions change the color of the air." She smiled to herself at the nice thought. The clipped lawn was damp and fresh with watering. The brilliant cinerarias threw little haloes of color into the air. The fuchsia trees were loaded with blooms. The buds, like little red Christmas tree ornaments, and the open blooms like ballet-skirted ladies. They were so right, the fuchsias, so absolutely right. And they discouraged the enemy on the other side, the brush and scrubby, untrimmed trees.

Mary walked across the lawn in the evening to her chair, and sat down. She could hear the birds gathering to come down to the pool. "Making up parties," she thought, "coming to my garden in the evening. How they must love it! How I would like to come to my garden for the first time. If I could be two people—'Good evening, come into the garden, Mary.' 'Oh, isn't it lovely.' 'Yes, I like it, especially at this time. Quiet, now, Mary. Don't frighten the birds.'" She sat as still as a mouse. Her lips were parted with expectancy. In the brush the quail twittered sharply. A yellowhammer dropped to the edge of the pool. Two little flycatchers flickered out over the water and stood still in the air, beating their wings. And then the quail ran out, with funny little steps. They stopped and cocked their heads, to see whether it was safe. Their leader, a big fellow with a crest like a black question mark, sounded the buglelike "All clear" call, and the band came down to drink.

And then it happened, the wonderful thing. Out of the brush ran a white quail. Mary froze. Yes, it was a quail, no doubt of it, and white as snow. Oh, this was wonderful! A shiver of pleasure, a bursting of pleasure swelled in Mary's breast. She held her breath. The dainty little white hen quail went to the other side of the pool, away from the ordinary quail. She paused and looked around, and then dipped her beak in the water.

"Why," Mary cried to herself, "she's like me!" A powerful ecstasy quivered in her body. "She's like the essence of me, an essence boiled down to utter purity. She must be the queen of the quail. She makes every lovely thing that ever happened to me one thing."

The white quail dipped her beak again and threw back her head to swallow.

The memories welled in Mary and filled her chest. Something sad, always something sad. The packages that came; untying the string was the ecstasy. The thing in the package was never quite——

The marvelous candy from Italy. "Don't eat it, dear. It's prettier than it's good." Mary never ate it, but looking at it was an ecstasy like this.

"What a pretty girl Mary is. She's like a gentian, so quiet." The hearing was an ecstasy like this.

"Mary dear, be very brave now. Your father has—passed away."
The first moment of loss was an ecstasy like this.

The white quail stretched a wing backward and smoothed down the feathers with her beak. "This is the me that was everything beautiful. This is the center of me, my heart."

6

The blue air became purple in the garden. The fuchsia buds blazed like little candles. And then a gray shadow moved out of the brush. Mary's mouth dropped open. She sat paralyzed with fear. A gray cat crept like death out of the brush, crept toward the pool and the drinking birds. Mary stared in horror. Her hand rose up to her tight throat. Then she broke the paralysis. She screamed terribly. The quail flew away on muttering wings. The cat bounded back into the brush. Still Mary screamed and screamed. Harry ran out of the house crying, "Mary! What is it, Mary?"

She shuddered when he touched her. She began to cry hysterically. He took her up in his arms and carried her into the house, and into her own room. She lay quivering on the bed. "What was it, dear? What frightened you?"

"It was a cat," she moaned. "It was creeping up on the birds." She sat up; her eyes blazed. "Harry, you must put out poison. To-night you simply must put out some poison for that cat."

"Lie back, dear. You've had a shock."

"Promise me you'll put out poison." She looked closely at him and saw a rebellious light come into his eyes. "Promise."

"Dear," he apologized, "some dog might get it. Animals suffer terribly when they get poison."

"I don't care," she cried. "I don't want any animals in my garden, any kind."

"No," he said. "I won't do that. No, I can't do that. But I'll get up early in the morning. I'll take the new air gun and I'll shoot that cat so he'll never come back. The air gun shoots hard. It'll make a hurt the cat won't forget."

It was the first thing he had ever refused. She didn't know how to combat it; but her head ached, terribly. When it ached its worst he tried to make it up to her for refusing the poison. He kept a little pad soaked with Florida Water, and he patted it on her forehead. She wondered whether she should tell him about the white quail. He wouldn't believe it. But maybe if he knew how important it was, he might poison the cat. She waited until her nerves were calm before she told him. "Dear, there was a white quail in the garden."

"A white quail? Are you sure it wasn't a pigeon?"

There it was. Right from the first he spoiled it. "I know quail," she cried. "It was quite close to me. A white hen quail."

"That would be a thing to see," he said. "I never heard of one."

"But I tell you I saw it."

He dabbed at her forehead. "Well, I suppose it was an albino. No pigment in the feathers, something like that."

She was growing hysterical again. "You don't understand. That white quail was me, the secret me that no one can ever get at, the me that's way inside." Harry's face was contorted with the struggle to understand.

"Can't you see, dear? The cat was after me. It was going to kill me. That's why I want to poison it." She studied his face. No, he didn't understand, he couldn't. Why had she told him? If she hadn't been so upset she never would have told him.

"I'll set my alarm clock," he assured her. "Tomorrow morning I'll give that cat something to remember."

At ten o'clock he left her alone. And when he had gone Mary got up and locked the door.

His alarm-clock bell awakened Mary in the morning. It was still dark in her room, but she could see the gray light of morning through the window. She heard Harry dressing quietly. He tiptoed past her door and went outside, closing the door silently for fear of awakening her. He carried the new shining air gun in his hand. The fresh gray morning air made him throw back his shoulders and step lightly over the damp lawn. He walked to the corner of the garden and lay down on his stomach in the wet grass.

The garden grew lighter. Already the quail were twittering metallically. The little brown band came to the edge of the brush and cocked their heads. Then the big leader called, "All's well," and his charges ran with quick steps to the pool. A moment later the white quail followed them. She went to the other side of the pool and dipped her beak and threw back her head. Harry raised the gun. The white quail tipped her head and looked toward him. The air gun spat with a vicious whisper. The quail flew off into the brush. But the white quail fell over and shuddered a moment, and lay still on the lawn.

Harry walked slowly over to her and picked her up. "I didn't

mean to kill it," he said to himself. "I just wanted to scare it away."
He looked at the white bird in his hand. Right in the head, right
under the eye the BB shot had gone. Harry stepped to the line of
fuchsias and threw the quail up into the brush. The next moment he
put down the gun and crashed up through the undergrowth. He found
the white quail, carried her far up the hill and buried her under a
pile of leaves.

Mary heard him pass her door. "Harry, did you shoot the cat?"

"It won't ever come back," he said through the door.

"Well, I hope you killed it, but I don't want to hear the details."

Harry walked on into the living-room and sat down in a big
chair. The room was still dusky, but through the big dormer window
the garden glowed and the tops of the lawn oaks were afire with sunshine.

"What a skunk I am," Harry said to himself. "What a dirty
skunk, to kill a thing she loved so much." He dropped his head and
looked at the floor. "I'm lonely," he said. "Oh, Lord, I'm so lonely!"

WINTER NIGHT

Although Kay Boyle now resides in the United States, she has spent more of her adult life in Europe than in this country. Despite the fact that her residence in foreign countries was not a matter of deliberate choice as it was with Henry James, it has given her fiction, as it did James', a strongly international character; in fact, she has said: "The longer I live and the more I write, the more completely am I convinced that my interest in people and in writing is of so unnational a character that, for me, the question of 'roots' in any particular soil or tradition is not of any moment."[1] Even though "unnational," the intermingled cultures of Europe nevertheless provide a singularly appropriate backcrop for the universal themes of love, marital maladjustment, and death with which her fiction is often concerned.

Miss Boyle was born in 1903, in St. Paul, Minnesota, but spent little time there, for during her childhood her family traveled widely in Europe and shifted their residence in America from St. Paul to Philadelphia, Atlantic City, Washington, and Cincinnati. Stimulated by her mother's encouragement, the interest she displayed from early youth in the creative arts—painting, music, and writing—was further developed at the Shipley School, Bryn Mawr, at the Ohio Mechanics Institute in Cincinnati, and at the Cincinnati Conservatory of Music. She then went to New York to begin her writing career and for a time did free lance reviewing, and worked on the staff of the magazine *Broom*. In 1922, Miss Boyle married Richard Brault, a French engineering student, and in 1923 went to France to live. From then until 1941 she continued to live abroad—in England, Austria, and Germany, but

[1]F. B. Millet, *Contemporary American Authors*, p. 256.

mainly in France. Subsequently, she has twice re-married; her last husband was Joseph M. Francken-stein, a native of Austria and a naturalized American. She is the mother of six children: two from the last marriage, and four from her former marriages. Among the honors she has won by her writing are a Guggen-heim fellowship in 1934 and the O. Henry Memorial first prize award in 1934 for the story "White Horses of Vienna." Her collections of short stories include *Wedding Day* (1930), *The First Lover* (1933), *The White Horses of Vienna* (1937), *Crazy Hunter* (1940), and *Thirty Stories* (1946). She has also published over a dozen novels and two volumes of poetry.

Personal suffering resulting from broken human ties and the dislocation of families by the alien forces of war and political conflicts provide the material for some of her best stories. In "Winter Night" the mother-daughter-babysitter relationship in the foreground re-ceives an ironic overtone from the background theme of the disruption of the normal order of things by war.

away of telling us now Felicia feels.

winter night

There is a time of apprehension which begins with the begin-ning of darkness, and to which only the speech of love can lend security. It is there, in abeyance, at the end of every day, not urgent enough to be given the name of fear but rather of concern for how the hours are to be reprieved from fear, and those who have forgotten how it was when they were children can remember nothing of this. It may begin around five o'clock on a winter afternoon when the light outside is dying in the windows. At that hour the New York apartment in which Felicia lived was filled with shadows, and the little girl would wait alone in the living room, looking out at the winter-stripped trees that stood black in the park against the isolated ovals of unclean snow. Now it was January, and the day had been a cold one; the water of the artificial lake was frozen fast, but because of the cold and the coming darkness, the skaters had ceased to move across its surface. The street that lay between the park and the apartment house was wide, and the two-way streams of cars and busses, some with their headlamps already shining, advanced and halted, halted and poured swiftly on to the tempo of the traffic signals' altering lights. The time of apprehension had set in, and Felicia, who was seven, stood at the window in the evening and waited before she asked the question. When the signals below would change from red to green again, or when the double-decker bus would turn the corner below, she would ask it. The words of it were already there, tentative in her mouth, when the answer came from the far end of the hall.

"Your mother," said the voice among the sound of kitchen things, "she telephoned up before you came in from nursery school. She won't be back in time for supper. I was to tell you a sitter was coming in from the sitting parents' place."

Felicia turned back from the window into the obscurity of the living room, and she looked toward the open door, and into the hall beyond it where the light from the kitchen fell in a clear yellow angle across the wall and onto the strip of carpet. Her hands were cold, and she put them in her jacket pockets as she walked carefully across the living-room rug and stopped at the edge of light.

"Will she be home late?" she said.

For a moment there was the sound of water running in the kitchen, a long way away, and then the sound of the water ceased, and the high, Southern voice went on:

"She'll come home when she gets ready to come home. That's all I have to say. If she wants to spend two dollars and fifty cents and ten cents' carfare on top of that three or four nights out of the week for a sitting parent to come in here and sit, it's her own business. It certainly ain't nothing to do with you or me. She makes her money, just like the rest of us does. She works all day down there in the office, or whatever it is, just like the rest of us works, and she's entitled to spend her money like she wants to spend it. There's no law in the world against buying your own freedom. Your mother and me, we're just buying our own freedom, that's all we're doing. And we're not doing nobody no harm."

"Do you know who she's having supper with?" said Felicia from the edge of the dark. There was one more step to take, and then she would be standing in the light that fell on the strip of carpet, but she did not take the step.

"Do I know who she's having supper with?" the voice cried out in what might have been derision, and there was the sound of dishes striking the metal ribs of the drainboard by the sink. "Maybe it's Mr. Van Johnson, or Mr. Frank Sinatra, or maybe it's just the Duke of Wincers for the evening. All I know is you're having soft-boiled egg and spinach and applesauce for supper, and you're going to have it quick now because the time is getting away."

The voice from the kitchen had no name. It was as variable as the faces and figures of the women who came and sat in the evenings. Month by month the voice in the kitchen altered to another voice, and the sitting parents were no more than lonely aunts of an evening or two who sometimes returned and sometimes did not to this apartment in which they had sat before. Nobody stayed anywhere very long any more, Felicia's mother told her. It was part of the time in which you lived, and part of the life of the city, but when the fathers came back, all this would be miraculously changed. Perhaps you would live in a house again, a small one, with fir trees on either side of the short brick walk, and Father would drive up every night from the station just after darkness set in. When Felicia thought of this, she stepped quickly into the clear angle of light, and she left the dark of the living room behind her and ran softly down the hall.

The drop-leaf table stood in the kitchen between the refrigerator and the sink, and Felicia sat down at the place that was set. The voice at the sink was speaking still, and while Felicia ate it did not cease to speak until the bell of the front door rang abruptly. The girl walked around the table and went down the hall, wiping her dark palms in her apron, and, from the drop-leaf table, Felicia watched her step from the angle of light into darkness and open the door.

"You put in an early appearance," the girl said, and the woman who had rung the bell came into the hall. The door closed behind her, and the girl showed her into the living room, and lit the lamp on the bookcase, and the shadows were suddenly bleached away. But when the girl turned, the woman turned from the living room too and followed her, humbly and in silence, to the threshold of the kitchen. "Sometimes they keep me standing around waiting after it's time for me to be getting on home, the sitting parents do," the girl said, and she picked up the last two dishes from the table and put them in the

500   boyle

sink. The woman who stood in the doorway was a small woman, and when she undid the white silk scarf from around her head, Felicia saw that her hair was black. She wore it parted in the middle, and it had not been cut, but was drawn back loosely into a knot behind her head. She had very clean white gloves on, and her face was pale, and there was a look of sorrow in her soft black eyes. "Sometimes I have to stand out there in the hall with my hat and coat on, waiting for the sitting parents to turn up," the girl said, and, as she turned on the water in the sink, the contempt she had for them hung on the kitchen air. "But you're ahead of time," she said, and she held the dishes, first one and then the other, under the flow of steaming water.

The woman in the doorway wore a neat black coat, not a new-looking coat, and it had no fur on it, but it had a smooth velvet collar and velvet lapels. She did not move, or smile, and she gave no sign that she had heard the girl speaking above the sound of water at the sink. She simply stood looking at Felicia, who sat at the table with the milk in her glass not finished yet.

"Are you the child?" she said at last, and her voice was low, and the pronunciation of the words a little strange.

"Yes, this here's Felicia," the girl said, and the dark hands dried the dishes and put them away. "You drink up your milk quick now, Felicia, so's I can rinse your glass."

"I will wash the glass," said the woman. "I would like to wash the glass for her," and Felicia sat looking across the table at the face in the doorway that was filled with such unspoken grief. "I will wash the glass for her and clean off the table," the woman was saying quietly. "When the child is finished, she will show me where her night things are."

"The others, they wouldn't do anything like that," the girl said, and she hung the dishcloth over the rack. "They wouldn't put their hand to housework, the sitting parents. That's where they got the name for them," she said.

Whenever the front door closed behind the girl in the evening, it would usually be that the sitting parent who was there would take up a book of fairy stories and read aloud for a while to Felicia; or else would settle herself in the big chair in the living room and begin to tell the words of a story in drowsiness to her, while Felicia took off her clothes in the bedroom, and folded them, and put her pajamas on, and brushed her teeth, and did her hair. But this time, that was not the way it happened. Instead, the woman sat down on the other chair at the kitchen table, and she began at once to speak, not of good fairies or bad, or of animals endowed with human speech, but to speak quietly, in spite of the eagerness behind her words, of a thing that seemed of singular importance to her.

"It is strange that I should have been sent here tonight," she said, her eyes moving slowly from feature to feature of Felicia's face, "for you look like a child that I knew once, and this is the anniversary of that child."

"Did she have hair like mine?" Felicia asked quickly, and she did not keep her eyes fixed on the unfinished glass of milk in shyness any more.

"Yes, she did. She had hair like yours," said the woman, and her glance paused for a moment on the locks which fell straight and thick on the shoulders of Felicia's dress. It may have been that she thought to stretch out her hand and touch the ends of Felicia's hair, for her fingers stirred as they lay clasped together on the table, and then they relapsed into passivity again. "But it is not the hair alone, it is the delicacy of your face, too, and your eyes the same, filled with the same spring lilac color," the woman said, pronouncing the words carefully. "She had little coats of golden fur on her arms and legs," she said, "and when we were closed up there, the lot of us in the cold, I used to make her laugh when I told her that the fur that was so pretty, like a little fawn's skin on her arms, would always help to keep her warm."

"And did it keep her warm?" asked Felicia, and she gave a little jerk of laughter as she looked down at her own legs hanging under the table, with the bare calves thin and covered with a down of hair.

"It did not keep her warm enough," the woman said, and now the mask of grief had come back upon her face. "So we used to take everything we could spare from ourselves, and we would sew them into cloaks and other kinds of garments for her and for the other children. . . ."

"Was it a school?" said Felicia when the woman's voice had ceased to speak.

"No," said the woman softly, "it was not a school, but still there were a lot of children there. It was a camp—that was the name the place had; it was a camp. It was a place where they put people until they could decide what was to be done with them." She sat with her hands clasped, silent a moment, looking at Felicia. "That little dress you have on," she said, not saying the words to anybody, scarcely saying them aloud. "Oh, she would have liked that little dress, the little buttons shaped like hearts, and the white collar——"

"I have four school dresses," Felicia said. "I'll show them to you. How many dresses did she have?"

"Well, there, you see, there in the camp," said the woman, "she did not have any dresses except the little skirt and the pullover. That was all she had. She had brought just a handkerchief of her belongings with her, like everybody else—just enough for three days away from home was what they told us, so she did not have enough to last the winter. But she had her ballet slippers," the woman said, and her clasped fingers did not move. "She had brought them because she thought during her three days away from home she would have the time to practice her ballet."

"I've been to the ballet," Felicia said suddenly, and she said it so eagerly that she stuttered a little as the words came out of her mouth. She slipped quickly down from the chair and went around the table to where the woman sat. Then she took one of the woman's hands away from the other that held it fast, and she pulled her toward the door. "Come into the living room and I'll do a pirouette for you," she said, and then she stopped speaking, her eyes halted on the woman's face. "Did she—did the little girl—could she do a pirouette very well?" she said.

"Yes, she could. At first she could," said the woman, and Felicia felt uneasy now at the sound of sorrow in her words. "But after that she was hungry. She was hungry all winter," she said in a low voice. "We were all hungry, but the children were the hungriest. Even now," she said, and her voice went suddenly savage, "when I see milk like that, clean, fresh milk standing in a glass, I want to cry out loud, I want to beat my hands on the table, because it did not have to be . . ." She had drawn her fingers abruptly away from Felicia now, and Felicia stood before her, cast off, forlorn, alone again in the time of apprehension. "That was three years ago," the woman was saying, and one hand was lifted, as in weariness, to shade her face. "It was somewhere else, it was in another country," she said, and behind her hand her eyes were turned upon the substance of a world in which Felicia had played no part.

"Did—did the little girl cry when she was hungry?" Felicia asked, and the woman shook her head.

"Sometimes she cried," she said, "but not very much. She was very quiet. One night when she heard the other children crying, she

503

said to me, 'You know, they are not crying because they want something to eat. They are crying because their mothers have gone away.' "

"Did the mothers have to go out to supper?" Felicia asked, and she watched the woman's face for the answer.

"No," said the woman. She stood up from her chair, and now that she put her hand on the little girl's shoulder, Felicia was taken into the sphere of love and intimacy again. "Shall we go into the other room, and you will do your pirouette for me?" the woman said, and they went from the kitchen and down the strip of carpet on which the clear light fell. In the front room, they paused hand in hand in the glow of the shaded lamp, and the woman looked about her, at the books, the low tables with the magazines and ash trays on them, the vase of roses on the piano, looking with dark, scarcely seeing eyes at these things that had no reality at all. It was only when she saw the little white clock on the mantelpiece that she gave any sign, and then she said quickly: "What time does your mother put you to bed?"

Felicia waited a moment, and in the interval of waiting the woman lifted one hand and, as if in reverence, touched Felicia's hair.

"What time did the little girl you knew in the other place go to bed?" Felicia asked.

"Ah, God, I do not know, I do not remember," the woman said.

"Was she your little girl?" said Felicia softly, stubbornly.

"No," said the woman. "She was not mine. At least, at first she was not mine. She had a mother, a real mother, but the mother had to go away."

"Did she come back late?" asked Felicia.

"No, ah, no, she could not come back, she never came back," the woman said, and now she turned, her arm around Felicia's shoulders, and she sat down in the low soft chair. "Why am I saying all this to you, why am I doing it?" she cried out in grief, and she held Felicia close against her. "I had thought to speak of the anniversary to you, and that was all, and now I am saying these other things to you. Three years ago today, exactly, the little girl became my little girl because her mother went away. That is all there is to it. There is nothing more."

Felicia waited another moment, held close against the woman, and listening to the swift, strong heartbeats in the woman's breast.

"But the mother," she said then in the small, persistent voice, "did she take a taxi when she went?"

"This is the way it used to happen," said the woman, speaking in hopelessness and bitterness in the softly lighted room. "Every week they used to come into the place where we were and they would read a list of names out. Sometimes it would be the names of children they would read out, and then a little later they would have to go away. And sometimes it would be the grown people's names, the names of the mothers or big sisters, or other women's names. The men were not with us. The fathers were somewhere else, in another place."

"Yes," Felicia said. "I know."

"We had been there only a little while, maybe ten days or maybe not so long," the woman went on, holding Felicia against her still, "when they read the name of the little girl's mother out, and that afternoon they took her away."

"What did the little girl do?" Felicia said.

"She wanted to think up the best way of getting out so that she could go find her mother," said the woman, "but she could not think of anything good enough until the third or fourth day. And then she tied her ballet slippers up in the handkerchief again, and she went up to the guard standing at the door." The woman's voice was gentle, controlled now. "She asked the guard please to open the door so that she could go out. 'This is Thursday,' she said, 'and every Tuesday and Thursday I have my ballet lessons. If I miss a ballet lesson, they do not count the money off, so my mother would be just be paying for nothing, and she cannot afford to pay for nothing. I missed my ballet lesson on Tuesday,' she said to the guard, 'and I must not miss it again today.'"

Felicia lifted her head from the woman's shoulder, and she shook her hair back and looked in question and wonder at the woman's face.

"And did the man let her go?" she said.

"No, he did not. He could not do that," said the woman. "He was a soldier and he had to do what he was told. So every evening after her mother went, I used to brush the little girl's hair for her," the woman went on saying. "And while I brushed it, I used to tell her the stories of the ballets. Sometimes I would begin with *Narcissus*," the woman said, and she parted Felicia's locks with her fingers, "so if you will go and get your brush now, I will tell it while I brush your hair."

"Oh, yes," said Felicia, and she made two whirls as she went quickly to the bedroom. On the way back, she stopped and held on to the piano with the fingers of one hand while she went up on her toes. "Did you see me? Did you see me standing on my toes?" she called to the woman, and the woman sat smiling in love and contentment at her.

"Yes, wonderful, really wonderful," she said. "I am sure I have never seen anyone do it so well." Felicia came spinning toward her, whirling in pirouette after pirouette, and she flung herself down in the chair close to her, with her thin bones pressed against the woman's soft, wide hip. The woman took the silver-backed, monogrammed brush and the tortoise-shell comb in her hands, and now she began to brush Felicia's hair. "We did not have any soap at all and not very much water to wash in, so I never could fix her as nicely and prettily as I wanted to," she said, and the brush stroked regularly, carefully down, caressing the shape of Felicia's head.

"If there wasn't very much water, then how did she do her teeth?" Felicia said.

"She did not do her teeth," said the woman, and she drew the comb through Felicia's hair. "There were not any toothbrushes or tooth paste, or anything like that."

Felicia waited a moment, constructing the unfamiliar scene of it in silence, and then she asked the tentative question.

"Do I have to do my teeth tonight?" she said.

"No," said the woman, and she was thinking of something else, "you do not have to do your teeth."

"If I am your little girl tonight, can I pretend there isn't enough water to wash?" said Felicia.

"Yes," said the woman, "you can pretend that if you like. You do not have to wash," she said, and the comb passed lightly through Felicia's hair.

"Will you tell me the story of the ballet?" said Felicia, and the rhythm of the brushing was like the soft, slow rocking of sleep.

"Yes," said the woman. "In the first one, the place is a forest glade with little pale birches growing in it, and they have green veils over their faces and green veils drifting from their fingers, because it is the springtime. There is the music of a flute," said the woman's voice softly, softly, "and creatures of the wood are dancing——"

"But the mother," Felicia said as suddenly as if she had been awaked from sleep. "What did the little girl's mother say when she didn't do her teeth and didn't wash at night?"

"The mother was not there, you remember," said the woman, and the brush moved steadily in her hand. "But she did send one little letter back. Sometimes the people who went away were able to do that. The mother wrote it in a train, standing up in a car that had no seats," she said, and she might have been telling the story of the ballet still, for her voice was gentle and the brush did not falter on Felicia's hair. "There were perhaps a great many other people standing up in the train with her, perhaps all trying to write their little letters on the bits of paper they had managed to hide on them, or that they had found in forgotten corners as they traveled. When they had written their letters, then they must try to slip them out through the boards of the car in which they journeyed, standing up," said the woman, "and these letters fell down on the tracks under the train, or they were blown into the fields or onto the country roads, and if it was a kind person who picked them up, he would seal them in envelopes and send them to where they were addressed to go. So a letter came back like this from the little girl's mother," the woman said, and the brush followed the comb, the comb the brush in steady pursuit through Felicia's hair. "It said good-by to the little girl, and it said please to take care of her. It said: 'Whoever reads this letter in the camp, please take good care of my little girl for me, and please have her tonsils looked at by a doctor if this is possible to do.'"

"And then," said Felicia softly, persistently, "what happened to the little girl?"

"I do not know. I cannot say," the woman said. But now the brush and comb had ceased to move, and in the silence Felicia turned her thin, small body on the chair, and she and the woman suddenly put their arms around each other. "They must all be asleep now, all of them," the woman said, and in the silence that fell on them again, they held each other closer. "They must be quietly asleep somewhere, and not crying all night because they are hungry and because they are cold. For three years I have been saying 'They must all be asleep, and the cold and the hunger and the seasons or night or day or nothing matters to them——'"

It was after midnight when Felicia's mother put her key in the lock of the front door, and pushed it open, and stepped into the hallway. She walked quickly to the living room, and just across the threshold she slipped the three blue foxskins from her shoulders and dropped them, with her little velvet bag, upon the chair. The room was quiet, so quiet that she could hear the sound of breathing in it, and no one spoke to her in greeting as she crossed toward the bedroom door. And then, as startling as a slap across her delicately tinted face, she saw the woman lying sleeping on the divan, and Felicia, in her school dress still, asleep within the woman's arms.

Eudora Welty

LIVVIE

Few contemporary writers of short fiction have enjoyed such high esteem as has Eudora Welty, and the various writing awards she has won are palpable evidence of this critical approbation. These include four O. Henry Memorial prizes, two Guggenheim awards, and a $1,000 award from the American Academy of Arts and Letters for her short stories, and, in 1955, the Howells Medal, given every five years by the Academy for the most distinguished work of American fiction written during that period. Although her output to date is slender—three short novels, four volumes of short stories, and a few scattered essays—she is firmly established in the front rank of today's creative artists.

Miss Welty was born in Jackson, Mississippi, in 1909, and, like William Faulkner, who exerted some influence on her early work, she has preferred to isolate herself from literary coteries and remain close to her materials. Thus, except for brief periods, she has continued to live in Jackson, which, along with the neighboring cities of Natchez and Vicksburg, is often used as the locale of her stories. She received her education at Mississippi State College for Women at Columbus, at the University of Wisconsin, from which she received the bachelor's degree in 1929, and at the Columbia University School of Advertising. She became interested in writing early in life, but she was twenty-five before her first story, "Death of a Traveling Salesman," appeared in *Manuscript* in June, 1936. Soon her stories began to appear in the distinguished but short-lived *Southern Review,* published at the Louisiana State University under the editorship of Cleanth Brooks and Robert Penn Warren, who from the first recognized her talent. Within a few years, she was reaching a wider audience through the pages of *Harper's Bazaar, Scholastic,* the *Atlantic Monthly,* and the *Yale Review.* Her first collection of stories, *A Curtain of Green,* appeared in 1941. It was followed in 1943 by *The Wide Net and Other Stories* and in 1949 by *The Golden Apples,* a book of connected stories which may be considered separately as individual stories or all together as a novel, a type of structure which bears a resemblance to Steinbeck's *Tortilla Flat,* Anderson's *Winesburg, Ohio,* and Faulkner's *Go Down, Moses.* Her most recent collection of stories is *The Bride of the Innisfallen* (1955). Miss Welty's three short novels are *The Robber Bridegroom* (1942), a fantasy based on American folklore; *Delta Wedding* (1946), a portrayal of three generations of one family; and *The Ponder Heart* (1954), a hilarious dramatic monologue.

Like any serious artist, Miss Welty warns against fixed formulae: "It is not rules as long as there is imagination . . . that calls forth and communicates," she writes in *On Stories* (p. 52). In her view, the most compelling quality a story can have—but also the one most difficult for the writer to achieve—is beauty, which "is of form, development of idea, of after-effect . . . ." In "Livvie" an "after-effect" results from the juxtapositions of youth and age, spring and winter, sunshine and shadow, and uncaged and caged. Thus a seemingly objective presentation of localized character and setting is transformed into a broad, poetic statement on life.

livvie

Solomon carried Livvie twenty-one miles away from her home when he married her. He carried her away up on the Old Natchez Trace into the deep country to live in his house. She was sixteen—an only girl, then. Once people said he thought nobody would ever come along there. He told her himself that it had been a long time, and a day she did not know about, since that road was a traveled road with *people* coming and going. He was good to her, but he kept her in the house. She had not thought that she could not get back. Where she came from, people said an old man did not want anybody in the world to ever find his wife, for fear they would steal her back from him. Solomon asked her before he took her, "Would she be happy?"—very dignified, for he was a colored man that owned his land and had it written down in the courthouse; and she said, "Yes, sir," since he was an old man and she was young and just listened and answered. He asked her, if she was choosing winter, would she pine for spring, and she said, "No indeed." Whatever she said, always, was because he was an old man . . . while nine years went by. All the time, he got old, and he got so old he gave out. At last he slept the whole day in bed, and she was young still.

It was a nice house, inside and outside both. In the first place, it had three rooms. The front room was papered in holly paper, with green palmettos from the swamp spaced at careful intervals over the walls. There was fresh newspaper cut with fancy borders on the mantelshelf, on which were propped photographs of old or very young men printed in faint yellow—Solomon's people. Solomon had a houseful of furniture. There was a double settee, a tall scrolled rocker and an organ in the front room, all around a three-legged table with a pink marble top, on which was set a lamp with three gold feet, besides a jelly glass with pretty hen feathers in it. Behind the front room, the other room had the bright iron bed with the polished knobs like a throne, in which Solomon slept all day. There were snow-white curtains of wiry lace at the window, and a lace bed-spread belonged on the bed. But what old Solomon slept so sound under was a big feather-stitched piece-quilt in the pattern "Trip Around the World," which had twenty-one different colors, four hundred and forty pieces, and a thousand yards of thread, and that was what Solomon's mother made in her life and old age. There was a table holding the Bible, and a trunk with a key. On the wall were two calendars, and a diploma from somewhere in Solomon's family, and under that Livvie's one possession was nailed, a picture of the little white baby of the family she worked for, back in Natchez before she was married. Going through that room and on to the kitchen, there was a big wood stove and a big round table always with a wet top and with the knives and forks in one jelly glass and the spoons in another, and a cut-glass vinegar bottle between, and going out from those, many shallow dishes of pickled peaches, fig preserves, watermelon pickles and blackberry jam always sitting there. The churn sat in the sun, the doors of the safe were always both shut, and there were four baited mouse-traps in the kitchen, one in every corner.

The outside of Solomon's house looked nice. It was not painted, but across the porch was an even balance. On each side there was one easy chair with high springs, looking out, and a fern basket hanging over it from the ceiling, and a dishpan of zinnia seedlings growing at its foot on the floor. By the door was a plow-wheel, just a pretty iron circle, nailed up on one wall and a square mirror on the other, a turquoise-blue comb stuck up in the frame, with the wash stand beneath it. On the door was a wooden knob with a pearl in the end, and Solomon's black hat hung on that, if he was in the house.

Out front was a clean dirt yard with every vestige of grass patiently uprooted and the ground scarred in deep whorls from the strike of Livvie's broom. Rose bushes with tiny blood-red roses blooming every month grew in threes on either side of the steps. On one side was a peach tree, on the other a pomegranate. Then coming around up the path from the deep cut of the Natchez Trace below was a line of bare crape-myrtle trees with every branch of them ending in a colored bottle, green or blue. There was no word that fell from Solomon's lips to say what they were for, but Livvie knew that there could be a spell put in trees, and she was familiar from the time she was born with the way bottle trees kept evil spirits from coming into the house— by luring them inside the colored bottles, where they cannot get out again. Solomon had made the bottle trees with his own hands over the nine years, in labor amounting to about a tree a year, and without a sign that he had any uneasiness in his heart, for he took as much pride in his precautions against spirits coming in the house as he took in the house, and sometimes in the sun the bottle trees looked prettier than the house did.

It was a nice house. It was in a place where the days would go by and surprise anyone that they were over. The lamplight and the firelight would shine out the door after dark, over the still and breathing country, lighting the roses and the bottle trees, and all was quiet there.

But there was nobody, nobody at all, not even a white person. And if there had been anybody, Solomon would not have let Livvie look at them, just as he would not let her look at a field hand, or a field hand look at her. There was no house near, except for the cabins of the tenants that were forbidden to her, and there was no house as far as she had been, stealing away down the still, deep Trace. She felt as if she waded a river when she went, for the dead leaves on the ground reached as high as her knees, and when she was all scratched and bleeding she said it was not like a road that went anywhere. One day, climbing up the high bank, she had found a graveyard without a church, with ribbon-grass growing about the foot of an angel (she had climbed up because she thought she saw angel wings), and in the sun, trees shining like burning flames through the great caterpillar nets which enclosed them. Scarey thistles stood looking like the prophets in the Bible in Solomon's house. Indian paint brushes grew over her head, and the mourning dove made the only sound in the world. Oh for a stirring of the leaves, and a breaking of the nets! But not by a ghost, prayed Livvie, jumping down the bank. After Solomon took to his bed, she never went out, except one more time.

Livvie knew she made a nice girl to wait on anybody. She fixed things to eat on a tray like a surprise. She could keep from singing when she ironed, and to sit by a bed and fan away the flies, she could be so still she could not hear herself breathe. She could clean up the house and never drop a thing, and wash the dishes without a sound, and she would step outside to churn, for churning sounded too sad to her, like sobbing, and if it made her home-sick and not Solomon, she did not think of that.

But Solomon scarcely opened his eyes to see her, and scarcely tasted his food. He was not sick or paralyzed or in any pain that he mentioned, but he was surely wearing out in the body, and no matter what nice hot thing Livvie would bring him to taste, he would only look at it now, as if he were past seeing how he could add anything more to himself. Before she could beg him, he would go fast asleep. She could not surprise him any more, if he would not taste, and she was afraid that he was never in the world going to taste another thing she brought him—and so how could he last?

But one morning it was breakfast time and she cooked his eggs and grits, carried them in on a tray, and called his name. He was sound asleep. He lay in a dignified way with his watch beside him, on his back in the middle of the bed. One hand drew the quilt up high, though it was the first day of spring. Through the white lace curtains a little puffy wind was blowing as if it came from round cheeks. All night the frogs had sung out in the swamp, like a commotion in the room, and he had not stirred, though she lay wide awake and saying "Shh, frogs!" for fear he would mind them.

He looked as if he would like to sleep a little longer, and so she put back the tray and waited a little. When she tiptoed and stayed so quiet, she surrounded herself with a little reverie, and sometimes it seemed to her when she was so stealthy that the quiet she kept was for a sleeping baby, and that she had a baby and was its mother. When she stood at Solomon's bed and looked down at him, she would be thinking, "He sleeps so well," and she would hate to wake him up. And in some other way, too, she was afraid to wake him up because even in his sleep he seemed to be such a strict man.

Of course, nailed to the wall over the bed—only she would forget who it was—there was a picture of him when he was young. Then he had a fan of hair over his forehead like a king's crown. Now his hair lay down on his head, the spring had gone out of it. Solomon had a lightish face, with eyebrows scattered but rugged, the way privet grows, strong eyes, with second sight, a strict mouth, and a little gold smile. This was the way he looked in his clothes, but in bed in the daytime he looked like a different and smaller man, even when he was wide awake, and holding the Bible. He looked like somebody kin to himself. And then sometimes when he lay in sleep and she stood fanning the flies away, and the light came in, his face was like new, so smooth and clear that it was like a glass of jelly held to the window, and she could almost look through his forehead and see what he thought.

She fanned him and at length he opened his eyes and spoke her name, but he would not taste the nice eggs she had kept warm under a pan.

Back in the kitchen she ate heartily, his breakfast and hers, and looked out the open door at what went on. The whole day, and the whole night before, she had felt the stir of spring close to her. It was as present in the house as a young man would be. The moon was in the last quarter and outside they were turning the sod and planting peas and beans. Up and down the red fields, over which smoke from the brush-burning hung showing like a little skirt of sky, a white horse and a white mule pulled the plow. At intervals hoarse shouts came through the air and roused her as if she dozed neglectfully in the shade, and they were telling her, "Jump up!" She could see how over each ribbon of field were moving men and girls, on foot and mounted on mules, with hats set on their heads and bright with tall hoes and forks as if they carried streamers on them and were going to some place on a journey—and how as if at a signal now and then they would all start at once shouting, hollering, cajoling, calling and answering back, running, being leaped on and breaking away, flinging to earth with a shout and lying motionless in the trance of twelve o'clock. The old women came out of the cabins and brought them the food they had ready for them, and then all worked together, spread evenly out. The little children came too, like a bouncing stream overflowing the fields, and set upon the men, the women, the dogs, the rushing birds, and the wave-like rows of earth, their little voices almost too high to be heard. In the middle distance like some white and gold towers were the haystacks, with black cows coming around to eat their edges. High above everything, the wheel of fields, house, and cabins, and the deep road surrounding like a moat to keep them in, was the turning sky, blue with long, far-flung white mare's-tail clouds, serene and still as high flames. And sound asleep while all this went around him that was his, Solomon was like a little still spot in the middle.

Even in the house the earth was sweet to breathe. Solomon had never let Livvie go any farther than the chicken house and the well. But what if she would walk now into the heart of the fields and take a hoe and work until she fell stretched out and drenched with her efforts, like other girls, and laid her cheek against the laid-open earth, and shamed the old man with her humbleness and delight? To shame him! A cruel wish could come in uninvited and so fast while she looked out the back door. She washed the dishes and scrubbed the table. She could hear the cries of the little lambs. Her mother, that she had not seen since her wedding day, had said one time, "I rather a man be anything, than a woman be mean."

So all morning she kept tasting the chicken broth on the stove, and when it was right she poured off a nice cup-ful. She carried it in to Solomon, and there he lay having a dream. Now what did he dream about? For she saw him sigh gently as if not to disturb some whole thing he held round in his mind, like a fresh egg. So even an old man dreamed about something pretty. Did he dream of her, while his eyes were shut and sunken, and his small hand with the wedding ring curled close in sleep around the quilt? He might be dreaming of what time it was, for even through his sleep he kept track of it like a clock, and knew how much of it went by, and waked up knowing where the hands were even before he consulted the silver watch that he never let go. He would sleep with the watch in his palm, and even holding it to his cheek like a child that loves a plaything. Or he might dream of journeys and travels on a steamboat to Natchez. Yet she thought he dreamed of her; but even while she scrutinized him, the rods of the foot of the bed seemed to rise up like a rail fence between them, and she could see that people never could be sure of anything as long as one of them was asleep and the other awake. To look at him dreaming of her when he might be going to die frightened her a little, as if he might carry her with him that way, and she wanted to run out of the room. She took hold of the bed and held on, and Solomon opened his eyes and called her name, but he did not want anything. He would not taste the good broth.

Just a little after that, as she was taking up the ashes in the front room for the last time in the year, she heard a sound. It was somebody coming. She pulled the curtains together and looked through the slit.

Coming up the path under the bottle trees was a white lady. At first she looked young, but then she looked old. Marvelous to see, a little car stood steaming like a kettle out in the field-track—it had come without a road.

Livvie stood listening to the long, repeated knockings at the door, and after a while she opened it just a little. The lady came in through the crack, though she was more than middle-sized and wore a big hat.

"My name is Miss Baby Marie," she said.

Livvie gazed respectfully at the lady and at the little suitcase she was holding close to her by the handle until the proper moment. The lady's eyes were running over the room, from palmetto to palmetto, but she was saying, "I live at home . . . out from Natchez . . . and get out and show these pretty cosmetic things to the white people and the colored people both . . . all around . . . years and years . . . Both shades of powder and rouge. . . . It's the kind of work a girl can do and not go clear 'way from home . . ." And the harder she looked, the more she talked. Suddenly she turned up her nose and said, "It is not Christian or sanitary to put feathers in a vase," and then she took a gold key out of the front of her dress and began unlocking the locks on her suitcase. Her face drew the light, the way it was covered with intense white and red, with a little patty-cake of white between the wrinkles by her upper lip. Little red tassels of hair bobbed under the rusty wires of her picture-hat, as with an air of triumph and secrecy she now drew open her little suitcase and brought out bottle after bottle and jar after jar, which she put down on the table, the mantel-piece, the settee, and the organ.

"Did you ever see so many cosmetics in your life?" cried Miss Baby Marie.

"No'm," Livvie tried to say, but the cat had her tongue.

"Have you ever applied cosmetics?" asked Miss Baby Marie next.

"No'm," Livvie tried to say.

"Then look!" she said, and pulling out the last thing of all, "Try this!" she said. And in her hand was unclenched a golden lipstick which popped open like magic. A fragrance came out of it like incense, and Livvie cried out suddenly, "Chinaberry flowers!"

Her hand took the lipstick, and in an instant she was carried away in the air through the spring, and looking down with a half-drowsy smile from a purple cloud she saw from above a chinaberry tree, dark and smooth and neatly leaved, neat as a guinea hen in the dooryard, and there was her home that she had left. On one side of the tree was her mama holding up her heavy apron, and she could see it was loaded with ripe figs, and on the other side was her papa holding a fish-pole over the pond, and she could see it transparently, the little clear fishes swimming up to the brim.

"Oh, no, not chinaberry flowers—secret ingredients," said Miss Baby Marie. "My cosmetics have secret ingredients—not chinaberry flowers."

"It's purple," Livvie breathed, and Miss Baby Marie said, "Use it freely. Rub it on."

Livvie tiptoed out to the wash stand on the front porch and before the mirror put the paint on her mouth. In the wavery surface her face danced before her like a flame. Miss Baby Marie followed her out, took a look at what she had done and said, "That's it."

Livvie tried to say "Thank you" without moving her parted lips where the paint lay so new.

By now Miss Baby Marie stood behind Livvie and looked in the mirror over her shoulder, twisting up the tassels of her hair. "The lipstick I can let you have for only two dollars," she said, close to her neck.

"Lady, but I don't have no money, never did have," said Livvie.

"Oh, but you don't pay the first time. I make another trip, that's the way I do. I come back again—later."

"Oh," said Livvie, pretending she understood everything so as to please the lady.

"But if you don't take it now, this may be the last time I'll call at your house," said Miss Baby Marie sharply. "It's far away from anywhere, I'll tell you that. You don't live close to anywhere."

"Yes'm. My husband, he keep the *money*," said Livvie, trembling. "He is strict as he can be. He don't know *you* walk in here—Miss Baby Marie!"

"Where is he?"

"Right now, he in yonder sound asleep, an old man. I wouldn't ever ask him for anything."

Miss Baby Marie took back the lipstick and packed it up. She gathered up the jars for both black and white and got them all inside the suitcase, with the same little fuss of triumph with which she had brought them out. She started away.

"Goodbye," she said, making herself look grand from the back, but at the last minute she turned around in the door. Her old hat wobbled as she whispered, "Let me see your husband."

Livvie obediently went on tiptoe and opened the door to the other room. Miss Baby Marie came behind her and rose on her toes and looked in.

"My, what a little tiny old, old man!" she whispered, clasping her hands and shaking her head over them. "What a beautiful quilt! What a tiny old, old man!"

"He can sleep like that all day," whispered Livvie proudly.

They looked at him awhile so fast asleep, and then all at once they looked at each other. Somehow that was as if they had a secret, for he had never stirred. Livvie then politely, but all at once, closed the door.

"Well! I'd certainly like to leave you with a lipstick!" said Miss Baby Marie vivaciously. She smiled in the door.

"Lady, but I told you I don't have no money, and never did have."

"And never will?" In the air and all around, like a bright halo around the white lady's nodding head, it was a true spring day.

"Would you take eggs, lady?" asked Livvie softly.

"No, I have plenty of eggs—plenty," said Miss Baby Marie.

"I still don't have no money," said Livvie, and Miss Baby Marie took her suitcase and went on somewhere else.

Livvie stood watching her go, and all the time she felt her heart beating in her left side. She touched the place with her hand. It seemed as if her heart beat and her whole face flamed from the pulsing color of her lips. She went to sit by Solomon and when he opened his eyes he could not see a change in her. "He's fixin' to die," she said inside. That was the secret. That was when she went out of the house for a little breath of air.

She went down the path and down the Natchez Trace a way, and she did not know how far she had gone, but it was not far, when she saw a sight. It was a man, looking like a vision—she standing on one side of the Old Natchez Trace and he standing on the other.

As soon as this man caught sight of her, he began to look himself over. Starting at the bottom with his pointed shoes, he began to look up, lifting his peg-top pants the higher to see fully his bright socks. His coat long and wide and leaf-green he opened like doors to see his high-up tawny pants and his pants he smoothed downward from the points of his collar, and he wore a luminous baby-pink satin shirt. At the end, he reached gently above his wide platter-shaped round hat, the color of a plum, and one finger touched at the feather, emerald green, blowing in the spring winds.

No matter how she looked, she could never look so fine as he did, and she was not sorry for that, she was pleased.

He took three jumps, one down and two up, and was by her side.

"My name is Cash," he said.

He had a guinea pig in his pocket. They began to walk along. She stared on and on at him, as if he were doing some daring spectacular thing, instead of just walking beside her. It was not simply the city way he was dressed that made her look at him and see hope in its insolence looking back. It was not only the way he moved along kicking the flowers as if he could break through everything in the way and destroy anything in the world, that made her eyes grow bright. It might be, if he had not appeared the way he did appear that day she would never have looked so closely at him, but the time people come makes a difference.

They walked through the still leaves of the Natchez Trace, the light and the shade falling through trees about them, the white irises shining like candles on the banks and the new ferns shining like green stars up in the oak branches. They came out at Solomon's house, bottle trees and all. Livvie stopped and hung her head.

Cash began whistling a little tune. She did not know what it was, but she had heard it before from a distance, and she had a revelation. Cash was a field hand. He was a transformed field hand. Cash belonged to Solomon. But he had stepped out of his overalls into this. There in front of Solomon's house he laughed. He had a round head, a round face, all of him was young, and he flung his head up, rolled it against the mare's-tail sky in his round hat, and he could laugh just to see Solomon's house sitting there. Livvie looked at it, and there was Solomon's black hat hanging on the peg on the front door, the blackest thing in the world.

"I been to Natchez," Cash said, wagging his head around against the sky. "*I* taken a trip, *I* ready for Easter!"

How was it possible to look so fine before the harvest? Cash must have stolen the money, stolen it from Solomon. He stood in the path and lifted his spread hand high and brought it down again and again in his laughter. He kicked up his heels. A little chill went through her. It was as if Cash was bringing that strong hand down to beat a drum or to rain blows upon a man, such an abandon and menace were in his laugh. Frowning, she went closer to him and his swinging arm drew her in at once and the fright was crushed from her body, as a little match-flame might be smothered out by what it lighted. She gathered the folds of his coat behind him and fastened her red lips to his mouth, and she was dazzled by herself then, the way he had been dazzled at himself to begin with.

In that instant she felt something that could not be told—that Solomon's death was at hand, that he was the same to her as if he were dead now. She cried out, and uttering little cries turned and ran for the house.

At once Cash was coming, following after, he was running behind her. He came close, and halfway up the path he laughed and passed her. He even picked up a stone and sailed it into the bottle trees. She put her hands over her head, and sounds clattered through the bottle trees like cries of outrage. Cash stamped and plunged zigzag up the front steps and in at the door.

When she got there, he had stuck his hands in his pockets and was turning slowly about in the front room. The little guinea pig peeped out. Around Cash, the pinned-up palmettos looked as if a lazy green monkey had walked up and down and around the walls leaving green prints of his hands and feet.

She got through the room and his hands were still in his pockets, and she fell upon the closed door to the other room and pushed it open. She ran to Solomon's bed, calling "Solomon! Solomon!" The little shape of the old man never moved at all, wrapped under the quilt as if it were winter still.

"Solomon!" She pulled the quilt away, but there was another one under that, and she fell on her knees beside him. He made no sound except a sigh, and then she could hear in the silence the light springy steps of Cash walking and walking in the front room, and the ticking of Solomon's silver watch, which came from the bed. Old Solomon was far away in his sleep, his face looked small, relentless, and devout, as if he were walking somewhere where she could imagine the snow falling.

Then there was a noise like a hoof pawing the floor, and the door gave a creak, and Cash appeared beside her. When she looked up, Cash's face was so black it was bright, and so bright and bare of pity that it looked sweet to her. She stood up and held up her head. Cash was so powerful that his presence gave her strength even when she did not need any.

Under their eyes Solomon slept. People's faces tell of things and places not known to the one who looks at them while they sleep, and while Solomon slept under the eyes of Livvie and Cash his face told them like a mythical story that all his life he had built, little scrap by little scrap, respect. A beetle could not have been more laborious or more ingenious in the task of its destiny. When Solomon was young, as he was in his picture overhead, it was the infinite thing with him, and he could see no end to the respect he would contrive and keep in a house. He had built a lonely house, the way he would make a cage, but it grew to be the same with him as a great monumental pyramid and sometimes in his absorption of getting it erected he was like the builder-slaves of Egypt who forgot or never knew the origin and meaning of the thing to which they gave all the strength of their bodies and used up all their days. Livvie and Cash could see that as a man might rest from a life-labor he lay in his bed, and they could hear how, wrapped in his quilt, he sighed to himself comfortably in sleep, while in his dreams he might have been an ant, a beetle, a bird, an Egyptian, assembling and carrying on his back and building with his hands, or he might have been an old man of India or a swaddled baby, about to smile and brush all away.

Then without warning old Solomon's eyes flew wide open under the hedge-like brows. He was wide awake.

And instantly Cash raised his quick arm. A radiant sweat stood on his temples. But he did not bring his arm down—it stayed in the air, as if something might have taken hold.

It was not Livvie—she did not move. As if something said "Wait," she stood waiting. Even while her eyes burned under motionless lids, her lips parted in a stiff grimace, and with her arms stiff at her sides she stood above the prone old man and the panting young one, erect and apart.

Movement when it came came in Solomon's face. It was an old and strict face, a frail face, but behind it, like a covered light, came an animation that could play hide and seek, that would dart and escape, had always escaped. The mystery flickered in him, and invited from his eyes. It was that very mystery that Cash with his quick arm would have to strike, and that Livvie could not weep for. But Cash only stood holding his arm in the air, when the gentlest flick of his great strength, almost a puff of his breath, would have been enough, if he had known how to give it, to send the old man over the obstruction that kept him away from death.

If it could not be that the tiny illumination in the fragile and ancient face caused a crisis, a mystery in the room that would not permit a blow to fall, at least it was certain that Cash, throbbing in his Easter clothes, felt a pang of shame that the vigor of a man would come to such an end that he could not be struck without warning. He took down his hand and stepped back behind Livvie, like a round-eyed schoolboy on whose unsuspecting head the dunce cap has been set.

"Young ones can't wait," said Solomon.

Livvie shuddered violently, and then in a gush of tears she stooped for a glass of water and handed it to him, but he did not see her.

"So here come the young man Livvie wait for. Was no prevention. No prevention. Now I lay eyes on young man and it come to be somebody I know all the time, and been knowing since he were born in a cotton patch, and watched grow up year to year, Cash McCord, growed to size, growed up to come in my house in the end—ragged and barefoot."

Solomon gave a cough of distaste. Then he shut his eyes vigorously, and his lips began to move like a chanter's.

"When Livvie married, her husband were already somebody. He had paid great cost for his land. He spread sycamore leaves over the ground from wagon to door, day he brought her home, so her foot would not have to touch ground. He carried her through his door. Then he growed old and could not lift her, and she were still young."

Livvie's sobs followed his words like a soft melody repeating each thing as he stated it. His lips moved for a little without sound, or she cried too fervently, and unheard he might have been telling his whole life, and then he said, "God forgive Solomon for sins great and small. God forgive Solomon for carrying away too young girl for wife and keeping her away from her people and from all the young people would clamor for her back." *giving Livvie his blessing she die.*

Then he lifted up his right hand toward Livvie where she stood by the bed and offered her his silver watch. He dangled it before her eyes, and she hushed crying; her tears stopped. For a moment the watch could be heard ticking as it always did, precisely in his proud hand. She lifted it away. Then he took hold of the quilt; then he was dead.

Livvie left Solomon dead and went out of the room. Stealthily, nearly without noise, Cash went beside her. He was like a shadow, but his shiny shoes moved over the floor in spangles, and the green downy feather shone like a light in his hat. As they reached the front room, he seized her deftly as a long black cat and dragged her hanging by the waist round and round him, while he turned in a circle, his face bent down to hers. The first moment, she kept one arm and its hand stiff and still, the one that held Solomon's watch. Then the fingers softly let go, all of her was limp, and the watch fell somewhere on the floor. It ticked away in the still room, and all at once there began outside the full song of a bird. *2 different ways of life.*

They moved around and around the room and into the brightness of the open door, then he stopped and shook her once. She rested in silence in his trembling arms, unprotesting as a bird on a nest. Outside the redbirds were flying and crisscrossing, the sun was in all the bottles on the prisoned trees, and the young peach was shining in the middle of them with the bursting light of spring.

Irwin Shaw

THE GIRLS IN THEIR SUMMER DRESSES

Irwin Shaw, who in attitude, method, and material aligns himself with the younger, "hard-boiled" fictional school, was born in Brooklyn, New York, in 1913, the son of a hat-trimmings salesman. After finishing high school he entered Brooklyn College, where he conducted a column in the college newspaper. Dropped from college during his freshman year for poor grades, he worked as truck driver and held other miscellaneous jobs before he re-entered Brooklyn College, this time to remain until he completed his degree in 1934. During this period he not only worked at a variety of jobs to support himself—tutoring, typing, assisting in the school library—but he also played football and wrote plays which were produced by the college dramatic society. After leaving college, he wrote radio scripts for a livelihood but found some time to devote to serious writing. In 1935, he wrote *Bury the Dead,* a one-act anti-war play, which was produced in New York with great success. He next went to Hollywood as a script writer but after finishing his contract with RKO Studios returned to New York to continue his play writing career. During his service in the Army in World War II, he saw action in North Africa, the Middle East, France, and Germany. Since the war he has lived abroad, chiefly in Paris, where he has concerned himself with both the writing of fiction and its adaptation for motion-picture production. His stories are collected in *Welcome to the City* (1942), *Act of Faith* (1946), *Mixed Company* (1950), and *Tip on a Dead Jockey, and Other Stories* (1957). He has also published four novels, *The Young Lions* (1948), *The Troubled Air* (1951), *Lucy Crown* (1956), and *Two Weeks in Another Town* (1960), but they have been less favorably received than his short stories.

Shaw's stories deal chiefly with metropolitan life,

involving all kinds of characters from school boys to taxi-drivers, from hooligans to veteran soldiers, and they center around themes ranging from the deadly serious to the ludicrous. Although "The Girls in Their Summer Dresses" is in the lighter vein, its serious undertone is unmistakable, for the problem it confronts seems increasingly urgent in modern society.

the girls in their summer dresses

Fifth Avenue was shining in the sun when they left the Brevoort. The sun was warm, even though it was February, and everything looked like Sunday morning—the buses and the well-dressed people walking slowly in couples and the quiet buildings with the windows closed.

Michael held Frances' arm tightly as they walked toward Washington Square in the sunlight. They walked lightly, almost smiling, because they had slept late and had a good breakfast and it was Sunday. Michael unbuttoned his coat and let it flap around him in the mild wind.

"Look out," Frances said as they crossed Eighth Street. "You'll break your neck." Michael laughed and Frances laughed with him.

"She's not so pretty," Frances said. "Anyway, not pretty enough to take a chance of breaking your neck."

Michael laughed again. "How did you know I was looking at her?"

Frances cocked her head to one side and smiled at her husband under the brim of her hat. "Mike, darling," she said.

"O.K.," he said. "Excuse me."

Frances patted his arm lightly and pulled him along a little faster toward Washington Square. "Let's not see anybody all day," she said. "Let's just hang around with each other. You and me. We're always up to our neck in people, drinking their Scotch or drinking our Scotch; we only see each other in bed. I want to go out with my husband all day long. I want him to talk only to me and listen only to me."

"What's to stop us?" Michael asked.

"The Stevensons. They want us to drop by around one o'clock and they'll drive us into the country."

"The cunning Stevensons," Mike said. "Transparent. They can whistle. They can go driving in the country by themselves."

"Is it a date?"

"It's a date."

Frances leaned over and kissed him on the tip of the ear.

"Darling," Michael said, "this is Fifth Avenue."

"Let me arrange a program," Frances said. "A planned Sunday in New York for a young couple with money to throw away."

"Go easy."

"First let's go to the Metropolitan Museum of Art," Frances suggested, because Michael had said during the week he wanted to go. "I haven't been there in three years and there're at least ten pictures I want to see again. Then we can take the bus down to Radio City and watch them skate. And later we'll go down to Cavanagh's and get a steak as big as a blacksmith's apron, with a bottle of wine, and after that there's a French picture at the Filmarte that everybody says— say, are you listening to me?"

"Sure," he said. He took his eyes off the hatless girl with the dark hair, cut dancer-style like a helmet, who was walking past him.

"That's the program for the day," Frances said flatly. "Or maybe you'd just rather walk up and down Fifth Avenue."

"No," Michael said. "Not at all."

"You always look at other women," Frances said. "Everywhere. Every damned place we go."

"No, darling," Michael said, "I look at everything. God gave me eyes and I look at women and men in subway excavations and moving pictures and the little flowers of the field. I casually inspect the universe."

"You ought to see the look in your eye," Frances said, "as you casually inspect the universe on Fifth Avenue."

"I'm a happily married man." Michael pressed her elbow tenderly. "Example for the whole twentieth century—Mr. and Mrs. Mike Loomis. Hey, let's have a drink," he said, stopping.

"We just had breakfast."

"Now listen, darling," Mike said, choosing his words with care, "it's a nice day and we both felt good and there's no reason why we have to break it up. Let's have a nice Sunday."

"All right. I don't know why I started this. Let's drop it. Let's have a good time."

They joined hands consciously and walked without talking among the baby carriages and the old Italian men in their Sunday clothes and the young women with Scotties in Washington Square Park.

"At least once a year everyone should go to the Metropolitan Museum of Art," Frances said after a while, her tone a good imitation of the tone she had used at breakfast and at the beginning of their walk. "And it's nice on Sunday. There're a lot of people looking at the pictures and you get the feeling maybe Art isn't on the decline in New York City, after all—"

"I want to tell you something," Michael said very seriously. "I have not touched another woman. Not once. In all the five years."

"All right," Frances said.

"You believe that, don't you?"

"All right."

They walked between the crowded benches, under the scrubby city-park trees.

"I try not to notice it," Frances said, "but I feel rotten inside, in my stomach, when we pass a woman and you look at her and I see that look in your eye and that's the way you looked at me the first time. In Alice Maxwell's house. Standing there in the living room, next to the radio, with a green hat on and all those people."

"I remember the hat," Michael said.

"The same look," Frances said. "And it makes me feel bad. It makes me feel terrible."

"Sh-h-h, please, darling, sh-h-h."

"I think I would like a drink now," Frances said.

They walked over to a bar on Eighth Street, not saying anything, Michael automatically helping her over curbstones and guiding her past automobiles. They sat near a window in the bar and the sun streamed in and there was a small, cheerful fire in the fireplace. A little Japanese waiter came over and put down some pretzels and smiled happily at them.

"What do you order after breakfast?" Michael asked.

"Brandy, I suppose," Frances said.

"Courvoisier," Michael told the waiter. "Two Courvoisiers."

The waiter came with the glasses and they sat drinking the brandy in the sunlight. Michael finished half his and drank a little water.

"I look at women," he said. "Correct. I don't say it's wrong or right. I look at them. If I pass them on the street and I don't look at them, I'm fooling you, I'm fooling myself."

"You look at them as though you want them," Frances said, playing with her brandy glass. "Every one of them."

"In a way," Michael said, speaking softly and not to his wife, "in a way that's true. I don't do anything about it, but it's true."

"I know it. That's why I feel bad."

"Another brandy," Michael called. "Waiter, two more brandies."

He sighed and closed his eyes and rubbed them gently with his fingertips. "I love the way women look. One of the things I like best about New York is the battalions of women. When I first came to New York from Ohio that was the first thing I noticed, the million wonderful women, all over the city. I walked around with my heart in my throat."

"A kid," Frances said. "That's a kid's feeling."

"Guess again," Michael said. "Guess again. I'm older now. I'm a man getting near middle age, putting on a little fat, and I still love to walk along Fifth Avenue at three o'clock on the east side of the street between Fiftieth and Fifty-seventh Streets. They're all out then, shopping, in their furs and their crazy hats, everything all concentrated from all over the world into seven blocks—the best furs, the best clothes, the handsomest women, out to spend money and feeling good about it."

The Japanese waiter put the two drinks down, smiling with great happiness.

"Everything is all right?" he asked.

"Everything is wonderful," Michael said.

"If it's just a couple of fur coats," Frances said, "and forty-five dollar hats—"

"It's not the fur coats. Or the hats. That's just the scenery for that particular kind of woman. Understand," he said, "you don't have to listen to this."

"I want to listen."

"I like the girls in the offices. Neat, with their eyeglasses, smart, chipper, knowing what everything is about. I like the girls on Forty-fourth Street at lunchtime, the actresses, all dressed up on nothing a week. I like the salesgirls in the stores, paying attention to you first because you're a man, leaving lady customers waiting. I got all this stuff accumulated in me because I've been thinking about it for ten years and now you've asked for it and here it is."

"Go ahead," Frances said.

"When I think of New York City, I think of all the girls on parade in the city. I don't know whether it's something special with me or whether every man in the city walks around with the same feeling inside him, but I feel as though I'm at a picnic in this city. I like to sit near the women in the theatres, the famous beauties who've taken six hours to get ready and look it. And the young girls at the football games, with the red cheeks, and when the warm weather comes, the girls in their summer dresses." He finished his drink. "That's the story."

Frances finished her drink and swallowed two or three times extra. "You say you love me?"

"I love you."

"I'm pretty, too," Frances said. "As pretty as any of them."

"You're beautiful," Michael said.

"I'm good for you," Frances said, pleading. "I've made a good wife, a good housekeeper, a good friend. I'd do any damn thing for you."

"I know," Michael said. He put his hand out and grasped hers.

"You'd like to be free to—" Frances said.

"Sh-h-h."

"Tell the truth." She took her hand away from under his.

Michael flicked the edge of his glass with his finger. "O.K.," he said gently. "Sometimes I feel I would like to be free."

"Well," Frances said, "any time you say."

"Don't be foolish." Michael swung his chair around to her side of the table and patted her thigh. _demeans her._

She began to cry silently into her handkerchief, bent over just enough so that nobody else in the bar would notice. "Someday," she said, crying, "you're going to make a move."

Michael didn't say anything. He sat watching the bartender slowly peel a lemon.

"Aren't you?" Frances asked harshly. "Come on, tell me. Talk. Aren't you?"

"Maybe," Michael said. He moved his chair back again. "How the hell do I know?"

"You know," Frances persisted. "Don't you know?"

"Yes," Michael said after a while, "I know."

Frances stopped crying then. Two or three snuffles into the handkerchief and she put it away and her face didn't tell anything to anybody. "At least do me one favor," she said.

"Sure."

"Stop talking about how pretty this woman is or that one. Nice eyes, nice breasts, a pretty figure, good voice." She mimicked his voice. "Keep it to yourself. I'm not interested."

Michael waved to the waiter. "I'll keep it to myself," he said.

Frances flicked the corners of her eyes. "Another brandy," she told the waiter.

"Two," Michael said.

"Yes, Ma'am, yes, sir," said the waiter, backing away.

Frances regarded Michael coolly across the table. "Do you want me to call the Stevensons?" she asked. "It'll be nice in the country."

"Sure," Michael said. "Call them."

She got up from the table and walked across the room toward the telephone. Michael watched her walk, thinking what a pretty girl, what nice legs.

deep ⟶ into
two very different people.
not speaking specifically
bv generally ℓ marriage.
Women not really doing
what they want.

Bernard Malamud

TAKE PITY

The number of strikingly original writers who emerge decade by decade testifies to the continuing variety and richness of the short story tradition in America. Bernard Malamud, who published his first collection of stories as recently as 1958, is a case in point. Writing in a manner he himself has described as the "realistic, expressionistic mode," and often making use of fantasy as well as special character types, he has developed a bold, fresh method of treating significant themes in emotionally powerful terms.

Born in Brooklyn in 1914, Malamud attended Erasmus High School, where he served on the staff of the school paper, *The Erasmian,* and contributed his early fiction to its columns. Continuing his education in the metropolitan area, he received the B.A. degree from the City College of New York in 1936 and the M.A. in English from Columbia University in 1942. He had held various jobs—as a factory hand and as a clerk in the Census Bureau in Washington—before he began teaching night classes at Erasmus High School in 1941. In 1949 he joined the faculty of Oregon State College, where he taught composition and literature for the next twelve years, with the exception of 1956, which he spent in Italy on a writing grant awarded him by the *Partisan Review* from funds supplied by the Rockefeller Foundation. Since 1961, he has been a member of the English faculty of North Bennington College. His published fiction includes three novels, *The Natural* (1952), *The Assistant* (1957), and *A New Life* (1961); and two collections of short stories, *The Magic Barrel and Other Stories* (1958), which won the National Book Award for 1958, and *Idiots First* (1963), which has drawn high critical praise.

Malamud sees the role of the literary artist as that of keeping civilization "from destroying itself,"

533

not by overt preachment, but by his artistry, which should "tell the truth about life." In his view, the artist may be able to reveal the truth more effectively by resorting to distortion and fantasy than he can by sticking to "pure, dead, documentary realism," a viewpoint his story "Take Pity" illustrates quite clearly. "Take Pity" also dramatizes his doctrine that effective creative writing must combine emotional depth and imaginative force so that it will "enflame, destroy, change the reader."

take pity

Davidov, the census-taker, opened the door without knocking, limped into the room and sat wearily down. Out came his notebook and he was on the job. Rosen, the ex-coffee salesman, wasted, eyes despairing, sat motionless, cross-legged, on his cot. The square, clean but cold room, lit by a dim globe, was sparsely furnished: the cot, a folding chair, small table, old unpainted chests—no closets but who needed them?—and a small sink with a rough piece of green, institutional soap on its holder—you could smell it across the room. The worn black shade over the single narrow window was drawn to the ledge, surprising Davidov.

"What's the matter you don't pull the shade up?" he remarked.

Rosen ultimately sighed. "Let it stay."

"Why? Outside is light."

"Who needs light?"

"What then you need?"

"Light I don't need," replied Rosen.

Davidov, sour-faced, flipped through the closely scrawled pages of his notebook until he found a clean one. He attempted to scratch in a word with his fountain pen but it had run dry, so he fished a pencil stub out of his vest pocket and sharpened it with a cracked razor blade.

Reprinted from *The Magic Barrel* by Barnard Malamud, by permission of Farrar, Straus & Company, Inc. Copyright © 1958 by Bernard Malamud.

Rosen paid no attention to the feathery shavings falling to the floor. He looked restless, seemed to be listening to or for something, although Davidov was convinced there was absolutely nothing to listen to. It was only when the census-taker somewhat irritably and with increasing loudness repeated a question, that Rosen stirred and identified himself. He was about to furnish an address but caught himself and shrugged.

Davidov did not comment on the salesman's gesture. "So begin," he nodded.

"Who knows where to begin?" Rosen stared at the drawn shade. "Do they know here where to begin?"

"Philosophy we are not interested," said Davidov. "Start in how you met her."

"Who?" pretended Rosen.

"Her," he snapped.

"So if I got to begin, how you know about her already?" Rosen asked triumphantly.

Davidov spoke wearily, "You mentioned before."

Rosen remembered. They had questioned him upon his arrival and he now recalled blurting out her name. It was perhaps something in the air. It did not permit you to retain what you remembered. That was part of the cure, if you wanted a cure.

"Where I met her—?" Rosen murmured. "I met her where she always was—in the back room there in that hole in the wall that it was a waste of time for me I went there. Maybe I sold them a half a bag of coffee a month. This is not business."

"In business we are not interested."

"What then you are interested?" Rosen mimicked Davidov's tone.

Davidov clammed up coldly.

Rosen knew they had him where it hurt, so he went on: "The husband was maybe forty, Axel Kalish, a Polish refugee. He worked like a blind horse when he got to America, and saved maybe two—three thousand dollars that he bought with the money this pisher grocery in a dead neighborhood where he didn't have a chance. He called my company up for credit and they sent me I should see. I recommended okay because I felt sorry. He had a wife, Eva, you know already about her, and two darling girls, one five and one three, little dolls, Fega and Surale, that I didn't want them to suffer. So right away I told him, without tricks, 'Kiddo, this is a mistake. This place is a grave. Here they will bury you if you don't get out quick!'"

Rosen sighed deeply.

"So?" Davidov had thus far written nothing, irking the ex-salesman.

"So?—Nothing. He didn't get out. After a couple months he tried to sell but nobody bought, so he stayed and starved. They never made expenses. Every day they got poorer you couldn't look in their faces. 'Don't be a damn fool,' I told him, 'go in bankruptcy.' But he couldn't stand it to lose all his capital, and he was also afraid it would be hard to find a job. 'My God,' I said, 'do anything. Be a painter, a janitor, a junk man, but get out of here before everybody is a skeleton.'

"This he finally agreed with me, but before he could go in auction he dropped dead."

Davidov made a note. "How did he die?"

"On this I am not an expert," Rosen replied. "You know better than me."

"How did he die?" Davidov spoke impatiently. "Say in one word."

"From what he died?—he died, that's all."

"Answer, please, this question."

"Broke in him something. That's how."

"Broke what?"

"Broke what breaks. He was talking to me how bitter was his life, and he touched me on my sleeve to say something else, but the next minute his face got small and he fell down dead, the wife screaming, the little girls crying that it made in my heart pain. I am myself a sick man and when I saw him laying on the floor, I said to myself, 'Rosen, say goodbye, this guy is finished.' So I said it."

Rosen got up from the cot and strayed despondently around the room, avoiding the window. Davidov was occupying the only chair, so the ex-salesman was finally forced to sit on the edge of the bed again. This irritated him. He badly wanted a cigarette but disliked asking for one.

Davidov permitted him a short interval of silence, then leafed impatiently through his notebook. Rosen, to needle the census-taker, said nothing.

"So what happened?" Davidov finally demanded.

Rosen spoke with ashes in his mouth. "After the funeral—" he paused, tried to wet his lips, then went on, "He belonged to a society that they buried him, and he also left a thousand dollars insurance, but after the funeral I said to her, 'Eva, listen to me. Take the money and your children and run away from here. Let the creditors take the store. What will they get?—Nothing.'

"But she answered me, 'Where will I go, where, with my two orphans that their father left them to starve?'

" 'Go anywhere,' I said. 'Go to your relatives.'

"She laughed like laughs somebody who hasn't got no joy. 'My relatives Hitler took away from me.'

" 'What about Axel—surely an uncle somewheres?'

" 'Nobody,' she said. 'I will stay here like my Axel wanted. With the insurance I will buy new stock and fix up the store. Every week I will decorate the window, and in this way gradually will come in new customers—'

" 'Eva, my darling girl—'

" 'A millionaire I don't expect to be. All I want is I should make a little living and take care of my girls. We will live in the back here like before, and in this way I can work and watch them, too.'

" 'Eva,' I said, 'you are a nice-looking young woman, only thirty-eight years. Don't throw away your life here. Don't flush in the toilet—you should excuse me—the thousand poor dollars from your dead husband. Believe me, I know from such stores. After thirty-five years' experience I know a graveyard when I smell it. Go better some place and find a job. You're young yet. Sometime you will meet somebody and get married.'

" 'No, Rosen, not me,' she said. 'With marriage I am finished. Nobody wants a poor widow with two children.'

" 'This I don't believe it.'

" 'I know,' she said.

"Never in my life I saw so bitter a woman's face.

" 'No,' I said. 'No.'

" 'Yes, Rosen, yes. In my whole life I never had anything. In my whole life I always suffered. I don't expect better. This is my life.'

"I said no and she said yes. What could I do? I am a man with only one kidney, and worse than that, that I won't mention it. When I talked she didn't listen, so I stopped to talk. Who can argue with a widow?"

The ex-salesman glanced up at Davidov but the census-taker did not reply. "What happened then?" he asked.

"What happened?" mocked Rosen. "Happened what happens."

Davidov's face grew red.

"What happened, happened," Rosen said hastily. "She ordered from the wholesalers all kinds goods that she paid for them cash. All week she opened boxes and packed on the shelves cans, jars, packages. Also she cleaned, and she washed, and she mopped with oil the floor.

With tissue paper she made new decorations in the window, everything should look nice—but who came in? Nobody except a few poor customers from the tenement around the corner. And when they came? When was closed the supermarkets and they needed some little item that they forgot to buy, like a quart milk, fifteen cents' cheese, a small can sardines for lunch. In a few months was again dusty the cans on the shelves, and her thousand was gone. Credit she couldn't get except from me, and from me she got because I paid out of my pocket the company. This she didn't know. She worked, she dressed clean, she waited that the store should get better. Little by little the shelves got empty, but where was the profit? They ate it up. When I looked on the little girls I knew what she didn't tell me. Their faces were white, they were thin, they were hungry. She kept the little food that was left, on the shelves. One night I brought in a nice piece sirloin, but I could see from her eyes that she didn't like that I did it. So what else could I do? I have a heart and I am human."

Here the ex-salesman wept.

Davidov pretended not to see though once he peeked.

Rosen blew his nose, then went on more calmly, "When the children were sleeping we sat in the dark there, in the back, and not once in four hours opened the door should come in a customer. 'Eva, for Godsakes, *run away*,' I said.

" 'I have no place to go,' she said.

" 'I will give you where you can go, and please don't say to me no. I am a bachelor, this you know. I got whatever I need and more besides. Let me help you and the children. Money don't interest me. Interests me good health, but I can't buy it. I'll tell you what I will do. Let this place go to the creditors and move into a two-family house that I own, which the top floor is now empty. Rent will cost you nothing. In the meantime you can go and find a job. I will also pay the downstairs lady to take care of the girls—God bless them—until you will come home. With your wages you will buy the food, if you need clothes, and also save a little. This you can use when you get married someday. What do you say?'

"She didn't answer me. She only looked on me in such a way, with such burning eyes, like I was small and ugly. For the first time I thought to myself, 'Rosen, this woman don't like you.'

" 'Thank you very kindly, my friend Mr. Rosen,' she answered me, 'but charity we are not needing. I got yet a paying business, and it will get better when times are better. Now is bad times. When comes again good times will get better the business.'

" 'Who charity?' I cried to her. 'What charity? Speaks to you your husband's a friend.'

" 'Mr. Rosen, my husband didn't have no friends.'

" 'Can't you see that I want to help the children?'

" 'The children have their mother.'

" 'Eva, what's the matter with you?' I said. 'Why do you make sound bad something that I mean it should be good?'

"This she didn't answer. I felt sick in my stomach, and was coming also a headache so I left.

"All night I didn't sleep, and then all of a sudden I figured out a reason why she was worried. She was worried I would ask for some kind payment except cash. She got the wrong man. Anyway, this made me think of something that I didn't think about before. I thought now to ask her to marry me. What did she have to lose? I could take care of myself without any trouble to them. Fega and Surale would have a father he could give them for the movies, or sometime to buy a little doll to play with, and when I died, would go to them my investments and insurance policies.

"The next day I spoke to her.

" 'For myself, Eva, I don't want a thing. Absolutely not a thing. For you and your girls—everything. I am not a strong man, Eva. In fact, I am sick. I tell you this you should understand I don't expect to live long. But even for a few years would be nice to have a little family.'

"She was with her back to me and didn't speak.

"When she turned around again her face was white but the mouth was like iron.

" 'No, Mr. Rosen.'

" 'Why not, tell me?'

" 'I had enough with sick men.' She began to cry. 'Please, Mr. Rosen. Go home.'

"I didn't have strength I should argue with her, so I went home. I went home but hurt me my mind. All day long and all night I felt bad. My back pained me where was missing my kidney. Also too much smoking. I tried to understand this woman but I couldn't. Why should somebody that her two children were starving always say no to a man that he wanted to help her? What did I do to her bad? Am I maybe a murderer she should hate me so much? All that I felt in my heart was pity for her and the children, but I couldn't convince her. Then I went back and begged her she should let me help them, and once more she told me no.

539

" 'Eva,' I said, 'I don't blame you that you don't want a sick man. So come with me to a marriage broker and we will find you a strong, healthy husband that he will support you and your girls. I will give the dowry.'

"She screamed, 'On this I don't need your help, Rosen!'

"I didn't say no more. What more could I say? All day long, from early in the morning till late in the night she worked like an animal. All day she mopped, she washed with soap and a brush the shelves, the few cans she polished, but the store was still rotten. The little girls I was afraid to look at. I could see in their faces their bones. They were tired, they were weak. Little Surale held with her hand all the time the dress of Fega. Once when I saw them in the street I gave them some cakes, but when I tried the next day to give them something else, the mother shouldn't know, Fega answered me, 'We can't take, Momma says today is a fast day.'

"I went inside. I made my voice soft. 'Eva, on my bended knee, I am a man with nothing in this world. Allow me that I should have a little pleasure before I die. Allow me that I should help you to stock up once more the store.'

"So what did she do? She cried, it was terrible to see. And after she cried, what did she say? She told me to go away and I shouldn't come back. I felt like to pick up a chair and break her head.

"In my house I was too weak to eat. For two days I took in my mouth nothing except maybe a spoon of chicken noodle soup, or maybe a glass tea without sugar. This wasn't good for me. My health felt bad.

"Then I made up a scheme that I was a friend of Axel's who lived in Jersey. I said I owed Axel seven hundred dollars that he lent me this money fifteen years ago, before he got married. I said I did not have the whole money now, but I would send her every week twenty dollars till it was paid up the debt. I put inside the letter two tens and gave it to a friend of mine, also a salesman, he should mail it in Newark so she would not be suspicious who wrote the letters."

To Rosen's surprise Davidov had stopped writing. The book was full, so he tossed it onto the table, yawned, but listened amiably. His curiosity had died.

Rosen got up and fingered the notebook. He tried to read the small distorted handwriting but could not make out a single word.

"It's not English and it's not Yiddish," he said. "Could it be in Hebrew?"

"No," answered Davidov. "It's an old-fashioned language that they don't use it nowadays."

"Oh?" Rosen returned to the cot. He saw no purpose to going on now that it was not required, but he felt he had to.

"Came back all the letters," he said dully. "The first she opened it, then pasted back again the envelope, but the rest she didn't even open."

" 'Here,' I said to myself, 'is a very strange thing—a person that you can never give her anything.—*But I will give.*'

"I went then to my lawyer and we made out a will that everything I had—all my investments, my two houses that I owned, also furniture, my car, the checking account—every cent would go to her, and when she died, the rest would be left for the two girls. The same with my insurance. They would be my beneficiaries. Then I signed and went home. In the kitchen I turned on the gas and put my head in the stove.

"Let her say now no."

Davidov, scratching his stubbled cheek, nodded. This was the part he already knew. He got up and before Rosen could cry no, idly raised the window shade.

It was twilight in space but a woman stood before the window.

Rosen with a bound was off his cot to see.

It was Eva, staring at him with haunted, beseeching eyes. She raised her arms to him.

Infuriated, the ex-salesman shook his fist.

"Whore, bastard, bitch," he shouted at her. "Go 'way from here. Go home to your children."

Davidov made no move to hinder him as Rosen rammed down the window shade.

Peter Taylor

RESERVATIONS: A LOVE STORY

Peter Taylor has made middle-class life of the urban South his special fictional province, the locale of his stories being typically such cities as Nashville, Memphis, and Chattanooga. Unlike some of his Southern as well as Northern contemporaries, he shuns violence and grostesquerie in his fiction and finds his subjects instead in the quieter, if none the less painful, dramas of domestic relationships and family affairs. Taylor's vivid character portrayal, flawless style, and subtle command of form place him among the foremost masters of the contemporary short story.

Born in Trenton, Tennessee, in 1919, Taylor received his early educational training at schools in Nashville, St. Louis, and Memphis. He continued his studies at Southwestern University in Memphis, Vanderbilt University, and Kenyon College, receiving his bachelor's degree from the last named school in 1940. In 1946, after spending two years in England during World War II as a sergeant in the Rail Transportation Corps, he joined the faculty of the University of North Carolina at Greensboro and has intermittently continued teaching creative writing at that institution. At various times he has also taught at Indiana University, Ohio State University, University of Chicago, and Kenyon College; and in 1955 he was a lecturer in The American Studies Institute of the University College, Oxford. Among the honors and awards his fiction have brought him are a Guggenheim Fellowship in 1950-1951, a $1,000 grant from the National Institute of Arts and Letters in 1952, and the first prize in the 1959 O. Henry Memorial awards. He has published a novel, *A Woman of Means* (1950); a play, *Tennessee Day in St. Louis* (1957); and four collections of short stories, *A Long Fourth and Other Stories* (1948), *The Widows of Thornton* (1954), *Happy Families Are All Alike*

543

(1959), and *Miss Leonora When Last Seen and 15 Other Stories* (1963).

"Reservations: A Love Story" shows Taylor in his best and most characteristic vein. The story maintains a consistent focus on two central characters, a bride and bridegroom, and develops fully a richly comic situation. In the process, however, it depicts an astonishing number of related minor characters, and the end result is a penetrating revelation not simply of the two main characters but of the whole stratum of middle-class society which they represent and which has shaped their values and standards of conduct. Not the least of the story's virtues is its subtly ironic exposure of the hollowness of those values, giving the title a double meaning in retrospect.

reservations: a love story

It was arranged, of all things, that the bride and groom should make their escape from the country club through the little boys' locker room! But this was very reasonable, really. At nine o'clock on a night in January, the exit from the little boys' locker room to the swimming-pool terrace was the exit least likely to be congested. It was the exit also most likely to be overlooked by mischievous members of the wedding party. Every precaution had to be taken! No one was to be trusted!

In the lounge of the women's locker room, the bride got out of her gown in exactly thirty seconds. (She had taken an hour, more or less, to get into it.) She pushed the wedding dress into the hands of one of the club's maids and from the hands of another accepted the tweed travelling suit—puce-brown tweed trimmed with black velvet. Because it was imperative that no suspicion of her departure be roused among the guests, the bride was not attended by her mother or by her maid of honor. Her mother and all the bridal attendants remained upstairs at the party, where there was dancing, and where waiters moved about balancing trays of stemmed glasses. At two minutes to nine the bride ran on tiptoe along a service passageway that connected most of the rooms on the ground floor. She was accompanied now by the elder of the two maids who had assisted in the change from white satin to tweed. This woman was one of the club's veteran maids, a large, rather middle-aged person who, though she dyed her hair a lemon yellow and rouged her cheeks excessively, was known for her stalwart character and her incorruptibility. In the passageway, the bride chattered nervously to this companion who had been assigned to her. She told how she had written her name in the club's bride's book as "Franny Crowell," having forgotten momentarily that she was now Mrs. Miles Miller. The maid was not a very responsive sort, and said nothing. But this didn't bother Franny; she went on to say, sometimes laughing while she spoke, that somehow she could not shake off the feeling that it was a pity and a shame to be slipping away from a party given in your own honor.

In one hand the maid held the key to a door down the passageway that would let the bride into the little boys' locker room. In the other hand she carried a pair of fur-trimmed galoshes. As they approached the locked door, the maid interrupted Franny's chatter. "Your father said tell you your fur coat's in the car, with your corsage pinned to it. He said be careful you don't sit on it." Simultaneously the maid held out the galoshes, giving them a little shake that indicated Franny should take them.

"What are those?" Franny chirped. "They're not mine."

"No, they're not yours, Mrs. Miller," said the maid, still pressing them on her.

"Well, I don't believe I'll want them," Franny said politely.

"Yes, your mother said so. It's snowing outside now—a nasty, wet snow, Mrs. Miller."

"But they're not mine, and they're not Mother's either. . . . How long has it been snowing?" She hoped to change the subject.

"Two hours off and on, Mrs. Miller. Ever since you got here from the church. It's not sticking, but there'll be slush underfoot."

"Well, whose are they?"

"Your mother snitched them from one of the guests—out of the cloakroom. She told me, 'Something borrowed.'"

Franny burst into laughter and took the galoshes. But she resolved not to put on the ugly things until after Miles had seen her and got the effect of her outfit.

545

While the maid fitted the key into the lock, Franny stood with her eyes lifted to the low basement ceiling. She heard the sound of the dancing overhead, and she speculated about which of the dancers upstairs these boots might belong to and thought of the pleasure it was sure to give some childhood friend of hers, or possibly some aunt or some woman friend of her parents, to learn that *she* had provided the bride with the one item that had been overlooked—the something borrowed.

Presently the door before her stood open. But Franny's eyes and thoughts were still directed toward the ceiling. "There you are," said the maid, obviously provoked by the bride's inattention.

Franny lowered her eyes. She looked at the woman beside her with a startled expression. Then she glanced briefly into the shadows of the unlighted locker room. And in the next moment she was clutching frantically at the starched sleeve of the maid's uniform. "But he is not here!" she exclaimed. Her tone was accusing; she eyed the maid suspiciously. Then, as if on further reflection, she spoke in a bewailing whisper: "He isn't hee-er!" According to the plan, he was to have been admitted to the little boys' locker room through a door from the adjoining men's locker room. But had he ever intended to be there? *He was gone! Of course he was! How else would it be?* Already Franny was thinking of what kind of poison she would administer to herself, of how she would manage to obtain the poison, of how she would look when they found her.

"What do you mean 'not here'?" said the maid, jerking her sleeve free.

Franny smiled coolly. She knew how she must carry it off. "Maybe I'll stay on for the party, after all," she said.

"What do you mean 'not here'?" the maid repeated. "He's standing there before your eyes."

Franny looked again, and of course there her bridegroom stood. "I didn't see him, it's so dark," she stammered.

But, instead of going to the bridegroom, suddenly the bride threw her arms about the woman with the lemon-yellow hair who had delivered her to him. This trustworthy woman had been known to Franny during most of her young life, but she was by no means a favorite of Franny's. And almost certainly Franny had never been a favorite of the woman's, either. . . . But still it seemed the thing to do. Somehow it was like embracing the whole wedding party or even the whole club membership, or possibly just simply her own mother. And, no doubt, in that moment this woman forgave Franny many an old score—forgave a little girl's criticism of sandwiches served toasted when they had been ordered untoasted, complaints about a bathing suit's not having been hung out to dry, and many another complaint besides. At any rate, the woman responded and returned the warm embrace. Then for an instant the two of them smiled at each other through the general mist of tears.

"Goodbye, little Miss 'Franny Crowell,' " the woman said.

"Goodbye, Bernice," said Franny, "and thanks for everything." Yes, the woman's name was Bernice. What a bother it had always been, trying to remember it, but now it had come out without Franny's having to try to think of it even.

Bernice took several steps backward, as if quitting a royal presence. At a respectful distance she turned her back, and in her white gum-soled shoes she retreated silently down the long service passageway.

While waiting for the bride to come through the doorway to him, the bridegroom had literally stood dangling his little narrow-brimmed hat, shifting it from one hand to the other. He did not know what to make of that blank look she had given him at first, didn't know what to make of her saying "He is not here," didn't know what to make of her throwing herself into the arms of the hired help instead of into his own. . . . The embrace perhaps he understood better than the look. But anyway, she had come to him at last, which was what he wanted most in the world at the moment. Presently he had seated her on one of the rough wooden benches in the locker room and, on his knees before her, he was struggling to push her feet into the borrowed galoshes. Franny had held on to the galoshes through both her embraces, and as soon as she had handed them to Miles and was seated on the bench, she began to chatter again—about the galoshes now, about how her mother had positively stolen "the ugly things" from somebody upstairs.

It wasn't easy getting the galoshes on. They were a near-perfect fit, but Franny seemed incapable of being any help. Her little ankles had gone limp, like an absent-minded child's. But finally Miles managed to force both galoshes on. He zipped them up neatly, and then lifted his face to Franny and smiled. Franny extended one of her tiny gloved hands to him, as if she were going to pull him to his feet. Miles seized it, but he remained on one knee before her, pressing the hand firmly between the two of his. While he knelt there, Franny made a vague gesture with her free hand, a gesture that indicated the whole of the dark locker room. "I've never been in here before, Miles," she said.

547

"Neither have I, you know," Miles said playfully.

"Oh," Franny breathed, thoughtfully. "No, you probably haven't, have you."

Now she felt she understood. . . . *That* was why she had not been able to see him there at first. She had never *imagined* him there. It was because Miles Miller was not one of the local boys she had grown up with, wasn't one of that familiar group from whose number she had always assumed she would someday accept a husband. He was better than any of *those,* of course; he was her own, beloved, blue-eyed, black-haired, fascinating Miles Miller, whom she had recognized the first moment she ever saw him as the best-looking man she had ever laid eyes on (or ever would), as the man she must have for *hers*—and the very same Miles, of course, that at least half a dozen other girls of her year had thought they must have for *theirs*. Moreover, he was the young man who doesn't turn up in *every*body's year: the young bachelor from out of town, brought in from a distant region by one of the big corporations to fill a place in its local office, a young man without any local history of teen-age romances to annoy and perhaps worry the bride. And in Miles' case the circumstances were enhanced still further. He was an only child, and his parents had died while he was still in college. For his bride there would be no parents or brothers and sisters to be visited and adjusted to, and, since he had lived always on the West Coast and gone to Stanford, no prep-school friends, not even—at such a distance—a college roommate to be won over. Once they were married, Franny's family would be *their* family, her friends *their* friends. Besides all this, her Miles was at once the most modest and most self-assured human being imaginable. With one gentle look—gentle and yet reasonable and terribly penetrating—he could make her aware of the utter absurdity of something she said or did, and make her simultaneously aware of how little such absurdities mattered to someone who loved you.

Franny bent forward and kissed her husband gently on his smiling lips. He came up beside her on the bench, no longer smiling, and took Franny in his arms. For Franny it was as it had always been before—every time he had ever held her in his tender, confident way. It was as though she possessed at last, or was about to possess at last, what she had always wanted above everything else and had never dreamed she wanted—or, that is, never dreamed she wanted in quite the same way she wanted everything else. That was what seemed so incredible to her about it: *This* desire and *this* happiness differed only in degree from the other longings and other satisfactions one experienced. There was nothing at all unreal about it. And somehow the most miraculous part was that the man she was going to marry was not the man she had ever imagined herself marrying. On the contrary, he was the frightening stranger of her girlish daydreams—the dark, handsome man she was always going to meet on a train coming home from boarding school at Christmas or during the summer at Lake Michigan. In her daydreams she sometimes even bore that man a child, but there had always had to be a barrier to their marrying. The man was already married (perhaps to an invalid!), or he was a Jew, he was a Catholic—a French Canadian—or he was the foreign agent of a country committed to the destruction of her own country, or (when she was still younger) there was insanity or even a strain of Negro blood in his family! Yet the stranger had turned up after all—after she had almost forgotten him—and there was no barrier.

Still holding Franny close to him, Miles got to his feet and for a moment lifted his bride completely off the floor. "Franny, oh, 'little Miss Franny,' let's go!" he said. Franny laughed aloud. And to Miles she sounded for all the world like a delighted little girl of four or five. "Let's be on our way," he said, still holding her there. "Let's get out of here."

"Carry me to the car, Miles," she whispered.

"I will," he said. "You bet I will. Not this way, though. I'll set you down and get a good hold and then we'll dash."

But just as Franny's feet touched the floor, there came a great rattling sound from over toward the door to the terrace. Franny gave a little shriek that came out almost "Aha!" And then, in a quiet voice, in a tone of utter resignation, she said, "They've found us." She meant, of course, that the mischief-makers had found them. "We'll never get away."

"No, they haven't, darling," Miles said impatiently.

Franny turned away from him. At the far end of the room she saw a man's figure silhouetted against the glass door to the terrace. She realized at once that the man must be one of the club's waiters. It was he, she surmised, who had let Miles in from the men's locker room. He had been present all the while, and actually he was now holding the terrace door a little way open. The rattling noise had, plainly, come from the long Venetian blind on that door. But the source of the rattling no longer interested Franny; she was too angry with Miles for not having told her they weren't alone.

Suddenly her impulse was to turn back and deliver Miles a slap across the face. His inference that the waiter's presence hadn't mattered was insulting both to herself and to this man who had so faithfully performed the duties assigned him. But before she could turn or speak, Miles had seized her by the hand and the waiter had thrown open the door. Hand in hand, the bride and groom ran the length of the little boys' locker room. In the excitement of the moment, Miles had forgotten that he was going to carry Franny to the car. It was well for him that he had. Franny consented to let him hold her hand only in order to keep from embarrassing the waiter. Halfway to the door she made out just which of the club's waiters he was, and she could easily have called him by name. But instead she dropped her eyes, and she kept them lowered even when Miles paused in the doorway to slip a bill into the hand at the end of the white sleeve. In her pique with Miles, she wondered if the bill was of as large a denomination as it ought to be.

Outside, they ran along the edge of the gaping swimming pool and on in the direction of the tennis courts. Beyond the courts, Miles' new car was hidden. The wet snow was falling heavily, and it was beginning to stick now. It seemed to Franny that the snow might fill the empty swimming pool before the night was over. They went through the gate into the area of the tennis courts. From there Franny glanced back once at the lighted windows of the low, sprawling club-house. Through the snow it seemed miles away. They ran on across the courts and through the white shrubbery. Neither of them spoke until they were in the car. By then their rendezvous in the locker room seemed like something that had happened too long ago to mention. As Miles was helping her into her coat, and she was carefully protecting the big white orchid that she knew her father had pinned on the coat with his own hands, Franny said, "What are we going to do, Miles? I'm terrified. I hate snow. We can't get even as far as Bardstown tonight."

"Of course we can't, honey," he said. He had switched on the car lights and was starting the motor. "We'll have to stay here in town tonight. I telephoned the hotel a while ago. We'll have to stay there."

They had planned to spend the first night at Bardstown, which in good weather was only a few hours away, down in Kentucky, and where there was an attractive old inn. They had planned to make it to Natchez by the second night, and to be at the Gulf Coast by the third. Franny's father had urged them to fly down, or to take a train. But they were able to think only of what fun it would be to have their own car once they got to Biloxi. It had been silly of them, they acknowledged now, driving into town through the snow, but they did have the satisfaction of knowing that all planes would be grounded on such a night, anyway. And to both of them the idea of spending their wedding night in a Pullman berth seemed grotesque.

It took Miles three-quarters of an hour to get them through the snow and the traffic to the downtown hotel where he had managed to make reservations. Along the way, he apologized to Franny for putting them up at this particular hotel—the hotel, that is, where he had himself been living during the past year and a half. "As luck would have it," he explained, "there are two big conventions in town this week. I was lucky to find a room anywhere at all. I hope you don't mind too much."

"Why in the world should I mind?" Franny laughed. "We're a bona-fide married couple now."

Yet the moment she had passed through the revolving door into the marble-pillared lobby of the hotel, Franny rested a gloved hand on the sleeve of Miles' overcoat and said, "I *do* feel a little funny about it, after all."

"I was afraid you might feel funny about it," Miles said. They stood there a moment waiting for the boy with their luggage to follow them through the revolving door, and Miles began to apologize all over again. "The other hotels were all full up," he said. "It's only because I happen to hit it off so well with Bill Carlisle that I was able to get a room here. It wasn't easy for him even; he's just the assistant manager. Your father, or almost any of the guys in the wedding, might have found us something better. But it seemed worse, somehow, to have any of them—even your father—know exactly where we're spending the night, since we can't get out of town. I guessed you would feel the same way about it."

But Franny was not listening to Miles. She had become aware that she was the only woman in the lobby, and the mention of the assistant manager's name had further distracted her. Bill Carlisle had been invited to the wedding—she recalled addressing his invitation—but he had not been invited to the reception and supper dance. As for her own acquaintance with him, it was very slight. She had known him for a long time, however, and she knew that he knew just about everyone that she did. She interrupted Miles' apologies to say, "Do we have to see Bill Collier?"

"Who?" asked Miles.

"You know—the assistant manager."

"Of course we don't, darling," he said. "We don't even have to register. That's all set."

The boy with their luggage had joined them now. Another boy had appeared with their key and was beckoning them to follow him to the elevator. As they crossed the lobby, Franny began laughing to herself. Miles noticed, and asked what was funny.

"I was wondering," she said, "do you think he'll have put us in your room?"

"Will who have?"

"You know, your friend Bill—the assistant manager."

"At least it won't be that," said Miles. "There was someone waiting to take it over when I got the last of my possessions out this morning."

"What a shame," Franny whispered. "It would have been kind of interesting, and no one but Bill Cook need ever have known."

"Bill Carlisle's his name," Miles said rather petulantly. Then he added, "He's a pretty nice fellow, in case you care to know."

"Certainly he is," Franny said with a wink. "I've known him for years."

Franny stepped into the elevator, followed by Miles. Then the boy with the luggage got in, then the one with the key. Franny observed that both the boys were mature men, and the key boy was even bald-headed. They kept their heads bowed, very courteously, not even looking up when presently they had occasion to speak to each other.

"Where's Jack?" the luggage boy asked quietly.

"He's coming," said the key boy.

"Who's Jack?" Franny asked Miles.

Thinking the question directed to him, the luggage boy replied, "He's the elevator boy." As he spoke, he glanced up at Franny. Probably he thought it was demanded of him. Unlike the key boy, he had a heavy head of hair, as dark and thick as Miles' own, and the face he lifted was youthful, almost handsome even, with a broad jaw and black, rather cruel eyes that seemed brimming with energy. As soon as he looked up he realized his mistake and bent his head again. But he had reminded Franny of someone—someone she didn't like. Or *did* like. Which was it? She couldn't think who it was, and felt vaguely that she didn't want to. And what would Jack, the elevator operator, be like, she wondered, when he turned up? Somehow she was sure he would be a redhead. Presently he would come running; he would hop into the elevator, close the door, push the button, and there she would be, locked in the elevator with Miles and with the three men in their dark-green livery and with the heap of luggage, and the elevator would shoot them up to their floor and stop with a sickening little bounce. She wished Miles would *say* something!

"Jack seems to have gotten lost," Miles said. Franny burst out laughing.

Immediately, Jack appeared, as if from nowhere. He was a Negro boy, but with light skin and a reddish tint to his hair.

Franny was conscious of Jack's arrival, and conscious of the color of his hair, but at the same time her real attention had been caught by a figure out in the lobby. It was the figure of a woman, and she was moving swiftly across the lobby toward this elevator, making her way between the heavier figures of the conventioners in their tweed overcoats and gray fedoras. (Most of them, it seemed to Franny, were smoking cigars, the way conventioners were supposed to.) The woman was wearing a navy-blue topcoat and hat, and carried an oversize handbag. "Wait!" Franny said to the elevator boy.

"What do you mean, 'Wait'?" Miles asked.

"Don't you see who that is trying to catch us?" Franny said, rising on her toes.

"I see who it is, but you don't know her, and I can promise you I don't either."

One of the hotel boys snorted, but he cut it off so short Franny couldn't tell for sure which of them it was. She suspected the bald-headed one.

"It's Bernice! The maid from the club!" Franny tried to recall whether she had forgotten anything essential. No, the woman must have an urgent message for her. Her father or her mother had been taken ill, or there had been some disaster at the club—a fire perhaps. She remembered distinctly having left a cigarette burning in the women's lounge.

"It's no such thing," Miles was saying. "Let's go, Jack!"

The woman was close enough now for Franny to see it was not Bernice. The long stride and the yellow hair sticking out from under the hat had deceived her. But she should have known, shouldn't she, that Bernice could not have worn such heels.

The elevator door was closing right in the woman's face, and even if the woman wasn't Bernice, this was more than Franny could bear. "Stop it!" she commanded, utterly outraged by the ungallant behavior of these men. "There's room for another person, easily!"

The boys looked at Miles. "Let the lady in," Miles thundered.

Jack slid the door open. But the woman hesitated. With a swift

553

glance she seemed to have taken in every aspect of the situation—that it was a bride and groom she was intruding upon, that the bride had insisted upon holding the car for her, that the groom had protested. She now signalled Jack to go on without her, but with Miles' thundering command still in his ears Jack made no move to do so. Miles kept silent. And so did Franny, who in a last-minute glance as swift as the woman's had taken in *her* total situation—that she was a middle-aged prostitute late for an engagement. There was but one solution to the awful silence and to the irresolution of the elevator boy. The woman stepped into the elevator and abruptly turned her back to the other passengers.

As the car shot upward, Jack asked with easy nonchalance, "Your floor, please?"

Again there was silence. Finally Miles said, "What's our floor?"

The key boy looked up, showing his full face for the first time—eyes set close together, a small, puffy nose, ears flat against the bald head. Franny thought it the stupidest, most brutal face she had ever set eyes on. *"Your* floor is eight, Mr. Miller," he said, barely opening his swollen lips when he spoke.

After a moment Jack repeated, "Your floor, please?"

The woman now turned her face toward the elevator boy so that Franny saw her profile. Her face was plain—neither homely nor otherwise, really—and seemed devoid of expression. Only the fact that she had turned her face toward him showed that she knew the boy expected an answer from her. It occurred to Franny that in her agitation this poor creature had forgotten what floor she was going to. At last, and as if with great effort, she did speak. "Seven for me," she said.

With a long, bony forefinger Jack stabbed the seventh-floor button. The elevator stopped almost at once, and the door slid open. The woman stepped out into the hallway, where there was a broad mirror facing her between two metal cigarette urns. Instead of turning to left or right she stopped there just outside the elevator, and for one instant her pale eyes met Franny's in the glass. Then the door closed quietly between them.

Franny had not been aware of a bouncing sensation when the elevator stopped at that floor. But when it stopped at the floor above, the sensation so upset her equilibrium that she felt positively faint. Her two feet in their fur-trimmed galoshes seemed chilled to numbness. She felt that if she tried to take one step down the hallway in the direction of the bridal chamber her knees might buckle underneath her. She wondered how she would ever manage it.

To Miles Miller, his bride had seemed not herself at all, from the time they met in the shadows of the locker room at the country club until at last they were alone in the hotel room. But her confusion and nervousness were very understandable, he reasoned, in view of the upsetting change in their plans. And once they were alone in the room, she was indeed very much herself again. She was once again the vivacious, unaffected, ingenuous little being he had decided to marry after talking to her for five minutes during an intermission at a big début party last year. From the beginning, Miles had felt that he appreciated her special brand of innocence and even artlessness as no one else ever before had. One thing he had determined when he left college and entered upon his career in business was that he would not be the sort—the type—to marry the boss's daughter and further his career that way. He detested that type. He extended this pledge to himself even to include the daughters of prominent and influential men who might indirectly help him in his career. He extended it even to cover all the débutantes he had ever met or would ever meet. He had had no definite ideas about where he *would* find his wife, except one idea that was so childish he laughed at it himself: He had thought of meeting a perfectly unspoiled girl while vacationing in an unspoiled countryside—perhaps in the highland South, perhaps even somewhere in Europe. He had thought particularly of Switzerland. But when thinking more realistically Miles told himself simply that he would not marry for the sake of his business or social advancement. His marriage and his family life must be something altogether apart from his career.

And then, in his twenty-sixth year, he had met Franny Crowell and had had a wonderful insight. Franny was, in a most important sense, as beautifully innocent and provincial as any little mountain girl might have been. She delighted in her surroundings, accepted her relation to them without question, and would be content to remain where she was and as she was for the rest of her life. She had been practically nowhere away from home. For two years she went to boarding school in Virginia but hated dormitory life and thought it silly of girls to go East to college when they could be so much more comfortable staying at home. She had herself attended the local city university for two years and had relished meeting different kinds of people from her own home town. True, she had spent most of her summers at a resort on Lake Michigan, but even there most of her companions had been the same people she went to school with at home during the winter. Miles Miller recognized in Franny Crowell the flaxen-haired mountain girl of his childish imaginings. Her outward appearance might deceive the world but never him. She arranged her golden-brown hair always in the very latest, most sophisticated fashions. Last summer she had even let the beauty parlor put a blond streak in her hair. She plucked her eyebrows, even pencilled them. The shade of her lipstick paled or darkened according to whatever was newest. But Miles perceived that all of this was as innocent and natural in his Franny as plaiting flaxen pigtails might have been.

Miles and Franny had agreed in advance that they should each have only one glass of champagne at the club on their wedding night. But among the bags that they had had brought into the hotel was Miles' genuine Gucci liquor case—a present from the men at his office. Packed with ice in the plastic compartment of the elaborate leather case were two bottles of champagne of a somewhat earlier and better year than that offered the guests by the bride's father. And into Franny's makeup bag she had managed to fit two of their very own champagne glasses. Together they had thought of everything.

In their hotel room, they spent the first half hour making toasts. They drank to Betty Manville's début ball, where they had met, drank to their first date, to their first kiss, to the night he first proposed, to the night she accepted, to the night of the announcement party. Each toast had to be followed by a kiss. Each kiss inspired and motivated another reminiscence. Finally they turned to toasting people whom they associated with events of their courtship. Since Franny was a talented and tireless mimic, Miles encouraged her to "do" each of these people. She "did" Betty Manville's mother, her own father, and then one of her bridesmaids, who had once upon a time imagined *she* was going to have Miles Miller for herself. This last was the funniest of all to Miles. He was seated on the side of the bed, leaning on one elbow, and when he had witnessed Franny's version of that poor, misguided girl he set his champagne glass on the floor and fell back on the bed in a spasm of laughter. He threshed about, still laughing aloud, and all the while wiping tears from his eyes and begging Franny to stop.

When Franny promised to stop, Miles got control of himself and sat up in the center of the bed. Wiping his eyes with his handkerchief, he looked up again and found Franny sitting on the side of the bed with her thumb pressed against her nose so hard that her little nose was flattened on her face. Her eyes were squinted up and her mouth, which was normally small and tight, was stretched and spread into a wide ribbon across her face. "You know who this is?" she asked, barely moving her lips.

"I'm glad to say I don't," Miles said, as if offended by her ugliness.

"Oh, you do," Franny insisted.

"I don't, and it's not very attractive."

"Of course it's not attractive," said Franny, keeping the thumb pressed against her nose. "It's that bald-headed bellboy, the one with the key."

"What's wrong with him?" Miles said, swinging his feet around to the other side of the bed and thus momentarily turning his back to Franny.

"You don't have to turn your back," Franny said. "See, it's still only me."

Miles looked around and smiled apologetically. Franny's face was her own again, and she was looking down at her hands very seriously. "Weren't all three of those bellboys grotesque?" she said.

"I don't think so," Miles said. "They're perfectly normal-looking human beings. I see them every day."

"Normal-looking!" Franny exclaimed, lifting her eyes to his. "How can you say so? The bald-headed one was really monstrous. And the one with the mop of hair had a really mad look in his eyes. And that pale Negro boy with the kinky red hair! How blind you are to people, Miles. You don't really *see* them."

"Maybe not," said Miles, meaning to dismiss the subject, since Franny seemed so emotional about it. Turning now, he let himself fall across the bed toward her, and again he took one of her hands between the two of his. But before he could speak the endearment he intended, something else occurred to him that he felt must be said first. It was in defense of his vision, or—he couldn't define it—in defense of something even more specially his own that had been disparaged. "Anyway," he said, "you must admit that not one of those bellhops was half as weird-looking as that painted-up creature you had your hug fest with when we were leaving the club. After the elevator ride, I don't have to tell you what *she* looked like." Though they had been in the room for more than half an hour, this was the first reference either of them had made to the woman in the elevator.

Franny withdrew her hand and stood up.

Miles said, "We're not going to quarrel about something so silly on our wedding night, are we?"

Franny was silent for a moment. Her eyes moved about the room as if taking it in for the first time. Then she bent over and kissed

Miles on the top of his head. "We aren't *ever* going to quarrel again, are we, Miles?"

"Never," he said. He reached out a hand, but she pulled away. "Come back," he said in a whisper.

"Not until I've slipped into something more—more right." She smiled vaguely.

Miles lay with his head propped on one hand and watched her go to her little overnight bag and take out the folds of lace and peach silk that were her negligee and gown. Suddenly he leaped from the bed with outstretched arms. But the bride dashed through the open doorway to the bathroom and closed the door.

Miles had long since changed into his blue silk pajamas with the white monogram on the pocket when he saw the first turning and twisting of the doorknob. When Franny failed to appear at once—that is, when the knob ceased its twisting and the bathroom door didn't open—his vexation showed itself momentarily in one little horizontal crease in his smooth forehead. But the moment was so brief that even his eyes didn't reflect it, and soon a sly little smile came to his lips. . . . He would give her a signal that all was ready and waiting, and at the same time give her motivation and courage. Stepping over to the dresser he uncorked the second bottle of champagne. He managed it very expertly, taking satisfaction in his expertness. The pop was loud enough for Franny to hear and comprehend, yet there was not one bubble of wasteful overflow. The tiny golden bubbles came just to the mouth of the champagne bottle and no further. Miles had not even taken the precaution of having the two glasses handy. He was expert and he was confident of his expertness.

He watched the first bubbles appear and then shot a glance across the room at the doorknob. It was turning again. He stepped over to where the two glasses were, on the bedside table, filled them, and then returned the bottle to its ice. Still no Franny. But the doorknob was now turning back and forth rather rapidly. Miles watched it as if hypnotized. Finally he uttered a tentative "Franny?" There was no response except in the acceleration of the knob's turning. "Franny?" he repeated, striding toward the door. "What's the matter?" Still no answer. The turning was frenzied now. "Franny, do you hear me? What are you doing?"

"Of course I hear you!" Franny exclaimed through the door. "I'm trying to get out of here, you fool!"

Miles seized the knob and gave it a forceful twist.

"That's not going to help," said Franny, resentful of the overpowering yank to the knob she had been holding on to.

"The thing must be locked," Miles said, astonished. "Why did you lock it?"

Franny was silent. Then she said, "*I* didn't lock it."

"Well, *I* didn't." Miles laughed. "Anyway, try unlocking it."

"Do you think I haven't already?"

"What kind of lock is it? Is there a key?"

"No. It's one of those damned little eggs you turn."

"But why on earth would you have locked it?"

"If I did it, Miles, I did it without thinking."

Miles was now trying to see the bolt through the crack of the door. "But why would you?" he said absently.

"Why would I what?"

"Lock it without thinking."

"All decent people lock bathroom doors," she said with conviction.

"We didn't at our house," Miles said. He could definitely see the bolt through the crack. "My father used to throw away the key to the bathroom door as soon as we moved into a place."

"Don't start on your father *now*, Miles."

"My father was all right."

"Who said he wasn't? *Do* something, Miles, for God's sake."

"There's nothing to do but call the desk and have them take down the door."

Franny who had for a moment been leaning against the rim of the washbowl, now straightened and grasped the doorknob again. "Miles, you *wouldn't!*"

"Don't go to pieces, Franny."

"You'd let them send up those three stooges—"

Miles burst into laughter.

"How coarse you are, Miles," Franny said, her voice deepening.

"Oh, honey, there's a regular maintenance crew, and—"

"Maybe so," she broke in, her voice climbing the scale till it was much higher than Miles had ever heard it before. "But don't you know, Miles, that Bill Carlisle would certainly know about it? Oh, God, everybody in this town would know about it before tomorrow morning!"

"In God's name, Franny, what do you propose I do?"

"What kind of man are you, Miles? Take the door down yourself. You've been living in this hotel so long you depend on them for everything. You seem to think the world's just one big hotel and that you call in the maintenance crew for any and every thing."

"O.K., Franny, I'll try," Miles said amiably. "But have you ever tried taking down a locked door?"

"Why did you have to bring me to this dump?" Franny wailed.

"And why did you have to lock the door?" he countered.

Now they were both silent as Miles went to the closet door where his Valpak hung, and dug out a small gold pocketknife. His first effort to remove the pin in the upper door hinge was fruitless. The pin wouldn't budge. Neither would the pin in the lower hinge. He decided he needed a hammer to drive the knife blade upward against the heads of the pins, and he was just turning to go and fetch his shoe for that purpose when Franny spoke again.

"Miles," she began, speaking very slowly and in a tone so grave that it stopped him, "do you remember that night at Cousin Jane Thompson's party?"

He listened, waiting for her to continue. Then he realized she expected some response from him. "Yes, Franny," he said.

"That night at Cousin Jane's," she now went on in the same sepulchral tone, "when you said Sue Maynard's date was drunk and that she asked you to take her home." Sue Maynard was the bridesmaid who had thought *she* would have Miles for herself. Miles had been a stag at the party that night.

"Yes, I remember."

"You were lying."

"In a way, Franny—"

"In the worst way," she said flatly. "You thought I would think it was just Sue's lie and that you didn't know better, or that you knew better but were too honorable to give her away."

"Maybe."

"That's how you *thought* I would think. But I knew even that night, Miles Miller, that you engineered it all. Her date was Puss Knowlton, and you had no trouble giving *him* the shove. And don't you think I know it's more than just necking that Sue Maynard goes in for? . . . And, Miles, the night last summer, *after* we were engaged, when you couldn't come for dinner at our house with Daddy's Aunt Caroline because of the report you had to write up—you didn't have any report to write up, Miles. You went someplace out on the South Side with a little creature named Becky Louise Johnson."

By the time Franny had finished, Miles had silently crossed the room to the bedside table and downed one of the two waiting glassfuls of champagne. He had listened intently to what she said, and the more he heard the more intent he had become on getting that damned door down. In his liquor case he found a bottle opener that he decided would work better than his knife. He returned to the door with his shoe and the bottle opener, and in no time he had the top pin out of its hinge.

"Miles—" Franny began again, still in the same tone.

"Shut up, Franny!" Miles said, and at once began hammering at the lower pin. It offered a little more resistance than the other, but was soon dislodged. The door was still firmly in place, however. Twice Miles jabbed the bottle opener into the crack on the hinge side, as though he might prize the door open. Then he laughed aloud at himself.

Franny heard him laugh, of course. "Is it funny? Is it really funny to you, Miles?" she said.

"Try giving it a push from in there, on the hinge side of the door," said Miles. Franny pushed. The door creaked, but that was all.

"Miles," Franny began once again, in a whisper now, and he could tell that she was leaning against the door and speaking into the crack. "I've thought of something else I've never confronted you with."

Miles felt the blood rush to his face. Suddenly he banged on the door with his fist. "Will you shut up, you little bitch! You know, I'm not above socking you in earnest if ever I get you out of there!"

"You would sock me just one time, Miles Miller."

"It would be the second time. Don't you forget that," he said.

They were really at it now, for he was reminding her of an occasion two days after their announcement party when he had found her kissing a college kid whose name he did not even know. He had struck her with his open hand on the back of her neck—not while she was kissing the kid but afterward, as he pushed her along the terrace there at the Polo Club. He had had too much to drink that night, and that was what saved them. Franny could claim that he had deserted her in favor of the bar. She also claimed that she had not really been kissing the boy and added that, anyway, he was an old, old, old friend and therefore meant nothing to her. They hardly spoke to each other during the week following, though of course they continued going about together. And until now they had neither of them ever referred to the incident, as if by mutual agreement.

"You're no gentleman, Miles," Franny pronounced, carefully keeping away from the door now. "As Daddy said of you to start with, you have all the outward signs of a gentleman but that's no evidence you're one inside."

"I've already settled your father's hash, Franny."

"You mean he's settled yours."

It was an unfortunate word—"settled." And both of them were aware of it immediately. It quieted both of them for some time. It referred to another incident that was assumed to be closed. Franny's father had apparently suspected Miles of being a fortune hunter, and before the engagement was announced he had asked Miles frankly what kind of "settlement" he expected. Miles had stormed out of the house, and was reconciled with Mr. Crowell only after having it hammered home to him by Franny that what her father had done was merely the conventional, old-fashioned thing for a man in Mr. Crowell's position to do. Miles had finally accepted Franny's explanation, but only a few weeks ago he had had another stormy session over a similar matter. This time it was with both the bride's parents. At that very late date he had learned about certain letters of inquiry that had been sent out concerning his "background." The letters had been written to various family friends and relatives of the Crowells who had lived for many years in Santa Barbara and Laguna Beach. When Miles learned of these letters through a remark of Franny's, it was many months after the letters had been written and replied to. The revelation sent Miles into a rage. He was in such a state that Franny feared he might do real violence to her father, or even to her mother, who had actually written the letters.

She had let the cat out of the bag inadvertently. She and he were just going out to a movie one night. Franny had come down to the living room already wearing her coat and even with her gloves on, but Miles had wanted to linger and talk awhile. Before she came down, he had wandered about the room studying some family photographs taken thirty years before. These "portraits," in their upright frames on the mantelshelf and on the various tables, had reminded him of pictures in his own family's living room when he was growing up. He commenced talking to Franny about how his mother always placed the same pictures on the same tables and bureaus no matter where they were living, and then he went on to speak, as he had on several previous occasions, of how restless his father had been after he left the service. (Miles' father had been a West Point graduate and had remained in the Army until he had his first heart attack, just a few months before Pearl Harbor.) And now, as Miles had already done several times before, he began listing for Franny the towns they had lived in during and after the war.

Franny, who was impatient to get on to the movie, didn't listen very carefully. When Miles hesitated, trying to think of which town it was he had omitted from his list, Franny absent-mindedly supplied "Palo Alto." But it was not Palo Alto he was trying to think of; it was San Jose.

"Palo Alto?" said Miles. "How did you know we ever lived in Palo Alto?"

"You've told me all this before," she answered.

But he had not told her about the spring in Palo Alto! It was then that his parents had quarrelled so endlessly, though he—and probably they—had never known just why. At any rate, he was always careful to leave Palo Alto out of his catalogue of towns. And he was not content now until he had wrung a confession of the whole business of the letters of inquiry out of Franny. Once she had confessed, he insisted upon taking the matter up with her parents that very night; he insisted upon *seeing* the letters. For a time, Mrs. Crowell maintained that she had already thrown away the letters. But at last she broke down. She went upstairs and returned with the packet of letters, all of which Miles read, sitting there in the family circle. He had known there couldn't be anything really bad in them, because just as there was nothing very good that could be said of his parents, there was nothing very bad, either. The worst the letters said of them was that they were "rootless people and apparently of restricted means." Miles found he could not even resent one lady's description of his mother as a "harmless little woman—pleasant enough—with a vague Southern background." The letters repeated each other with phrases like "thoroughly nice" and "well bred" and "well behaved." The sole reference to Palo Alto was "I think they lived at Palo Alto for a time. John's sister Laura met them there. She thought Major Miller very handsome. He had a small black mustache, if I recall."

The memory of all this and of the "settlement" episode occupied Miles' mind as he crossed the hotel room and picked up the glass of champagne that he had poured for Franny. The champagne had gone flat already, but he relished its flatness. He sipped it slowly, as if tasting in each sip a different unpleasant incident or aspect of their courtship and engagement—tasting all they had not tasted and toasted with the first bottle. Suddenly he put down the glass, leaving still a sip or two in the bottom, and stepped quickly over to the bathroom door. "Franny," he said, "it has just occurred to me! It wasn't your father's idea to talk about a settlement with me. You put him up to it! It was you who thought I might be after your family's money! If it had been your father's idea, he wouldn't have been so meek and mild when I called his hand. And, by God, you put your mother up to writing those letters, or she never would have given in and shown them to me."

He waited for Franny's denial, but none came. "And, Franny," he went on after a moment, "there's one more thing I know that you didn't know I knew. Your father went down to my office and asked about the likelihood of my staying on here or being transferred."

"I knew he did that, Miles."

"Darn right you knew it. You put him up to that, too. You didn't even want to take a chance on my moving you away from here." But before he had finished his last sentence, Miles heard the water running full force into the bathtub. "Franny, I'm not finished!" he shouted. "What are you doing?"

"If you don't get this door down within ten minutes"—she was speaking through the crack again—"and get it down without having Bill Carlisle up here to witness it, I'm going to drown myself in the damned bathtub."

As a matter of fact, she had begun running the water to drown out Miles' accusations, but as she spoke she became convinced that suicide really had been her original intention.

"Yes," Miles boomed, "you drown yourself in the bathtub and I'll jump out our eighth-floor window! Romeo and Juliet, that's us!"

Franny shut off the water. She opened her mouth to reply, but no words came. She burst into tears. And the poor little bride could not herself have said whether her tears were brought on by the heavy irony and sarcasm of her groom or by the thought of her dear Miles and her dear self lying dead in their caskets with their love yet unfulfilled.

Almost at once Miles began pleading with her not to cry. But it seemed that his every word brought increased volume to the wailing beyond the bathroom door. It was as if she had decided she could more effectively drown out the sound of his voice with tears than with the rush of bath water. But actually it wasn't the sound of her bridegroom's voice alone that she wished not to hear. There was the sound of another voice—other voices. She had first become aware of the other voices during one of hers and Miles' silences. Which silence she couldn't have said, because for some time afterward she tried to believe that she had only imagined hearing the other voices, or at least imagined that they sounded as near to her as they did. Finally, though, the persistence of the voices drew her attention to the fact of the other door. The other door, she finally acknowledged, must certainly lead into an adjoining room. And the voices—a man's and a woman's—came to her from that room. And now the ever-increasing volume of her own wailing was meant to conceal from herself that the woman's voice was addressing her directly through that door.

"Honey, I think we can help you." The offer was unmistakable.

"No, you can't, no, you can't!" Franny wailed.

"The gentleman in here thinks he is pretty good with locks."

"No, no, please don't come in here," Franny begged, too frightened, too perplexed for more tears now.

"Franny, what's going on?" Miles seemed on the verge of tears himself. "Darling, I'll get a doctor, you'll be all right!"

"Miles, there's another door."

"Yes?"

"And there's someone over there. Oh, Miles, make them go away."

"Keep your head, Franny. What do they want?"

"It's a woman. She says there's a man in there who can get me out of here."

"You do want to get out, don't you, Franny?" It was as though he were speaking to someone on a window ledge.

"Not that way, I don't," said Franny. Now she was whispering through the door crack. "Miles, their voices sound familiar!"

"Now, Franny, cut it out!" scolded Miles, and Franny understood his full meaning. For a moment she listened to the other voices. From the start the man's voice had been no more than a low mumbling. He didn't want his voice recognized! The woman spoke more distinctly. Franny could hear them now discussing the problem. Presently the man said something and laughed. And the woman said, "Hush, the kid will hear you." Somehow this gave Franny courage. She stepped over to the other door and said bravely, "*Will* you help me?"

Hearing her, Miles gave a sigh of relief. Then he said, "Ask them to let me come around into their room—and help."

"Will you let my—my husband come around into your room?"

She heard them deliberating. The man was opposed. Finally, the woman said, "No. He can come and meet you outside our hall door if we get this one open."

She repeated this to Miles.

"Tell them O.K.," he commanded.

"O.K.," said Franny softly.

Now the man and woman were at the door. The man was still mumbling. "Is there a latch on your side?" the woman asked.

"Yes," said Franny. "A little sort of knob."

565

"Tell her to turn it," the man muttered.

"Turn it," said the woman.

Franny turned it. It moved easily. "I have," she said. She watched the big doorknob revolving, but the door didn't open. There was more discussion on the other side of the door.

"It's locked with a key," said the woman to Franny. "But that's how he's going to make hisself useful." Franny's deliverer was hard at work. She couldn't tell whether it was a skeleton key or some makeshift instrument he was using. Presently, she heard the click of the lock and heard the man say, "That's got it."

"Miles!" Franny called out. But Miles didn't answer. He was already waiting at their neighbors' hall door. There was the sound of footsteps hurriedly retreating, and then the door opened. The room itself was in darkness, but in the light from the bathroom Franny could see the man's figure outlined on the bed. The sheet was pulled up over his face. Franny looked at the woman. She was fully dressed, though barefoot, and she stood smiling at the ridiculous sight in the bed and probably at the memory of the male figure's racing across the room and jumping into the bed and pulling the sheet over its head.

"You're an angel," Franny said, without having known she was going to say it.

The woman acknowledged the compliment only by allowing the smile to fade from her lips. "He'll get up from there and try to open the other door for you in a minute," she said.

Franny gave her a grateful smile, and then she turned and walked with perfect poise toward the hall door. Her peach negligee was floor-length and its little train of lace swept gracefully along the dark carpet. When her hand was on the doorknob, she turned and said simply, "Good night." She might have been at home, turning to say a casual good night to her mother.

In the hallway, Miles had waited, fully expecting to have to carry his bride back to their room in his arms. When she appeared he was stunned by her radiance and self-possession. He had never seen her so beautiful. And Franny was equally stunned by Miles' manly beauty as he stood before her in his blue silk pajamas. For a moment they stood there beaming at one another. Finally Miles slipped his arm gently about his bride's waist and hurried her off to their room.

They found their bathroom door standing half open, and the door beyond it tightly closed. The two heavy pins still lay on the floor, but Miles quickly slipped them into the hinges. The door was now in perfect working order. Miles stood a moment gazing into the bright bathroom where Franny's clothes were heaped in one corner like a child's. "Well," he said at last, "that fellow worked fast."

"Miles," said Franny, also looking into the bathroom but with her eyes focussed on the door opposite, "did you see who it was?"

"What do you mean?"

"The woman over there—she was the woman on the elevator."

"Franny, Franny! . . . She got off at the seventh floor! How could you forget?"

"And the man—" Franny began.

"Franny, Franny, Franny," Miles interrupted, already having left her side to fetch the champagne glasses and refill them. "The man in that room is one of the conventioners from out of town. You never heard his voice or saw him before in your life."

She had been going to say that the man in the bed was Bill Carlisle. But she saw it was useless. And she knew she would never say it now. Miles came toward her slowly with the two glasses filled to the brim. They sipped their champagne, looking at one another over the glasses. In their hearts both of them were glad they had said all the things that they said through the door. As they gazed deep into each other's eyes, they believed that they had got all of that off their chests once and for all. There was nothing in the world to come between them now. They believed, really and truly, that neither of them would ever deceive or mistrust the other again. Silently they were toasting their own bliss and happiness, confident that it would never again be shadowed by the irrelevances of the different circumstances of their upbringings or by the possibly impure and selfish motives that had helped to bring them together.

J. F. Powers

THE FORKS

James Farl Powers was born in Jacksonville, Illinois, on July 18, 1917. After attending various public and parochial grade schools, he received his high school training at Quincy College Academy, a Franciscan school. Later he took some college work, mostly English, at the Chicago campus of Northwestern University, where he says he "actually learned something about writing from one of my teachers . . . Bergen Evans." He then served as an editor on the Historical Records Survey, compiling a calendar of manuscripts dealing with early American Methodist circuit-riders, and worked in Chicago book stores. His first story appeared in *Accent* in 1943, and other stories, articles, and reviews have been published in such magazines as *The Commonweal, The Western Review, The New Mexico Quarterly, Tomorrow, The New Yorker,* and *The Partisan Review.* A collection of stories, *The Prince of Darkness,* published in 1943, drew wide critical praise. In 1948 he received both a Guggenheim fellowship and a grant from the National Institute of Arts and Letters. Since 1948, he has been teaching writing courses at Marquette University and winning further plaudits with *The Presence of Grace* (1956), another collection, and with *Morte D'Urban* (1962), a brilliant novel that won the National Book Award.

Powers has an intimate knowledge of the Catholic Church that enables him to write about priests and their problems with real insight, as "The Forks" illustrates. One basic issue which this story presents is the endless struggle between religious idealism and selfish, worldly interests. The reader can best approach an understanding of the complex treatment of this problem by examining the significance of the conflict between the Monsignor and Father Eudex, the function in the story of the bonus checks, and the meaning

569

of the interview between the woman and Father Eudex. "The Forks," however, is more than a commentary on the church: in a broader sense it suggests that the problems of the church are the problems of society at large.

the forks

That summer when Father Eudex got back from saying Mass at the orphanage in the morning, he would park Monsignor's car, which was long and black and new like a politician's, and sit down in the cool of the porch to read his office. If Monsignor was not already standing in the door, he would immediately appear there, seeing that his car had safely returned, and inquire:

"Did you have any trouble with her?"

Father Eudex knew too well the question meant, Did you mistreat my car?

"No trouble, Monsignor."

"Good," Monsignor said, with imperfect faith in his curate, who was not a car owner. For a moment Monsignor stood framed in the screen door, fumbling his watch fob as for a full-length portrait, and then he was suddenly not there.

"Monsignor," Father Eudex said, rising nervously, "I've got a chance to pick up a car."

At the door Monsignor slid into his frame again. His face expressed what was for him intense interest.

"Yes? Go on."

"I don't want to have to use yours every morning."

"It's all right."

"And there are other times." Father Eudex decided not to be maudlin and mention sick calls, nor be entirely honest and admit he was tired of busses and bumming rides from parishioners. "And now I've got a chance to get one—cheap."

From *Prince of Darkness and Other Stories* by J. F. Powers. Copyright 1943, 1944, 1946, 1947 by J. F. Powers, reprinted by permission of Doubleday & Company, Inc.

Monsignor, smiling, came alert at *cheap*.

"New?"

"No, I wouldn't say it's new."

Monsignor was openly suspicious now. "What kind?"

"It's a Ford."

"And not new?"

"Not new, Monsignor—but in good condition. It was owned by a retired farmer and had good care."

Monsignor sniffed. He *knew* cars. "V-Eight, Father?"

"No," Father Eudex confessed. "It's a Model A."

Monsignor chuckled as though this were indeed the damnedest thing he had ever heard.

"But in very good condition, Monsignor."

"You said that."

"Yes. And I could take it apart if anything went wrong. My uncle had one."

"No doubt." Monsignor uttered a laugh at Father Eudex's rural origins. Then he delivered the final word, long delayed out of amusement. "It wouldn't be prudent, Father. After all, this isn't a country parish. You know the class of people we get here."

Monsignor put on his Panama hat. Then, apparently mistaking the obstinacy in his curate's face for plain ignorance, he shed a little more light. "People watch a priest, Father. *Damnant quod non intelligunt*. It would never do. You'll have to watch your tendencies."

Monsignor's eyes tripped and fell hard on the morning paper lying on the swing where he had finished it.

"Another flattering piece about that crazy fellow. . . . There's a man who might have gone places if it weren't for his mouth! A bishop doesn't have to get mixed up in all that stuff!"

Monsignor, as Father Eudex knew, meant unions, strikes, race riots—all that stuff.

"A parishioner was saying to me only yesterday it's getting so you can't tell the Catholics from the Communists, with the priests as bad as any. Yes, and this fellow is the worst. He reminds me of that bishop a few years back—at least he called himself a bishop, a Protestant—that was advocating companionate marriages. It's not that bad, maybe, but if you listened to some of them you'd think that Catholicity and capitalism were incompatible!"

"The Holy Father—"

"The Holy Father's in Europe, Father. Mr. Memmers lives in this parish. I'm his priest. What can I tell him?"

"Is it Mr. Memmers of the First National, Monsignor?"

"It is, Father. And there's damned little cheer I can give a man like Memmers. Catholics, priests, and laity alike—yes, and princes of the Church, all talking atheistic communism!"

This was the substance of their conversation, always, the deadly routine in which Father Eudex played straight man. Each time it happened he seemed to participate, and though he should have known better he justified his participation by hoping that it would not happen again, or in quite the same way. But it did, it always did, the same way, and Monsignor, for all his alarums, had nothing to say really and meant one thing only, the thing he never said—that he dearly wanted to be, and was not, a bishop.

Father Eudex could imagine just what kind of bishop Monsignor would be. His reign would be a wise one, excessively so. His mind was made up on everything, excessively so. He would know how to avoid the snares set in the path of the just man, avoid them, too, in good taste and good conscience. He would not be trapped as so many good shepherds before him had been trapped, poor souls—caught in fair-seeming dilemmas of justice that were best left alone, like the first apple. It grieved him, he said, to think of those great hearts broken in silence and solitude. It was the worst kind of exile, alas! But just give him the chance and he would know what to do, what to say, and, more important, what not to do, not to say—neither yea nor nay for him. He had not gone to Rome for nothing. For him the dark forest of decisions would not exist; for him, thanks to hours spent in prayer and meditation, the forest would vanish as dry grass before fire, his fire. He knew the mask of evil already—birth control, indecent movies, salacious books—and would call these things by their right names and dare to deal with them for what they were, these new occasions for the old sins of the cities of the plains.

But in the meantime—oh, to have a particle of the faith that God had in humanity! Dear, trusting God forever trying them beyond their feeble powers, ordering terrible tests, fatal trials by nonsense (the crazy bishop). And keeping Monsignor steadily warming up on the side lines, ready to rush in, primed for the day that would perhaps never dawn.

At one time, so the talk went, there had been reason to think that Monsignor was headed for a bishopric. Now it was too late; Monsignor's intercessors were all dead; the cupboard was bare; he knew it at heart, and it galled him to see another man, this *crazy* man, given the opportunity, and making such a mess of it.

Father Eudex searched for and found a little salt for Monsignor's wound. "The word's going around he'll be the next archbishop," he said.

"I won't believe it," Monsignor countered hoarsely. He glanced at the newspaper on the swing and renewed his horror. "If that fellow's right, Father, I'm"—his voice cracked at the idea—"*wrong!*"

Father Eudex waited until Monsignor had started down the steps to the car before he said, "It could be."

"I'll be back for lunch, Father. I'm taking her for a little spin."

Monsignor stopped in admiration a few feet from the car—her. He was as helpless before her beauty as a boy with a birthday bicycle. He could not leave her alone. He had her out every morning and afternoon and evening. He was indiscriminate about picking people up for a ride in her. He kept her on a special diet—only the best of gas and oil and grease, with daily rubdowns. He would run her only on the smoothest roads and at so many miles an hour. That was to have stopped at the first five hundred, but only now, nearing the thousand mark, was he able to bring himself to increase her speed, and it seemed to hurt him more than it did her.

Now he was walking around behind her to inspect the tires. Apparently O.K. He gave the left rear fender an amorous chuck and eased into the front seat. Then they drove off, the car and he, to see the world, to explore each other further on the honeymoon.

Father Eudex watched the car slide into the traffic, and waited, on edge. The corner cop, fulfilling Father Eudex's fears, blew his whistle and waved his arms up in all four directions, bringing traffic to a standstill. Monsignor pulled expertly out of line and drove down Clover Boulevard in a one-car parade; all others stalled respectfully. The cop, as Monsignor passed, tipped his cap, showing a bald head. Monsignor, in the circumstances, could not acknowledge him, though he knew the man well—a parishioner. He was occupied with keeping his countenance kindly, grim, and exalted, that the cop's faith remain whole, for it was evidently inconceivable to him that Monsignor should ever venture abroad unless to bear the Holy Viaticum, always racing with death.

Father Eudex, eyes baleful but following the progress of the big black car, saw a hand dart out of the driver's window in a wave. Monsignor would combine a lot of business with pleasure that morning, creating what he called "good will for the Church"—all morning in the driver's seat toasting passers-by with a wave that was better than a blessing. How he loved waving to people!

Father Eudex overcame his inclination to sit and stew about things by going down the steps to meet the mailman. He got the usual handful for the Monsignor—advertisements and amazing offers, the unfailing crop of chaff from dealers in church goods, organs, collection schemes, insurance, and sacramental wines. There were two envelopes addressed to Father Eudex, one a mimeographed plea from a missionary society which he might or might not acknowledge with a contribution, depending upon what he thought of the cause—if it was really lost enough to justify a levy on his poverty—and the other a cheque for a hundred dollars.

The cheque came in an eggshell envelope with no explanation except a tiny card, "Compliments of the Rival Tractor Company," but even that was needless. All over town clergymen had known for days that the cheques were on the way again. Some, rejoicing, could hardly wait. Father Eudex, however, was one of those who could.

With the passing of hard times and the coming of the fruitful war years, the Rival Company, which was a great one for public relations, had found the best solution to the excess-profits problem to be giving. Ministers and even rabbis shared in the annual jack pot, but Rival employees were largely Catholic and it was the cheques to the priests that paid off. Again, some thought it was a wonderful idea, and others thought that Rival, plagued by strikes and justly so, had put their alms to work.

There was another eggshell envelope, Father Eudex saw, among the letters for Monsignor, and knew his cheque would be for two hundred, the premium for pastors.

Father Eudex left Monsignor's mail on the porch table by his cigars. His own he stuck in his back pocket, wanting to forget it, and went down the steps into the yard. Walking back and forth on the shady side of the rectory where the lilies of the valley grew and reading his office, he gradually drifted into the back yard, lured by a noise. He came upon Whalen, the janitor, pounding pegs into the ground.

Father Eudex closed the breviary on a finger. "What's it all about, Joe?"

Joe Whalen snatched a piece of paper from his shirt and handed it to Father Eudex. "He gave it to me this morning."

He—it was the word for Monsignor among them. A docile pronoun only, and yet when it meant the Monsignor it said, and concealed, nameless things.

The paper was a plan for a garden drawn up by the Monsignor in his fine hand. It called for a huge fleur-de-lis bounded by smaller crosses—and these Maltese—a fountain, a sundial, and a cloister walk running from the rectory to the garage. Later there would be birdhouses and a ten-foot wall of thick grey stones, acting as a moat against the eyes of the world. The whole scheme struck Father Eudex as expensive and, in this country, Presbyterian.

When Monsignor drew the plan, however, he must have been in his medieval mood. A spouting whale jostled with Neptune in the choppy waters of the fountain. North was indicated in the legend by a winged cherub huffing and puffing.

Father Eudex held the plan up against the sun to see the watermark. The stationery was new to him, heavy, simulated parchment, with the Church of the Holy Redeemer and Monsignor's name embossed, three initials, W. F. X., William Francis Xavier. With all those initials the man could pass for a radio station, a chancery wit had observed, or if his last name had not been Sweeney, Father Eudex added now, for high Anglican.

Father Eudex returned the plan to Whalen, feeling sorry for him and to an extent guilty before him—if only because he was a priest like Monsignor (now turned architect) whose dream of a monastery garden included the overworked janitor under the head of "labour."

Father Eudex asked Whalen to bring another shovel. Together, almost without words, they worked all morning spading up crosses, leaving the big fleur-de-lis to the last. Father Eudex removed his coat first, then his collar, and finally was down to his undershirt.

Toward noon Monsignor rolled into the driveway.

He stayed in the car, getting red in the face, recovering from the pleasure of seeing so much accomplished as he slowly recognized his curate in Whalen's helper. In a still, appalled voice he called across the lawn, "Father," and waited as for a beast that might or might not have sense enough to come.

Father Eudex dropped his shovel and went over to the car, shirtless.

Monsignor waited a moment before he spoke, as though annoyed by the everlasting necessity, where this person was concerned, to explain. "Father," he said quietly at last, "I wouldn't do any more of that—if I were you. Rather, in any event, I wouldn't."

"All right, Monsignor."

575

"To say the least, it's not prudent. If necessary"—he paused as Whalen came over to dig a cross within earshot—"I'll explain later. It's time for lunch now."

The car, black, beautiful, fierce with chromium, was quiet as Monsignor dismounted, knowing her master. Monsignor went around to the rear, felt a tire, and probed a nasty cinder in the tread.

"Look at that," he said, removing the cinder.

Father Eudex thought he saw the car lift a hoof, gaze around, and thank Monsignor with her headlights.

Monsignor proceeded at a precise pace to the back door of the rectory. There he held the screen open momentarily, as if remembering something or reluctant to enter before himself—such was his humility—but then called to Whalen with an intimacy that could never exist between them.

"Better knock off now, Joe."

Whalen turned in on himself. "*Joe*—is it!"

Father Eudex removed his clothes from the grass. His hands were all blisters, but in them he found a little absolution. He apologized to Joe for having to take the afternoon off. "I can't make it, Joe. Something turned up."

"Sure, Father."

Father Eudex could hear Joe telling his wife about it that night—yeah, the young one got in wrong with the old one again. Yeah, the old one, he don't believe in it, work, for them.

Father Eudex paused in the kitchen to remember he knew not what. It was in his head, asking to be let in, but he did not place it until he heard Monsignor in the next room complaining about the salad to the housekeeper. It was the voice of dear, dead Aunt Hazel, coming from the summer he was ten. He translated the past into the present: I can't come out and play this afternoon, Joe, on account of my monsignor won't let me.

In the dining room Father Eudex sat down at the table and said grace. He helped himself to a chop, creamed new potatoes, pickled beets, jelly, and bread. He liked jelly. Monsignor passed the butter.

"That's supposed to be a tutti-frutti salad," Monsignor said, grimacing at his. "But she used green olives."

Father Eudex said nothing.

"I said she used green olives."

"I like green olives all right."

"*I* like green olives, but *not* in tutti-frutti salad."

Father Eudex replied by eating a green olive, but he knew it could not end there.

"Father," Monsignor said in a new tone. "How would you like to go away and study for a year?"

"Don't think I'd care for it, Monsignor. I'm not the type."

"You're no canonist, you mean?"

"That's one thing."

"Yes. Well, there are other things it might not hurt you to know. To be quite frank with you, Father, I think you need broadening."

"I guess so," Father Eudex said thickly.

"And still, with your tendencies . . . and with the universities honeycombed with Communists. No, that would never do. I think I meant seasoning, not broadening."

"Oh."

"No offence?"

"No offence."

Who would have thought a little thing like an olive could lead to all this, Father Eudex mused—who but himself, that is, for his association with Monsignor had shown him that anything could lead to everything. Monsignor was a master at making points. Nothing had changed since the day Father Eudex walked into the rectory saying he was the new assistant. Monsignor had evaded Father Eudex's hand in greeting, and a few days later, after he began to get the range, he delivered a lecture on the whole subject of handshaking. It was Middle West to shake hands, or South West, or West in any case, and it was not done where he came from, and—why had he ever come from where he came from? Not to be reduced to shaking hands, you could bet! Handshaking was worse than foot washing and unlike that pious practice there was nothing to support it. And from handshaking Monsignor might go into a general discussion of Father Eudex's failings. He used the open forum method, but he was the only speaker and there was never time enough for questions from the audience. Monsignor seized his examples at random from life. He saw Father Eudex coming out of his bedroom in pyjama bottoms only and so told him about the dressing gown, its purpose, something of its history. He advised Father Eudex to barber his armpits, for it was being done all over now. He let Father Eudex see his bottle of cologne, "Steeple," special for clergymen, and said he should not be afraid of it. He suggested that Father Eudex shave his face oftener, too.

He loaned him his Rogers Peet catalogue, which had sketches of clerical blades togged out in the latest, and prayed that he would stop going around looking like a rabbinical student.

He found Father Eudex reading *The Catholic Worker* one day and had not trusted him since. Father Eudex's conception of the priesthood was evangelical in the worst sense, barbaric, gross, foreign to the mind of the Church, which was one of two terms he used as sticks to beat him with. The other was taste. The air of the rectory was often heavy with The Mind of the Church and Taste.

Another thing. Father Eudex could not conduct a civil conversation. Monsignor doubted that Father Eudex could even think to himself with anything like agreement. Certainly any discussion with Father Eudex ended inevitably in argument or sighing. Sighing! Why didn't people talk up if they had anything to say? No, they'd rather sigh! Father, don't ever, ever sigh at me again!

Finally, Monsignor did not like Father Eudex's table manners. This came to a head one night when Monsignor, seeing his curate's plate empty and all the silverware at his place unused except for a single knife, fork, and spoon, exploded altogether, saying it had been on his mind for weeks, and then descending into the vernacular he declared that Father Eudex did not know the forks—now perhaps he could understand that! Meals, unless Monsignor had guests or other things to struggle with, were always occasions of instruction for Father Eudex, and sometimes of chastisement.

And now he knew the worst—if Monsignor was thinking of recommending him for a year of study, in a Sulpician seminary probably, to learn the forks. So this was what it meant to be a priest. *Come, follow me. Going forth, teach ye all nations. Heal the sick, raise the dead, cleanse the lepers, cast out devils.* Teach the class of people we get here? Teach Mr. Memmers? Teach Communists? Teach Monsignors? And where were the poor? The lepers of old? The lepers were in their colonies with nuns to nurse them. The poor were in their holes and would not come out. Mr. Memmers was in his bank, without cheer. The Communists were in their universities, awaiting a sign. And he was at table with Monsignor, and it was enough for the disciple to be as his master, but the housekeeper had used green olives.

Monsignor inquired, "Did you get your cheque today?"

Father Eudex looked up, considered. "I got *a* cheque," he said.

"From the Rival people, I mean?"

"Yes."

"Good. Well, I think you might apply it on the car you're want-

ing. A decent car. That's a worthy cause." Monsignor noticed that
he was not taking it well. "Not that I mean to dictate what you shall
do with your little windfall, Father. It's just that I don't like to see
you mortifying yourself with a Model A—and disgracing the Church."

"Yes," Father Eudex said, suffering.

"Yes. I dare say you don't see the danger, just as you didn't
a while ago when I found you making a spectacle of yourself with
Whalen. You just don't see the danger because you just don't think.
Not to dwell on it, but I seem to remember some overshoes."

The overshoes! Monsignor referred to them as to the Fall.
Last winter Father Eudex had given his overshoes to a freezing picket.
It had got back to Monsignor and—good Lord, a man could have
his sympathies, but he had no right clad in the cloth to endanger the
prestige of the Church by siding in these wretched squabbles. Monsignor said he hated to think of all the evil done by people doing
good! Had Father Eudex ever heard of the Albigensian heresy, or
didn't the seminary teach that any more?

Father Eudex declined dessert. It was strawberry mousse.

"Delicious," Monsignor said. "I think I'll let her stay."

At that moment Father Eudex decided that he had nothing to
lose. He placed his knife next to his fork on the plate, adjusted them
this way and that until they seemed to work a combination in his mind,
to spring a lock which in turn enabled him to speak out.

"Monsignor," he said. "I think I ought to tell you I don't
intend to make use of that money. In fact—to show you how my mind
works—I have even considered endorsing the cheque to the strikers'
relief fund."

"So," Monsignor said calmly—years in the confessional had
prepared him for anything.

"I'll admit I don't know whether I can in justice. And even if
I could I don't know that I would. I don't know why . . . I guess hush
money, no matter what you do with it, is lousy."

Monsignor regarded him with piercing baby blue eyes. "You'd
find it pretty hard to prove, Father, that *any* money *in se* is . . .
what you say it is. I would quarrel further with the definition 'hush
money.' It seems to me nothing if not rash that you would presume to
impugn the motive of the Rival Company in sending out those cheques.
You would seem to challenge the whole concept of good works—not
that I am ignorant of the misuses to which money can be put." Monsignor, changing tack, tucked it all into a sigh. "Perhaps I'm just a
simple soul, and it's enough for me to know personally some of the

people in the Rival Company and to know them good people. Many of them Catholic . . ." A throb had crept into Monsignor's voice. He shut it off.

"I don't mean anything that subtle, Monsignor," Father Eudex said. "I'm just telling you, as my pastor, what I'm going to do with the cheque. Or what I'm not going to do with it. I don't know what I'm going to do with it. Maybe send it back."

Monsignor rose from the table, slightly smiling. "Very well, Father. But there's always the poor."

Monsignor took leave of Father Eudex with a laugh. Father Eudex felt it was supposed to fool him into thinking that nothing he had said would be used against him. It showed, rather, that Monsignor was not winded, that he had broken wild curates before, plenty of them, and that he would ride again.

Father Eudex sought the shade of the porch. He tried to read his office, but was drowsy. He got up for a glass of water. The saints in Ireland used to stand up to their necks in cold water, but not for drowsiness. When he came back to the porch a woman was ringing the doorbell. She looked like a customer for rosary beads.

"Hello," he said.

"I'm Mrs. Klein, Father, and I was wondering if you could help me out."

Father Eudex straightened a porch chair for her. "Please sit down."

"It's a German name, Father. Klein was German descent," she said, and added with a silly grin, "It ain't what you think, Father."

"I beg your pardon."

"Klein. Some think it's a Jew name. But they stole it from Klein."

Father Eudex decided to come back to that later. "You were wondering if I could help you?"

"Yes, Father. It's personal."

"Is it matter for confession?"

"Oh no, Father." He had made her blush.

"Then go ahead."

Mrs. Klein peered into the honeysuckle vines on either side of the porch for alien ears.

"No one can hear you, Mrs. Klein."

"Father—I'm just a poor widow," she said, and continued as though Father Eudex had just slandered the man. "Klein was awful good to me, Father."

"I'm sure he was."

"So good . . . and he went and left me all he had." She had begun to cry a little.

Father Eudex nodded gently. She was after something, probably not money, always the best bet—either that or a drunk in the family—but this one was not Irish. Perhaps just sympathy.

"I come to get your advice, Father. Klein always said, 'If you got a problem, Freda, see the priest.' "

"Do you need money?"

"I got more than I can use from the bakery."

"You have a bakery?"

Mrs. Klein nodded down the street. "That's my bakery. It was Klein's. The Purity."

"I go by there all the time," Father Eudex said, abandoning himself to her. He must stop trying to shape the conversation and let her work it out.

"Will you give me your advice, Father?" He felt that she sensed his indifference and interpreted it as his way of rejecting her. She either had no idea how little sense she made or else supreme faith in him, as a priest, to see into her heart.

"Just what is it you're after, Mrs. Klein?"

"He left me all he had, Father, but it's just laying in the bank."

"And you want me to tell you what to do with it?"

"Yes, Father."

Father Eudex thought this might be interesting, certainly a change. He went back in his mind to the seminary and the class in which they had considered the problem of inheritances. Do we have any unfulfilled obligations? Are we sure? . . . Are there any impedimenta?

"Do you have any dependents, Mrs. Klein—any children?"

"One boy, Father. I got him running the bakery. I pay him good—too much, Father."

"Is 'too much' a living wage?"

"Yes, Father. He ain't got a family."

"A living wage is not too much," Father Eudex handed down, sailing into the encyclical style without knowing it.

Mrs. Klein was smiling over having done something good without knowing precisely what it was.

"How old is your son?"

"He's thirty-six, Father."

"Not married?"

"No, Father, but he's got him a girl." She giggled, and Father Eudex, embarrassed, retied his shoe.

"But you don't care to make a will and leave this money to your son in the usual way?"

"I guess I'll have to . . . if I die." Mrs. Klein was suddenly crushed and haunted, but whether by death or charity, Father Eudex did not know.

"You don't have to, Mrs. Klein. There are many worthy causes. And the worthiest is the cause of the poor. My advice to you, if I understand your problem, is to give what you have to someone who needs it."

Mrs. Klein just stared at him.

"You could even leave it to the archdiocese," he said, completing the sentence to himself: but I don't recommend it in your case . . . with your tendencies. You look like an Indian giver to me.

But Mrs. Klein had got enough. "Huh!" she said, rising. "Well! You *are* a funny one!"

And then Father Eudex realized that she had come to him for a broker's tip. It was in the eyes. The hat. The dress. The shoes. "If you'd like to speak to the pastor," he said, "come back in the evening."

"You're a nice young man," Mrs. Klein said, rather bitter now and bent on getting away from him. "But I got to say this—you ain't much of a priest. And Klein said if I got a problem, see the priest—huh! You ain't much of a priest! What time's your boss come in?"

"In the evening," Father Eudex said. "Come any time in the evening."

Mrs. Klein was already down the steps and making for the street.

"You might try Mr. Memmers at the First National," Father Eudex called, actually trying to help her, but she must have thought it was just some more of his nonsense and did not reply.

After Mrs. Klein had disappeared Father Eudex went to his room. In the hallway upstairs Monsignor's voice, coming from the depths of the clerical nap, halted him.

"Who was it?"

"A woman," Father Eudex said. "A woman seeking good counsel."

He waited a moment to be questioned, but Monsignor was not awake enough to see anything wrong with that, and there came only a sigh and a shifting of weight that told Father Eudex he was simply turning over in bed.

Father Eudex walked into the bathroom. He took the Rival cheque from his pocket. He tore it into little squares. He let them flutter into the toilet. He pulled the chain—hard.

He went to his room and stood looking out the window at nothing. He could hear the others already giving an account of their stewardship, but could not judge them. I bought baseball uniforms for the school. I bought the nuns a new washing machine. I purchased a Mass kit for a Chinese missionary. I bought a set of matched irons. Mine helped pay for keeping my mother in a rest home upstate. I gave mine to the poor.

And you, Father?

Truman Capote

JUG OF SILVER

From the beginning of his writing career to the present, the work of Truman Capote has received a mixed critical reception. There are those, on the one hand, who accuse him of celebrating in his fiction the sensational and grotesque phases of life for their own sake and of being too prone to escape into a contrived narcissistic fictional world, peopled with psychological deviates and other misfits, which bears little relationship to the real world. But there are those, on the other hand, who praise him as the possessor of a bold and strikingly original talent, whose fiction is notable for its range of moods from nightmarish horror to hilarious comedy and for its unerring sense of style. The moderate critic will indeed concede that Capote's fiction has its faults as well as its merits, as is true of nearly any writer who has sought his own personal solution to the timeless problems of his art. But he will also insist that Capote's work commands respect.

Truman Capote, whose real name is Truman S. Persons, was born in New Orleans, Louisiana, in 1925, but spent a portion of his childhood in Alabama. He attended Trinity School in New York City and public school in Greenwich, Connecticut. Encouraged in his early writing efforts by a high school English teacher, he began publishing stories in magazines when he was only seventeen. His first book, however, was a novel, *Other Voices, Other Rooms* (1948). This work, published when he was twenty-three, drew instant notice and promptly established him in the public eye as a precocious *enfant terrible* of literature, a reputation he has not yet fully outlived. His next book, *The Tree of Night and Other Stories* (1949), is his most noteworthy collection of stories. Subsequently, he has published another novel, *The Grass Harp* (1951), which was adapted to the stage in 1952; a second collection of stories, *Breakfast at Tiffany's* (1958); and two volumes of essays, *Local Color* (1950) and *The Muses Are Heard* (1956). The *Selected Writings of Truman Capote* (1963) reprints some of his representative stories and essays. Capote has twice won the O. Henry Memorial Short Story Prize, and in 1959 he received an award from the National Institute of Arts and Letters.

In a perceptive article, "Truman Capote: The Revelation of the Broken Image" (*Virginia Quarterly Review,* Autumn, 1958), Paul Levine notes that ". . . Capote's stories inhabit two worlds—that of the realistic, colloquial, often humorous daytime and that of the dreamlike, detached, and inverted nocturnal world." Whether "Jug of Silver" belongs wholly to one or the other of these worlds—or perhaps to both—should be a matter of some interest to students of Capote's work. In either case the story offers convincing proof of his maturity in the management of characterization and point of view.

jug of silver

After school I used to work in the Valhalla drugstore. It was owned by my uncle, Mr. Ed Marshall. I call him Mr. Marshall because everybody, including his wife, called him Mr. Marshall. Nevertheless he was a nice man.

This drugstore was maybe old-fashioned, but it was large and dark and cool: during summer months there was no pleasanter place in town. At the left, as you entered, was a tobacco-magazine counter behind which, as a rule, sat Mr. Marshall: a squat, square-faced, pink-fleshed man with looping, manly, white mustaches. Beyond this counter stood the beautiful soda fountain. It was very antique and made of fine, yellowed marble, smooth to the touch but without a trace of cheap glaze. Mr. Marshall bought it at an auction in New Orleans in 1910 and was plainly proud of it. When you sat on the high, delicate stools and looked across the fountain you could see yourself reflected softly, as though by candlelight, in a row of ancient, mahogany-framed mirrors. All general merchandise was displayed in glass-doored, curiolike cabinets that were locked with brass keys. There was always in the air the smell of syrup and nutmeg and other delicacies.

The Valhalla was the gathering place of Wachata County till a certain Rufus McPherson came to town and opened a second drugstore directly across the courthouse square. This old Rufus McPherson was a villain; that is, he took away my uncle's trade. He installed fancy equipment such as electric fans and colored lights; he provided curb service and made grilled-cheese sandwiches to order. Naturally, though some remained devoted to Mr. Marshall, most folks couldn't resist Rufus McPherson.

For a while, Mr. Marshall chose to ignore him: if you were to mention McPherson's name he would sort of snort, finger his mustaches and look the other way. But you could tell he was mad. And getting madder. Then one day toward the middle of October I strolled into the Valhalla to find him sitting at the fountain playing dominoes and drinking wine with Hamurabi.

Hamurabi was an Egyptian and some kind of dentist, though he didn't do much business as the people hereabouts have unusually strong teeth, due to an element in the water. He spent a great deal of his time loafing around the Valhalla and was my uncle's chief buddy. He was a handsome figure of a man, this Hamurabi, being dark-skinned and nearly seven feet tall; the matrons of the town kept their daughters under lock and key and gave him the eye themselves. He had no foreign accent whatsoever, and it was always my opinion that he wasn't any more Egyptian than the man in the moon.

Anyway, there they were swigging red Italian wine from a gallon jug. It was a troubling sight, for Mr. Marshall was a renowned teetotaler. So naturally, I thought: Oh, golly, Rufus McPherson has finally got his goat. That was not the case, however.

"Here, son," said Mr. Marshall, "come have a glass of wine."

"Sure," said Hamurabi, "help us finish it up. It's store-bought, so we can't waste it."

Much later, when the jug was dry, Mr. Marshall picked it up and said, "Now we shall see!" And with that disappeared out into the afternoon.

"Where's he off to?" I asked.

"Ah," was all Hamurabi would say. He liked to devil me.

A half-hour passed before my uncle returned. He was stooped and grunting under the load he carried. He set the jug atop the fountain and stepped back, smiling and rubbing his hands together. "Well, what do you think?"

"Ah," purred Hamurabi.

"Gee . . ." I said.

It was the same wine jug, God knows, but there was a wonderful difference; for now it was crammed to the brim with nickels and dimes that shone dully through the thick glass.

"Pretty, eh?" said my uncle. "Had it done over at the First National. Couldn't get in anything bigger-sized than a nickel. Still, there's lotsa money in there, let me tell you."

"But what's the point, Mr. Marshall?" I said. "I mean, what's the idea?"

Mr. Marshall's smile deepened to a grin. "This here's a jug of silver, you might say. . . ."

"The pot at the end of the rainbow," interrupted Hamurabi.

". . . and the idea, as you call it, is for folks to guess how much money is in there. For instance, say you buy a quarter's worth of stuff—well, then you get to take a chance. The more you buy, the more chances you get. And I'll keep all guesses in a ledger till Christmas Eve, at which time whoever comes closest to the right amount will get the whole shebang."

Hamurabi nodded solemnly. "He's playing Santa Claus—a mighty crafty Santa Claus," he said. "I'm going home and write a book: *The Skillful Murder of Rufus McPherson.*" To tell the truth, he sometimes did write stories and send them out to the magazines. They always came back.

It was surprising, really like a miracle, how Wachata County took to the jug. Why, the Valhalla hadn't done so much business since Station Master Tully, poor soul, went stark raving mad and claimed to have discovered oil back of the depot, causing the town to be overrun with wildcat prospectors. Even the pool-hall bums who never spent a cent on anything not connected with whiskey or women took to investing their spare cash in milk shakes. A few elderly ladies publicly disapproved of Mr. Marshall's enterprise as a kind of gambling, but they didn't start any trouble and some even found occasion to visit us and hazard a guess. The school kids were crazy about the whole thing, and I was very popular because they figured I knew the answer.

"I'll tell you why all this is," said Hamurabi, lighting one of the Egyptian cigarettes he bought by mail from a concern in New York City. "It's not for the reason you may imagine; not, in other words, avidity. No. It's the mystery that's enchanting. Now you look at those nickels and dimes and what do you think: ah, *so* much! No, no. You think: ah, *how* much? And that's a profound question, indeed. It can mean different things to different people. Understand?"

And oh, was Rufus McPherson wild! When you're in trade, you count on Christmas to make up a large share of your yearly profit, and he was hard pressed to find a customer. So he tried to imitate the jug; but being such a stingy man he filled his with pennies. He also wrote a letter to the editor of *The Banner,* our weekly paper, in which he said that Mr. Marshall ought to be "tarred and feathered and strung up for turning innocent little children into confirmed gamblers and sending them down the path to Hell!" You can imagine what kind of laughing stock he was. Nobody had anything for McPherson but scorn. And so by the middle of November he just stood on the sidewalk outside his store and gazed bitterly at the festivities across the square.

At about this time Appleseed and sister made their first appearance.

He was a stranger in town. At least no one could recall ever having seen him before. He said he lived on a farm a mile past Indian Branches; told us his mother weighed only seventy-four pounds and that he had an older brother who would play the fiddle at anybody's wedding for fifty cents. He claimed that Appleseed was the only name he had and that he was twelve years old. But his sister, Middy, said he was eight. His hair was straight and dark yellow. He had a tight, weather-tanned little face with anxious green eyes that had a very wise and knowing look. He was small and puny and high-strung; and he wore always the same outfit: a red sweater, blue denim britches and a pair of man-sized boots that went clop-clop with every step.

It was raining that first time he came into the Valhalla; his hair was plastered round his head like a cap and his boots were caked with red mud from the country roads. Middy trailed behind as he swaggered like a cowboy up to the fountain where I was wiping some glasses.

"I hear tell you folks got a bottle fulla money you fixin' to give 'way," he said, looking me square in the eye. "Seein' as you-all are givin' it away, we'd be obliged iffen you'd give it to us. Name's Appleseed, and this here's my sister, Middy."

Middy was a sad, sad-looking kid. She was a good bit taller and older-looking than her brother: a regular bean pole. She had tow-colored hair that was chopped short, and a pale pitiful little face. She wore a faded cotton dress that came way up above her bony knees. There was something wrong with her teeth, and she tried to conceal this by keeping her lips primly pursed like an old lady.

"Sorry," I said, "but you'll have to talk with Mr. Marshall."

So sure enough he did. I could hear my uncle explaining what he would have to do to win the jug. Appleseed listened attentively, nodding now and then. Presently he came back and stood in front of the jug and, touching it lightly with his hand, said, "Ain't it a pretty thing, Middy?"

Middy said, "Is they gonna give it to us?"

"Naw. What you gotta do, you gotta guess how much money's inside there. And you gotta buy two bits' worth so's even to get a chance."

"Huh, we ain't got no two bits. Where you 'spec we gonna get us two bits?"

Appleseed frowned and rubbed his chin. "That'll be the easy part, just leave it to me. The only worrisome thing is: I can't just take a chance and guess. . . . I gotta *know*."

Well, a few days later they showed up again. Appleseed perched on a stool at the fountain and boldly asked for two glasses of water, one for him and one for Middy. It was on this occasion that he gave out the information about his family: ". . . then there's Papa Daddy, that's my mamma's papa, who's a Cajun, an' on accounta that he don't speak English good. My brother, the one what plays the fiddle, he's been in jail three times. . . . It's on accounta him we had to pick up and leave Louisiana. He cut a fella bad in a razor fight over a woman ten years older'n him. She had yellow hair."

Middy, lingering in the background, said nervously, "You oughtn't to be tellin' our personal private fam'ly business thataway, Appleseed."

"Hush now, Middy," he said, and she hushed. "She's a good little gal," he added, turning to pat her head, "but you can't let her get away with much. You go look at the picture books, honey, and stop frettin' with your teeth. Appleseed here's got some figurin' to do."

This figuring meant staring hard at the jug, as if his eyes were trying to eat it up. With his chin cupped in his hand, he studied it for a long period, not batting his eyelids once. "A lady in Louisiana told me I could see things other folks couldn't see 'cause I was born with a caul on my head."

"It's a cinch you aren't going to see how much there is," I told him. "Why don't you just let a number pop into your head, and maybe that'll be the right one."

"Uh, uh," he said, "too darn risky. Me, I can't take no sucha chance. Now, the way I got it figured, there ain't but one sure-fire thing and that's to count every nickel and dime."

"Count!"

"Count what?" asked Hamurabi, who had just moseyed inside and was settling himself at the fountain.

"This kid says he's going to count how much is in the jug," I explained.

Hamurabi looked at Appleseed with interest. "How do you plan to do that, son?"

"Oh, by countin'," said Appleseed matter-of-factly.

Hamurabi laughed. "You better have X-ray eyes, son, that's all I can say."

"Oh, no. All you gotta do is be born with a caul on your head. A lady in Louisiana told me so. She was a witch; she loved me and when my ma wouldn't give me to her she put a hex on her and now my ma don't weigh but seventy-four pounds."

"Ve-ry in-ter-esting," was Hamurabi's comment as he gave Appleseed a queer glance.

Middy sauntered up, clutching a copy of *Screen Secrets*. She pointed out a certain photo to Appleseed and said: "Ain't she the nicest-lookin' lady? Now you see, Appleseed, you see how pretty her teeth are? Not a one outa joint."

"Well, don't you fret none," he said.

After they left Hamurabi ordered a bottle of orange Nehi and drank it slowly, while smoking a cigarette. "Do you think maybe that kid's o.k. upstairs?" he asked presently in a puzzled voice.

Small towns are best for spending Christmas, I think. They catch the mood quicker and change and come alive under its spell. By the first week in December house doors were decorated with wreaths, and store windows were flashy with red paper bells and snowflakes of glittering isinglass. The kids hiked out into the woods and came back dragging spicy evergreen trees. Already the women were busy baking fruitcakes, unsealing jars of mincemeat and opening bottles of blackberry and scuppernong wine. In the courthouse square a huge tree was trimmed with silver tinsel and colored electric bulbs that were lighted up at sunset. Late of an afternoon you could hear the choir in the Presbyterian church practicing carols for their annual pageant. All over town the japonicas were in full bloom.

The only person who appeared not the least touched by this heartwarming atmosphere was Appleseed. He went about his declared business of counting the jug-money with great, persistent care. Every day now he came to the Valhalla and concentrated on the jug, scowling and mumbling to himself. At first we were all fascinated, but after a while it got tiresome and nobody paid him any mind whatsoever. He never bought anything, apparently having never been able to raise the two bits. Sometimes he'd talk to Hamurabi, who had taken a tender interest in him and occasionally stood treat to a jawbreaker or a penny's worth of licorice.

"Do you still think he's nuts?" I asked.

"I'm not so sure," said Hamurabi. "But I'll let you know. He doesn't eat enough. I'm going to take him over to the Rainbow Café and buy him a plate of barbecue."

"He'd appreciate it more if you'd give him a quarter."

"No. A dish of barbecue is what he needs. Besides, it would be better if he never was to make a guess. A high-strung kid like that, so unusual, I wouldn't want to be the one responsible if he lost. Say, it would be pitiful."

I'll admit that at the time Appleseed struck me as being just funny. Mr. Marshall felt sorry for him, and the kids tried to tease him, but had to give it up when he refused to respond. There you could see him plain as day sitting at the fountain with his forehead puckered and his eyes fixed forever on that jug. Yet he was so withdrawn you sometimes had this awful creepy feeling that, well, maybe he didn't exist. And when you were pretty much convinced of this he'd wake up and say something like, "You know, I hope a 1913 buffalo nickel's in there. A fella was tellin' me he saw where a 1913 buffalo nickel's worth fifty dollars. Or, "Middy's gonna be a big lady in the picture shows. They make lotsa money, the ladies in the picture shows do, and then we ain't gonna never eat another collard green as long as we live. Only Middy says she can't be in the picture shows 'less her teeth look good."

Middy didn't always tag along with her brother. On those occasions when she didn't come, Appleseed wasn't himself; he acted shy and left soon.

Hamurabi kept his promise and stood treat to a dish of barbecue at the café. "Mr. Hamurabi's nice, all right," said Appleseed afterward, "but he's got peculiar notions: has a notion that if he lived in this place named Egypt he'd be a king or somethin'."

And Hamurabi said, "That kid has the most touching faith. It's a beautiful thing to see. But I'm beginning to despise the whole business." He gestured toward the jug. "Hope of this kind is a cruel thing to give anybody, and I'm damned sorry I was ever a party to it."

Around the Valhalla the most popular pastime was deciding what you would buy if you won the jug. Among those who participated were: Solomon Katz, Phoebe Jones, Carl Kuhnhardt, Puly Simmons, Addie Foxcroft, Marvin Finkle, Trudy Edwards and a colored man named Erskine Washington. And these were some of their answers: a trip to and a permanent wave in Birmingham, a second-hand piano, a Shetland pony, a gold bracelet, a set of *Rover Boys* books and a life insurance policy.

Once Mr. Marshall asked Appleseed what he would get. "It's a secret," was the reply, and no amount of prying could make him tell. We took it for granted that whatever it was, he wanted it real bad.

Honest winter, as a rule, doesn't settle on our part of the country till late January, and then is mild, lasting only a short time. But in the year of which I write we were blessed with a singular cold spell the week before Christmas. Some still talk of it, for it was so terrible: water pipes froze solid; many folks had to spend the days in bed snuggled under their quilts, having neglected to lay in enough kindling for the fireplace; the sky turned that strange dull gray as it does just before a storm, and the sun was pale as a waning moon. There was a sharp wind: the old dried-up leaves of last fall fell on the icy ground, and the evergreen tree in the courthouse square was twice stripped of its Christmas finery. When you breathed, your breath made smoky clouds. Down by the silk mill where the very poor people lived, the families huddled together in the dark at night and told tales to keep their minds off the cold. Out in the country the farmers covered their delicate plants with gunny sacks and prayed; some took advantage of the weather to slaughter their hogs and bring the fresh sausage to town. Mr. R. C. Judkins, our town drunk, outfitted himself in a red cheesecloth suit and played

Santa Claus at the five 'n' dime. Mr. R. C. Judkins was the father of a big family, so everybody was happy to see him sober enough to earn a dollar. There were several church socials, at one of which Mr. Marshall came face to face with Rufus McPherson: bitter words were passed but not a blow was struck.

Now, as has been mentioned, Appleseed lived on a farm a mile below Indian Branches; this would be approximately three miles from town; a mighty long and lonesome walk. Still, despite the cold, he came every day to the Valhalla and stayed till closing time which, as the days had grown short, was after nightfall. Once in a while he'd catch a ride partway home with the foreman from the silk mill, but not often. He looked tired, and there were worry lines about his mouth. He was always cold and shivered a lot. I don't think he wore any warm drawers underneath his red sweater and blue britches.

It was three days before Christmas when out of the clear sky, he announced: "Well, I'm finished. I mean I know how much is in the bottle." He claimed this with such grave, solemn sureness it was hard to doubt him.

"Why, say now, son, hold on," said Hamurabi, who was present. "You can't know anything of the sort. It's wrong to think so: you're just heading to get yourself hurt."

"You don't need to preach to me, Mr. Hamurabi. I know what I'm up to. A lady in Louisiana, she told me . . ."

"Yes yes yes—but you got to forget that. If it were me, I'd go home and stay put and forget about this goddamned jug."

"My brother's gonna play the fiddle at a wedding over in Cherokee City tonight and he's gonna give me the two bits," said Appleseed stubbornly. "Tomorrow I'll take my chance."

So the next day I felt kind of excited when Appleseed and Middy arrived. Sure enough, he had his quarter: it was tied for safe-keeping in the corner of a red bandanna.

The two of them wandered hand in hand among the showcases, holding a whispery consultation as to what to purchase. They decided finally on a thimble-sized bottle of gardenia cologne which Middy promptly opened and partly emptied on her hair. "It smells like . . . oh, darlin' Mary, I ain't never smelled nothin' as sweet. Here, Appleseed, honey, let me douse some on your hair." But he wouldn't let her.

Mr. Marshall got out the ledger in which he kept his records, while Appleseed strolled over to the fountain and cupped the jug between his hands, stroking it gently. His eyes were bright and his cheeks flushed from excitement. Several persons who were in the drugstore at that moment crowded close. Middy stood in the background quietly scratching her leg and smelling the cologne. Hamurabi wasn't there.

Mr. Marshall licked the point of his pencil and smiled. "Okay, son, what do you say?"

Appleseed took a deep breath. "Seventy-seven dollars and thirty-five cents," he blurted.

In picking such an uneven sum he showed originality, for the run-of-the-mill guess was a plain round figure. Mr. Marshall repeated the amount solemnly as he copied it down.

"When'll I know if I won?"

"Christmas Eve," someone said.

"That's tomorrow, huh?"

"Why, so it is," said Mr. Marshall, not surprised. "Come at four o'clock."

During the night the thermometer dropped even lower, and toward dawn there was one of those swift, summerlike rainstorms, so that the following day was bright and frozen. The town was like a picture postcard of a Northern scene, what with icicles sparkling whitely on the trees and frost flowers coating all windowpanes. Mr. R. C. Judkins rose early and, for no clear reason, tramped the streets ringing a supper bell, stopping now and then to take a swig of whiskey from a pint which he kept in his hip pocket. As the day was windless, smoke climbed lazily from various chimneys straightway to the still, frozen sky. By midmorning the Presbyterian choir was in full swing; and the town kids (wearing horror masks, as at Hallowe'en) were chasing one another round and round the square, kicking up an awful fuss.

Hamurabi dropped by at noon to help us fix up the Valhalla. He brought along a fat sack of Satsumas, and together we ate every last one, tossing the hulls into a newly installed potbellied stove (a present from Mr. Marshall to himself) which stood in the middle of the room. Then my uncle took the jug off the fountain, polished and placed it on a prominently situated table. He was no help after that whatsoever, for he squatted in a chair and spent his time tying and retying a tacky green ribbon around the jug. So Hamurabi and I had the rest to do alone: we swept the floor and washed the mirrors and dusted the cabinets and strung streamers of red and green crepe paper from wall to wall. When we were finished it looked very fine and elegant.

But Hamurabi gazed sadly at our work, and said: "Well, I think I better be getting along now."

"Aren't you going to stay?" asked Mr. Marshall, shocked.

"No, oh, no," said Hamurabi, shaking his head slowly. "I don't want to see that kid's face. This is Christmas and I mean to have a rip-roaring time. And I couldn't, not with something like that on my conscience. Hell, I wouldn't sleep."

"Suit yourself," said Mr. Marshall. And he shrugged, but you could see he was really hurt. "Life's like that—and besides, who knows, he might win."

Hamurabi sighed gloomily. "What's his guess?"

"Seventy-seven dollars and thirty-five cents," I said.

"Now I ask you, isn't that fantastic?" said Hamurabi.

He slumped in a chair next to Mr. Marshall and crossed his legs and lit a cigarette. "If you got any Baby Ruths I think I'd like one; my mouth tastes sour."

As the afternoon wore on, the three of us sat around the table feeling terribly blue. No one said hardly a word and, as the kids had deserted the square, the only sound was the clock tolling the hour in the courthouse steeple. The Valhalla was closed to business, but people kept passing by and peeking in the window. At three o'clock Mr. Marshall told me to unlock the door.

Within twenty minutes the place was jam full; everyone was wearing his Sunday best, and the air smelled sweet, for most of the little silk-mill girls had scented themselves with vanilla flavoring. They scrunched up against the walls, perched on the fountain, squeezed in wherever they could; soon the crowd had spread to the sidewalk and stretched into the road. The square was lined with team-drawn wagons and Model T Fords that had carted farmers and their families into town. There was much laughter and shouting and joking—several outraged ladies complained of the cursing and the rough, shoving ways of the younger men, but nobody left. At the side entrance a gang of colored folks had formed and were having the most fun of all. Everybody was making the best of a good thing. It's usually so quiet around here: nothing much ever happens. It's safe to say that nearly all of Wachata County was present but invalids and Rufus McPherson. I looked around for Appleseed but didn't see him anywhere.

Mr. Marshall harumphed, and clapped for attention. When things quieted down and the atmosphere was properly tense, he raised his voice like an auctioneer, and called: "Now listen, everybody, in this here envelope you see in my hand"—he held a manila envelope above his head—"well, in it's the *answer*—which nobody but God and the First National Bank knows up to now, ha, ha. And in this book"—he held up the ledger with his free hand—"I've got written down what you folks guessed. Are there any questions?" All was silence. "Fine. Now, if we could have a volunteer . . ."

Not a living soul budged an inch: it was as if an awful shyness had overcome the crowd, and even those who were ordinarily natural-born show-offs shuffled their feet, ashamed. Then a voice, Appleseed's, hollered, "Lemme by . . . Outa the way, please, ma'am." Trotting along behind as he pushed forward were Middy and a lanky, sleepy-eyed fellow who was evidently the fiddling brother. Appleseed was dressed the same as usual, but his face was scrubbed rosy clean, his boots polished and his hair slicked back skin tight with Stacomb. "Did we get here in time?" he panted.

But Mr. Marshall said, "So you want to be our volunteer?"

Appleseed looked bewildered, then nodded vigorously.

"Does anybody have an objection to this young man?"

Still there was dead quiet. Mr. Marshall handed the envelope to Appleseed who accepted it calmly. He chewed his under lip while studying it a moment before ripping the flap.

In all that congregation there was no sound except an occasional cough and the soft tinkling of Mr. R. C. Judkins' supper bell. Hamurabi was leaning against the fountain, staring up at the ceiling; Middy was gazing blankly over her brother's shoulder, and when he started to tear open the envelope she let out a pained little gasp.

Appleseed withdrew a slip of pink paper and, holding it as though it was very fragile, muttered to himself whatever was written there. Suddenly his face paled and tears glistened in his eyes.

"Hey, speak up, boy," someone hollered.

Hamurabi stepped forward and all but snatched the slip away. He cleared his throat and commenced to read when his expression changed most comically. "Well, Mother o' God . . ." he said.

"Louder! Louder!" an angry chorus demanded.

"Buncha crooks!" yelled Mr. R. C. Judkins, who had a snootful by this time. "I smell a rat and he smells to high heaven!" Whereupon a cyclone of catcalls and whistling rent the air.

Appleseed's brother whirled round and shook his fist. "Shuddup, shuddup 'fore I bust every one a your goddamn heads together so's you got knots the size a musk melons, hear me?"

"Citizens," cried Mayor Mawes, "citizens—I say, this is Christmas . . . I say . . ."

And Mr. Marshall hopped up on a chair and clapped and stamped till a minimum of order was restored. It might as well be noted here that we later found out Rufus McPherson had paid Mr. R. C. Judkins to start the rumpus. Anyway, when the outbreak was quelled, who should be in possession of the slip but me . . . don't ask how.

Without thinking, I shouted, "Seventy-seven dollars and thirty-five cents." Naturally, due to the excitement, I didn't at first catch the meaning; it was just a number. Then Appleseed's brother let forth with his whooping yell, and so I understood. The name of the winner spread quickly, and the awed, murmuring whispers were like a rainstorm.

Oh, Appleseed himself was a sorry sight. He was crying as though he was mortally wounded, but when Hamurabi lifted him onto his shoulders so the crowd could get a gander, he dried his eyes with the cuffs of his sweater and began grinning. Mr. R. C. Judkins yelled, "Gyp! Lousy gyp!" but was drowned out by a deafening round of applause.

Middy grabbed my arm. "My teeth," she squealed. "Now I'm gonna get my teeth."

"Teeth?" said I, kind of dazed.

"The false kind," says she. "That's what we're gonna get us with the money—a lovely set of white false teeth."

But at that moment my sole interest was in how Appleseed had known. "Hey, tell me," I said desperately, "tell me, how in God's name did he know there was just exactly seventy-seven dollars and thirty-five cents?"

Middy gave me this *look*. "Why, I thought he told you," she said, real serious. "He counted."

"Yes, but how—how?"

"Gee, don't you even know how to count?"

"But is that all he did?"

"Well," she said, following a thoughtful pause, "he did do a little praying, too." She started to dart off, then turned back and called, "Besides, he was born with a caul on his head."

And that's the nearest anybody ever came to solving the mystery.

Thereafter, if you were to ask Appleseed "How come?" he would smile strangely and change the subject. Many years later he and his family moved to somewhere in Florida and were never heard from again.

But in our town his legend flourishes still; and, till his death a year ago last April, Mr. Marshall was invited each Christmas Day to tell the story of Appleseed to the Baptist Bible class. Hamurabi once typed up an account and mailed it around to various magazines. It was never printed. One editor wrote back and said that "If the little girl really turned out to be a movie star, then there might be something to your story." But that's not what happened, so why should you lie?

Flannery O'Connor

GOOD COUNTRY PEOPLE

With the publication in 1955 of *A Good Man Is Hard to Find and Other Stories,* Flannery O'Connor won immediate recognition as one of the most talented members of the younger generation of American story writers. Though her fiction has a strong Southern accent, she is a regionalist only in the sense that the artist concerned with reality must anchor his fiction firmly in the life he has observed and knows best. Actually, her larger aim is to depict the distortions which the writer with "Christian concerns" can find existing everywhere in modern life. To make these distortions recognizable as such to the reader used to accepting them as normal, she believes the writer must accentuate real life—if need be even to the extent of shocking the reader into an awareness of the distortions. As the means to this end she sometimes resorts to the use of grotesque characters and violent action in her stories, which enables her to create powerful effects otherwise unattainable. Despite the fact that she writes from the vantage point of a person who has a strong commitment to the Christian doctrine, she is an artist, not a propagandist.

Miss O'Connor was born in Savannah, Georgia, in 1925. After early educational training in Savannah, she attended Peabody High School in Milledgeville, Georgia, earned her bachelor's degree at the Georgia State College for Women in 1945, and then continued her education at the State University of Iowa, where she studied creative writing in Paul Engle's Writers Workshop for two years and earned an M.F.A. degree in 1947. Her fiction began appearing in 1946, first in *Accent* and then in the *Sewanee, Partisan,* and *Kenyon Reviews* as well as in various other periodicals such as *Harper's Bazaar, Mademoiselle,* and *New World Writing.* Her first book, chapters of which had received prior publication in periodicals, was a novel, *Wise Blood* (1952). Neither this first novel nor her second, *The Violent Bear It Away* (1960), however, has drawn the high praise that her short stories have consistently received, both those reprinted in *A Good Man Is Hard to Find* (1955) and those so far uncollected. Since 1954, the editors of the two best-stories-of-the-year collections have regularly included her work in their volumes, and she has twice won the first prize story citation, first in 1957 and again in 1963. Other honors her fiction has brought her include two *Kenyon Review* writing fellowships, a grant from the National Academy of Arts and Letters in 1957, and a $10,000 grant from the Ford Foundation in 1959—this last being one of three such awards given to American writers that year. Miss O'Conner died in August 1964.

"Good Country People" is a noteworthy example of Miss O'Connor's art. Thematically, it reflects her deep concern with the "heart condition" or spiritual barrenness which afflicts members of modern society and is more terrifying than mere physical illness. Structurally, it illustrates her characteristic method of writing wherein a seemingly casual flow of events culminates suddenly in an explosive and—in this case—bizarre climax.

good country people

Besides the neutral expression that she wore when she was alone, Mrs. Freeman had two others, forward and reverse, that she used for all her human dealings. Her forward expression was steady and driving like the advance of a heavy truck. Her eyes never swerved to left or right but turned as the story turned as if they followed a yellow line down the center of it. She seldom used the other expression because it was not often necessary for her to retract a statement, but when she did, her face came to a complete stop, there was an almost imperceptible movement of her black eyes, during which they seemed to be receding, and then the observer would see that Mrs. Freeman, though she might stand there as real as several grain sacks thrown on top of each other, was no longer there in spirit. As for getting anything across to her when this was the case, Mrs. Hopewell had given it up. She might talk her head off. Mrs. Freeman could never be brought to admit herself wrong on any point. She would stand there and if she could be brought to say anything, it was something like, "Well, I wouldn't of said it was and I wouldn't of said it wasn't," or letting her gaze range over the top kitchen shelf where there was an assortment of dusty bottles, she might remark, "I see you ain't ate many of them figs you put up last summer."

They carried on their most important business in the kitchen at breakfast. Every morning Mrs. Hopewell got up at seven o'clock and lit her gas heater and Joy's. Joy was her daughter, a large blonde girl who had an artificial leg. Mrs. Hopewell thought of her as a child though she was thirty-two years old and highly educated. Joy would get up while her mother was eating and lumber into the bathroom and slam the door, and before long, Mrs. Freeman would arrive at the back door. Joy would hear her mother call, "Come on in," and then they would talk for a while in low voices that were indistinguishable in the bathroom. By the time Joy came in, they had usually finished the weather report and were on

© 1955 by Flannery O'Connor. Reprinted from her volume *A Good Man Is Hard to Find and Other Stories* by permission of Harcourt, Brace & World, Inc.

one or the other of Mrs. Freeman's daughters, Glynese or Carramae. Joy called them Glycerin and Caramel. Glynese, a redhead, was eighteen and had many admirers; Carramae, a blonde, was only fifteen but already married and pregnant. She could not keep anything on her stomach. Every morning Mrs. Freeman told Mrs. Hopewell how many times she had vomited since the last report.

Mrs. Hopewell liked to tell people that Glynese and Carramae were two of the finest girls she knew and that Mrs. Freeman was a *lady* and that she was never ashamed to take her anywhere or introduce her to anybody they might meet. Then she would tell how she had happened to hire the Freemans in the first place and how they were a godsend to her and how she had had them four years. The reason for her keeping them so long was that they were not trash. They were good country people. She had telephoned the man whose name they had given as a reference and he had told her that Mr. Freeman was a good farmer but that his wife was the nosiest woman ever to walk the earth. "She's got to be into everything," the man said. "If she don't get there before the dust settles, you can bet she's dead, that's all. She'll want to know all your business. I can stand him real good," he had said, "but me nor my wife neither could have stood that woman one more minute on this place." That had put Mrs. Hopewell off for a few days.

She had hired them in the end because there were no other applicants but she had made up her mind beforehand exactly how she would handle the woman. Since she was the type who had to be into everything, then, Mrs. Hopewell had decided, she would not only let her be into everything, she would *see to it* that she was into everything—she would give her the responsibility of everything, she would put her in charge. Mrs. Hopewell had no bad qualities of her own but she was able to use other people's in such a constructive way that she never felt the lack. She had hired the Freemans and she had kept them four years.

Nothing is perfect. This was one of Mrs. Hopewell's favorite sayings. Another was: that is life! And still another, the most important, was: well, other people have their opinions too. She would make these statements, usually at the table, in a tone of gentle insistence as if no one held them but her, and the large hulking Joy, whose constant outrage had obliterated every expression from her face, would stare just a little to the side of her, her eyes icy blue, with the look of someone who has achieved blindness by an act of will and means to keep it.

When Mrs. Hopewell said to Mrs. Freeman that life was like that, Mrs. Freeman would say, "I always said so myself." Nothing had been arrived at by anyone that had not first been arrived at by her. She was quicker than Mr. Freeman. When Mrs. Hopewell said to her after they had been on the place a while, "You know, you're the wheel behind the wheel," and winked, Mrs. Freeman had said, "I know it. I've always been quick. It's some that are quicker than others."

"Everybody is different," Mrs. Hopewell said.

"Yes, most people is," Mrs. Freeman said.

"It takes all kinds to make the world."

"I always said it did myself."

The girl was used to this kind of dialogue for breakfast and more of it for dinner; sometimes they had it for supper too. When they had no guest they ate in the kitchen because that was easier. Mrs. Freeman always managed to arrive at some point during the meal and to watch them finish it. She would stand in the doorway if it were summer but in the winter she would stand with one elbow on top of the refrigerator and look down on them, or she would stand by the gas heater, lifting the back of her skirt slightly. Occasionally she would stand against the wall and roll her head from side to side. At no time was she in any hurry to leave. All this was very trying on Mrs. Hopewell but she was a woman of great patience. She realized that nothing is perfect and that in the Freemans she had good country people and that if, in this day and age, you get good country people, you had better hang onto them.

She had had plenty of experience with trash. Before the Freemans she had averaged one tenant family a year. The wives of these farmers were not the kind you would want to be around you for very long. Mrs. Hopewell, who had divorced her husband long ago, needed someone to walk over the fields with her; and when Joy had to be impressed for these services, her remarks were usually so ugly and her face so glum that Mrs. Hopewell would say, "If you can't come pleasantly, I don't want you at all," to which the girl, standing square and rigid-shouldered with her neck thrust slightly forward, would reply, "If you want me, here I am—LIKE I AM."

Mrs. Hopewell excused this attitude because of the leg (which had been shot off in a hunting accident when Joy was ten). It was hard for Mrs. Hopewell to realize that her child was thirty-two now and that for more than twenty years she had had only one leg. She thought of her still as a child because it tore her heart to think instead of the poor stout girl in her thirties who had never danced a step or had any *normal* good times. Her name was really Joy but as soon as she was twenty-one and away from home, she had had it legally changed. Mrs. Hopewell was certain that she had thought and thought until she had hit upon the ugliest name in any language. Then she had gone and had the beautiful name, Joy, changed without telling her mother until after she had done it. Her legal name was Hulga.

When Mrs. Hopewell thought the name, Hulga, she thought of the broad blank hull of a battleship. She would not use it. She continued to call her Joy to which the girl responded but in a purely mechanical way.

Hulga had learned to tolerate Mrs. Freeman who saved her from taking walks with her mother. Even Glynese and Carramae were useful when they occupied attention that might otherwise have been directed at her. At first she had thought she could not stand Mrs. Freeman for she had found that it was not possible to be rude to her. Mrs. Freeman would take on strange resentments and for days together she would be sullen but the source of her displeasure was always obscure; a direct attack, a positive leer, blatant ugliness to her face—these never touched her. And without warning one day, she began calling her Hulga.

She did not call her that in front of Mrs. Hopewell who would have been incensed but when she and the girl happened to be out of the house together, she would say something and add the name Hulga to the end of it, and the big spectacled Joy-Hulga would scowl and redden as if her privacy had been intruded upon. She considered the name her personal affair. She had arrived at it first purely on the basis of its ugly sound and then the full genius of its fitness had struck her. She had a vision of the name working like the ugly sweating Vulcan who stayed in the furnace and to whom, presumably, the goddess had to come when called. She saw it as the name of her highest creative act. One of her major triumphs was that her mother had not been able to turn her dust into Joy, but the greater one was that she had been able to turn it herself into Hulga. However, Mrs. Freeman's relish for using the name only irritated her. It was as if Mrs. Freeman's beady steel-pointed eyes had penetrated far enough behind her face to reach some secret fact. Something about her seemed to fascinate Mrs. Freeman and then one day Hulga realized that it was the artificial leg. Mrs. Freeman had a special fondness for the details of secret infections, hidden deformities, assaults upon children. Of diseases, she preferred the lingering or incurable. Hulga had heard Mrs. Hopewell give her the details of the hunting accident, how the leg had been literally blasted off, how she had never lost consciousness. Mrs. Freeman could listen to it any time as if it had happened an hour ago.

When Hulga stumped into the kitchen in the morning (she could walk without making the awful noise but she made it—Mrs. Hopewell was certain—because it was ugly-sounding), she glanced at them and did not speak. Mrs. Hopewell would be in her red kimono with her hair tied around her head in rags. She would be sitting at the table, finishing her breakfast and Mrs. Freeman would be hanging by her elbow outward from the refrigerator, looking down at the table. Hulga always put her eggs on the stove to boil and then stood over them with her arms folded, and Mrs. Hopewell would look at her—a kind of indirect gaze divided between her and Mrs. Freeman—and would think that if she would only keep herself up a little, she wouldn't be so bad looking. There was nothing wrong with her face that a pleasant expression wouldn't help. Mrs. Hopewell said that people who looked on the bright side of things would be beautiful even if they were not.

Whenever she looked at Joy this way, she could not help but feel that it would have been better if the child had not taken the Ph.D. It had certainly not brought her out any and now that she had it, there was no more excuse for her to go to school again. Mrs. Hopewell thought it was nice for girls to go to school to have a good time but Joy had "gone through." Anyhow, she would not have been strong enough to go again. The doctors had told Mrs. Hopewell that with the best of care, Joy might see forty-five. She had a weak heart. Joy had made it plain that if it had not been for this condition, she would be far from these red hills and good country people. She would be in a university lecturing to people who knew what she was talking about. And Mrs. Hopewell could very well picture her there, looking like a scarecrow and lecturing to more of the same. Here she went about all day in a six-year-old skirt and a yellow sweat shirt with a faded cowboy on a horse embossed on it. She thought this was funny; Mrs. Hopewell thought it was idiotic and showed simply that she was still a child. She was brilliant but she didn't have a grain of sense. It seemed to Mrs. Hopewell that every year she grew less like other people and more like herself—bloated, rude, and squint-eyed. And she said such strange things! To her own mother she had said—without warning, without excuse, standing up in the middle of a meal with her face purple and her mouth half full—"Woman! do you ever look inside? Do you ever look inside and see what you are *not*? God!" she had cried sinking down again and staring at her plate, "Malebranche was right: we are not our own light. We are not our own light!" Mrs. Hopewell had no idea to this day what brought that on. She had only made the remark, hoping Joy would take it in, that a smile never hurt anyone.

The girl had taken the Ph.D. in philosophy and this left Mrs. Hopewell at a complete loss. You could say, "My daughter is a nurse," or "My daughter is a school teacher," or even, "My daughter is a chemical engineer." You could not say, "My daughter is a philosopher." That was something that had ended with the Greeks and Romans. All day Joy sat on her neck in a deep chair, reading. Sometimes she went for walks but she didn't like dogs or cats or birds or flowers or nature or nice young men. She looked at nice young men as if she could smell their stupidity.

One day Mrs. Hopewell had picked up one of the books the girl had just put down and opening it at random, she read, "Science, on the other hand, has to assert its soberness and seriousness afresh and declare that it is concerned solely with what-is. Nothing—how can it be for science anything but a horror and a phantasm? If science is right, then one thing stands firm: science wishes to know nothing of nothing. Such is after all the strictly scientific approach to Nothing. We know it by wishing to know nothing of Nothing." These words had been underlined with a blue pencil and they worked on Mrs. Hopewell like some evil incantation in gibberish. She shut the book quickly and went out of the room as if she were having a chill.

This morning when the girl came in, Mrs. Freeman was on Carramae. "She thrown up four times after supper," she said, "and was up twict in the night after three o'clock. Yesterday she didn't do nothing but ramble in the bureau drawer. All she did. Stand up there and see what she could run up on."

"She's got to eat," Mrs. Hopewell muttered, sipping her coffee, while she watched Joy's back at the stove. She was wondering what the child had said to the Bible salesman. She could not imagine what kind of a conversation she could possibly have had with him.

He was a tall gaunt hatless youth who had called yesterday to sell them a Bible. He had appeared at the door, carrying a large black suitcase that weighted him so heavily on one side that he had to brace himself against the door facing. He seemed on the point of collapse but he said in a cheerful voice, "Good morning, Mrs. Cedars!" and set the suitcase down on the mat. He was not a bad-looking young man though he had on a bright blue suit and yellow socks that were not pulled up far enough. He had prominent face bones and a streak of sticky-looking brown hair falling across his forehead.

"I'm Mrs. Hopewell," she said.

"Oh!" he said, pretending to look puzzled but with his eyes sparkling, "I saw it said 'The Cedars,' on the mailbox so I thought you was Mrs. Cedars!" and he burst out in a pleasant laugh. He picked up the satchel and under cover of a pant, he fell forward into her hall. It was rather as if the suitcase had moved first, jerking him after it. "Mrs.

Hopewell!" he said and grabbed her hand. "I hope you are well!" and he laughed again and then all at once his face sobered completely. He paused and gave her a straight earnest look and said, "Lady, I've come to speak of serious things."

"Well, come in," she muttered, none too pleased because her dinner was almost ready. He came into the parlor and sat down on the edge of a straight chair and put the suitcase between his feet and glanced around the room as if he were sizing her up by it. Her silver gleamed on the two sideboards; she decided he had never been in a room as elegant as this.

"Mrs. Hopewell," he began, using her name in a way that sounded almost intimate, "I know you believe in Chrustian service."

"Well yes," she murmured.

"I know," he said and paused, looking very wise with his head cocked on one side, "that you're a good woman. Friends have told me."

Mrs. Hopewell never liked to be taken for a fool. "What are you selling?" she asked.

"Bibles," the young man said and his eye raced around the room before he added, "I see you have no family Bible in your parlor, I see that is the one lack you got!"

Mrs. Hopewell could not say, "My daughter is an atheist and won't let me keep the Bible in the parlor." She said, stiffening slightly, "I keep my Bible by my bedside." This was not the truth. It was in the attic somewhere.

"Lady," he said, "the word of God ought to be in the parlor."

"Well, I think that's a matter of taste," she began. "I think . . ."

"Lady," he said, "for a Chrustian, the word of God ought to be in every room in the house besides in his heart. I know you're a Chrustian because I can see it in every line of your face."

She stood up and said, "Well, young man, I don't want to buy a Bible and I smell my dinner burning."

He didn't get up. He began to twist his hands and looking down at them, he said softly, "Well lady, I'll tell you the truth—not many people want to buy one nowadays and besides, I know I'm real simple. I don't know how to say a thing but to say it. I'm just a country boy." He glanced up into her unfriendly face. "People like you don't like to fool with country people like me!"

"Why!" she cried, "good country people are the salt of the earth! Besides, we all have different ways of doing, it takes all kinds to make the world go 'round. That's life!"

"You said a mouthful," he said.

"Why, I think there aren't enough good country people in the world!" she said, stirred. "I think that's what's wrong with it!"

His face had brightened. "I didn't inraduce myself," he said. "I'm Manley Pointer from out in the country around Willohobie, not even from a place, just from near a place."

"You wait a minute," she said. "I have to see about my dinner." She went out to the kitchen and found Joy standing near the door where she had been listening.

"Get rid of the salt of the earth," she said, "and let's eat."

Mrs. Hopewell gave her a pained look and turned the heat down under the vegetables. "*I* can't be rude to anybody," she murmured and went back into the parlor.

He had opened the suitcase and was sitting with a Bible on each knee.

"You might as well put those up," she told him. "I don't want one."

"I appreciate your honesty," he said. "You don't see any more real honest people unless you go way out in the country."

"I know," she said, "real genuine folks!" Through the crack in the door she heard a groan.

"I guess a lot of boys come telling you they're working their way through college," he said, "but I'm not going to tell you that. Somehow," he said, "I don't want to go to college. I want to devote my life to Chrustian service. See," he said, lowering his voice, "I got this heart condition. I may not live long. When you know it's something wrong with you and you may not live long, well then, lady . . ." He paused, with his mouth open, and stared at her.

He and Joy had the same condition! She knew that her eyes were filling with tears but she collected herself quickly and murmured, "Won't you stay for dinner? We'd love to have you!" and was sorry the instant she heard herself say it.

"Yes mam," he said in an abashed voice, "I would sher love to do that!"

Joy had given him one look on being introduced to him and then throughout the meal had not glanced at him again. He had addressed several remarks to her, which she had pretended not to hear. Mrs. Hopewell could not understand deliberate rudeness, although she lived with it, and she felt she had always to overflow with hospitality to make up for Joy's lack of courtesy. She urged him to talk about himself and he did. He said he was the seventh child of twelve and that his father had been crushed under a tree when he himself was eight year old. He had been crushed very badly, in fact, almost cut in two and was practically not recognizable. His mother had got along the best she could by hard working and she had always seen that her children went to Sunday School and that they read the Bible every evening. He was now nineteen year old and he had been selling Bibles for four months. In that time he had sold seventy-seven Bibles and had the promise of two more sales. He wanted to become a missionary because he thought that was the way you could do most for people. "He who losest his life shall find it," he said simply and he was so sincere, so genuine and earnest that Mrs. Hopewell would not for the world have smiled. He prevented his peas from sliding onto the table by blocking them with a piece of bread which he later cleaned his plate with. She could see Joy observing sidewise how he handled his knife and fork and she saw too that every few minutes, the boy would dart a keen appraising glance at the girl as if he were trying to attract her attention.

After dinner Joy cleared the dishes off the table and disappeared and Mrs. Hopewell was left to talk with him. He told her again about his childhood and his father's accident and about various things that had happened to him. Every five minutes or so she would stifle a yawn. He sat for two hours until finally she told him she must go because she had an appointment in town. He packed his Bibles and thanked her and prepared to leave, but in the doorway he stopped and wrung her hand and said that not on any of his trips had he met a lady as nice as her and he asked if he could come again. She had said she would always be happy to see him.

Joy had been standing in the road, apparently looking at something in the distance, when he came down the steps toward her, bent to the side with his heavy valise. He stopped where she was standing and confronted her directly. Mrs. Hopewell could not hear what he said but she trembled to think what Joy would say to him. She could see that after a minute Joy said something and that then the boy began to speak again, making an excited gesture with his free hand. After a minute Joy said something else at which the boy began to speak once more. Then to her amazement, Mrs. Hopewell saw the two of them walk off together, toward the gate. Joy had walked all the way to the gate with him and Mrs. Hopewell could not imagine what they had said to each other, and she had not yet dared to ask.

Mrs. Freeman was insisting upon her attention. She had moved from the refrigerator to the heater so that Mrs. Hopewell had to turn and face her in order to seem to be listening. "Glynese gone out with Harvey Hill again last night," she said. "She had this sty."

"Hill," Mrs. Hopewell said absently, "is that the one who works in the garage?"

"Nome, he's the one that goes to chiropracter school," Mrs. Freeman said. "She had this sty. Been had it two days. So she says when he brought her in the other night he says, 'Lemme get rid of that sty for you,' and she says, 'How?' and he says, 'You just lay yourself down acrost the seat of that car and I'll show you.' So she done it and he popped her neck. Kept on a-popping it several times until she made him quit. This morning," Mrs. Freeman said, "she ain't got no sty. She ain't got no traces of a sty."

"I never heard of that before," Mrs. Hopewell said.

"He ast her to marry him before the Ordinary," Mrs. Freeman went on, "and she told him she wasn't going to be married in no *office*."

"Well, Glynese is a fine girl," Mrs. Hopewell said. "Glynese and Carramae are both fine girls."

"Carramae said when her and Lyman was married Lyman said it sure felt sacred to him. She said he said he wouldn't take five hundred dollars for being married by a preacher."

"How much would he take?" the girl asked from the stove.

"He said he wouldn't take five hundred dollars," Mrs. Freeman repeated.

"Well we all have work to do," Mrs. Hopewell said.

"Lyman said it just felt more sacred to him," Mrs. Freeman said. "The doctor wants Carramae to eat prunes. Says instead of medicine. Says them cramps is coming from pressure. You know where I think it is?"

"She'll be better in a few weeks," Mrs. Hopewell said.

"In the tube," Mrs. Freeman said. "Else she wouldn't be as sick as she is."

Hulga had cracked her two eggs into a saucer and was bringing them to the table along with a cup of coffee that she had filled too full. She sat down carefully and began to eat, meaning to keep Mrs. Freeman there by questions if for any reason she showed an inclination to leave. She could perceive her mother's eye on her. The first roundabout question would be about the Bible salesman and she did not wish to bring it on. "How did he pop her neck?" she asked.

Mrs. Freeman went into a description of how he had popped her neck. She said he owned a '55 Mercury but that Glynese said she would rather marry a man with only a '36 Plymouth who would be married by a preacher. The girl asked what if he had a '32 Plymouth and Mrs. Freeman said what Glynese had said was a '36 Plymouth.

Mrs. Hopewell said there were not many girls with Glynese's common sense. She said what she admired in those girls was their common sense. She said that reminded her that they had had a nice visitor yesterday, a young man selling Bibles. "Lord," she said, "he bored me to death but he was so sincere and genuine I couldn't be rude to him. He was just good country people, you know," she said, "—just the salt of the earth."

"I seen him walk up," Mrs. Freeman said, "and then later—I seen him walk off," and Hulga could feel the slight shift in her voice, the slight insinuation, that he had not walked off alone, had he? Her face remained expressionless but the color rose into her neck and she seemed to swallow it down with the next spoonful of egg. Mrs. Freeman was looking at her as if they had a secret together.

"Well, it takes all kinds of people to make the world go 'round," Mrs. Hopewell said. "It's very good we aren't all alike."

"Some people are more alike than others," Mrs. Freeman said.

Hulga got up and stumped, with about twice the noise that was necessary, into her room and locked the door. She was to meet the Bible salesman at ten o'clock at the gate. She had thought about it half the night. She had started thinking of it as a great joke and then she had begun to see profound implications in it. She had lain in bed imagining dialogues for them that were insane on the surface but that reached below to depths that no Bible salesman would be aware of. Their conversation yesterday had been of this kind.

He had stopped in front of her and had simply stood there. His face was bony and sweaty and bright, with a little pointed nose in the center of it, and his look was different from what it had been at the dinner table. He was gazing at her with open curiosity, with fascination, like a child watching a new fantastic animal at the zoo, and he was breathing as if he had run a great distance to reach her. His gaze seemed somehow familiar but she could not think where she had been regarded with it before. For almost a minute he didn't say anything. Then on what seemed an insuck of breath, he whispered, "You ever ate a chicken that was two days old?"

The girl looked at him stonily. He might have just put this question up for consideration at the meeting of a philosophical association. "Yes," she presently replied as if she had considered it from all angles.

"It must have been mighty small!" he said triumphantly and shook all over with little nervous giggles, getting very red in the face, and subsiding finally into his gaze of complete admiration, while the girl's expression remained exactly the same.

"How old are you?" he asked softly.

She waited some time before she answered. Then in a flat voice she said, "Seventeen."

His smiles came in succession like waves breaking on the surface of a little lake. "I see you got a wooden leg," he said. "I think you're real brave. I think you're real sweet."

The girl stood blank and solid and silent.

"Walk to the gate with me," he said. "You're a brave sweet little thing and I liked you the minute I seen you walk in the door."

Hulga began to move forward.

"What's your name?" he asked, smiling down on the top of her head.

"Hulga," she said.

"Hulga," he murmured, "Hulga. Hulga. I never heard of anybody name Hulga before. You're shy, aren't you, Hulga?" he asked.

She nodded, watching his large red hand on the handle of the giant valise.

"I like girls that wear glasses," he said. "I think a lot. I'm not like these people that a serious thought don't ever enter their heads. It's because I may die."

"I may die too," she said suddenly and looked up at him. His eyes were very small and brown, glittering feverishly.

"Listen," he said, "don't you think some people was meant to meet on account of what all they got in common and all? Like they both think serious thoughts and all?" He shifted the valise to his other hand so that the hand nearest her was free. He caught hold of her elbow and shook it a little. "I don't work on Saturday," he said. "I like to walk in the woods and see what Mother Nature is wearing. O'er the hills and far away. Pic-nics and things. Couldn't we go on a pic-nic tomorrow? Say yes, Hulga," he said and gave her a dying look as if he felt his insides about to drop out of him. He had even seemed to sway slightly toward her.

During the night she had imagined that she seduced him. She imagined that the two of them walked on the place until they came to the storage barn beyond the two back fields and there, she imagined, that things came to such a pass that she very easily seduced him and that then, of course, she had to reckon with his remorse. True genius can get an idea across even to an inferior mind. She imagined that she took his remorse in hand and changed it into a deeper understanding of life. She took all his shame away and turned it into something useful.

She set off for the gate at exactly ten o'clock, escaping without drawing Mrs. Hopewell's attention. She didn't take anything to eat, forgetting that food is usually taken on a picnic. She wore a pair of slacks and a dirty white shirt, and as an afterthought, she had put some Vapex on the collar of it since she did not own any perfume. When she reached the gate no one was there.

She looked up and down the empty highway and had the furious feeling that she had been tricked, that he had only meant to make her walk to the gate after the idea of him. Then suddenly he stood up, very tall, from behind a bush on the opposite embankment. Smiling, he lifted his hat which was new and wide-brimmed. He had not worn it yesterday and she wondered if he had bought it for the occasion. It was toast-colored with a red and white band around it and was slightly too large for him. He stepped from behind the bush still carrying the black valise. He had on the same suit and the same yellow socks sucked down in his shoes from walking. He crossed the highway and said, "I knew you'd come!"

The girl wondered acidly how he had known this. She pointed to the valise and asked, "Why did you bring your Bibles?"

He took her elbow, smiling down on her as if he could not stop. "You can never tell when you'll need the word of God, Hulga," he said. She had a moment in which she doubted that this was actually happening and then they began to climb the embankment. They went down into the pasture toward the woods. The boy walked lightly by her side, bouncing on his toes. The valise did not seem to be heavy today; he even swung it. They crossed half the pasture without saying anything and then, putting his hand easily on the small of her back, he asked softly, "Where does your wooden leg join on?"

She turned an ugly red and glared at him and for an instant the boy looked abashed. "I didn't mean you no harm," he said. "I only meant you're so brave and all. I guess God takes care of you."

"No," she said, looking forward and walking fast, "I don't even believe in God."

At this he stopped and whistled. "No!" he exclaimed as if he were too astonished to say anything else.

She walked on and in a second he was bouncing at her side, fanning with his hat. "That's very unusual for a girl," he remarked, watching her out of the corner of his eye. When they reached the edge of the wood, he put his hand on her back again and drew her against him without a word and kissed her heavily.

The kiss, which had more pressure than feeling behind it, produced that extra surge of adrenalin in the girl that enables one to carry a packed trunk out of a burning house, but in her, the power went at once to the brain. Even before he released her, her mind, clear and detached and ironic anyway, was regarding him from a great distance, with amusement but with pity. She had never been kissed before and she was pleased to discover that it was an unexceptional experience and all a matter of the mind's control. Some people might enjoy drain water if they were told it was vodka. When the boy, looking expectant but uncertain, pushed her gently away, she turned and walked on, saying nothing as if such business, for her, were common enough.

He came along panting at her side, trying to help her when he saw a root that she might trip over. He caught and held back the long swaying blades of thorn vine until she had passed beyond them. She led the way and he came breathing heavily behind her. Then they came out on a sunlit hillside, sloping softly into another one a little smaller. Beyond, they could see the rusted top of the old barn where the extra hay was stored.

The hill was sprinkled with small pink weeds. "Then you ain't saved?" he asked suddenly, stopping.

The girl smiled. It was the first time she had smiled at him at all. "In my economy," she said, "I'm saved and you are damned but I told you I didn't believe in God."

Nothing seemed to destroy the boy's look of admiration. He gazed at her now as if the fantastic animal at the zoo had put its paw through the bars and given him a loving poke. She thought he looked as if he wanted to kiss her again and she walked on before he had the chance.

"Ain't there somewheres we can sit down sometime?" he murmured, his voice softening toward the end of the sentence.

"In that barn," she said.

They made for it rapidly as if it might slide away like a train. It was a large two-story barn, cool and dark inside. The boy pointed up the ladder that led into the loft and said, "It's too bad we can't go up there."

"Why can't we?" she asked.

"Yer leg," he said reverently.

The girl gave him a contemptuous look and putting both hands on the ladder, she climbed it while he stood below, apparently awestruck. She pulled herself expertly through the opening and then looked down at him and said, "Well, come on if you're coming," and he began to climb the ladder, awkwardly bringing the suitcase with him.

"We won't need the Bible," she observed.

"You never can tell," he said, panting. After he had got into the loft, he was a few seconds catching his breath. She had sat down in a pile of straw. A wide sheath of sunlight, filled with dust particles, slanted over her. She lay back against a bale, her face turned away, looking out the front opening of the barn where hay was thrown from a wagon into the loft. The two pink-speckled hillsides lay back against a dark ridge of woods. The sky was cloudless and cold blue. The boy dropped down by her side and put one arm under her and the other over her and began methodically kissing her face, making little noises like a fish. He did not remove his hat but it was pushed far enough back not to interfere. When her glasses got in his way, he took them off of her and slipped them into his pocket.

The girl at first did not return any of the kisses but presently she began to and after she had put several on his cheek, she reached his lips and remained there, kissing him again and again as if she were trying to draw all the breath out of him. His breath was clear and sweet like a child's and the kisses were sticky like a child's. He mumbled about loving her and about knowing when he first seen her that he loved her, but the mumbling was like the sleepy fretting of a child being put to sleep by his mother. Her mind, throughout this, never stopped or lost itself for a second to her feelings. "You ain't said you loved me none," he whispered finally, pulling back from her. "You got to say that."

She looked away from him off into the hollow sky and then down at a black ridge and then down farther into what appeared to be two green swelling lakes. She didn't realize he had taken her glasses but this landscape could not seem exceptional to her for she seldom paid any close attention to her surroundings.

"You got to say it," he repeated. "You got to say you love me."

She was always careful how she committed herself. "In a sense," she began, "if you use the word loosely, you might say that. But it's not a word I use. I don't have illusions. I'm one of those people who see *through* to nothing."

The boy was frowning. "You got to say it. I said it and you got to say it," he said.

The girl looked at him almost tenderly. "You poor baby," she murmured. "It's just as well you don't understand," and she pulled him by the neck, face-down, against her. "We are all damned," she said, "but some of us have taken off our blindfolds and see that there's nothing to see. It's a kind of salvation."

The boy's astonished eyes looked blankly through the ends of her hair. "Okay," he almost whined, "but do you love me or don'tcher?"

"Yes," she said and added, "in a sense. But I must tell you something. There mustn't be anything dishonest between us." She lifted his head and looked him in the eye. "I am thirty years old," she said. "I have a number of degrees."

The boy's look was irritated but dogged. "I don't care," he said. "I don't care a thing about what all you done. I just want to know if you love me or don'tcher?" and he caught her to him and wildly planted her face with kisses until she said, "Yes, yes."

"Okay then," he said, letting her go. "Prove it."

She smiled, looking dreamily out on the shifty landscape. She had seduced him without even making up her mind to try. "How?" she asked, feeling that he should be delayed a little.

He leaned over and put his lips to her ear. "Show me where your wooden leg joins on," he whispered.

The girl uttered a sharp little cry and her face instantly drained of color. The obscenity of the suggestion was not what shocked her. As a child she had sometimes been subject to feelings of shame but education had removed the last traces of that as a good surgeon scrapes for cancer; she would no more have felt it over what he was asking than she would have believed in his Bible. But she was as sensitive about the artificial leg as a peacock about his tail. No one ever touched it but her. She took care of it as someone else would his soul, in private and almost with her own eyes turned away. "No," she said.

"I known it," he muttered, sitting up. "You're just playing me for a sucker."

"Oh no no!" she cried. "It joins on at the knee. Only at the knee. Why do you want to see it?"

The boy gave her a long penetrating look. "Because," he said, "it's what makes you different. You ain't like anybody else."

She sat staring at him. There was nothing about her face or her round freezing-blue eyes to indicate that this had moved her; but she felt as if her heart had stopped and left her mind to pump her blood. She decided that for the first time in her life she was face to face with real innocence. This boy, with an instinct that came from beyond wisdom, had touched the truth about her. When after a minute, she said in a hoarse high voice, "All right," it was like surrendering to him completely. It was like losing her own life and finding it again, miraculously, in his.

Very gently he began to roll the slack leg up. The artificial limb, in a white sock and brown flat shoe, was bound in a heavy material like canvas and ended in an ugly jointure where it was attached to the stump. The boy's face and his voice were entirely reverent as he uncovered it and said, "Now show me how to take it off and on."

She took it off for him and put it back on again and then he took it off himself, handling it as tenderly as if it were a real one. "See!" he said with a delighted child's face. "Now I can do it myself!"

"Put it back on," she said. She was thinking that she would run away with him and that every night he would take the leg off and every morning put it back on again. "Put it back on," she said.

"Not yet," he murmured, setting it on its foot out of her reach. "Leave it off for a while. You got me instead."

She gave a little cry of alarm but he pushed her down and began to kiss her again. Without the leg she felt entirely dependent on him. Her brain seemed to have stopped thinking altogether and to be about some other function that it was not very good at. Different expressions raced back and forth over her face. Every now and then the boy, his eyes like two steel spikes, would glance behind him where the leg stood. Finally she pushed him off and said, "Put it back on me now."

"Wait," he said. He leaned the other way and pulled the valise toward him and opened it. It had a pale blue spotted lining and there were only two Bibles in it. He took one of these out and opened the cover of it. It was hollow and contained a pocket flask of whiskey, a pack of cards, and a small blue box with printing on it. He laid these out in front of her one at a time in an evenly-spaced row, like one presenting offerings at the shrine of a goddess. He put the blue box in her hand. THIS PRODUCT TO BE USED ONLY FOR THE PREVENTION OF DISEASE, she read, and dropped it. The boy was unscrewing the top of the flask. He stopped and pointed, with a smile, to the deck of cards. It was not an ordinary deck but one with an obscene picture on the back of each card. "Take a swig," he said, offering her the bottle first. He held it in front of her, but like one mesmerized, she did not move.

Her voice when she spoke had an almost pleading sound. "Aren't you," she murmured, "aren't you just good country people?"

The boy cocked his head. He looked as if he were just beginning to understand that she might be trying to insult him. "Yeah," he said, curling his lip slightly, "but it ain't held me back none. I'm as good as you any day in the week."

"Give me my leg," she said.

He pushed it farther away with his foot. "Come on now, let's begin to have us a good time," he said coaxingly. "We ain't got to know one another good yet."

"Give me my leg!" she screamed and tried to lunge for it but he pushed her down easily.

"What's the matter with you all of a sudden?" he asked, frowning as he screwed the top on the flask and put it quickly back inside the Bible. "You just a while ago said you didn't believe in nothing. I thought you was some girl!"

Her face was almost purple. "You're a Christian!" she hissed. "You're a fine Christian! You're just like them all—say one thing and do another. You're a perfect Christian, you're . . ."

The boy's mouth was set angrily. "I hope you don't think," he said in a lofty indignant tone, "that I believe in that crap! I may sell Bibles but I know which end is up and I wasn't born yesterday and I know where I'm going!"

"Give me my leg!" she screeched. He jumped up so quickly that she barely saw him sweep the cards and the blue box back into the Bible and throw the Bible into the valise. She saw him grab the leg and then she saw it for an instant slanted forlornly across the inside of the suitcase with a Bible at either side of its opposite ends. He slammed the lid shut and snatched up the valise and swung it down the hole and then stepped through himself.

When all of him had passed but his head, he turned and regarded her with a look that no longer had any admiration in it. "I've gotten a lot of interesting things," he said. "One time I got a woman's glass eye this way. And you needn't to think you'll catch me because Pointer ain't really my name. I use a different name at every house I call at and don't stay nowhere long. And I'll tell you another thing, Hulga," he said, using the name as if he didn't think much of it, "you ain't so smart. I been believing in nothing ever since I was born!" and then the toast-colored hat disappeared down the hole and the girl was left, sitting on the straw in the dusty sunlight. When she turned her churning face toward the opening, she saw his blue figure struggling successfully over the green speckled lake.

Mrs. Hopewell and Mrs. Freeman, who were in the back pasture, digging up onions, saw him emerge a little later from the woods and head across the meadow toward the highway. "Why, that looks like that nice dull young man that tried to sell me a Bible yesterday," Mrs.

Hopewell said, squinting. "He must have been selling them to the Negroes back in there. He was so simple," she said, "but I guess the world would be better off if we were all that simple."

Mrs. Freeman's gaze drove forward and just touched him before he disappeared under the hill. Then she returned her attention to the evil-smelling onion shoot she was lifting from the ground. "Some can't be that simple," she said. "I know I never could."

THE DOCTOR'S WIFE

The youngest author represented in this volume, John Updike already has firmly established a reputation as a gifted and versatile writer. Preferring, as Peter Taylor does, to concentrate on the quieter, more ordinary phases of life, Updike places less emphasis on plot and dramatic physical conflicts in his fiction than on the tensions, dilemmas, and frustrations members of the human family experience in their daily involvements with one another. He is the master of a facile style which is characterized by a graphic clarity of imagery and diction and, at its best, by a brilliant intensity and terseness.

Updike was born in West Reading, Pennsylvania, in 1932. After attending public school in Shillington, Pennsylvania, he entered Harvard University, where he majored in English and became president of the Harvard *Lampoon*. Graduating *summa cum laude* in 1954, he spent a year studying art at the Ruskin School of Drawing and Fine Art in Oxford, England. Returning to the United States, he worked from 1955 to 1957 for *The New Yorker* magazine, to which he contributed stories, parodies, essays, and verse. His first published volume, *The Carpentered Hen and Other Tame Creatures* (1958) was a collection of verse. In rapid succession thereafter, he published *The Same Door* (1959), a collection of short stories; *The Poorhouse Fair* (1959), a novel which won the Hilda Rosenthal Foundation Award; *Rabbit, Run* (1960), a second novel, written on a Guggenheim Fellowship; *Pigeon Feathers and Other Stories* (1962), a second collection of short stories; and *The Centaur* (1963), a third novel, which won the fifteenth Annual Book Award. He lives with his wife and their four children at Ipswich, Massachusetts.

As is true of many twentieth-century writers,

Updike uses with particular effectiveness the fictional technique of developing his story situations dramatically and objectively through the dialogue of the characters, with a central character serving as a focal point, or "center of consciousness." Typically, the dialogue occurs within a brief time interval and in one locality, while the characters are often shown engaged in some incidental—even inconsequential—activity. But whatever the action may be—as well as the setting which provided the context for characters, action, and dialogue—every part of the story is rendered with a graphic clarity of detail. As in "The Doctor's Wife," the overall effect is somewhat like that of an impressionistic painting in which people, caught in a particular posture and setting, momentarily confront each other before the fluid movement of life separates and rearranges them into new postures, moods, and settings. "The Doctor's Wife" further resembles an impressionistic painting in the unified atmospheric quality which arises from the deliberate fusion of the characters, land, sea, and air into a unified whole.

the doctor's wife

"Sharks?" The tip of the doctor's wife's freckled nose seemed to sharpen in the sparkling air. Her eyes, momentarily rendered colorless by thought, took up the green of the Caribbean; the plane of the water intersected her throat. "Yes, we have some. Big dark fellows, too."

Ralph, hanging beside her, squatting on buoyance, straightened up, splashing, and tried to survey the beryl depths around him. His

Reprinted from *Pigeon Feathers and Other Stories* by John Updike, by permission of Alfred A. Knopf, Inc. Copyright 1961 © 1962 by John Updike. "The Doctor's Wife" first appeared in *The New Yorker*.

sudden movements rendered even the immediate water opaque. The doctor's wife's surprisingly young laughter rang out.

"You Americans," she said, "so nervy," and with complacence pushed a little deeper into the sea, floating backwards while the water gently bubbled around her mouth. She had a small face, gone freckled and rosy in this climate; her stringy auburn hair had been dulled by daily sea-bathing. "They rarely come in this far," she said, tilting her face upward and speaking to the sky. "Only in the turtle-killing season, when the blood draws them in. We're fortunate. Our beaches go out shallowly. Over in St. Martin, now, the offshore water is deep, and they must be careful."

She turned and, with the casual paddling stroke of a plump woman who floats easily, swam smiling toward him. "A shame," she said, her voice strained by the effort of curving her throat to keep her lips free, "Vic Johnson is gone. He was a dear soul. The old Anglican vicar." She pronounced "vicar" rather harshly, perhaps humorously. She stood up beside Ralph and pointed to the horizon. "Now *he*," she said, "used to swim far out into the bay, he and his great black dog Hooker. Vic would swim straight out, until he couldn't move a muscle, and then he would float, and grab Hooker's tail, and the dog would pull him in. Honestly, it was a sight, this fat old English gentleman, his white hair streaming, coming in on the tail of a dog. He never gave a thought to sharks. Oh, he'd swim *way* out, until he was just a dot."

They were waist-deep in the sea and at a motion from Ralph they walked toward shore together. The calm warm water leaped from their strides. She was small beside him, and her voice piped at his shoulder. "I'm sorry he's gone," she said. "He was a lovely old gentleman. He had been here forty years. He loved the island."

"I can see why he would," Ralph said. He turned his head to review the crescent of landscape around the beach, as if through his fresh eyes the doctor's wife could renew—what obscurely seemed to him to need renewing—her sense of the island's beauty. The white beach was empty. The natives used it only as a path. Their homes were set behind the ragged hedge of sea grape that rimmed the sand. Bits of tarpaper, pink-painted cement, corrugated roofing reddened by rust, wooden walls weathered to silver and patched by flattened kerosene tins, shacks on stilts, and unfinished cinder-block shells peeped above the dull, low foliage. There were few flowers. This was January. But the clusters of coconuts nested under the shuffling branches of the palms, and the high, small, soft clouds, like the quick clouds of spring in his own climate, suggested that here the season of bloom and the season of harvest were parallel and perpetual: germination and fruition ceaselessly intertwined. There were no mountains in the view. The island was low; when they came in on the airplane, it seemed a two-dimensional twin, or sketch, of St. Martin, which thrust from the sea like a set of Vermont mountaintops. There, the beaches were steep and dangerous; here, they were safe. There, Dutchmen and Frenchmen built bustling hotels and restaurants to entice American dollars; here, strangers rarely came. Here, even the place names were bestowed without enterprise or effort. East End, West End, The Road, The Forest—thus the island was geographically divided. The uninhabited ridge of scrub and coral rubble that formed one side of the bay was named High Hill. The village was called The Bay. The orange cliffs on the other side of the bay were called The Cliffs. During these short winter days the sun set on a diagonal above them and, between six and seven o'clock, touched the sea at the fingertips of the most distant arm of land. Yet after the sun had drowned, light, itself lazy, lingered among the huts and the olean-der bushes. Now it was late afternoon; the tiny tropical sun, not yet swollen to red, patiently poured white brilliance down through the hushed air. The air was as soft, as kind, as the water; there was no hostility in either. The two elements, as Ralph came out of one into the other, seemed tints of a single enveloping benevolence.

"Oh, yes, but not merely that," the doctor's wife said. "He loved the people. He built them three churches and, oh, did all manner of good works. We're talking of Reverend Johnson," she explained to Eve, who had remained on the beach with the children. "The Anglican padre. He retired last year and went back to England. Sussex, I think."

"He loved the people?" Eve asked. She had heard. Voices carried well in the air, disturbed, during the day, by only the whispering beat of the surf and infrequent voices calling in English made musical by an unintelligible lilt.

The doctor's wife dropped down on the sand. "These are my children," she intoned gruffly. She chased the abrupt parody away with her sharp laughter. "Oh, yes, he loved them. He gave his life to them." The youthful excitement of her voice and the innocent clarity of her eyes went queerly with her body, which was middle-aged. Her plump legs had gone lumpy and sodden, and her small face was finely wrin-kled, each wrinkle accented by a line of white where the pinched skin had evaded the sun. "He didn't have any children of his own," she thought to add. "Just this dreadful dog Hooker. Such a funny old man. You might have liked him. I'm sure you never see his kind in Amer-ica."

"I know we would have liked him," Eve said. "Hannah often mentions Reverend Johnson." Hannah was their cook, a woman of over thirty yet as shy and subtle as a girl. Her skin was always shining as if in embarrassment, but she had a jaunty way of crooning hymns to herself in the kitchen. The children, at first timid of her color, adored her, and listened with eyes rounded by delight when she held up a two-tone forefinger and told them to be good. Goodness had never before been presented to them seriously. Ralph and Eve had not expected a servant. They had picked the most obscure island they could find. But Hannah came with the house; the owner, a svelte widow who had children in Florida, Peru, and Antigua, assumed they would need her. As it turned out, they did. They could never have unravelled alone all the riddles of this novel world. Eve could never have managed the shopping, which was carried on by gossip—invisible voices as liquid as the wind, telling who had just slaughtered a pig, and whose fishing boat had come in with a catch. The village was full of stores; almost every shack at least sold—for disturbingly discrepant prices—American cigarettes smuggled from St. Martin. But even the business hours of the most official store, a cement corridor of shelves attached to the customs office, had proved a mystery the Americans were unable to crack. They always found barred the large green door bearing in wobbly chalk script the ancient announcement "Attention Members! Attention Friends! This Store will be CLOSED Thursday afternoon."

"Oh, Hannah. She's a good girl," the doctor's wife said, and rolled over on her stomach. The corrugated backs of her thighs were frosted with sand like wet sugar.

"She is, you know," Eve said. "She's lovely. I think they're all lovely. They've all been lovely to us." Such insistence was unlike his wife. Ralph wondered what was between the two women, who had just met a day ago. "I can see why Reverend Johnson loved the people," Eve added in a deliberate, though cautiously soft, voice. "The people" were all around them; their huts came down to the edge of the sand, and, windows shuttered, the patched walls seemed to be listening raptly.

The doctor's wife rolled over again and returned to a sitting position. What was making her so restless?

"Yes," she said, and an especially heavy curl of surf foamed up the white slope and soaked in just short of their feet. The sand was porous; innumerable punctures dotted it, the breathing-holes of crabs. The doctor's wife's eyes fixed on the horizon and became, from the side, colorless lenses. Her nose in profile turned acute. "They're simple souls," she said.

The doctor's wife was a queen here. She was the only fully white woman resident on the island. When the rare British official and the rarer, fantastically minor member of royalty came to grace this most remote and docile scrap of empire with a visit, she was the hostess. When she roared along the dirt roads in her spattered English Ford—its muffler had long ago rotted away—the older natives touched their foreheads ironically and the children flapped their arms in her wake of dust. When she and the doctor condescended to call upon the American family staying three weeks in The Bay, Hannah had trembled with pride and broken a cup in the kitchen. The doctor was a slight, rapid-voiced man with a witty air of failure. His fingertips were dyed deep yellow by smuggled cigarettes. He preferred Camels, but Chesterfields were all that were coming through now. Camels had more scratch in them. He had never seen a filtered cigarette. He and his wife had been ten years in the tropics—B.G., Trinidad, Barbados, now this. He had some vague scheme of getting to America and making a fortune and retiring to a Yorkshire village. He was off for the day to St. Martin.

"In America, now," the doctor's wife said, vehemently brushing sand from her knees, "are the coloreds well cared for?"

"How do you mean?" Eve asked.

"Are they well off?"

"Not really," Ralph said, because he sensed that it would be better if he, rather than Eve, answered. "In some parts better than others. In the South, of course, they're openly discriminated against; in the North they by and large have to live in the city slums but at least they have full legal rights."

"Oh, dear," the doctor's wife said. "It is a problem, isn't it?"

Eve's face flashed up from studying a shell. "Whose problem?" she asked. She was a graduate of one of those female colleges where only a member of a racial minority or a cripple can be elected class president. News from South Africa made her voice thrash, and she was for anyone—Castro, Ben-Gurion, Martin Luther King—who in her mind represented an oppressed race. That such automatic sympathy was itself condescending had not occurred to her. Of English blood, enriched by remote and aristocratic injections of French and Russian, she denied the less favored even the compliment of fearing them.

The doctor's wife returned her gaze to the horizon, and Ralph wondered if they had been rude. In the woman's pointed profile there was a certain perhaps deliberately noble thrust. But, the hostess, she relented and tried to make the conversation go again. She turned her head, shading her eyes with a quick hand and exposing her neat white teeth in a tense smile. "The schools," she said. "Can they go to your schools?"

"Of course," Ralph said swiftly, at the same time realizing that for her there was no "of course" to it. She knew nothing about his country. He felt firmer, having gauged her ignorance, and having moved to the hard ground of information. "Nobody denies them schools. In the South the schools are segregated. But in the North, and the West, and so on, there's no problem." He hunched his shoulders, feeling at his back Eve's disapproval of his saying "problem."

"But"—the doctor's wife's freckles gathered under her eyes as she squinted into the focus of the issue—"would *your* children go to school with them?"

"Sure. Good heavens. Why not?" He was relieved to clear this up, to lock this door. He hoped the doctor's wife would now turn away and talk of something else.

She sighed. "Of course, you in America have lived with the problem so long. In England, now, they're just waking up; the blacks are *pouring* into London."

A wave, pushed by one behind it, slid so far up the slant of sand their feet were delicately shocked and soaked. For a few seconds their ankles glittered in rippling sleeves of retreating water. Eve said slowly, "You talk as if they had asked to be made slaves and brought here."

"Mommy, look! Mommy, look!" Kate's voice, mingling with Larry's babyish yips of excitement, came from far down the beach. Their little silhouettes were jiggling around something dark at their feet, and out of the sea grape an old woman in a kerchief and a young sailor with a naked chest had emerged to watch them, amused to see what amused these strange children. Eve rose, casting down, for Ralph to see, a startled and indignant look at the doctor's wife's body, as if it were an offensive piece of rubbish washed up on the pure sands of her mind.

As Eve walked away, the doctor's wife said, "Doesn't she take a tan beautifully?"

"Yes, she always does. She's part French." With his wife out of earshot, Ralph relaxed into the sand. Mediating between the two women had demanded an exhausting equilibrium. He resigned himself to listening; he knew the doctor's wife's tongue would be loosened. The presence of another white queen inhibited her, diluted her authority.

"Do you want to hear a frightening story?"

"Sure." He acquiesced uneasily. The attention of the houses

behind them seemed to grow more intense. He felt that he and his family were liked in the village; the doctor's wife, driving down from the center of the island to enjoy their beach, assumed an incriminating alliance which he did not wish to exist. For when the sun went down, she would go home, leaving them alone in the village with the night and its noises. Their tilly lamps hissed; black bugs droned into their heat and fell crackling to the floor; far up the road a boy practiced on his lonely steel drum and next door, in an unpainted cabin that was never unshuttered, a woman wailed and a man infrequently growled a brief, hurt complaint.

"When Vic Johnson left," the doctor's wife said, lowering her voice and sinking back on her elbow, to bring her face closer to Ralph's, "they had a party to greet the new parson, a very nice young colored boy from St. Kitts. *Very* nice, I must say, and they say very intelligent, though I haven't heard him preach. Well, the Warden—you haven't met him, and I dare say you won't, a big smooth Jamaican, takes himself oh *ever* so seriously—the Warden makes this little speech. He of course mentions Vic, forty years and so on, but right at the end he says that he knows we will not miss Reverend Johnson, because the new vicar is such a fine young man, comes to us with such an excellent record of study, and the rest of it, and furthermore, *furthermore,* what makes us especially happy and proud, he is one of us. Imagine! One of us! Of course, the young parson was embarrassed to death. It made me so mad I would have jumped up and left if the doctor hadn't held my hand. *One of us!* Vic had given his life to these people."

Her voice had become shrill; Ralph spoke in the hope of restraining it. "It seems unnecessary; but natural," he said.

"I don't see anything natural about it. *Un*natural, in my book. Unnatural, childish ingratitude. You just don't know how unnatural these people are. If you could see one-tenth of the antics, and then the selfishness, the doctor puts up with. At two in the morning, 'Doctor, Doctor, come save my child,' and then a week later, when he tries to collect his poor little dollar or two, they don't *remember*. They don't remember at all. And if he insists—'The white people are stealing our money.' Oh. I hate them. God forgive me, I've come to hate them. They're *not* natural. They're not fully human." Seeing his hand begin a protesting movement, she added, "And for that matter, do you know what they say about you and your wife?" It was as if a shadow cruising through her words now made its lunge.

"No. Do they say something?"

"This is just to show how malicious they are. They say your wife has a touch of the brush." It took Ralph a moment to expand "brush" into "tarbrush." He laughed; what else?

The doctor's wife laughed, too; but under the blond eyebrows her blue eyes, the pupils pinpricks in the sun, were fixed on his face. She expected his face to crack and the truth to escape. "You see how dark she is," she explained. "How tan." He watched her tongue tick as she suspensefully pronounced the last two words. Girlish curiosity gave a taut surface to her mature malice.

Blood rushed through his body; the wound was confused; his anger entangled him with his attacker. He was supplying an absurd assault with teeth out of himself. "She just naturally gets that brown."

"And you see," the doctor's wife went on, still not unpinning her eyes from his face, "that's why they say you came here. No tourists come here, least of all with children. They say your wife's being part Negro has kept you out of the hotels on the better islands."

He felt certain that this ingenious argument was wholly her own. "We came here because it was cheap," he said.

"Of *course*," she said, "of *course*," and giggled, sensing that she had exposed herself to his defense. "But they can't believe that. They believe, you see, that all Americans are *rich*." Which was just what, Ralph knew, she and the doctor believed.

He stood up, wet sand collapsing from his legs. In an effort to rein his excitement, he threw several unrelated laughs, as if out of a renewed apprehension of absurdity, outward into the air. He looked down at the woman and said, "Well, that explains why they seem to like her better than me."

The doctor's wife, having strained her neck to squint up at him, collapsed the rest of the way. She pillowed her head with one arm and threw the other over her eyes. Without her eyes her lips seemed vague and numb. "Oh, no," she said. "They hate her for getting away with it."

His laughter this time was totally vacant; it humiliated him. "I think I'll go in again," he said. "Before the sun fades."

"It won't fade," was the faint answer.

From the safety of the water he watched his dark wife herd his two pale, burned children up the beach. The distance between them and the doctor's wife's inert body diminished; he had an urge to shout a warning, then smiled, picturing the laughter that would greet this story when they were home, at a cocktail party, secure among their own. Abruptly, he felt guilty in relation to his wife. He had betrayed her. His seriousness had been unworthy of her. She would have wanted him to say yes, her grandfather picked cotton in Alabama, in America these things are taken for granted, we have no problem. But he saw, like something living glimpsed in a liquid volume, that the comedy of this response depended upon, could only live within, a vast unconscious pride of race. That since this medium was poisoned all its creatures must be evil. That he and the doctor's wife were immersed together; he hated her blue eyes because they were pinned to his face, hated the taste of her because—could it be?—she was dying. His guilt could not be mapped. Its intricacy was as dense as a simple mass. He moved backward in the ocean, touching the ribbed bottom with his toes, until the water wrapped around his throat. Something—seaweed or the pulse of a current—touched his calf. He thrashed, and peered down, but saw nothing. He was afraid of the sharks, and he was afraid of the doctor's wife, so he hung there between them, bleeding shame, while the water forgave him.